THE YEAR'S BEST DARK FANTASY AND HORROR

2010 EDITION

THE YEAR'S BEST DARK FANTASY AND HORROR

2010 EDITION

EDITED BY
PAULA GURAN

PRIME BOOKS

THE YEAR'S BEST DARK FANTASY
AND HORROR 2010 EDITION

Prime Books
www.prime-books.com

ISBN: 978-1-60701-233-7

To Ellen Datlow
who has always been and always will be
the best.

TABLE OF CONTENTS

TABLE OF CONTENTS

WHAT THE HELL DO YOU MEAN BY "DARK FANTASY AND HORROR?"

PAULA GURAN

> "I shall not today attempt further to define the kinds of material I understand to be embraced within that shorthand description [hard-core pornography]; and perhaps I could never succeed in intelligibly doing so. But I know it when I see it . . . "
>
> —Justice Potter Stewart,
> *Jacobellis v. Ohio*, 378 U.S. 184 (1964)

Like Justice Potter Stewart with pornography, I can't intelligibly define "dark fantasy."

But I know it when I read it.

Of course, *you* might not agree with what I "see" as dark fantasy. I might not agree with what you "see."

There's no single definition. "Dark fantasy" isn't universally defined—the definition depends on the context in which the phrase is used or who is elucidating it. It has, from time to time, even been considered as nothing more than a marketing term for various types of fiction.

Darkness itself can be many things: nebulous, shadowy, tenebrous, mysterious, paradoxical (and thus illuminating) . . .

A dark fantasy story might be only a bit unsettling or perhaps somewhat eerie. It might be revelatory or baffling. It can be simply a small glimpse of life seen "through a glass, darkly." Or, in more literary terms (all of which are debatable), it might be any number of things—as long as the darkness is there: weird fiction (new or old) or supernatural fiction or magical realism or surrealism or the *fantastique* or the ever-ambiguous horror fiction.

As for defining horror: Since horror is something we feel—it's an emotion, an affect—what each of us experiences, responds or reacts to differs.

What you feel may not be what I feel. Maybe you can't stand the thought of, oh . . . spiders. Understandably, one doesn't want to encounter one of the poisonous types, but I think of spiders, for the most part, as helpful arachnids that eat harmful insects. You, however, might shiver at the very thought of eight spindly legs creeping down your wall.

Once upon a time I felt the term "horror" could be broadened, accepted, and generally regarded as a fiction [to quote Douglas E. Winter who wrote in *Revelations* (1997)] that was "evolving, ever-changing—because it is about our relentless need to confront the unknown, the unknowable, and the emotion we experience while in its thrall."

One reason Winter was reminding us of that in the introduction to his anthology was because the word "horror" had already been devalued. He was right about what horror literature is, but the word itself had been slapped on a generic marketing category and, by 1997, the word had become a pejorative. The appellation was hijacked even more completely in the years thereafter and became associated in the public hive mind—an amorphous organism far more frequently influenced by the seductive images, motion, sounds, and effects that appear on a screen of any size than by written words (even when they are on a screen)—with entertainments that depend on shock for any value they may (or may not) possess rather than eliciting the more subtle emotion of fear.

And while fine and highly diverse horror literature—some of the best ever created—continues to be written in forms short and long, the masses for the most part have identified "horror" as either a certain kind of cinema or a generic type of fiction (of which they have certain expectations or ignore entirely because it delivers only a specific formula.)

So, the term "horror" has been expropriated, and I doubt we'll ever be able to convince the world it means what we alleged horror mavens might want it to mean.

For this anthology, I might have just stuck with just "dark fantasy" for the title, but there are stories here with nothing supernatural in them at all. I mean, fantasy of any type must have a supernatural element. Doesn't it?

Of course some people insist that "horror" has to have a supernatural element for it to be "horror." Without the woo-woo, they insist, you are deal ing with a psychological thriller or . . . something or other.

Seems we're back to "What the hell . . . ?"

I'm not offering any definitions. I'm merely offering you, the reader, a diverse selection of stories—all published within the calendar year 2009—that struck me as fitting the title of this tome. Each of them—no matter the style of the writing, theme, or shade of darkness—grabbed me from the start and kept me reading.

You may find yourself abruptly jerked from one reality and thrust into another as you read. I have eclectic tastes. I hope you do, too, or are at least willing to try a taste of something new.

Or, considering the size of this tome, even if you don't care for a certain percentage of the stories, I sincerely hope you find enough you do like to have made it worth your while.

If you are interested in my own shallow musings on the selections, I've included comments at the end of each. But don't read the notes until after you've read the story! If you do, well . . .

You never know what might find *you* in the dark.

Paula Guran
June 2010

THE HORRID GLORY OF ITS WINGS

ELIZABETH BEAR

—◆—

> "Speaking of livers," the unicorn said. "Real magic can never be made by offering up someone else's liver. You must tear out your own, and not expect to get it back. The true witches know that."
>
> —Peter S. Beagle, *The Last Unicorn*

My mother doesn't know about the harpy.

My mother, Alice, is not my *real* mom. She's my foster mother, and she doesn't look anything like me. Or maybe I don't look anything like her. Mama Alice is plump and soft and has skin like the skin of a plum, all shiny dark purple with the same kind of frosty brightness over it, like you could swipe it away with your thumb.

I'm sallow—Mama Alice says olive—and I have straight black hair and crooked teeth and no real chin, which is okay because I've already decided nobody's ever going to kiss me.

I've also got *lipodystrophy*, which is a fancy doctor way of saying I've grown a fatty buffalo hump on my neck and over each shoulder blade from the antiretrovirals, and my butt and legs and cheeks are wasted like an old lady's. My face looks like a dog's muzzle, even though I still have all my teeth.

For now. I'm going to have to get the wisdom teeth pulled this year while I still get state assistance, because my birthday is in October and then I'll be eighteen. If I start having problems with them after then, well forget about it.

There's no way I'd be able to afford to get them fixed.

The harpy lives on the street, in the alley behind my building, where the Dumpster and the winos live.

I come out in the morning before school, after I've eaten my breakfast and taken my pills (nevirapine, lamivudine, efavirenz). I'm used to the pills. I've been taking them all my life. I have a note in my file at school, and excuses for my classmates.

I don't bring friends home.

Lying is a sin. But Father Alvaro seems to think that when it comes to my sickness, it's a sin for which I'm already doing enough penance.

Father Alvaro is okay. But he's not like the harpy.

The harpy doesn't care if I'm not pretty. The harpy is beyond not pretty, way into ugly. Ugly as your mama's warty butt. Its teeth are snaggled and stained piss-yellow and char-black. Its claws are broken and dull and stink like rotten chicken. It has a long droopy blotchy face full of lines like Liv Tyler's dad, that rock star guy, and its hair hangs down in black-bronze rats over both feathery shoulders. The feathers look washed-out black and dull until sunlight somehow finds its way down into the grubby alley, bounces off dirty windows and hits them, and then they look like scratched bronze.

They are bronze.

If I touch them, I can feel warm metal.

I'd sneak the harpy food, but Mama Alice keeps pretty close track of it—it's not like we have a ton of money—and the harpy doesn't seem to mind eating garbage. The awfuller the better: coffee grounds, moldy cake, meat squirming with maggots, the stiff corpses of alley rats.

The harpy turns all that garbage into bronze.

If it reeks, the harpy eats it, stretching its hag face out on a droopy red neck to gulp the bits, just like any other bird. I've seen pigeons do the same thing with a crumb too big to peck up and swallow, but their necks aren't scaly naked, ringed at the bottom with fluffy down as white as a confirmation dress.

So every morning I pretend I'm leaving early for school—Mama Alice says "Kiss my cheek, Desiree"—and then once I'm out from under Mama Alice's window I sneak around the corner into the alley and stand by the Dumpster where the harpy perches. I only get ten or fifteen minutes, however much time I can steal. The stink wrinkles up my nose. There's no place to sit. Even if there were, I couldn't sit down out here in my school clothes.

The harpy says, I want you.

I don't know if I like the harpy. But I like being wanted.

The harpy says, We're all alone.

It's six thirty in the morning and I hug myself in my new winter coat from the fire department giveaway, my breath streaming out over the top of the scratchy orange scarf Mama Alice knitted. I squeeze my legs together, left knee in the hollow of the right knee like I have to pee, because even tights don't help too much when the edge of the skirt only comes to the middle of your kneecap. I'd slap my legs to warm them, but these are my last pair of tights and I don't want them to snag.

The scarf scrapes my upper lip when I nod. It's dark here behind the Dumpster. The sun won't be up for another half hour. On the street out front, brightness pools under streetlights, but it doesn't show anything warm—just cracked black snow trampled and heaped over the curb.

"Nobody wants me," I say. "Mama Alice gets paid to take care of me."

That's unfair. Mama Alice didn't have to take me or my foster brother Luis. But sometimes it feels good to be a little unfair. I sniff up a drip and push my chin forward so it bobs like the harpy swallowing garbage.

"Nobody would want to live with me. But I don't have any choice. I'm stuck living with myself."

The harpy says, There's always a choice.

"Sure," I say. "Suicide is a sin."

The harpy says, Talking to harpies is probably a sin, too.

"Are you a devil?"

The harpy shrugs. Its feathers smell like mildew. Something crawls along a rat of its hair, greasy-shiny in the street light. The harpy scrapes it off with a claw and eats it.

The harpy says, I'm a heathen monster. Like Celaeno and her sisters, Aello and Ocypete. The sisters of the storm. Your church would say so, that I am a demon. Yes.

"I don't think you give Father Alvaro enough credit."

The harpy says, I don't trust priests, and turns to preen its broken claws.

"You don't trust anybody."

That's not what I said, says the harpy—

You probably aren't supposed to interrupt harpies, but I'm kind of over that by now. "That's why I decided. I'm never going to trust anybody. My birth mother trusted somebody, and look where it got her. Knocked up and dead."

The harpy says, That's very inhuman of you.

It sounds like a compliment.

I put a hand on the harpy's warm wing. I can't feel it through my glove. The gloves came from the fire department, too. "I have to go to school, Harpy."

The harpy says, You're alone there too.

I want to prove the harpy wrong.

The drugs are really good now. When I was born, a quarter of the babies whose moms had AIDS got sick too. Now it's more like one in a hundred. I could have a baby of my own, a healthy baby. And then I wouldn't be alone.

No matter what the harpy says.

It's a crazy stupid idea. Mama Alice doesn't have to take care of me after I turn eighteen, and what would I do with a baby? I'll have to get a job. I'll have to get state help for the drugs. The drugs are expensive.

If I got pregnant now, I could have the baby before I turn eighteen. I'd have somebody who was just mine. Somebody who loved me.

How easy is it to get pregnant, anyway? Other girls don't seem to have any problem doing it by accident.

Or by "accident."

Except whoever it was, I would have to tell him I was pos. That's why I decided I would sign the purity pledge and all that. Because then I have a reason not to tell.

And they gave me a ring. Fashion statement.

You know how many girls actually keep that pledge? I was going to. I meant to. But not just keep it until I got married. I meant to keep it forever, and then I'd never have to tell anybody.

No, I was right the first time. I'd rather be alone than have to explain. Besides, if you're having a baby, you should have the baby for the baby, not for you.

Isn't that right, Mom?

The harpy has a kingdom.

It's a tiny kingdom. The kingdom's just the alley behind my building, but it has a throne (the Dumpster) and it has subjects (the winos) and it has me. I know the winos see the harpy. They talk to it sometimes. But it vanishes when the other building tenants come down, and it hides from the garbage men.

I wonder if harpies can fly.

It opens its wings sometimes when it's raining as if it wants to wash off the filth, or sometimes if it's mad at something. It hisses when it's mad like that, the only sound I've ever heard it make outside my head.

I guess if it can fly depends on if it's magic. Miss Rivera, my bio teacher sophomore year, said that after a certain size things couldn't lift themselves with wings anymore. It has to do with muscle strength and wingspan and gravity. And some big things can only fly if they can fall into flight, or get a *headwind*.

I never thought about it before. I wonder if the harpy's stuck in that alley. I wonder if it's too proud to ask for help.

I wonder if I should ask if it wants some anyway.

The harpy's big. But condors are big, too, and condors can fly. I don't know if the harpy is bigger than a condor. It's hard to tell from pictures, and it's not like you can walk up to a harpy with a tape measure and ask it to stick out a wing.

Well, maybe you could. But I wouldn't.

Wouldn't it be awful to have wings that didn't work? Wouldn't it be worse to have wings that do work, and not be able to use them?

After I visit the harpy at night, I go up to the apartment. When I let myself in the door to the kitchen, Mama Alice is sitting at the table with some mail open in front of her. She looks up at me and frowns, so I lock the door behind me and shoot the chain. Luis should be home by now, and I can hear music from his bedroom. He's fifteen now. I think it's been three days since I saw him.

I come over and sit down in my work clothes on the metal chair with the cracked vinyl seat.

"Bad news?"

Mama Alice shakes her head, but her eyes are shiny. I reach out and grab her hand. The folded up paper in her fingers crinkles.

"What is it, then?"

She pushes the paper at me. "Desiree. You got the scholarship."

I don't hear her right the first time. I look at her, at our hands, and the rumply paper. She shoves the letter into my hand and I unfold it, open in, read it three times as if the words will change like crawly worms when I'm not looking at it.

The words are crawly worms, all watery, but I can see *hardship* and *merit* and *State*. I fold it up carefully, smoothing out the crinkles with my fingertips. It says I can be anything at all.

I'm going to college on a scholarship. Just state school.

I'm going to college because I worked hard. And because the State knows I'm full of poison, and they feel bad for me.

The harpy never lies to me, and neither does Mama Alice.

She comes into my room later that night and sits down on the edge of my bed, with is just a folded-out sofa with springs that poke me, but it's mine and better than nothing. I hide the letter under the pillow before she turns on the light, so she won't catch on that I was hugging it.

"Desiree," she says.

I nod and wait for the rest of it.

"You know," she says, "I might be able to get the State to pay for liposuction. Doctor Morales will say it's medically necessary."

"Liposuction?" I grope my ugly plastic glasses off the end table, because I need to see her. I'm frowning so hard they pinch my nose.

"For the hump," she says, and touches her neck, like she had one too. "So you could stand up straight again. Like you did when you were little."

Now I wish I hadn't put the glasses on. I have to look down at my hands. The fingertips are all smudged from the toner on the letter. "Mama Alice," I say, and then something comes out I never meant to ask her. "How come you never adopted me?"

She jerks like I stuck her with a fork. "Because I thought . . . " She stops, shakes her head, and spreads her hands.

I nod. I asked, but I know. Because the state pays for my medicine. Because Mama Alice thought I would be dead by now.

We were all supposed to be dead by now. All the HIV babies. Two years, maybe five. AIDS kills little kids really quick, because their immune systems haven't really happened yet. But the drugs got better as our lives got longer, and now we might live forever. Nearly forever.

Forty. *Fifty.*

I'm dying. Just not fast enough. If it were faster, I'd have nothing to worry about. As it is, I'm going to have to figure out what I'm going to do with my life.

I touch the squishy pad of fat on my neck with my fingers, push it in until it dimples. It feels like it should keep the mark of my fingers, like Moon Mud, but when I stop touching it, it springs back like nothing happened at all.

I don't want to get to go to college because somebody feels bad for me. I don't want anybody's pity.

The next day, I go down to talk to the harpy.

I get up early and wash quick, pull on my tights and skirt and blouse and sweater. I don't have to work after school today, so I leave my uniform on the hanger behind the door.

But when I get outside, the first thing I hear is barking. Loud barking, lots of it, from the alley. And that hiss, the harpy's hiss. Like the biggest maddest cat you ever heard.

There's junk all over the street, but nothing that looks like I could fight with it. I grab up some hunks of ice. My school shoes skip on the frozen sidewalk and I tear my tights when I fall down.

It's dark in the alley, but it's city dark, not real dark, and I can see the dogs okay. There's three of them, dancing around the Dumpster on their hind legs. One's light colored enough that even in the dark I can see she's all scarred up from fighting, and the other two are dark.

The harpy leans forward on the edge of the Dumpster, wings fanned out like a cartoon eagle, head stuck out and jabbing at the dogs.

Silly thing doesn't know it doesn't have a beak, I think, and whip one of the ice rocks at the big light-colored dog. She yelps. Just then, the harpy sicks up over all three of the dogs.

Oh, God, the smell.

I guess it doesn't need a beak after all, because the dogs go from growling and snapping to yelping and running just like that. I slide my backpack off one shoulder and grab it by the strap in the hand that's not full of ice.

It's heavy and I could hit something, but I don't swing it in time to stop one of the dogs knocking into me as it bolts away. The puke splashes on my leg. It burns like scalding water through my tights.

I stop myself just before I slap at the burn. Because getting the puke on my glove and burning my hand too would just be smart like that. Instead, I scrub at it with the dirty ice in my other hand and run limping towards the harpy.

The harpy hears my steps and turns to hiss, eyes glaring like green torches, but when it sees who's there it pulls its head back. It settles its wings like a nun settling her skirts on a park bench, and gives me the same fishy glare.

Wash that leg with snow, the harpy says. Or with lots of water. It will help the burning.

"It's acid."

With what harpies eat, the harpy says, don't you think it would have to be?

I mean to say something clever back, but what gets out instead is, "Can you fly?"

As if in answer, the harpy spreads its vast bronze wings again. They stretch from one end of the Dumpster to the other, and overlap its length a little.

The harpy says, Do these look like flightless wings to you?

Why does it always answer a question with a question? I know kids like that, and it drives me crazy when they do it, too.

"No," I say. "But I've never seen you. Fly. I've never seen you fly."

The harpy closes its wings, very carefully. A wind still stirs my hair where it sticks out under my hat.

The harpy says, There's no wind in my kingdom. But I'm light now, I'm empty. If there were wind, if I could get higher—

I drop my pack beside the Dumpster. It has harpy puke on it now anyway. I'm not putting it on my back. "What if I carried you up?"

The harpy's wings flicker, as if it meant to spread them again. And then it settles back with narrowed eyes and shows me its snaggled teeth in a suspicious grin.

The harpy says, What's in it for you?

I say to the harpy, "You've been my friend."

The harpy stares at me, straight on like a person, not side to side like a bird. It stays quiet so long I think it wants me to leave, but a second before I step back it nods.

The harpy says, Carry me up the fire escape, then.

I have to clamber up on the Dumpster and pick the harpy up over my head to put it on the fire escape. It's heavy, all right, especially when I'm holding it up over my head so it can hop onto the railing. Then I have to jump up and catch the ladder, then swing my feet up like on the uneven bars in gym class.

That's the end of these tights. I'll have to find something to tell Mama Alice. Something that isn't exactly a lie.

Then we're both up on the landing, and I duck down so the stinking, heavy harpy can step onto my shoulder with her broken, filthy claws. I don't want to think about the infection I'll get if she scratches me. Hospital stay. IV antibiotics. But she balances there like riding shoulders is all she does for a living, her big scaly toes sinking into my fat pads so she's not pushing down on my bones.

I have to use both hands to pull myself up the fire escape, even though I left my backpack at the bottom. The harpy weighs more, and it seems to get heavier with every step. It's not any easier because I'm trying to tiptoe and not wake up the whole building.

I stop to rest on the landings, but by the time I get to the top one my calves shake like the mufflers on a Harley. I imagine them booming like that too, which makes me laugh. Kind of, as much as I can. I double over with my hands on the railing and the harpy hops off.

"Is this high enough?"

The harpy doesn't look at me. It faces out over the empty dark street. It spreads its wings. The harpy is right: I'm alone, I've always been alone. Alone and lonely.

And now it's also leaving me.

"I'm dying," I yell, just as it starts the downstroke. I'd never told anybody. Mama Alice had to tell me, when I was five, but *I* never told anybody.

The harpy rocks forward, beats its wings hard, and settles back on the railing. It cranks its head around on its twisty neck to stare at me.

"I have HIV," I say. I press my glove against the scar under my coat where I used to have a G-tube. When I was little.

The harpy nods and turns away again. The harpy says, I know.

It should surprise me that the harpy knows, but it doesn't. Harpies know things. Now that I think about it, I wonder if the harpy only loves me because I'm garbage. If it only wants me because my blood is poison. My scarf's come undone, and a button's broken on my new old winter coat.

It feels weird to say what I just said out loud, so I say it again. Trying to get used to the way the words feel in my mouth. "Harpy, I'm dying. Maybe not today or tomorrow. But probably before I should."

The harpy says, That's because you're not immortal.

I spread my hands, cold in the gloves. Well *duh*. "Take me with you."

The harpy says, I don't think you're strong enough to be a harpy.

"I'm strong enough for this." I take off my new old winter coat from the fire department and drop it on the fire escape. "I don't want to be alone any more."

The harpy says, If you come with me, you have to stop dying. And you have to stop living. And it won't make you less alone. You are human, and if you stay human your loneliness will pass, one way or the other. If you come with me, it's yours. Forever.

It's not just empty lungs making my head spin. I say, "I got into college."

The harpy says, It's a career path.

I say, "You're lonely too. At least I decided to be alone, because it was better."

The harpy says, I am a harpy.

"Mama Alice would say that God never gives us any burdens we can't carry."

The harpy says, Does she look you in the eye when she says that?

I say, "Take me with you."

The harpy smiles. A harpy's smile is an ugly thing, even seen edge-on. The harpy says, You do not have the power to make me not alone, Desiree.

It's the first time it's ever said my name. I didn't know it knew it. "You have sons and sisters and a lover, Celaeno. In the halls of the West Wind. How can you be lonely?"

The harpy turns over its shoulder and stares with green, green eyes. The harpy says, I never told you my name.

"Your name is Darkness. You told me it. You said you *wanted* me, Celaeno."

The cold hurts so much I can hardly talk. I step back and hug myself tight. Without the coat I'm cold, so cold my teeth buzz together like gears stripping, and hugging myself doesn't help.

I don't want to be like the harpy. The harpy is disgusting. It's *awful*.

The harpy says, And underneath the filth, I shine. I *salvage*. You choose to be alone? Here's your chance to prove yourself no liar.

I don't want to be like the harpy. But I don't want to be me any more, either. *I'm stuck living with myself.*

If I go with the harpy, I will be stuck living with myself *forever.*

The sky brightens. When the sunlight strikes the harpy, its filthy feathers will shine like metal. I can already see fingers of cloud rising across the horizon, black like cut paper against the paleness that will be dawn, not that you can ever see dawn behind the buildings. There's no rain or snow in the forecast, but the storm is coming.

I say, "You only want me because my blood is rotten. You only want me because I got thrown away."

I turn garbage into bronze, the harpy says. I turn rot into strength. If you came with me, you would have to be like me.

"Tell me it won't always be this hard."

I do not lie, child. What do you want?

I don't know my answer until I open my mouth and say it, but it's something I can't get from Mama Alice, and I can't get from a scholarship. "Magic."

The harpy rocks from foot to foot. I can't give you that, she says. You have to make it.

Downstairs, under my pillow, is a letter. Across town, behind brick walls, is a doctor who would write me another letter.

Just down the block in the church beside my school is a promise of maybe heaven, if I'm a good girl and I die.

Out there is the storm and the sunrise.

Mama Alice will worry, and I'm sorry. She doesn't deserve that. When I'm a harpy will I care? Will I care forever?

Under the humps and pads of fat across my shoulders, I imagine I can already feel the prickle of feathers.

I use my fingers to lift myself onto the railing and balance there in my school shoes on the rust and tricky ice, six stories up, looking down on the streetlights. I stretch out my arms.

And so what if I fall?

Elizabeth Bear *was born on the same day as Frodo and Bilbo Baggins, but in a different year. She lives in Connecticut, and her hobbies include rock climbing, cooking, kayaking, taking her giant ridiculous dog for long walks, playing some of the worst guitar ever heard, neglecting her garden, annoying her cat, and finding all sorts of things to do besides write. She is a recipient of several genre awards, including two Hugos and the Sturgeon. Her most recent novels are* Chill *(2010) and* By the Mountain Bound *(2009), and she is involved in an awesome ongoing narrative experiment at www.shadowunit.org.*

It's a very *real* story, isn't it?

Now, tell me again about how fantasy is about *escapism* . . .

LOWLAND SEA

SUZY McKEE CHARNAS

Miriam had been to Cannes twice before. The rush and glamour of the film festival had not long held her attention (she did not care for movies and knew the real nature of the people who made them too well for that magic to work), but from the windows of their festival hotel she could look out over the sea and daydream about sailing home, one boat against the inbound tide from northern Africa.

This was a foolish dream; no one went to Africa now—no one could be paid enough to go, not while the Red Sweat raged there (the film festival itself had been postponed this year till the end of summer on account of the epidemic). She'd read that vessels wallowing in from the south laden with refugees were regularly shot apart well offshore by European military boats, and the beaches were not only still closed but were closely patrolled for lucky swimmers, who were also disposed of on the spot.

Just foolish, really, not even a dream that her imagination could support beyond its opening scene. Supposing that she could survive long enough to actually make it home (and she knew she was a champion survivor), noth-ing would be left of her village, just as nothing, or very close to nothing, was left to her of her childhood self. It was eight years since she had been taken.

Bad years; until Victor had bought her. Her clan tattoos had caught his attention. Later, he had had them reproduced, in make-up, for his film, *Hearts of Light* (it was about African child-soldiers rallied by a brave, warm-hearted American adventurer—played by Victor himself—against Islamic terrorists).

She understood that he had been seduced by the righteous outlawry of buying a slave in the modern world—to free her, of course; it made him feel bold and virtuous. In fact, Victor was accustomed to buying people. Just since Miriam had known him, he had paid two Russian women to carry babies for him because his fourth wife was barren. He already had children but, edging toward sixty, he wanted new evidence of his potency.

Miriam was not surprised. Her own father had no doubt used the money he had been paid for her to buy yet another young wife to warm his cooling bed; that was a man's way. He was probably dead now or living in a refugee camp somewhere, along with all the sisters and brothers and aunties from his compound: wars, the Red Sweat, and fighting over the scraps would leave little behind.

She held no grudge: she had come to realize that her father had done her a favor by selling her. She had seen a young cousin driven away for witchcraft by his own father, after a newborn baby brother had sickened and died. A desperate family could thus be quickly rid of a mouth they could not feed.

Better still, Miriam had not yet undergone the ordeal of female circumcision when she was taken away. At first she had feared that it was for this reason that the men who bought her kept selling her on to others. But she had learned that this was just luck, in all its perverse strangeness, pressing her life into some sort of shape. Not a very good shape after her departure from home, but then good luck came again in the person of Victor, whose bed she had warmed till he grew tired of her. Then he hired her to care for his new babies, Kevin and Leif.

Twins were unlucky back home: there, one or both would immediately have been put out in the bush to die. But this, like so many other things, was different for all but the poorest of whites.

They were pretty babies; Kevin was a little fussy but full of lively energy and alertness that Miriam rejoiced to see. Victor's actress wife, Cameron, had no use for the boys (they were not hers, after all, not as these people reckoned such things). She had gladly left to Miriam the job of tending to them.

Not long afterward Victor had bought Krista, an Eastern European girl, who doted extravagantly on the two little boys and quickly took over their care. Victor hated to turn people out of his household (he thought of himself as a magnanimous man), so his chief assistant, Bulgarian Bob found a way to keep Miriam on. He gave her a neat little digital camera with which to keep a snapshot record of Victor's home life: she was to be a sort of documentarian of the domestic. It was Bulgarian Bob (as opposed to French Bob, Victor's head driver) who had noticed her interest in taking pictures during an early shoot of the twins.

B. Bob was like that: he noticed things, and he attended to them.

Miriam felt blessed. She knew herself to be plain next to the diet-sculpted, spa-pampered, surgery-perfected women in Victor's household, so she could hardly count on beauty to secure protection; nor had she any outstanding talent of the kind that these people valued. But with a camera like this Canon G9, you needed no special gift to take attractive family snapshots. It was certainly better than, say, becoming someone's lowly third wife, or being bonded for life to a wrinkled shrine-priest back home.

Krista said that B. Bob had been a gangster in Prague. This was certainly possible. Some men had a magic that could change them from any one thing into anything else: the magic was money. Victor's money had changed Miriam's status from that of an illegal slave to, of all wonderful things, that of a naturalized citizen of the U.S.A. (although whether her new papers could stand serious scrutiny she hoped never to have to find out). Thus she was cut off from her roots, floating in Victor's world.

Better not to think of that, though; better not to think painful thoughts.

Krista understood this (she understood a great deal without a lot of palaver). Yet Krista obstinately maintained a little shrine made of old photos, letters, and trinkets that she set up in a private corner wherever Victor's household went. Despite a grim period in Dutch and Belgian brothels, she retained a sweet naiveté. Miriam hoped that no bad luck would rub off on Krista from attending to the twins. Krista was an *East* European, which seemed to render a female person more than normally vulnerable to ill fortune.

Miriam had helped Krista to fit in with the others who surrounded Victor—the coaches, personal shoppers, arrangers, designers, bodyguards, publicists, therapists, drivers, cooks, secretaries, and hangers-on of all kinds. He was like a paramount chief with a great crowd of praise singers paid to flatter him, out-shouting similar mobs attending everyone significant in the film world. This world was little different from the worlds of Africa and Arabia that Miriam had known, although at first it had seemed frighteningly strange—so shiny, so fast-moving and raucous! But when you came right down to it here were the same swaggering, self-indulgent older men fighting off their younger competitors, and the same pretty girls they all sniffed after; and the lesser court folk, of course, including almost-invisible functionaries like Krista and Miriam.

One day, Miriam planned to leave. Her carefully tended savings were nothing compared to the fortunes these shiny people hoarded, wasted, and squabbled over; but she had almost enough for a quiet, comfortable life in some quiet, comfortable place. She knew how to live modestly and thought she might even sell some of her photographs once she left Victor's orbit.

It wasn't as if she yearned to run to one of the handsome African men she saw selling knock-off designer handbags and watches on the sidewalks of great European cities. Sometimes, at the sound of a familiar language from home, she imagined joining them—but those were poor men, always on the run from the local law. She could not give such a man power over her and her savings.

Not that having money made the world perfect: Miriam was a realist, like any survivor. She found it funny that, even for Victor's followers with their light minds and heavy pockets, contentment was not to be bought. Success itself eluded them, since they continually redefined it as that which they had not yet achieved.

Victor, for instance: the one thing he longed for but could not attain was praise for his film—his first effort as an actor-director.

"They hate me!" he cried, crushing another bad review and flinging it across the front room of their hotel suite, "because I have the balls to tackle grim reality! All they want is sex, explosions, and the new Brad Pitt! Anything but truth, they can't stand truth!"

Of course they couldn't stand it. No one could. Truth was the desperate lives of most ordinary people, lives often too hard to be borne; mere images on a screen could not make that an attractive spectacle. Miriam had known boys back home who thought they were "Rambo." Some had become killers, some had been become the killed: doped-up boys, slung about with guns and bullet-belts like carved fetish figures draped in strings of shells. Their short lives were not in the movies or like the movies.

On this subject as many others, however, Miriam kept her opinions to herself.

Hearts of Light was scorned at Cannes. Victor's current wife, Cameron, fled in tears from his sulks and rages. She stayed away for days, drowning her unhappiness at parties and pools and receptions.

Wealth, however, did have certain indispensable uses. Some years before Miriam had joined his household, Victor had bought the one thing that turned out to be essential: a white-walled mansion called La Bastide, set high on the side of a French valley only a day's drive from Cannes. This was to be his retreat from the chaos and crushing boredom of the cinema world, a place where he could recharge his creative energies (so said B. Bob).

When news came that three Sudanese had been found dead in Calabria, their skins crusted with a cracked glaze of blood, Victor had his six rented Mercedes loaded up with petrol and provisions. They drove out of Cannes before the next dawn. It had been hot on the Mediterranean shore. Inland was worse. Stubby planes droned across the sky trailing plumes of retardant and water that they dropped on fires in the hills.

Victor stood in the sunny courtyard of La Bastide and told everyone how lucky they were to have gotten away to this refuge before the road from Cannes became clogged with people fleeing the unnerving proximity of the Red Sweat.

"There's room for all of us here," he said (Miriam snapped pictures of his confident stance and broad, chiefly gestures). "Better yet, we're prepared and we're *safe*. These walls are thick and strong. I've got a rack of guns downstairs, and we know how to use them. We have plenty of food, and all the water we could want: a spring in the bedrock underneath us feeds sweet, clean water into a well right here inside the walls. And since I didn't have to store water, we have lots more of everything else!"

Oh, the drama; already, Miriam told Krista, he was making the movie of all this in his head.

Nor was he the only one. As the others went off to the quarters B. Bob assigned them, trailing an excited hubbub through the cool, shadowed spaces of the house, those who had brought their camcorders dug them out and began filming on the spot. Victor encouraged them, saying that this adventure must be recorded, that it would be a triumph of photojournalism for the future.

Privately he told Miriam, "It's just to keep them busy. I depend on your stills to capture the reality of all this. We'll have an exhibition later, maybe even a book. You've got a good eye, Miriam; and you've had experience with crisis in your part of the world, right?"

"La Bastide" meant "the country house" but the place seemed more imposing than that, standing tall, pale, and alone on a crag above the valley. The outer walls were thick, with stout wooden doors and window-shutters as Victor had pointed out. He had had a wing added on to the back in matching stone. A small courtyard, the one containing the well, was enclosed by walls between the old and new buildings. Upstairs rooms had tall windows and sturdy iron balconies; those on the south side overlooked a French village three kilometers away down the valley.

Everyone had work to do—scripts to read, write, or revise, phone calls to make and take, deals to work out—but inevitably they drifted into the ground floor salon, the room with the biggest flat-screen TV. The TV stayed on. It showed raging wildfires. Any place could burn in summer, and it was summer most of the year now in southern Europe.

But most of the news was about the Red Sweat. Agitated people pointed and shouted, their expressions taut with urgency: "Looters came yesterday. Where are the police, the authorities?"

"We scour buildings for batteries, matches, canned goods."

"What can we do? They left us behind because we are old."

"We hear cats and dogs crying, shut in with no food or water. We let the cats out, but we are afraid of the dogs; packs already roam the streets."

Pictures showed bodies covered with crumpled sheets, curtains, bedspreads in many colors, laid out on sidewalks and in improvised morgues—the floors of school gyms, of churches, of automobile showrooms.

My God, they said, staring at the screen with wide eyes. Northern Italy now! So *close*!

Men carrying guns walked through deserted streets wearing bulky, outlandish protective clothing and facemasks. Trucks loaded with relief supplies waited for roads to become passable; survivors mobbed the trucks when they arrived. Dead creatures washed up on shorelines, some human, some not. Men in robes, suits, turbans, military uniforms, talked and talked and talked into microphones, reassuring, begging, accusing, weeping.

All this had been building for months, of course, but everyone in Cannes had been too busy to pay much attention. Even now at La Bastide they seldom talked about the news. They talked about movies. It was easier.

Miriam watched TV a lot. Sometimes she took pictures of the screen images. The only thing that could make her look away was a shot of an uncovered body, dead or soon to be so, with a film of blood dulling the skin.

On Victor's orders, they all ate in the smaller salon, without a TV.

On the third night, Krista asked, "What will we eat when this is all gone?"

"I got boxes of that paté months go." Bulgarian Bob smiled and stood back with his arms folded, like a waiter in a posh restaurant. "Don't worry, there's plenty more."

"My man," said Victor, digging into his smoked Norwegian salmon.

Next day, taking their breakfast coffee out on the terrace, they saw military vehicles grinding past on the roadway below. Relief convoys were being intercepted now, the news had said, attacked and looted.

"Don't worry, little Mi," B. Bob said, as she took snaps of the camouflage-painted trucks from the terrace. "Victor bought this place and fixed it up in the Iranian crisis. He thought we had more war coming. We're set for a year, two years."

Miriam grimaced. "Where food was stored in my country, that is where gunmen came to steal," she said.

B. Bob took her on a tour of the marvelous security at La Bastide, all controlled from a complicated computer console in the master suite: the heavy steel-mesh gates that could be slammed down, the metal window shutters, the ventilation ducts with their electrified outside grills.

"But if the electricity goes off?" she asked.

He smiled. "We have our own generators here."

After dinner that night Walter entertained them. Hired as Victor's Tae Kwan Do coach, he turned out to be a conservatory-trained baritone.

"No more opera," Victor said, waving away an aria. "Old country songs for an old country house. Give us some ballads, Walter!"

Walter sang "Parsley Sage," "Barbara Ellen," and "The Golden Vanity."

This last made Miriam's eyes smart. It told of a young cabin boy who volunteered to swim from an outgunned warship to the enemy vessel and sink it, single-handed, with an augur; but his Captain would not to let him back on board afterward. Rather than hole that ship too and so drown not just the evil Captain but his own innocent shipmates, the cabin boy drowned himself: "He sank into the lowland, low and lonesome, sank into the lowland sea."

Victor applauded. "Great, Walter, thanks! You're off the hook now, that's enough gloom and doom. Tragedy tomorrow—comedy tonight!"

They followed him into the library, which had been fitted out with a big movie screen and computers with game consoles. They settled down to watch Marx Brothers movies and old romantic comedies from the extensive film library of La Bastide. The bodyguards stayed up late, playing computer games full of mayhem. They grinned for Miriam's camera lens.

In the hot and hazy afternoon next day, a green mini-Hummer appeared on the highway. Miriam and Krista, bored by a general discussion about which gangster movie had the most swear words, were sitting on the terrace painting each other's toenails. The Hummer turned off the roadway, came up the hill, and stopped at La Bastide's front gates. A man in jeans, sandals, and a white shirt stepped out on the driver's side.

It was Paul, a writer hired to ghost Victor's autobiography. The hot, cindery wind billowed his sleeve as he raised a hand to shade his eyes.

"Hi, girls!" he called. "We made it! We actually had to go off-road, you wouldn't believe the traffic around the larger towns! Where's Victor?"

Bulgarian Bob came up beside them and stood looking down.

"Hey, Paul," he said. "Victor's sleeping; big party last night. What can we do for you?"

"Open the gates, of course! We've been driving for hours!"

"From Cannes?"

"Of course from Cannes!" cried Paul heartily. "Some Peruvian genius won the Palme D'Or, can you believe it? But maybe you haven't heard—the jury made a special prize for *Hearts of Light*. We have the trophy with us—Cammie's been holding it all the way from Cannes."

Cameron jumped out of the car and held up something bulky wrapped in a towel. She wore party clothes: a sparkly green dress and chunky sandals that laced high on her plump calves. Miriam's own thin, straight legs shook a little with the relief of being up here, on the terrace, and not down there at the gates.

Bulgarian Bob put his big hand gently over the lens of her camera. "Not this," he murmured.

Cameron waved energetically and called B. Bob's name, and Miriam's, and even Krista's (everyone knew that she hated Krista).

Paul stood quietly, staring up. Miriam had to look away.

B. Bob called, "Victor will be very happy about the prize."

Krista whispered, "He looks for blood on their skin; it's too far to see, though, from up here." To Bob she said, "I should go tell Victor?"

B. Bob shook his head. "He won't want to know."

He turned and went back inside without another word. Miriam and Krista took their bottles of polish and their tissues and followed.

Victor (and, therefore, everyone else) turned a deaf ear to the pleas, threats, and wails from out front for the next two days. A designated "security team" made up of bodyguards and mechanics went around making sure that La Bastide was locked up tight.

Victor sat rocking on a couch, eyes puffy. "My God, I hate this; but they were too slow. *They could be carrying the disease.* We have a responsibility to protect ourselves."

Next morning the Hummer and its two occupants had gone.

Television channels went to only a few hours a day, carrying reports of the Red Sweat in Paris, Istanbul, Barcelona. Nato troops herded people into make-shift "emergency" camps: schools, government buildings, and of course that trusty standby of imprisonment and death, sports arenas.

The radio and news sites on the Web said more: refugees were on the move everywhere. The initial panicky convulsion of flight was over, but smaller groups were reported rushing this way and that all over the continent. In Eastern Europe, officials were holed up in mountain monasteries and castles, trying to subsist on wild game. Urbanites huddled in the underground malls of Canadian cities. When the Red Sweat made its lurid appearance in Montreal, it set off a stampede for the countryside.

They said monkeys carried it; marmots; stray dogs; stray people. Ravens, those eager devourers of corpses, must carry the disease on their claws and beaks, or they spread it in their droppings. So people shot at birds, dogs, rodents, and other people.

Krista prayed regularly to two little wooden icons she kept with her. Miriam had been raised pagan with a Christian gloss. She did not pray. God had never seemed further away.

After a screaming fight over the disappearance of somebody's stash of E, a sweep by the security squad netted a hoard of drugs. These were locked up, to be dispensed only by Bulgarian Bob at set times.

"We have plenty of food and water," Victor explained, "but not an endless supply of drugs. We don't want to run through it all before this ends, do we?" In compensation he was generous with alcohol, with which La Bastide's cellar was plentifully stocked. When his masseuse (she was diabetic) and one of the drivers insisted on leaving to fend for themselves and their personal requirements outside, Victor did not object.

Miriam had not expected a man who had only ever had to act like a leader onscreen to exercise authority so naturally in real life.

It helped that his people were not in a rebellious mood. They stayed in their rooms playing cards, sleeping, some even reading old novels from the shelves under the window seats downstairs. A running game of trivia went on in the games room ("Which actors have played which major roles in green body make-up?"). People used their cell phones to call each other in different parts of the building, since calls to the outside tended not to connect (when they did, conversations were not encouraging).

Nothing appeared on the television now except muay thai matches from Thailand, but the radio still worked: "Fires destroyed the main hospital in Marseilles; fire brigades did not respond. Refugees from the countryside who were sheltering inside are believed dead."

"Students and teachers at the university at Bologna broke into the city offices but found none of the food and supplies rumored to be stored there."

Electricity was failing now over many areas. Victor decreed that they must only turn on the modern security system at night. During daylight hours they used the heavy old locks and bolts on the thick outer doors. B. Bob posted armed lookouts on the terrace and on the roof of the back wing. Cell phones were collected, to stop them being recharged to no good purpose.

But the diesel fuel for Victor's vastly expensive, vastly efficient German generators suddenly ran out (it appeared that the caretaker of La Bastide had sold off much of it during the previous winter). The ground floor metal shutters that had been locked in place by electronic order at nightfall could not be reopened.

Unexpectedly, Victor's crew seemed glad to be shut in more securely. They moved most activities to the upper floor of the front wing, avoiding the shuttered darkness downstairs. They went to bed earlier to conserve candles. They partied in the dark.

The electric pumps had stopped, but an old hand-pump at the basement laundry tubs was rigged to draw water from the well into the pipes in the house. They tore up part of the well yard in the process, getting dust everywhere, but in the end they even got a battered old boiler working over a wood-fire in the basement. A bath rota was eagerly subscribed to, although Alicia, the wig-girl, was forbidden to use hot water to bathe her Yorkie any more.

Victor rallied his troops that evening. He was not a tall man but he was energetic and his big, handsome face radiated confidence and determination. "Look at us—we're movie people, spinners of dreams that ordinary people pay money to share! Who needs a screening room, computers, TV? We can entertain ourselves, or we shouldn't be here!"

Sickly grins all around, but they rose at once to his challenge.

They put on skits, plays, take-offs of popular TV shows. They even had concerts, since several people could play piano or guitar well and Walter was not the only one with a good singing voice. Someone found a violin in a display case downstairs, but no one knew how to play that. Krista and the youngest of the cooks told fortunes, using tea leaves and playing cards from the game room. The fortunes were all fabulous.

Miriam did not think about the future. She occupied herself taking pictures. One of the camera men reminded her that there would be no more recharging of batteries now; if she turned off the LCD screen on the Canon G9 its picture-taking capacity would last longer. Most of the camcorders were already dead from profligate over-use.

It was always noisy after sunset now; people fought back this way against the darkness outside the walls of La Bastide. Miriam made earplugs out of candle wax and locked her bedroom door at night. On an evening of lively revels (it was Walter's birthday party) she quietly got hold of all the keys to her room that she knew of, including one from Bulgarian Bob's set. B. Bob was busy at the time with one of the drivers, as they groped each other urgently on the second floor landing.

There was more sex now, and more tension. Fistfights erupted over a card game, an edgy joke, the misplacement of someone's plastic water bottle. Victor had Security drag one pair of scuffling men apart and hustle them into the courtyard.

"What's this about?" he demanded.

Skip Reiker panted, "He was boasting about some Rachman al Haj concert he went to! That guy is a goddamn A-rab, a crazy damn Muslim!'

"Bullshit!" Sam Landry muttered, rubbing at a red patch on his cheek. "Music is music."

"Where did the god damned Sweat start, jerk? Africa!" Skip yelled. "The ragheads passed it around among themselves for years, and then they decided to share it. How do you think it spread to Europe? They brought it here on purpose, poisoning the food and water with their contaminated spit and blood. Who could do that better than musicians 'on tour'?"

"Asshole!" hissed Sam. "That's what they said about the Jews during the Black Plague, that they'd poisoned village wells! What are you, a Nazi?"

"Fucker!" Skip screamed.

Miriam guessed it was withdrawal that had him so raw; coke supplies were running low, and many people were having a bad time of it.

Victor ordered Bulgarian Bob to open the front gates.

"Quit it, right now, both of you," Victor said, "or take it outside."

Everyone stared out at the dusty row of cars, the rough lawn, and the trees shading the weedy driveway as it corkscrewed downhill toward the paved road below. The combatants slunk off, one to his bed and the other to the kitchen to get his bruises seen to.

Jill, Cameron's hair stylist, pouted as B. Bob pushed the heavy front gates shut again. "Bummer! We could have watched from the roof, like at a joust."

B. Bob said, "They wouldn't have gone out. They know Victor won't let them back in."

"Why not?" said the girl. "Who's even alive out there to catch the Sweat from anymore?"

"You never know." B. Bob slammed the big bolts home. Then he caught Jill around her pale midriff, made mock-growling noises, and swept her back into the house. B. Bob was good at smoothing ruffled feathers. He needed to be. Tensions escalated. It occurred to Miriam that someone at La Bastide might attack her, just for being from the continent on which the disease had first appeared. Mike Bellows, a black script doctor from Chicago, had vanished the weekend before; climbed the wall and ran away, they said.

Miriam saw how Skip Reiker, a film editor with no film to edit now, stared at her when he thought she wasn't looking. She had never liked Mike Bellows, who was an arrogant and impatient man; perhaps Skip had liked him even less, and had made him disappear.

What she needed, she thought, was to find some passage for herself, some unwatched door to the outside, that she could use to slip away if things turned bad here. That was how a survivor must think. So far, the ease of life at La Bastide—the plentiful food and sunshine, the wine from the cellars, the scavenger hunts and skits, the games in the big salon, the fancy-dress parties—had bled off the worst of people's edginess. Everyone, so far, accepted Victor's rules. They knew that he was their bulwark against anarchy.

But: Victor had only as much authority as he had willing obedience. Food rationing, always a dangerous move, was inevitable. The ultimate loyalty of these bought-and-paid-for friends and attendants would be to themselves (except maybe for Bulgarian Bob, who seemed to really love Victor).

Only Jeff, one of the drivers, went outside now, tinkering for hours with the engines of the row of parked cars. One morning Miriam and Krista sat on the front steps in the sun, watching him.

"Look," Krista whispered, tugging at Miriam's sleeve with anxious, pecking fingers. Down near the roadway a dozen dogs, some with chains or leads dragging from their collars, harried a running figure across a field of withered vines in a soundless pantomime of hunting.

They both stood up, exclaiming. Jeff looked where they were looking. He grabbed up his tools and herded them both back inside with him. The front gates stayed closed after that.

Next morning Miriam saw the dogs again, from her balcony. At the foot of the driveway they snarled and scuffled, pulling and tugging at something too mangled and filthy to identify. She did not tell Krista, but perhaps someone else saw too and spread the word (there was a shortage of news in La Bastide these days, as even radio signals had become rare).

Searching for toothpaste, Miriam found Krista crying in her room. "That was Tommy Mullroy," Krista sobbed, "that boy that wanted to make computer games from movies. He was the one with those dogs."

Tommy Mullroy, a minor hanger-on and a late riser by habit, hadn't made it to the cars on the morning of Victor' hasty retreat from Cannes. Miriam was doubtful that Tommy could have found his way across the plague-stricken landscape to La Bastide on his own, and after so much time.

"How could you tell, from so far?" Miriam sat down beside her on the bed and stroked Krista's hand. "I didn't know you liked him."

"No, no, I hate that horrible monkey-boy!" Krista cried, shaking her head furiously. "Bad jokes, and pinching! But now he is dead." She buried her face in her pillow.

Miriam did not think the man chased by dogs had been Tommy Mullroy, but why argue? There was plenty to cry about in any case.

Winter had still not come; the cordwood stored to feed the building's six fireplaces was still stacked high against the courtyard walls. Since they had plenty of water everyone used a lot of it, heated in the old boiler. Every day a load of wood ash had to be dumped out of the side gate.

Miriam and Krista took their turns at this chore together.

They stood a while (in spite of the reeking garbage overflowing the alley outside, as no one came to take it away any more). The road below was empty today. Up close, Krista smelled of perspiration and liquor. Some in the house were becoming neglectful of themselves.

"My mother would use this ash for making soap," Krista said, "but you need also—what is it? Lime?"

Miriam said, "What will they do when all the soap is gone?"

Krista laughed. "Riots! Me, too. When I was kid, I thought luxury was change bedsheets every day for fresh." Then she turned to Miriam with wide eyes and whispered, "We must go away from here, Mimi. They have no Red Sweat in my country for sure! People are farmers, villagers, they live healthy, outside the cities! We can go there and be safe."

"More safe than in here?" Miriam shook her head. "Go in, Krista, Victor's little boys must be crying for you. I'll come with you and take some pictures."

The silence outside the walls was a heavy presence, bitter with drifting smoke that tasted harsh; some of the big new villas up the valley, built with expensive synthetic materials, smoldered slowly for days once they caught fire. Now and then thick smoke became visible much further away. Someone would say, "There's a fire to the west," and everyone would go out on the terrace to watch until the smoke died down or was drifted away out of sight on the wind. They saw no planes and no troop transports now. Dead bodies appeared on the road from time to time, their presence signaled by crows calling others to the feast.

Miriam noticed that the crows did not chase others of their kind away but announced good pickings far and wide. Maybe that worked well if you were a bird.

A day came when Krista confided in a panic that one of the twins was ill.

"You must tell Victor," Miriam said, holding the back of her hand to the forehead of Kevin, who whimpered. "This child has fever."

"I can't say anything! He is so scared of the Sweat, he'll throw the child outside!"

"His own little boy?" Miriam thought of the village man who drove out his son as a witch. "That's just foolishness," she told Krista; but she knew better, having known worse.

Neither of them said anything about it to Victor. Two days later, Krista jumped from the terrace with Kevin's small body clutched to her chest. Through tears, Miriam aimed her camera down and took a picture of the slack, twisted jumble of the two of them. They were left there on the driveway gravel with its fuzz of weeds and, soon after, its busy crows.

The days grew shorter. Victor's crowd partied every night, never mind about the candles. Bulgarian Bob slept on a cot in Victor's bedroom, with a gun in his hand: another thing that everyone knew but nobody talked about.

On a damp and cloudy morning Victor found Miriam in the nursery with little Leif, who was on the floor playing with a dozen empty medicine bottles. Leif played very quietly and did not look up. Victor touched the child's head briefly and then sat down across the table from Miriam, where Krista used to sit. He was so cleanshaven that his cheeks gleamed. He was sweating.

"Miriam, my dear," he said, "I need a great favor. Walter saw lights last night in the village. The army must have arrived, at long last. They'll have medicine. They'll have news. Will you go down and speak with them? I'd go myself, but everyone depends on me here to keep up some discipline, some hope. We can't have more people giving up, like Krista."

"I'm taking care of Leif now—" Miriam began faintly.

"Oh, Cammie can do that."

Miriam quickly looked away from him, her heart beating hard. Did he really believe that he had taken his current wife into La Bastide after all, in her spangly green party dress?

"This is so important," he urged, leaning closer and blinking his large, blue eyes in the way that (B. Bob always said) the camera loved. "There's a very, very large bonus in it for you, Miriam, enough to set you up very well on your own when this is all over. I can't ask anyone else, I wouldn't trust them to come back safe and sound. But you, you're so levelheaded and you've had experience of bad times, not like some of these spoiled, silly people here. Things must have gotten better outside, but how would we know, shut up in here? Everyone agrees: we need you to do this.

"The contagion must have died down by now," he coaxed. "We haven't seen movement outside in days. Everyone has gone, or holed up, like us. Soldiers wouldn't be in the village if it was still dangerous down there."

Just yesterday Miriam had seen a lone rider on a squeaky bicycle peddling down the highway. But she heard what Victor was *not* saying: that he needed to be able to convince others to go outside, convince them that it was safe, as the more crucial supplies (dope, toilet paper) dwindled; that he controlled those supplies; that he could, after all, have her put out by force.

Listening to the *tink* of the bottles in Leif's little hands, she realized that she could hardly wait to get away; in fact, she *had* to go. She would find amazing prizes, bring back news, and they would all be so grateful that she would be safe here forever. She would make up good news if she had to, to please them; to keep her place here, inside La Bastide.

But for now, go she must.

Bulgarian Bob found her sitting in dazed silence on the edge of her bed.

"Don't worry, Little Mi," he said. "I'm very sorry about Krista. I'll look out for your interest here."

"Thank you," she said, not looking him in the eyes. *Everyone agrees*. It was hard to think; her mind kept jumping.

"Take your camera with you," he said. "It's still working, yes? You've been sparing with it, smarter than some of these idiots. Here's a fresh card for it, just in case. We need to see how it is out there now. We can't print anything, of course, but we can look at your snaps on the LCD when you get back."

The evening's feast was dedicated to "our intrepid scout Miriam." Eyes glittering, the beautiful people of Victor's court toasted her (and, of course, their own good luck in not having been chosen to venture outside). Then they began a boisterous game: who could remember accurately the greatest number of deaths in the *Final Destination* movies, with details?

To Miriam, they looked like crazy witches, cannibals, in the candlelight. She could hardly wait to leave.

Victor himself came to see her off early in the morning. He gave her a bottle of water, a ham sandwich, and some dried apricots to put in her red ripstop knapsack. "I'll be worrying my head off until you get back!" he said.

She turned away from him and looked at the driveway, at the dust-coated cars squatting on their flattened tires, and the shrunken, darkened body of Krista.

"You know what to look for," Victor said. "Matches. Soldiers. Tools, candles; you know."

The likelihood of finding anything valuable was small (and she would go out of her way *not* to find soldiers). But when he gave her shoulder a propulsive pat, she started down the driveway like a wind-up toy.

Fat dogs dodged away when they saw her coming. She picked up some stones to throw but did not need them.

She walked past the abandoned farmhouses and vacation homes on the valley's upper reaches, and then the village buildings, some burned and some spared; the empty vehicles, dead as fossils; the remains of human beings. Being sold away, she had been spared such sights back home. She had not seen for herself the corpses in sun-faded shirts and dresses, the grass blades growing up into empty eye sockets, that others had photographed there. Now she paused to take her own carefully chosen, precious pictures.

There were only a few bodies in the streets. Most people had died indoors, hiding from death. Why had her life bothered to bring her such a long way round, only to arrive where she would have been anyway had she remained at home?

Breezes ruffled weeds and trash, lifted dusty hair and rags fluttering from grimy bones, and made the occasional loose shutter or door creak as it swung. A few cows—too skittish now to fall easily to roaming dog packs—grazed watchfully on the plantings around the village fountain, which still dribbled dispiritedly.

If there were ghosts, they did not show themselves to her.

She looked into deserted shops and houses, gathering stray bits of paper, candle stubs, tinned food, ballpoint pens. She took old magazines from a beauty salon, two paperback novels from a deserted coffee house. Venturing into a wine shop got her a cut on the ankle: the place had been smashed to smithereens. Others had come here before her, like that dead man curled up beside the till.

In a desk drawer she found a chocolate bar. She ate it as she headed back up the valley, walking through empty fields to skirt the village this time. The chocolate was crumbly and dry and dizzyingly delicious.

When she arrived at the gates of La Bastide, the men on watch sent word to Bulgarian Bob. He stood at the iron balustrade above her and called down questions: What had she seen, where exactly had she gone, had she entered the buildings, seen anyone alive?

"Where is Victor?" Miriam asked, her mouth suddenly very dry.

"I'll tell you what; you wait down there till morning," Bulgarian Bob said. "We must be sure you don't have the contagion, Miriam. You know."

Miriam, not Little Mi. Her heart drummed painfully. She felt injected into her own memory of Cammie and Paul standing here, pleading to come in. Only now she was looking up at the wall of La Bastide, not down from the terrace.

Sitting on the bonnet of one of one of the cars, she stirred her memory and dredged up old prayers to speak or sing softly into the dusk. Smells of food cooking and wood smoke wafted down to her. Once, late, she heard squabbling voices at a second floor window. No doubt they were discussing who would be sent out the next time Victor wanted news of the world and one less mouth to feed.

In the morning, she held up her arms for inspection. She took off her blouse and showed them her bare back.

"I'm sorry, Miriam," Victor called down to her. His face was full of compassion. "I think I see a rash on your shoulders. It may be nothing, but you must understand—at least for now, we can't let you in. I really do want to see your pictures, though. You haven't used up all your camera's battery power, have you? We'll lower a basket for it."

"I haven't finished taking pictures," she said. She aimed the lens up at him. He quickly stepped back out of sight. Through the viewfinder she saw only the parapet of the terrace and the empty sky.

She flung the camera into the ravine, panting with rage and terror as she watched it spin on its way down, compact and clever and useless.

Then she sat down and thought.

Even if she found a way back in, if they thought she was infected they would drive her out again, maybe just shoot her. She imagined Skip Reiker throwing a carpet over her dead body, rolling her up in it, and heaving her outside the walls like rubbish. The rest of them would not approve, but anger and fear would enable their worst impulses ("See what you made us do!").

She should have thought more before, about how she was a supernumerary here, acquired but not really *needed*, not *talented* as these people reckoned such things; not important to the tribe.

"Have I have stopped being a survivor?" she asked Krista's withered back.

In the house Walter was singing. "Some Enchanted Evening!" Applause. Then, "The Golden Vanity."

Miriam sat with her back against the outside wall, burning with fear, confusion, and scalding self-reproach.

When the sun rose again she saw a rash of dark blisters on the backs of her hands. She felt more of them rising at her hairline, around her face. Her joints ached. She was stunned: Victor was right. It was the Red Sweat. But how had she caught it? Through something she had touched—a doorknob, a book, a slicing shard of glass? By merely breathing the infected air?

Maybe—the *chocolate*? The idea made her sob with laughter.

They wouldn't care one way or the other. She was already dead to them. She knew they would not even venture out to take her backpack, full of scavenged treasures, when she was dead (she threw its contents down the ravine after the camera, to make sure). She'd been foolish to have trusted Bulgarian Bob, or Victor either.

They had never intended to let the dove back into the ark.

She knelt beside Krista's corpse and made herself search the folds of reeking, sticky clothing until she found Krista's key to the rubbish gate, the key they had used to throw out the ashes. She sat on the ground beside Krista and rubbed the key bright on her own pant-leg.

Let them try to keep her out. Let them try.

Krista was my shipmate. Now I have no shipmates.

At moonrise she shrugged her aching arms through the straps of the empty pack and walked slowly around to the side alley gate. Krista's key clicked minutely in the lock. The door sprang outward, releasing more garbage that had been piled up inside. No one seemed to hear. They were roaring with song in the front wing and drumming on the furniture, to drown out the cries and pleadings they expected to hear from her.

Miriam stepped inside the well yard, swallowing bloody mucus. She felt the paving lurch a little under her.

A man was talking in the kitchen passageway, set into the ground floor of the back wing at an oblique angle across the well yard. She thought it was Edouard, a camera tech, pretending to speak on his cell as he sometimes did to keep himself company when he was on his own. Edouard, as part of Security, carried a gun.

Her head cleared suddenly. She found that she had shut the gate behind her, and had slid down against the inside wall, for she was sitting on the cool pavement. Perhaps she had passed out for a little. By the moon's light she saw the well's raised stone lip, only a short way along the wall to her left. She was thirsty, although she did not think she could force water down her swollen throat now.

The paving stones the men had pried up in their work on the plumbing had not been reset. They were still piled up out of the way, very near where she sat.

Stones, water. Her brain was so clogged with hot heaviness that she could barely hold her head up.

"Non, non!" Edouard shouted. "Ce n'est pas vrai, ils sont menteurs, tous!"

Yes, all of them; menteurs. She sympathized, briefly.

Her mind kept tilting and spilling all its thoughts into a turgid jumble, but there were constants: *stones. Water.* The exiled dove, the brave cabin boy. Krista and little Kevin. She made herself move, trusting to the existence of an actual plan somewhere in her mind. She crawled over to the stacked pavers. Slowly and with difficulty she took off her backpack and stuffed it with some of the smaller stones, one by one. Blood beaded black around her fingernails. She had no strength to pull the loaded pack onto her back again, so she hung it from her shoulder by one broad strap, and began making her painful way toward the well itself.

Edouard was deep in his imaginary quarrel. As she crept along the wall she heard his voice echo angrily in the vaulted passageway.

The thick wooden well cover had been replaced with a lightweight metal sheet, back when they had had to haul water by hand before the old laundry pump was reconnected. She lifted the light metal sheet and set it aside. Dragging herself up, she leaned over the low parapet and peered down.

She could not make out the stone steps that descended into the water on the inside wall, left over from a time when the well had been used to hide contraband. Now . . . something. Her thoughts swam.

Focus.

Even without her camera there was a way to bring home to Victor all the reality he had sent her out to capture for him in pictures.

She could barely shift her legs over the edge, but at last she felt the cold roughness of the top step under her feet. She descended toward the water, using the friction of her spread hands, turning her torso flat against the curved wall like a figure in an Egyptian tomb painting. The water winked up at her, glossy with reflected moonlight. The backpack, painful with hard stone edges, dragged at her aching shoulder. She paused to raise one strap and put her head through it; she must not lose her anchor now.

The water's chill lapped at her skin, sucking away her last bit of strength. She sagged out from the wall and slipped under the surface. Her hands and feet scrabbled dreamily at the slippery wall and the steps, but down she sank anyway, pulled by the bag of stones strapped to her body.

Her chest was shot through with agony, but her mind clung with bitter pleasure to the fact that in the morning all of Victor's tribe would wash themselves and brush their teeth and swallow their pills down with the water Victor was so proud of, water pumped by willing hands from his own wonderful well.

Head craned back, she saw that dawn pallor had begun to flush the small circle of sky receding above her. Against that light, black curls of the blood that her body wept from every seam and pore feathered out in secret silence, into the cool, delicious water.

Suzy McKee Charnas *is the author of over a dozen works of science fiction, fantasy, and horror. Her novels include the The Vampire Tapestry, the Holdfast series, and the Sorcery Hall series of books for young adults. A selection of her short fiction was collected in Stagestruck Vampires and Other Phantasms. She has been awarded a Hugo, a Nebula, and has won the James Tiptree, Jr. Award twice. Charnas took a joint major at Barnard College—Economic History—because she "wanted tools to build convincing societies to set fantastic stories in." She lives in New Mexico with her lawyer-husband.*

This finely crafted, beautifully executed story is one example of why "horror" is in the title of this book. There's no fantasy here. Not a whit of the supernatural. It may have been inspired by Edgar Allan Poe, but it steps into a speculative day-after-tomorrow that could most certainly happen.

COPPING SQUID

MICHAEL SHEA

Ricky Deuce, twenty-eight and three years sober, was the night clerk at Mahmoud's Mom and Pop Market. He was a small, leanly muscled guy, and as he sat there, the darkness outside deepening toward midnight, his tight little Irish face looked pleased with where he was. Behind Ricky on his stool, the whole wall was bottles of every kind of Hard known to man.

This job was easy money—a sit-down after his day forklifting at the warehouse. He already owned an awesomely restored sixty-four Mustang, and had near ten K saved, and by rights he ought to be casting around for where he might take off to next. But the fact was, he got a kick out of clerking here till two AM each night.

A kick that was not powder nor pill nor smoke nor booze, that was not needing any of them, especially not booze, which could shine and glint in its bottles and surround him all night long, and he not give a shit. He never got tired of sitting here immune, savoring the unadorned adventure of being alive.

Not that the job lacked irritants. There were obnoxious clientele, and these preponderated toward the deep of night.

Ricky thought he heard one even now.

Single cars shushed past outside, long silences falling between, and a scuffy tread advanced along the sidewalk. A purposeful tread that nonetheless staggered now and then. It reminded Ricky that he was It, the only island of comfort and light for a half a mile in all directions, in a big city, in the dead of night.

Then, there in Mahmoud's Mom and Pop Market's entryway, stood a big gaunt black guy. Youngish, but with a strange, outdated look, his hair growing weedily out towards a 'fro. His torso and half his legs were engulfed in an oversize nylon athletic jacket that looked like it might have slept in an alley or two, and which revealed the chest of a dark T-shirt that said something indecipherable RULES. The man had a drugged look, but he also had wide-arched, inquiring brows. His glossy black eyes checked you out, as if maybe the real him was somewhere back in there, smarter than he looked.

But then, as he lurched inside the store, and into the light, he just looked drunk.

"Evening," Ricky said smiling. He always opened by giving all his clientele the benefit of the doubt.

The man came and planted his hands of the counter, not aggressively, it seemed, but in the manner of someone tipsily presenting a formal proposition.

"Hi. I'm Andre. I need your money, man."

Ricky couldn't help laughing. "What a coincidence! So do I!"

"Okay, Bro," Andre said calmly, agreeably. As if he was shaping a counter-proposal, he straightened and stepped back from the counter. "Then I'ma cut your fuckin ass to *ribbons* till you *give* me your fuckin money!"

The odd picture this plan of action presented almost made Ricky laugh again, but then the guy whipped out and flipped open—with great expertise—a very large gravity knife, which he then swept around by way of threat, though still out of striking range. Ricky was so startled that he half fell off his stool.

Getting his legs under him, furious at having been galvanized like that, Ricky shrieked, "A knife? You're gonna to rob me with a fucking *knife*? *I've* got a fucking knife!"

And he unpocketed his lock-back Buck knife, and snapped it open. All this while he found himself once again trying to decipher the big, uncouthly lettered word on the guy's T-shirt above the word RULES.

Andre didn't seem drunk at all now. He swept a slash over the counter at Ricky's head, which Ricky had to recoil from right smartly.

"You shit! You do that again and I'm gonna slice your—"

Here came the gravity knife again, as quick as a shark, and, snapping his head back out of the way, Ricky counter-slashed at the sweeping arm, and felt the rubbery tug of flesh unzipped by the tip of his Buck's steel.

Andre abruptly stepped back and relaxed. He put his knife away, and held up his arm. It had a nice bloody slash across the inner forearm. He stood there letting it bleed for Ricky. Ricky had seen himself and others bleed, but not a black man. On black skin, he found, blood looked more opulent, a richer red, and so did the meat underneath the skin. That cut would take at least a dozen stitches. They both watched the blood soak the elastic cuff of Andre's jacket.

"So here's what it is," said Andre, and dipped his free hand in the jacket and pulled out a teensy, elegant little silver cellphone. "Ima call the oinkers, and say I need an ambulance because this mad whacked white shrimp—that's you—slashed me when I just axed him for some spare change, and then Ima ditch the shit outta this knife before they show up, and it won't matter if they believe me or not, when they see me bleedin like this they gonna take us both down for questioning and statements. How's your rap sheet, Chief, hey? So look. Just give me a little money and I'm totally outta your face. It don't have to be much. Ten dollars would do it!"

This took Ricky aback. "Ten dollars? You make me cut you for ten dollars?"

"You wanna give me a hundred, give me a hundred! Ten's all you gotta give me—and a ride. A short ride, over to the Hood."

"You want money and a ride! You think I'm outta my mind? You wanna ride to your connection to score, and when we get there, you're gonna try an get more money out of me. And that's the *best* case scenario." Ricky was dismayed to hear a hint of negotiation in his own words. It was true, he'd had a number of contacts with the San Francisco Police Department, as the result of alcohol-enhanced conflicts here and there. But also, he felt intrigued by the guy. Something fascinating burned in this Andre whack. Intensity came off him in waves, along with his faint scent of street-funk. The man was consumed by a passion. In the deformed letters on his T-shirt, Ricky thought he could make out a T-H-U.

"What could I be coppin for ten bucks?" crowed Andre. "I'm not out to harm you! This just has to do with *me*. See, it's *required*. I have to get these two things from someone else, the money and the ride."

"Explain that. Explain why you *have* to get these two things from someone else."

Andre didn't answer for a moment. He stared and stared, not exactly at Ricky, but at something he seemed to see in Ricky. He seemed to be weighing this thing he detected. He had eyes like black opals, and strange slow thoughts seemed to move within their shiny hemispheres . . .

"The reason is," he said at last, "that's the *procedure*. There are these particular rules for seeing the one I want to see."

"And who is that?"

"I can't tell you. I'm not allowed."

It was almost time to close up anyway. Ricky became aware of a powerful tug of curiosity, and aware of the fact that Andre saw it in his eyes. This put Ricky's back up.

"No. You gotta give me something. You gotta tell me at least—"

"Thassit! Fuck you!" And Andre flipped open the cellphone. His big spatulate fingertips made quick dainty movements on the minute keys. Ricky heard the bleep, minuscule but crystal clear, of the digits, and then a microvoice saying, "Nine-one-one emergency."

"I been stabbed by a punk in a liquor store! I been stabbed!"

Ricky violently shook his head, and held up his hands in surrender. With a bleep, Andre clicked off. "Believe me! You're not makin a mistake. It's something I can't talk about, but you can *see* it. You can see it yourself. But the thing is, it's got to be now. We can't hem an haw. And Ima tell you now, now that you're in, that there's something *in* it for you, something good as gold. Trust me, you'll see. Help me with this knot," he said, pulling a surprisingly clean looking handkerchief from his jacket pocket. He folded it—rather expertly, Ricky thought—into a bandage. Ricky wrapped it round the wound, and tied the ends in a neat, tight squareknot, feeling as his fingers pressed against flesh that he was forming a bond with this whack by stanching his blood. He was accepting a dangerous complicity with his whack aims, whatever they might be . . .

Bandaged, Andre held out his hand. Ricky put a ten in it.

"Thanks," said Andre. "So. Where's your ride?"

The blue Mustang boomed down Sixteenth through the Mission. All the signals were on blink. Here and there under the streetlights, there was a wino or two, or someone walking fast, shoulders hunched against the emptiness, but mostly the Mustang rolled through pure naked City, a vacant concrete stage.

Ricky liked driving around at this hour, and often did it on his own for fun. When he was a kid, he'd always felt sorcery in the midnight streets, in the mosaic of their lights, and he'd never lost the sense of unearthly shapes stirring beneath their web, stirring till they almost cohered, as the stars did for the ancients into constellations. Tonight, with mad, bleeding Andre riding shotgun, the lights glittered wilder possibilities, and a sinister grandeur seemed to lurk in them.

They passed under the freeway, and down to the Bayside, hanging south on Third. After long blocks of big blank buildings, Third took a snaky turn, and they were rolling through the Hood.

Pawn shops and thrift stores and liquor stores. A whiff of Mad Dog hung over it, Mad Dog with every other drug laced through it. The Hood was lit, was like a long jewel. The signals were working here.

The signals stretched out of sight ahead, like a python with scales of red and green, their radiance haloed in a light fog that was drifting in off the Bay. And people were out, little knots of them near the corners. They formed isolated clots of gaudy life, like tide pools, all of them dressed in baggy clothes of bright-colored nylon, paneled and logo-ed with surreal pastels under the emerald-and-ruby signal glare. And as they stood and talked together, they moved in a way both fitful and languid, like sealife bannering in a restless sea.

The signals changed in pattern to a slow tidal rhythm. It seemed a rhythm meant to accommodate rush-hour traffic. You got a green for two blocks max, and then you got a red. A long, long red. Ricky's blue Mustang was almost the only car on the road in this phantom rush-hour, creeping down the long bright python two blocks at a time, and then idling, idling interminably, while the sealife on the corners seemed astir with interest and attention.

Ricky had no qualms about running red lights on deserted streets, but here it seemed dangerous, a declaration of unease.

"Fuck this!" he said at their fourth red light, and slipped the brake, and rolled forward. At a stroll though, under twenty. The Mustang lounged along, taking green and red alike, as if upon a scenic country road. The bright languid people on the corners threw laughter at them now, a shout or two, and it seemed as if the whole great submarine python stirred to quicker currents. Ricky felt a ripple of hallucination, and saw here, for just a moment, a vast inked mural, the ink not dry, themselves and all around them still half-liquid entities billowing in an aqueous universe . . .

Out of nowhere, for the first time in three years, Ricky had the thought that he would like a drink. He was amazed at this thought. He was frightened. Then he was angry.

"I'm not drivin much farther, Andre. Spit out where we're going, and it better be nearby, or you can call nine-one-one and I'll take my chances. I'll bet you got a longer past with the SFPD than I do."

"*Damn* you! Whip in here, then."

This cross street was mostly houses—some abandoned—with a liquor store on the next corner, and a lot of sealife lounging out in front of it. "Pull up into some light where you can *see* this."

They idled at the curb. The people on the main drag were two-thirds of a block behind them, the liquor store tide pool much closer ahead of them. Andre leaned his fanatic's face close to Ricky. The intensity of the man was an almost tactile experience; Ricky seemed to feel the muffled crackling of his will through the inches of air that separated them. "Here," hissed Andre. "I'm gonna give you *this*, just to drive me another coupla miles up into these hills. Look at it. Count it. Take it." He shoved a thick roll of bills into Ricky's ribs.

It was in twenties and fifties and hundreds . . . It was over five thousand dollars.

"You're . . . you're batshit, Andre! You make me cut you to get ten bucks, and now you—"

"Just listen." Some people from the liquor store tide pool were drifting their way, and Ricky saw similar movement from Third Street in his rearview mirror. "What I needed," said Andre, "was money that blood was spilt for—it didn't matter how much blood, it didn't matter how much money. Your ten-spot? It's worth that much to me there in your hand. Your ten-spot and another couple miles in your car."

The locals were flowing closer to the Mustang at both ends. Ricky fingered the money. The gist of it was, he decided, that if he didn't follow this waking dream to its end, he would never forgive himself. "Okay," he said.

"Another couple miles in your car," said Andre, "an one more thing. You gotta come in."

"You fuck! You shit! Where does it *end* with you? You just keep—"

"You come in, you watch me connect, and you go out again, scott-free, no harm, no strings attached! I gotta bring blood money, and I gotta bring a *witness*. I lied to you. It wasn't the ride I needed. It was a *witness*."

A huge shape in lavender running-sweats, and a gaunt one wearing a lime-green jumpsuit, stood beside the Mustang, smiling and making roll-down-the-window gestures. Behind the car, shapes from the main drag were moving laterally out into the street to come up to the driver's side . . .

But in that poised moment what Ricky saw most vividly was Andre's face, his taut narrow face within its weedy 'fro. This man was in the visionary's trance. His eyes, his soul were locked upon something that filled him with awe. What he pursued had nothing to do with Ricky, nor with anything Ricky could imagine, and Ricky wanted to know what that thing was.

Andre said, "Ima show you—what's your name again?"

"Ricky."

"Ima show you, Richie, the power and the glory. They are right here *among* you, man, an you don't even see it! Hell, even these fools out here can *see* it!"

The Mustang was surrounded now. From behind it sprouted shapes in crimson hoods, with fists bulging inside gold velvet jacket pockets. Up to Ricky's door (its window already open, his elbow thrust out, and five K in cash on his lap) stepped two men with thundercloud hair, wearing shades, their cheeks and brows all whorled with Maori tattooing like ink-black flames. A trio of gaudy nylon scarecrows leaned on his hood, conferring, the side-thrust bills of their caps switching like blades. But Ricky also noted that all this audience, every one of them, had eyes strictly for Andre sitting there at his side. Ricky was free to scan all those exotic, piratical faces as though he were invisible . . .

All their eyes were grave. They showed awe, and they showed loathing too, as if they abhorred something Andre had done, but just as piercingly, longed for his nerve to do it. Ricky realized he had embarked on a longer journey than he'd thought.

Andre scanned all these buccaneer faces, his fellow mariners of the Hood. A remote little grin was hanging slantwise across his jaw. "Check this out Rocky," he growled, "an learn from these fools. Learn their *awe*, man, cause what I'ma show you, up in those hills, is *awe*."

He shouldered his door open, and thrust himself up onto the sidewalk. He towered just as tall as the giant in lavender sweats, but he was narrow as a reed. Yet his voice fairly boomed:

"Yo! Alla you! Listen up! Looka here! Looka me! You all wanna see something? Wanna see something *about* something besides *shit*!? See something *real*, just for a *change*? See the ice-cold, spine-crawlin, hair-stirrin *truth*? Looka here! Looka here, at the power! Looka here! Looka here, at the glory!"

Ricky scanned all the dark faces that ringed them round, and every eye was locked upon that wild gaunt man in his rapture, who now, with a powerful shrug, shouldered off his nylon jacket. It flopped down on the sidewalk with a slither and a sigh, and lay there on the concrete like a sloughed cocoon. He stretched the fabric of his T-shirt, displaying it to every locked-on eye.

Rickey's angle was still too acute to let him decipher exactly who it was who "ruled." But all these encircling faces, *they* seemed to know. They shared a vision of awe and terror and . . . something like hope. A frosty hope, endlessly remote . . . but hope. Ricky realized that there prevailed on these mean streets a consensus of vision. He clearly saw that all these eyes had seen, and understood, a catastrophic spectacle beyond his own imagining.

Andre barked, hoarse and brutish as a sea-lion, "Jus *look* at me here! I have gone up to see Him, and I have looked through His eyes, and I have *been* where He *is*, time without end! An I'm here to tell you, all you dearly beloved mongrel dogs of mine, I'm here to tell you that it's *consumed* me! My flesh, and my time, have been blown off my bones, by the searing winds of His breath! I'm not far off now from eternity! Not far off from infinity now!"

The raving seer then hiked up his T-shirt to his chest. What Ricky, from behind, saw there, was like a blow to his own chest, an impact of terror and dizziness, for Andre's thorax on its left side was normal, gauntly fleshed and sinewed, but along its right side, his spine was denuded bone, and midriff was there none, and just below his hoisted shirt-hem, a lathed bracket looped down: a fleshless rib, as clean and bare as sculpture . . .

His rapt audience recoiled like a single person, some lifting their arms convulsively, as in a reflex of self-protection, or acclaim . . .

Ricky dropped the Mustang into gear, and launched it from the curb, but in that selfsame instant Andre dropped into his seat again, and slammed his door, and so he was snatched deftly away, as if he were a prize that Ricky treasured, and not a horror that Ricky had been trying to flee.

Moonsilvered, lightless blocks floated past, yet Ricky never took his eyes from the gaunt shape whose T-shirt he could now, uncomprehending, read: CHTHULU RULES.

Somehow he drove, and, shortly, pulled again to a more deserted curb, and killed the engine. On this block, a sole dim streetlight shone. Half the houses were doorless, windowless . . .

He sat with only silence between himself and a man who had, at the least, submitted to a grave surgical mutilation in the service of his deity. Ricky looked into Andre's eyes.

That was the first challenge, to establish that he dared to look into Andre's eyes—and he found that he did dare.

"For all you've lost, "Ricky said, queasily referencing the gruesome marvel, " . . . you seem very . . . alive."

"I'm more alive than you will ever be, and when I'm all consumed, I'll be far *more* alive, and I will live forever!"

Ricky fingered the little bale of cash in his hand. "If you want me to go on, you have to tell me this. *Why* do you have to have a witness?"

"Because the One I'm gonna see wants someone new to see Him. He doesn't wanna know you. He wants *you* to know *Him*." In the darkness, Andre's polished eyes seemed to burn with this thing that he knew, and Ricky did not.

"He wants me to know him. And then?"

"And then it's up to you. To walk away, or to see him like I do."

"And how is that? How do you see him?"

"All the way."

Ricky's hand absently stroked the gearshift knob. "The choice is absolutely mine?"

"Your will is your own! Only your knowledge will be changed!"

Ricky slipped the Mustang into gear, and once more the blue beast growled onward. "Take a right here," purred Andre. "We going up to the top of the hills."

It was the longest "couple miles" that Ricky had ever driven. The road poured down past the Mustang like time itself, a slow stream of old, and older houses, on steepening blocks gapped by vacant lots, or by derelict cottages whose windows and doors were coffined in grafittied plywood.

They began to wind, and a rising sense of peril woke in Ricky. He was charging up into the sinister unknown! There was just too much missing from this man's body! You couldn't lose all that and still walk around, still fight with knives . . . could you?

But you could. Just look at him.

The houses thinned out even more, big old trees half-shrouding them. Dead cars slept under drifts of leaves, and dim bedroom lights showed life just barely hanging on, here in the hungry heights.

As they mounted this shoulder of the hills, Ricky saw glimpses of other ridges to the right and left, rooftop-and-tree-encrusted like this one. All these crestlines converged toward the same summit, and when Ricky looked behind, it seemed that these ridges poured down like a spill of titanic tentacles. They plunged far below into a thick, surprisingly deep fog that drowned and dimmed the jeweled python of the Hood.

Near the summit, their road entered a deepening gully. At the apex stood a municipal watertank, the dull gloss of its squat cylinder half-sunk in trees and houses.

"We goin to that house there right upside the tank. See that big gray roof pokin from the trees? The driveway goes down through the trees, it's steep an dark. Just roll down slow and easy, kill the engine, an let me get out first an talk to her."

"Her?"

Andre didn't answer. The road briefly crested before plunging, and Ricky had a last glimpse below of the tentacular hills rooted in the fogbank—and rooted beyond that, he imagined, more deeply still into the black floor of the Bay, as if the tentacles rummaged there for their deep-sunk food . . .

"Right there," said Andre, pointing ahead. "See the gap in the bushes?"

The Mustang crept muttering down the dark leafy tunnel, just as a wind rose, rattling dry oak foliage all around them.

A dim grotto of grassy ground opened below. There was a squat house on it, so dark it was almost a shadow-house. It showed one dim yellow light on the floor of its porch. A lantern, it looked like. A large dark shape loomed on one side of this lantern, and a smaller dark shape lay on the other.

Ricky cut his engine. Andre drew a long, slow breath, and got out. Leaves whispered in the silence. Andre's feet crackled across the yard. Ricky could hear the creak of his weight on the porch-steps as he climbed them, halfway up to the two dark shapes and their dim shared light. And Ricky could also hear . . . a growly breathing, wasn't it? Yes . . . A slow, phlegmy purr of big lungs.

Andre's voice was a new one to Ricky: low and implacable. "I'm back again, Mamma Hagg. I got the toll. I got the witness." Then he looked back and said, "Stand on out here . . . what's your name again?"

Ricky got out. How dangerous it suddenly seemed to declare himself in this silence, this place! Well, shit. He was here. He might as well say who he was. Loudly: "Ricky Deuce."

When he'd said it, he found his eyes could suddenly decipher the smaller dark shape by the lantern: it was a seated black dog, a big one, with the hint of aging frost on his lower jaw, and with his red tongue hanging and gently pulsing by that frosted jaw. The dog was looking steadily back at him, its tongue a bright spoon of greedy tissue scooping up the taste of the night . . .

It was not the brute's breathing Ricky had heard. It was Momma Hagg's, her voice deep now from the vault of her cave-like lungs:

"Then show the toll, fool."

Andre bent slightly to hold something towards the hound. And above his bent back, the woman in her turn became visible to Ricky. Within a briarpatch of dreads as pale as mushrooms, her monolithic black face melted in its age, her eyes two tarpools in this terrain of gnarled ebony. The shadowy bulk of her body eclipsed the mighty chair she sat in, though its armrests jutted into view, dark wood intricately carven into the coils and claws and thews of two heraldic monsters. Ricky couldn't make out what they were, but they seemed to snarl beneath the fingers of Momma Hagg's immense hands.

The dog's tongue was licking what Andre held up to it—Ricky's tenspot. The mastiff sniffed and sniffed, then snorted, and licked the bill again, and licked his chops.

"Come on up," said Momma. "The two of you." The big woman's voice had a strange kind of pull to it. Like surf at your legs, its growl dragged you towards her. Ricky approached. Andre mounted to the porch, and Ricky climbed after him. He had the sensation with each step up that he entered a bigger and emptier kind of space. When he stood on the porch, Momma Hagg seemed farther off than he had expected. From her distance wafted the smell of her—an ashen scent like the drenched coals of a bonfire that had included flesh and bones in its fuel. The dog rose.

The porch took too long to cross as they followed the hound. His bright tongue lolling like a casually held torch, with just one back-glance of one crimson eye, the brute led them through a wide, doorless doorframe, and into a high dark interior that gusted out dank salty breath in their faces.

A cold gray light leaked in here, as if the fog that had swallowed the Hood had now climbed the hills, and its glow was seeping into this gaunt house. They trod a rambling, unpartitioned space, the interior all wall-less, while the outer walls were irregularly recessed in alcoves, nooks and grottos. In some of these stood furniture, oddly forlorn, bulky antique pieces—an armchair, a settee, an escritoire crusted with ancient papers. These stranded little settings—like fossils of foregone transactions whose participants had blown to dust long since—seemed to mark the passage of generations through this rambling gloom.

Ricky had the disorienting sense they had been trekking for a long, long time. He realized that the stranded furniture had a delicately furred and crusted profile in the gray light, like tide pool rocks, and a cold tidal scent touched his nostrils. Realized too, that here and there in those recesses, there were windows. Beyond their panes lay a different shade of darkness, where weedy and barnacled shadows stirred, and glinted wetly . . .

And throughout this shadowy passage, Ricky noted, on every stretch of wall he could discern, wooden wainscottings densely carved. The misty glow put a sheen on the sinuous saliences of this dark chiselwork, which seemed to depict bulbous, serpentine knots of tail and claw and thew—or perhaps woven Cephalopodia, braided greedy tentacles, and writhing prey in ragged beaks . . .

But now the walls had narrowed in, and here were stairs, and up these steep, worn stairs the hound, not pausing, led them. The air of this stairwell was slightly dizzying. The labor of the black beast climbing before them seemed to pull the two men after, as if the beast drew them in an executioner's tumbrel. They were lifted, Ricky suddenly felt, by a might far greater than theirs, and Andre, ahead of him, seemed to shiver and quake in the flux of that dire energy. It gave Ricky the sensation of walking in Andre's lee, and being sheltered by his body from a terror that streamed around him like a solar wind.

From the head of the stairs, a great moldy vacancy breathed down on them. They emerged into what seemed a simpler and far older structure. High-beamed ceiling, carven walls . . . it was no more than a grand passage ending at a high dark archway. The floorplanks faintly drummed, as if this was a bridgeway, unfoundationed. That great black arch ahead . . . it was inset in a wall that bowed. A metallic wall.

"The tank!" said Ricky. It jumped out of him. "That's that big water tank!"

The Hound halted and turned. Andre too turned, gave him eyes of wild reproof, but the Hound, raising to Ricky his crimson eyes, gave him a red-tongued leer, gave him the glinty-pupiled mockery of a knowing demon. This look set the carved walls to seething, set the sculpted thews rippling, limbs lacing, beaks butchering, all brutally busy beneath their fur of dust . . .

The Hound turned again, and led them on. Now they could smell the water in the great tank—an odor both metallic and marine—and the hound's breathing began to echo, to grow as cavernous as Mamma Hagg's had been. Within that archway was a blackness absolute, a darkness far more perfect than the gloom that housed them. As they closed with it, the hound's nails echoed as on a great oaken drum above a jungle wilderness. The beast dropped to its belly, lay panting, whining softly. The two men stood behind.

Within the portal, a huge glossy black surface confronted them, a great shield of glass, a mirror as big as a house. There they were in it: Ricky, Andre, the hound. The brightest feature of their tiny, distorted reflection was the bright red dot of the hound's tongue.

Andre paused for a few heartbeats only. Then he stepped through the arch, with an odd ceremonial straightness to his posture. He gestured and Ricky followed him, seeing, as he did so, that the aperture was cut through a double metal wall that showed a cross-section of struts between.

They stood on a narrow balcony just within the tank, and felt a huge damp breath of the steel-clad lake below them, and gazed into the immense glass that was to afford them their Revelation of the Power and the Glory . . .

Andre stared some moments at his reflection, then turned to Ricky. "Now I tell you what it is . . . you say your name was Rocky?"

"Ricky."

"Ricky, now Ima tell you what it is. I came to see, and be seen by Him. When He really sees *you*, you can see through *His* eyes, and you can live His mind."

"But what if I don't want to live his mind?"

"You can't! You didn't pay the toll! You'll *see* some shit though! You'll see enough, you'll know that if you got any adventure in your soul, you got to *pay* that toll! But that's up to you! Now look, an learn!"

He faced the mirror again, and in a cracked voice he cried, "Ia! Ia! Ia fthagn!"

And the mirror, ever so slightly, contracted, and the faintest circumference of white showed round its great rim, and encompassing that ring of pallor, something black and scaly like a sea-beast's hide crinkled into view . . . and Ricky realized that they stood before the pupil of an immense eye.

And Ricky found his feet were rooted, and he could not turn to flee.

And he beheld a dizzying mosaic of lights flashing to life within the mighty pupil. A grand midnight vision crystallized: the whole San Francisco Bay lay within the black orb, bordered by the whole bright oroboros of coastal lights . . .

He and Andre gazed on the vista, on the Bridges' glittering spines transecting it, all their lengths corpuscled with fleeing lights red and white. The two men gazed on the panorama and it drank their minds. Rooted, they inhabited its grandeur, even as it began a subtle distortion. The vista seemed tugged awry, torqued towards the very center of the giant's pupil. And within that grand, slow distortion, Ricky saw strange movements. Across the Bay Bridge, near its eastern end, the cargo cranes of West Oakland—tracked monsters, each on four mighty legs—raised and bowed their cabled booms in a dinosaurian salute— obeisance, or acclaim . . . While to their left, the giant tanks on Benecia's tarry hills, and the Richmond tanks too in the West, began a ponderous rotation on their bases, a slow spin like planets obeying the pupil's gathering vortex.

Andre cried out, to Ricky, or just to the world he was about to leave, "I see it all coming apart! In detail! Behold!"

This last word reverberated in a brazen basso far larger than the lean man's lungs could shape. And the knell of that voice awoke winds in the night, and the winds buffeted Ricky as though he hung in the night sky within the eye, and Ricky *knew*. He knew this being into whose view he'd come! Knew this monster was the King of a vast migration of titans across the eons of the countless Space-Times! Over the gale-swept universe they moved, these Great Old Ones. Across the cracked continents they trawled, they plundered! Worlds were the pastures that they grazed, and the broken bodies of whole races were the pavement that they trod!

It astonished him, the threshold to which this Andre, night-walking zealot, had brought him. He looked at Andre now, saw the man utterly alone at the brink of his apotheosis. How high he seemed to hang in the night winds! Look at the frailty of that skinny frame! The mad greed of his adventure!

Andre seemed to shudder, to gather himself. He looked back at Ricky. He looked like he was seeing in Ricky some foreigner in a far, quaint land, some backward Innocent, unknowing of the very world he stood in.

"On squid, man," he said, " . . . on squid, *Ricky*, you get big! All hell breaks loose in the back of your brain, and you can *hold* it, you can *contain* it! And then you get to watch Him *feed*. And now *you'll* see. Just a little! Not too much! But you going to *know*."

Andre turned, and faced the eye. He gathered himself, gathered his voice for a great shout:

"Here's my witness! Here I come!"

And he vaulted from the balcony, out into the pupil—impacted it for an instant, seemed to freeze in mid-leap as if he had struck glass—but in the instant after, was within the vast inverted cone of light-starred night, and hung high, tiny but distinct, above the slowly twisting panorama of the great black Bay all shoaled and shored and spanned with light. That galactic metropolis, round its core of abyss, was—less slowly now—still contorting, twisting toward the center of the pupil . . .

And Ricky found that he too hung within it, he stood on the wide cold air in the night sky, he felt against his face the winds' slow torque towards the the the center of the Old One's sight.

And now all Hell, with relentless slow acceleration, broke loose. The City's blazing architected crown began to discohere, brick fleeing brick in perfect pattern, in widening pattern, till they all became pointillist buildings snatched away in the whirlwind, and from the buildings, all the people too like flung seed swirled up into the night, their evaporating arms raised as in horror, or salute, crying out their being from clouding faces that the black winds sucked to tatters . . .

He saw the great bridges braided with—and crumpling within—barnacle-crusted tentacles as thick as freeway tunnels, saw the freeways themselves—pillared rivers of light—unravelling, their traffic like red and white stars fleeing into the air, into the cyclone of the Great Old One's attention.

And an inward vision was given to Ricky, simultaneous with this meteoric overview. For he also knew the Why of it. He knew the hunger of the nomad titans, their unappeasable will to consume each bright busy outpost they could find in the universal Black and Cold. Knew that many another world had fled, as this one fled, draining into the maw of the grim cold giants, each world's collapsing roofs and walls bleeding a smoke of souls, all sucked like spume into the mossy curvature of His colossal jaws . . .

It was perfectly dark. It was almost silent, except for a rattle of leaves. The cold against his face had the wet bite of fog . . .

Ricky shook his head, and the dark grew imperfect. He put out his hand and touched rough wooden siding. He was alone on the porch, no lantern now, no armchair, no one else. Just dead leaves in crackly little drifts on the floorboards as—slowly and unsteadily—he started across them.

He had *seen* some shit. Stone cold sober, he had *seen*. And now the question was, who was he?

He crossed the leaf-starred grass, on legs that felt increasingly familiar. Yes . . . here was this Ricky-body that he knew, light and quick. And here was his Mustang, blown oak leaves chittering across its polished hood. And still the question was, who was he?

He was this car, for one thing, had worked long to buy it and then to perfect it. He got behind the wheel and fired it up, felt his perfect fit in this machine. Flawlessly it answered to his touch, and the blue beast purred up through the leaf-tunnel as the house—a doorless, glassless derelict—fell away behind him. But this Ricky Deuce . . . who was he now?

He emerged from the foliage, and dove down the winding highway. There was the fog-banked Bay below, the jewelled snake of the Hood glinting within its gray wet shroud, and Ricky took the curves just like his old self, riding one of the hills' great tentacles down, down towards the sea they rooted in . . .

There was something Ricky had to do. Because in spite of his body, his nerves being his, he didn't *know* who he was now, had just had a big chunk torn out of him. And there was something terrible he had to do, to locate, by desperate means, the man he had lost, to find at least a piece of him he was sure of.

His hands and arms knew the way, it seemed. Diving down into the thicker fog, he smoothly threw the turns required . . . and slid up to the curb before the liquor store they'd parked near . . . when? A universe ago. Parked and jumped out.

Ricky was terrified of what he was going to do, and so he moved swiftly to have it done with, just nodding to his recent companions as he hastened into the store—nodding to the Maoris in shades, to the guys with the switchblade cap-bills, to the guys with the crimson hoods and the golden pockets. But rushed though he was, it struck him that they were all looking at him with a kind of fascination . . .

At the counter he said, "Fifth of Jack." He didn't even look to see what he peeled off his wad to pay for it, but there were a lot of twenties in his change. The Arab bagged him his bottle, his eyes fixed almost raptly on Ricky's, so Ricky was moved to ask in simple curiosity, "Do I look strange?"

"No," the man said, and then said something else, but Ricky had already turned, in haste to get outside where he could take a hit. Had the man said *no, not yet*?

Ricky got outside, cracked the cap, and hammered back a stiff, two-gurgle jolt.

He scarcely could wait to let it roll down and impact him. He felt the hot collision in his body's center, the roil of potential energy glowing there, then poked down a long, three-gurgle chaser. Stood reeling inwardly, and outwardly showing some impact as well . . .

And there it was: a heat, a turmoil, a slight numbing. No more. No magic. No rising trumpets. No wheels of light . . . The half-pint of Jack he'd just downed had no marvel to show like the one he'd just seen.

And so Ricky knew that he was someone else now, someone he had not yet fully met.

"'Sup?" It was the immense guy in the lavender sweats. He had a solemn Toltec-statue face, but an incongruously merry little smile.

"'S happnin," said Ricky. "Hey. You want this?"

"That Jack?"

"Take the rest. Keep it. Here's the cap."

"No thanks." This to the cap. The man drank. As he chugged, he slanted Ricky an eye with something knowing, something *I thought so* in it. Ricky just stood watching him. He had no idea at all of what would come next in his life, and for the moment, this bibulous giant was as interesting a thing as any to stand watching . . .

The man smacked his lips. "It ain't the same, is it?" he grinned at Ricky, gesturing the bottle. "It just don't matter any more. I mean, so I *understand*. I like the glow jus fine myself. But you . . . see, you widdat Andre. You've been a *witness*."

"Yeah. I have. So . . . tell me what that means."

"You the one could tell me. AIs I know is *I'd* never do it, and a whole lotta folks around here *they'd* never do it—but you didn't know that, did you?"

"So tell me what it *means*."

"It means what you make of it! And speakin of which, man, of what you might make of it, I wanna show you something right now. May I?"

"Sure. Show me."

"Let's step round here to the side of the building . . . just round here . . . " Now they stood in the shadowy weed-tufted parking lot, where others lounged, but moved away when they appeared.

"I'm gonna show you somethin," said the man, drawing out his wallet, and opening it.

But opening it for himself at first, for he brought it close to his face as he looked in, and a pleased, proprietary glow seemed to beam from his Olmec features. For a moment, he gloated over the contents of his billfold.

Then he extended and spread the wallet open before Ricky. There was a fat sheaf of bills in it, hand-worn bills with a skinlike crinkle. It seemed the money, here and there, was stained.

Reverently, Olmec said, "I bought this from the guy that capped the guy it came from. This is as pure as it gets. Blood money with the blood right on it! An you can have a bill of it for five hundred dollars! I *know* that Andre put way more than that in your hand. I *know* you know what a great deal this is!"

Ricky . . . had to smile. He saw an opportunity at least to *gauge* how dangerously he'd erred. "Look here," he told Olmec. "Suppose I did buy blood money. I'd still need a witness. So what about *that* man? Will *you* be my witness for . . . almost five grand?"

Olmec did let the sum hang in the air for a moment or two, but then said, quite decisive, "Not for twice that."

"So Andre got me cheap?"

"Just by my book. You could buy witnesses round here for half that!"

"I guess I need to think it over."

"You know where I hang. Thanks for the drink."

And Ricky stood there for the longest time, thinking it over . . .

Michael Shea *learned to love the "genres" from the great Jack Vance's* Eyes of the Overworld, *chance-discovered in a flophouse in Juneau when Shea was twenty-one. He tilled the field of sword-and-sorcery for more than a decade* (Quest for Simbilis, In Yana the Touch of Undyine, Nifft the Lean). *Concurrently he wallowed in the delights of supernatural/extraterrestrial horror, primarily in the novella form, and this remains his genre of choice (as can be seen in the collections* Polyphemus *and* The Autopsy and Other Tales). *In the last decade or so he has added* hommages *to H.P. Lovecraft to his novella work (as in collection* Copping Squid.) *Currently he is writing a trilogy of near-future thrillers:* The Extra, Assault on Sunrise, *and* Fortress Hollywood.

This particular tale was written for S.T. Joshi's *Black Wings: New Tales of Lovecraftian Horror,* an anthology that wasn't published until 2010. Luckily (for us) Shea included it as the title story of his most recent collection which was published in 2009. As for the San Francisco setting: If there were anywhere one might cop squid, it would be there.

MONSTERS

STEWART O'NAN

They were going to be monsters, for the church—Creatures from the Black Lagoon. Mark wanted to be Dracula, but Father Don said only one person could, and Derek convinced him it would be more fun. You got to wear a suit with a zipper up the back and a head that fit like a diving helmet. They could scare the little kids and gross out the girls. No one would know who they were.

"Plus it's boring by yourself," Derek said. "You just sit there."

"You don't need fangs," Derek said. "There's already teeth in the head."

It was Mark's only argument. It was like that with Derek, he was always in charge, which was all right, because Mark was shy and terribly aware and ashamed of it. Plus Derek never ditched him like Peter did. Peter was his brother; he was only two years older than Mark. They'd always played together, ever since they were little, but since Peter started at the high school this fall, he was never home after school. At dinner when Mark brought it up, his father just sighed. "Why don't you go next door?" he said. "You and Derek should be able to find something to do."

That's what they were doing, just messing around. It was a Thursday after school and there was nothing to do, so Derek brought out his Daisy and they took turns plinking the same six pop bottles off some old railroad ties Derek's stepfather had piled in the back lot. The gun was so weak they didn't even fall over sometimes, just tinked and wobbled.

It was Derek's idea to play Shooting Gallery. One of them hid behind the ties and then popped up and you had to shoot him. You only pumped the gun once, and they had their jackets on; it only stung if it hit bare skin. You crawled around behind the ties and then popped up and the other person tried to shoot you.

They did that for ten minutes but it was boring. Then Mark came up with Moving Target. In this one, you jumped up and ran and then dove behind the ties. This was even more boring because no one got shot.

Then Derek made up Ambush. The guy with the gun hid somewhere behind the piles of woodchips and gravel, and the guy who popped up threw hand grenades—just round stones Derek's stepfather used to edge the little goldfish ponds he built.

Mark had the gun. He pumped it once and crouched behind a sharp pallet of bricks, waiting for Derek to lob one of the stones. They were a little smaller than baseballs, and he didn't want to get hit with one. He peeked around the corner and saw Derek start to pop up and toss the grenade like a soldier, like a hook shot—saw the stone leave his hand and arc towards him.

He'd have time to think about this later: how impossible it all was. He saw the stone was going to miss, so he ducked around the corner, firing without even bringing the gun up. From the hip, just like in the movies.

He expected Derek to run but he was watching the grenade like it might really explode.

It was just one shot, from the hip.

Derek grabbed his face and bent over, holding it.

Mark thought he was faking. He loved death scenes on TV, dropping to the carpet in their rec room, one hand clutching his heart as he gasped out his last words, the other reaching for Mark's sneaker. But then he was screaming—high and loud and over and over—and walking fast toward his backdoor, his hand still there, as if he were trying to keep the eye in.

Mark dropped the gun and ran over and walked along with him. "Are you okay?"

"No."

"Let me see."

"No." He was walking slower now, and Mark could have stopped him, but there was blood coming out between his fingers and Mark couldn't think. He went up the porch stairs in front of him and opened the storm door. He saw his own hands were empty, and thought: I shouldn't leave the gun out there.

"Sarah!" he called inside, because Derek's sister was the only one home. He went through the kitchen into the front hall and called her, and she came running down, asking what had happened. When she saw the blood she grabbed Derek and hauled him to the sink and started running water. Mark had a crush on her—her lip gloss, her purple scrunchy, the way she bowed down and then reared up and flung her hair over her head—and her taking charge made her seem heroic, older, even more unreachable.

"What happened?" she asked.

"It was my fault," Mark said. "We were playing with the gun—"

"God damn it," she said. "I can't believe it, you're so stupid, both of you."

Sarah ran some water on a dishcloth and got right up next to Derek. She told him it was okay, everything was okay. They needed to see how bad it was. Derek wasn't screaming anymore, it was more like crying, trying to breathe in too fast. She had her arm over his shoulders, her face so close they could have been kissing. "Yeah, I know," she said, "it's all right, we just need to see."

He nodded and Sarah took his hand away from his eye.

"Oh my God," she said, "Go get your mom," and Mark ran.

There was a path worn between their backdoors. He dodged the kitchen table, gave it the same move he did when Peter was chasing him in from something. "Mom!" he called, "Mom!"

She was upstairs sewing costumes for the haunted house, pins between her teeth. She was so used to him screaming she didn't even get up. She talked out of the side of her mouth. "What is it now?"

"I shot him," Mark said, and tried to explain, but suddenly he couldn't talk, and then he was crying just like Derek, trying to get enough air.

His mother spit the pins out and grabbed his arm, dragged him along behind her as she ran down the stairs. He couldn't believe she was so fast, banging out the storm door and flying across the yard and into the Rotas'.

Derek was sitting at the kitchen table with Sarah holding a baggie of ice on his eye. He still had his jacket on. He wasn't crying, just hunched over, rocking back and forth, saying, "Ow, ow, ow."

"Is he all right?" Mark's mom asked.

"No," Sarah said. "It's his eye. I called 911, they said they'd send an ambulance."

"Let me take a look at it." His mother plucked the bag away and put it back fast. "When did they say they'd get here?"

"Five minutes."

His mother sat down, then got up again and walked around the room, biting her thumbnail and looking out the windows.

"I'm sorry," Mark said, and again he began to cry, right in front of Sarah.

"It was an accident," his mom said.

"It's okay," Derek said, but this only made it worse, and Mark ran out into the yard and didn't stop until he reached the back lot.

There was the gun next to the pallet of bricks, and there on a yellow leaf was a dark spot of blood, and another.

"Mark," his mom called. "Mark, get in here now!"

He picked up the gun and the BBs shifted and clicked in the barrel. He loved the Daisy, the afternoons they spent winging cans and bottles and old archery targets Derek's stepfather kept in the shed, but now as he walked across the yard, he promised—honestly, to God—that this was the last time he'd ever touch a gun.

It wasn't even a real gun.

"Give me that," his mom said on the porch, and snatched it by the barrel, something you weren't supposed to do. He knew to just keep quiet.

The kitchen was empty. They'd moved Derek to the front porch to wait for the ambulance. He sat on the glider, still nodding and rocking, making it move. "It hurts," he said.

"I know," Mark's mom said. "It'll be here soon." To Mark, she said, "I'm not mad at you, no one's mad at you, just don't run off like that."

"I'm sorry," Mark said.

"We know you are," she said. "It was an accident, everyone knows that, now just calm down."

"Here it comes," Sarah said, pointing at the ambulance.

It didn't even have its lights on, or its siren. It pulled into the drive and the EMTs jumped out. One looked at Derek while the other talked with Mark's mom. The one with Derek knelt down by the glider and pulled out a mini-flashlight and waved it in front of his face.

"Can you see it now?"

"No," Derek said.

"How about over here?'

"Yeah."

The EMT stood up and told Mark's mom they were taking him to Butler Memorial and that she should contact his parents.

"I already have," his mom said.

They put him in the back, and the one got in with him.

"You can follow us if you want," the other one said.

The nurse at the emergency room said Mark's mom could go in with Derek but Mark and Sarah would have to wait outside. Sarah lost herself in Cosmopolitan and Mark got up and looked at everything in the vending machines. The hospital had taped up the same cardboard decorations his Sunday school class had—the same pickle-nosed witches and rearing black cats and ogling, wide-eyed pumpkins. Mark tried to read a Sports Illustrated but it was too old. The last time he'd been here was when he broke his wrist trying a grind on a concrete bench in the back lot, and now he wondered if he was bad luck, if the rest of his life would be like this. It would be okay, he thought.

Derek's stepfather showed up first, his work gloves stuffed in his back pockets. He was small but he had a huge mustache; he wore his Steeler cap everywhere except church, where he played guitar up front with Mark's dad.

Mark stood up but he went straight to Sarah.

"They were messing around with the BB gun," she said, pointing to Mark.

"Is that right?"

"Yes sir."

"I thought I showed you two how to handle that thing."

Mark just nodded.

"Well, accidents will happen, I guess. Are you all right?"

"Yeah," Mark said.

"Okay," he said, and put his hand on Mark's shoulder and gave it a squeeze before he went off to find the nurse.

Ten minutes later, Derek's mom ran through the electric doors. She was dressed for the mill, still wearing her clip-on nametag, and she smelled like pencil lead. She had steeltoed boots like Mark's father and a line of grease across the front of her uniform. It looked like a costume on her.

"How is he?" she asked Sarah, and when she didn't like her answer, stalked right past Mark to the nurse.

Mark's mom came out after a while and said the doctors weren't sure. He might lose the eye or it might get better, only time would tell. He'd probably have to stay in the hospital for a day or two, they'd see. While she was explaining everything to them, Mark's dad walked in.

The first thing he did was sit down. It was a thing he had; anytime they had to discuss something serious, he made everyone sit down. His other rule was no shouting, no matter how angry you were. His mom told him the whole thing, and then he stood up and took Mark's hand and then his mom's and then Sarah joined the circle and they all bowed their heads and they prayed.

"Amen," his father said, and gave a little squeeze which Mark returned out of habit.

Sarah suddenly broke into tears, and his mom held her for a while, and then Derek's stepfather came back out and gave his father a hug. Derek was resting, they'd given him something; Derek's mom would stay with him tonight. Meanwhile it was probably best if they all went home.

"Can we visit him later?" Mark asked.

"Tomorrow," his mom said.

It was night out now, the moon almost full. In the parking lot they split up. "Why don't you go with dad?" his mom said, so Mark climbed into the pick-up and buckled himself in.

His dad would tell him a story, Mark knew that. It would be something from the Bible, a parable Mark could learn from, and he waited for it as they got on the highway and headed out of town. It wasn't until they passed the salvage yard by the firehouse that his dad cleared his throat and said, "You know something?"

"What?" Mark said.

"It could have just as easily been you. You know that."

"Yeah."

"Do you remember what it says in John about the two farmers?"

"No," Mark said, because he never knew what the Bible said. In Sunday school they read stories together that everyone had heard before, but his father knew all of it, pulled it out like a favorite wrench.

"There were two farmers who lived next to each other, and one day a plague, of locusts came along, so thick they could hardly see. When the locusts flew off, the one farmer's crop was all gone, bitten down to the roots. But the other farmer's crop wasn't touched at all. It was like a sign, people said." His dad looked to him, and Mark said, "Uh-huh."

"The farmer who lost his crop thought it was the work of sorcery. The farmer whose crop wasn't touched thought it was the hand of God. The two of them accused each other of being in league with the devil. Each of them set about to prove it in the courts. In the meantime no one was tending the fields and it was high summer. And you know what happened?"

"What?" Mark said.

"The whole crop burned up and was lost."

His dad looked to him again as if to make sure he understood, and then they drove along, nothing but the truck's engine and the tires whining over the road.

It was past supper so Mark's mom heated up some lasagna from yesterday. Peter was home, and they had to tell him what happened.

"Your brother and Derek were playing around out back," his mom said. "And somehow . . ."

Every time Mark heard someone tell it, he could feel them blaming him. That was fine, it was his fault; he just wondered if it would get better. He hoped so.

Peter washed while he dried and put the dishes away.

"You weren't trying to hit him," Peter asked

"No," Mark said, angry at him. But was that really true?

It was just a game. Now the crop was gone, the fields burnt.

"He'll be okay," Peter said. "Plus he's still got the other one, it's not like he's blind."

"Shut up."

"I'm just saying," he said.

It was a school night, and they had homework to do, and then when they were done they were allowed an hour of TV. His dad went over to the Rotas' during Seinfeld and came back during Suddenly Susan. Nothing had changed; Derek's mom was still at the hospital. Maybe they'd know something in the morning.

In bed, Mark pictured the celebration they'd have when they found out Derek was okay. His dad would call for a prayer circle and they'd bow their heads and all of them—Mark, especially—would thank God.

But in the morning Derek's stepfather said the doctors still couldn't say one way or the other. Derek's mom was taking the day off to stay with him. Peter and Sarah walked together to the bus stop; the grass was frosted and they left footprints. Mark's bus came later. He scuffed through the drifted leaves, his backpack a load on his shoulder. It was the last stop on the route, which was good in the morning but bad after school. On a regular day, he and Derek would jag around, maybe play kill-the-man-with-the-ball until the bus came. Today it was just him, and he waited outside the shelter, kicking stones across the road and thinking how impossible the shot was, the terrible odds of it, and how unlucky it was that the person firing the rifle had been him. Sometimes he couldn't believe it was real, he could pretend it never happened. But it did.

In school he didn't mention it.

"Is Derek sick, do you know?" Mrs. Albright asked him, and he said yes.

After school he had haunted house practice, but his mom called Father Don, who said it was okay if he missed it to visit the hospital. The Creature from the Black Lagoon suits weren't in yet anyway, and they knew what to do, they didn't have to practice being monsters.

"Do you not want to go?" his mom said in the car.

"No, I do"

"He's not going to be mad at you, if that's what you're worried about."

"I know," Mark said but he was thinking about the farmer who'd lost his crop. How could you not be angry?

Derek's room was on a floor just for children; the halls were crowded with parents, and the decorations were the same as downstairs. The shades were down and Derek was asleep. His stepfather and mom were both there. His roommate had just been released, so there was an empty bed next to his. Derek's mom took them out in the hall to talk to them.

"They say the eye itself isn't as bad as they thought, but the thing is lodged in there. They're going to try to get it out but they say there's a chance the retina might detach."

"Is there any way to reattach it?" Mark's mom asked.

"No, if it detaches you lose the eye."

The surgery was scheduled for tomorrow morning. That night they prayed for him, Mark's father talking about the mystery of God's purpose and their acceptance of His will. Mark thought it was wrong, that there must be something they could do to fix things. It felt like giving up to him.

And then after the surgery they still had to wait another day to see if it worked. The doctors said everything went well but with something like this there was no guarantee.

Sunday before church Derek's mom came over; she was in the same clothes as yesterday and said she hadn't slept. They weren't going to be there, so she wanted Mark to say Derek's name during the Prayers for the People. Everyone thought it was a good idea, and Mark did too. Maybe this would help a little. He'd already planned what he was going to say during the Confession. It would be like an offering. He didn't think it would change anything, but still, it was something.

His mom laid out his good white shirt and Mark buttoned it till it pinched his neck. His hair was still wet; it combed down dark in the mirror so you wouldn't know he was blond. He fixed his part and leaned close to his own reflection, looking at his eyes, one and then the other. The black part and the green around it and then the white was like a bullseye, three rings. He put his hand over his right eye and everything off to that side disappeared.

It wasn't that much different, was it?

But he could always take his hand away, he thought. Derek couldn't.

His mom drove and he and Peter sat in the back, his dad's guitar case across their laps. Even the new part of the parking lot was full; Mr. Jenner waved people in with a blaze orange vest and parked them on the grass. Mark waited for his dad to slide his guitar out, then followed him around the car to where Peter and his mom were waiting. He saw the Tates across the lot, all dressed up, and Mrs. Lerner in her white gloves, carrying a lily in purple foil. The bells were playing from the loudspeakers above the front doors, and everyone was headed for them. It wouldn't be hard, Mark thought. All he had to do was stand up and say Derek's name.

Inside, it was warm with voices. Since Derek's stepfather wasn't there, Charlie Wycoff was up front tuning up, and Mark's dad needed to go over some changes with him.

"Play well," his mom said, and gave him a kiss.

She let Mark into the pew first and sat down with Peter on the other side of her, on the aisle. They shared the pew with the Rotas, and Mark wasn't used to all the space. His slacks slid on the wood, and he pushed himself side to side like a goalie fixing his crease, his feet on the kneeler. "Stop," his mom said, a hand on his leg. "Now are you all set with what you're going to say?"

"Yes."

"Here." She had her prayer book open to where they said it. "Right after Father Don says this here."

She marked the place with a white ribbon and gave him the book.

His dad and Charlie Wycoff started playing and people stopped talking. Father Don came out in his robes with his old Bible and raised his arms to welcome everyone, and Mark wondered what Father Don would say to him. It wouldn't be like his dad and his farmer story, it would be different. If Derek's eye was all right, then it was a chance for Mark to learn something. In school, Mrs. Albright drew a minus sign on the board, then waited a second till they all saw it and made it into a plus. "Make a positive," she said, "out of a negative." Now Mark wondered how that fit with the two farmers. What could you make from a burnt up field?

Not much.

It was just a story, it wasn't something that actually happened.

They stood to sing and knelt to pray, and he read the whole program, seeing who donated the flowers for the altar this week, whose birthday was coming up. During the announcements before the sermon, Father Don reminded everyone that there would be a sneak preview of the haunted house this Wednesday for church members only, so it would be a good time to beat the lines. Last year they raised over five thousand dollars, so how about a big hand for all those folks who helped put it together?

"That's us," Mark's mom said as they clapped.

And then the sermon, which seemed long, and the offering, and another hymn, until finally Father Don raised his arms and said, "Let us pray," and lowered them for everyone to kneel down.

Mark had the book turned to the right page. They prayed for the president and they prayed for the bishop and for Father Don. They prayed for all those struggling against injustice and oppression and for the poor and the unfortunate. And then they prayed for the sick and infirm, and Father Don asked God to especially keep in mind those members of the congregation in special need of His healing

It was quiet then, and Mark's mom touched his arm. He stood up.

The church was a field of heads bent down, and he was taller than all of them, except Father Don, who turned to look at him, as if he expected this.

"Derek Rota," Mark said, and Father Don nodded.

He wasn't loud enough, he thought, but it was too late and he knelt dawn again.

"Eileen Covington," someone else said, and then it was quiet.

"Gertrude Wheeler."

"Jan Tomczak."

It went on for eight names. Mark thought it was a lot, all of those people in the hospital, and all their families worried about them. Some of them were probably going to die. He'd barely noticed this part of the service before, and now it seemed terrible to him, proof of something gone wrong.

But none of the other people had shot anyone, had they?

They finished and everyone sat up with a rumble of kneelers. "You did very well," his mom said, and then his dad stepped to the center and played and they all stood up to watch the altar boys take the cross away.

In the receiving line, Father Don shook his hand in both of his. "Are you ready to be the Creature?" he said, because the suits had come in yesterday.

"Sure."

He'd have to come by and try it on tomorrow. Mark's mom said it wasn't a problem.

Outside, the little kids were running around on the new sod, one girl crying because she'd gotten grass stains on her white dress. They waited for Mark's dad, who had to pack up his stuff. When he came out he was still talking with Charlie Wycoff.

"He's pretty good," Mark's dad said in the car. "He's really been practicing a lot."

"I thought Mark did a nice job too," his mom said.

"I heard. Good projection."

In the back seat, Peter made a face, and Mark elbowed him, and Peter went to hit him but stopped short just to make him flinch.

Outside the fields went by, long harvested, the stubble white and bent down by the reaper. He could smell someone burning leaves; you weren't supposed to but people still did.

Nothing had changed, Mark thought. Nothing had happened. He'd just said his name, that was all.

But what if saying his name saved his eye? That was possible, wasn't it?

That's what faith was. If the two farmers had had faith—was that the meaning of it? He wanted to ask his dad: What were the farmers supposed to do?

It was dumb thinking about it; it was just made-up.

At home they changed clothes and ate lunch and put on the Steeler game. It was dumb; they were beating up on Houston. Mark was thinking about going out and raking the yard when Derek's stepfather came over.

Mark answered the door. Usually he'd just let him in, but Derek's stepfather asked if his dad was around.

"I'll go get him," Mark said.

His dad was lying on the couch with the football in his lap. He looked surprised and got up and handed off to Peter, and Mark knew not to follow him.

His dad didn't come right back. He closed the door and went upstairs where his mom was working on the costumes, and then in a while the two of them came down together. Peter looked at Mark like this was about him.

His dad clicked the set off and had everyone sit down.

"Take hands," he said, and they did.

"Mrs. Rota just called. The doctors said Derek's eye was just too badly damaged."

He went on, but Mark had stopped listening, concentrating on the shot, that one stupid moment with the gun. It was Derek who made up the game, it was Derek's rifle. Derek had shot at him a million times, even shooting one of his mom's cigarettes out of his mouth on three tries. But none of that mattered. Now, bending his head in prayer again, his dad's hand strong in his, all that mattered was that one shot. It was his fault, and he was sorry, but that wasn't enough.

"Amen," his dad said, and there was the squeeze, like a reminder.

Later he went out and raked the yard by himself until he saw his mom at her sewing room window looking down at him. She'd bought a huge trash bag that looked like a pumpkin, and he stuffed it with leaves and faced it toward the road so you could see it when you came around the curve. Then he went in and watched the late game, or sat there not watching, startled when Peter called out, "Nice! Nice!"

No one told him it wasn't his fault. After the dishes, his mom took him into the living room and said he hadn't meant for this to happen. Tucking him in, his dad told him he shouldn't blame himself, that what was done was done. He was a good guy, everyone knew that. Derek knew that, Derek's parents knew it. Okay?

"Okay," Mark said.

His door closed, blocking out the hall light, leaving him alone. He wondered if Derek was awake in the hospital, if he'd gotten a new roommate. He closed both his eyes and tried to see. Blue dots floated, then shifted when he tried to look at them, drifted like galaxies, little soft stars. He opened his eyes and the room grew back. No, he thought, that wasn't what it was like at all.

It was just one, he still had the other. Peter said that to be mean, but it was true too.

The wind was in the trees. It was only two weeks till Halloween; his mom had already bought candy and hid it where his dad couldn't get at it, set out bowls of candy corn around the house. Would Derek be able to be a Creature? Mark wanted to see him, to say he was sorry to his face. He couldn't remember if he did when he shot him. It was funny: he thought he would never forget it, but already, like his part in the service this morning, the Steeler game, the leaves, the two farmers—like the blue stars under his eyelids, it was all fading away.

The next day his mom picked him up after school and drove him over to church. Father Don had the two suits hung over folding chairs in the parish hall. They were greenish-black, the color of snakes, and sagged like empty skins. They were so fake it made Mark want to laugh. Their claws came to sharp points. On the table sat the two heads, the eyes bugged out under angry brows, flipperlike gills behind the jaw.

"You look out of the mouth," Father Don explained, and fit it over his head.

"Can you see?" his mom asked.

He could, but just a wedge between two even rows of ridiculous fangs. He'd have to remember to tell Derek.

"Okay," Father Don said, "take that off and let's try the body."

It was heavy, and the webbed hands went on separately, like rubber gloves. The feet went over his shoes, kept on with a gumband. It was like wearing armor, he thought, everything covered up.

"How does it feel?" Father Don asked him.

"Good," Mark said.

They had him move around some; it wasn't easy.

"Okay," Father Don said, "get that off and try on the other one. They're supposed to be the same size but it never hurts to check."

So then Derek was going to do it. For some reason, it made Mark afraid the suit wouldn't fit.

It did. Father Don zipped him up, and Mark put the head on and stumped around.

"Growl," his mother said. "Look like you're going to drag someone overboard and take them to your secret cave."

"Graaaahhhh," Mark tried, claws raised, and his mother screamed like she was the girl in the movie. Father Don stepped between them to protect her, and he knocked him aside with one blow.

"Very convincing," Father Don said. "Okay, let's get it off."

Mark wondered if Dracula would have been better. Probably not. It all seemed cheesy now, dumb.

After that they visited Derek. He was awake, drinking ginger ale through a straw. He smiled when he saw Mark. He had a patch over the eye, otherwise he was fine. He turned so his good one was aimed at him. It was brown; Mark hadn't noticed it before.

"Hey," he said.

"Hey," Mark said. "How's it going?"

"All right. Got to miss school. It would have been great but they don't have cable, just the regular stations."

Mark didn't have anything else to say.

"Randy took the gun apart," Derek said. "Did you know that?"

"No."

"He unscrewed all the parts and put them in this plastic bag. He says I can have it back when I'm fifteen."

"Wow."

"Yeah. That's all right, he said we might get a Nintendo 64 for my birthday."

"Cool," Mark said. It was good to hear Derek talk like he always did. It was only bad when he looked at the patch. "Hey, I'm sorry."

"That's okay," Derek said. "Did you know there's a club for people with one eye? Yeah, it's called Singular Vision. A lot of famous people are in it, like Wesley Walker, the receiver for the Jets."

Mark didn't mention that he was retired; Derek knew that. He thought he should say he was sorry again. It was like saying his name; he expected it to do something, but it didn't.

Derek was coming home tomorrow. He could have come home today but they had to fit him with a prosthetic eye.

"It's not glass," Derek insisted. "It's a special kind of plastic they did experiments with on the Space Shuttle. You can drop it fifty feet onto concrete and it won't chip."

"Huh," Mark said.

It was dinner time; a man with a hairnet was rolling a cart down the hall, bringing trays into the rooms. Derek's had plastic wrap over some kind of chicken. Derek's mom peeled the plastic off and steam came up.

"I guess we ought to be heading out," Mark's mom said, and Derek's mom walked them out into the hall. "We'll see you tomorrow, I guess."

"Oh yeah," Derek's mom said. "We're having a little welcome home party for him."

"We'll be there."

"Thanks for coming," Derek's mom said to Mark.

"Sure," Mark said. Because what else was he supposed to say? You're welcome?

He thought about all this in bed—which was dumb, he thought. There was nothing he could do about it then.

Tuesday after school Mark helped his mom hang a banner from the porch. It was one she rented out. It said WELCOME HOME and then had a patch where you spelled out the name of the person. Mark handed her the scratchy, Velcro-backed letters from the plastic bin and then held the ladder.

They were all waiting on the porch for him, and then when the Rotas' truck pulled into the drive they all ran down to the yard. Derek was sitting in the passenger seat; he waited until his stepfather came around to open the door for him.

The patch was gone. At first Mark couldn't see because his mom was hugging him, and then Sarah, her hair pulled back in a black velvet scrunchy. Derek's mom was crying a little, and trying to laugh at how sappy she was, and then Derek turned to get a hug from Mark's dad and Mark could see the eye.

It seemed big, maybe because the lid was puffed-up, and Mark tried not to watch for it to move. It couldn't, he thought, but he couldn't be sure, and he didn't want Derek to catch him staring. But it didn't look right.

No, because inside when they sat down to have cake, they sat Mark right beside him, on that side. It was like they did it on purpose, so he had to see what he'd done, and so close it was impossible not to see the eye was plastic, and stuck looking straight ahead, no matter who Derek was talking to. To talk to Mark he had to twist around in his chair and look at him over his nose.

"Good cake, huh?"

"Great," Mark said.

"My mom said you tried on the costumes."

"Yeah."

"So, are they like amazing?"

"They have teeth just like you said."

"Cool."

"Are you boys ready for the big night?" Mark's dad asked. "You got your act down?"

"Oh, forget it," Derek's mom joked. "I'm not going anywhere near that place. I've had my scare for the year, thank you."

They all laughed and pitched in to convince her.

"All right," she said, "but just once."

It was decided; Mark's mom would drop them off and then the rest of them would all go together, even Peter and Sarah.

The next morning Derek and Mark got on the bus together. Derek's eye wasn't as puffed up, but Philip Dawkins across the aisle wouldn't stop looking at him.

"What are you staring at?" Derek said.

"You. Your eye."

And before he knew what he was doing, Mark shot across the aisle and was smashing Philip Dawkins in the face, driving his fist in again and again and growling as Philip's friends tried to drag him off.

"I'll kill you," Philip was saying, but now everyone was staring at him, then looking away, embarrassed for him because blood was coming from his lip and he was crying, even his ears red.

Mark sat rigid in his seat, ready to hit him again if he didn't shut up. He wouldn't say anything, he'd just hit him. And when Philip said it again, Mark did. And then no one would look at him.

"What are you doing?" Derek asked.

"He was looking at you."

"Yeah, so? People are gonna look."

"I didn't like what he said either."

"You didn't have to hit him again," Derek said, and the rest of the way they didn't talk.

"What's this I hear about a fight on the bus?" his mom said when he got home.

"Nothing," Mark said. "Someone was making fun of Derek."

"So you split his lip, is that right?"

"We got in a fight."

"That's not the way I heard it. The way I heard it it sounds like you attacked him."

"It was a fight," Mark said.

"You make it sound like you've been in fights before. Have you?"

"No."

"Then why now?"

"I don't know."

"Well," his mom said, "why don't you go up to your room and think about it, and I'll think about whether you should do your haunted house tonight."

He didn't argue, he just went up and closed the door. It was starting to get dark, the sun behind the trees, turning the sky orange. He thought of the gun in pieces in Derek's basement, in a plastic bag. He still wanted to hit Philip Dawkins, and he would tomorrow if he said anything, he didn't care.

"Well, have you thought about it?" his mom said when she looked in.

"Yes."

"And?"

"And I'm sorry," he said, and this really was a lie.

"You should be," his mom said, "and if you think you're sorry now, you just wait till your father hears about this." She told him to get ready, they were leaving in five minutes.

Derek must have told on him, but on the way over neither of them mentioned the fight. They talked about the Ghost Mine at Kennywood and all the things that jumped out at you, the hiss of air that made your hair stand up just before the end. This was going to be better, Derek said, because there it was the same ride every time; here things could jump out at you from anywhere. Mark was on the side with his good eye but couldn't stop thinking of the other, the wall of black there, not even blue stars, just nothing.

The haunted house used to be the main building of the old hospital. There was already a long line outside, teenagers and parents with little kids. The fence around the parking lot was covered with giant spiders Mark's mom made from black garbage bags and old socks. From the trees in front hung ghosts and grinning skeletons. The porch was done up in cobwebs, and speakers on the roof blasted out eerie laughter. Mr. Jenner waved them through to the back lot with a flashlight. Father Don's mini-van was there, and a bunch of other cars. Mark's mom got out and came in with them to check on her work.

The hallways were wide but the ceilings were low, and they'd crammed in as much as they could. There were bats that flittered on nylon fishing line, and zombies that peered at you from the rooms, and a mummy who swung down from the ceiling. "Whoa!" Derek said. "Man!" There was an operating room in the real operating room where the doctor cut off the patient's head, and a torture chamber with an iron maiden and a victim stretched hideously on the rack—all his mom's work. She bent over the displays, straightening things, touching up. Right now it looked stupid, but in the dark with the dry ice fog sliding along the floor it would be scary, or that was the idea. Last year when they went through, Mark had stayed close to his dad, hoping he wouldn't notice. None of it was really scary, it was all fake; it was just that he didn't like being frightened. It was stupid to be frightened of that stuff, he thought; there were real things to be afraid of.

Father Don was putting on his costume—the lab coat and wire glasses of Dr. Frankenstein. Mark's mom told him everything looked okay and that she'd see them later and left them with him.

"Let me show you where you are," Father Don said, and took them upstairs.

They had a room of their own, made up to look like the ocean, the walls covered in wavy, mirrored paper with a blue light shining on it, an inflatable shark in one corner, fake sea- weed and cardboard starfish everywhere. There were mossy papier-mâché rocks with a crack you had to squeeze through to get to the next room; that's where they'd scare people.

"Cool," Derek said when he saw the suits, and Mark wished he'd stop being so stupid.

"Okay, I'll let you two get settled. We should be starting in about ten minutes. They'll be an announcement on the PA."

"Wow," Derek said, and looked around the room, turning in a circle. The foil and the blue light made the room seem bigger. He went to the stairs and then came back. "Check this out," he whispered, and pulled a small white tube from his pocket and handed it to Mark.

It was Vampire Blood, Mark had seen some in the novelty shop downtown, thin runny stuff the color of maraschino cherries.

"What are you going to do with it?" Mark asked.

"We'll put it on, it'll be scarier."

"You shouldn't put it on the costumes."

"Look," Derek said, and pointed to where it said Does Not Stain Clothing. "Okay?"

"Whatever."

"Whatever," Derek echoed him.

"Shut up," Mark said, and threw the tube at him.

As soon as it left his hand, he was sure it would hit him in the other eye. He didn't mean it; he didn't know why he was angry. Everything.

The tube flew past Derek and skittered under the shark.

"What was that for?" Derek said.

"Nothing. I'm sorry."

"You should be," Derek said, and retrieved it.

They didn't say anything while they hauled their suits on.

"Here," Mark said, and zipped him up, helped him settle the head.

"It's heavy," Derek said. "Can you see anything?"

"Not much."

The announcement came over the PA and someone's dad ran up the stairs and left a bucket with a chunk of dry ice steaming in the corner. Derek held up the Vampire Blood.

"You want some?"

"Sure," Mark said, more to be nice than anything. It would probably look cheesy; all that stuff did.

Derek held the front of the mask and for a minute all Mark could see were his hands and the tube. The lights flickered and finally stayed on, but just barely. With the blue light it almost looked liked they were underwater.

"How about your claws?"

"Why not," Mark said, and held out his arms. He waited inside the suit and then Derek let go of one hand and took the other.

"Well," Mark said, "how's it look?"

"See for yourself." Derek led him forward a few steps and then turned him toward the wall.

There in the wavy mirror stood the Creature from the Black Lagoon, its lips bright with blood. Mark raised his claws and growled, then did it again, leaning closer, and again, till he was inches from it, his breath coming back off the wall. The foil distorted his face, made the Creature's eyes bulge and slither, his fangs grow. Mark tilted his chin until he could see himself inside the mouth, his eyes looking back at the monster that had devoured him. In the mirror, in the dim light, with the fog rolling all around him, Mark thought it looked very real.

Stewart O'Nan *was born in Pittsburgh on George A. Romero's and Alice Cooper's birthday. His darker novels include* The Speed Queen, A Prayer for the Dying, *and* The Night Country. *His screenplay* Poe *was recently published in a limited edition by Lonely Roads Books.*

No hint of the fantastic or supernatural, nothing truly shocking, just a quietly brilliant story with its own singular darkness. Stewart O'Nan's "Monsters," is a slice of everyday life. But it's also, among other things, about learning there are "real things to be afraid of" and that no one's life is entirely ordinary or free of shadows.

THE BRINK OF ETERNITY

BARBARA RODEN

———◆———

The knife is long and lethal yet light, both in weight and appearance; a thing precise and definite, which he admires for those reasons. It has not been designed for the task at hand, but it will suffice.

The sound of a heart beating fills his ears, and he wonders if it is his heart or the other's. He will soon know.

The knife is raised, and then brought down in a swift movement. A moment of resistance, and then the flesh yields, and vivid spatters spread, staining the carpet of white, bright and beautiful.

He brings the knife down again, and again. He can still hear the beating, and knows it for his own heart, for the other's has stopped. He fumbles for a moment, dropping the knife, pulling off his gloves, then falls to his knees and plunges his bare hand into the bruised and bloody chest, pulling out the heart, warm and red and raw.

He eats.

WALLACE, William Henry (1799–?1839) was born in Richmond, Virginia. His family was well-to-do, and William was almost certainly expected to follow his father, grandfather, and two uncles into the legal profession. However, for reasons which remain unknown he abandoned his legal studies, and instead began work as a printer and occasional contributor of letters, articles, and reviews to various publications. In this respect there are interesting parallels between Wallace and Charles Francis HALL (q.v.), although where Hall's Arctic explorations were inspired by the fate of the Franklin Expedition, Wallace appears to have been motivated by the writings of John Cleve Symmes, Jr. (1779–1829), particularly Symmes's "hollow earth" theory—popular through the 1820s—which postulated gateways in the Polar regions which led to an underground world capable of sustaining life.

From *We Did Not All Come Back: Polar Explorers, 1818–1909*
by Kenneth Turnbull
(HarperCollins Canada, 2005)

He could not remember a time when he did not long for something which he could not name, but which he knew he would not find in the course laid out for him. The best tutors and schools, a career in the law which would be eased by his family's name and wealth, marriage to one of the eligible young ladies whose mamas were so very assiduous in calling on his own mother, and whose eyes missed nothing, noting his manners, his well-made figure, strong and broad-shouldered, his prospects and future, of which they were as sure as he; surer, for his was an old story which they had read before.

But he chafed under his tutors, a steady stream of whom were dismissed by his father, certain that the next one would master the boy. School was no better; he was intelligent, even gifted, yet perpetually restless, dissatisfied, the despair of his teachers, who prophesied great things for him if he would only apply himself fully. He was polite to the mamas and their daughters, but no sparkling eyes enchanted him, no witty discourse ensnared him; his heart was not touched. He studied law because it was expected of him and he saw no other choice.

And then . . . and then came the miracle that snapped the shackles, removed the blinders, showed him the path he was to follow. It came in the unprepossessing form of a pamphlet, which he was later to discover had been distributed solely to institutes of higher learning throughout America, and which he almost certainly would never have seen had he not, however reluctantly, wearily, resignedly, followed the dictates of his family, if not his head and heart. Proof, if it were needed, that the Fate which guides each man was indeed watching over him.

The pamphlet had no title, and was addressed, with a forthright simplicity and earnestness Wallace could only admire, "To All The World." The author wrote:

> I declare the earth is hollow, and habitable within; containing a number of solid concentrick spheres, one within the other, and that it is open at the poles 12 or 16 degrees; I pledge my life in support of this truth, and am ready to explore the hollow, if the world will support and aid me in the undertaking.
>
> JOHN CLEVES SYMMES
> Of Ohio, Late Captain of Infantry.

He opened the pamphlet, his hands trembling. A passage caught his eye:

> I ask one hundred brave companions, well equipped, to start from Siberia in the fall season, with Reindeer and slays, on the ice of the frozen sea: I engage we find warm and rich land, stocked with thrifty vegetables and animals if not men, on reaching one degree northward of latitude 62; we will return in the succeeding spring.

The words seemed to inscribe themselves on his heart. "One hundred brave companions"; "start from Siberia"; "find warm and rich land"; "return in the succeeding spring."

In an instant he knew what it was that he had to do. After long years of wandering and searching, his restless feet were halted and pointed in the only true direction.

It is his first food in—how long? He has lost count of the days and weeks; all is the same here in this wasteland of white. He remembers Symmes's "warm and rich land" and a laugh escapes his throat. It is a rough, harsh, scratched sound, not because its maker is unamused, but because it has been so long since he has uttered a sound that it is as if he has forgotten how.

The remains of the seal lie scattered at his feet; food enough to last for several days if carefully husbanded. There will be more seals now, further south, the way he has come, the way he should go. Salvation lies to the south; reason tells him this. But that would be salvation of the body only. If he does not continue he will never know. He fears this more than he fears the dissolution of his body.

He grasps the knife firmly in his hand—he can at least be firm about this—and begins to cut up the seal, while all around the ice cracks and cries.

One of the earliest pieces of writing identified as being by Wallace is a review of James McBride's *Symmes' Theory of Concentric Spheres* (1826), in which Wallace praises the ingenuity and breadth of Symmes's theory, and encourages the American government to fund a North Polar expedition "with all due speed, to investigate those claims which have been advanced so persuasively, by Mr. Symmes and Mr. Reynolds, regarding the Polar Regions, which endeavor can only result in the advancement of knowledge and refute the cant, prejudice, ignorance, and unbelief of those whose long-cherished, and wholly unfounded, theories would seek to deny what they themselves can barely comprehend."

From *We Did Not All Come Back*

His path was set. He threw over his legal studies, to the anger of his father and the dismay of his mother, and waited anxiously for further word of Symmes's glorious expedition. How could anyone fail to be moved by such passion, such selfless determination, such a quest for knowledge that would surely be to the betterment of Mankind?

Yet no expedition was forthcoming. Symmes's words had, it seemed, fallen on the ears of people too deaf to hear, too selfish to abandon their petty lives and transient pleasures. Wallace had fully expected to be a part of the glorious expedition; now, faced with its failure, he cast round for something that would enable him to dedicate his life—or a large part of it—to those Polar realms which now haunted him, in preparation for the day when Symmes's vision would prevail, and he could fulfil the destiny which awaited him.

He became a printer, for it seemed that his only connection with that region which so fascinated him was through words; so words would become his trade. He found work with a printer willing—for a consideration—to employ him as an apprentice, and learned the trade quickly and readily. When he was not working he was reading, anything and everything he could to prepare himself. He read Scoresby's two volume *Account of the Arctic Regions* and found, for the first time, pictures of that region of snow and ice, and of the strange creatures living there, seals and whales and the fearsome Polar Bear and, strangest of all, the Esquimaux who, in their furs, resembled not so much men as another type of animal. It was true that Scoresby scorned the idea of a "hollow earth"; yet he was only a whaling captain, and could not be expected to appreciate, embrace the ideas of someone like Symmes, a man of vision, of thought. Wallace expected more from Parry, that great explorer, and was heartened to find that the captain believed firmly in the idea of an Open Polar Sea, although he, like Scoresby, declined to accept a hollow earth.

Wallace knew that it existed, knew with his whole heart and soul that such a thing must be; those who denied it, even those who had been to the North, were either wilfully blind, or jealous that they had not yet managed to discover it, and thereby accrue to themselves the glory which belonged to Symmes. When Symmes came to Richmond on a speaking tour Wallace obtained a ticket to the lecture and sat, enthralled, while Symmes and his friend Joshua Reynolds preached their doctrine, hanging on to every word, eyes greedily devouring the wooden globe which was used by way of illustration, and displayed the hollows in the earth at the Polar extremities which led to a fantastic world of pale beings and weak sunlight.

In 1823 he heard that Symmes's friend, the businessman James McBride, had submitted a proposal to Congress, asking for funding to explore the North Polar region expressly to investigate Symmes's theory. Here at last was his opportunity; and he waited in a fever of excitement for the passing of the proposal, the call to arms, the expedition, the discovery, the triumphant return, the vindication.

The proposal was voted down.

He has been living thus for so long that his body now works like a thing independent of his mind, an automaton. The seal meat is still red, but no longer warm; the strips are hardening, freezing. He must . . . what must he do? Build a snow house for the night; yes. And then he must load the seal meat on to his sledge, in preparation for the next day's travel. In which direction that will be he can not say. He does not know what lies ahead, what awaits, and it frightens him as much as it elates him; he does know what lies behind, what awaits there, and that frightens him even more, with no trace of elation whatever.

Following Symmes's death in 1829 his theory largely fell out of favor, as a wave of Polar exploration failed to find any evidence of a "hollow earth." Symmes's adherents gradually deserted him, or turned their attentions elsewhere; Joshua Reynolds successfully lobbied Congress for funding for a South Seas expedition which would also, as an aside, search for any traces of a "Symmes hole," as it came to be known, in the Antarctic. Although no sign of such a hole was found, the voyage did have far-reaching literary consequences, inspiring both Edgar Allan Poe's *The Narrative of Arthur Gordon Pym* and Herman Melville's *Moby-Dick*.

Poe published an article in praise of Reynolds, and the South Sea expedition, in the *Southern Literary Messenger* in January 1837; a reply to this article, penned by Wallace, appeared in the March 1837 issue. Wallace commends Poe on his "far-sighted and clear-headed praise of what will surely be a great endeavor, and one which promises to answer many of the questions which, at present, remain beyond our understanding," but laments the abandonment of American exploration in the North. "A golden opportunity is slipping through our fingers; for while the British Navy must needs sail across an ocean and attack from the east, through a maze of channels and islands which has defied all attempts and presents one of the most formidable barriers on Earth, the United States need only reach out along our western coast and sail through Bering's Strait to determine, for once and all, the geography of the Northern Polar regions."

Elsewhere in the article Wallace writes of the Arctic as "this Fearsome place, designed by Nature to hold and keep her secrets" and of "the noble Esquimaux, who have made their peace with a land so seemingly unable to support human existence, and who have much to teach us." These references make it clear that Wallace had, by 1837, already spent time in the Eastern Arctic, a fact borne out by the logbook of the whaling ship *Christina*, covering the period 1833–5. On board when the ship left New London in May 1833 was one "Wm. H. Wallace, gent., late of Richmond," listed as "passenger." In late August the log notes starkly that "Mr. Wallace disembarked at Southampton Island."

Where he lived, and what he did, between August 1833 and March 1837 remains a mystery; Wallace left behind few letters, no journals or diaries that have been discovered, and did not publish any accounts of his travels. It has been assumed that he, like later explorers such as Hall and John RAE (q.v.), spent time living among the Inuit people and learning their way of life; if so, it is unfortunate that Wallace left no account of this time, as his adoption of the traditional Inuit way of life, in the 1830s, would mark him as one of the first white men to do so.

From *We Did Not All Come Back*

Even when Symmes died, and his theory looked set to die with him, Wallace kept faith. There would, he now knew, be no government-backed venture in search of the hollow earth; it would be up to one man of vision, daring, resolve to make his own way north. That man, he swore, would be William Henry Wallace, whose name would ever after ring down the annals of history.

Yet it was not fame, or the thought of fame, which spurred him on; rather, it was the rightness of the cause, the opportunity to prove the naysayers wrong, and a chance to break truly free from the shackles of his life and upbringing and venture, alone, to a place which was shrouded in mystery, to see for himself the wonders which were, as yet, no more than etchings in books, tales told by travellers. He had lived frugally, not touching the allowance still provided by his father, who hoped that the Prodigal Son would one day return to the family home; and with this he set out, early in 1833, for New England, where he persuaded a reluctant—until he saw the banknotes in the stranger's pocketbook—whaling captain to let him take passage on board his ship. Only when the *Christina* had set sail for the north did William Henry Wallace, for the first time in many years, know a kind of peace.

But it was a restless peace, short-lived. He spent the days pacing the deck with anxious feet, eyes ever northward, scanning the horizon for any signs of that frozen land for which he longed. When the first icebergs came in sight he was overcome with their terrible beauty, so imperfectly captured in the drawings he had pored over until he knew their every detail as well as if he himself had been the artist. Soon the ice was all around, and while captain and crew kept a fearful eye on it always, Wallace drank in its solemn majesty, and rejoiced that each day brought him closer to his goal.

When the *Christina* left him at Southampton Island he was oblivious to the crew's concern for a man whom they obviously thought mad. Yet they did not try to dissuade him; they had business to attend to, and only a short time before the ice closed in and either forced them home or sealed them in place for long, dreary months. The captain did try, on one occasion, to stop Wallace; but after a few moments he ceased his efforts, for the look in the other's eyes showed that no words the captain could muster would mean anything. At least the man was well provisioned; whatever qualms the captain might have about his mental state, his physical well-being was assured for a time. And once off the ship he was no longer the captain's concern.

Wallace had studied well the texts with which he had provided himself. In addition to clothing and food and tools, he had purchased numerous small trinkets—mirrors, knives, sewing needles, nails—and they paid handsome dividends amongst the Esquimaux, who were at first inclined to laugh at the *kabloona* come to live among them, but soon learned that he was in earnest about learning their ways. Before long Wallace had shed the outward garb of the white man and adopted the clothing of the Esquimaux, their furs and skins so much better suited to the land than his own cotton and wool garments. Their food he found more difficult, at first, to tolerate; it took many attempts before his stomach could accept the raw blubber and meat without convulsing, but little by little he came to relish it. His first clumsy attempts at building a snow house, or igloo, were met with good-natured laughter, but before long he was adept at wielding the snow knife, a seemingly delicate instrument carved from a single piece of bone which ended in a triangular blade of surprising sharpness. He learned to judge the snow needed for blocks, neither too heavy nor too light, and fashion the bricks so they were tapered where necessary. He learned to make windows of clear ice, and of the importance not only of a ventilation hole at the top of the structure, but of ensuring that it was kept free of the ice that formed from the condensation caused by breath and body warmth, lest it become a tomb for those inside.

The casual way in which the Esquimaux men and women shared their bodies with each other shocked him, at first; after a time he came to see the practicality of sleeping, unclothed under furs, in a group, but he remained aloof from the women who plainly showed that they would welcome him as a partner. In all other ways he admired the natives of that cold land: what other travellers remarked on as their cruelty he saw as a necessity. Illness or frailty in one could mean death for all; there was no room in that place for pity, or sentiment, and he abandoned without regret the last traces of those feelings within his own soul.

He became skilled at traversing the fields of ice and snow, and would often set out alone. The Esquimaux, who only ventured across the ice when necessity compelled them in search of food, were puzzled by his expeditions, which seemed to serve no purpose. In reality he was searching, always searching, for any indication that he was drawing closer to the proof he sought, the proof that would vindicate Symmes, and his own life. He did not mark, in that realm of endless snow, how long he searched; but eventually he realized that he would not find the answers he was seeking in this place of maze-like channels. Symmes had been correct when he said that the answer lay from the west, not the east; and if he had been correct in this, why should he not be correct in much else?

When the *Christina* put in at Southampton Island in 1836 he had been cut off from his own kind for three years. The captain—the same man who had left him there—was astounded when he recognised, among the natives who crowded to the ship to trade for goods, the figure whom he had long thought dead. He was even more astounded when Wallace indicated—in the halting tones of one mastering a foreign tongue—that he sought passage back to New London. He spoke vaguely of business, but further than that he would not be drawn, except to say, of his time in the north, that he did not know whether he had found heaven on earth or an earthly heaven.

His igloo is finished. Small as it is, he has had difficulty lifting the last few blocks into place. He is vaguely surprised that the seal meat, coming as it did to revive him after his body's stores had been depleted, has not given him more energy. Instead, it seems almost as if his body, having achieved surfeit in one respect, is now demanding payment in another regard. After days, weeks, months of driving his body ever onward, all he can think of now is sleep; of the beauty of

*lying down under his fur robes and drifting into slumber even as the ice bearing
him drifts closer to those unknown regions about which he has dreamed for so
long.*

Wallace's reference, in his article, to the west coast of America and
"Bering's Strait" suggests that he felt an attempt on the Arctic should
be made from that side of the continent, and this would have been
in keeping with Symmes's own beliefs. No such formal expedition
along the west coast was to be made until 1848, when the first of the
expeditions in search of the Franklin party set out, but it is clear
that Wallace undertook an informal—and ultimately fatal—journey
of his own more than a decade earlier. An open letter from Wallace,
published in the Richmond *Enquirer* in April 1837, states his intention
of travelling via Honolulu to Hong Kong and thence to Siberia, "which
location is ideally placed as a base for the enterprising Polar traveller,
and has inexplicably been ignored as such by successive governments,
which have declined to take the sound advice of men such as Mr.
Symmes, whose work I humbly continue, and whose theories I shall
strive to prove to the satisfaction of all save those who are immune to
reason, and who refuse to acknowledge any thing with which they do
not have personal acquaintance."

Wallace's letter continues, "I shall be travelling without companions, and with a minimum of provisions and the accoutrements
of our modern existence, for I have no doubt that I shall be able to
obtain sustenance and shelter from the land, as the hardy Esquimaux
do, until such time as I reach my journey's end, where I shall doubtless
be shown the hospitality of those people who are as yet a mystery
to us, but from whom we shall undoubtedly learn much which is
presently hidden."

It is not known when Wallace left Virginia, but the diary of
the Rev. Francis Kilmartin—now in the possession of the Mission
Houses Museum in Honolulu—confirms that he had arrived in the
Sandwich Islands, as they were then known, by March 1838, when he
is mentioned in Kilmartin's diary. "Mr. Wallace is a curious mixture
of the refined gentleman and the mystic, at one moment entertaining
us all with his vivid and stirring tales of life among the Esquimaux,
at another displaying an almost painful interest in any news from
the ships' Captains arriving in port from eastern realms. His theories
about the Polar region seem scarcely credible, and yet he appears to
believe in them with every fiber of his being." In an entry from April
1838 Kilmartin writes "We have said our farewells and God speeds
to Mr. Wallace, who departed this day on board the *Helena* bound
for Hong Kong. While I am, I confess, loath to see him go—for I do
not foresee a happy outcome to his voyage—it is also a relief that he

has found passage for the next stage of his journey, which he has been anticipating for so long, and which consumes his mind to the exclusion of all else."

From *We Did Not All Come Back*

He had not wanted to return to Virginia, but there was that which needed to be done, preparations he needed to make, before setting out once more. He was uncomfortable with his parents, although not as uncomfortable as they with him. His father declared, publicly, that he would wash his hands of the boy, as if Wallace were still the feckless lad who had abandoned his studies so long ago; his mother thought, privately, that she would give much to have that feckless lad back once more if only for a moment, for she found herself frightened of the man who had returned from a place she could barely imagine.

He left Richmond—which he had long since ceased to think of as home—in early summer of 1837, and made his way to the Sandwich Islands, thence to Hong Kong, and thence—but later he could hardly remember the route by which he had attained the frozen shore of that far country about which he had dreamed for so long. He seemed to pass through his journey as one travels through a dream world, the people and places he saw like little more than ghosts, pale and inconsequent shadows. It was not until he stood on that northern coast, saw once more the ice stretching out before him, that he seemed to awaken. All that he had passed through was forgotten; all that existed now was the journey ahead, through the ice which stretched as far as his eyes could see.

The ice moves, obeying laws which have existed since the beginning of time. Currents swirl in the dark depths below, carrying the ice floe upon which he has erected his igloo, carrying it—where? He does not know. It is carrying him onward; that is all he knows.

Kilmartin's fears were well founded, for it is at this point that William Henry Wallace disappears from history. What befell him after he left Honolulu is one of the minor mysteries of Arctic exploration, for no further word is heard of him; we do not even know if he successfully reached Hong Kong, and from there north his passage would have been difficult. His most likely course would have been to travel the sea trading route north to the Kamtschatka Peninsula and then across the Gulf of Anadyr to Siberia's easternmost tip and the shore of the Chukchi Sea, from whence he would have been able to start out across the treacherous pack ice toward the North Pole.

Whether or not he made it this far is, of course, unknown, and likely to remain so at this remove, although one tantalising clue exists. When the crew of the *Plover* were forced to spend the winter of 1848–9 in Chukotka, on the northeast tip of the Gulf of Anadyr, they heard many tales of the rugged coastline to the west, and met many of the inhabitants of the villages, who came to Chukotka to trade. One of the party—Lieutenant William Hulme Hooper—later wrote *Ten Months Among the Tents of the Tuski* about the *Plover's* experience, and in one chapter touches on the character of these hardy coastal people. "They are superstitious almost to a fault," he wrote, "and signs and events that would be dismissed by most are seized on by them as omens and portents of the most awful type. . . . One native told of a man who appeared like a ghost from the south, who had no dogs and pulled his own sledge, and whose wild eyes, strange clothes, and terrible demeanor so frightened the villagers that they—who are among the most hospitable people on Earth, even if they have but little to offer—would not allow him a space in their huts for the night. When day came they were much relieved to find that he had departed, across the ice in the direction of Wrangel Land to the north, where the natives do not venture, upon seeing which they were convinced that he was come from—and gone to—another world."

Historians have debated the meaning behind Hooper's "a man who appeared like a ghost from the south." The author would, of course, have been hearing the native's words through an interpreter, who might himself have been imprecise in his translation. Hooper's phraseology, if it is a faithful transcription of what he was told, could mean that the stranger appeared in ghost-like fashion; that is, unexpectedly. However, another interpretation is that the man appeared pale, like a ghost, to the dark-skinned Chukchi people; this, when taken with the direction from which the man appeared (which is the course Wallace would almost certainly have taken) and his decision to head northeast toward Wrangel, means that Hooper's description of "the man like a ghost" might be our last glimpse of William Henry Wallace, who would have gone to certain death in the treacherous ice field; although whether before, or after, finding that Symmes's theory was just that—a theory only—will never be known.

From We Did Not All Come Back

The land ice—the shelf of ice permanently attached to the shore—was easy enough to traverse. He towed a light sledge of his own devising behind him; he had no need of dogs, and now laughed at Symmes's idea that reindeer would have been a practical means of transport. Here there was one thing, and one thing only, on which he could depend, and that was himself.

An open lead of water separated the land ice from the pack ice, and it was with difficulty that he traversed it. From that moment his journey became a landscape of towering ice rafters and almost impenetrable pressure ridges, formed by the colliding sheets of ice. On some days he spent more time hacking a trail through the pressure ridges, or drying himself and his clothes after falling through young ice or misjudging his way across a lead, than he did travelling, and would advance less than a mile; on other days, when his progress seemed steady, he would find that the currents carrying the ice had taken him further forward than he anticipated.

He headed ever northward. He passed Wrangel Land on his left, and could have confirmed that it was an island, not a land bridge across the Pole connecting with Greenland; but by now such distinctions were beyond him. All was one here, the ice and snow and he himself, a tiny dot in the landscape of white. Did he believe, still, in Symmes? Would he have recalled the name, had there been anyone to mention it? But there was no one, and with every step forward he left the world, and his part in it, further behind.

Each night he built his house of snow. The Esquimaux had built their igloos large enough to accommodate several people; his own houses were small, large enough to accommodate only one, and consequently he had had to train himself to wake every hour or so, to clear the ventilation hole of ice so that he could breathe. It was not difficult to wake at regular intervals; the ice cracked and groaned and spoke almost as a living person, and more than once he sat in the Arctic night, listening to the voices, trying to discern what they were saying. One day, perhaps; one day.

His provisions, despite careful husbanding, gave out eventually, and for several days he subsisted on melted snow, and by chewing on the leather traces of the harness which connected him to his sledge, his only remaining link with his past. In reality, he was almost beyond bodily needs; he only remembered that it was time to eat when the increasing darkness reminded him that another day was drawing to a close. The seal was the first living thing that he had seen in—how long? He did not remember; yet instinct took over, and he killed it and ate it, and when he had sated his hunger he had a moment of clarity, almost, when his course seemed laid out, stark and level. Either he hoarded the seal meat, turned, and set back for the coast, or he continued, onward through the ice, toward: what? An Open Polar Sea? Symmes's hollow earth?

It did not matter.

Nothing mattered.

His destiny was here, in the north, in the ice. It was all he had wanted, since—he could not remember when. Time meant nothing. The life he had left behind was less than dust. This was the place that he was meant to be.

He would go on.

He crawls into the igloo and fastens the covering over the opening, making a tight seal. His fur-covered bed beckons, and he pulls the robes over himself. Around and below him the ice cracks and cries, a litany lilting as a lullaby which slowly, gradually, lulls him to sleep.

The ventilation hole at the top of the igloo becomes crusted with ice, condensed from his own breath.

He does not wake to clear it.

And the ice carries him, ever onward.

Barbara Roden *is a World Fantasy Award-winning editor and publisher, whose short stories have appeared in numerous publications, including* Year's Best Fantasy and Horror: Nineteenth Annual Collection, Horror: Best of the Year 2005, Bound for Evil, Strange Tales 2, Gaslight Grimoire, Gaslight Grotesque, *and* Poe: 19 New Tales Inspired by Edgar Allan Poe. *Her first collection,* Northwest Passages, *was published in October 2009; the title story was nominated for the Stoker, International Horror Guild, and World Fantasy awards. "The Brink of Eternity," which originally appeared in* Poe, *gave her a welcome opportunity to put her love of Arctic exploration to good use; she only wishes that the reference book cited in the story,* We Did Not All Come Back: Polar Explorers, 1818–1909, *actually existed, as it would have been a useful research tool.*

Barbara Roden has also written of "The Brink of Eternity":

It incorporates Poe's belief that at one time mankind was united with the Godhead, and that there was a subsequent division, with man getting further away; at some point man will start to return towards the Godhead, and at the moment of collision, there will be ultimate knowledge, as well as annihilation. We see this in the protagonists of [Poe's "Ms. in a Bottle" and "A Descent Into the Maelström,"] I mentioned, who fear their ultimate destiny, but also embrace it, realizing they will gain knowledge they desire, even at the cost of their own death.

As an editor/publisher, Roden has long been an advocate of classic supernatural fiction and ghost stories. Although she frequently evokes the style of an earlier age with her writing, there's nothing old-fashioned about its effect. Her Poe-influenced theme reminds me of one of my personal theories about horror, which was best summed up by Kurt J. Schneider: "Ecstasy is a glimpse of the infinite; terror is full disclosure."

FROST MOUNTAIN PICNIC MASSACRE

SETH FRIED

—◆—

Last year, the people in charge of the picnic blew us up. Every year it gets worse. That is, more people die. The Frost Mountain Picnic has always been a matter of uncertainty in our town and the massacre is the worst part. Even the people whose picnic blankets were not laid out directly upon the bomb line were knocked unconscious by the airborne limbs of their neighbors, or at least had the black earth at the foot of Frost Mountain driven under their eyelids and fingernails and up into their sinuses. The apple dumpling carts and cotton candy stands and guess-your-weight booths that were not obliterated in the initial blasts leaned slowly into the new-formed craters, each settling with a limp, hollow crumple. The few people along the bombline who survived the blast were at the very least blown into the trees.

The year before that, the boom of the polka band had obscured the scattered reports of far-off rifles. A grown man about to bite a caramel apple suddenly spun around wildly, as if propelled by the thin spray of blood from his neck. An old woman, holding her stomach, stumbled into a group of laughing teenagers. Someone fell forward into his funnel cake and all day long we walked around as if we weren't aware of what was happening.

One year, the muskets of the Revolutionary War Reenactment Society were somehow packed with live ammunition. Another year, all the children who played in the picnic's Bouncy Castle died of radiation poisoning. Yet another year, it was discovered halfway through the picnic that a third of the port-a-potties contained poisonous snakes. The year we were offered free hot air balloon rides, none of the balloons that left—containing people laughing and waving from the baskets, snapping pictures as they ascended—ever returned.

Nevertheless, every year we still turn out in the hundreds to the quaint river quay in our marina district to await the boats that will take us to Frost Mountain But we still turn out in the hundreds to the quaint river quay in our marina district to await the boats that will take us to Frost Mountain.

In a hilltop parking lot, we apply sunscreen to the noses of our children. We rifle through large canvas carryalls, taking inventory of fruit snacks, extra jelly sandals, Band-Aids, and juice boxes, trying to anticipate our children's inevitable needs and restlessness in the twenty minutes that they will have to wait for the boats to be readied. Anxious to claim our place in line, we head down the hill in a rush toward the massive white boats aloft in the water.

We wait in a long, roped queue that doubles back on itself countless times before reaching the loading platform with its blue vinyl awning. Once it's time to depart, the line will move forward, leading us to the platform, where the deckhands will divide us up evenly between the various boats. From there, we will be moved up river, to the north of our city, where Frost Mountain looms. From the decks, we will eventually see a lush, green field interrupted by brightly colored tents and flashing carnival rides, the whole scene contained by the incredible height of Frost Mountain, reaching into the sky with its cold, blue splendor.

The sight of the picnic at the foot of Frost Mountain is so appealing that most of us will, once again, convince ourselves that this year will be different, that all we have in store for us is a day full of leisure and amusements—but sooner or later, one of the rides will collapse, or a truck of propane will explode near one of the food tents, killing dozens.

Of course, every year more people say they won't come. Every year, there are town meetings during which we all condemn the Frost Mountain Picnic. We meet in the empty tennis courts of the Constituent Metro Park where we vow to forsake the free bags of peanuts, the free baked butternut squashes, the free beer, the free tractor rides and firework expositions.

We grow red in the face, swearing our eternal alignment against all the various committees, public offices, and obscure private interests in charge of organizing the picnic. Every year, there are more people at the meetings who are walking on crutches and wearing eye patches from the injuries they sustained the previous year. Every year, there are more people holding up pictures of dead loved ones and beating their chests. Every year, there are more people getting angry, interrupting one another, and asking the gathered crowd if they might be allowed to speak first. Every year, loyalty oaths are signed. Every year, pledges to abstain from the Frost Mountain Picnic are given and received freely and every single year, without exception, everyone ends up going to the picnic anyway.

Often, the people who are the most vocally opposed to the picnic are also the most eager to get there, the people most likely to cut in line for the boats, the people most disdainful toward the half-dozen zealots picketing in the parking lot.

Waiting in line for the boats, our children rub their chins in the dirt and push their foreheads against our feet. They roll around on the ground and shout obscenities, then run in circles, screaming nonsense, while we play with the car keys in our pockets and gawk passively at the massive boats. Typically, we don't allow our children to our children to misbehave in this way. However, we do our best to understand. Their faces are in pain.

Our children's cheeks begin to ache as they wait in line for the boats, and continue to ache until their faces are painted at the Frost Mountain Picnic. We've come to understand that all children are born with phantom cat whiskers. All children are born with phantom dog faces. All children are born with phantom American flag foreheads, rainbow-patterned jawbones and deep, curving pirate scars, the absence of which haunts them throughout their youth. We understand that all children are born with searing and trivial images hidden in their faces, the absence of which causes them a great deal of discomfort. It is a pain that only the brush of a face painter can alleviate, each stroke revealing the cryptic pictures in our children's faces. Any good parent knows this.

Ten years ago, the massacre came in the form of twenty-five silverback gorillas set loose at the height of the picnic. Among the fatalities, a young girl by the name of Louise Morris was torn to pieces. Perhaps it was Louise's performance as Mary in the Christmas pageant of the preceding winter, or perhaps it was the grim look on the faces of the three silverback gorillas that tugged her arms and legs in opposite directions, or perhaps it was just that she was so much prettier and more well-behaved than the other children who were killed that day—but whatever the case, Louise Morris's death had a profound impact on the community.

That year, the town meetings grew into full-blown rallies. Louise Morris's picture ran on the front page of local newspapers every day for a month. We wore yellow ribbons to church and a local novelty shop began selling Remember Louise T-shirts, which were quickly fashionable. Under extreme pressure from the city council, the local zoo was forced to rid itself of its prized gorilla family, Gigi, Taffy and their newborn baby Jo-Jo, who were sold to the St. Louis Zoo, Calgary Zoo, and Cleveland Zoo, respectively.

The school board added a three-day weekend to the district calendar in memoriam of Louise and successfully carried out a protest campaign against a school two districts away, demanding that they change their mascot from the Brightonville Gorillas to the Brightonville Lightning Bolts. Without any formal action from the school board, the opposition to teaching evolution in public schools began to enjoy a sudden, regional popularity. Without any written mandate, with only the collective moral outcry of the community to guide them, teachers slowly began removing from their classrooms the laminated posters that pictured our supposed, all-too-gorilla-like ancestors as they lumbered their way across the primordial landscape.

The community's reaction to Louise's death was so strong that, in time, it was hard to keep track of all the changes it had engendered. It was difficult to know where one change ended and another began. Perhaps it was our hatred of gorillas that eventually gave way to our distrust of large men with bad posture, which led to the impeachment of Mayor Castlebach. Perhaps our general fear of distant countries, the forests of which were either known or suspected to support gorilla populations, had more to do with the deportation of those four Kenyan exchange students than any of us cared to admit. With all the changes connected to Louise's death, there were many ins and outs, many complexities and half-attitudes, which made it difficult to calculate. In fact, the only thing that seemed at all the same was the Frost Mountain Picnic.

When the public meetings die down, we begin to see advertisements for next year's picnic. Naturally, the initial reaction is always more outrage. But after the advertisements persist for months and months, after we see them on more billboards and on the sides of buses, after we hear the radio jingles and watch the fluff pieces about the impending picnic on the local news, our attitudes invariably begin to soften. Though no one ever comes out and says it, the collective assumption seems to be that if the picnic can be advertised with so little reservation, then the problems surrounding it must have been solved. If such a pleasant jingle can be written for it, if the news anchor can discuss it with the meteorologist so vapidly, the picnic must be harmless. Our oaths against the impending picnic becomes difficult to maintain. Through the sheer optimism of those advertisements, the unfortunate events of the previous year are exorcized.

Those few citizens holding onto their anger are inevitably viewed as people who refuse to move on, people who thrive on discord. When they canvas neighborhoods and approach others on the streets with brochures containing facts about previous massacres, they are called conspiracy theorists and cranks. They're accused of remembering events creatively, of cherry-picking facts in order to accommodate their paranoid fantasies. Or else, it might be said of them that they have some valid points, which would bear consideration, if only their methods weren't so obnoxious, if only they didn't insist on holding up signs at street corners and putting fliers under our windshield wipers, if only they didn't look so self-righteous and affirmed in their opinions. Ultimately, the only thing that these dissenters ever manage to convince us is that to not attend the picnic is to exist outside of what is normal.

Waiting in line for the boats, we wear our Remember Louise T-shirts. We stand in line and busily anticipate the free corndogs, the free ice cream cones, and the free party hats.

Our children bark and grab at the passing legs of the deckhands as they move through the line in their crisp uniforms. Pale-blue pants neatly pressed, matching ties tucked into short-sleeve button-downs, the men acknowledge our children with exaggerated smiles. A deckhand drops to one knee and places his flat, white cap on a child's head. When the child screams, takes off the cap, and tries to tear it in half, the deckhand begins to laugh, as if the child has just said something delightful.

The charm of the deckhands is made all the more unbelievable by our children's outrageous behavior. Desperate to have their faces painted, our children writhe on the ground and moan after the deckhands as they make their way to the loading platform. Once they reach their place beneath the awning, the deckhands occasionally look back at the long line and flash those same exaggerated smiles. They wave excitedly, a gesture that sends our children into a revitalized frenzy.

On various occasions, it has been suggested that perhaps the trouble with our children's faces is only that we indulge them in it, that perhaps what they feel is not actually a physical discomfort, but an emotional discomfort similar to that of any child whose whims might be occasionally frustrated. It has been suggested that perhaps, as a rule, it may be better to do without face painting or, for that matter, anything that would cause them to act so wildly in its absence. It has been suggested that perhaps it would give our children more character if we were to let them suffer under the burden of the hidden images in their faces, forcing them to bring those images out gradually through the development of personal interests and pleasant dispositions, rather than having them only crudely painted on.

Though, in the end, it's difficult for any of us to see it that way. After all, when the children wear their painted faces to school the next day, already smudged and fading, none of us wants our children to be the ones whose faces are bare. None of us wants our children to be the ones excluded or ridiculed. As good parents, we want our children to be successful, even if only in the most superficial way, as such small successes, we hope, might eventually lead to deeper, more meaningful ones. None of us wants our children to be accused of something arbitrary and most likely untrue due to the lack of some item of social significance. None of us has the confidence in our children to endure that type of thing. None of us wants our children to become outcasts. None of us wants our children to become criminals or perverts. None of us wants our children to begin smoking marijuana or masturbating excessively. None of us wants our children to become homeless or adopt strange fetishes, driving away perfectly good mates who simply don't want to be peed on or tied down or have cigarettes put out on their backsides. None of us wants our children to begin hanging around public parks in order to steal people's dogs for some dark, unimaginable purpose. None of us wants our children to wait around outside churches after morning mass in black trench coats in order to flash the departing congregation their bruised, over-sexed genitals, genitals which were once tiny and adorable to us, genitals which we had once tucked lovingly into cloth diapers. None of us wants our children dispersing crowds of elderly churchgoers with their newly-wretched privates, sending those churchgoers screaming, groaning in disgust, fumbling with the keys to their Cadillacs, shielding their eyes in vain.

It isn't a judgment against people who have produced such children. It just isn't something we would want for our own. Even the parents who are less involved in their children's well-being are sick of paying the hospital bills when their unpainted children are pushed off the jungle gym or have their heads shoved into their jacket cubbies. Even those parents are sick of their kids getting nicknames like paintless, bare-face, and faggy-faggy-no-paint. Even those parents, for the most part, seem to understand.

Though the organizations and public offices in charge of the picnic remain vague and mysterious to us, it should be said that we are never directly denied information. It's simply a matter of our not knowing the right questions to ask or where to ask them.

One year, after twenty young couples were electrocuted to death in the Tunnel of Love, many of us showed up to public and private offices in groups and demanded explanations. But in each instance, we were simply informed by a disinterested clerk that the office in question had nothing to do with the picnic, and so could offer no information. Or else we were told that it had played such a small part that the only document on hand was a form reserving the park site for that particular date or a carbon copy of the event's temporary liquor license or some other trivial article.

When one of us asked where we could obtain more information or which office bore the most responsibility, the clerks offered us only a helpless look, as if to suggest that we were being unreasonable. And, truly, once we began to realize the gigantic apparatus of which each office was apparently only an incredibly small part, we had to admit that we were being unreasonable. It became clear that we were not dealing with an errant official or an ineffective ordinance, but an intersection between local government and private interests so complex that it was as if it was none of our business.

At the very most, a clerk referenced some huge, multi-national corporation said to be the primary orchestrator of the picnic. But what could be done with such information? Like that other apparatus, only on a much larger scale, such entities were too big to be properly held accountable for anything. The power of the people in charge of them was so far-reaching that by the time any one of their decisions had run its course, it was like trying to blame them for the weather. Also, because we already sensed ourselves to be a nuisance, we were reminded—a clerk pinching the bridge of his nose, and then replacing his glasses—that the walls of communication were built high around such people, and for good reason.

We wandered out of those offices in silence, our anger abated by our own embarrassment. Suddenly, we were afraid that the clerks had mistaken us for more conspiracy theorists and cranks. Mortified, we returned to those offices to apologize.

Truth be told, as compelled as each of us is to attend the Frost Mountain Picnic, for our own sake as much as for our children's, few of us ever really end up enjoying the aspects of the picnic which originally drew us there.

The craft tables, the petting zoos, the scores of musicians and wandering performers in their festively colored jerkins. Once obtained, all the much-anticipated amusements tend to seem a little trite. Even a thing as difficult to disapprove of as free food doesn't usually satisfy any of us as much as we might pretend. The fried ice creams and elephant ears are all inevitably set aside by those of us who find ourselves feeling suddenly queasy, those of us who, while waiting in line for the boats, had only recently bragged of our hunger.

On the old, wilting merry-go-round, large groups of us sit with our tongues in our cheeks and almost before the ride starts, we wish for it to be over. Even the ironic enjoyment of a child's ride seems belabored and fake. On the merry-go-round, we look to our fellow horsemen and strain forward, feigning attempts to pull ahead. Leaning dramatically from our horses, we clap hands, cheer and force out laughter so awkward and shapeless that it makes our throats ache, so high-toned and weak that it makes our eyes water.

We understand that the amusements of the Frost Mountain Picnic are supposed to entertain us. We understand that when we talk about the picnic's amusements with others, we pretend as if they do. Around water coolers and in restaurants, we repeat stories about unfinished tins of caramel corn and slow, creaking rides on the witch's wheel as if they are deeply cherished memories.

In anticipation of the free such and such, and the free such and such, we manage to convince ourselves that we are indeed looking forward to the picnic. In our minds, we falsely attach value to the items that will be given so generously. Or else, we attempt to see our participation as paying homage to something long past and romantic, a matter of heritage.

Among the difficulties we face in attempting to extricate ourselves from the Frost Mountain Picnic, a problem which is never fully addressed at the town meetings is the fact that—just as all those offices throughout the city perform simple tasks for the picnic, but then can claim no real knowledge or responsibility—most of us are involved with the picnic on many different levels, some of which might not even be completely known to us.

Any number of local businesses, social clubs, volunteer groups, local radio stations, television stations, and departments of municipal utility are either sponsored or underwritten or provided endowments by those in charge of the Frost Mountain Picnic. If we were to buy a bag of oranges from a local grocer, if we were to drop a quarter into the milk jug of the young boy standing by the automatic doors in his soccer uniform, if we were to listen to the Top 40 radio droning from the store's speakers, if we were to flip on a light switch in our own home or flush a toilet, we would be contributing in one fashion or another to the Frost Mountain Picnic. Our role is not limited to our attendance, but extends to include our inclination to drink tap water, eat fresh fruit and go to the bathroom.

Moreover, even if we could deny ourselves these things, everywhere there are peculiar inconsistencies and non sequiturs, which, taken together, are ominous. Periodic bank errors are reported on our checking statements next to the letters FMP and, every week, strange, superfluous deductions are made from our paychecks by an unknown entity.

A Rotary Club, attempting to raise money for childhood leukemia, will later check their records only to find that a majority of the proceeds were somehow accidentally sent to a cotton candy distributor in New Jersey. When the highway patrol calls two weeks before the picnic to ask us if we'd care to donate to the Officers' Widows Fund, the call, routed through Philadelphia, Mexico City, and Anchorage, appears on our phone bills as a $17 charge.

We might volunteer to take part in a committee to discuss the repair of potholes throughout the city only to wind up somehow duped into preparing large mailings in the basements of public buildings, mailings which have nothing to do with potholes, but which include brochures in foreign languages with pictures of families laughing, eating corndogs and playing carnival games next to large, boldly colored words like *lustig* and *glücklich*.

Several times a year, men in dark blue suits flood the city. Without notice, without any noticeable regularity in their visits, they turn up everywhere. They drive slowly across town in large motorcades of black sedans with tinted windows. Dozens of them stand in line at the post office, mailing identical packages wrapped neatly in brown paper and fixed with small blue address labels. They stand outside office buildings and talk into the sleeves of their suit coats. Large groups of them sit in restaurants amid clouds of hushed laughter and cigarette smoke. The men are mostly older, but well-groomed and tan, with magnificently white teeth and expensive watches. They sit three to a bench in public parks and are seen hunched over surveyor's levels outside churches and hospitals and elementary schools. The men walk in and out of every imaginable type of building at every imaginable hour for days. Then, with even less warning than their arrival, they disappear.

One hardly knows what to do with such subtleties, such phenomena. One hardly knows how to combine them or how to separate them or how to consider them in relation to one another. But whatever their sum or difference, such occurrences tend to intensify the sensation that the Frost Mountain Picnic is, in fact, unavoidable. Though it's never expressly stated, the general consensus seems to be that there's nothing we can do which would ever come to any final good, which would ever change the picnic or the massacre or whatever machinations lie beneath either.

While we ourselves feel powerless to avoid it, many of us often hope that our children might eventually outgrow the picnic. After the town meetings, most of us are already well aware that we will betray our own pledges and loyalty oaths. We leave the meetings, feeling sheepish and impotent. Though, some of us do take the opportunity to stop and talk quietly with one another about the possibility that the next generation might eventually rise up and break the pattern of our complacency.

On the way home from the picnic, with the ring of mortar fire still in our ears or the stink of gorillas or gun powder in our noses, we steal glances at our sleeping children in the back seats of our station wagons and minivans. Typically, we are bandaged from some close brush with the massacre, our arms in slings improvised out of our torn and battered Remember Louise T-shirts. Our lips split, our noses are bloodied, our palms, sweaty on the steering wheel. We recall the first moments of the massacre, the first explosion, the first gunshot, the first creeping hum of the planes, the earth moving beneath our feet. We watch our children sleeping in the rear-view, moonlight passing over their peaceful faces. Through the unsightly globs of paint, we catch a glimpse of how our children seemed before the picnic endowed them with such an eager, selfish spirit.

When it comes time to leave the highway, as we drift slowly toward our exit, we are tempted to jerk the wheel in the other direction and speed off to some distant city, a place untouched by picnics. We know our husbands and wives wouldn't say a word, wouldn't ask for an explanation, wouldn't even turn their heads to watch our exit as it passes, but would keep their eyes forward, like ours, a look of exhilaration on their faces.

However, these fantasies are as appealing as they are unlikely, and so our hope remains tied into our children. Our children, who took their first steps while waiting in line for the boats, who muttered their first words to the face painters and jugglers, who lost their first teeth in the picnic's salt water taffy and red-rope licorice. Our children, who, as they grow older, begin to explain the picnic to us as if we don't understand it. Our children, who have begun to scorn and mock us if we so much as mention Frost Mountain, snap their gum and laugh with their friends, as if our old age and presumed irrelevance threatens the very existence of the picnic.

A horn sounds, signaling the line to move forward. No matter how long we wait for the boats, or how eager we might seem, there is always a slight pause between the sounding of the horn and the eventual lurching forward of the crowd. It is a moment in which we recall the year some of the boats sank as they left the picnic, how everyone aboard trusted the surprisingly bulky lifejackets and sank to the bottom of the river like stones. It is a moment of looking from side to side, a moment of coughing and shrugging.

On the opposite shore, a small orchestra of men in dark suits begins to play the second movement of Beethoven's *Eroica*. Assembled under a large carnival tent, the men play expertly, ploddingly. Those whose parts have not yet come stand perfectly still or adjust the dark glasses on the bridge of their noses or speak slowly into the sleeves of their suit coats. The music sounds strange over the noise of the river and weighs heavily in the air.

It is a moment of clarity and anxiety, in which we hope that something will deliver us from our sense of obligation toward the picnic, the sense of embarrassment that would proceed from removing our children from the line, evoking tantrums so fierce as to be completely unimaginable. It is a moment in which we wait for some old emotion to well up in us, some passion our forefathers possessed that made them unafraid of change, no matter how radical or how dangerous or—the deckhands gesturing for us to move forward, their faces suddenly angry and impatient—how impossible.

Seth Fried's *stories have either appeared or are forthcoming in* McSweeney's, The Kenyon Review, The Missouri Review, One Story, Tin House, Vice Magazine, *and many others. He also has a bachelor's degree in Latin from a state university, and can therefore pretty much write his own ticket. He is the recipient of the William Peden Prize in Fiction and "Frost Mountain Picnic Massacre" won a Pushcart Prize. His debut short story collection will be published next year.*

The folks who are annually obliged to attend the Frost Mountain picnic seem incapable of changing the inevitable fatal pattern of their lives. But then aren't most of us are more afraid of change than we'd like to think? Is there an ominous unknown something in Fried's story that keeps the townspeople from breaking away? Or is it simply the same inertia that can ultimately bind us all?

SEA-HEARTS

MARGO LANAGAN

There's never silence, is there? There's always the sea, sucking and sighing. However many doors you like to close between yourself and it, when all other bustlings and conversations cease or pause, always it whispers: *Still I am here. Hear me?*

"That oul witch Messkeletha is down there again," said Raditch.

"'t's all right. We're plenty," said Grinny.

"We're plenty and we have business," James said with some bluster—he was as scared of her as anyone. He shook his empty sack. "We have been sent by our mams. We're to provide for our famblies."

"Yer."

"Hear."

And down the cliff we went. It was a poisonous day. Every now and again the naughty wind would take a rest from pressing us to the wall, and try to pull us off it instead. We would grab together and sit, then, making a bigger person's weight that it could not remove. The sea was gray with white bits of temper all over it; the sky sailed full of different clouds, torn into strips, very ragged.

We spilled out onto the sand. There are two ways you can fetch sea-hearts. You can go up the tide-wrack; you will find more there, but they will be harder, dryer for lying there, and many of them dead. You can still eat them, but they will take more cooking, and unless you bile them through the night more chewing. They are altogether more difficult.

Those of us whose mams had sighed or dads had smacked their heads for bringing them went down the water. Grinny ran ahead and picked up the first heart, but nobody raced him; we could see them all along the sea-shined sand there, plenty for all our families. They do not keep, once collected. They can lie drying in the wrack for days and still be tolerable eating, but put them in a house and they'll do any number of awful things: collapse in a smell, sprout white fur, explode themselves all over your pantry-shelf. So there is no point grabbing up more than you need.

Along we went, in a bunch because of the witch. She sat halfway along the distance we needed to go, and exactly halfway between tideline and water, as if she meant to catch the lot of us. She had a grand pile of weed that she was knitting up beside her, and another of blanket she had already made, and the knobs of her iron needles jittered and danced as she made more, and the rest of her was immovable as rocks, except her swiveling head, which watched us, watched the sea, swung to face us again.

"Oh," breathed James. "Maybe we can come back later."

"Come now, look at this catch," I said. "We will just gather all up and run home and it will be done. Think how pleased your mam will be! Look at this!" I lifted one; it was a doubler, one sea-heart clammed upon another like hedgehogs in the spring.

"She spelled Duster Kimes dotty," he whimpered.

"Kimeses are all dotty," I said. How like my dad I sounded, so sensible, knowing everything. "Duster is just more frightenable than the rest. Come, look." And I thrust a good big heart into his hands, sharp with barnacles to wake him up.

The ones as still floats is the best, most tender, though the ones that's landed, leaning in the wet with sea-spit still around them, is still good, and so even are those that have sat only a little, up there along the drying rime, beginning to dry themselves. The others were dancing along the wrack, gathering too much, especially lad Cawdron. He was too little; why hadn't Raditch told him? We would have to tip most that sack out, or he'd stink up half the town with the waste.

"They'll not need to go as far as us," said Grinny at my elbow.

I dropped a nice wet-heavy heart in my sack. "We can call them down here, make us up some numbers . . . "

No more had I said it than Grinny was off up the beach fetching them. He must have been scareder than he looked.

I preoccupied myself catching floating ones without sogging my trouser-edges. Some people eat the best ones raw, particularly mams; they drink up the liquor inside, and if there is more than one mam there they will exclaim how delicious, and if not they will go quiet and stare away from everyone. If it is only dads, they will say to each other, "I cannot see the 'traction, myself," and smack their lips and toss the heartskin in the pot for biling with the rest. If you bile the heart up whole, that clear liquor goes curdish; we were all brung up on that, spooned and spooned into us, and some kids never lose the taste. I quite like it myself, but only when I am ailing. It is bab-food, and a growing lad needs bread and meat, mostly.

Anyway, the wrack-hunters came down and made a big crowd with us. Harper picked up a wet heart and weighed and turned it, and emptied his sack of dry ones to start again. Cawdron watched him, in great doubt now.

"Why'n't you take a few o' these, Cawdron?" I said. "'Stead of all them jaw-breakers. Your mam will think you a champion."

He stared at the heart glistening by his foot, and then came alive and upended his sack. Oh, he had some dross in there; they bounced down the shore dry as pompons.

I picked up a few good hearts, if small, to encourage him. "See how all the shells is closed on it? And the thready weed still has some juice in it, see? Those is the signs, if you want to make mams happy."

"Do they want small or big?" he says, taking one.

"Depends on her taste. Does she want small and quicker to cook, or fat and full of juice? My mam likes both, so I take a variety."

And now we were quite close to the witch, in the back of the bunch, which was closer, quieter, and not half so dancey as before, oh no. And she was fixed on us, the face of our night-horrors, white and creased and greedy.

"Move along past," I muttered. "Plenty on further."

"Oh, *plenty*!" says Messkeletha, making me jump and stiffen. "Naught want to pause by oul Messkel and be knitted up, eh? Naught want to become piglets in a blanket!" Her eyes bulged in their cavities like glisteny rockpool creatures; I'd have wet myself had I had any in me to wet with.

"We is only c'lecting sea-hearts, Messkeletha," says Grinny politely, and I was grateful to him for dragging her sights off me.

"Only!" she says, and her voice would tear tinplate. "*Only* collecting!"

"That's right, for our mams' dinners."

She snorted, and matter flew out one of her nostrils and into the blanket. She knitted on savagely, the iron needles noising as would send your boy-sacks up inside you like started mice to their hole. "That's right. Keep 'em sweet, keep 'em sweet, those pretty mams."

There was a pause, she sounded so nasty, but Grinny took his life in his hands and went on. "That's what we aim to do, ma'am."

"Don't 'ma'am' me, sprogget!"

We all jumped.

"Move along, all ye, and stop your gawking," spat the witch. So I'm ugly and unmanned! So's I make my own living! What's the fascination? Staring there like folk at a hanging. Get out my sight, 'fore I emblanket youse and tangle you up to drown!"

Well, we didn't need her to tell us twice.

"You can never tell which way she'll go," muttered Grinny.

"You did grand, Grin," said Raditch. "I don't know how you found a voice." And Cawdron, I saw, was making sure to keep big Batton Baker between himself and the old crow.

"Sometimes she's all sly and coaxy? Sometimes she loses her temper like now."

"Sometimes all she does is sit and cry and not say a word or be frightening at all," says Raditch. "Granted, that's when she's had a pot or two."

We collected most efficiently after that, and when we were done we described a wide circle way round the back of her on our way to the foot of the path. "From behind she ain't nearly so bad," I said, for she was a dark lump almost like a third mound of weed, only smoother-edged, and with her needle-knobs bobbing beyond her elbows.

It was wintertime when we ruined everything. It was Cawdron, really, but he would not have said it had we not put a coat on him and got him overexcited.

The weather was all over the place: that was why we were back of the pub. The first snow had fallen, but that was days ago, and it lay only little rotten bits in the shade of walls, nothing useful. We had made a man of what was available in the yard at back, but he was more of a snow-blob, it had gone to such slop—although he had a fine rod on him made of the brace of a broken bar stool Raditch's dad had put back for mending, so you knew at least he was a man-blob.

Anyway, it was beastly cold and the wind had begun to nip and numb us, so we came in the back, and it felt like heaven just the little heat that had leaked out into the hall from the snug, and there was no one to tell us to hie on out again before our ears turned blue from the language we might hear, so we milled there thawing out and being quiet.

And then Jakes Trumbell found the coatroom door unlocked.

"How is that?" he said, the door a crack open in his hand. He looked up and down it as if it must be broken somewhere.

We were all standing just as shocked. The sea-smell came spilling out the crack, sour and cold.

"Wholeman must have left it," said Raditch. "Wholeman must store other stuff in there."

"What other?" said Baker. "Would there be food, mebbe? Would they notice a little gone? Crisps or summink?"

At the word "crisps" the door went wider and our fright dissolved into hope and naughtiness. And as none of us had ever seen in there we went in, several at a time because there was not much room; the coats crowded it up pretty thorough.

"Ain't they strange?" said Angast ahead of me. "Like people theirselves."

"They're *thick*," said Raditch. "Have a feel. And smooth."

"Just like a mam," said Jakes from the door, and some giggled and some jumped on him and started quietly fighting.

"I wish I could *see*," said Raditch, because it was afternoon and the most we could make out was glooming shapes, and hung up very tall. "I want to know how the heads go."

"Bring one out," suggested Angast, "to the better light."

I was glad to go out ahead of him; that room was too much for me, the heavy things pressing at us, hung so closely they pushed out wide at the bottom. And the smell was the smell my mam got when she lay abed unhappy. It was like being suffocated.

We managed to get one of the smaller ones out, and each tried it on awhile, except Cawdron, who would not.

"How do they *swim* in these things?" said Raditch, lifting his sealie arm.

"It is all bonded to them, proper," said Angast. "And the water holds them up, *you* know."

Jakes was the only one put the hood over, and we made him stop when he looked out the eyes and lurched at us—he has dark mam-type eyes, and it was too eerie.

"It *smells*," he said, taking it off. I sniffed the arm of my woolly to see if the smell had stuck. I was worried Mam would smell it on me later, and go into a mood. It was hard to tell. The whole air, the whole hall there, was greenish with that sad smell.

"Cawn, Kit," said Jakes to Cawdron, "let us see you in it; you will make a great little mam, you're so pretty."

"Not on your nelly," Cawdron said. "It'll flatten me, that will."

"We will hold up the weight of it, from the shoulders, so you can stand. Come on; it will suit you so well."

And seeing as there was nothing else to do but persuade him, we set to it, and Jakes hauled out another bigger coat and put it on, and urged some more, and before too long we had weakened the poor lad sufficient to drape the thing dark and gleaming and—I cannot describe to you the feeling of putting it on. It was as if you found yourself suddenly swimming right down the bottom of the sea, a weight of black water above you.

The snug door opened and there was a scramble. Somehow the coatroom door got pulled and the coats got hid behind legs and we were all lounging idle and innocent when Batton Baker's dad passed us on his way out the back pisser.

"What you lads brewing?" he says, swaying back when he sees all our eyes.

But none of us need answer, 'cause he opens the yard door then, and the wind hits him to staggering.

"It's perishin' out there, Mister Baker," says Grinny in just the right voice, dour and respectful.

"I'll freeze my man off, pissing in that." He squints into the darkening yard. "I see a chap who's frozen out there already," he adds jocular. "A fine upstanding chap, if I'm not mistaken."

And he laughs and out he goes, leaving the door banging.

"He sees so much of a sleeve-edge, we are beaten," says Grinny, into the quiet of our relief. "Beaten and put in our rooms and no suppers for *ever*—and our mams *so* disappointed."

We had time to hide them better before Baker came back. He swayed and looked at us, all in our same places. "Don't do anything I wouldn't do," he finally said, and tapped his nose and went off.

And that might have ended it there and then, and all been tip-top and usual.

Except, "Come, Kit," whispers Jakes. "You looked the perfect mam."

So we lumped the coat on Cawdron again, and Jakes put the other one on, and then they made us laugh, trying to walk about like mams, trying to move their hands all delicate and their heads all thoughtful. Cawdron was the best at it, of course, being so delicate anyway, and with the coloring. Jakes was funnier, though, being more dad-like, all freckles and orange hair and hands like sausage-bunches.

"I of been abed for days, so mis'rable, Missis Cawdron," he said, and the way he leaned and rolled his eyes, and his voice trying and failing to trill and sing—we were holding each other up, it was so funny.

And then Kit Cawdron joined in and, my, he was good, because his voice was not yet begun to go, and he could really sound the part. "Because I'm to have another bair-beh," he says, and we were all just about rolling on the slates there, but as quiet as we could.

"I thought you just had one, missis?" says Jakes, through laughing.

"Oh'm, I did. But 'twas only a girl, so I took her down and drowned her."

"Grand!" says Jakes. "Another sea-wife for our lads to net, come sixteen summers."

"Oh no," says Cawdron proudly—proudly because he was doing such a fine job of imitating, proudly because he was playing a proud mam. "I tied the cross on her breast just like you done, so she cannot be caught," he said, and gave Jakes a stage-wink, whose face was already falling. "She'll never suffer like we've had to, Missis Trumbell."

And he was just overacting a suffering mam, staggering, with the back of his hand to his forehead, when he realized how still we all were, how puzzled our faces.

He looked beyond us, and up. His hand snatched to his side and he tripped at his coat-edge and banged up against the wall. His face was not mammish no more, and not at all playful; he was the littlest of us, and the most frightened. He had the most to lose, after all, with Baker's dad there at the back of us, and Mister Grinny, too, come soundless from the snug to catch us at whatever.

We all of us shrank together and back, all around Cawdron and Jakes against the wall there, staring at those men. They were red already in their natural coloring, but the drinking had enflamed them, and now the rage tided up across their faces and they scarcely looked human. Baker's dad—jolly Mister Baker, who would toss a flour-roll out his shop door at a quiet time, to any boy, and mustle your hair as soon as look at you—honest, I thought his head were going to burst, it swelled and trembled so, and stared.

"What did you say, lad," he hissed into the utter silence. Someone gave a little peeping fart at the sound of such rage, and nobody even snickered, we were all so close to shitting ourselves, every lad of us.

Cawdron didn't whimper or sniff; I could *hear* behind me how he was applied, how *glued*, to the wall, trying to melt away into it.

I expected Baker to wade in. Everyone expected it. I saw Grinny's dad expect it, and decide it must not happen, and put a hand on Baker's arm.

"Take that off, lad," he said to Kit Cawdron, gentle as gentle.

The crowd of us loosened, but only a little, at the immediate danger's easing. "Here," Raditch muttered, helping Cawdron behind. Silence except for the fumbling, Cawdron's unsteady breathing, the clop and slide of the coat.

"Come," said Mister Grinny, holding out his hand. I could not tell what he might be thinking—how does anyone else's dad think, and what might he want?—but he was not so red now and I was relieved. I thought, Good, they'll not thrash Cawdron, then. It is too bad even for that. "Hang them coats up, lads," he says, and he stands there one freckly hand ensausaging Kit's little white slip of a paw, and the other on Baker's sleeve who was steaming and readying to roar and punch something, as we hauled the flemming things into the coatroom, and manage to re-hang them. Everybody was shaking like the leaves of the poplars on Watch-Out Hill; everyone was clumsy and needed each other's help.

When it was done and the door closed, whisper-quiet, Mister Grinny was still there holding Cawdron, but Baker was gone, the snug door slamming and beyond it his hard voice spreading a silence through the snug.

"You'll not touch them things again, all right?" says Mister Grinny, still gently.

"No, sir."

"No, Mister Grinny."

"We won't. Promise."

"Even if you find it unlocked," he says. "Even if the door is swinging wide open, you will not go in. You will not lay a finger on your mams' coats."

"Not a finger, sir." We all shook our heads.

"Shan," he says to his boy, "you go on home to your mam. All you boys, go on home. Look to your mams and see if they need aught. Bring in some coal. Make them a tea. Rub their poor feet. Or just sit and talk to them the way they like, about nice things, the spring, mebbe, or the fishing. Go home and do something nice for your mams, each lad of you, because things will go not-so-nice for them for a while. And Shan? On your way? Fetch up Jod Cawdron. The lad should have his father by him, for this."

Out into the cold street we scattered.

"What will they do to Kit?" said Raditch shiveringly to me as we ran. "They will kill him!"

"They will kill his mam," I said. "They will kill all the mams—all those who's had girl-babies, anyhow."

"Oh gawd, you think?"

"Not kill,' I said. "But I don't know what they will do to them."

"Still, I would not be Kit, for all the tea in china."

"I would not be Jakes," I said. "It is all his fault and he will feel it. I know I will knuckle him, for one."

"I don't know," said Raditch. "I don't think a knuckling is going to set this right."

"No," I said over my shoulder, leaving him on his house-step, "but I must hurt *something*."

And I ran on home.

For a while Mam paced back and forth, muttering, the shaggy blanket dragging out behind her like a king's cloak. From one window, past the door, to the other window, and muttering as I say, no words that I could hear.

My dad had gone, the door banged behind him and the bang seeming still to ring, on and on throughout our house. All the swish and scratch of her blanket could not still it, all her hissing whispering, or the pad of her foot soles on the gray boards.

Then she paused by one of the windows, fenced off from me by the chair backs, a seaweedy hummock of her shoulders and then her head, against the glary cloudlight, her hair pushed and pulled a little, a few strands waving in the wind of her warmth. She stood there applying herself to the view and silent, and I stood at the kitchen door silent, listening to the distress.

I went to her, stood at the sill as if I were interested, innocently interested, also in the view. The same lanes slanted away: the one up, the one down. The same front steps shone whitewashed like lamps up and down the lane. The same tedious cat sat in Sacks' window, now blinking out at us, now dozing again. And through the gaps and over some of the roofs, the sea rode charcoal to the horizon, flat-colored as a piece of slate, with neither sail nor dragon nor dinghy to relieve the emptiness.

She was turning and turning her silver wedding ring, which she did when she was upset sometimes, to the point of reddening the spare flesh around it. She pressed and turned, as if to work free the stuck lid of a jar.

I laid my hands on hers, paler than hers. She looked down from the view.

"What is it, Daniel?"

I took her hands one from the other. I turned to the window again, and draped the ring hand over my shoulder, down to my chest, and I held it and took from her the task of turning the warm silver, moving it much more gently upon her finger than she had been doing. It was loose; let it go and it would slide down to the first joint. If you held it higher and quite careful it need not touch her finger-skin at all. But I did not play so with it, only continued the turning of it for her.

She laughed very softly, deep in her throat. "Sweetest boy," she said. She kissed the top of my head and then laid her other hand there. And so we stood, she in her cloak blanket and me wearing her like a cloak, turning the ring on her finger while outside the steps glowed and the cat dozed and the sea sat flat behind it all, nothing of anything changing.

My mam had never had daughters—only me, and a couple of those seal-things that did not live more than a few minutes outside of her. So after that first unpleasantness—which was all about did she know, and why had she not said, and how could they do this to the men who loved them so—our peaceful life went on. But Lonna Trumbell, across the lane, she had drowned six—"Daughters-in-law for all of ye," Marcus Trumbell had boasted up at Wholeman's. Trumbell woke us up every night now, rolling down the hill when Wholeman turned him out, bellowing foulness. He would force into his house, and sometimes in his rage and hurry to hit her he would forget closing the door, and the whole dire scene would pour straight into our woken ears. Sometimes it was surprising when morning came up and the house there looked quite the same as always, after the smashings and roarings that had come from it in the night.

I would get up and go to my dad in the front room, at the moonsilver lace at the window, his face and front patterned with its flowers. We would stand and flinch there together awhile—we had had the conversation about how Dad could do nothing, having lost no daughters himself. *I have lost as many wives for my boy as has anyone,* he had said to them, but still he had not the same rights to misery. He would stand there, his great hand on my shoulder and arm, his thumb at my hair and ear, and I would hold to his leg as to a big warm tree, while Trumbell's shouts, and the wife's, and sometimes Jakes' and Kerry's as well, made a kind of awful weather over there, that might yet blow across the lane, and break something of ours.

When Dad patted and sent me off I would go in to Mam, curled tight as a hedgehog in their bed, sometimes sea-blanketed and sometimes wool. There! If you want to be held tight, clamber up next to your sea-mam when she is alarmed; she will pull you into the knot of herself where nothing can get at you. Her breath will change from uneven and muttering to slow, steady, sea-like as your presence consoles her, and behind the rushing of it and the beat-beat of her pulses calming, Trumbell's rage is nothing, Trumbell's blows, Jakes's pleas; it is all happening in another house, another world, as separate from us as a birds' duel among the clouds, as fish-monsters' battling away down in the sea.

They spoiled their wives' faces, some of them. Some men made the women stay home and not show anyone, until they were not so swollen; others took them out on their arms, and very gentlemanly escorted them about the streets and in the lanes around. If you came upon the men they would greet you gruesome heartily, and say how they and their lady-wife were out for a stroll and weren't it lovely weather?

And you would not be able to *not* glance just a little at the wife. You needed to know—although what good did it do, to know a tooth was gone, to marvel how tight and shiny and bright purple eye-skin could swell up?

And then you were caught; somehow you felt again as if you were abandoning the woman to her bully man by walking on. But my, the most thing you wanted to do was run from this awful game, from the two faces, one so wrong-colored and-shaped, the other a skin of mawkish friendliness over a red-biling rage.

They used all to go down together, the mams, and wash their blankets in the sea. They would sit about on the rocks at the start of the south mole, with their feet hooked in the seaweed, and the water would rush up, and fizz and shush in the blankets, and rush away again. It seemed to soothe them , and we liked to be with them then, clambering about at our own play among them while they joked to one another. "I've a mind to let it go," Grinny's mam might say, "the way he's been treating me. I've a mind to lift my feet and let it float away, free as a summer cloud." Or my own mam: "Not many sea-hearts down the washing-beach this year, anyone find? Usually there is a good lot coming up by now." They sat so solid there, and watched the crowding sea so attentive, you could imagine them not getting up from there ever, sitting like sea-rocks all night even, searching the black waves as the water and knitted weed bobbed and sucked around them.

Messkeletha would walk along the mole above; the mams always ignored her. She would climb down now and again muttering, and wade out to one woman's blanket and another's. From her belt-string she took a length of weed for mending, and worked there scowling a while. Then she knotted and bit off the shining weed, and waded back, climbed back, and paced and stared again above.

When the washing was done and the mending, she would loose one of her two-finger whistles up to Wholeman's Inn—which would set us boys to practicing our own whistles, none of us achieving anything like the witch's piercingness except sometimes by luck. Dads would file out of Wholeman's—not all the dads, maybe six or seven—and gather along the rail there and watch while the mams dragged their blankets up, and spread them on the mole-top, some of them, or carried the great wet bundles in their arms or on their heads, up to their own clotheslines to dry.

"Bye, Sal, then."

"Bye, Peachy. Don't you take no nonsense now."

That was how it was done, before Titch Cawdron let slip. Now Messkeletha came to your door and took out your mam individual—which was terrifying, that she knew where you lived and might come back of a night and snatch you out through your dreams. It was horrible; everyone seemed blamed.

Some mams went tall and proud ahead of her pretending their weed was not such a burden; others, particularly ones whose dads had beaten them, walked as if smacked low, or expecting to be, bobbed along gathering up corners and turning their faces from all the windows as they went.

"My dad watches them go by," I heard Grinny say to Asham. "Every one, and he's not a good word to say of any of them. My mam will be scrubbing and scrubbing over the sound of him, but he'll just talk louder—the sly look of that one, the three girls that one stole away, how Martyr walloped the smile off that one's face. It's shocking, and he will not let me go, not out into the yard, even. He makes me stay and listen."

We were none of us let out at that time, even the sons of the mam called to washing. We were a distraction, the town said, and it would grow from there: a lad would have his friend, and then his friend's friend would tag along, and before you knew it the lot of them would all be down there, arrayed on rocks and scheming again.

We lived high enough in the town that not many women were brought by. But when they were, Mam or Dad would hurry to close the door, and open the lace so as to show no one was looking from behind it, and find works to do in yard and scullery, and ways for me to help them. When the knock came for my mam, Dad would always have some job ready. "Here, take the other end of this, Dan'l; save your old man's back." Or, "Is that ash-bin still out the back lane, I'm wondering?" So that I should never see her go, never see Messkeletha take her. Or maybe that *he* shouldn't see. Perhaps he was as frightened of the oul witch as I was.

They used—and it seemed so foolish to me now, but it wasn't then, in those accepting days when we all ran about among our mams' skirts—they used to be allowed to gather, in this house and that, the mams and children, by themselves without men or Messkeletha. At first there would be talk and tea and sitting upright and eyes everywhere. They would talk of their men and their men's tempers; they would talk of us, and how we were coming on, how we ate and grew.

Then one of them would sigh and cross from table to armchair, or settee or fireside stool. All their movements would suddenly change, slowing and swaying, and their voices would lower from so bright and brittle, and someone might laugh low, too. As we ran in and out we would see more of them gather at the seated one, leaning to her or pulling her to lean on them. Hairs would be unpinned and fall, and combs brought out and combing begin, and there is nothing happier than the sight of a mam's face when her hair is being combed. When we were littler we would run in from our play and lie among them, patted and tutted over and our own hairs combed and compared, the differences in wave and redness. Sometimes we were allowed the combing, but our arms were never long enough to do it as well as they did for each other, long slow silky sweeps from scalp to tips, the combed mam dreamy, the comber thoughtful above.

But of course that came to an end once the daughter-matter were out. Mam combed her own hair now, and if Dad or I saw her at it we would take it on too, and it was always a pleasant time, but it was not the same, though I didn't like to say, as a room full of warm mams murmurous by the fire, and several hairs to plait and play with as you would, and any number of bosoms to lay your head upon, and doze away an afternoon.

Nobody expected Aggie Bannister, after all her time hid away from us, so no one stopped her. They were too astounded seeing this white creature in midst of the clouds and gray, among coats and wool hats and clumpy boots this naked thing, all that bared skin in the cold air, the wobbling nipple-eyes mad below her determined face, and then the wobbling bottom behind, the feet that we remembered from summer, toenails and bunions and cracked heels freed of the shoes that so pained them, the slap of cobbles against foot-soles. Wrong, so wrong, for this season, for this place.

Down she ran, Aran's mam, through the dark gray town like a running flare, through the streets like an animal gone wild, like someone's stock got out and not knowing about towns and hard surfaces and cold. Or about real people, and their eyes and their laughter and their cruel words. *Oh, gracious who was that! Aggie Bannister! It's Aggie!* Her name, which was not her name at all but Bannister's chosen name for her, his own name with a girl's name that he liked tied on before like the front end of a horse costume—her name got passed all down the streets and back over shoulders into the houses, and from being on so many lips, it became soiled so badly that the woman might never be able to lift her head in Potshead streets again, nor Bannister pass by without laughter breaking out behind him, nor Aran nor Timmy nor Cornelius neither.

It was clear where she was headed, and while she was not thinking straight, we were. Or at least, she was after a different aim: to reach the sea, whereas we only needed the view of it, so we all headed down Totting Lane and Fishhead Lane straight down, while she ran the full ramp length of the main street and across to the mole and then she clambered, all white bottom and—you could see every fold of her if your eyes were good as mine, while the young men whooped and whistled and the women and the married men turned their faces away behind their hands, and glanced again and groaned and laughed. She clambered, slipped, clambered down and then turned and with one bloodied knee ran limping, ran clumsy as if she were transforming back right there, down the pebbly gray sand towards the water.

And then she was in it, a naked back and bottom in the middle of a white fan of water. And then the green-white froth passed over her and her hair wasn't wild any more but pasted flat to her head. *Thank goodness!* I thought. *The seals will come and fetch her and she never will have to flounder ashore and face our kindness and our ridicule.* And she was embracing the waves, and swimming there so strongly, you could tell they were her home; she was not clumsy there.

"She want to stay within the lee of the mole," said Prentice Meehan above me. "It's dirty farther out."

A howl of the wind turned to the howl of a man, the howl of Bannister running out the house ends. "Aggie!"

"Look at him! He has her coat!" Which made him look somewhat octopus -ish, all its arms and flaps a-flapping.

"Don't you expect me to do that for you," muttered Arthur Sack to his missus. He was standing his hand locked around hers, glaring at her, while she gazed now towards lumbering woeful Bannister, now out to the water, where Aggie was a dot of black, a momentary shining white haunch, a white foot splashing, and now hidden behind the green glass upshelving of a wave.

Along the mole ran Bannister. All our men is taciturn, when not angry; I cannot describe to you the uncomfortableness of seeing him so come out of himself, his mouth wide in his face like a bawling bab's, his arms reaching. His bellows were torn up by the wind and waves and thrown at us in shreds, some strange animal's cry, not a man's, not a grown man's.

Right out to the end he got, and still he yearned farther. He made to clamber down the end point.

"Don't be daft, man!" said some man.

"He will be swept away!" a woman said dreamily.

But the sea jumped up and smacked the mole-end, a great fanfare of spray, and Bannister staggered back in it, soaked with it. And there he stood a moment, clutching her coat and staring out to where she came and went, came and went, bobbing and struggling now among the wilder, dirtier waves.

A spot of sun came then, poked a hole in the clouds and cut a bar through the spume and lighted on them both as he flung the coat, as it flew—not far, it was so heavy—as it lumped out into the air and splatted on the water and was gone there, then was there again, struggling, just as she was, to stay above water.

And the laugh-and-chattering here against the rail stopped, because coat and Aggie were so far apart, and neither of them were swimming towards the other. We saw the coat edge at the surface, the shadow of the coat within a big sunlit wave; we saw her face, her mouth, her arm and breast, and a different wave crash down, folding her down into the sea. Bannister knew not to dive in; even mad with grief he knew. He stood instead a little way down from the mole-top, stood with legs bent and red hands claws upon his knees, bellowing out to Aggie not to die.

She did not obey him. She lay slumped in the water when next we saw her, only her back, and then the sun went away and the sea brought her in behind the mole again. Through the gray rain-beginning, through the green-gray waters, the rows and curling rows of them, up and down it brought her slow— mams ushered some of the littler boys away. It deposited her not three yards from where it had thrown up the empty coat, a welter of black flesh and stirred pebbles, onto Potshead beach.

"It is all our faults," shivered little Thomas Davven, left behind with me on the rail while the men ran, while the woman pushed children away, while here came Messkeletha with one of her blankets for a shroud. "If we had not faddle-arsed around in that coat room . . . "

"It is all *their* faults," I said and savagely. The witch cast me a look in passing, and I waited till she had gone, one blanket-corner dragging as she went. "Stealing our mams out of the sea in the first place," I hissed to Thomas.

"Oh, you cannot blame them that." He clutched himself and bowed and bent in the cold wind, without the shelter of the crowd any more. "You had the choice between women like that raddle-witch and our beautiful mams, which would you choose?"

He had me. That was no fair choice, that was. "Still," I said through my teeth, clamping them tight against their chattering. "Still, they never ought to done it. They dint belong here. They belonged under the waves."

Down there, we could see it all well; we were like birds stopped above them in the wind. Only Aggie Bannister was normal length, white and awash until they pulled her by wrists and ankles up out of the shadows; the rest of them were all cap-tops and coat-shoulders, with boot toes popping out, popping away again. And Messkeletha hurried up, a snarl of red-streaked white hair above a trailing clump of knitted seaweed, and her feet were bare and blue, the toenails long as the teeth of some old neglected dog.

I went home to Mam. I did not care if she talked or wept of slept or hid from me under her seaweed; I wanted only to be in the room with her, to see the mound of her and know she was not drowned and naked before the Potshead populace.

I sat by the window and the sun now and again broke through and lit the sea silver, and lit the ceiling with silver reflections, and the wind outside was one breath and the sea, rushing, pausing, falling, was another, and Mam's was another—though mostly I could only see it in her rise and fall, not hear it among all the others. And then there was my own breathing, which at first when I sat was all raggy and half into speech, and after a while was soothed, by Mam's ongoingness, by the wind's being outside and by the distance of the dirty sea and of the people round Aggie Bannister, to something that fit, that fell into peaceful pace, with all the other beings'. The furniture sat plain and hard in its place; the rug that I remembered her making—her twisting fingers with her singing face above—lay finished and in place by the bed, and her hair was a black salty tangle on the pillow, beyond the table where lay her shells, and her stones that meant something, and her sea-glass, red and blue and powdery white, smoothed to harmlessness, beaten to something beautiful by the sea, taken from the sea before it were quite beaten away into nothing but more sand.

I was not waiting for anything. I had forgot I was there; I had forgot, indeed, who I was. Being with Mam often made me this way—how much did it matter, after all, that I was crossed of land-man and sea-woman? Time could pass unwatched; it need not lead away from good times so that I yearned back, or push me towards a future that I dreaded. I could just lounge, and breathe like this, and the silver lights of water and winter could move above me.

There is labor in getting a boat through the sea. Either you pull it with oars, digging and hauling the water back, or you dance and scrabble with sails and sheets, begging the wind to cooperate with your work. Or some men engage with grease and metal, propellers, stinking fuel, and carve up the sea behind them with an engine.

Looking from that labor to the seals, you can tell they are magical. All they have is those slender hands, those fine feet like a limp plant hanging off their back end, like a tail. I have watched men struggle with the washed-up body of one of those, reduced to cutting it to pieces and moving it with hooks. They are such a stubborn, slippery weight. And yet they fly under water, and spin and sport and somersault, all the while we chug and beat and swear above.

First the mainland was a black fingernail's-edge between the pale sea and the pale sky. I pulled Dad's sleeve as he talked to Mr. Fisher, who was coming over to buy some tins and vegetables for the store.

"There, yes," Dad said to me, and gazed at it a little, first to satisfy me and then because some thought had caught him about it.

"Don't you be fooled, young Dan'l," Fisher said around Dad's front. "It may look like the land of promise, but Killy's best, home is best."

Dad squeezed my shoulder, invisibly to Fisher. I didn't know whether he meant me to listen carefully to Fisher or ignore him and flee to mainland as soon as I ever could. Mam had combed my hair—I had watched in the mirror—so that it was two slick curves either side of a raw white parting. My whole head still felt scraped and chilled.

Slowly the land grew; slowly it rose and unrolled out of the horizon: two main rounded hills with others either side like attendants. The sea slopped and danced below us. The sky blued as the sun got up higher, and we began to see shapes on the land, forested parts and fielded, and the glint of roofs and roads, and the black cliffs with the dazzling break between them, where we would chug in and find safe harbor.

"We will catch the bus in to Knocknee," said Dad. "It goes right from the pier."

"So we'll not see this town, so much?" I said, disappointed because it seemed so rich, with its warehouses along the front like a wall, with its several steeples, with its shining vehicles gliding along by the water.

"Can you not let the lad at the fleshpots of Cordlin Harbor, Mallet?" laughed Fisher. "Even to the 'stent of a raspberry lollipop at Mrs. Hedly's shop?"

"We've business." My dad shook his head and smiled. "Knocknee Market will have to be excitement enough for the boy."

I did not see how anything could be more exciting than motoring in between the heads. Cordlin Harbor spread and spread out, serene and glossy after the tumbled sea, after the beating of the waves at the cliffs' feet. Rank after rank of boats was moored here, alongside the piers and also punctuating the more open water, each little pleasure motor, each ketch and trawler, kissing its morning reflection. Cordlin Town lay as if spilled in the valley, thickening towards us in the bottom, thinning away to skerricks, a cottage here, a barn there, higher up the hills like drops of milk around porridge in a bowl. Windows winked at us and the great granaries and woolstores stood all barred windows and red-and-white brickwork, and I saw for the first time the humbleness of my home island, in contrast to this center of wealth and commerce.

"There's our bus," said Dad, and I noticed the marvelous thing, painted and polished, a crest on the side of it and a number-plate behind, and with people, Cordlin people, people who did this every day, already in it waiting, for our boat to come alongside, for Dad and me to walk up the gangplank with the other islanders, for us to climb on to the little glinting box of the bus, and pay our fares, and sit.

I held fast to Dad's hand. Mr. Fisher clapped my shoulder, and the surprise of the blow made my heart jump hard in my chest, and ran across my scalp like a wind-gust through damp grass.

The trip to Knocknee was all events, one piled on the next so that my telling of them, which at first I tried to rehearse to Mam in my head, fast became garbled and then fell to silence. I hung onto the windowsill, grateful that Dad looked over me, and would see the important things, would collect any details that I might miss. Presently the overwhelming town with its too-many faces, its too many curtains and gates and window boxes, sank away and we were in fields, flying among fields on the back of our grinding, squashy-wheeled monster, and this I could bear more easily, fields being more like the sea in their emptiness, in their roundness and billowyness, Cordlin fields being very much like Killy fields, such as those were.

I turned to Dad: "Such a noisy way to get about." I thought the engine must be right below our seat, it juddered at our bums so.

"It is indeed," he said. "Noisier than a boat, and certainly noisier than a man's own legs. But fast," he added. "And fast is what we're wanting, to reach inland and back in a day."

And to see numerous people, not all of them friendly, and to ask them questions that made their eyes slide aside, made them shake their heads and turn away. I ran about after my striding dad, and the running, and the ways of people, eventually tired me. He put me on a sunny bench in the market square and bid me wait while he searched on.

Before long someone else was put there, at the other end of the bench, someone in skirts, with hair. I had got my breath by then, and when we had caught each other glancing several times, "I know what you are," I said to her.

She stopped swinging her legs. She looked at me and narrowed her eyes, which were pale like a dad's looking blue in this light but possibly green, possibly gray. "Well, what?"

"You are a girl-child," I said.

She gave a small hiccup of a laugh. "No joking!" she said. "Good thing that you told me." And she swung her legs some more and looked about at the legs and bums and baskets and bustle.

"You are, aren't you," I said.

She looked me up and down. Her breath was white on the cold air. "Are you touched, or what?"

"I ant never seen one before," I said.

She snorted.

"It's true," I said. "We don't have them on Killy."

Her face got more startled, and prettier. "You're from Killy Isle?"

"I am," I said. "My dad brang me over this morning."

"For the first-ever time?" Now I was interesting, and she seemed to have stopped disliking me, which was good.

"First ever," I said.

"You been on that one island all your life?"

"I've been to St. Mark's, and Ogben also. And on lots of sea."

"I never seen the sea yet," she said. "My mam and dad won't take me. Say it sends men potty. Is your dad potty?"

"I don't know," I said, not sure what she meant, and not sure about Dad. None of these legs were recognizable as his, none of these hats, fuzzy-outlined against the sunshine.

"Are *you* potty?" said the girl. What a *lot* of hair she had, and it was not straight and silky like a mam's. It looked as if, you take that band off, undo that ribbon, loose it from those plaits, it would stand straight out from her head, or possibly get up and walk right off her, or flame up and away, burn away in the sunlight, from the heat in its wires, from the combination of so many hot red strands together.

"*I'm* not potty." I knew that much.

She laughed at me, but not all unkindly. "You might be anything," she said, "you look so strange, with your great eyes."

I turned my face from her embarrassed, and again she laughed. These girl-children were certainly unsettling.

"What brings you, then?" she said as if she had a perfect right to know. "You and your dad, to Knocknee?"

"I ant sure," I said. "He has business here, he said." Again I searched the crowd, for I rather wished he would burst out now, perhaps with something for me to eat, some mainland fancy.

"Cloth, mebbe?"

"I don't think so. He said he had to talk to someone."

"Hmm," she said considering. "Private, like, then, if he put you here. Was it a woman?"

"I think so," I said, knowing for certain so, but not liking, somehow, to confirm what this girl might be thinking.

"Don't you have womens there, on Killy? Is it all potty boys and men?"

"We have women," I said, stung. "We have very beautiful women, all our mams."

She narrowed her eyes at me again, and breathed more breath-smoke. "Ye-es," she said and frowned. "That is your specialty out there, is it?"

"What?"

"I'm trying to remember. I've heard mams talking. There's something about those Killy women, isn't there?"

"Maybe," I said. "But they're our mams, so don't you say anything that might get you popped on the snout."

"Well, they must be unusual, to've got an unusual like you," she said commonsensically, looking me up and down again.

I turned back to the crowd, to the sun, not knowing what to say to that. *They're usual for our town,* I wanted to assert. *Perfectly usual.* But I could not say it. She would not find that convincing, and I did not want to feel more foreign than she had already made me.

We had come to bring home a girl, but not the girl from the market. This other girl we fetched from a smelly part of the town; there was some kind of offal piled and straggling in the drain outside her family's house.

I thought her mam was her grandma, she had so few teeth and was so weathered. All the time they talked the woman watched my dad as if he might snap at and bite her, as if he were there to trick her and she ought to be very careful.

The girl herself was orange-haired like all of them, but not so clean as the market girl, and she had something of the twitchiness of the mam about her, and something a little sneaky, I thought. She sat there all pursed lips, her glance flicking from Dad to the mam to Dad, listening close and clearly understanding everything they exchanged, although to my ears it made no more sense than murmurings in someone's sleep.

They were talking about money; the mam wanted some, and Dad was saying how he oughtn't to have to pay, giving board and accommodations to this girl as he would. He seemed to be buying her, buying something she could do. Truth tell, she didn't look capable of a lot, so skinny and gray-fleshed. Looked more like the sort to skip quick smart out of any job going.

Dad sighed. "You have eleven of her, missis. Ain't you glad to get the burden of even the one of them off your shoulder?"

"This one eats mouse-rations," snapped the mam. "Why don't you take one of the big girls, my Gert or my Lowie, great heffers that they are?"

"You know why, Mrs. Callisher. This is the one with the touch on her. As can be taught up useful by our Messkeletha." Ah, that was what he wanted. For when the oul witch died, of her awful coughing, or perhaps just the strength of her own evil.

"Useful for what? Useful for living on Killy, is what. Useful for catching and keeping mermaids. And stuck in that God-hole for the rest of her life, the amount she'll be useful elsewhere." She slid a glance at me. "I don't want grandsons with *tails*," she said. "Granddaughters with *fins*."

"We will pay her a yearly journey here, how about that? Boat and carriage to visit you every spring."

The mam sucked at the inside of her discontented face. "And no one to marry."

"She might well meet a man here, one of her visits. I don't know, missis. These terms is reasonable. I'm sure Trudle would be very content, a room of her own built special onto the oul-woman's, and a livelihood."

The girl Trudle gave a kind of a whinny, and were no prettier for laughing. If anything she looked more weaselish or rattish, creased up like that.

Her mam looked at her and shook her head. "She'd be happy on a dungheap, that one. She's touched more ways than the one."

"Ask Fan Dowser how touched I am," said Trudle in a rasping voice.

Swiftly the mam stepped over and smacked Trudle's head. The girl rubbed the spot and glared up at her through her eyebrows.

"Very well, take her," said the mam with great carelessness. "Don't come blubbing back to me, though, what she gets up to with your pretty lads." She spared me something of a sneer, but there was fear in it, too. "As I say, there's not a lot up her top. Why a person cannot have magic *and* intelligence I do not know."

"'Tis straightforward enough work," said Dad.

"Hmph. Nothing of this nature is straight. Go fetch your box, girl."

I did not like traveling with this girl. We were an odd little couple, her and me, her in some ancient hand-me-down ruffles and a big dark-blue bonnet, her weasely face in the middle looking everywhere. She walked in a funny rocking way, her legs wide as if she had discovered herself wet. People glanced at us going by, and glanced away when they saw me watching. My dad preceded us, Trudle's box on his shoulder, her best-dress pillowing up at the top. He was walking quite fast, making Trudle rocky-rock along ridiculous. It was a nightmare, this big town and the hurrying, people's eyes and opinions peppering us as we walked, and the sun lost behind the flare-edged house rows. Trudle did not speak to me nor I to her; we only struggled along separate and together, both after Dad.

Then the crowds cleared, and the bus was there waiting for us alongside its shelter. The door was just hissing shut, but my dad hoyed and waved and ran, and it opened for us again.

Trudle got up first very bustling. She chose a seat halfway down and sat very straight and pleased there, sparing Dad a glare when he made to sit by her, so that he came with me to the seat behind her instead.

"That was close," he said as the bus threw him back into his seat. "Any more bargaining with that mam and we'd have been stuck here the night."

I could smell Trudle Callisher; I could smell the oldness of her clothes, and the fact that she had not bathed in a while.

"I seen you got talking to a maid?" says my dad politely when we had got our breaths.

I nodded, watching the last of Knocknee town whirl by: a cottage with a yard full of rubbish, a dog with a plume-y tail, water shining in bootprinted mud.

"What was that like?" he said.

I shrugged—it had not been like anything, and I did not know what to think of it, what to say.

"Did you like her?"

I slid my bottom back, to sit straighter in the seat. Cows flew by, some of them watching us with their great heads raised. "She was fine, I suppose." Did

I have the right to like or dislike such a stranger? Today I was just a big empty trawler-hold, with the world's fish and sea-worms tumbling into me. "We only talked a little while."

There's something about those Killy women, isn't there? I saw the girl's narrow eyes, her hair-wires around her head as she asked. *Those Killy women.* I wished I was among those Killy women suddenly, sharply; I was sick of this adventure. I wished I was tiny again, and curled in Mam's lap with her singing buzzing and burring around me in the quiet room, Dad gone to fish or to Wholeman's. Or among the mams on their sea-washed stones, their blankets trailing and pulling at their legs as they called to each other, as they laughed, grown-up jokes that we didn't need to understand, and me with my fellows at play.

Trudle watched everything out the window across the mainland countryside. She boarded the boat ahead of us as if she owned it, and kept similar straightness and cheer all across the Bite.

When we reached Killy my dad sent me up home, and I did not see what happened then and nor did I mind. I went home with a lemon for my mam, given me by Mr. Fisher. I dug my fingernail in the rind a little and sniffed lemon all the way up the town, to clear the Trudle-smell out of my head.

From what I gathered she were given over to Messkeletha just as promised and no fussing. And after that the two of them went about a pair, like a flour-caddy and a tea. They both wore witch-dresses, tight to their tops to the waist, then springing out like flower-bells, nearly to the ground. Cages and flowers, like all those women at Knocknee and at Cordlin Harbortown wore, so *presenting* of themselves, so insisting on your looking.

The one's hair was dirty orange in the sunlight, the other's mostly frost, only a few reddish stains in it to hint what it once was. And Messkeletha's was thin in places; as Trudle stayed longer, she grew her hair, as if to make the point that she alone had such color, and could bear it about in such quantity.

Messkeletha never was polite, never greeted you even did she meet your eye, and this one learned the same ways quite fast, or at least towards mams and children. For men she would raise what might be called a smile if it were not so sly and ambiguous. "Mister Paige," she would say, but it would come out *Pay-eesh,* too lingering, and Paige would seem to dodge and weave without taking a step in any direction, would seem to bow and tug a forelock without taking his hands from his pockets. In all her interactions with our men Trudle got herself this chopped-about reaction, and enjoyed herself with the getting, anyone could see.

But, as I say, she followed her mistress about the town and there was something powerful in there being the two of them, the small caddy tripping after the big one, taking on and giving new notes to the oul-witch's herbaceous, privy-aceous smell. Two bells on feet, they were, ringing unpleasant thoughts out the men's memories. Two ragged flower shadows, they crept along the sky on Watch-Out Hill. Messkeletha would stand peering to sea and town on the south mole while Trudle bent bum-up collecting fish-scales for their magics. Or the two of them would be horrors together on Marksman Road, glowering ahead, pretending not to see us boys as we hugged the hedge opposite, greeting them feebly.

You stand there against the boat rail with your small warmth hugged to you inside the stiff coat. The seals break out of the endlessness of the sea, they make all that space less anguishing, all that drowned world beneath. Their round head-tops, their whiskery-ness, the humdrummery of their rough breath, the shiver of ripples around the landforms of their heads, their seeming to smile—you cannot help but love them.

And the eyes, oh the eyes. The eyes are the magic of them, seals and mams: deep as night but starless, starless and kind—or at least not calculating the way pale eyes are. They are dark and glossy as any sea-washed stone, still magic while wetted, still live.

Water flowing over a rock, over a seal, curves and curls to the rock's shape—or the seal's—clinging. The skirts around mams' thighs are like that, the curves of them, the cloth. Follow a mam down the town and you cannot keep your eyes off her beskirted bum, what it does with that skirt, shaking and shuddering it, turning it almost to liquid.

They have beautiful faces, too, not like dad faces all pinched and pale and suspicious. Mams' faces are open, the eyes wide and all-seeing, the mouths ready always to kiss you, their salty kisses. *My baby,* they call you, even if you are someone else's. They gather up anyone little and kiss them better, they encircle them in their strong arms, the skin so cool, the flesh beneath so warm. Strands of their loose hair catch in their lips, and in yours, and their eyes blink over you, and their mouths smile. They love children, mams. It doesn't matter whose; they love all of us.

I found Toddy Martyr the far side the northern mole, where you can see forever and not be seen, where the town might not exist, for all you can see or hear of it.

I saw him because I looked up from my moody walking, from my plodding boots, and in among the mole-rocks one of those rocks lifted an arm and dropped it again. Then I worked out a head, with hair flopping about on it in the wind a bit of black, a bit of shine, and a pale boy-face. I didn't care who it was; it was someone out here with me not a mam or a dad, not a witch, and greeting this someone would provide me a path away from my thoughts.

By his swaying and by his singing which I now separated out of the wind's other strings as I clambered, Toddy was off in his own land, or his own private ocean and swimming. Then he wrenched something up and lifted—ah, it was a spirit-bottle—and drank from it. He was headed for trouble, wasn't he? That bottle was quite full, the way he had to heft it.

"Dan'l Mallett!" he cried as he distinguished me from all the other rocks climbing towards him. "What brings you here this fine morning sirrah?" And he bonked the cork back in and held out his hand like an old gaffer from the village seat.

I shook it, cold frog that it was. "Your dad will give you a thrashing, no mistake."

"Rather me than my mam. And this here is the fuel of his thrash-motor, so I am doubly saving her."

"You could've only emptied it, into the sea or otherwise," I said.

"That's what I intended. But then I got seated here and I thought what a waste. And here, have a slosh of it, Dan'l; it is like carrying hot coals in your stomach. It warms all of you, right out to the toenails." He twisted out the cork and offered me the bottle.

"There's a quantity," I said in wonder. I lifted and tipped. The air off the stuff rushed out the neck and nipped my nose; the spirit itself ran cold and evil and stinging across my tongue; a little ran out the side and dripped to my collar, leaving a line of cold burning. "Who-hoah." I gave it back to him, and wiped my chin, and crouched in the cavity next to him.

"How is this, Dan'l? It is in-*suff*'rable the way things are, do you not think?"

"With the mams, you mean?" I was still negotiating the spirit into myself; it felt as if it were eating my gullet lining to lacework.

"With the mams, with the dads, with *all* the people of our world." He spread his arms extravagantly, as if the people were out there seaward, not behind us.

"None of us is happy any more," I conceded.

"Happy!" He shook his head, pointed his face to the wind to clear it of hair. "I *hate* my dad. I could *kill* my dad, had I stren'th. And he hates me. And he hates my mam so wild, he's like a madman at her. He can. Not. Let. Up. And the only reason she don't hate him is, she's so dispirited. She hardly have life to lift her head, let alone raise a good temper."

I sat my bottom to the wet sand among the rocks and hugged my knees and nodded miserable.

"I don't see why everyone's fussing so," said Toddy. "Who wants girls anyway? What are they good for?"

"I don't know," I said. "I han't ever known any." Except that red girl at Knocknee, her hair fizzing and flaming, her inquisitive eyes looking me up and down.

"And babies. Gawd, that last one! Yawped all day and night until Mam took her down. He was glad to be rid of it as much as I was, the racketing. We could all get some sleep."

We listened to his cruel words in our shelter there. Then *doik!*, he pulled out the cork again, thrust the bottle at me, as much apologizing as daring me to drink more.

The second pull of it was gentler; it soothed the damages caused by the first.

Watching Toddy's throat jump around his next swallow, I told myself I must not do this again too soon. It was far too pleasant, too warming against the weather. Enough of it, and I should be agreeing Toddy Martyr; I should be agreeing all the Toddy Martyrs of this town; I should be loosing everything about my own mam and how she lived alone in her room under her weed, and about Trumbells opposite—though the town knew most of that already.

I drank myself hot-faced, though—that didn't take much. And I kept Toddy company while he sickened himself. When next he could anyway stand I helped him up and along to Fishers, because he wouldn't be taken to his home. Then I went hill-walking, not wanting to present myself at my house with spirit on my breath. Right to the top of Watch-Out I went and down and across the Spine and to Windaway Peak, all that way, and stood in the rain there and listened to the chattering of my teeth. The drink was gone from me by then, and it was a trudge home, and more of a trudge. I thought I would never get there.

I woke warm in the morning knowing what I must do. I ached all over, from my hair-ends in to my heart. I sat up and looked around at the ordinariness of my room, at the spills of light across the wall around my window-blind, and at all sides of my proposition to myself.

That night I walked up home from Wholeman's hearth with the first part, the main part, accomplished. Dad had stayed behind, with his pipe and pals awhile, to talk that special make of eldermen's talk that makes no sense to young ones with its boringness, but seems to gratify dads so.

Into our little house I broke, the seaweedy silence of it. I hummed, a twiddling tune such as Jerrolt Harding had been whistling up in the snug, but without so much direction as he.

I went in to her. She was a great dark dune there. She was awake, though, because you couldn't hear her breathing.

I sat at her pillow edge and tried to distinguish the tear-salted hair from the knitted weed. A scooped sea-heart lay beginning rancid in a saucer on the sill; the spoon was licked clean, almost polished in its shine.

"Mam," I said, "I have some news for you."

She burrowed a little deeper into the blanket.

"Your son," I said, "has got himself a position, as bottlewash at Whole-man's."

I had thought her still before, but now she was all listening; not a leaf of seaweed moved.

"I'm a good lad, says Mister Wholeman. He says they can trust me. Cannot they."

The dune quaked and her white face rolled up from under. There was not much light. "Did they bully you?"

"A little," I said. "I had to weep some and show proper remorse for that day last winter." I thought perhaps she could hear my smile, if she could not see it.

She crawled up to me. Powerful out from under the blanket came her warmth and the smell of the warmed weed. "They would kill you, Daniel, even for thinking this."

"Yes," I said, with an odd satisfaction. "It's different, though, when you are our mams. Mams is different from wives."

She swayed there on her hands and knees, accustoming herself to the thought. Fears and realizations stopped and started her breath. Even with their little window-shine her eyes were indistinct; holes in her floating pale face through which her attention poured and poured at me.

"I know I don't need to tell you," she said low. And then she whispered, half-strangled, "You must not say a word."

"Not to anyone," I said to her, as earnest as she could wish. "Don't you worry. Not even to *myself*."

She laughed suddenly, and knocked me to the bed, and squashed the breath out of me the way we had always liked to fight. She was still the stronger yet, though I might be bottle-boy, but I was beginning to see that I might soon have a chance against her. It was all darkness and strain and struggle a little while, and stifled laughter and threats.

She pinned and then released me, sprang back onto her haunches and the fight was over. "They will know it was you, Daniel," she said. "And no other."

"I don't care," I said panting. "You will be home by then."

"Foolish boy," she said fondly, and her thin hand reached through the dark, pushed my hair behind my ear, tickled down my neck and along the shelf of my collarbone. Then she slapped my cheek twice, lightly. "Let me think on this. Out of here, laddy-lad. Just a glance at us and he'll know we were plotting and scheming. Go."

I went to bed happy. I washed and undressed and lay down untroubled, and my sleep closed over me like sun-warmed water.

Things fast went out of my control, of course, as they will when you tell a secret. First, it was that Kit's mam must come too, and then all the mams. Then, Kit's mam must bring Kit, and then, yes, all the other mams must bring their boys too. "Particularly you, Daniel," said Mam, "who is up for the greatest punishment. The only way I can protect you is have you with me."

"I can protect myself," I said, as stoutly as I could, but truth to tell a mad hope had been lit in me when she said that Kit was to be coming. Was that possible, then? For us to go under and be seals with our happy mams?

It turned out there was work involved, much secret work, difficultly organized because the mams could not have with each other, and must send coded and sometimes garbled messages along of their boys, house to house under the guise of playing. This work involved witchery of a kind, though not Trudle-spells nor Messkeletha, and skins, fish skins and sheep-skins and any kind of skins that could be got. The stories we span about skins, to our dads, when they happened on our hoards! The only way to get over the terror of it was to pretend it were all a great game, a great secret costume-play for the dads, and some of them were entirely silly with it, conducting false rehearsals of carefully crafted song-and-dances so as on purpose to be discovered and scramble to hidings in their skin patchworks.

"Stand still, Daniel." Mam's hands were at my face, pinching, pinning. "Or I'll have your eye out."

"It's tight as tight," I said. "A boy cannot breathe in it."

"Not here," she agreed. "But once you touch water, it will all soften, and you'll grow great underwater lungs, for to swim full minutes on a single breath. You've seen us."

"I have. And will my nose work the same, close-and-openable on top of my snout?"

"Exactly that way, my sweet."

I tried it within the hood. She tut-tutted. "Wretched boy." She sounded quite fond all the same.

"There," she said eventually. "Now, don't dislodge my pins, getting it off. It must be sewn aright if it's to fit and form you."

Time came for the thefts from the coat-room. I don't know what they had planned for the red-witches; some things they kept from me, so as I could not confess them if pressured by the men. Down at Wholeman's I was bottlewash and guard and keeper-at-bay of our dads, stopping them going the pisser while the coats were taken out the back, between elf-fifteen and elf-thirty by the snug clock, which had a chime that could be heard in the hall. Grinny and Batton had been locked in the room all afternoon, taking down the coats and tying them, and the whole operation went like a game of fire-buckets along a chain of children to Lonna Trumbell, who only had to sniff one coming to say whose it was and where to send the runner. I pictured it all happening as Jerrolt held the men steady and somnolent in the snug with the tunes I had requested, which were all the slow and funereal ones it would be rude to get up and piss through: "The Night My Mother Died" and "Low Lay the Boat in the Harbor" and "The Fiercest Storm."

"I could just about hear the thunder in that," said Baker to my horror as Jerrolt finished and the snug clock chimed. Straightaway Fernly Asham and Michael Cleft got up and went out. I hurried to the scullery with my tray of bottles and began to wash and wash, waiting for the fiercest storm to break over our heads.

Which it did not. Thank heaven, I thought, something has got in the way of it and we must wait another several nights. I have been sweating on nothing; the coats are still in their rows, the hall and yard are empty and cold as always.

But no, the key was where I had told Grinny to leave it. And walking up home, the town was different. The secrets gusted about the streets with the leaves and litter, thick enough in the air to choke me.

Run along home, Wholeman had said. *No, lad*—when I'd protested—*you done a fine night's work. Like some kind of little steam engine you are, getting through them bottles. The rest can wait'll tomorrow.*

But no one will be here tomorrow to do them, I almost said, then went obedient home.

There I found my mam pacing. She scooped me up and squeezed me. "While I have arms to do this," she said.

"Did it all happen, then?" I said, hardly believing, into her black hair. "Did you all do?"

Out from under the table she pulled the bag, and from it she tugged a coat-edge, very thick and smooth, dark, with not a lot of freckle. She unslid the whole skin and held it up beside herself by the hood, the exact height, though the ragged face-holes were nothing like my pretty mam. The closed air of our front room soured and went salty.

"Do you remember it, from back then?" I held the slithery skin to my lips; it seemed to defy my bottlewashed fingers to purchase on it and feel it properly.

"No," she said. "but it smells of me and mine, very distinct. Let's get on, then." She fell to whispering. "Everyone else is gone, Daniel, hours ago."

Close she came and folded the coat, the ragged-faced floppy person, down to bag size. "Slippery thing," she said flusteredly, as the sleeves misbehaved. Surely that smell would be smelt, out in the street where we carried it? Surely someone would stop us: *Neme Mallett, what are you out for, this time of night? And what do you think you have there, that can only be one thing?* And pluck the bag from my fingers, open it and bring the trouble down on our heads.

"There, done." She met my eyes and huffed. "Let us shut up and follow, then."

Off we went, coated but unbuttoned. She took my hand once we were out on the street, and hers was cold and tight.

"I do love him," she said to the cobbles, to the passing front steps. "I am breaking his heart."

"He ought never have caught you, Mam," I said severely. I didn't want to think of Dad. "None of them ought. They should have left you in your home."

I thought she smiled down on me out of the stars, but the light was not good and her hair shadowed her face, she might have winced just as easy.

Down slippy-slop we went, the wind skirling and twiddling around us, caught in the narrow ways. Every now and again a strong breath from the sea would push at our faces, smelling green and live and massive. When that happened, Mam would almost run a few steps, as if the sea were summoning her more peremptory.

The water was rucked-up and difficult looking between the moles. I thought I saw seal-heads awaiting, a couple, but when I looked again they were not there. They may have been only wave-shadows, mistakes of my eyes, wishings perhaps if I but knew what I wished.

"Come-come." Mam let go my hand and preceded me down the steps to the beach. I hurried after her, frightened and not knowing why but needing to be right by her for my own peace.

We ran out from the wall, the town hunkering behind us, its eyes tightening the skin of my back. Out across the scraping pebbles we went, impatient water smashing its hands at the edge of them, the wind frothing and flapping our hairs at our ears.

Let us run home, I would have said, *and all go on as before.* But she knelt before me and her face in the moonlight was clear—alight as the moon, it was—and I was too busy admiring the clean arches of her eyebrows to voice my doubts.

"Step in," she said and then I was preoccupied, wasn't I, with fitting myself—for truth, I had grown a tiny bit since she sewed the thing—into the sheepskin suit. I gasped but did not complain as she tied and tied me into it, and then she pulled the ragged hood-mask down over my face and it was as if she sewed my mouth shut and my chin to my chest. I stood there with my neck pulled into an ache behind, my little sounds nothing against the sea's impatience.

Through the eyeholes I watched her as well as I could, for though she was being indecent there was such joy in it, such spirit, I could not but follow her every move, privileged to see. White she emerged out of her scratchy land-clothing, out of its wrinkles and seams.

"Ah!" She flung her drawers up on the pebbles, and she was animal within, all flesh and fur uncluttered by all those trappings.

Next she took up the coat-bag, drew out the coat, wrestled it open and slid it on. All of a sudden the air was cold and thick as water. I gasped inside my dry leather mask, and my flatted hair crawled.

She did not don the coat like any man-garment; rather, she began, and then the thing sank upon and encompassed her, clung on close, clung to its own edges around her. *Clap* and *clop* and *zip*, it went, and *snick*, and then she fell, from standing foot-fins together, straight into the wavelets, where she was now seal, and flang herself down towards the deeper water.

She turned and there was enough of her left that I could not refuse to follow, so I too fell and floundered through the curdled cold air and into the sea through its foamy edge. There the water, and the magic, overtook me, and what was seal of me supplanted what was boy, and I ceased to think and to intend or decide, in any way that makes sense in a story, but only followed my mam, crying after her into our dark world, all alive to the tides now and temperatures, to the bubbling trail of her that I sought and followed with my whiskers, to the depths and wonders and fellows and foes disposed on all sides of us, and before us, and below.

I will not tell you much about that time. It is not the kind of thing that can be caught in words, human words out of our subtle mouths: sunlight shafting into the green; the mirrory roof; the women racing ahead through the halls of the sea, the cathedrals; boat bellies, and the mumble and splash of man-business disturbing the water above; the seal-men, the sea-men, spun light as wooden tops by the delicate tail, pressing out the water behind them, impelling their bulk forward, upward, outward— It is very much like flying, through a green air flocking with tiny sunlit flecks of life.

Seal-men I found to be very like our dads on land, all possessiveness and anxiety, patrolling the borders of the clan. When we went up on a beach, they must always be seeing other seal-men off, coming back blown and bloodied. It seemed a savage way of work to me, this knocking of heads together. Sometimes me and my fellows had a play at it, but it were two rubber heads bouncing off each other, no teeth and no purpose, and the mams laughed lounging around us.

And then there were those sister-seals, our size but not fighters, but only slipping alongside us through the sun shafts, blinking beside us through the roof of the world, into the windy air and the rasp of breath in both of ours' opening nostrils. Those whiskery sea-maids, the ones with the spell on them to keep them seals, to keep them safe from human men. Like animate seeds or stones, they moved, like bullets leaping through the water, like weed undulating away along the tide or teasing your face with a leaf-end.

I don't know how to tell you. Seal feelings are different from human ones, seal-affections, seal-ties with other seals. The best I can do is overlay a skin of man-words on the grunt and urge and song and flight and slump of seal-being.

Our mams belonged better here than they ever had belonged above. Our mams found their wings, is how you might put it. Our mams did not glory or revel or make any particular celebration, but only slipped back to rightness, went back about their business. The bulk of our mams was not beautiful as a man sees beautiful, but to seal-eyes their beautiful black teardrops of being fell fast, flew fast, twisted through the home depths.

The sea was at our ears and against our sensitive faces, all its cavities and their echoes like a giants' city, this castle, that market and that cluster of tiny homes. Braided through, it was, with tidal temperatures, underlain with colder harder depths, with darkness-fish and the skeletons that fell out of everyone's feeding. Here above we were a multitude, in ranks of size and ferocity; I cannot explain to you, if you are a fisherman, the beauty and panic of a shining mass of herded fish, the whole school flashing back and forth looking for the no-way-out among my darting fellows, the topmost swimming out into the air in their terror.

The days were long and unformed; the seasons beckoned us, then pushed us away behind them; stars rode over us, and moons in their boatishness and bulbousness; towns were a crust at the edge of our world's eye and people were mites that crawled there. If I saw my father in that time, I don't recall it, or recognizing any man of Potshead—or woman, because Messkeletha was still there for a long while, and Trudle stayed all that time, and is still here now.

I don't recall particularly the landscape of our island, not above its rocks or above the beach-sand that as men we called Crescent Corner. As the sea to men, beyond the point that they can see bottom, becomes only the plumblined depths full of loves and livelihoods, so to seals the heights become only wastes of dry blaring light from which weather and occasional dangers descend.

I felt no pull to the land; I barely knew that I knew the land; I barely thought; I didn't feel the way a person feels. I only was, following flurries of instinct, flurries of friends and of fish.

"It happened by accident," says my dad. "Shorten Thomas found it out, enraging 'cross an ice floe one winter—all those cold nights without light nor woman will set a man to clubbing. Only he was using a hacker-pick that sealers have, cutting them, you see. Well, he was in a fine way—up to his ears in hotpunch too, no doubt. And he says it like this, that he turned at the end of the crowd of them, and weeping and looking back down the path of his butchery he saw a boy—all long and lanky, he says, much like you were extracted as, Dan'l. Writhing on the ice, he said, just like a seal does, only not managing to move as they do, for he was not built the same. And when the boy realizes, up onto hands and knees he goes, and quick as he can but clumsy—because he has forgot, in all that time, how to progress such a body—he crawls for the edge of the ice.

"Shorten went after him, calling: 'Boy, boy! What is your name?' But not fast enough, and the boy gets to the rim and looks back once, and falls in, all messy like an accident, not like seals do, like a brine-drop back into the ocean. And of course there drowns, doesn't come up even the once, for all Shorten's pleading. The cold catches him, and his first breath of the North Sea, and all that is left to Shorten is a few bubbles among the bobbing ice."

"He looked around, you say, the boy?"

Dad shakes his head. "You press Shorten on that, he will break and blub at you like you charged him with holding the boy's head under. He says he was all emotional, and you all look the same, you boys. He says he couldn't tell, that he might even have been looking his own Vernar in the eye and not known, the boy would have grown so much. But it might have been any of you, any of the ones we've not recovered yet: Snow, or Toll Hardy, Harold Roman, or the Gormlin twins who knows?" In the windowlight my dad is worn and clean; even the smoke from his brier-pipe is clean and white as his hair. Evening is coming; that light is cool, gray-blue. I am glad of the fire against its lack of cheer.

"So, then," he begins into the crackling silence with the sea behind it.

"Yes." The light fades on his face even as I watch, all crags of frail flesh.

"Well, he is struck horrorful with the thought he may have butchered other sons, he says, but mainly he's wondering, How did I cut that seal, to free the boy inside? And he goes back and finds the skin—and this is not hard among six-seven slaughtered beasts, because it has all shrunk and thinned, don't you know. It's one of those wee coats, you see, that your mams made to spirit you away in. Wi' the hoods, you remember? All of rabbit or lambskin."

I nod. "They stank to be inside, and were so tight. We had to put them on there in the shallows, else we were trapped tight in them, unable to walk, and too big for them to carry as well as their own coat."

"And Shorten sees that with this pick he's managed to cut, neat as a tailor, all the front stitches down the middle, so as to open the thing just like the coat that it is, and out has come the boy. And he brings the skin home and tells the tale, and we're all there handling this wee coat and weeping, like it were a holy relic, a roomful of grown men brought to nothing by this garment, all of us trying to recognize our wife's hand in the stitching, all of us desperate to see it, yet not to see it, so as not to lose hope of our son."

There is a slight crack in his voice on that last word, and I look up in time to see him surprised, and embarrassed, and straightaway recovered. "So then the hunt was on, every man for his boy," he says almost jovial, lifting pipe and paws and letting them drop to his blanketed lap, a fleck of ash stirred out of the bowl by the movement and falling beside.

I was born again and I came out crying—a lot of us did, they say. There never was such a race as the seals for mawking and mowing. I came out crying into a driving rain, and all sounds hurt my ears, rain-hiss on the decks and hatches and the sealers' celebrations: "Daniel Mallett! Welcome back to the world, boy!" They lifted me into the confusion and there with my big bony shoulders pulling my ragged coat apart up the back I stood and choked and took their embraces, that each was like an assault on me but which I did not rebuff. I had not the strength; I had forgot how to use arms.

They laid me down on the deck; it was not comfortable. Some man had put a rope-coil under my head for pillowing and it pressed in hard enough to hurt. I was accustoming myself—and it was difficult—to the frontwaysed eyes seeing two things for every one and putting them together. My bony body was less massy than before; how could it be so much heavier? Everything was heavier around me, glued to the deck; the men as they moved must cling to it; anything that fell must roll or slide to any lower point.

Around me was airy noise, every movement light and startling, every contact a concussion, throwing out more noise. Unpredictable, to no rhythm, they moved and swore and fumbled, the men of my town, of my land-world, and the sea-birds stuttered in the sky. And I was glued here myself, to these coat-remnants beneath me, pressed to the damp wood by this blanket, its heavy knots of sea-grass. All the wind could do was push the damp hair back and forth on my brow; it could not lift and return me to the water; it could not lift even this knotted knitted thing, that held the little left of my warmth around me in the absence of my seal-flesh.

It was an ill-making dream, and the men came by, smiling and patting me, to console me for it, all the way home. They asked me nothing; they did not expect me to speak, out of this strange-packed mouth, out of this flat face with its new framework of jaw. They muttered and crooned, and as the sky went on and the illness, their noises slipped together, interlocked into items of sense.

Welcoming me, they were, welcoming me back; their words were all about their gladness and our preciousness, their sons'. They were changed men from the ones I was beginning to remember.

"You'll be heavy to yourself awhile," said one, over the grinding of the boatside into the jetty, over the hard explosions of sound in my back, in the back of my head. He lifted the weed-blanket off me, and I waited to fly up into the air. But I did not. I lay helpless.

They hooked my arms over two men's necks and taught me walking, across the deck all cluttered with box and bolt and reel; across the frail plank that was all that kept me from a dirty corner of water, a corner of my home below. And to the land, locked unmoving, the jetty standing firm against the water that slapped and fought it below. My feet dragged and my legs attempted rescuing them—how was I to support myself and balance, on these two stalkish things? The men had put a shirt on me and trousers but still the foreign knees swung and braced below my poor-focusing eyes, my heavy head. I knew that they belonged to me, but I could not see how ever I was to control them.

My father was brought down the street to me, but I did not see him, only heard clomping boots and men saying, "See, Dominic? There he is!" And then a voice out of years ago, out of my bones, saying, "Is that him? Is that my Daniel? Are you sure?"

Then space opened before me and I heaved up my head. Some boots swam there and his familiar belt-buckle, and then the rest of him was there, sharp-edged and astounding, his big hands out wide at me and in between them his awakening face.

"Dan'l," he said, and "Dad," I said, and even words were heavy here, all burdened with the years, and my head sagged again and there was nothing but wet greeny-black-blue cobbles ringed by boot-toes and marveling men.

"Here, let me take him," said my father to the man at my right, and they un-hooked and re-hooked me and I seemed to walk worse than ever, leaning onto him with my head swung fast into his shoulder.

"You will be fine, my boy," he said. "Fine and good." And he held me up and walked me. A splash appeared a brighter blue on his shirt and I had not known it was raining, or he was crying, and I tried to say, I did not know what, that I knew him, that I was surprised, that I was sorry, that I had found my way somehow into this strange, long, wrong-grown body—but all I could manage for the moment was seal-cries, that said nothing, that had to say everything for me.

"We found out various as they came back," my dad says, "a little by little. But that first boy, Willem Canker, no. He came in, shocked and shivering, eyes all over the place, and as they brought him on the boat all the men were at him, question-and-poking, weeping on him and embracing, each asking after his own sons.

"Some thought Willem had gone simple, there under the waters all that time, or perhaps half-drowned on the way up and it had affected his brain, because he did not utter a proper word all the way, only moaned somewhat and seemed to suffer to be with us.

"We put him away in his house. Joel Canker laid him in his bed, and milk-and-breaded him back to life, and every now again he would come out and say, *Oh he is coming good, every day a wee bit more our lad.* He was sitting by the boy, talking and talking whenever he was awake to usen him to the sound of words again, to bring him back his memory. *And today he answered me,* he might say. *Today he said yes, when I asked him did he want for milk.*

"Which the rest of us found little consolation of, one word here or there when such bright little buttons you'd been all of you, never stopped rattling and singing morning to night, every one of you, questions questions. And the last five years along at Wholeman's every word you had spoke we had turned over and wet with our tears and polished with our examinations and nostalgias. Besides which, Canker might be imagining, from the strength of his own wishing, and Willem truly damaged and never to think a clear thought nor speak a clear word again.

"But then the boy came out. I remember the day. 'Twas a whole new weather and season, bright and blowy, and suddenly there was color in the sky and flowers on the hills around town.

"And the boy come out, good as new, Willem Canker, good as gold; I opened my curtains and there he was walking up the town long and limber with his easy man-stride—just like yours, Dan'l, only of course I'd not seen yours then. Had no surety of ever seeing it, always I reminded myself. I remember he looked up—not at me nor no one but just up, at the town, at walls, and maybe at hill and sky above, and the look of him—of all our boys and our wives and our selves rolled into the one—the sight of him near split me down the middle. And Canker out ahead—he did not need to sing, just his face was singing, the joy of it. They say it is a sin, envy. You must not covet, they say. Well, your old man, Dan'l, he's a sinner I hope you don't mind, cloven by envy, hating Joel Canker for having what I had not."

He beams around his pipe; takes the thing from between his teeth with one rheumaticky hand, reaches out the other and bats my face with it, softly, and takes it purple-gray away, trailing soap-scent.

Then a thought scoops his smile away and he's a codger again, all belligerent, his eyes a-swim with window-light. "'Course, there's some that only got that ever, only ever got that envy and no more. Corris Snow, bless his soul, and the Greens, none o' theirs came back." His gaze is like a pressure on my face, feasting on me and guilting about it.

Sometimes it can be simple pleasure seeing each other, but not often; net after net of past event and slippery feelings drops between us, until sometimes I can barely make him out through the masses.

When that happens I will up and sigh, and fetch us teas, maybe, that the two of us can sip staring out over the roofs and water, while it all dissipates. You cannot have that stuff drawn in on yourself too close and constant. It will

drive you mad; it will drive you off Chisel Top like Corris Snow, into the arms
of your wife as you think, into the rocks, crushed cold there forever. Sometimes
you must just stand, upright on the earth as you are or cupped in an armchair
like Dad or propped on a barstool; sometimes you must just breathe and be,
with your small land-lungs and your stuck body. You must cease your wishing
for things you cannot have, and just proceed towards the grave, kind as you can
be to your fellow travelers, not raising any great hopes or moaning any great
miseries.

This is the truest way for us boys, and the hardest, bred as we are from two
great tribes-ful of yearning. Not all of us can steady ourselves so, and none of
us are balanced aright all of the time.

We were all put to fishing, of course. Gratefully the older men passed us their
places on the boats, while the ones with still a little fire in them leaped to
ordering and instructing us with almost glee.

It was good for us. It was better than sitting at home net-mending with the
sadder dads. The sea was the best place for us, halfway between our two homes
and with a job to do. And it tired us properly, all that hauling and winding. And
you never knew what curious-familiar thing would come up squirming in the
net and make you wonder.

This was going to be our lives then, these the components, unless Grinny
enacted his scheme of starting Trudle knitting again, unless Raditch and
Cawdron took up theirs, of rowing to the mainland for a look at the women
there.

I am not much for venturing. I had no such schemes. I tend to stop where I
am brought or put, and endure whatever yearning is my lot there. It has been
before me all my life in my mam, and now it is in me, and in my dad, and that
is only natural, the whole town with its head full of sea and seals, enraged or
grief-ridden or both. Us boys—well, I did not know about the others, it was
not as if we named things to each other. For myself I felt too freshly arrived,
too newly born yet to do more than walk and work from day to day. I thought
if I waited, equanimity might come, my father's slow eating of himself, after
all these years, notwithstanding.

I came home early from helping at Fisher's store. The smell was all through the
house: wild salt sweat of mams, caverns of ocean, turning the air blue-green. I
walked through it with my arms out; it all but swirled about them.

In the kitchen, at the heart of the smell, at the heart of the home, Dad sat at
the slab table with his white plate and a spoon and a caught-red-handed look
disguised as normal every-dayness up at me.

"What brings you so early?" he accused me.

"Done all I had to do." His chin was tilted up, his eyes craven, and then there
was the thing on the plate—hairy, with a rubbery inner lining with a blob of
orange curd on the lip. The spoon hovered.

"Here," he says. "There's another." Points with his thumb to the pot on the stove. As if this were an ordinary dinner.

I tried for both our sakes to pretend it was. Crossed and spooned it from the pot, clanked out a plate and rattled a spoon from the drawer. Cut the cap off, with my big capable hands—last time I et one of these, my mam had to open it for me, that tough skin.

The steam flooded up and the smell: bodies, wet hair, boiled shellfish, sour seawater, the coziest of winter nights, her clear pale skin with a hint of green; her hair like black water made thread, made silk.

I spooned up a bit and there it was in my mouth now, all my childhood, warm and free of worry, before the future came down out of its scratchy gray cloud and began to bother and itch me. Days of play and safety, our mothers laughing together, my mam and dad laughing, too, looking to each other, leaning arm to arm. I would do things; I would perform; I would stand on my hands against the wall so they would look at me again, include me with them. Always it was my fight when Dad was there, to have her eyes and her mind on me.

Well, I got that, did I not. The curd sat cooling on my tongue; it slid down my throat, soaking my head with the sweet-saltness. Up sprang tears, but not so far as to fall.

I saw what we had done to them, the mams and boys to the dads. It weren't necessarily worse than what the dads done in the beginning. What a thing to weigh up: would you rather be born of redheads both, or would you be silky-dark and big-eyed? Would you prefer another mother? There is no way of trying that out. Maybe mainland children love their scour-haired mams just as fiercely as we love our silkies, maybe they learn to lose themselves in pale eye-depths whereas here with our mams' darknesses beside them, our dads' blues and greens revealed no more than blue-or-greenpainted curves of china.

Anyway we took all that away, the polish off the china, the shine of purpose and determination. I had not known what we were doing back then. I did not know, looking back now, whether we ought not to've, with Dad there across from me, head bent over the rubbish-looking heart, scooping up more orange.

And once we'd gone, us and the mams, each man had a choice, either to go like Bannister into breakage and mourning, and slope around Potshead like a sprite lost between this world and the next, or to go rocklike with rage like Martyr or Green, and shout and rally everyone, and proclaim how things were all right, an improvement in fact, now that those sly enchantresses had loosed their holds on our hearts.

But they had not, of course. They never would. You could not be free if you were born of them, and looking at our dads the husbanding of them was much the same: you thought *you* had caught and confined *them*, but really it was you as was tangled in the weed nets; you could not breathe properly either in air or in water, were the seal-women not there to encourage the life in and out of you.

Raditch ran up, and stood all outlined in the sunny doorway. "Ho, Daniel. There looks to be another witch coming in."

"What do we want one for?" I did not stop sweeping. "Trudle is young yet, and when she goes there is all those daughters." All wall-eyed skitterish four of them.

"She's here unaxed," said Raditch. "Come down and watch. I'm going to."

"Someone told Trudle?"

"Jakes and Wretch." The names floated back to me through the empty doorway.

Dad would be down there already; it was something the dads did, watch the unloading, some of them swap worldly words with the lumping-men. I propped the broom by the door and walked down through the sunshine.

Between the cottages I could see the *Fleet Fey* cutting towards us, the spot of red hair at her prow. A very straight figure, I thought, not like our Trudle, who had hunched into Messkeletha's old shape by now, taken over the posture as well as the witching, so as we should know it at a distance—know to turn and run, in good time, before she could enchant another daughter out of our loins.

Everyone gathered to meet the boat, just about: such men as would leave their houses and most of us long-shanked boys, trickling down from the streets and the men already on their bench and bollards on the front. "What is this, then, eh? What is this?" said Grinny's dad happily, taking up position against the warmed storehouse wall.

Trudle came down out the town at the moment the gangway-end clacked to the cobbles. Her daughters preceded her wild in their grubby print frocklets, all of the same flowers; she carried the boy against her shoulder who anyone could tell would grow up simple, he stared so slack-mouthed.

She met the visitor with the little suitcase at the plank-end, stood fast there so that the girl could not step off.

"What do you think you are about, young miss?" At the sound all the daughters swilled in around her and stared.

The girl looked Trudle over, and all the eyes around her. "Who are you," she said, "that I should account to you?" She asked it plain, with no sneering. "Are you mayor or police or officialdom?"

"What business has you in this place?" Trudle pointed her chin at her. "We've all the women we want here and no more."

The girl's gaze traveled from one end the crew of us behind the witch to the other. "Are you sure? It seems a touch unwomaned to me. But I have property here," she said, "if you must know my business, though it is none of yours, as far as I know you yet." She stepped neatly around Trudle and the daughters in her skirts.

"Property? What property?" Trudle swung and followed her, as if she were attached with string.

The girl crossed half the dock and stood there surveying us. "This is the way you welcome strangers, then?" she said, not loud but we could hear her, every syllable. "Let them be harassed and harridaned even before they've set foot?"

"What property would a mainland girl have here?" said Trudle at the girl's elbow and fear all over her.

"Quieten, woman," said old Baker.

Trudle bristled and chin-poked at him, drew herself up as much as she might.

But he went on, to the visitor, "Now I see you, you must be Dully Winch's girl, of his wife Mary."

"You have it," she said. "Lory Winch, I am."

"Lory, that's right." The woman-name was uncertain in his mouth.

"My mother died in the winter." No one looked or offered anything, so she went on. "She has left me a cottage here, she said." And straightway I saw it in my mind, the house called Winch's, a boarded-up box on the road out to the Hill. It was the first time I realized it belonged to anyone, and was not there just to say *out beyond Winch's* with, a landmark only.

We followed them up, Lory Winch and Baker, with Trudle there too, in close, still suspicious, and the daughters flowing around, and the boy staring dumbly at us over Trudle's shoulder. Up the sunshiny lanes we went, after those red hairs—for all the witch's girls had piles of it too, flags of it, bunches of it haphazardly pinned. The visitor's was all tied in, two plaits clambering back over her head from her temples and joining to one down her back. I had seen such plaiting on mams' dark heads, but theirs had lain obedient, while this seemed on the point of bursting its bindings did it but get half the chance.

Winch's stopped where it always had, only I saw it for the first time in a long time. It was black boards; it seemed to lean, the slope threw your eyes off so much, to lean back into the hill, for a better hold, maybe. The yard was thick angelweed up to the fencetop, up to the windows, like a bowl of wild salads, and sea pinks clumped and sea rocket trailed off through the pickets into Asham's fields around.

I thought she would be disappointed, a town girl like her. I had seen Knocknee houses. But "Yes," she said into our silences. "It is exactly as Mam said. I could have found my way alone with her directions, and a little black house is what she said."

We stood in the road and watched the creature encounter the gate. Raditch stepped forward to help. "No, I have it," she said. She opened it to the extent it could be opened, by which she could sidle onto the broken path, and then she waded up to the door. She took a key from her belt that was all the bigger and blacker for being in her small white hand, and she slid it into the keyhole and turned it, and we heard from the sound of that the house had insides, as well as the outsides we knew.

And we saw them, when she pushed the door wide into an upcurl of dust: papered walls, with pictures, and beyond the far door some furniture-back looming, shadow on shadow.

The miss put her case on the floor, a little way into the hall. She looked at us all out there with our stares on.

"Thank you for your help, gentlemen," she said, and it was hard to say how much she was laughing at us. "Let me settle myself here awhile, and then I'll out with a thousand questions, I'm sure."

"Did you want them battens taken off your winders, miss?" said Raditch. "I can fetch a claw and have it done soon as looking."

"Maybe in a while,' she said. "For now, I need the place to myself, if you don't mind."

She turned her back on us and darkened away down the hall, an upright young woman. We were not used to seeing that type of figure.

"Well," said Grinny as we walked slow away, hoping rather she would call us back for some question or favour. "That has livened up our morning."

"What's she want here?" fretted Trudle among us. "Who would want a-coming to this place?"

"You heard. She inherited. She wanted to see what she had," said Baker's dad. "I don't reckon she means to take your place, Trudle. She isn't got a spelling look about her."

"Why did her mam go, though? The widder?" This was Cawdron, gormless still. I didn't know the answer, but I knew it was one of those questions no one wanted asked.

"Sem reason they all went," snapped Martyr, Toddy's dad that had beat his wife, and to whom Toddy had not returned.

And what was that? Cawdron's face said it, but he didn't allow it out of his mouth. All of a sudden the older men found the spirit to walk, and closed their faces down, and went preoccupied with important and worrisome thoughts, so that they did not have to answer him.

"And so she is up there now, settling herself." I laughed. "Like a little red hen."

My dad had not come up to Winch's with the crowd. He bit into his breakfast bread and dealt with it, nodding and nodding to keep me quiet.

But she'd done something, that little hen; she'd pushed something over in my brain that now was falling, stone by stone. "They used to be all red, didn't they?"

He nodded towards the door.

"Why did they go? Widow Winch? Everyone?"

I saw him realize that I would not be put off. "There were no prospects here for them."

"Prospects?"

"Norn to *wed*, boy," he said crossly, and bit the bread again.

"Ha, there is nothing *but* men here. Was there such a crowd of red girls, then? Too many to go round? Couldn't some of them have stayed?"

But he was shaking his head and chewing.

"How did it happen, then? You tell. Then I'll not bother you by guessing wrong over and over."

He dabbed his bread at his plate. He chewed as long as he could and then swallowed, and did not bite again, only sat there dabbing, picking up crumbs with the damp bread-edge.

Stubborn old coot, he would not say, all that morning. I did not sit and badger him; now and then in passing I would say. "You are going to have to tell me some day. Well, it may as well be today, no?" or the like. But all he would do was chew at his teeth and look as if I had smacked him.

I know what you need, I thought, and after our dinner I went down to Fisher's and got us a bottle of spirit.

"Cold nights, these," said Doby Fisher just as his dad would, cold weather or hot, to anyone who bought such a bottle. "Man needs a tot."

I carried it up home. Dad watched me cross to the hall with it.

"I know what you're at," he said after me.

"Good," I threw back. "I should not like to deceive you."

"Impertinent."

Well, it took that night a bit of hoo-ing and hawing, and a long disquisition on whiskies the land over, but we reached a time after all the nonsense, late in the night, when all lamps outside were gone excepting the sky's own, when anything could be said between a son and his father; we'd taken on the perfect amount of liquoring to make the tongue loose but not yet the tears.

"Oh, Daniel," he began, out of nothing, out of my questioning way back this morning, "she were so beautiful. You know it," he said. "You remember. She come out the skin and none of our misery had touched her yet; none of the cruelties of this world had marked her. She was sad, yes, she was desperate to go home, but you could distract her from that, you could fascinate her with any small thing—the way an auger worked, maybe, or a swallow-nest in the eaves. And when she laughed—well, you remember, don't you? You made her laugh enough. We were all envious of our sons, that could make their mams laugh just by breathing, or playing stones, or asking where the sky ended, or eating up a fresh bowl of porridge. None of us husbands could do that, not so readily. We were always their imprisoners as well as the men they loved, and the fathers of their children."

He put out his glass, and I filled it for him, with candlelight and the sweet-woody smell of truth-telling. He slid it back to himself and looked into its dark-gold eye.

"I've had a plenty of time to go over this. While she was here I did not think it, but when she went, and you with her—why, then we all had time, didn't we? *Years* we had, to meditate upon it. There were some men all afire to fetch up more women from the sea, but with their few tries they had no luck, and the rest of us, we wanted the wives we'd had and no other; we wanted our own lads back that we knew.

"I remember when Jon Fisher brought the very first one in, and we all went down the storehouse to see her. Tricked up in Lucy Fisher's dress, she was, and my, wasn't she uncomfortable. She stared, one way and another; she would not look at you. She had been crying, all botched about the eyes, you could see. Jon Fisher's mam sat by her, looking so fierce, no one was bold enough to say a word, to ask the seal-girl anything."

He sipped his drink. "I thought she would die if she stayed here, and she must have thought the same, for she made herself bleed breaking into the cupboard where the skin was that night, and fighting her way out of Fishers'. In the morning she was just footprints across the wharf, blood-prints. I was glad for her, and I was blistering angry with Fishers the same, for not locking her up better, or setting any kind of guard on her, so's we could look some more in the morning.

"We know Martyr is not an admirable fellow, and we knew he wasn't then, yet when he showed at market with his new girl on his arm, that he called Ivy, just as if she belonged on dry land among us, the thing we wanted most to know was how he had come by and kept her. And one by one from him and each other we found out, and one by one we went and had a sea-blanket knitted up. Some went by water and netted their wives there. Some waited until the seals come up for sunbasking in Crescent Corner. And some went well away and took theirs from icebergs up north or other islands. There was no stopping us. Even the women threatening to go did not stop us."

"But I always thought the women went first, and left the men in need."

"Oh no, lad. They were here all the time. They saw it all. They said and said: *You don't stop this, you will lose all the real-wives of the town, and then you will see what it's like, being married to magic.* Which they did, and which we did. Which we are seeing still."

He took almost a bite of the spirit, to bring himself back to me and this room a moment.

"Anyway, I did same as all of them—I was no stronger nor better at the sight of those lovely women. You know the story from there."

"I do not," I said. "Did you go down Crescent Corner or what, for instance?"

"No, I was not brave enough. Crescent was for lads who could do it alone, and I wanted others around me. You always had to have Messkeletha there, of course, but I wanted fellows, too. Make me feel I was on the right path, that it was not against nature, what I was doing." He snorted and looked at the window. "Yes, so I just went out on our boats, with the wife-net the witch had spelled for us and that first blanket she had knitted me from seaweed and a good portion of my money, and up come your mam." He gave this last an end-of-story flourish.

I did not let up with my eyes, though. He paused and added a little water to the spirit, then shot me a glance. Then—it was a relief, I could tell. He fell into the next part, and his face flowered open. He had never told it before, and he knew he was doing right by telling me, and I saw expressions on him he had never worn before, except when my mam herself were in this very room with the two of us.

"Then the seal would be fighting trapped in the blanket, and most unladylike noises it would make. Messkeletha was at your elbow muttering: *Keep her covered, keep her covered.* But even through the knitted weed you could see the split in the seal-flesh, the crimson that did not bleed, the whiteness of the woman that came out clean, not touched or at all smudged or smelling of seal from inside. Clean as a peeled onion she came out, and soon you had all whiteness bucking in there like a mad maggot and you thought, *Whoa, Messkeletha's got me a bent one; how will I get my money back?*

"But then she told me: *Right, my work is done now. I am going for sleep before I throw my stomach*—for she was always on border of seasick, out there on the boat with us doing this work. All our money in the world could not settle her stomach.

"And she's gone, and it's only you—all the other lads are up beyond the deckhouse so as not to catch the silky's first eye and become her master instead of you.

"I found which end was her head and I held her down and I whispered her calm. Her eyes through the netting, through the blanket—I had seen enough seal-women by then to know them, yet this was a new beast, of course, among us, and I was her first close person.

"All the time whispering, I drew back the blanket, just from her face first and then her hair, untangling as I went. One white shoulder.

"*What have you done?* she said to me, at a pause in my whispering. *Why have you taken me from my home?* Her voice grew stronger later, and clearer, but that first utterance it was rusty and bubbly, and did not know how to pitch itself.

"*To take care of you,* I told her, *the best you have ever been cared for. To make you my wife.*

"By now we had run out of girl-clothing left to us by our own mams and sisters. But Grinny and Ewart had proved themselves neat at stitching up shifts that covered a woman decent, and I had me one of these, which I gave to her: *Here, put this on. It's kinder than that rough blanket.*

"And I will not forget her in it: lost, white-armed and white-footed and white-faced, sitting on a bollard in the gray shift with the world gray around her, boat and boy and sea and sky of it, looking up to me for—"

He drained his glass, put it down and examined the table either side of it. "Well, back then I liked to think it were love and comforting she looked for, but she may as easily have been reproaching me, for taking her up from everything she knew, and landing her here in my strange world, for my strange pleasures, for the rest of our lives, as I thought."

He sat a long time with that sour expression, thinking. Then his mind moved on, and his face softened.

"I hope you have a wedding night half like it, though, Dan'l. I hope you hold someone to your heart with only a shred of what I felt for that animal-woman. It is not something you can give back to the sea, after that. You put your full self, your full soul into them narrow hands, and afterwards you cannot be far from her, for fear of becoming nothing. When you all went, Dan'l—ahh, can you imagine? Can you imagine the—the—" He grinned over the candle at me. "The ghosts we were, the objects! We bare had strength to eat—and some did not, of course, and died that way, Errol Curse was one. We did not manage a funeral even for Errol, just put him away in the earth where he would not smell and interrupt our miseries, though Baker was all for throwing him in the sea, to make the point to Curse's wife, and Frederick and Batton, what they had done to him."

Then the tears started, and I will not show him to you that way. I stayed out the weeping with him, though, and the talking; I poured him more spirit when he asked for it; I agreed with him and soothed him as I could.

I lifted my head from my arms some time after midnight. He was staring into and addressing his drink.

"A night like this, it were," he said, "with the night breeze drabbling in the window just so, with not much to it."

I did not know if he meant the wedding night, or the night he met Mam, or the night they all went down to Fishers' store and saw the first seal-woman, and began the whole thing—or indeed another night of his story, that I had not been awake for.

I was washing the breakfast plates next morning when Dad came to me, which was unusual of him. Just his approaching, out of his chair when I knew he had already performed all the rituals of his morning, threw the day unusual. Was he poorly some way?

He came up close. "The Winch girl is here," he said to my shoulder.

"Here?"

His blue eyes swam as surprised as I felt. "She wants to speak to Daniel." As if Daniel were a third person—which almost he might be, a Daniel that Miss Lory Winch summoned.

I dried my hands. Dad watched me, watched me go, as if I were become that third man, another creature suddenly.

She flamed in the street outside. She had her hair different today, tied back still but exploding out beyond her shoulders. But very demure underneath it, with her arms folded.

"Good morning," I said.

Her face was so white it seemed lit from inside. She considered me until my greeting had erased itself from the air into foolishness. "You *don't* remember, then," she said, disappointed.

Which immediately I did. There was only the one red girl to remember, after all, other than Trudle and Trudle's girls. "Knocknee Market," I said.

She beamed.

"I went home and bothered my mam about you Killy men. I had not even realized she came from here. I suppose it is not something you boast of, that you were no prospect in a town full of beautiful mer-women.'

In my head Dad said, *Did you like her?* And I heard his tone now as I'd not when he said it, the great restraint in it, over the shyness, over the interest. I hid one-third of myself by leaning behind the doorpost. How could she stand so cheerfully in the sunlight and talk so?

"I am very disappointed not to have seen them," she said. "From the looks of the lads, they must have been quite a different make."

She wore neat mainland shoes, with an odd strap on them that seemed not entirely necessary.

"Were there any pictures painted of them, or photographs taken?"

"Cawdron drew some, of his mam, when he was little, that his dad has still on their wall. Grinny's dad brought a picture from the mainland—not of a wife, but a woman who looked like a wife. Some old painting; this was a picture of the painting. She had quite the look. That is at their place, sometimes on the wall, sometimes behind an armchair."

"Come walking?' she said. "You can only footle about on a doorstep so long."

"I've dishes to finish."

"Those can wait, Daniel," said my dad up the hall. "Or even I could do them, at a pinch. Think of that. You go."

"Come down the water?" said Lory Winch. "I have barely seen anything, there was such a crowd around me yesterday."

"Are you sure?" I said to Dad.

"Of course." He waved me away. "Go. Go. A walk in the sunshine with a pretty girl can only do you good."

So out we walked, and down the town, and as we walked and conversed—as she questioned me and I showed her the shapes of my ignorance, as I filled their emptinesses from Dad's memories and brought them back to her—without hardly being noticed, the rest of that summer went by. By the time we reached the water the air was chill and the sky gray. Graceless the waves moved, chop-chopping where they ought to have been smooth, a field of moving thorns against the underside of the land-world.

Lory and I walked along the mole between them, the littler water to our left an apron for the town; then to our right and forward the larger sea, busy all the way to the horizon and who knew how far beyond? Foam smeared it here and there, like whiteness being combed out; apart from that, the surface was dark and opaque; nothing splashed or surfaced, and no boat cut through the chop.

We did not hold hands; we were too secret for that. I did not even look at her, though her orange hair burned as bright now in my heart as it did at my shoulder-height over there. I could see it out the corner of my eye, crawling up into the air, unraveling from its ponytail, the frizzy bits at her forehead and temples flinging themselves away from their tetherment, always sprung back by their curliness. I could see, even as I chewed my lip and looked out at the nothing overriding our mothers, Lory's curve of white forehead; Lory's round-tipped white nose spattered with pale freckles; Lory's mouth that I intended kissing, soon as I could summon myself, the palest apology for color; Lory's soft girl-chin. All of these were neat and clear-edged against the dirty ocean, and her mainland hair, her dads' hair, smoked orange into the sky, curled and tumbled down her back like brookwater tightened between rocks.

The moment passed when we could stand any longer without awkwardness. Still I stood and stared, not knowing what else to do, but Lory turned and eyed the town, and went to the stones at the path edge and examined among them—for sheltering birds, maybe, or for things washed up. Her curiosity would make something arrive there, make the right thing happen now, any moment, and carry her on out of her shyness, and me with her.

Margo Lanagan *published poetry in her teens and twenties, then began publishing prose with novels for teens in the early nineties. She attended Clarion West in 1999, and her first collection of speculative-fiction short stories,* White Time, *appeared the following year. Her 2006 collection,* Black Juice, *was widely acclaimed, winning two World Fantasy Awards, two Ditmar Awards, two Aurealis Awards, and a Michael L. Printz Honor from the Young Adult Library Services Association. It was also shortlisted for the Los Angeles Times Book Prize. Stories from* Black Juice *were nominated for a Hugo, a Nebula, a Theodore Sturgeon, a Bram Stoker, an International Horror Guild Award, and a Tiptree Award. Her third collection,* Red Spikes, *was the Children's Book Council of Australia Book of the Year for older readers, and was shortlisted for the Commonwealth Writers Prize and the World Fantasy Award, and longlisted for the Frank O'Connor International Short Story Award. Her novel,* Tender Morsels, *won a World Fantasy Award and was also a Michael L. Printz Honor Book. Her fourth collection,* Yellowcake, *and another novel,* The Brides of Rollrock Island, *will be published in 2011. Lanagan taught at Clarion South in Brisbane in 2005, 2007, and 2009. She lives in Sydney and is currently working as a technical writer and an arts bureaucrat, and writing a lot of short stories.*

The selkie myth has often been used as a motif in fiction, but few have handled it as well as Lanagan does in this novella. Other than the gorgeous prose, wealth of atmosphere, and clear characterization, she offers a balanced, poignant view from all sides . . . and even what is probably a happy ending.

Originally published in *X6* by Coeur de Lion, this is *Sea-Heart*'s first publication outside of Australia.

A HAUNTED HOUSE OF HER OWN

KELLEY ARMSTRONG

Tanya couldn't understand why realtors failed to recognize the commercial potential of haunted houses. This one, it seemed, was no different.

"Now, these railings need work," the woman said as she led Tanya and Nathan out onto one of the balconies. "But the floor is structurally sound, and that's the main thing. I'm sure these would be an attractive selling point to your bed-and-breakfast guests."

Not as attractive as ghosts.

"You're sure the house doesn't have a history?" Tanya prodded again. "I thought I heard something in town. . . . "

She hadn't, but the way the realtor stiffened told Tanya that she was onto something. After pointed reminders about disclosing the house's full history, the woman admitted there was, indeed, something. Apparently a kid had murdered his family here, back in the seventies.

"A tragedy, but it's long past," the realtor assured her. "Never a spot of trouble since."

"Damn," Tanya murmured under her breath, and followed the realtor back inside.

Nathan wanted to check out the coach house, to see if there was any chance of converting it into a separate "honeymoon hideaway."

Tanya was thrilled to see him taking an interest. Opening the inn had been her idea. An unexpected windfall from a great-aunt had come right after she'd lost her teaching job and Nathan's office-manager position teetered under end-of-year budget cuts. It seemed like the perfect time to try something new.

"You two go on ahead," she said. "I'll poke around in here, maybe check out the gardens."

"Did I see a greenhouse out back?" Nathan asked the realtor.

She beamed. "You most certainly did."

"Why don't you go take a look, hon? You were talking about growing organic vegetables."

"Oh, what a wonderful idea," the realtor said. "That is so popular right now. Organic local produce is all the rage. There's a shop in town that supplies all the . . . "

As the woman gushed, Tanya backed away slowly, then escaped.

The house was perfect—a six-bedroom, rambling Victorian perched on a hill three miles from a suitably quaint village. What more could she want in a bed-and-breakfast? Well, ghosts. Not that Tanya believed in such things, but haunted inns in Vermont were all the rage, and she was determined to own one.

When she saw the octagonal Victorian greenhouse, though, she decided that if it turned out there'd never been so much as a ghostly candle spotted on the property, she'd light one herself. She had to have this place.

She stepped inside and pictured it with lounge chairs, a bookshelf, maybe a little woodstove for winter. Not a greenhouse, but a sunroom. First, though, they'd need to do some serious weeding. The greenhouse *conservatory*, she amended—sat in a nest of thorny vines dotted with red. Raspberries? She cleaned a peephole in the grime and peered out.

A head popped up from the thicket. Tanya fell back with a yelp. Sunken brown eyes widened, and wizened lips parted in a matching shriek of surprise.

Tanya hurried out as the old woman made her way from the thicket, a basket of red berries in one hand.

"I'm sorry, dear," she said. "We gave each other quite a fright."

Tanya motioned at the basket. "Late for raspberries, isn't it?"

The old woman smiled. "They're double-blooming. At least there's one good thing to come out of this place." She looked over at the house. "You aren't . . . looking to buy, are you?"

"I might be."

The woman's free hand gripped Tanya's arm. "No, dear. You don't want to do that."

"I hear there's some history."

"History?" The old woman shivered. "Horrors. Blasphemies. Murders. Foul murders. No, dear, you don't want this house, not at all."

Foul murders? Tanya tried not to laugh. If they ever did a promotional video, she was hiring this woman.

"Whatever happened was a tragedy," Tanya said. "But it's long past, and it's time—"

"Long past? Never. At night, I still hear the moans. The screams. The chanting. The chanting is the worst, as if they're trying to call up the devil himself."

"I see. "Tanya squinted out at the late-day sun, dropping beneath the horizon. "Do you live around here, then?"

"Just over there."

The woman pointed, then shuffled around the conservatory; still pointing. When she didn't come back, Tanya followed, wanting to make note of her name. But the yard was empty.

Tanya poked around a bit after that, but the sun dropped fast over the mountain ridge. As she picked her way through the brambles, she looked up at the house looming in the twilight—a hulking shadow against the night, the lights inside seeming to flicker like candles behind the old glass.

The wind sighed past and she swore she heard voices in it, sibilant whispers snaking around her. A shadow moved across an upper window. She'd blame a drape caught in a draft . . . only she couldn't see any window coverings.

She smiled as she shivered. For someone who didn't believe in ghosts, she was quite caught up in the fantasy. Imagine how guests who did believe would react.

She found Nathan still in the coach house, measuring tape extended. When she walked up, he grinned, his boyish face lighting up.

"It's perfect," he said. "Ten grand and we'd have ourselves a honeymoon suite."

Tanya turned to the realtor. "How soon can we close?"

The owners were as anxious to sell as Tanya was to buy, and three weeks later, they were in the house, with the hired contractors hard at work. Tanya and Nathan were working, too, researching the house's background, both history and legend.

The first part was giving them trouble. The only online mention Nathan found was a secondary reference. But it proved that a family had died in their house, so that morning he'd gone to the library in nearby Beamsville, hoping a search there would produce details.

Meanwhile, Tanya would try to dig up the less-tangible ghosts of the past.

She started in the gardening shop, and made the mistake of mentioning the house's history. The girl at the counter shut right down, murmuring, "We don't talk about that," then bustled off to help the next customer. That was fine. If the town didn't like to talk about the tragedy, she was free to tweak the facts and her guests would never hear anything different.

Next, she headed for the general store, complete with rocking chairs on the front porch and a tub of salty pickles beside the counter. She bought supplies, then struck up a conversation with the owner. She mentioned that she'd bought the Sullivan place, and worked the conversation around to, "Someone over in Beamsville told me the house is supposed to be haunted."

"Can't say I ever heard that," he said, filling her bag. "This is a nice, quiet town."

"Oh, that's too bad." She laughed. "Not the quiet part but . . . " She lowered her voice. "You wouldn't believe the advertising value of ghosts."

His wife poked her head in from the back room. "She's right, Tom. Folks pay extra to stay in those places. I saw it on TV."

"A full house for me means more customers for you," Tanya said.

"Well, now that you mention it, when my boys were young, they said they saw lights . . . "

And so it went. People might not want to talk about the true horrors of what had happened at the Sullivan place, but with a little prodding they spun tales of imagined ones. Most were secondhand accounts, but Tanya didn't even care if they were true. Someone in town said it, and that was all that mattered. By the time she headed home, her notebook was filled with stories.

She was at the bottom of the road when she saw the postwoman putting along in her little car, driving from the passenger seat so she could stuff the mailboxes. Tanya got out to introduce herself. As they chatted, Tanya mentioned the raspberry-picking neighbor, hoping to get a name.

"No old ladies around here," the postwoman said. "You've got Mr. McNally to the north. The Lee gang to the south. And to the back, it's a couple of new women. Don't recall the names—it isn't my route—but they're young."

"Maybe a little farther? She didn't exactly say she was a neighbor. Just pointed over there."

The woman followed her finger. "That's the Lee place."

"Past that, then."

"Past that?" The woman eyed her. "Only thing past that is the cemetery."

Tanya made mental notes as she pulled into the darkening drive. She'd have to send Nathan to the clerk's office, see if he could find a dead resident who resembled a description of the woman she'd seen.

Not that she thought she'd seen a ghost, of course. The woman probably lived farther down the hill. But if she found a similar deceased neighbor, she could add her own spooky tale to the collection.

She stepped out of the car. When a whisper snaked around her, she jumped. Then she stood there, holding the car door, peering into the night and listening. It definitely sounded like whispering. She could even pick up a word or two, like come and join. Well, at least the ghosts weren't telling her to get lost, she thought, her laugh strained and harsh against the quiet night.

The whispers stopped. She glanced up at the trees. The dead leaves were still. No wind. Which explained why the sound had stopped. As she headed for the house, she glanced over her shoulder, checking for Nathan's SUV. It was there, but the house was pitch black.

She opened the door. It creaked. Naturally. No oil for that baby, she thought with a smile. No fixing the loose boards on the steps, either. Someone was bound to hear another guest sneaking down for a midnight snack and blame ghosts. More stories to add to the guest book.

She tossed her keys onto the table. They hit with a jangle, the sound echoing through the silent hall. When she turned on the light switch, the hall stayed dark. She tried not to shiver as she peered around. *That's quite enough ghost stories for you*, she told herself as she marched into the next room, heading for the lamp. She tripped over a throw rug and stopped.

"Nathan?"

No answer. She hoped he wasn't poking around in the basement. He'd been curious about some boxes down there, but she didn't want to get into that. There was too much else to be done.

She eased forward, feeling the way with her foot until she reached the lamp. When she hit the switch, light flooded the room. Not a power outage, then. Good; though it reminded her they had to pick up a generator. Blackouts would be a little more atmospheric than guests would appreciate.

"Nathan?"

She heard something in the back rooms. She walked through, hitting lights as she went—for safety, she told herself.

"Umm-hmm." Nathan's voice echoed down the hail. "Umm-hmm.

On the phone, she thought, too caught up in the call to realize how dark it had gotten and turn on a light. She hoped it wasn't the licensing board. The inspector had been out to assess the ongoing work yesterday. He'd seemed happy with it, but you never knew.

She let her shoes click a little harder as she walked over the hardwood floor, so she wouldn't startle Nathan. She followed his voice to the office. From the doorway, she could see his back in the desk chair.

"Umm-hmm."

Her gaze went to the phone on the desk. Still in the cradle. Nathan's hands were at his sides. He was sitting in the dark, looking straight ahead, at the wall.

Tanya rubbed down the hairs on her neck. He was using his cell phone earpiece, that was all. Guys and their gadgets. She stepped into the room and looked at his ear. No headset.

"Nathan?"

He jumped, wheeling so fast that the chair skidded across the floor. He caught it and gave a laugh, shaking his head sharply as he reached for the desk lamp.

"Must have dozed off. Not used to staring at a computer screen all day anymore."

He rubbed his eyes, and blinked up at her.

"Everything okay, hon?" he asked.

She said it was and gave him a rundown of what she'd found, and they had a good laugh at that, all the shopkeepers rushing in with their stories once they realized the tourism potential.

"Did you find anything?"

"I did indeed." He flourished a file folder stuffed with printouts. "The Rowe family. Nineteen seventy-eight. Parents, two children, and the housekeeper, all killed by the seventeen-year-old son."

"Under the influence of Satan?"

"Rock music. Close enough." Nathan grinned. "It was the seventies. Kid had long hair, played in a garage band, partial to Iron Maiden and Black Sabbath. Clearly a Satanist."

"Works for me."

Tanya took the folder just as the phone started to ring. The caller ID showed the inspector's name. She set the pages aside and answered as Nathan whispered that he'd start dinner.

There was a problem with the inspection—the guy had forgotten to check a few things, and he had to come back on the weekend, when they were supposed to be away scouring estate auctions and flea markets to furnish the house. The workmen would be there, but apparently that wasn't good enough. And on Monday, the inspector would leave for two weeks in California with the wife and kids.

Not surprisingly, Nathan offered to stay. Jumped at the chance, actually. His enthusiasm for the project didn't extend to bargain hunting for Victorian beds. He joked that he'd have enough work to do when she wanted her treasures refinished. So he'd stay home and supervise the workers, which was probably wise anyway.

It was an exhausting but fruitful weekend. Tanya crossed off all the necessities and even a few wish-list items, like a couple of old-fashioned washbasins.

When she called Nathan an hour before arriving home, he sounded exhausted and strained, and she hoped the workers hadn't given him too much trouble. Sometimes they were like her grade-five pupils, needing a watchful eye and firm, clear commands. Nathan wasn't good at either. When she pulled into the drive and found him waiting on the porch, she knew there was trouble.

She wasn't even out of the car before the workmen filed out, toolboxes in hand.

"We quit," the foreman said.

"What's wrong?" she asked.

"The house. Everything about it is wrong."

"Haunted," an older man behind him muttered.

The younger two shifted behind their elders, clearly uncomfortable with this old-man talk, but not denying it, either.

"All right," she said slowly. "What happened?"

They rhymed off a litany of haunted-house tropes—knocking inside the walls, footsteps in the attic, whispering voices, flickering lights, strains of music.

"Music?"

"Seventies rock music," Nathan said, rolling his eyes behind their backs. "Andy found those papers in my office, about the Rowe family.

"You should have warned us," the foreman said, scowling. "Working where something like that happened? It isn't right. The place should be burned to the ground."

"It's evil," the older man said. "Evil soaked right into the walls. You can feel it."

The only thing Tanya felt was the recurring sensation of being trapped in a B movie. Did people actually talk like this? First the old woman. Then the townspeople. Now the contractors.

They argued, of course, but the workmen were leaving. When Tanya started to threaten, Nathan pulled her aside. The work was almost done, he said. They could finish up themselves, save some money, and guilt these guys into cutting their bill even more.

Tanya hated to back down, but he had a point. She negotiated 20 percent off for the unfinished work and another 15 for the inconvenience—unless they wanted her spreading the word that grown men were afraid of ghosts. They grumbled, but agreed.

The human mind can be as impressionable as a child. Tanya might not believe in ghosts, but the more stories she heard, the more her mind began to believe, with or without her permission. Drafts became cold spots. Thumping pipes became the knocks of unseen hands. The hisses and sighs of the old furnace became the whispers and moans of those who could not rest. She knew better: that was the worst of it. She'd hear a pipe thump and she'd jump, heart pounding, even as she knew there was a logical explanation.

Nathan wasn't helping. Every time she jumped, he'd laugh. He'd goof off and play ghost, sneaking into the bathroom while she was in the shower and writing dirty messages in the condensation on the mirror. She was spooked; he thought it was adorable.

The joking and teasing she could take. It was the other times, the ones when she'd walk into a room and he'd be standing or sitting, staring into nothing, confused, when he'd start out of his reverie, laughing about daydreaming, but nervously, like he didn't exactly know what he'd been doing.

They were three weeks from opening when she returned from picking up the brochures and, once again, found the house in darkness. This time, the hall light worked—it'd been nothing more sinister than a burned-out bulb before. And this time she didn't call Nathan's name, but crept through the halls looking for him, feeling silly, and yet . . .

When she approached the kitchen, she heard a strange rasping sound. She followed it and found Nathan standing in the twilight, staring out the window, hands moving, a *skritch-skritch* filling the silence.

The fading light caught something in his hands—a flash of silver that became a knife, a huge butcher's knife moving back and forth across a whetting stone.

"N-Nathan?"

He jumped, nearly dropping the knife, then stared down at it, frowning. A sharp shake of his head and he laid the knife and stone on the counter, then flipped on the kitchen light.

"Really not something I should be doing in the dark, huh?" He laughed and moved a carrot from the counter to the cutting board, picked up the knife, then stopped. "Little big for the job, isn't it?"

She moved closer. "Where did it come from?"

"Hmm?" He followed her gaze to the unfamiliar knife. "Ours, isn't it? Part of the set your sister gave us for our anniversary? It was in the drawer." He grabbed a smaller knife from the wooden block. "So, how did the brochures turn out?"

Two nights later, Tanya was startled awake and bolted up, blinking hard, hearing music. She rubbed her ears, telling herself it was a dream, but she could definitely hear something. She turned to Nathan's side of the bed. Empty.

Okay, he couldn't sleep, so he'd gone downstairs. She could barely hear the music, so he was being considerate, keeping it low, probably doing paperwork in the office.

Even as she told herself this, though, she kept envisioning the knife. The big butcher's knife that seemed to have come from nowhere.

Nonsense. Her sister *had* given them a new set, and Nathan did most of the cooking, so it wasn't surprising that she hadn't recognized it. But as hard as she tried to convince herself, she just kept seeing Nathan standing in the twilight, sharpening that knife, the *skritch-skritch* getting louder, the blade getting sharper.

Damn her sister. And not for the knives, either. Last time they'd been up, her sister and boyfriend had insisted on picking the night's video. *The Shining.* New caretaker at inn is possessed by a murderous ghost and hacks up his wife. There was a reason Tanya didn't watch horror movies, and now she remembered why.

She turned on the bedside lamp, then pushed out of bed and flicked on the overhead light. The hall one went on, too. So did the one leading downstairs. Just being careful, of course. You never knew where a stray hammer or board could be lying around.

As she descended the stairs, the music got louder, the thump of the bass and the wail of the singer. Seventies' heavy-metal music. Hadn't the Rowe kid—? She squeezed her eyes shut and forced the thought out. Like she'd know seventies heavy metal from modern stuff anyway. And hadn't Nathan picked up that new AC/DC disk last month? *Before* they came to live here. He was probably listening to that, not realizing how loud it was.

When she got downstairs, though, she could feel the bass vibrating through the floorboards. Great. He couldn't sleep, so he was poking through those boxes in the basement.

Boxes belonging to the Rowe family. To the Rowe kid.

Oh, please. The Rowes had been gone for almost thirty years. Anything in the basement would belong to the Sullivans, a lovely old couple now living in Florida.

On the way to the basement, Tanya passed the kitchen. She stopped. She looked at the drawer where Nathan kept the knife, then walked over and opened it. Just taking a look, seeing if she remembered her sister giving it to them, not making sure it was still there. It was. And it still didn't look familiar.

She started to leave, then went back, took out the knife, wrapped it in a dishtowel, and stuck it under the sink. And, yes, she felt like an idiot. But she felt relief even more.

She slipped down to the basement, praying she wouldn't find Nathan sitting on the floor, staring into nothing, nodding to voices she couldn't hear. Again, she felt foolish for thinking it, and again she felt relief when she heard him digging through boxes, and more relief yet when she walked in and he looked up, grinning sheepishly like a kid caught sneaking into his Christmas presents.

"Caught me," he said. "Was it the music? I thought I had it low enough."

She followed his gaze and a chill ran through her. Across the room was a record player, an album spinning on the turntable, more stacked on the floor.

"Found it down here with the albums. Been a while since you've seen one of those, I bet."

"Was it . . . his? The Rowe boy?"

Nathan frowned, as if it hadn't occurred to him. "Could be, I guess. I didn't think of that."

He walked over and shut the player off. Tanya picked up an album. Initials had been scrawled in black marker in the corner. T.R. What was the Rowe boy's name? She didn't know and couldn't bring herself to ask Nathan, would rather believe he didn't know, either.

She glanced at him. "Are you okay?"

"Sure. I think I napped this afternoon, while you were out. Couldn't get to sleep."

"And otherwise . . . ?"

He looked at her, trying to figure out what she meant, but what could she say? *Have you had the feeling of being not yourself lately? Hearing voices telling you to murder your family?*

She had to laugh at that. Yes, it was a ragged laugh, a little unsure of itself; but a laugh nonetheless. No more horror movies for her, however much her sister pleaded.

"Are you okay?" Nathan asked.

She nodded. "Just tired."

"I don't doubt it, the way you've been going. Come on. Let's get up to bed." He grinned. "See if I can't help us both get to sleep."

The next day, she was in the office, adding her first bookings to the ledger when she saw the folder pushed off to the side, the one Nathan had compiled on the Rowe murders. She'd set it down that day and never picked it up again. She could tell herself she'd simply forgotten, but she was never that careless. She hadn't read it because her newly traitorous imagination didn't need any more grist for its mill.

But now she thought of that album cover in the basement. Those initials. If it didn't belong to the Rowe boy, then this was an easy way to confirm that and set her mind at ease.

The first report was right there on top, the names listed, the family first, then the housekeeper, Madelyn Levy, and finally, the supposed killer, seventeen-year-old Timothy Rowe.

Tanya sucked in a deep breath, then chastised herself. What did that prove? She'd known he listened to that kind of music, and that's all Nathan had been doing—listening to it, not sharpening a knife, laughing maniacally.

Was it so surprising that the Rowes' things were still down there? Who else would claim them? The Sullivans had been over fifty when they moved in—maybe they'd never ventured down into the basement. There had certainly been enough room to store things upstairs.

And speaking of the Sullivans, they'd lived in this house for twenty-five years. If it was haunted, would they have stayed so long?

If it was *haunted*? Was she really considering the possibility? She squeezed her eyes shut. She was not that kind of person. She would not become that kind of person. She was rational and logical, and until she saw something that couldn't be explained by simple common sense, she was sending her imagination to the corner for a time-out.

The image made her smile a little, enough to settle back and read the article, determined now to prove her fancies wrong. She found her proof in the next paragraph, where it said that Timothy Rowe shot his father. *Shot.* No big, scary butcher—

Her gaze stuttered on the rest of the line. She went back to the beginning, rereading. Timothy Rowe had apparently started his rampage by shooting his father, then continued on to brutally murder the rest of his family with a ten-inch kitchen carving knife.

And what did that prove? Did she think Nathan had dug up the murder weapon with those old LPs? Of course not. A few lines down, it said that both the gun and knife had been recovered.

What if Nathan bought a matching one? Compelled to reenact—

She pressed her fists against her eyes. Nathan possessed by a killer teen, plotting to kill her? Was she losing her mind? It was Nathan—the same good-natured, carefree guy she'd lived with for ten years. Other than a few bouts of confusion, he was his usual self, and those bouts were cause for a doctor's appointment, not paranoia.

She skimmed through the rest of the articles. Nothing new there, just the tale retold again and again, until—the suspect dead—the story died a natural death, relegated to being a skeleton in the town's closet.

The last page was a memorial published on the first anniversary of the killings, with all the photos of the victims. Tanya glanced at the family photo and was about to close the folder when her gaze lit on the picture of the housekeeper: Madelyn Levy.

When Nathan came in a few minutes later, she was still staring at the picture.

"Hey, hon. What's wrong?"

"I—" She pointed at the housekeeper's photo. "I've seen this woman. She—she was outside, when we were looking at the house. She was picking raspberries."

The corners of Nathan's mouth twitched, as if he was expecting—hoping—that she was making a bad joke. When her gaze met his, the smile vanished and he took the folder from her hands, then sat on the edge of the desk.

"I think we should consider selling," he said.

"Wh-what? No. I—"

"This place is getting to you. Maybe—I don't know. Maybe there is something. Those workers certainly thought so. Some people could be more susceptible—"

She jerked up straight. "I am not susceptible—"

"You lost a job you loved. You left your home, your family, gave up everything to start over, and now it's not going the way you dreamed. You're under a lot of stress and it's only going to get worse when we open."

He took her hands and tugged her up, his arms going around her. "The guy who owns the Beamsville bed-and-breakfast has been asking about this place. He'd been eyeing it before, but with all the work it needed, it was too much for him. Now he's seen what we've done and, well, he's interested. Very interested. You wouldn't be giving up; you'd be renovating an old place and flipping it for a profit. Nothing wrong with that."

She stood. "No. I'm being silly, and I'm not giving in. We have two weeks until opening, and there's a lot of work to be done."

She turned back to her paperwork. He sighed and left the room.

It got worse after that, as if in refusing to leave, she'd issued a challenge to whatever lived there. She'd now stopped laughing when she caught herself referring to the spirits as if they were real. They were. She'd come to accept that. Seeing the housekeeper's picture had exploded the last obstacle. She'd wanted a haunted house and she'd gotten it.

For the last two nights, she'd woken to find herself alone in bed. Both times, Nathan had been downstairs listening to that damned music. The first time, he'd been digging through the boxes, wide awake, blaming insomnia. But last night . . .

Last night, she'd gone down to find him talking to someone. She'd tried to listen, but he was doing more listening than talking himself, and she caught only a few *um-hmms* and *okays* before he'd apparently woken up, startled and confused. They'd made an appointment to see the doctor after that. An appointment that was still a week away, which didn't do Tanya any good now, sitting awake in bed alone on the third night, listening to the strains of distant music.

She forced herself to lie back down. Just ignore it. Call the doctor in the morning, tell him Nathan would take any cancellation.

But lying down didn't mean falling asleep. As she lay there, staring at the ceiling, she made a decision. Nathan was right. There was no shame in flipping the house for a profit. Tell their friends and family they'd decided small-town life wasn't for them. Smile coyly when asked how much they'd made on the deal.

No shame in that. None at all. No one ever needed to know what had driven her from this house.

She closed her eyes and was actually on the verge of drifting off when she heard Nathan's footsteps climbing the basement stairs. Coming to bed? She hoped so, but she could still hear the boom and wail of the music. Nathan's steps creaked across the first level. A door opened. Then the squeak of a cupboard door. A *kitchen* cupboard door.

Grabbing something to eat before going back downstairs.

Only he didn't go downstairs. His footsteps headed upstairs.

He's coming up to bed—just forgot to turn off the music.

All very logical, but logical explanations didn't work for Tanya anymore. She got out of bed and went into the dark hall. She reached for the light switch, but stopped. She didn't dare announce herself like that.

Clinging to the shadows, she crept along the wall until she could make out the top of Nathan's blond head as he slowly climbed the stairs. Her gaze dropped, waiting for his hands to come into view.

A flash of silver winked in the pale glow of a nightlight. Her breath caught. She forced herself to stay still just a moment longer, to be sure, and then she saw it, the knife gripped in his hand, the angry set of his expression, the emptiness in his eyes, and she turned and fled.

A room. Any room. Just get into one, lock the door, and climb over the balcony.

The first one she tried was locked. She wrenched on the doorknob, certain she was wrong.

"Mom?" Nathan said, his voice gruff, unrecognizable. "Are you up here, Mom?"

Tanya turned. She looked down the row of doors. All closed. Only theirs was open, at the end. She ran for it as Nathan's footsteps thumped behind her.

She dashed into the room, slammed the door, and locked it. As she raced for the balcony, she heard the knob turn behind her. Then the creak of the door opening. But that couldn't be. She'd locked—

Tanya glanced over her shoulder and saw Nathan, his face twisted with rage.

"Hello, Mom. I have something for you."

Tanya grabbed the balcony door. It was already cracked open, since Nathan always insisted on fresh air. She ran out onto the balcony and looked down to the concrete patio twenty feet below. No way she could jump that, not without breaking both legs, and then she'd be trapped. Maybe if she could hang from it, then drop—

Nathan stepped onto the balcony. Tanya backed up. She called his name, begged him to snap out of it, but he just kept coming, kept smiling, knife raised. She backed up, leaning against the railing.

"Nathan. Plea—"

There was a tremendous crack, and the railing gave way. She felt herself falling, dropping backward so fast that she didn't have time to twist, to scream, and then—

Nothing.

Nathan escorted the innkeeper from Beamsville to the door.

"You folks did an incredible job," the man said. "But I really do hate to take advantage of a tragedy . . . "

Nathan managed a wan smile. "You'd be doing me a favor. The sooner I can get away, the happier I'll be. Every time I drive in, I see that balcony, and I—" His voice hitched. "I keep asking myself why she went out there. I know she loved the view; she must have woken up and seen the moon and wanted a better look." He shook his head. "I meant to fix that balcony. We did the others, but she said ours could wait, and now . . . "

The man laid a hand on Nathan's shoulder. "Let me talk to my real estate agent and I'll get an offer drawn up, see if I can't take this place off your hands."

"Thank you."

Nathan closed the door and took a deep breath. He was making good use of those community-theater skills, but he really hoped he didn't have to keep this up much longer.

He headed into the office, giving it yet another once-over, making sure he'd gotten rid of all the evidence. He'd already checked, twice, but he couldn't be too careful.

There wasn't much to hide. The old woman had been an actor friend of one of his theater buddies, and even if she came forward, what of it? Tanya had wanted a haunted house and he'd hired her to indulge his wife's fancy.

Adding the woman's photo to the article had been simple Photoshop work, the files—paper and electronic—long gone now. The workmen really had been scared off by the haunting, which he'd orchestrated. The only person who knew about his "bouts" was Tanya. And he'd been very careful with the balcony, loosening the nails just enough that her weight would rip them from the rotting wood.

Killing Tanya hadn't been his original intention. But when she'd refused to leave, he'd been almost relieved. As if he didn't mind having to fall back on the more permanent solution, get the insurance money as well as the inheritance, go back home, hook up with Denise again—if she'd still have him—and open the kind of business he wanted. There'd been no chance of that while Tanya was alive. Her money. Her rules. Always.

He opened the basement door, stepped down, and almost went flying, his foot sending a hammer clunking down a few stairs. He retrieved it, wondering how it got there, then shoved it into his back pocket and—

The ring of the phone stopped his descent. He headed back up to answer it.

"Restrictions?" Nathan bellowed into the phone. "What do you mean *restrictions*? How long—?"

He paused.

"A year? I have to live here a year?"

Pause.

"Look, can't there be an exception under the circumstances? My wife died in this house. I need to get out of here."

Tanya stepped up behind Nathan and watched the hair on his neck rise. He rubbed it down and absently looked over his shoulder, then returned to his conversation. She stepped back, caught a glimpse of the hammer in his pocket, and sighed. So much for that idea. But she had plenty more, and it didn't sound like Nathan was leaving anytime soon.

She slid up behind him, arms going around his waist, smiling as he jumped and looked around. Her house might not have been haunted when she'd bought it. But it was now.

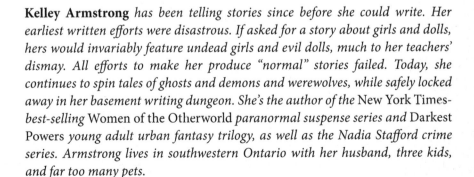

Kelley Armstrong has been telling stories since before she could write. Her earliest written efforts were disastrous. If asked for a story about girls and dolls, hers would invariably feature undead girls and evil dolls, much to her teachers' dismay. All efforts to make her produce "normal" stories failed. Today, she continues to spin tales of ghosts and demons and werewolves, while safely locked away in her basement writing dungeon. She's the author of the New York Times-*best-selling* Women of the Otherworld *paranormal suspense series and* Darkest Powers *young adult urban fantasy trilogy, as well as the Nadia Stafford crime series. Armstrong lives in southwestern Ontario with her husband, three kids, and far too many pets.*

When we moved to a house built in 1918, my daughter really wanted it to be haunted. She thought it would be *so cool*. I've lived here more than twenty years now, and we've still never seen a ghost.

One of two tales selected from a fiftieth anniversary *Twilight Zone* tribute anthology, Kelly Armstrong's story provided not only the twists one might expect from such a theme, but delved into our modern fascination with "real" ghosts and hauntings: We watch "paranormal investigations" on TV and haunted locales attract tourism. We have a notion that supernatural intrusion raises a few goosebumps but ultimately spooks are fun.

When things get a little too scary for Tanya, the cause is all-too-human. For Nathan, though . . .

HEADSTONE IN YOUR POCKET

PAUL TREMBLAY

The sun is high but it feels low, its heat close and heavy enough to push heads down and slump shoulders. Border Patrol Agent Joe Marquez runs his hand along the tractor-trailer and chips of white paint break off and crumble to dust under his fingertips like dried leaves from a dead houseplant. There are rustling noises inside the truck, trapped spirits, humanity in a tin can. He wonders if they'll emerge in any better shape than the trailer's paint job.

Two agents pin the driver against the truck's chrome grille. He yells, claiming the hot chrome burns his skin. The agents don't care, don't say anything, and handcuff him. The smuggler is priority one. The cargo can wait.

Joe jogs the length of the trailer and yells ahead, "Let's go, get those doors open, now!"

Local commuters and smugglers and immigrants know the Tubac checkpoint's schedule. The checkpoint is thirty miles south of Tucson and thirty miles north of Nogales and the Mexico-U.S. border. It was supposed to be closed at this mid-afternoon hour, but the Border Patrol office in Tucson, which prominently features a photo of John Wayne (circa *The Alamo*) on its wall, received an anonymous tip, a tip that turned out to be true.

One agent turns the rusted handle and throws open the trailer's doors while another agent aims his automatic rifle. Heat, sweat, and a low, desperate collected conversation rush out of the trailer and into the surrounding desert. There is no air conditioning and the temperature inside is over one hundred and ten degrees. Flashlights penetrate the darkness and reveal a mass of bodies, scores of men picking up their heads but hiding their eyes, holding out empty hands.

They'll be unarmed, they will not hurt anyone, and they'll have nothing on them. All will be processed for deportation. Joe has been a Border Patrol Agent for two years and has witnessed the same sorry scene at least twice a month.

The Tubac checkpoint is a temporary one, with its portable lights and generators resting on the shoulder of I-19, alongside its incendiary local politics. The suburbanites don't want a fixed checkpoint because checkpoint towns become a de facto second border, fearing smugglers and immigrants and other dangerous (non-white) criminals would use their sleepy little towns as way stations, drug factories, and shoot 'em ups. The Border Patrol's Tucson sector comprises almost the entire Arizona-Mexico border and is the only sector without at least one fixed checkpoint.

Agents separate the fifty men into groups of ten. The men are a task to be divvied up. They are sweaty, exhausted, and frightened, but everyone makes it out of the trailer alive and conscious. Joe's ten stand in a line and with their hands held out and open although he did not tell them to do so. Joe pats them down. The third in line has something in the front left pocket of his jeans. Joe says, "¿Cuál es su nombre?" being rigidly formal in the request, an attempt to give a measure of respect and dignity, but he knows it could very well be interpreted as one of la migra flaunting his position.

The man says, "Guillermo." He's tall and skinny, a piece of string hanging from the leg of his cut-off jean shorts. Guillermo has thick beard stubble overwriting a map of acne scars and he is likely a full decade older than Joe is, but there's no way to tell. He doesn't have a passport.

Joe says, "Guillermo, dame lo que tienes un tu bolsillo. Por favor."

"No es nada. No son drogas." *It is nothing. It is not drugs.* His speech pattern is as formal as Joe's. The two men are actors afraid of forgetting their lines. He reaches into his pocket and gives Joe what he wants. It's a folded rectangle of tinfoil.

"Entonces, ¿qué es?"

"Es de m'hijo."

Joe unwraps the tinfoil slowly. It sits open on his palm, a metal flower with petals dancing in the warm breeze. In the middle, there's a small, clear plastic baggie, and inside the baggie is a white rock. Joe takes it out and realizes it is a tooth, a baby tooth, small as a pebble, so inconsequential and fragile that it might blow away in the scalding desert winds, or simply disintegrate.

The lights are dim. Local country songs alternate with Johnny Cash standards on the jukebox, one that still plays scratchy 45 records. Joe is purposefully early, sitting at their usual booth for two at Zula's, a restaurant in the small and impoverished border town of Nogales, their hometown. He stirs his second screwdriver with a red swizzle stick, counterclockwise, as if he can turn back the clock. The tinfoil, folded up with its secret tooth inside, is on the chipped wooden table-top. *Es de m'hijo. It's from my son.* Joe kept it by mistake. Before he could give the tooth back to Guillermo, he was called away to help with the smuggler's arrest and processing, and then Joe forgot he'd pocketed the tooth. The other agents deported Guillermo and the rest of the immigrants before Joe could return the harmless keepsake. There's no way he can get the tooth back to Guillermo. He can't even create a fantasy scenario where he meets the ragged man unexpectedly to return the memento, the little white tooth. The scenario that's easy to conjure is Guillermo's return home as a failure being unbearably brief and then him attempting an even more dangerous and desperate route to the U.S., hiking through the desert around Nogales, where the past two years have seen an over twenty percent increase in immigrant fatalities. Security improvements are forcing more immigrants to attempt border crossings in further remote areas, forcing them to take their chances in the desert. Joe imagines Guillermo struggling through the barren, unforgiving landscape, then falling, twisting an ankle, getting lost, dying of heat exposure, or as has been increasingly the case, he sees Guillermo falling prey to bandits, armed Mexican nationals, or a double-crossing smuggler he paid as a guide, his body never to be found. Last winter, bandits shot a group of immigrants in an area just west of Nogales, inside the expansive and desolate Tohono-O'odham Reservation. Joe helped carry one of the rescued survivors to an ambulance, an older Nicaraguan woman who had her left ear blown off. After receiving baseline medical care she was sent back to Nicaragua.

Joe checks his watch. She's late. He turns the swizzle stick again. Today was another worst day in a litany of worst days; still his job has an inexplicable hold on him, a job that says more about him than he cares to hear. He orders a third screwdriver, which means he likely won't be driving back to his Tucson apartment tonight.

Jody Fernandez finally arrives, forty minutes late, limping to their booth. "Sorry, Joe. I had a hard time escaping from my parents' house." Her voice is rough but dampened, a crinkling paper bag as it's shaped into a ball. She wears a black long-sleeved T-shirt to cover her skinny arms and jeans that are supposed to be tight, but hang off her gaunt frame like elephant skin. Her black hair is tied up in a ponytail and her skin is pale. She's in her late twenties like Joe but looks like she could be his older sister, or an aunt. Still, she's in better shape than she was a few short months ago, before the rehab stint.

Joe gets the sense that she's not telling him the truth, but he's okay with it. Despite everything and the relapse warning signs he's supposed to watch for, they're close enough that the little lies don't equate to betrayal. Not yet, anyway. He says, "De nada. I've had a long day and I'm just sitting here. Unwinding."

Jody smiles, but won't show her teeth, which were ravaged by the year-plus of meth addiction. Meth is acidic, dries up the protective saliva, and while in the throes of the drug, the heavy users grind and clench their teeth to dust. She explained it to him once, saying *meth mouth* was like a neglected and abused engine being empty of oil but still redlining and chewing up its own gears. She says, "I see that. I guess you'll be sleeping on the couch tonight, then?"

As children, they were neighbors and best friends. Their mothers taught biology and chemistry at the regional high school and their fathers commuted to Tucson together. Joe and Jody, their names and lives almost the same until college, where both went to the University of Arizona. Jody married a physics Ph.D. student and upon graduation got a job teaching special-ed for elementary-aged children. Two years ago, after visiting her mother in Nogales, she and her husband were hit by a pest exterminator who fell asleep at the wheel and drifted over the center lines. Her husband died. Jody's right leg shattered in three places and her skull fractured, requiring a plate. She suffered from debilitating headaches for months and wasn't able to work, living but not living on disability insurance, so, like many of the hopeless locals of Nogales, she turned to meth.

Joe says, "Yeah, I think I might need to crash on your couch. Will that be okay?"

"Of course, but no puking allowed. I just cleaned the goddamn bathroom."

"How are you feeling?"

A waiter appears with a beer that she must've ordered before she sat down. She takes a sip big enough for the both of them, then says, "Shitty, like I was last week. But I can deal with it."

Joe fights a growing impatience. Her lateness, her short answers that aren't really answers; he knows he can't rush her back. He wants the Jody he knew before the addiction, before the accident. He might never get her back, and that's something he needs to deal with, not her.

They both order light meals, garden salads and appetizer-sized quesadillas. Joe orders another screwdriver. He says, "How's your mother?"

"Fine. Same old stuff. Bugging me to move back home until I get back on my feet. God, I hate that fucking phrase. Like me being able to simply walk around on my broken leg has anything to do with improving my shitty days."

Joe says, "I hate it when people say *cut a check*." As soon as he says it, he thinks the quip ill-timed and a terrible, miserable mistake. But she laughs, and he's flooded with relief, then shame because he shouldn't be so nervous around her.

Jody stops laughing, then leans forward, her head in the spotlight of the black pewter pot light fixture that hangs above their table like a bat. Her deep, brown eyes grow too big for her face. "All right, Joe, I wasn't at my mom's house. I'm late because I found an old note from Steve, today." She smirks; a child caught doing something wrong, but not caring at all. But that's not right. She's no child and hasn't been one for a lifetime.

Joe says, "I'm sorry."

"Don't be. I'm not sure if I am. It was folded inside an old textbook, *Educational Philosophy*. My therapist keeps saying work is still a year or two away, but I've been looking through my old notes and textbooks, reading until the headaches take over."

Joe nods. He knows that's enough.

"I opened up to the chapter on cognitive disorders, and there it was, one of his wiseass notes. De-motivational aphorisms, he called them." She smiles but covers her mouth with a hand. The hand tremors and it's not enough to cover everything. "He slipped them into my notebooks and textbooks; the gloomy physics geek that he was, thinking his clever was so cute."

"What'd the note say?"

"I'll tell you if you show me what you're hiding?"

"What? I'm not hiding anything?"

"You had something out on the table and you stuffed it into your pocket when I walked over. I want to see it."

He says, "Okay. Deal. But you tell me first." Joe doesn't look forward to explaining why he has the tinfoil and what it means, but he'll play along. It's good to see her willing to play games with him, even if the game pieces aren't exactly silly.

"It said, 'Evil is a consequence of good. Cheers! Steve.'"

"That's nice. Should be a Hallmark card."

"I know. This was the only note I confronted him about. Was he implying that a gig serving special needs students was somehow a bad thing in his warped little world? He could be snotty about his field of study putting him in the supreme strata of society." Jody is talking fast, manic with her words. "If he was honest with me, if he didn't back down, he would've said something like my helping the helpless only delayed and prolonged their suffering and the suffering of their loved ones, making it all worse in the long run. He used to say shit like that at parties just to get a rise out of people. But he didn't say any of that, didn't let me put those words in his mouth. I played at being super pissed and he backed off real quick, apologizing up and down. It was the last of those notes he left in my books. Him backing down, that was my small victory, our relationship was always a competition, but now I wish he'd given me more of his pithy lovenotes of doom. Isn't that sad? I spent the afternoon and early evening staring at it and thinking it was all quite sad."

"It is sad. But I'm glad you can talk about it."

"Stop it. You sound like my fucking therapist when you say shit like that."

"Does she say 'cut a check' too?"

"No, but I'll insist she do so from now on. Now pay up, Marquez. What are you hiding from me?"

"Oh oh. Using the last name, she means business."

"All business all the time."

"Okay, let's take a look." Joe takes out the tinfoil and lays it on the table. Jody furrows her brow and cocks her head to the side, and Joe panics, almost spilling his drink as he pleads with opens his hands over the tinfoil, a bumbling magician with nothing up his sleeves. He says, "Now, hold on a second. It's not what you think it is." He won't say drugs. He quickly launches into the story of Guillermo, fumbles through their roadside conversation, how this belonged to his son, and then how everything got so crazy that he forgot to give it back. The story already sounds rehearsed. Joe talks while slowly unwrapping the package, careful not to make any new folds or marks in the tinfoil, preservation somehow being of the upmost importance.

Jody leans over the table. "Well, what is it?"

He lifts the plastic bag, dangles it from his finger, and holds it across the table. "It's a tooth. His son's baby tooth. See? I feel bad, it's probably the first tooth he . . . "

Jody stands up, jumps out of her seat, and her head crashes into the pewter pot light fixture, sending its weak light arcing elsewhere into the restaurant.

"Whoa. You okay?"

She turns away from the flickering light and from him, and says, "I need to go to the bathroom." The light shines directly in his eyes, then away, then back, and Joe is unable to watch her progress through the restaurant and bar.

The waiter appears with their food, and steadies the swaying light fixture. The quesadillas are smoking and hissing on the pan. Joe wraps the little tooth back into the foil. Jody didn't just go to the bathroom; she fled from the table. He's not sure what he did, but clearly it was wrong, and he's not sure if Jody is coming back. He waits, elbows on the table, hands making a steeple, and now she has been gone long enough that he considers going to the bathroom or the parking lot to find her.

She does come back, walking as fast as her limp allows, and she sits down abruptly, the final word to some inner conversation. She stabs her fork around the salad, into the cherry tomatoes, and doesn't place her napkin on her lap.

Joe says, "Hey, everything okay? I'm sorry if . . . "

"Jim Dandy," she says, but doesn't look at him.

Everything has become so difficult between them. He knows he's not being fair, but these bi-weekly dinners are becoming as tedious and futile as his job. He isn't helping anyone, isn't improving lives, if anything he's making everything worse; he is that note from Steve. He orders another screwdriver.

For now, Joe won't ask Jody what's wrong because he's afraid of making it worse, and he's also being selfish. He drank too much to drive home and he needs her couch tonight, not further complications.

They walk the two blocks to Jody's one-bedroom apartment. It's late, a weeknight, and no one else is out, the streets as desolate and windswept as the desert. They don't talk. She doesn't ask Joe why he still has that tooth, why hasn't he just pitched it and moved on. Joe assumes she's just accepted it, like he has.

Her apartment is maniacally clean, antiseptic, and it smells of cleanser and airfreshener. The hardwood floor in the living room gives way to yellowed and curling linoleum tile in the kitchen. Joe falls onto the couch in front of the TV and turns it on. Jody says that she has a headache, and disappears into her bedroom, closing and locking the door.

Joe kills the lights and tries watching a baseball game between two teams he doesn't like, then shuts off the TV and reclines, sinking into the couch, and stares at the stucco ceiling. The buzz of alcohol fills the sensory void, droning in his ears and jostling his equilibrium. He closes his eyes, the room spins, he sinks deeper into the couch, and he can't sleep. He's always had trouble sleeping. As a kid, he'd lie awake for hours and obsess over his nightmares. Then he learned to trick himself to sleep. He created and choreographed his own waking-dream, some simple innocuous scene on which to focus and loop in his head until it relaxed him enough and he fell sleep.

Tonight, in Joe's crafted dream, he gets off the couch and walks into the kitchen, first pausing above the room's borderline, where the hardwood meets the cracked linoleum. He fills a glass with tap water and drinks half, dumps the rest in the sink, then walks back to the couch, lies down, then starts it all up again, past the borderline and back to the kitchen again for his same glass of water. On one of his return trips to the sink, Joe stops filling his glass. To his right and next to Jody's bedroom is the study, and its door is open. There's no light, everything is dark, but inside the study is somehow darker than the rest of the apartment. A child, a little boy, stands in the doorway, his hands in the pockets of his jeans, hangdog in his posture. It's too dark to see any facial features, but he knows this boy. Then Joe is standing in the doorway although he doesn't want to be there, just wants to be back at the sink, filling his glass of water and make it half-empty. The boy is still in the doorway too, and he wraps his arms around Joe's legs. The embrace is brief and weak, a butterfly wing hug, and then the boy puts his hand inside Joe's and it feels like a small, cool stone. The boy leads Joe back to the couch. There's more light here, stray neon and streetlight amber filter through the windows. The boy has thick, black hair and eyes like Jody's but not Jody's. Joe lies on the couch. He doesn't want to lie on the couch. He's tired of doing so many things that he doesn't want to do, that he can't do. The boy smiles like Jody too, hiding his mouth behind quivering lips. It's not a smile, it's something else, recognition maybe, or acceptance, whatever it is, it's filled with more despair than the tears to come. Then the boy does part his lips, those rusted hinges, and opens his mouth, and the teeth, an angler fish at the bottom of the deep, black ocean, his *teeth*, the stalactites and stalagmites of nightmare, angry shards of glass with thick tips curved in awkward and dangerous directions, teeth just spilling out of the boy's mouth. He climbs on top of Joe, sits on his lap, and tears the size of gumdrops fall from the boy's eyes as if he doesn't know he's a monster, and it's not fair because he's not supposed to be the monster, does not deserve to be the monster. But the teeth, the teeth.

Two weeks pass like most time does, without any acknowledgement. It's the night before Joe is to return to active duty. He is again at their booth at Zula's. He sits, a tumbleweed without a breeze, and he stares at his empty screwdriver and empty cup of coffee.

After he fled her apartment for his car and I-19, Joe was stopped at the Tubac checkpoint, his non-permanent checkpoint. The agents shined flashlights in his face. He knew they initially only saw a Mexican behind the wheel, and Joe knew he looked just like the men in that decaying trailer, dark skin, squinting and hands held empty and up. The agents were going to pat him down and take the tinfoil away, but the flashlights turned off as they did recognize their coworker. Yeah, they knew him, and they knew he was drunk. They didn't arrest him, but they didn't allow him to drive home and there was an incident report filed with the Tucson office. His immediate two-week suspension was the result.

Joe's drink and coffee cup remain empty no matter how hard he stares at them, as empty as his booth at Zula's. He knows Jody isn't coming. He didn't really expect her to show.

For two weeks, he only left his apartment to go the liquor store. He ate meals only when he wasn't drinking, and the meals consisted of slices of American cheese, cold hot dogs, dry cereal, pretzel sticks. He removed all of the curtains and shades from his windows, and at night, turned on all the lights. He drank himself into unconsciousness, and then didn't wake until late afternoon. He lay on the couch or on the floor and wouldn't sleep in his bedroom, convinced he'd find the little boy sitting at the foot of his bed, and the boy wouldn't say anything and wouldn't look at Joe, but he also wouldn't leave, not this time. He kept the tinfoil. He called Jody when he was awake past midnight. She didn't answer and didn't return his calls.

Joe leaves the booth and the restaurant, and walks to her apartment. This night is hotter than all the previous nights, and Joe sweats through his white T-shirt. Her door isn't locked and he lets himself in without knocking. Inside, the apartment is dark and a disaster of clothes and food and trash. It's as though the spotless apartment he saw two weeks ago never existed, or maybe the duration between visits was longer than those arbitrary and government-assigned weeks, time enough for the apartment to fall into such an advanced state of decay, maybe a collection of years, lost years, had passed, or epochs only measurable by fossilized bodies, bones, and teeth.

"What are you doing here?" Jody's voice is frayed, an exposed wire, quick with its electricity but weak enough that it'll break or flame out at any moment.

Joe steps over the rubble of her apartment. The place smells of sweat and burnt chemicals. Joe walks inside the study. Jody sits on the floor, cross-legged, huddled next to a small fire, a mini-pyre set up on the hardwood floor stained black. Mounds of papers, books, and photographs surround her and the fire. She wears a white bra and black underwear along with black marks that are either bruises or smudged ash. She's too thin. Her bones are a story written in Braille, but the story is too big and horrible to be contained by her skin. Joe puts a hand into his pocket, touches the tinfoil, and he knows how she spent their time apart, and he knows this is all his fault.

Jody's eyes can't focus, and they roll around the room. Her breaths are fast and irregular as are her twitchy movements. She says, "You still have it, don't you, Joe. You still have it . . . " Her voice trails into whispers, and the words come too fast, fumbling over each other, letters placed inside of letters, making new sounds.

He says, "I do."

"You didn't forget to give the tooth back, you kept it on purpose, you made it all up, that story you told me is bullshit, all bullshit, you kept it on purpose. You didn't forget, no way, no way you forgot."

"I did forget, Jody."

She laughs. Then says, "Look at this. Another note. Misery is manifold, Joe. It's true. Steve wrote that on this letter over here, and stuck it in my English Lit book, it's right over here. There. You wanna read it?" Jody picks up a slip of paper and drops it into the fire. Jody turns toward him, and her hair is frayed thread. She smiles, shows her meth mouth, her teeth, blackened and decayed, pieces missing, an incomplete jigsaw puzzle, jagged and eroded canyon boulders, each tooth or what was a tooth is a bombed and burnt-out building that cannot be repaired.

"You know what? A tooth fell out last night, Joe. It was cracked and loose, and I played with it, wiggled it around with my tongue and fingers, like we did when we were kids, I wiggled it, pulled on it, and it hurt a little but not much, nothing I couldn't take, nothing I couldn't deal with, and it just kinda popped out. Do you wanna see it, Joe? I saved it for you because you're collecting teeth now, right?"

Joe needs to do something, say something, anything that will close her terrible mouth. "I don't know why I kept the tooth. I don't know why I do what I do, anymore."

"You're a junkie, just like me." She smiles again, flashes her intimate, private devastation. "Like me, Joe. See? Get that fuckin' tooth out of your pocket, you fucking junkie, the worst kind, the one who won't ever admit there's a problem even when the signs, the signs, the signs are there, big as fucking billboards, billboards in your pocket, fuck billboards, a headstone, headstone in your pocket, Joe, you have a headstone in your pocket, Joe. Joe, fucking, Joe, take it out, tell me what is says, what does it say? I know what it says but I want you to tell me, I want you to tell me tell me tell me tell me . . . "

Joe says, "I'm sorry, Jody. I didn't mean to do this to you, to us. I'd forgotten about him. Really, I did."

He isn't strong enough to tell her that he forgot on purpose and that he worked at it and that he was good at it, better than she was, and it's why she's like she is now and it's why he's like he is now. He wants to run out of her apartment, to run away, as he's always been running away even if he never left home, where there's still room enough to hide, there's an all-encompassing desert in which to hide.

At the southwest edge of Nogales, there was a stretch of desert near the border—and at the time, almost twenty years ago, a generally unsupervised border—where local teens would ride their dirt bikes and mountain bikes during the day and then later reconvene at night to light fires and bottle rockets and drink cheap six-packs. Joe and Jody were only eight and not allowed to go to there, but they went anyway. They told each set of parents they were riding to the playground for the afternoon and then would ride their bikes to the edge of the desert.

It was late afternoon, the sun low and lazy in the west, a half-shut eye, and they were knee deep in their summer routine; climbing on rocks, turning over smaller stones looking for scorpions and small lizards, filling small burrows with sand and dried grass. Two high school-aged kids on dirt bikes showed up in their desert, kicking up dirt and filling the air with their engines' whine. Jody pulled Joe behind a rock, their roles shifting from desert explorers to spies, skulking around and hiding behind boulders and saguaro cactus.

The dirt bikes were chipped-paint and dented metal. The riders didn't wear helmets. One kid was white, short and pudgy, wore a sleeveless black T-shirt with a bald eagle that was all talons and beak, and he had a mop of unkempt, dark hair, like a dead tarantula on his head. The other teen was a blond beanpole with a crew cut, wearing a baggy white T-shirt with large, slashing letters and baggier shorts that hung down to his shins when he stood up on his pegs. The teens rode up a ridge that was one hundred yards or so away, a ridge that may or may not have been a part of Mexico, and then back down.

Joe and Jody didn't say anything or do anything, afraid of the teens, but both secretly wished for the thrill of being caught, of having to jump on their bikes and then somehow outrun the dirt bikes, cutting through yards and short cuts that only they knew. They moved carefully, exchanging cactus for boulder, and crept closer to the ridge.

While tearing through another run, the chubby kid grabbed his left shoulder like it'd been stung, then swerved, and jumped off his bike, which landed on its side and slid halfway down the ridge. Three Mexican boys popped up from behind a boulder at the ridge's crest; two kids threw rocks and a third pointed and shouted something, then they all took off running down the other side of the ridge. The blond sped over and helped get his friend's bike back on its wheels. Their conversation was animated and brief. The bikes' engines were too loud for Jody and Joe to hear anything.

The teens went over the ridge. Jody pulled Joe from out of their hiding spot and said, "Come on!" She ran ahead, and he followed her up the ridge. They stopped at the top and could see everything below.

The three boys alternated fleeing with throwing their small stones at the circling dirt bikes. The teens swore and shouted epithets from the top of their mechanical steeds, and they both cradled a rock in the crook of one arm. The smallest and presumably the youngest trailed far behind the other two retreating boys. The teens focused on the straggler, tightening their circle, revving their engines and spraying dirt on the boy with their spinning, angry tires. The boy was trapped and crying, and scrambled onto a large, jagged boulder. He shouted to his friends, cupping his hands over his small mouth, but they hadn't stopped running, were too far ahead to hear his pleas. The chubby kid, the one with the eagle T-shirt, threw his rock and hit the boy in the back of his thigh. There wasn't much behind the throw, but the boy lost his balance, windmilled his arms, and fell off, behind the craggy rock, out of view of Jody and Joe.

The teens didn't stop to investigate. They tightened their formation, parallel to each other, shared an awkward high-five, and rode triumphantly back up the ridge. Joe and Jody crouched, praying they wouldn't be seen, or they'd be next, chased down the ridge, into Mexico, and then knocked off a boulder, but the teens didn't see them and didn't stop. They sped away, out of the sand, and onto the main drag and out of sight.

Silence, the voice of the desert, replaced the screaming boys and dirt bikes. Joe and Jody listened and watched for a sign from the boy who fell and there was none. They waited. The sun drooped lower in the west. The other two boys did not come back for their friend.

Jody and Joe climbed down the ridge. They crept behind the jagged boulder and found his body, lying adjacent to the flat rock upon which he landed. The boy looked like Joe and the boy looked like Jody, but only smaller, younger. The left side of his head was dented, caved-in, and was missing a flap of scalp. His left arm was held out stiffly and twitched, beating like one wing of a broken hummingbird. The lower half of his face had crumbled, ice cream melting over a cone. He was breathing, but irregularly. They crouched, hands over their mouths, but not over their eyes. His chest inflated sharply, then deflated slowly, a sagging balloon. The right side of his face was perfect, asleep. His left eye was swollen shut, or missing. It was hard to know for sure with the orbital socket broken, pushed in, along with the area around his temple. Everything leaked slowly. There were too many colors on his face. And his teeth, his teeth, they were baby teeth, as small as seeds, and they peppered the sand and dirt around his head, miniature headstones in the sand. Then there was one long sigh and the boy stopped breathing and his arm stopped moving.

His suspension is over but Joe does not report to the Tucson office in the morning. He manages to drive his Jeep into the Tohono-O'odham Reservation and into its desert despite his near total exhaustion, his being purposefully drunk, and the pain that fills his head. He deposits a mix of aspirin, ibuprofen, and little blue pills he took from Jody's apartment into his dry, copper mouth, and grinds them up as best he can. It hurts to chew, but he won't use his water yet; he needs to conserve it.

He stops the Jeep in approximately the same area where he helped rescue the Nicaraguan woman, but he didn't save her. He knows he hasn't saved anyone and can't save anyone. This trip into the desert isn't about saving anyone. He's going to find Guillermo and give the man back his son's tooth. Joe crawls out of his Jeep and walks, slowly, due south, toward the border. He doesn't have a compass, but he thinks he knows where the border is.

Joe allows himself to remember that day in the desert. He remembers the slow walk back to their bikes, their pile of metal and chains, and the ride home. They didn't tell anyone about what had happened, didn't tell anyone about the boy. They were afraid of the teens, afraid people would think it was their fault, afraid because they were only eight and didn't know what to do. They didn't tell anyone about their desert silence.

The sun is only beginning its climb in the east, but it's midday hot. Joe's pulse throbs in his temples and inside his cheeks. His backpack of meager supplies already feels too heavy.

There was never any word or news about the little boy. They did not go back over the ridge and to that boulder. They didn't talk about it, didn't make up stories about coyotes dragging the boy away, didn't fool themselves into believing he was alive, didn't discuss the possibilities or probabilities of the police finding him or the teens coming back for the body or the boy's friends and family laying belated claim and bringing him back to Mexico. They didn't turn the boy into a legend for the neighborhood kids, didn't tell anyone that the boy might still be there. They agreed to forget their secret, bury it inside themselves, beneath as much passed time as they could.

Despite the heat and his headache, which is a fire inside his brain, Joe walks for hours until the sun is directly above him and discerning direction becomes impossible. He finds a Desert Ironwood and sits under its thin canopy, desperate for shade. Half of his water supply is already gone. Joe takes off his small backpack, drinks, and again goes back to that day all those years ago in another part of the same desert. Joe remembers the urge to pick up the boy's teeth, those headstones, and put them in his pocket, an urge as inexplicable now as it was then.

There are teeth in his pocket now; a small one lovingly wrapped in tinfoil, and another tooth, it's adult and big and ugly with roots like talons, and that tooth is not wrapped in tinfoil or anything that would protect it. Neither tooth is his.

Joe fights waves of dizziness and nausea. His fistful of pills isn't helping. His gums are still bleeding and his right bicuspid is loose. If he pushes on the tooth with enough force there's a wet sucking sound inside his mouth. There are pliers in his backpack. Earlier this morning, the pain was too much. Unlike Jody, he couldn't deal with the pain, to where it went, and he stopped pulling on the tooth. He'll try the pliers again later, maybe when the sun goes down and when the pills kick in.

Joe falls in and out of sleep throughout the afternoon and the temperature begins to drop. Maybe a quarter of a mile beyond his tree is a ridge, and just beyond that ridge is Mexico, he's sure of it, and despite everything, he's sure he can make it over that ridge. And maybe he'll be strong enough to make it through the desert, his desert, and give back the teeth.

Paul Tremblay *is the author of the novels* The Little Sleep *and* No Sleep Till Wonderland, *the fiction collections* In the Mean Time *and* Compositions for the Young and Old, *and the novellas* The Harlequin & The Train *and* City Pier: Above and Below.

His fiction has appeared in Razor Magazine, Last Pentacle of the Sun, *and* Best American Fantasy 3.

He has served as fiction editor of ChiZine, *as co-editor of* Fantasy Magazine, *and as co-editor of the anthologies* Fantasy, Bandersnatch, *and* Phantom.

To each his or her own nightmare.

The tooth in this story casts both Joe and Jody into personal nightmares. Might give you a nightmare or two as well.

On a completely different nightmare-note, S. Baring Gould, published a story in 1905 called "Dead Man's Teeth." The narrator, a quarryman, innocently comes across a skeleton. As he suffers from toothache and believes a dead man's tooth will cure the pain, he takes a tooth. The tooth, however, gives the man—an upright, working class, teetotaler—three nights of terrifying nightmares. The first night he dreams he is wearing "a red coat, and galloping after the hounds"; the next dream involves drinking, swearing, and kissing a barmaid. In the final and most ghastly nightmare he finds himself voting Conservative. He gets rid of the tooth and is never again haunted by the "spirit of unrighteousness and drinking and Consarvatism [sic]."

THE COLDEST GIRL IN COLDTOWN

HOLLY BLACK

Matilda was drunk, but then she was always drunk anymore. Dizzy drunk. Stumbling drunk. Stupid drunk. Whatever kind of drunk she could get.

The man she stood with snaked his hand around her back, warm fingers digging into her side as he pulled her closer. He and his friend with the open-necked shirt grinned down at her like underage equaled dumb, and dumb equaled gullible enough to sleep with them.

She thought they might just be right.

"You want to have a party back at my place?" the man asked. He'd told her his name was Mark, but his friend kept slipping up and calling him by a name that started with a D. Maybe Dan or Dave. They had been smuggling her drinks from the bar whenever they went outside to smoke—drinks mixed sickly sweet that dripped down her throat like candy.

"Sure," she said, grinding her cigarette against the brick wall. She missed the hot ash in her hand, but concentrated on the alcoholic numbness turning her limbs to lead. Smiled. "Can we pick up more beer?"

They exchanged an obnoxious glance she pretended not to notice. The friend—he called himself Ben—looked at her glassy eyes and her cold-flushed cheeks. Her sloppy hair. He probably made guesses about a troubled home life. She hoped so.

"You're not going to get sick on us?" he asked. Just out of the hot bar, beads of sweat had collected in the hollow of his throat. The skin shimmered with each swallow.

She shook her head to stop staring. "I'm barely tipsy," she lied.

"I've got plenty of stuff back at my place," said MarkDanDave. *Mardave*, Matilda thought and giggled.

"Buy me a 40," she said. She knew it was stupid to go with them, but it was even stupider if she sobered up. "One of those wine coolers. They have them at the bodega on the corner. Otherwise, no party."

Both of the guys laughed. She tried to laugh with them even though she knew she wasn't included in the joke. She was the joke. The trashy little slut. The girl who can be bought for a big fat wine cooler and three cranberry-and-vodkas.

"Okay, okay," said Mardave.

They walked down the street and she found herself leaning easily into the heat of their bodies, inhaling the sweat and iron scent. It would be easy for her to close her eyes and pretend Mardave was someone else, someone she wanted to be touched by, but she wouldn't let herself soil her memories of Julian.

They passed by a store with flat-screens in the window, each one showing different channels. One streamed video from Coldtown—a girl who went by the name Demonia made some kind of deal with one of the stations to show what it was really like behind the gates. She filmed the Eternal Ball, a party that started in 1998 and had gone on ceaselessly ever since. In the background, girls and boys in rubber harnesses swung through the air. They stopped occasionally, opening what looked like a modded hospital tube stuck on the inside of their arms just below the crook of the elbow. They twisted a knob and spilled blood into little paper cups for the partygoers. A boy who looked to be about nine, wearing a string of glowing beads around his neck, gulped down the contents of one of the cups and then licked the paper with a tongue as red as his eyes. The camera angle changed suddenly, veering up, and the viewers saw the domed top of the hall, full of cracked windows through which you could glimpse the stars.

"I know where they are," Mardave said. "I can see that building from my apartment."

"Aren't you scared of living so close to the vampires?" she asked, a small smile pulling at the corners of her mouth.

"We'll protect you," said Ben, smiling back at her.

"We should do what other countries do and blow those corpses sky high," Mardave said.

Matilda bit her tongue not to point out that Europe's vampire hunting led to the highest levels of infection in the world. So many of Belgium's citizens were vampires that shops barely opened their doors until nightfall. The truce with Coldtown worked. Mostly.

She didn't care if Mardave hated vampires. She hated them too.

When they got to the store, she waited outside to avoid getting carded and lit another cigarette with Julian's silver lighter—the one she was going to give back to him in thirty-one days. Sitting down on the curb, she let the chill of the pavement deaden the backs of her thighs. Let it freeze her belly and frost her throat with ice that even liquor couldn't melt.

Hunger turned her stomach. She couldn't remember the last time she'd eaten anything solid without throwing it back up. Her mouth hungered for dark, rich feasts; her skin felt tight, like a seed thirsting to bloom. All she could trust herself to eat was smoke.

When she was a little girl, vampires had been costumes for Halloween.

They were the bad guys in movies, plastic fangs and polyester capes. They were Muppets on television, endlessly counting.

Now she was the one who was counting. Fifty-seven days. Eighty-eight days. Eighty-eight nights.

"Matilda?"

She looked up and saw Dante saunter up to her, earbuds dangling out of his ears like he needed a soundtrack for everything he did. He wore a pair of skintight jeans and smoked a cigarette out of one of those long, movie-star holders. He looked pretentious as hell. "I'd almost given up on finding you."

"You should have started with the gutter," she said, gesturing to the wet, clogged tide beneath her feet. "I take my gutter-dwelling very seriously."

"*Seriously.*" He pointed at her with the cigarette holder. "Even your mother thinks you're dead. Julian's crying over you."

Maltilda looked down and picked at the thread of her jeans. It hurt to think about Julian while waiting for Mardave and Ben. She was disgusted with herself, and she could only guess how disgusted he'd be. "I got Cold," she said. "One of them bit me."

Dante nodded his head.

That's what they'd started calling it when the infection kicked in—Cold—because of how cold people's skin became after they were bitten. And because of the way the poison in their veins caused them to crave heat and blood. One taste of human blood and the infection mutated. It killed the host and then raised it back up again, colder than before. Cold through and through, forever and ever.

"I didn't think you'd be alive," he said.

She hadn't thought she'd make it this long either without giving in. But going it alone on the street was better than forcing her mother to choose between chaining her up in the basement or shipping her off to Coldtown. It was better, too, than taking the chance Matilda might get loose from the chains and attack people she loved. Stories like that were in the news all the time; almost as frequent as the ones about people who let vampires into their homes because they seemed so nice and clean-cut.

"Then what are you doing looking for me?" she asked. Dante had lived down the street from her family for years, but they didn't hang out. She'd wave to him as she mowed the lawn while he loaded his panel van with DJ equipment. He shouldn't have been here.

She looked back at the store window. Mardave and Ben were at the counter with a case of beer and her wine cooler. They were getting change from a clerk.

"I was hoping you, er, *wouldn't* be alive," Dante said. "You'd be more help if you were dead."

She stood up, stumbling slightly. "Well, screw you too."

It took eighty-eight days for the venom to sweat out a person's pores. She only had thirty-seven to go. Thirty-seven days to stay so drunk that she could ignore the buzz in her head that made her want to bite, rend, devour.

"That came out wrong," he said, taking a step toward her. Close enough that she felt the warmth of him radiating off him like licking tongues of flame. She shivered. Her veins sang with need.

"I can't help you," said Matilda. "Look, I can barely help myself. Whatever it is, I'm sorry. I can't. You have to get out of here."

"My sister Lydia and your boyfriend Julian are gone," Dante said. "Together. She's looking to get bitten. I don't know what he's looking for . . . but he's going to get hurt."

Matilda gaped at him as Mardave and Ben walked out of the store. Ben carried a box on his shoulder and a bag on his arm. "That guy bothering you?" he asked her.

"No," she said, then turned to Dante. "You better go."

"Wait," said Dante.

Matilda's stomach hurt. She was sobering up. The smell of blood seemed to float up from underneath their skin.

She reached into Ben's bag and grabbed a beer. She popped the top, licked off the foam. If she didn't get a lot drunker, she was going to attack someone.

"Jesus," Mardave said. "Slow down. What if someone sees you?"

She drank it in huge gulps, right there on the street. Ben laughed, but it wasn't a good laugh. He was laughing at the drunk.

"She's infected," Dante said.

Matilda whirled toward him, chucking the mostly empty can in his direction automatically. "Shut up, asshole."

"Feel her skin," Dante said. "Cold. She ran away from home when it happened, and no one's seen her since."

"I'm cold because it's cold out," she said.

She saw Ben's evaluation of her change from *damaged enough to sleep with strangers* to *dangerous enough to attack strangers.*

Mardave touched his hand gently to her arm. "Hey," he said.

She almost hissed with delight at the press of his hot fingers. She smiled up at him and hoped her eyes weren't as hungry as her skin. "I really like you."

He flinched. "Look, it's late. Maybe we could meet up another time." Then he backed away, which made her so angry that she bit the inside of her own cheek.

Her mouth flooded with the taste of copper and a red haze floated in front of her eyes.

Fifty-seven days ago, Matilda had been sober. She'd had a boyfriend named Julian, and they would dress up together in her bedroom. He liked to wear skinny ties and glittery eye shadow. She liked to wear vintage rock T-shirts and boots that laced up so high that they would constantly be late because they were busy tying them.

Matilda and Julian would dress up and prowl the streets and party at lockdown clubs that barred the doors from dusk to dawn. Matilda wasn't particularly careless; she was just careless enough.

She'd been at a friend's party. It had been stiflingly hot, and she was mad because Julian and Lydia were doing some dance thing from the musical they were in at school. Matilda just wanted to get some air. She opened a window and climbed out under the bobbing garland of garlic.

Another girl was already on the lawn. Matilda should have noticed that the girl's breath didn't crystallize in the air, but she didn't.

"Do you have a light?" the girl had asked.

Matilda did. She reached for Julian's lighter when the girl caught her arm and bent her backwards. Matilda's scream turned into a shocked cry when she felt the girl's cold mouth against her neck, the girl's cold fingers holding her off balance.

Then it was as though someone slid two shards of ice into her skin.

The spread of vampirism could be traced to one person—Caspar Morales. Films and books and television had started romanticizing vampires, and maybe it was only a matter of time before a vampire started romanticizing *himself.*

Crazy, romantic Caspar decided that he wouldn't kill his victims. He'd just drink a little blood and then move on, city to city. By the time other vampires caught up with him and ripped him to pieces, he'd infected hundreds of people. And those new vampires, with no idea how to prevent the spread, infected thousands.

When the first outbreak happened in Tokyo, it seemed like a journalist's prank. Then there was another outbreak in Hong Kong and another in San Francisco.

The military put up barricades around the area where the infection broke out. That was the way the first Coldtown was founded.

Matilda's body twitched involuntarily. She could feel the spasm start in the muscles of her back and move to her face. She wrapped her arms around herself to try and stop it, but her hands were shaking pretty hard. "You want my help, you better get me some booze."

"You're killing yourself," Dante said, shaking his head.

"I just need another drink," she said. "Then I'll be fine."

He shook his head. "You can't keep going like this. You can't just stay drunk to avoid your problems. I know, people do. It's a classic move, even, but I didn't figure you for fetishizing your own doom."

She started laughing. "You don't understand. When I'm wasted I don't crave blood. It's the only thing keeping me human."

"What?" He looked at Matilda like he couldn't quite make sense of her words.

"Let me spell it out: if you don't get me some alcohol, I am going to bite you."

"Oh." He fumbled for his wallet. "Oh. Okay."

Matilda had spent all the cash she'd brought with her in the first few weeks, so it'd been a long time since she could simply overpay some homeless guy to go into a liquor store and get her a fifth of vodka. She gulped gratefully from the bottle Dante gave her in a nearby alley.

A few moments later, warmth started to creep up from her belly, and her mouth felt like it was full of needles and Novocain.

"You okay?" he asked her.

"Better now," she said, her words slurring slightly. "But I still don't understand. Why do you need me to help you find Lydia and Julian?"

"Lydia got obsessed with becoming a vampire," Dante said, irritably brushing back the stray hair that fell across his face.

"Why?"

He shrugged. "She used to be really scared of vampires. When we were kids, she begged Mom to let her camp in the hallway because she wanted to sleep where there were no windows. But then I guess she started to be fascinated instead. She thinks that human annihilation is coming. She says that we all have to choose sides and she's already chosen."

"I'm not a vampire," Matilda said.

Dante gestured irritably with his cigarette holder. The cigarette had long burned out. He didn't look like his usual contemptuous self; he looked lost. "I know. I thought you would be. And—I don't know—you're on the street. Maybe you know more than the video feeds do about where someone might go to get themselves bitten."

Matilda thought about lying on the floor of Julian's parents' living room. They had been sweaty from dancing and kissed languidly. On the television, a list of missing people flashed. She had closed her eyes and kissed him again.

She nodded slowly. "I know a couple of places. Have you heard from her at all?"

He shook his head. "She won't take any of my calls, but she's been updating her blog. I'll show you."

He loaded it on his phone. The latest entry was titled: *I Need a Vampire.* Matilda scrolled down and read. Basically, it was Lydia's plea to be bitten. She wanted any vampires looking for victims to contact her. In the comments, someone suggested Coldtown and then another person commented in ALL CAPS to say that everyone knew that the vampires in Coldtown were careful to keep their food sources alive.

It was impossible to know which comments Lydia had read and which ones she believed.

Runaways went to Coldtown all the time, along with the sick, the sad, and the maudlin. There was supposed to be a constant party, theirs for the price of blood. But once they went inside, humans—even human children, even babies born in Coldtown—weren't be allowed to leave. The National Guard patrolled the barbed wire–wrapped and garlic-covered walls to make sure that Coldtown stayed contained.

People said that vampires found ways through the walls to the outside world. Maybe that was just a rumor, although Matilda remembered reading something online about a documentary that proved the truth. She hadn't seen it.

But everyone knew there was only one way to get out of Coldtown if you were still human. Your family had to be rich enough to hire a vampire hunter. Vampire hunters got money from the government for each vampire they put in Coldtown, but they could give up the cash reward in favor of a voucher for a single human's release. One vampire in, one human out.

There was a popular reality television series about one of the hunters, called *Hemlok*. Girls hung posters of him on the insides of their lockers, often right next to pictures of the vampires he hunted.

Most people didn't have the money to outbid the government for a hunter's services. Matilda didn't think that Dante's family did and knew Julian's didn't. Her only chance was to catch Lydia and Julian before they crossed over.

"What's with Julian?" Matilda asked. She'd been avoiding the question for hours as they walked through the alleys that grew progressively more empty the closer they got to the gates.

"What do you mean?" Dante was hunched over against the wind, his long skinny frame offering little protection against the chill. Still, she knew he was warm underneath. Inside.

"Why did Julian go with her?" She tried to keep the hurt out of her voice. She didn't think Dante would understand. He DJed at a club in town and was rumored to see a different boy or girl every day of the week. The only person he actually seemed to care about was his sister.

Dante shrugged slim shoulders. "Maybe he was looking for you."

That was the answer she wanted to hear. She smiled and let herself imagine saving Julian right before he could enter Coldtown. He would tell her that he'd been coming to save her and then they'd laugh and she wouldn't bite him, no matter how warm his skin felt.

Dante snapped his fingers in front of Matilda and she stumbled.

"Hey," she said. "Drunk girl here. No messing with me."

He chuckled.

Melinda and Dante checked all the places she knew, all the places she'd slept on cardboard near runaways and begged for change. Dante had a picture of Lydia in his wallet, but no one who looked at it remembered her.

Finally, outside a bar, they bumped into a girl who said she'd seen Lydia and Julian. Dante traded her the rest of his pack of cigarettes for her story.

"They were headed for Coldtown," she said, lighting up. In the flickering flame of her lighter, Melinda noticed the shallow cuts along her wrists. "Said she was tired of waiting."

"What about the guy?" Matilda asked. She stared at the girl's dried garnet scabs. They looked like crusts of sugar, like the lines of salt left on the beach when the tide goes out. She wanted to lick them.

"He said his girlfriend was a vampire," said the girl, inhaling deeply. She blew out smoke and then started to cough.

"When was that?" Dante asked.

The girl shrugged her shoulders. "Just a couple of hours ago."

Dante took out his phone and pressed some buttons. "Load," he muttered. "Come on, *load*."

"What happened to your arms?" Matilda asked.

The girl shrugged again. "They bought some blood off me. Said that they might need it inside. They had a real professional set-up too. Sharp razor and one of those glass bowls with the plastic lids."

Matilda's stomach clenched with hunger. She turned against the wall and breathed slowly. She needed a drink.

"Is something wrong with her?" the girl asked.

"Matilda," Dante said, and Matilda half-turned. He was holding out his phone. There was a new entry up on Lydia's blog, entitled: *One-Way Ticket to Coldtown*.

"You should post about it," Dante said. "On the message boards."

Matilda was sitting on the ground, picking at the brick wall to give her fingers something to do. Dante had massively overpaid for another bottle of vodka and was cradling it in a crinkled paper bag.

She frowned. "Post about what?"

"About the alcohol. About it helping you keep from turning."

"Where would I post about that?"

Dante twisted off the cap. The heat seemed to radiate off his skin as he swigged from the bottle. "There are forums for people who have to restrain someone for eighty-eight days. They hang out and exchange tips on straps and dealing with the begging for blood. Haven't you seen them?"

She shook her head. "I bet sedation's already a hot topic of discussion. I doubt I'd be telling them anything they don't already know."

He laughed, but it was a bitter laugh. "Then there's all the people who want to be vampires. The Web sites reminding all the corpsebait out there that being bitten by an infected person isn't enough; it has to be a vampire. The ones listing gimmicks to get vampires to notice you."

"Like what?"

"I dated a girl who cut thin lines on her thighs before she went out dancing so if there was a vampire in the club, it'd be drawn to her scent." Dante didn't look extravagant or affected anymore. He looked defeated.

Matilda smiled at him. "She was probably a better bet than me for getting you into Coldtown."

He returned the smile wanly. "The worst part is that Lydia's not going to get what she wants. She's going become the human servant of some vampire who's going to make her a whole bunch of promises and never turn her. The last thing they need in Coldtown is new vampires."

Matilda imagined Lydia and Julian dancing at the endless Eternal Ball. She pictured them on the streets she'd seen in pictures uploaded to Facebook and Flickr, trying to trade a bowl full of blood for their own deaths.

When Dante passed the bottle to her, she pretended to swig. On the eve of her fifty-eighth day of being infected, Matilda started sobering up.

Crawling over, she straddled Dante's waist before he had a chance to shift positions. His mouth tasted like tobacco. When she pulled back from him, his eyes were wide with surprise, his pupils blown and black even in the dim streetlight.

"Matilda," he said and there was nothing in his voice but longing.

"If you really want your sister, I am going to need one more thing from you," she said.

His blood tasted like tears.

Matilda's skin felt like it had caught fire. She'd turned into lit paper, burning up. Curling into black ash.

She licked his neck over and over and over.

The gates of Coldtown were large and made of consecrated wood, barbed wire covering them like heavy, thorny vines. The guards slouched at their posts, guns over their shoulders, sharing a cigarette. The smell of percolating coffee wafted out of the guardhouse.

"Um, hello," Matilda said. Blood was still sticky where it half-dried around her mouth and on her neck. It had dribbled down her shirt, stiffening it nearly to cracking when she moved. Her body felt strange now that she was dying. Hot. More alive than it had in weeks.

Dante would be all right; she wasn't contagious and she didn't think she'd hurt him too badly. She hoped she hadn't hurt him too badly. She touched the phone in her pocket, his phone, the one she'd used to call 911 after she'd left him.

"Hello," she called to the guards again.

One turned. "Oh my god," he said and reached for his rifle.

"I'm here to turn in a vampire. For a voucher. I want to turn in a vampire in exchange for letting a human out of Coldtown."

"What vampire?" asked the other guard. He'd dropped the cigarette, but not stepped on the filter so that it just smoked on the asphalt.

"Me," said Matilda. "I want to turn in me."

They made her wait as her pulse thrummed slower and slower. She wasn't a vampire yet, and after a few phone calls, they discovered that technically she could only have the voucher after undeath. They did let her wash her face in the bathroom of the guardhouse and wring the thin cloth of her shirt until the water ran down the drain clear, instead of murky with blood.

When she looked into the mirror, her skin had unfamiliar purple shadows, like bruises. She was still staring at them when she stopped being able to catch her breath. The hollow feeling in her chest expanded and she found herself panicked, falling to her knees on the filthy tile floor. She died there, a moment later.

It didn't hurt as much as she'd worried it would. Like most things, the surprise was the worst part.

The guards released Matilda into Coldtown just a little before dawn. The world looked strange—everything had taken on a smudgy, silvery cast, like she was watching an old movie. Sometimes people's heads seemed to blur into black smears. Only one color was distinct—a pulsing, oozing color that seemed to glow from beneath skin.

Red.

Her teeth ached to look at it.

There was a silence inside her. No longer did she move to the rhythmic drumming of her heart. Her body felt strange, hard as marble, free of pain. She'd never realized how many small agonies were alive in the creak of her bones, the pull of muscle. Now, free of them, she felt like she was floating.

Matilda looked around with her strange new eyes. Everything was beautiful. And the light at the edge of the sky was the most beautiful thing of all.

"What are you doing?" a girl called from a doorway. She had long black hair, but her roots were growing in blond. "Get in here! Are you crazy?"

In a daze, Matilda did as she was told. Everything smeared as she moved, like the world was painted in watercolors. The girl's pinkish-red face swirled along with it.

It was obvious the house had once been grand, but it looked like it'd been abandoned for a long time. Graffiti covered the peeling wallpaper and couches had been pushed up against the walls. A boy wearing jeans but no shirt was painting make-up onto a girl with stiff pink pigtails, while another girl in a retro polka-dotted dress pulled on mesh stockings.

In a corner, another boy—this one with glossy brown hair that fell to his waist—stacked jars of creamed corn into a precarious pyramid.

"What is this place?" Matilda asked.

The boy stacking the jars turned. "Look at her eyes. She's a vampire!" He didn't seem afraid, though; he seemed delighted.

"Get her into the cellar," one of the other girls said.

"Come on," said the black-haired girl and pulled Matilda toward a doorway. "You're fresh-made, right?"

"Yeah," Matilda said. Her tongue swept over her own sharp teeth. "I guess that's pretty obvious."

"Don't you know that vampires can't go outside in the daylight?" the girl asked, shaking her head. "The guards try that trick with every new vampire, but I never saw one almost fall for it."

"Oh, right," Matilda said. They went down the rickety steps to a filthy basement with a mattress on the floor underneath a single bulb. Crates of foodstuffs were shoved against the walls, and the high, small windows had been painted over with a tarry substance that let no light through.

The black-haired girl who'd waved her inside smiled. "We trade with the border guards. Black-market food, clothes, little luxuries like chocolate and cigarettes for some ass. Vampires don't own everything."

"And you're going to owe us for letting you stay the night," the boy said from the top of the stairs.

"I don't have anything," Matilda said. "I didn't bring any cans of food or whatever."

"You have to bite us."

"What?" Matilda asked.

"One of us," the girl said. "How about one of us? You can even pick which one."

"Why would you want me to do that?"

The girl's expression clearly said that Matilda was stupid. "Who doesn't want to live forever?"

I don't, Matilda wanted to say, but she swallowed the words. She could tell they already thought she didn't deserve to be a vampire. Besides, she wanted to taste blood. She wanted to taste the red, throbbing, pulsing insides of the girl in front of her. It wasn't the pain she'd felt when she was infected, the hunger that made her stomach clench, the craving for warmth. It was heady, greedy desire.

"Tomorrow," Matilda said. "When it's night again."

"Okay," the girl said, "but you promise, right? You'll turn one of us?"

"Yeah," said Matilda, numbly. It was hard to even wait that long.

She was relieved when they went upstairs, but less relieved when she heard something heavy slide in front of the basement door. She told herself that didn't matter. The only thing that mattered was getting through the day so that she could find Julian and Lydia.

She shook her head to clear it of thoughts of blood and turned on Dante's phone. Although she didn't expect it, a text message was waiting: *I cant tell if I luv u or if I want to kill u.*

Relief washed over her. Her mouth twisted into a smile and her newly sharp canines cut her lip. She winced. Dante was okay.

She opened up Lydia's blog and posted an anonymous message: *Tell Julian his girlfriend wants to see him . . . and you.*

Matilda made herself comfortable on the dirty mattress. She looked up at the rotted boards of the ceiling and thought of Julian. She had a single ticket out of Coldtown and two humans to rescue with it, but it was easy to picture herself saving Lydia as Julian valiantly offered to stay with her, even promised her his eternal devotion.

She licked her lips at the image. When she closed her eyes, all her imaginings drowned in a sea of red.

Waking at dusk, Matilda checked Lydia's blog. Lydia had posted a reply: *Meet us at the Festival of Sinners.*

Five kids sat at the top of the stairs, watching her with liquid eyes.

"Are you awake?" the black-haired girl asked. She seemed to pulse with color. Her moving mouth was hypnotic.

"Come here," Matilda said to her in a voice that seemed so distant that she was surprised to find it was her own. She hadn't meant to speak, hadn't meant to beckon the girl over to her.

"That's not fair," one of the boys called. "I was the one who said she owed us something. It should be me. You should pick me."

Matilda ignored him as the girl knelt down on the dirty mattress and swept aside her hair, baring a long, unmarked neck. She seemed dazzling, this creature of blood and breath, a fragile manikin as brittle as sticks.

Tiny golden hairs tickled Matilda's nose as she bit down.

And gulped.

Blood was heat and heart running-thrumming-beating through the fat roots of veins to drip syrup slow, spurting molten hot across tongue, mouth, teeth, chin.

Dimly, Matilda felt someone shoving her and someone else screaming, but it seemed distant and unimportant. Eventually the words became clearer.

"Stop," someone was screaming. "Stop!"

Hands dragged Matilda off the girl. Her neck was a glistening red mess. Gore stained the mattress and covered Matilda's hands and hair. The girl coughed, blood bubbles frothing on her lip, and then went abruptly silent.

"What did you do?" the boy wailed, cradling the girl's body. "She's dead. She's dead. You killed her."

Matilda backed away from the body. Her hand went automatically to her mouth, covering it. "I didn't mean to," she said.

"Maybe she'll be okay," said the other boy, his voice cracking. "We have to get bandages."

"She's *dead*," the boy holding the girl's body moaned.

A thin wail came from deep inside Matilda as she backed toward the stairs. Her belly felt full, distended. She wanted to be sick.

Another girl grabbed Matilda's arm. "Wait," the girl said, eyes wide and imploring. "You have to bite me next. You're full now so you won't have to hurt me—"

With a cry, Matilda tore herself free and ran up the stairs—if she went fast enough, maybe she could escape from herself.

By the time Matilda got to the Festival of Sinners, her mouth tasted metallic and she was numb with fear. She wasn't human, wasn't good, and wasn't sure what she might do next. She kept pawing at her shirt, as if that much blood could ever be wiped off, as if it hadn't already soaked down into her skin and her soiled insides.

The Festival was easy to find, even as confused as she was. People were happy to give her directions, apparently not bothered that she was drenched in blood. Their casual demeanor was horrifying, but not as horrifying as how much she already wanted to feed again.

On the way, she passed the Eternal Ball. Strobe lights lit up the remains of the windows along the dome, and a girl with blue hair in a dozen braids held up a video camera to interview three men dressed all in white with gleaming red eyes.

Vampires.

A ripple of fear passed through her. She reminded herself that there was nothing they could do to her. She was already like them. Already dead.

The Festival of Sinners was being held at a church with stained-glass windows painted black on the inside. The door, papered with pink-stenciled posters, was painted the same thick tarry black. Music thrummed from within and a few people sat on the steps, smoking and talking.

Matilda went inside.

A doorman pulled aside a velvet rope for her, letting her past a small line of people waiting to pay the cover charge. The rules were different for vampires, perhaps especially for vampires accessorizing their grungy attire with so much blood.

Matilda scanned the room. She didn't see Julian or Lydia, just a throng of dancers and a bar that served alcohol from vast copper distilling vats. It spilled into mismatched mugs. Then one of the people near the bar moved and Matilda saw Lydia and Julian. He was bending over her, shouting into her ear.

Matilda pushed her way through the crowd, until she was close enough to touch Julian's arm. She reached out, but couldn't quite bring herself to brush his skin with her foulness.

Julian looked up, startled. "Tilda?"

She snatched back her hand like she'd been about to touch fire.

"Tilda," he said. "What happened to you? Are you hurt?"

Matilda flinched, looking down at herself. "I ... "

Lydia laughed. "She ate someone, moron."

"Tilda?" Julian asked.

"I'm sorry," Matilda said. There was so much she had to be sorry for, but at least he was here now. Julian would tell her what to do and how to turn herself back into something decent again. She would save Lydia and Julian would save her.

He touched her shoulder, let his hand rest gingerly on her blood-stiffened shirt. "We were looking for you everywhere." His gentle expression was tinged with terror; fear pulled his smile into something closer to a grimace.

"I wasn't in Coldtown," Matilda said. "I came here so that Lydia could leave. I have a pass."

"But I don't want to leave," said Lydia. "You understand that, right? I want what you have—eternal life."

"You're not infected," Matilda said. "You have to go. You can still be okay. Please, I need you to go."

"One pass?" Julian said, his eyes going to Lydia. Matilda saw the truth in the weight of that gaze—Julian had not come to Coldtown for Matilda. Even though she knew she didn't deserve him to think of her as anything but a monster, it hurt savagely.

"I'm not leaving," Lydia said, turning to Julian, pouting. "You said she wouldn't be like this."

"*I killed a girl,*" Matilda said. "I killed her. Do you understand that?"

"Who cares about some mortal girl?" Lydia tossed back her hair. In that moment, she reminded Matilda of her brother, pretentious Dante who'd turned out to be an actual nice guy. Just like sweet Lydia had turned out cruel.

"You're a girl," Matilda said. "You're mortal."

"I know that!" Lydia rolled her eyes. "I just mean that we don't care who you killed. Turn us and then we can kill lots of people."

"No," Matilda said, swallowing. She looked down, not wanting to hear what she was about to say. There was still a chance. "Look, I have the pass. If you don't want it, then Julian should take it and go. But I'm not turning you. I'm never turning you, understand."

"Julian doesn't want to leave," Lydia said. Her eyes looked bright and two feverish spots appeared on her cheeks. "Who are you to judge me anyway? You're the murderer."

Matilda took a step back. She desperately wanted Julian to say something in her defense or even to look at her, but his gaze remained steadfastly on Lydia.

"So neither one of you want the pass," Matilda said.

"Fuck you," spat Lydia.

Matilda turned away.

"Wait," Julian said. His voice sounded weak.

Matilda spun, unable to keep the hope off her face, and saw why Julian had called to her. Lydia stood behind him, a long knife to his throat.

"Turn me," Lydia said. "Turn me, or I'm going to kill him."

Julian's eyes were wide. He started to protest or beg or something and Lydia pressed the knife harder, silencing him.

People had stopped dancing nearby, backing away. One girl with red-glazed eyes stared hungrily at the knife.

"Turn me!" Lydia shouted. "I'm tired of waiting! I want my life to begin!"

"You won't be alive—" Matilda started.

"I'll be alive—more alive than ever. Just like you are."

"Okay," Matilda said softly. "Give me your wrist."

The crowd seemed to close in tighter, watching as Lydia held out her arm. Matilda crouched low, bending down over it.

"Take the knife away from his throat," Matilda said.

Lydia, all her attention on Matilda, let Julian go. He stumbled a little and pressed his fingers to his neck.

"I loved you," Julian shouted.

Matilda looked up to see that he wasn't speaking to her. She gave him a glittering smile and bit down on Lydia's wrist.

The girl screamed, but the scream was lost in Matilda's ears. Lost in the pulse of blood, the tide of gluttonous pleasure and the music throbbing around them like Lydia's slowing heartbeat.

Matilda sat on the blood-soaked mattress and turned on the video camera to check that the live feed was working.

Julian was gone. She'd given him the pass after stripping him of all his cash and credit cards; there was no point in trying to force Lydia to leave since she'd just come right back in. He'd made stammering apologies that Matilda ignored; then he fled for the gate. She didn't miss him. Her fantasy of Julian felt as ephemeral as her old life.

"It's working," one of the boys—Michael—said from the stairs, a computer cradled on his lap. Even though she'd killed one of them, they welcomed her back, eager enough for eternal life to risk more deaths. "You're streaming live video."

Matilda set the camera on the stack of crates, pointed toward her and the wall where she'd tied a gagged Lydia. The girl thrashed and kicked, but Matilda ignored her. She stepped in front of the camera and smiled.

My name is Matilda Green. I was born on April 10, 1997. I died on September 3, 2013. Please tell my mother I'm okay. And Dante, if you're watching this, I'm sorry.

You've probably seen lots of video feeds from inside Coldtown. I saw them too. Pictures of girls and boys grinding together in clubs or bleeding elegantly for their celebrity vampire masters. Here's what you never see. What I'm going to show you.

For eighty-eight days you are going to watch someone sweat out the infection. You are going to watch her beg and scream and cry. You're going to watch her throw up food and piss her pants and pass out. You're going to watch me feed her can after can of creamed corn. It's not going to be pretty.

You're going to watch me, too. I'm the kind of vampire that you'd be, one who's new at this and basically out of control. I've already killed someone and I can't guarantee I'm not going to do it again. I'm the one who infected this girl.

This is the real Coldtown.

I'm the real Coldtown.

You still want in?

⎯⎯◈⎯⎯

Holly Black *is the best-selling author of contemporary fantasy novels for teens and children. Her first book,* Tithe: A Modern Faerie Tale *(2002) was included* *in the American Library Association's Best Books for Young Adults. Black has since written two other books in the same universe,* Valiant *(2005), and* Ironside *(2007).* Valiant *was a finalist for the Mythopoeic Award for Young Readers and the recipient of the Andre Norton Award for Excellence in Young Adult Literature. Black collaborated artist Tony DiTerlizzi, to create the Spiderwick Chronicles. The Spiderwick Chronicles were adapted into a film by Paramount Pictures in conjunction with Nickelodeon Films and released in February 2008. Black is a frequent contributor to anthologies, and has co-edited three of them:* Geektastic *(with Cecil Castellucci, 2009),* Zombies vs. Unicorns *(with Justine Larbalestier, 2010), and* Bordertown *(with Ellen Kushner, 2011). Her first collection of short fiction,* Poison Eaters and Other Stories, *came out in 2010. She has just finished the third book in her Eisner-nominated graphic novel series,* The Good Neighbors, *and is working on* Red Glove, *the second novel in* The Curse Workers *series.* White Cat, *the first in the series, was published in May 2010. The author lives in Massachusetts with her husband, Theo, in a house with a secret library.*

And "they"—whoever *they* are—keep telling us there's nothing original left to do with the vampire mythos. (This fallacy is disproved in an entirely different way with another story in this anthology: John Langan's novella, *The Wide, Carnivorous Sky.*) With "The Coldest Girl in Coldtown" Black provides more characterization, world building, social commentary, and emotion in this irony-rich short story than many novels can manage with a dozen times as many words . . . and I bet you'd like to read more about Coldtown, hmm?

STRANGE SCENES FROM AN UNFINISHED FILM

GARY MCMAHON

The sticky label had peeled off the videocassette, leaving behind only thin ragged scraps of dirty white paper. I peered at the stains on the paper trying to make out what had once been written there, but could make no sense of the faint striations which remained.

The wind moved heavily across the walls, pressing against the outside of the house. The window creaked, the glass shifting fractionally in old frames. I glanced outside, across the jagged tops of the trees in the park opposite, and towards the brightly lit expanse of the city.

"It's a third generation copy," the man in the pub had promised me. "One of Reef's last short films, made before he died."

I fingered the spools, turning one of them with my thumb jammed into the gap. The plastic groaned; the tape encased within the slim box whispered as it wound around its inner cogs.

"It doesn't have a title, not that I can find. It's just a short show reel, meant as a teaser to attract finance for a longer project he wanted to direct." The man's face had been covered in acne scars; his big square hands swallowed the pint glass I'd brought him from the bar.

I didn't know the man's name, but we'd been introduced by a petty criminal named Billy Talbot, a mutual friend and fellow cinema enthusiast. Billy and I shared a love of obscure horror films, if not much else, and Derek Reef was one of the few directors we both admired—although my own admiration for the oddball director far outweighed Talbot's own.

For the uninitiated, Reef had made a handful of films in the 1970s, and had been assassinated in New York before even having the chance to make a name for himself with his short body of work.

After the renegade director's death, there had been a small groundswell of interest in his output: a few independent cinemas ran retrospective seasons, a documentary was funded by the BBC but never shown because of unquoted legal reasons, and various film magazines ran one-page features on his debauched lifestyle rather than the films he left behind.

None of that interested me to any great degree; I simply wanted to see the films. None of them were particularly great in the conventional sense, but they were at least technically proficient. My favorite was *Flowers For Flora's Grave*, which had been based on a cult novel by a pulp horror writer (also dead), but even that suffered from a lack of budget and the inability of the director to extract decent performances from anyone but his voluptuous star and sometime lover, the infamous Vanna St. Clair.

My own interest in the films was due mainly to the fact that my late father had appeared as an extra in one of Reef's early mainstream shorts, and after I found a copy of it when sorting through his particulars after his death, I became intrigued by the somewhat cheesy and certainly controversial films subsequently made by Reef.

The tape given to me by the man in the pub was allegedly one of the few copies in circulation of a ten-minute sequence Reef had put together a few weeks before his murder by a mumbling vagrant with an obscure axe to grind. I'd read about the rumored existence of the film, but had given up any hope of actually seeing it until Billy Talbot rang me, drunk and breathless, one evening to tell me that he'd tracked down a copy.

The conversation had been stilted; Billy was obviously stoned on something, and judging by the background noise he was calling from a party or somewhere equally as chaotic. He was a strange and often dangerous man, but for some reason our relationship had lasted a number of years. I vicariously enjoyed the risky nature of his subculture lifestyle; he liked to be associated with a nerd, just to give him what he always called "layers."

I crouched before the old VHS machine I kept wired to the television in my bedroom. I hadn't used the thing in over a year, and wasn't even sure if it was still in working order. Everything worthwhile was available on DVD these days, usually downloaded and converted from the Internet.

Pressing the power button, I experienced a brief and oddly enjoyable moment of panic when nothing happened . . . but then the green light came on and I hit eject. The shelf shuddered out of the front of the machine, and I slipped in the tape.

"Okay, Reef. Let's see what you've got."

I moved to the armchair in the center of the room, cracked open the can of lager I'd brought up from the fridge, and settled down in front of a screen full of grizzled static. Lifting the remote control, I pressed play, and waited to be disappointed

I wasn't quite prepared to believe that this was actually what the man in the pub had claimed it to be; not for the relatively measly sum of one hundred pounds and a few pints of bitter. If this were the real thing, it would be worth several times that sum on the Internet, sold to a private collector. But the man had been adamant that he was not in it for the money: he wanted the recording to go to someone who would appreciate it, and apparently Billy Talbot had vouched for me in that capacity.

The static began to clear. I narrowed my eyes in the dark room and struggled to make out a picture. After a short while, a scene resolved on the screen. A young bearded man sat in an armchair at the center of a grubby room. There was a television before him, but it was impossible to make out what he was watching—to me, it looked like a reflection of himself, or perhaps another scene featuring a similar figure in an armchair, but this one slovenly and unkempt.

The man stared at the screen, sipping something from a glass. I took a drink of my beer. On the screen the man seemed nervous, almost pensive. His face was blurred, but he seemed to be frowning.

I leaned forward, eager to see more.

The man on the screen leaned forward.

I experienced then a moment of déjà vu tinged with acute vertigo, as if I were falling through a space I'd once dreamed of, and knew that what waited for me at the bottom would possess a familiar face.

Suddenly, as if speakers had just been turned on, the film's badly overdubbed soundtrack came into play. Through a storm of static, I heard what sounded like loud clapping but soon realized was, in fact, the beating of huge wings.

The young man left his chair and went to the window. The bare boards he trod upon were stained and worn; the peeling walls of the room were angled inwards, patches of plaster showing signs of dampness and decay.

When he reached the window the man stretched out and unlatched the clasp, then slid the sash upward. The sound grew louder; whatever was making it was outside, and drawing near.

The camera swung around fluidly, a vertiginous precursor to modern jerky shooting techniques, and I was able to see over the man's shoulder and out of the window. The trees in the park opposite shuddered and the lights of the city beyond were smeared, like a bad oil painting done by the hand of a madman.

Something was approaching.

It flew low, gliding for a moment just above the level of the trees, and although it was far away it grew larger as it closed in on the young man in the window. He clutched the wooden frame, rotten wood splintering and breaking off in his hands. Then, panicking, he pulled down the sash and retreated, backing into the center of the room. His backside collided with the raggedy armchair and he stopped.

The camera then offered another view of the window, but this time the sky was empty of everything but the stars and the seedy reflected lights from the city below. Even the trees had vanished, leaving behind an emptiness that seemed somehow pregnant with meaning.

I sat in my chair and stared at the small gray screen, attempting to make sense of what I'd seen. Was it some kind of elaborate joke concocted by Billy

Talbot, perhaps as revenge for some imaginary hurt? But Billy possessed neither the imagination nor the funds for such an ambitious enterprise; he was currently out of work (legal or otherwise), claiming benefits, and could barely put together enough cash for a couple of pints in the local pub.

"The man?" What about him? The nameless scarface who'd sold me the tape.

I stood, went to the window, and looked out at the view. The sky was dark: gossamer scraps of clouds bled across a flat gray canvas. In the distance, just about visible, a dark speck hung on the horizon. As I watched, I could imagine that speck was drawing closer, as if borne by great leathery wings.

I put on my coat and left the house. The pub was still open—it never closed, not since the drinking laws had changed to allow all-day service.

The cold air hit me like a slap in the face as I made my way past crumbling blocks of empty flats, burned-out warehouses and the remains of shops closed down years ago. The council regeneration program had not yet reached my district; we were still waiting for the work to be done. My surroundings consisted mainly of crumbling brickwork, steel security shutters and exposed concrete foundations.

The man was standing at the bar when I entered the pub, his big hands resting on the scarred wooden surface. An empty glass stood before him, but he made no move to have it refilled.

I approached him without speaking. He glanced at me, and then returned his apathetic gaze to the empty glass.

"Two pints," I said to the barman—a fat man who rarely ever spoke yet still managed to attract a regular crowd to his premises. Perhaps his lack of chitchat was the main draw.

"Have you watched it?"

The barman served our drinks and retreated to the far end of the bar, where he stared at the repeat of an earlier football match on a tiny wall-mounted TV.

"Yes. I've just sat through it."

"Good," said the man, before taking a drink. "That'll save us a lot of pointless discussion."

I watched his hands. They moved slowly, but with little finesse. The knuckles were badly damaged, covered in small cuts and swellings, as if he'd been in a fight.

"What is it?" I waited for him to answer.

"It's a film. Just a bit of film." His swollen lips writhed across the lower half of his face; a thick band of shadow lengthened his chin, making it look as if his head were too large for his stocky body.

"Yes, I know that. But what is it?"

He turned to me then, finally gracing me with his full attention. There were tears in his eyes and his forehead was freshly scabbed. Fresh blood was smeared across one eyebrow, mingling with the dark hairs. "I don't know. I haven't even watched it. The people I got it from told me not to: they said it only works on one person, and I wasn't fit to be exposed to its glory. Fucking nutters." He looked away, blinking.

"Who were they, these people?"

"Religious types. Met them at a film fair in Cleveland. I was selling homemade porn and they had all these DVDs supposed to be a recording of angels. Bullshit. All I saw was a few retarded children in a Romanian orphanage dressed up in paper fairy costumes."

He paused to take another drink.

"I bought a job lot of other crap off them, though. A load of old horror films, some rare stuff I already had a customer for, and the thing I sold you. That Reef thing."

I licked my lips. Behind me, the door opened and heavy footsteps entered the bar, pausing at my back; when I turned to look, there was no one there and the door was closed to keep out the night. "How can I contact these people? Do you have an address, a telephone number? Anything. I would make it worth your while."

Again he turned to face me, a look of fear in those wide, wet eyes. "They came to see me earlier this evening, after I gave you the tape. They said they were watching me, and that if I ever tried to contact them, they'd kill me." He raised his hand, opened his fist to show me the marks I'd noticed earlier. "I'm a hard man, but they were harder. They showed me photographs of the last person who crossed them." He picked up his pint glass and drained it, not a flicker of distaste crossing his face.

I thought about Billy Talbot, and how he'd been involved with certain groups in the past—neo Nazis, right wing protest parties, obscure pseudo-religious cults. I'd thought he'd put all that behind him, but perhaps I was wrong.

Was I the money-shot finale to some insane ritual, or maybe a debt owed by Billy to a crowd he should not have messed with—people far more dangerous than he had expected? None of this seemed real. It was like the plot of one of the films I loved.

When I left the pub I felt as if I were being followed. Shadows stirred in every corner, sounds came from each dark doorway I passed. Whenever I looked up at the sky, I expected to catch sight of something gliding down towards me, reaching for me like a bird of prey claiming a field mouse.

I locked myself indoors, climbed the stairs, and knelt before the VCR, once more pressing the eject button. The tape was not inside. I'd left it there when I returned to the pub, but now it was gone. I should have expected it, really: I'm not a stupid man.

I tried to eat a sandwich but it tasted like cardboard. Water from the tap had a coppery bite. I drank whisky, lots of it: my only recourse was to get blindingly drunk. Perhaps that way I would be unable to see whatever it was when finally it came for me . . .

Finally, I return to the armchair in my upstairs room to stare at the dead television screen. The whisky is dwindling, but I cannot get drunk enough to turn off my mind.

The screen flares up suddenly, a bright light accompanied by a faint popping sound. Despite the lack of a videocassette, the picture is almost the same as before: a young man sitting in a filthy armchair, a drink in his hand. I raise my glass; the man raises his glass. I sit forward; the man shuffles forward in his chair.

"No." We speak the dialogue in unison, twin performers on a darkened set. "Please."

Then, eventually, the sound of great flapping wings approaches, unhindered by the layer of glass and the thin walls of my/his dwelling.

We—the actor and I—stand and run to the window. The thing is closer now, and I can see that it is gaunt and leathery, like a corpse whose skin has dried out and adhered to yellowed bone. Its head is massive, like the skull of a skinned lion, and its eye sockets are filled with a glow that burns like the bulbs from a set of arc lights in the film of my destruction.

But the whole thing resembles a shoddy costume, a lazy special effect. Its details are shabby. I can almost see the stitches holding together the frayed seams of its outline. For some reason I find this idea even more disturbing than if the creature looked real.

I turn to the television screen; my counterpart turns his back on me.

Then, horrified, I watch the screen as the thing crashes soundlessly through the window, grasping the man's back, and begins to tear at his head and upturned face. He throws up his hands, trying to bat it away, but it is far too powerful and pins him easily to the dusty boards, its lolloping, oversized head lowering over his screaming features.

It is over in seconds: the beast drags the bloody remains to the window and carries them away, perhaps to some terrible nest located far off, in another place, made up of discarded scraps of celluloid.

I turn stiffly to the window, but there is nothing to be seen. Like a coming attraction, what I have witnessed on the screen is merely a precursor, a clip of what is meant to happen next. I step to the window. The night beyond is completely black, like a cinema screen between shows. Then, one by one, tiny lights flash on in the darkness, and I am shocked by the sight of a million television screens flickering like childhood nightlights.

"Why me? Why choose me?"

There is no answer but the gentle pulsing of television light.

I once again have the sense that I am being watched, or perhaps maneuvered by hidden personalities: writer and director, linking up for a final collaboration, something that will eventually reach out across the cosmos towards a brand new audience . . .

"I'm not important. I have nothing to offer . . . I have no story to tell."

My words break off into the darkness, a trail of confusion I will soon follow towards my annihilation. These words, I now realize, are no longer part of the shooting script.

I stare at the screens that are really eyes; they are suspended in the void, hung from unseen stars and the tails of strange comets that remain invisible to my eyes. I turn around and grab the armchair, hauling it across to the window, where I sit and stare out at the digital congregation, waiting for the often-tricky third act to unspool.

Calmly, I wonder which of the screens will be big enough to contain my soul.

Gary McMahon's *fiction has appeared in magazines and anthologies in the U.K. and U.S and has been reprinted in both* The Mammoth Book of Best New Horror *and* Year's Best Horror and Fantasy. *He is the British-Fantasy-Award-nominated author of* Rough Cut, All Your Gods Are Dead, Dirty Prayers, *and* How to Make Monsters, Rain Dogs, Different Skins, Pieces of Midnight, Hungry Hearts. *He has edited an anthology of original novelettes titled* We Fade to Grey. *Forthcoming are several reprints in "Best of" anthologies, a story in the mass market anthology* The End of the Line, *novels* Pretty Little Dead Things *and* Dead Bad Things *from Angry Robot/Osprey, and* The Concrete Grove *trilogy from Solaris. His Web site: www.garymcmahon.com.*

The narrator says: "I'm not important. I have nothing to offer . . . I have no story to tell."

Perhaps we all should hope this is true because—to my mind—at the end of this story, one gets the feeling that he will soon have all too many stories to offer . . . and they will be tales we might not survive the telling of.

A DELICATE ARCHITECTURE

CATHERYNNE M. VALENTE

My father was a confectioner. I slept on pillows of spun sugar; when I woke, the sweat and tears of my dreams had melted it all to nothing, and my cheek rested on the crisp sheets of red linen. Many things in my father's house were made of candy, for he was a prodigy, having at the age of five invented a chocolate trifle so dark and rich that the new emperor's chocolatier sat down upon the steps of his great golden kitchen and wept into his truffle-dusted mustache. So it was that when my father found himself in possession of a daughter, he cut her corners and measured her sweetness with no less precision than he used in his candies.

My breakfast plate was clear, hard butterscotch, full of oven-bubbles. I ate my soft-boiled marzipan egg gingerly, tapping its little cap with a toffee-hammer. The yolk within was a lemony syrup that dribbled out into my egg-cup. I drank chocolate in a black vanilla-bean mug. But I ate sugared plums with a fork of sparrow bones; the marrow left salt in the fruit and the strange, thick taste of a thing once alive in all that sugar. When I asked my father why I should taste these bones along with the sweetness of the candied plums, he told me very seriously that I must always remember that sugar was once alive. It grew tall and green and hard as my own knuckles in a far-away place, under a red sun that burned on the face of the sea. I must always remember that children just like me cut it down and crushed it up with tan and strong hands, and that their sweat, which gave me my sugar, tasted also of salt.

"If you forget that red sun and those long, green stalks, then you are not truly a confectioner, you understand nothing about candy but that it tastes good and is colorful—and these things a pig can tell, too. We are the angels of the cane, we are oven-magicians, but if you would rather be a pig snuffling in the leaves—"

"No, Papa."

"Well then, eat your plums, magician of my heart."

And so I did, and the tang of marrow in the sugar-meat was rich and disturbing and sweet.

Often I would ask my father where my mother had gone, if she had not liked her fork of sparrow bones, or if she had not wanted to eat marzipan eggs every day. These were the only complaints I could think of. My father ruffled my hair with his sticky hand and said:

"One morning, fine as milk, when I lived in Vienna and reclined on turquoise cushions with the empress licking my fingers for one taste of my sweets, I went walking past the city shops, my golden cane cracking on the cobbles, peering into their frosted windows and listening to the silver bells strung from the doors. In the window of a competitor who hardly deserved the name, being but a poor maker of trifles which would hardly satisfy a duchess, I saw the loveliest little crystal jar. It was as intricately cut as a diamond and full of the purest sugar I have ever seen. The little shopkeeper, bent with decades of hunching over trays of chocolate, smiled at me with few enough teeth and cried:

'Alonzo! I see you have cast your discerning gaze upon my little vial of sugar! I assure you it is the finest of all the sugars ever made, rendered from the tallest cane in the isles by a fortunate virgin snatched at the last moment from the frothing red mouth of her volcano! It was then blanched to the snowy shade you see in a bath of lion's milk and ground to sweetest dust with a pearl pestle, and finally poured into a jar made from the glass of three church windows. I am no emperor's darling, but in this I exceed you at last!'

The little man did a shambling dance of joy, to my disgust. But I poured out coins onto his scale until his eyes gleamed wet with longing, and took that little jar away with me." My father pinched my chin affectionately. "I hurried back home, boiled the sugar with costly dyes and other secret things, and poured it into a Constanze-shaped mold, slid it into the oven, and out you came in an hour or two, eyes shining like caramels!"

My father laughed when I pulled his ear and told him not to tease me, that every girl has a mother, and an oven is no proper mother! He gave me a slice of honeycomb, and shooed me into the garden, where raspberries grew along the white gate.

And thus I grew up. I ate my egg every morning, and licked the yolk from my lips. I ate my plums with my bone fork, and thought very carefully about the tall cane under the red sun. I scrubbed my pillow from my cheeks until they were quite pink. Every old woman in the village remarked on how much I resembled the little ivory cameos of the emperor, the same delicate nose, high brow, thick red hair. I begged my father to let me go to Vienna, as he had done when he was a boy. After all, I was far from a dense child. I had my suspicions—I wanted to see the emperor. I wanted to hear the violas playing in white halls with green and rose checkered floors. I wanted to ride a horse with long brown reins. I wanted to taste radishes and carrots and potatoes, even a chicken, even a fish on a plate of real porcelain, with no oven-bubbles in it.

"Why did we leave Vienna, Papa?" I cried, over our supper of marshmallow crèmes and caramel cakes. "I could have learned to play the flute there; I could have worn a wig like spun sugar. You learned these things—why may I not?"

My father's face reddened and darkened all at once, and he gripped the sides of the butcher's board where he cut caramel into bricks. "I learned to prefer sugar to white curls," he growled, "and peppermints to piccolos, and cherry creams to the emperor. You will learn this, too, Constanze." He cleared his throat. "It is an important thing to know."

I bent myself to the lesson. I learned how to test my father's syrups by dropping them into silver pots of cold water. By the time I was sixteen I hardly needed to do it, I could sense the hard crack of finished candy, feel the brittle snap prickling the hairs of my neck. My fingers were red with so many crushed berries; my palms were dry and crackling with the pale and scratchy wrapping papers we used for penny sweets. I was a good girl. By the time my father gave me the dress, I was a better confectioner than he, though he would never admit it. It was almost like magic, the way candies would form, glistening and impossibly colorful, under my hands.

It was very bright that morning. The light came through the window panes like butterscotch plates. When I came into the kitchen, there was no egg on the table, no toffee-hammer, no chocolate in a sweet black cup. Instead, lying over the cold oven like a cake waiting to be iced, was a dress. It was the color of ink, tiered and layered like the ones Viennese ladies wore in my dreams, floating blue to the floor, dusted with diamonds that caught the morning light and flashed cheerfully.

"Oh, Papa! Where would I wear a thing like that?"

My father smiled broadly, but the corners of his smile were wilted and sad.

"Vienna," he said. "The court. I thought you wanted to go, to wear a wig, to hear a flute?"

He helped me on with the dress, and as he cinched in my waist and lifted my red hair from bare shoulders, I realized that the dress was made of hard blue sugar and thousands of blueberry skins stitched together with syrupy thread. The diamonds were lumps of crystal candy, still a bit sticky, and at the waist were icing flowers in a white cascade. Nothing of that dress was not sweet, was not sugar, was not my father's trade and mine.

Vienna looked like a Christmas cake we had once made for a baroness: all hard, white curls and creases and carvings, like someone had draped the city in vanilla cream. There were brown horses, and brown carriages attached to them. In the emperor's palace, where my father walked as though he had built it, there were green and rose checkered floors, and violas playing somewhere far off. My father took my hand and led me to a room which was harder and whiter than all the rest, where the emperor and the emperor sat frowning on terrible silver thrones of sharpened filigree, like two demons on their wedding day. I gasped, and shrank behind my father, the indigo train of my dress showing so dark against the floor. I could not hope to hide from those awful royal eyes.

"Why have you brought us this thing, Alonzo?" barked the emperor, who had a short blond mustache and copper buttons running down his chest. "This thing which bears such a resemblance to our wife? Do you insult us by dragging this reminder of your crimes and hers across our floor like a dust broom?"

The emperor blushed deeply, her skin going the same shade as her hair, the same shade as my hair. My father clenched his teeth.

"I told you then, when you loved my chocolates above all things, that I did not touch her, that I loved her as a man loves God, not as he loves a woman."

"Yet you come back, begging to return to my grace, towing a child who is a mirror of her! This is obscene, Alonzo!"

My father's face broke open, pleading. It was terrible to see him so. I clutched my icing flowers, confused and frightened.

"But she is not my child! She is not the emperor's child! She is the greatest thing I have ever created, the greatest of all things I have baked in my oven. I have brought her to show you what I may do in your name, for your grace, if you will look on me with love again, if you will give me your favor once more. If you will let me come back to the city, to my home."

I gaped, and tears filled my eyes. My father drew a little silver icing-spade from his belt and started toward me. I cried out and my voice echoed in the hard, white hall like a sparrow cut into a fork. I cringed, but my father gripped my arms tight as a tureen's handles, and his eyes were wide and wet. He pushed me to my knees on the emperor's polished floor, and the two monarchs watched impassively as I wept in my beautiful blue dress, though the emperor let a pale hand flutter to her throat. My father put the spade to my neck and scraped it up, across my skin, like a barber giving a young man his first shave.

A shower of sugar fell glittering across my chest.

"I never lied to you, Constanze," he murmured in my ear.

He pierced my cheek with the tip of the spade, and blood trickled down my chin, over my lips. It tasted like raspberries.

"Look at her, your majesty. She is nothing but sugar, nothing but candy, through and through. I made her in my own oven. I raised her up. Now she is grown—and so beautiful! Look at her cinnamon hair, her marzipan skin, her tears of sugar and salt! And you may have her, you may have the greatest confection made on this earth, if you will but let me come home, and make you chocolates as I used to, and put your hand to my shoulder in friendship again."

The emperor rose from her throne and walked toward me, like a mirror gliding on a hidden track, so like me she was, though her gown was golden, and its train longer than the hall. She looked at me, her gaze pointed and deep, but did not seem to hear my sobbing, or see my tears. She put her hand to my bleeding cheek, and tasted the blood on her palm, daintily, with the tip of her tongue.

"She looks so much like me, Alonzo. It is a strange thing to see."

My father flushed. "I was lonely," he whispered. "And perhaps a man may be forgiven for casting a doll's face in the image of God."

I was kept in the kitchens, hung up on the wall like a copper pot, or a length of garlic. Every day a cook would clip my fingernails to sweeten the emperor's coffee, or cut off a curl of my scarlet hair to spice the Easter cakes of the emperor's first child—a boy with brown eyes like my father's. Sometimes, the head cook would lance my cheek carefully and collect the scarlet syrup in a hard white cup. Once, they plucked my eyelashes, ever so gently, for a licorice comfit the emperor' new daughter craved. They were kind enough to ice my lids between plucking.

They tried not to cause me any pain. Cooks and confectioners are not wicked creatures by nature, and the younger kitchen girls were disturbed by the shape of me hanging there, toes pointed at the oven. Eventually, they grew accustomed to it, and I was no more strange to them than a shaker of salt or a pepper-mill. My dress sagged and browned, as blueberry skins will do, and fell away. A kind little boy who scrubbed the floors brought me a coarse black dress from his mother's closet. It was made of wool, real wool, from a sheep and not an oven. They fed me radishes and carrots and potatoes, and sometimes chicken, sometimes even fish, on a plate of real porcelain, with no heat-bubbles in it, none at all.

I grew old on that wall, my marzipan-skin withered and wrinkled no less than flesh, helped along by lancings and scrapings and trimmings. My hair turned white and fell out, eagerly collected. As I grew old, I was told that the emperor liked the taste of my hair better and better, and soon I was bald.

But emperors die, and so do fathers. Both of these occurred in their way, and when at last the emperor died, there was no one to remember that the source of the palace sugar was not a far off isle, under a red sun that burned on the face of the sea. On the wall, I thought of that red sun often, and the children cutting cane, and the taste of the bird's marrow deep in my plum. That same kind floor-scrubber, grown up and promoted to butler, cut me down when my bones were brittle, and touched my shorn hair gently. But he did not apologize. How could he? How many cakes and teas had he tasted which were sweetened by me?

I ran from the palace in the night, as much as I could run, an old, scraped-out crone, a witch in a black dress stumbling across the city and through, across and out. I kept running and running, my sugar-body burning and shrieking with disuse. I ran past the hard white streets and past the villages where I had been a child who knew nothing of Vienna, into the woods, into the black forest with the creeping loam and nothing sweet for miles. Only there did I stop, panting, my spiced breath fogging in the air. There were great dark green boughs arching over me, pine and larch and oak. I sank down to the earth, wrung dry of weeping, safe and far from anything hard, anything white, anything with accusing eyes and a throne like a demon's wedding. No one would scrape me for teatime again. No one would touch me again. I put my hands to my head and stared up at the stars though the leaves. It was quiet, at last, quiet, and dark. I curled up on the leaves and slept.

When I woke, I was cold. I shivered. I needed more than a black dress to cover me. I would not go back, not to any place which had known me, not to Vienna, not to a village without a candy-maker. I would not hang a sign over a door and feed sweets to children. I would stay, in the dark, under the green. And so I needed a house. But I knew nothing of houses. I was not a bricklayer or a thatcher. I did not know how to make a chimney. I did not know how to make a door-hinge. I did not know how to stitch curtains.

But I knew how to make candy.

I went begging in the villages, a harmless old crone—was it odd that she asked for sugar and not for coins? Certainly. Did they think it mad that she begged for berries and liquors and cocoa, but never alms? Of course. But the elderly are strange and their ways inexplicable to the young. I collected, just as they had done from me all my years on the wall, and my hair grew. I went to my place in the forest, under the black and the boughs, and I poured a foundation of caramel. I raised up thick, brown gingerbread walls, with cinnamon for wattle and marshmallow for daub. Hard-crack windows clear as the morning air, a smoking licorice chimney, stairs of peanut brittle and carpets of red taffy, a peppermint bathtub. And a great black oven, all of blackened, burnt sugar, with a yellow flame within. Gumdrops studded my house like jewels, and a little path of molasses ran liquid and dark from my door. And when my hair had grown long enough, I thatched my roof with cinnamon strands.

It had such a delicate architecture, my house, that I baked and built. It was as delicately made as I had been. I thought of my father all the while, and the red sun on waving green cane. I thought of him while I built my pastry-table, and I thought of him while I built my gingerbread floors. I hated and loved him in turns, as witches will do, for our hearts are strange and inexplicable. He had never come to see me on the wall, even once. I could not understand it. But I made my caramel bricks and I rolled out sheets of toffee onto my bed, and I told his ghost that I was a good girl, I had always been a good girl, even on the wall.

I made a pillow of spun sugar. I made plates of butterscotch. Each morning I tapped a marzipan egg with a little toffee-hammer. But I never caught a sparrow for my plums. They are so very quick. I was always hungry for them, for something living, and salty, and sweet amid all my sugar. I longed for something alive in my crystalline house, something to remind me of the children crushing up cane with tan, strong hands. There was no marrow in my plums. I could not remember the red sun and the long, green stalks, and so I bent low in my lollipop rocking-chair, weeping and whispering to my father that I was sorry, I was sorry, I was no more than a pig snuffling in the leaves, after all.

And one morning, when it was very bright, and the light came through the window like a viola playing something very sweet and sad, I heard footsteps coming up my molasses-path. Children: a boy and a girl. They laughed, and over their heads blackbirds cawed hungrily.

I was hungry, too.

Born in the Pacific Northwest in 1979, Catherynne M. Valente is the author of over a dozen books of fiction and poetry, including Palimpsest, *the Orphan's Tales series,* and The Girl Who Circumnavigated Fairyland in a Ship of Own Making. *She is the winner of the Tiptree Award, the Andre Norton Award, the Lambda Award, the Mythopoeic Award, the Rhysling Award, and the Million Writers Award. She was a finalist for the World Fantasy Award in 2007 and 2009, and the Locus and Hugo Awards in 2010. She lives on an island off the coast of Maine with her partner, two dogs, an enormous cat, and an accordion.*

Like Kelly Link's story, Catherynne M. Valente's "A Delicate Architecture," was written for *Troll's Eye View: A Book of Villainous Tales.* Unlike Link, Valente stays closer to the anthology's stated theme: the backstories of fairy tale villains. Although written for younger readers, the vividly descriptive imagery; her twisted uses of the standard fairy tale tropes, trappings, and characters; and the final revelation of exactly who our sweet protagonist turns out to be all make the story a deliciously dark treat for their elders as well.

THE MYSTERY

PETER ATKINS

—◆—

"For upwards of two hours, the sky was brilliant with lights."
—*The Liverpool Daily Post*, Sept 8th 1895

There's actually no mystery at all.

Not if you went to the Bluey, anyway.

It used to be the grounds of a house, a big one. No Speke Hall or anything, but still technically a Stately Home. It had been called The Grange and was pulled down in May of 1895.

Four months later, minus an ornamental lake which had been filled in, the grounds were opened as a park for the children of Liverpool by the city council. It was officially named Wavertree Playground but was almost immediately dubbed "The Mystery" by local people, because the person who bought the land and donated it to the city had asked for anonymity.

The Bluecoat School, a boys' Grammar, backed onto The Mystery and if you were a pupil there, even seventy-five years later, it was made pretty damn clear to you that it was one of our old Governors who'd forked up for the park. Philip Holt—one of our four school houses was named for him—was a maritime magnate in the days of the great ships and the Cast Iron Shore. The money needed to clear the land and create the park was probably no more than loose change to the man whose Blue Funnel Line practically owned the tea trade between Britain and China.

So. No mystery there.

I'll tell you what *was* a mystery, though. The fucking state of the Gents' bogs.

The Liverpool of the mid-sixties was a city suffering a dizzying drop into recession. No more ships, no more industry, no more Beatles—*Tara, Mum. Off to London to shake the world. Don't wait up*—but even so, the public toilets at the northwest corner of the Mystery were astonishingly disgusting. "Derelict" didn't even come close. They'd been neither bricked up nor pulled down. It was more like they'd been simply forgotten, as if a file had been lost somewhere in the town hall and nobody with any responsibility knew they even existed. Utterly unlooked-after in a third world sort of way and alarming to enter, let alone use. No roof, no cubicle doors, no paper, what was left of the plaster over the ancient red bricks completely covered with graffiti of an obsessive and sociopathic nature, and last mopped out sometime before Hitler trotted into Poland.

But, you know, if you had to go you had to go, and I'd had many a piss there back in the day. If you didn't actually touch anything, you had a fighting chance of walking out without having contracted a disease.

But to see that soiled shed-like structure still there on an autumn afternoon thirty years later was more than a little surprising.

I had some business to attend to and shouldn't really have allowed myself to be distracted, but I felt a need to check it out. The boys appeared just as I approached the stinking moss-scarred walkway entrance.

There were two of them, both about thirteen, though one at least a head taller than his friend. Although they weren't actually blocking the path—standing just off to the side, ankle-deep in the overgrown grass—they nevertheless gave the impression of being self-appointed sentries, as if they were there to perhaps collect a toll or something.

"Where are you going, then?" The first one said. His hair was russet and looked home-cut and his face was patchily rosy with the promise of acne.

"The bog," I said.

They looked at each other, and then back at me.

"*This* bog?" said the first.

"Fuckin' 'ell," said the second. He was the shorter one, black Irish pale, unibrowed and sullen.

"You don't wanna go in *there*," said the first.

"Why would you go in *there*?" said his mate.

I shrugged, but I wasn't sure they noticed. They were staring at me with the kind of incipient aggression you'd expect, but weren't actually meeting my eyes. Instead, they were both looking at me at about mid-chest height, as if looking at someone smaller and younger.

"Why wouldn't I?" I said.

"He might get ya," said the black-haired one.

"Who?"

"The feller," said the redhead.

"What feller?" I asked him.

He looked surprised. "Yerav'n 'eard of 'im?" he said.

"No."

"Fuckin' 'ell," said the shorter one.

"He's there all the time," his friend said. "Nights, mostly."

"Yeah," Blackie nodded in support. "Nights."

"Yeah?" I said to the taller one, the redhead, who seemed to be the boss. "What does he do?"

"Waits there for lads," he said.

"What for?"

"You know."

I didn't. He shook his head off my blank look, in pity for my ignorance. "He bums them," he said.

"Shags them up the bum," said his companion helpfully.

"Why?"

"Fuckin' 'ell," said the first one, and looked at his friend with a *we've got a right idiot here* expression. "Because he's an 'omo, that's why."

"A Hom," said the second.

The first looked thoughtful. Came to a decision. "We better go in with ya," he said.

"For safety, like," said the second, with only a trace of his eagerness betraying itself. "He might be in there now."

"Oh, I think I'll be all right," I said. "If he's in there, I'll tell him I'm not in the mood."

My tone was confusing to them. It wasn't going the way it was meant to, the way it perhaps usually did.

"Yeah, burrit's worse than we said," the first one told me, as if worried some opportunity was slipping away. He looked to his friend. "Tell him about the, you know, the thing."

"Yeah, he's gorra nutcracker," Blackie said. "You know warramean?" He mimed a plier-like action in order to help me visualise what he was talking about. "After he's bummed ya, he crushes yer bollocks."

I remembered that. It was a story I'd first heard when I was much younger than them. An urban legend, though the phrase hadn't been coined at the time, conjured into being in the summer of 1965 and believed by nearly every nine year old boy who heard it.

They were still looking at my chest, as if staring down a smaller con-temporary.

"How old am I?" I asked them.

"You wha'?" the redhead said.

"How old do you think I am?"

They shared a look, and the taller one shrugged. "Dunno," he said. "About eight?"

"Might be ten," the other one said, not to me but to his friend, and the redhead shot him an angry look as if he didn't want to be bothered with details or sidetracked by debate.

I snapped my fingers loudly, close to my face, and drew their eyes upwards.

They looked confused. Their eyes weren't quite focussing on mine, and I still wasn't sure they could really see me. There was something else hovering behind their confusion; an anxiety, perhaps, as if they feared they might be in trouble, as if something would know they were being distracted from their duty and wouldn't be very pleased with them. As far as they were concerned, this was a day like every other and *needed* to be a day like every other, and any disruption in the pattern was alarming to them, in however imprecise a way.

I didn't doubt that this was how they'd spent a fair portion of their time, back when it was linear. Having a little chat and preparing some eight year old victim for a good battering. They'd probably done it before, and more than once. Done it regularly, perhaps, until their belief in the very predator they used as bait had become their undoing.

"Take a look at this," I said and took something out of my pocket to show them.

A few minutes later, back on the main footpath, I took a look back over my shoulder. It was very dark now and neither the toilets nor the boys were anywhere in sight. The moon had risen in the cloudless sky and I took a glance at my watch. It was an old fashioned watch and its dial was un-illuminated, but I was fairly certain it said it was still four in the afternoon.

I'd kept up a brisk pace while checking the time and, when I looked up again, the house was directly ahead of me, though I hadn't noticed it earlier. Its size alone suggested it was probably magnificent in the daylight, but its lawns were unlit and its windows shuttered and it appeared simply as a great black shape, a mass of deeper darkness against the midnight blue of the sky.

Just outside its black iron gates, half-open as if in tentative invitation, a little girl was standing on the gravel of the driveway.

She was dressed in a simple knee-length smock dress and didn't look up at me as I walked towards her. She was concentrating on her game, her mouth opening and closing in recitation of something. It was a skipping song, as best I remembered it, but she was using it as accompaniment for the rapid bouncing of a small rubber ball between the gravel and her outstretched palm.

"Dip dip dip,
My blue ship.
Sailing on the water
Like a cup and saucer.
O, U, T spells—"

Oh, that's right. Not a skipping song at all. A rhyme of selection or exclusion, a variant of eeny meeny miney mo. The little girl, long and ringleted hair pulled back from her forehead by a wide black ribbon, seemed to remember that at the same moment I did and, just as she mouthed the word *out*, her hand snapped shut around the ball, her eyes flicked up to meet mine, and she thrust her other hand out to point its index finger dramatically at me. Her eyes were jet black and her now silent mouth was pulled in a tight unsmiling line.

"I'm out?" I asked her.

She didn't say anything, and nor did her fixed expression waver. I let the silence build for a few moments as we stared at each other, though I blinked deliberately several times to let her know that if it was a contest it was one she was welcome to win.

"Your concentration's slipping," I said eventually. "Where did the ball go?"

Her little brow furrowed briefly and she looked down at her empty hand. She pulled an annoyed face and then looked back at me.

"Are you going into the house?" she asked.

"In a manner of speaking," I said.

She gave a small *tut* of derision. "Is that supposed to be clever?" she said.

"No," I said. "Not really."

"Good," she said. "Because it's *not* clever. It's just stupid. Are you going into the house or not?"

"The house isn't really here," I told her.

"Then where are you standing?" she said. "And who are you talking to?"

Without waiting for an answer, and keeping her eyes fixed on mine, she began to lean her head sideways and down. Keeping her unblinking eyes fixed on mine, she continued the movement, slowly and steadily, with no apparent difficulty or discomfort, until her pale little cheek rested flat against her right shoulder and her head was at an impossible right-angle to her neck. At the same time, in some strange counterpoint, her hair rose up into the air, stately and unhurried, until the ringlets were upright and taut, quivering against the darkness like mesmerised snakes dancing to an unheard piper.

I grinned at her. She was good at this.

We exchanged a few more words before I walked through the gates without her, following the wide and unbending path to the house itself. The imposingly large front door was as unlit as the rest of the exterior and was firmly closed. But I knew that others had come to this house before me, and that the door, despite its size and its weight and its numerous locks, had opened as easily for them as it would for me.

The rest of the vast reception room was pretty impressive, but the portrait over the fireplace was magnificent.

The picture itself was at least eight feet tall, allowing for some grass below and some sky above its life-size and black-suited central figure, who stared out into the room with the confident Victorian swagger of those born to wealth and empire. A foxhound cowered low at its master's feet and, in the far background, which appeared to be the grounds of the house, a group of disturbingly young children were playing Nymphs and Shepherds.

The room, like the long hall along which I'd walked to come to it, was illuminated by many candles, though I'd yet to see anyone who might have lit them. Through a half-open door at the far end of the room, though, I could see a shadow flicking back and forth, back and forth, as if somebody was about their business in a repeated pattern of movements.

As I came into the anteroom, the young woman who was pacing up and down looked up briefly from the clipboard she was holding. She appeared to be barely twenty, dressed in what I guessed to be the kind of nurse's uniform women might have worn when they were dressing wounds received in the Crimea, and the stern prettiness of her face and the darkness of her eyes said she could have been an older sister of the little girl I'd met outside the gates.

There was a single bed in the room and, though it was unoccupied, its sheets were rumpled, as if the woman's patient had just recently gone for a little walk. There were wires and cables and drip-feeds lying on the sheets and the other ends of some of them were connected to a black and white television monitor that attempted to hide its anachronism by being cased within a brass and mahogany housing of a Victorian splendor and an H.G. Wells inventiveness.

The young woman, having registered my presence with neither surprise nor welcome, was back to her job of glancing at the monitor and then marking something on her clipboard.

The image on the monitor—grainy and distorted, washed-out like a barely-surviving kinescope of some long ago transmission—was a fixed-angle image of moonlight-bathed waves, deep-water waves, no shore in sight, as if a single camera were perched atop an impossible tower standing alone in some vast and distant ocean.

I looked at the image for a moment or two while she continued to pace and to make checkmarks on her clipboard.

"So what does that do?" I asked eventually, nodding at the monitor.

She stopped pacing and turned to look at me again. Her expression, while not unfriendly, was conflicted, as if she were both grateful for the break in routine and mildly unsettled by it.

"It used to show his dreams," she said, and turned her head briefly to look again at the endless and unbreaking waves. "But it's empty now."

She looked back at me and tilted her head a little, like she was deciding if I was safe enough to share a confidence with. "It's frightening, isn't it?" she said.

"Frightening?" I said. "I don't know. Perhaps it just means he's at peace."

"No, no," she said, her voice rising in a kind of nervous excitement. "You've misunderstood. That isn't what I meant." And then she caught herself and her voice went flat as if she feared lending emotion to what she said next. "I mean we might be having his dreams *for* him."

She looked at me half-expectantly, her eyes wide, like she was hoping I might tell her that she was wrong, but before I could answer a bell began to ring from a room somewhere deeper in the house.

"Teatime," she said. "You'd best hurry."

The children sat at trestle tables and ate without enthusiasm and there were far too many of them.

Their clothes were a snapshot history lesson; tracksuits and trainers, pullovers and short pants, britches and work-shirts, smocks and knickerbockers. The ones who'd been here longest were an unsettling monochrome against the colors of the more recent arrivals, and it wasn't only their outfits that were fading to gray.

Despite the dutiful shovelling of gruel into their mouths, I knew that they weren't hungry—there was only one inhabitant of this house who was hungry—and I wondered briefly why they even needed to pretend to eat, but figured that habit and routine were part of what helped him chain them here. Not a one of them spoke. Not a one of them smiled. I decided against joining them and headed back down the corridor to which the nurse had pointed me.

I saw something unspeakable in one of the rooms I passed and felt no need to look in any of the others.

The reception room was still empty when I got there. Patience is encouraged in these situations but, you know, fuck it. I decided to break something. There was an exquisite smoked glass figurine resting on top of the piano. I didn't even pick it up, just swept it away with the back of my hand and listened to it shatter against the parquet floor.

I hadn't intended to look, but a rapid skittering caught my eye and I bent down, barely in time to see a tiny something, wretched and limbless, slithering wetly beneath the sofa. I was still crouched down when there was a noise from somewhere behind me, unusually loud for what it most sounded like; the sticky gossamer ripping of a blunder through an unseen spider's web.

I stood up quickly, turning around to look. There was still nobody in the room but, though the large picture over the fireplace was intact and undamaged, its central figure was missing.

"You're a little older than my usual guests," the master of the house said from immediately behind me.

I span back around, very successfully startled. There was nothing overtly threatening about his posture, but he was standing uncomfortably close to me and I wasn't at all fond of his smile.

"A little older," he repeated. "But I'm sure we can find you a room."

"I won't be staying," I said. My voice was steady enough, but I was pissed off at how much he'd thrown me and pissed off more at how much he'd enjoyed it.

"You're very much mistaken," he said. "My house is easy to enter but not so easy to leave."

I understood his confidence. He had a hundred years of experience to justify his thinking that I was one of his usual guests. He could see me, so I had to be dead. Just as most ghosts are invisible to people, most people are invisible to ghosts. But, just as there are a few anomalous ghosts who *can* be seen by people, so are there a few anomalous people who can be seen by ghosts. And he'd just met one.

"Do you know what this is?" I said, and brought the tesseract out of my pocket. They've been standard issue at the department for the last couple of years. Fuck knows where they get them made, but I have a feeling it isn't Hong Kong.

I let it rest in my palm and he looked at it. He tried to keep his expression neutral but I could tell his curiosity was piqued. It always is.

"What does it do?" he said.

"Well, it doesn't really *do* anything," I said. "It just is."

"And what do you want me to do about it?"

"Nothing," I said. "Just look at it for a while."

I gave it a little tap and it slid impossibly through itself.

The room shivered in response, but I don't think he noticed. His eyes were fixed on the little cube and its effortless dance through dimensions.

"There's something wrong with it," he said, but the tone of his voice was fascinated rather than dismissive. "I can't see it properly."

"It's difficult," I agreed. "Because part of it shouldn't be here. Doesn't mean it's not real. Just means it doesn't belong in the space it's in."

The metaphor hit home, as it always did. I don't know why the tesseract works so well on them—I mean, it's utterly harmless, more wake-up call than weapon—but it's definitely made the job easier. He looked up at me. His face was already a little less defined than it had been, but I could still read the fear in it. He was smart, though. Went straight for the important questions and fuck the nuts and bolts.

"Will I be judged?" he said.

"Nobody's judged."

"Will I be hurt?"

"Nobody's hurt."

"Will I be—" He stopped himself then, as an unwilled understanding came to him, and he repeated what he'd just said. Same words. Different stress. "Will I *be*?"

I looked at him.

"Nobody'll be." I said.

It was too late for him to fight, but the animal rage for identity made him try, his imagined flesh struggling against its dissolution and his softening arms reaching out for me uselessly.

"You know who hangs around?" I said. "People with too little will of their own, and people with too much. Let it go. We're just lights in the sky, and their shadows."

"I'll miss it!" he shouted, his disappearing mouth twisting into a final snarl of appetite and terror.

"You won't miss a thing," I said, and watched him vanish.

I'd been in there longer than I thought and, as I walked back through the park towards the Hunter's Lane gate, true night was falling. But it was far from dark. There'd been so many souls in the house, young and old, predator and prey, that the cascade of their dissolution was spectacular and sustained.

For upwards of two hours, the sky was brilliant with lights.

Like an anniversary. Like a half remembered dream. Like a mystery.

Peter Atkins *was born in Liverpool, England and now lives in Los Angeles.
He is the author of the novels* Morningstar, Big Thunder, *and* Moontown
and the screenplays Hellraiser II, Hellraiser III, Hellraiser IV, Wishmaster,
and Prisoners of the Sun. *His short fiction has appeared in such best-selling
anthologies as* The Museum of Horrors, Dark Delicacies II, *and* Hellbound
Hearts. *He is the co-founder, with Dennis Etchison and Glen Hirshberg, of The
Rolling Darkness Revue, who tour the west coast annually bringing ghost stories
and live music to any venue that'll put up with them.* "The Mystery" *comes
from* Spook City, *a three-author collection which featured Atkins alongside his
fellow Liverpudlians Clive Barker and Ramsey Campbell. A new collection of
his short fiction is forthcoming.*

Other than its fine writing, several things drew me to Peter Atkins' story: The
narrator's sheer Liverpudlian matter-of-factness about encountering spirits
and consequent explanation for them: "People with too little will of their own,
and people with too much. Let it go. We're just lights in the sky, and their
shadows." And the other mystery of the story, one just tossed in: "I . . . brought
the tesseract out of my pocket. They've been standard issue at the department
for the last couple of years . . . "

I've got a good guess about that tesseract, but I'd like to know more about
"the department."

VARIATIONS ON A THEME FROM *SEINFELD*

PETER STRAUB

⟨glyph⟩

Statement of Theme (from "Bizarro World" Episode):
One may discover the existence of a parallel world in which the characters and situations of our own are strangely echoed, and experience will demonstrate that this world is not only profoundly unsatisfying, but probably dangerous.

1

Three days before his fiftieth birthday, Clyde Mortar, once a Peace Corps volunteer to Mali and ever after officially a faithful servant of USAID and its august parent body, the United States Government's Department of State, tilted forward over the expansive sink of the master bathroom in his Georgetown row house and examined the ornate little chamber reflected in the bathroom mirror. Everything present and available to be seen echoed back from its proper place: the towels briskly refolded on the towel-rack; the powerful toothbrush erect on its charging stand; on the back of the enamel-white bedroom door, the curving brass hook holding taut the fabric strip sewn just below the collar of a spotless white pajama top; the translucent glass flank and inset door of the spacious shower cabinet. When he canted forward another half-inch, there came into view three of the flat, shining footprints he had left on the floor's dark blue tiles in the brief journey from shower to sink. Of Clyde Mortar himself, however, nothing at all was to be seen. The image before him in the mirror's rectangular surface depicted an unusually orderly bathroom empty of humanity, especially as represented by himself. Clyde Mortar—to speak with greater accuracy, OtherClyde—had done a bunk, slipped his traces, downed tools, declared a holiday.

Had it been the first time his double's waywardness had presented him with a mirror absent of his reflection, Mortar might well have fainted away, accused himself of vampirism or mental illness, or committed some other indecorous solecism; as it was in fact the fourth time Good Old Clyde, Clydie

Boy (to use two of the names by which he liked to be known) had by failing to report to his customary station left but a Clyde-shaped vacancy in his place, Mortar experienced a great deal more of dismay and irritation than shock though of course shock was not altogether avoidable. To a great extent, he understood exactly what had happened and what he had to do to set it right; what he did not and could not know, however, were the depths of Clydie Boy's grievances, whatever they were, and what, after he had wiggled through the uncomfortably narrow mirror and entered the world he called De Land, he would be forced to do to redress them. Adding to the complexities of the task before him, his careful, inspection of the mirror's bathroom yielded no hints whatsoever as to where his wayward double might have gone.

When Mortar had been a child of six, the absent six-year-old Clydie Boy had left at least a small clue to his whereabouts, though the creature's Primary, his Original, would never have noticed a thing but for the presence, the in fact astoundingly prescient presence, of his footloose Uncle Budgie.

2

"Budgie," originally Budgen Mortar, Clyde's father's older brother, a man of wandering habits, no fixed abode, and an impenetrable temperament, timed his lengthy visits precisely to the maximum period his brother's wife found it possible to tolerate his company. This period generally worked out to be within the two-to-three week range.

It so fell out that in the manner of children everywhere little Clyde responded not as his parents wished, negatively, but entirely in reaction to his Uncle Budgie's treatment of him, which although sometimes forgetful tended toward a grave kindly courtesy, as though the young Clyde happened to be a small Asian potentate who had dropped in on a ceremonial round of visits.

And it was with exactly such a kindly courteous gravity that Uncle Budgie met his six-year-old nephew's stricken approach to the Mortar family kitchen, for it was in that room they took their family breakfasts, at nine o'clock of the mid-fifties Saturday morning when his nephew's reflection first failed to make its scheduled post-urination appearance in the mirror of the upstairs family bathroom.

And it was Uncle Budgie's kind and grave courtesy, the very gravitas of his courteous kindliness, that led the stricken boy to edge near to his uncle instead of his mother or father, who in fact, had barely noticed his entrance, and to Budgie alone describe the terrifying phenomenon of the failure of the top of his head, all at the time that was ordinarily visible to him, to appear in the mirror above the sink in the upstairs bathroom.

"You, too, hmmm?" observed the sympathetic uncle, and arranged a rendez-vous, five minutes hence, upstairs.

And, "Oh, you, hmmm?" spoke the OtherClyde, when tracked down to the soda fountain where the prominent drawing of a yummy hamburger visible in an *Archie* comic visible just beyond the reflected bathroom door had directed the Primary and Original. Budgie had gently lifted him above the sink and guided him, outstretched hands exploring first, through the mirror's suddenly vaporous surface. "The drugstore, boy, the drugstore," Budgie had whispered a moment before young Clydie passed through entire, and so it had been: the drugstore, boy, the drugstore down on the corner of 44th and Auer, that's where he found his rhyme.

In a cluttered little corner or alcove of this same drugstore, six-year-old Clyde had noticed a forlorn little girl with a sallow face and dust-colored hair nibbling a paper-cone cornet of cotton candy that appeared to have been rained upon, briefly.

Ever after, Clyde Mortar thought of this other world as De Land ob Cotton.

3

After the first time followed three others: at ages thirteen (a rebellion on behalf of principle, quelled by Mortar's promise to enjoy long, probing philosophical discussions with himself in front of the very same bathroom mirror); twenty-two (Peace Corps, the bleak northern reaches of Mali; disappeared to escape the perpetual sandstorms by dozing off under a truck belonging to a sadistic tribal chief); thiry-five (Beirut, even dicier, and turned on a bribe: a long search through the bazaars of flesh merchants officially Not to Be Visited, Not Ever, and resolved only by the young officer of the United States Government's Department of State agreeing to surround his bed on at least two sides, plus the surface overhead, with mirrors, that Clydie Boy might enjoy actual sex for a change.) The increasingly cautious and circumspect man Mr. Mortar had become detested the growing seediness of these unwelcome encounters with De Land ob Cotton.

After the first time, Uncle Budgie had pledged him to silence. This silence he kept, along with others.

His initial wife, Evelyn, the one who buggered off like the mirror-self, asked, "Clyde, are you in the CIA, really?"

His brother said, "Clyde, the other day Dad and I were saying that you travel so much and we can never figure out what you're doing, we think you're in the CIA. Are we right?

A girl of no consequence said, "Clydie-baby, just tell me the truth for once, okay? Are you one of those god-damned spooks?"

4

De Land ob Cotton had rolled a long way downhill since Mortar had been obliged to stalk his double through the honky-tonks and bordellos of the Other Beirut. Then, the degenerates and lowlifes who had taken so great an interest in his progress had at least maintained a respectful distance, and what he glimpsed of the world beyond the forbidden quarter seemed only a bit seedier and run-down than the one in which he led his already deeply doubled life. Now, everything in De Land seemed poisoned. In the real-world Washington, DC, an all-night café where, in the gloom and chiaroscuro of a high-walled rear booth, he had garroted a man at the time named Pluckrose had been unsavory enough, but nothing like the leprous ruin inhabited by smear drunken shadows who were now tracking his progress past its filthy windows. All traces of gaiety and high life, of cigarette holders and lowslung cars with detachable ragtops had departed, leaving streets flecked with garbage and dark, tough stains that looked like blood. Bullet holes and ricochet chips. scarred the brick walls. Most of the windows he saw were broken or boarded. Wearing the protective, Ninja-like garb of black trousers, black sweatshirt, a black cap, and sunglasses, and in his right front pocket carrying the faithful garrote, Mortar still felt unreasonably threatened, as if Clydie Boy might at any second launch himself, .9mm in hand, from one of the darkened doorways lining the dreary street.

Of course he would not. His mirror-self had merely drifted into despair or a half-hearted rebellion, not into a crazed homicidal hostility. As far as Mortar knew, that never happened. How could it? In the first place, whatever would these poor creatures do without their masters?

On a search such as Mortar's, instinct, "gut feeling," is the best guide possible, and after a half-hour of aimless wandering through the littered, brick-strewn, ever-slummier streets of De Land, he discovered that his wandering had not been aimless after all, for only a short distance from De Land's grim, rat-infested Dupont Circle, he had come to rest on the cracked sidewalk before a tenement with crumbling steps leading up to a peeling door badly out of plumb. With every cell in his body our hero knew that Clydie Boy, Good Old Clyde, lived in the ugly rat-trap before him. The question of how long the fellow had been stuck in this hovel and the issue of what had brought him to this pass were mysteries to which Good Old Clyde's Primary and Original was completely indifferent.

Mortar wondered what he would have to do to get into the building, and was just concocting a variation upon a scheme he had used some years before in Caracas when he placed his hand experimentally on the rough surface of the peeling door and felt it yield before him, scraping the ground as it swung inward. He stepped inside. Feathers and broken bits of white tile lay like dust on the floor of the little lobby. His target lived, of course, on the fifth floor, way at the top. Where else, but the place it would cost him most effort to reach? Otherwise, the building struck him as almost empty. Then for the first time it occurred to Clyde Mortar that his double may have seen him as he stood deliberating on the sidewalk.

Up and up Mortar climbed, step upon step, unworried, meeting no one and hearing no voices genuine or broadcast as he toiled upward. When at last he had attained the fifth floor, he paused panting and wheezing, confident in the supposition that no one but Good Old Clyde lived in the building. His fieldwork days were long behind him, but he still knew how to draw an inferential conclusion.

He knocked on an ugly door; his own voice called out, *Come in, Clyde*, and when he did so, he detected motion behind him and heard the lock click shut.

Calmly, he turned and regarded OtherClyde, who as ever in these odd moments appeared both to resemble him exactly and to be at least twenty percent more handsome than himself. The double was holding a long knife in his hand, the grip flat in his hand and the sharp side of the blade facing up.

"You won't need that," he said.

I've been thinking about us.

The double moved closer, forcing Clyde to walk backwards toward the center of the room. In his eyes was a handsome flare of passionate determination that had now and again surprised Clyde Mortar when he came upon it in his mirror.

"There is no us," Clyde said.

Oh yes, there is. Just look at things from my perspective.

"I need you to put down the knife," Clyde said.

I need you to hand over the garrote.

Clyde pulled the instrument from his pocket and gripped its handles, pulling the wire taut. "This little thing?"

The blade flashed up, and without Mortar feeling any sense of motion or pressure whatsoever, the separated halves of the wire flopped down like loose strings.

"Why don't you tell me what you want?" Clyde asked. "I'm sure we'll be able to work out a reasonable agreement."

There is something I want, Clyde. OtherClyde moved closer, then closer again. *I'll be happy to tell you what it is.*

I want your life.

O, Uncle Budgie, Clyde thought, what did you do to me? O, my first wife, O my brother and my father, O my onetime mistress, yes, you were right, for yes, it's true, you would have hated most of the things I had to do, I've been thinking about us, and it's true, but you'd damn well better take care around me in the future.

Peter Straub *is the author of seventeen novels which have been translated into more than twenty languages. They include* Ghost Story, Koko, Mr. X, In the Night Room, *and two collaborations with Stephen King,* The Talisman *and* Black House. *He has written two volumes of poetry and two collections of short fiction. Straub edited the Library of America's edition of* H.P. Lovecraft's Tales *and the forthcoming Library of America's two-volume anthology,* American Fantastic Tales. *He has won the British Fantasy Award, eight Bram Stoker Awards, two International Horror Guild Awards, and two World Fantasy Awards. In 1998, he was named Grand Master at the World Horror Convention. In 2006, he was given the HWA's Life Achievement Award and, in 2008, both the International Horror Guild's Living Legend Award and the Barnes & Noble Writers for Writers Award by Poets & Writers.*

Peter Straub is, without doubt, a master of the dark. This strange little gem plays on the idea of the doppelgänger, a theme the author addresses with stunning originality in his novel *Mr. X* (1999). Although Clyde here is not one of them, Straub has several fictional alter-egos for himself as well: novelist Tim Underhill (who appears in or even "authors" Straubian fiction) and, most recently, in Lee Harwood, the narrator of Straub's latest novel, the superb *A Dark Matter* (2010).

Then there's the late Professor Putney Tyson Ridge, chair and sole member of the Department of Popular Culture at Popham College, who sees Straub as a dismal failure, "a case study in the destructive effects of misguided praise and vulgar popularity upon a writer too foolish to accept his limitations." Perhaps even the professor would find literary merit in this story

THE WIDE, CARNIVOROUS SKY

JOHN LANGAN

⇥

I

9:13 PM

From the other side of the campfire, Lee said, "So it's a vampire."

"I did not say vampire," Davis said. "Did you hear me say vampire?"

It was exactly the kind of thing Lee would say, the gross generalization that obscured more than it clarified. Not for the first time since they'd set out up the mountain, Davis wondered at their decision to include Lee in their plans.

Lee held up his right hand, index finger extended. "It has the fangs."

"A mouthful of them."

Lee raised his middle finger. "It turns into a bat."

"No—its wings are like a bat's."

"Does it walk around with them?"

"They—it extrudes them from its arms and sides."

"'Extrudes'?" Lee said.

Han chimed in: "College."

Not this shit again, Davis thought. He rolled his eyes to the sky, dark blue studded by early stars. Although the sun's last light had drained from the air, his stomach clenched. He dropped his gaze to the fire.

The Lieutenant spoke. "He means the thing extends them out of its body."

"Oh," Lee said. "Sounds like it turns into a bat to me."

"Uh-huh," Han said.

"Whatever," Davis said. "It doesn't—"

Lee extended his ring finger and spoke over him. "It sleeps in a coffin."

"Not a coffin—"

"I know, a flying coffin."

"It isn't—it's in low-Earth orbit, like a satellite."

"What was it you said it looked like?" the Lieutenant asked. "A cocoon?"

"A chrysalis," Davis said.

"Same thing," the Lieutenant said.

"More or less," Davis said, unwilling to insist on the distinction because, even a year and three-quarters removed from Iraq, the Lieutenant was still the Lieutenant and you did not argue the small shit with him.

"Coffin, cocoon, chrysalis," Lee said, "it has to be in it before sunset or it's in trouble."

"Wait," Han said. "Sunset."

"Yes," Davis began.

"The principle's the same," the Lieutenant said. "There's a place it has to be and a time it has to be there by."

"Thank you, sir," Lee said. He raised his pinky. "And, it drinks blood."

"Yeah," Davis said, "it does."

"Lots," Han said.

"Yeah," the Lieutenant said.

For a moment, the only sounds were the fire popping and, somewhere out in the woods, an owl prolonging its question. Davis thought of Fallujah.

"Okay," Lee said, "how do we kill it?"

II

2004

There had been rumors, stories, legends of the things you might see in combat. Talk to any of the older guys, the ones who'd done tours in Vietnam, and you heard about a jungle in which you might meet the ghosts of Chinese invaders from five centuries before; or serve beside a grunt whose heart had been shot out a week earlier but who wouldn't die; or find yourself stalked by what you thought was a tiger but had a tail like a snake and a woman's voice. The guys who'd been part of the first war in Iraq—"The good one," a sailor Davis knew called it—told their own tales about the desert, about coming across a raised tomb, its black stone worn free of markings, and listening to someone laughing inside it all the time it took you to walk around it; about the dark shapes you might see stalking through a sandstorm, their arms and legs a child's stick-figures; about the sergeant who swore his reflection had been killed so that, when he looked in a mirror now, a corpse stared back at him. Even the soldiers who'd returned from Afghanistan talked about vast forms they'd seen hunched at the crests of mountains; the street in Kabul that usually ended in a blank wall, except when it didn't; the pale shapes you might glimpse darting into the mouth of the cave you were about to search. A lot of what you heard was bullshit, of course, the plot of a familiar movie or TV show adapted to new location and cast of characters, and a lot of it started off sounding as if it were headed somewhere interesting then ran out of gas halfway through.

But there were some stories about which, even if he couldn't quite credit their having happened, some quality in the teller's voice, or phrasing, caused him to suspend judgment.

During the course of his Associate's Degree, Davis had taken a number of courses in psychology—preparation for a possible career as a psychologist—and in one of these, he had learned that, after several hours of uninterrupted combat (he couldn't remember how many, had never been any good with numbers), you would hallucinate. You couldn't help it; it was your brain's response to continuous unbearable stress. He supposed that at least some of the stories he'd listened to in barracks and bars might owe themselves to such cause, although he was unwilling to categorize them all as symptoms. This was not due to any overriding belief in either organized religion or disorganized superstition; it derived more from principle, specifically, a conclusion that an open mind was the best way to meet what continually impressed him as an enormous world packed full of many things.

By Fallujah, Davis had had no experiences of the strange, the bizarre, no stories to compare with those he'd accumulated over the course of basic and his deployment. He hadn't been thinking about that much as they took up their positions south of the city; all of his available attention had been directed at the coming engagement. Davis had walked patrol, had felt the crawl of the skin at the back of your neck as you made your way down streets crowded with men and women who'd been happy enough to see Saddam pulled down from his pedestal but had long since lost their patience with those who'd operated the crane. He'd ridden in convoys, his head light, his heart throbbing at the base of his throat as they passed potential danger after potential danger, a metal can on the right shoulder, what might be a shell on the left, and while they'd done their best to reinforce their Hummers with whatever junk they could scavenge, Davis was acutely aware that it wasn't enough, a consequence of galloping across the Kuwaiti desert with The Army You Had. Davis had stood checkpoint, his mouth dry as he sighted his M-16 on an approaching car that appeared full of women in black burkas who weren't responding to the signs to slow down, and he'd wondered if they were suicide bombers, or just afraid, and how much closer he could allow them before squeezing the trigger. However much danger he'd imagined himself in, inevitably, he'd arrived after the sniper had opened fire and fled, or passed the exact spot an IED would erupt two hours later, or been on the verge of aiming for the car's engine when it screeched to a halt. It wasn't that Davis hadn't discharged his weapon; he'd served support for several nighttime raids on suspected insurgent strongholds, and he'd sent his own bullets in pursuit of the tracers that scored the darkness. But support wasn't the same thing as kicking in doors, trying to kill the guy down the hall who was trying to kill you. It was not the same as being part of the Anvil.

That was how the Lieutenant had described their role. "Our friends in the United States Marine Corps are going to play the Hammer," he had said the day before. "They will sweep into Fallujah from east and west and they will drive what hostiles they do not kill outright south, where we will be waiting to act as the Anvil. The poet Goëthe said that you must be either hammer or anvil. We will be both, and we are going to crush the hostiles between us."

After the Lieutenant's presentation, Han had said, "Great—so the jarheads have all the fun," with what Davis judged a passable imitation of regret, a false sentiment fairly widely held. Davis had been sure, however, the certainty a ball of lead weighting his gut, that this time was going to be different. Part of it was that the Lieutenant had known one of the contractors who'd been killed, incinerated, and strung up at the Saddam Bridge last April. Davis wasn't clear exactly how the men had been acquainted, or how well, but the Lieutenant had made no secret of his displeasure at not being part of the first effort to (re)take the city in the weeks following the men's deaths. He had been—you couldn't say happy, exactly, at the failure of that campaign—but he was eager for what was shaping up to be a larger-scale operation. Though seven months gone, the deaths and dishonorings of his acquaintances had left the Lieutenant an appetite for this mission. Enough to cause him to disobey his orders and charge into Fallujah's southern section? Davis didn't think so, but there was a reason the man still held the rank of Lieutenant when his classmates and colleagues were well into their Captaincies.

The other reason for Davis's conviction that, this time, something was on its way to him was a simple matter of odds. It wasn't possible—it was not possible that you could rack up this much good luck and not have a shitload of the bad bearing down on you like a SCUD on an anthill. A former altar boy, he was surprised at the variety of prayers he remembered—not just the Our Father and the Hail Mary, but the Apostles' Creed, the Memorare, and the Hail, Holy Queen. As he disembarked the Bradley and ran for the shelter of a desert-colored house, the sky an enormous, pale blue dome above him, Davis mumbled his way through his prayers with a fervency that would have pleased his mother and father no end. But even as his lips shaped the words, he had the strong sense that this was out of God's hands, under the control of one of those medieval demi-goddesses, Dame Fortune or something.

Later, recovering first in Germany, then at Walter Reed, Davis had thought that walking patrol, riding convoy, standing checkpoint, he must have been saved from something truly awful each and every time, for the balance to be this steep.

III

10:01PM

"I take it stakes are out," the Lieutenant said.

"Sir," Lee said, "I unloaded half a clip easy into that sonovabitch, and I was as close to him as I am to you."

"Closer," Han said.

"The point is, he took a half-step backwards—maybe—before he tore my weapon out of my hands and fractured my skull with it."

"That's what I'm saying," the Lieutenant said. "I figure it has to be . . . what? Did you get your hands on some kind of major ordnance, Davis? An rpg? A Stinger? I'll love you like a son—hell, I'll adopt you as my own if you tell me you have a case of Stingers concealed under a bush somewhere. Those'll give the fucker a welcome he won't soon forget."

"Fucking-A," Han said.

"Nah," Lee said. "A crate of Willy Pete oughta just about do it. Serve his ass crispy-fried!"

Davis shook his head. "No Stingers and no white phosphorous. Fire isn't going to do us any good."

"How come?" Lee said.

"Yeah," Han said.

"If I'm right about this thing spending its nights in low-Earth orbit—in its 'coffin'—and then leaving that refuge to descend into the atmosphere so it can hunt, its skin has to be able to withstand considerable extremes of temperature."

"Like the Space Shuttle," the Lieutenant said. "Huh. For all intents and purposes, it's fireproof."

"Oh," Lee said.

"Given that it spends some of its time in the upper atmosphere, as well as actual outer space, I'm guessing substantial cold wouldn't have much effect, either."

"We can't shoot it, can't burn it, can't freeze it," Lee said. "Tell me why we're here, again?" He waved at the trees fringing the clearing. "Aside from the scenery, of course."

"Pipe down," the Lieutenant said.

"When we shot at it," Davis said, "I'm betting half our fire missed it." He held up his hand to the beginning of Lee's protest. "That's no reflection on anyone. The thing was fast, cheetah-taking-down-a-gazelle fast. Not to mention, it's so goddamned *thin* . . . Anyway, of the shots that connected with it, most of them were flesh wounds." He raised his hand to Lee, again. "Those who connected with it," a nod to Lee, "were so close their fire passed clean through it."

"Which is what I was saying," Lee said.

"There's a lot of crazy shit floating around space," Davis said, "little particles of sand, rock, ice, metal. Some of them get to moving pretty fast. If you're doing repairs to the Space Station and one of those things hits you, it could ruin your whole day. Anything that's going to survive up there is going to have to be able to deal with something that can punch a hole right through you."

"It's got a self-sealing mechanism," the Lieutenant said. "When Lee fired into it, its body treated the bullets as so many dust-particles."

"And closed right up," Davis said. "Like some kind of super-clotting-factor. Maybe that's what it uses the blood for."

"You're saying it's bulletproof, too?" Lee said.

"Shit," Han said.

"Not—more like, bullet-resistant."

"Think of it as a mutant healing ability," the Lieutenant said, "like Wolverine."

"Oh," Han said.

"Those claws it has," Lee said, "I guess Wolverine isn't too far off the mark."

"No," Han said. "Sabertooth."

"What?" Lee said. "The fuck're you going on about?"

"Sabertooth's claws." Han held up his right hand, fingers splayed. He curled his fingers into a fist. "Wolverine's claws."

"Man has a point," the Lieutenant said.

"Whatever," Lee said.

"Here's the thing," Davis said, "it's bullet-resistant, but it can still feel pain. Think about how it reacted when Lee shot it. It didn't tear his throat open: it took the instrument that had hurt it and used that to hurt Lee. You see what I'm saying?"

"Kind of," Lee said.

"Think about what drove it off," Davis said. "Remember?"

"Of course," the Lieutenant said. He nodded at Han. "It was Han sticking his bayonet in the thing's side."

For which it crushed his skull, Davis could not stop himself from thinking. He added his nod to the Lieutenant's. "Yes he did."

"How is that different from shooting it?" Lee said.

"Your bullets went in one side and out the other," Davis said. "Han's bayonet stuck there. The thing's healing ability could deal with an in-and-out wound no problem; something like this, though: I think it panicked."

"Panicked?" Lee said. "It didn't look like it was panicking to me."

"Then why did it take off right away?" Davis said.

"It was full; it heard more backup on the way; it had an appointment in fucking Samara. How the fuck should I know?"

"What's your theory?" the Lieutenant said.

"The type of injury Han gave it would be very bad if you're in a vacuum. Something opening you up like that and leaving you exposed . . . "

"You could vent some or even all of the blood you worked so hard to collect," the Lieutenant said. "You'd want to get out of a situation like that with all due haste."

"Even if your healing factor could seal the wound's perimeter," Davis said, "there's still this piece of steel in you that has to come out and, when it does, will reopen the injury."

"Costing you still more blood," the Lieutenant said.

"Most of the time," Davis said, "I mean, like, nine hundred and ninety-nine thousand, nine hundred and ninety-nine times out of a million, the thing would identify any such threats long before they came that close. You saw its ears, its eyes."

"Black on black," Lee said. "Or, no—black over black, like the corneas had some kind of heavy tint and what was underneath was all pupil."

"Han got lucky," Davis said. "The space we were in really wasn't that big. There was a lot of movement, a lot of noise—"

"Not to mention," Lee said, "all the shooting and screaming."

"The right set of circumstances," the Lieutenant said.

"Saved our asses," Lee said, reaching over to pound Han's shoulder. Han ducked to the side, grinning his hideous smile.

"If I can cut to the chase," the Lieutenant said. "You're saying we need to find a way to open up this fucker and keep him open so that we can wreak merry havoc on his insides."

Davis nodded. "To cut to the chase, yes, exactly."

"How do you propose we do this?"

"With these." Davis reached into the duffel bag to his left and withdrew what appeared to be a three foot piece of white wood, tapered to a point sharp enough to prick your eye looking at it. He passed the first one to the Lieutenant, brought out one for Lee and one for Han.

"A baseball bat?" Lee said, gripping near the point and swinging his like a Louisville Slugger. "We gonna club it to death?"

Neither Davis nor the Lieutenant replied; they were busy watching Han, who'd located the grips at the other end of his and was jabbing it, first underhand, then overhand.

"The people you meet working at Home Depot," Davis said. "They're made out of an industrial resin, inch-for-inch, stronger than steel. Each one has a high-explosive core."

"Whoa," Lee said, setting his on the ground with exaggerated care.

"The detonators are linked to this," Davis said, fishing a cell phone from his shirt pocket. "Turn it on." Pointing to the Lieutenant, Han, Lee, and himself, he counted, "One-two-three-four. Send. That's it."

"I was mistaken," the Lieutenant said. "It appears we will be using stakes, after all."

IV

2004

At Landstuhl, briefly, and then at Walter Reed, at length, an impressive array of doctors, nurses, chaplains, and other soldiers whose job it was encouraged Davis to discuss Fallujah. He was reasonably sure that, while under the influence of one of the meds that kept his body at a safe distance, he had let slip some detail, maybe more. How else to account for the change in his nurse's demeanor? Likely, she judged he was a psych case, a diagnosis he half-inclined to accept. Even when the Lieutenant forced his way into Davis's room, banging around in the wheelchair he claimed he could use well enough, Goddamnit, Davis was reluctant to speak of anything except the conditions of the other survivors. Of whom he had been shocked—truly shocked, profoundly shocked, almost more so than by what had torn through them—to learn there were only two, Lee and Han, Manfred bled out on the way to be evac'd, everyone else long gone by the time the reinforcements had stormed into the courtyard. According to the Lieutenant, Han was clinging to life by a thread so fine you couldn't see it. He'd lost his helmet in the fracas, and the bones in his skull had been crushed like an eggshell. Davis, who had witnessed that crushing, nodded. Lee had suffered his own head trauma, although, compared to Han's, it wasn't anything a steel plate couldn't fix. The real problem with Lee was that, if he wasn't flooded with some heavy-duty happy pills, he went fetal, thumb in his mouth, the works.

"What about you?" the Lieutenant said, indicating the armature of casts, wires, weights, and counterweights that kept Davis suspended like some overly-ambitious kid's science project.

"Believe it or not, sir," Davis said, "it really is worse than it looks. My pack and my helmet absorbed most of the impact. Still left me with a broken back, scapula, and ribs—but my spinal cord's basically intact. Not that it doesn't hurt like a motherfucker, sir. Yourself?"

"The taxpayers of the United States of America have seen fit to gift me with a new right leg, since I so carelessly misplaced the original." He knocked on his pajama leg, which gave a hollow, plastic sound.

"Sir, I am so sorry—"

"Shut it," the Lieutenant said. "It's a paper cut." Using his left foot, he rolled himself back to the door, which he eased almost shut. Through the gap, he surveilled the hallway outside long enough for Davis to start counting, *One Mississippi, Two Mississippi*, then wheeled himself to Davis's head. He leaned close and said, "Davis."

"Sir?"

"Let's leave out the rank thing for five minutes, okay? Can we do that?"

"Sir—yes, yes we can."

"Because ever since the docs have reduced my drugs to the point I could string one sentence after another, I've been having these memories—dreams—I don't know what the fuck to call them. Nightmares. And I can't decide if I'm losing it, or if this is why Lee needs a palm full of M&Ms to leave his bed. So I need you to talk to me straight, no bullshit, no telling the officer what you think he wants to hear. I would genuinely fucking appreciate it if we could do that."

Davis looked away when he saw the Lieutenant's eyes shimmering. Keeping his own focused on the ceiling, he said, "It came out of the sky. That's where it went, after Han stuck it, so I figure it must have dropped out of there, too. It explains why, one minute we're across the courtyard from a bunch of hostiles, the next, that thing's standing between us."

"Did you see it take off?"

"I did. After it had stepped on Han's head, it spread its arms—it kind of staggered back from Han, caught itself, then opened its arms and these huge wings snapped open. They were like a bat's, skin stretched over bone—they appeared so fast I'm not sure, but they shot out of its body. It tilted its head, jumped up, high, ten feet easy, flapped the wings, which raised it another ten feet, and turned—the way a swimmer turns in the water, you know? Another flap, two, and it was gone."

"Huh."

Davis glanced at the Lieutenant, whose face was smooth, his eyes gazing across some interior distance. He said, "Do you—"

"Back up," the Lieutenant said. "The ten of us are in the courtyard. How big's the place?"

"I'm not very good with—"

"At a guess."

"Twenty-five feet wide, maybe fifty long. With all of those jars in the way—what were they?"

"Planters."

"Three-foot-tall stone planters?"

"For trees. They were full of dirt. Haven't you ever seen those little decorative trees inside office buildings?"

"Oh. All right. What I was going to say was, With the row of planters at either end, the place might have been larger."

"Noted. How tall were the walls?"

"Taller than any of us—eight feet, easy. They were thick, too, a foot and a half, two feet." Davis said, "It really was a good spot to attack from. Open fire from the walls, then drop behind them when they can't maintain that position. The tall buildings are behind it, and we don't hold any of them, so they don't have to worry about anyone firing down on them. I'm guessing they figured we didn't know where we were well enough to call in any artillery on them. No, if we want them, we have to run a hundred feet of open space to a doorway that's an easy trap. They've got the planters for cover near and far, not to mention the doorway in the opposite wall as an exit."

"Agreed."

"To be honest, now that we're talking about it, I can't imagine how we made it into the place without losing anyone. By all rights, they should have tagged a couple of us crossing from our position to theirs. And that doorway: they should have massacred us."

"We were lucky. When we returned fire, they must have panicked. Could be they didn't see all of us behind the wall, thought they were ambushing three or four targets, instead of ten. Charging them may have given the impression there were even more of us. It took them until they were across the courtyard to get a grip and regroup."

"By which time we were at the doorway."

"So it was Lee all the way on the left—"

"With Han beside him."

"Right, and Bay and Remsnyder. Then you and Petit—"

"No—it was me and Lugo, then Petit, then you."

"Yes, yes. Manfred was to my right, and Weymouth was all the way on the other end."

"I'm not sure how many—"

"Six. There may have been a seventh in the opposite doorway, but he wasn't around very long. Either he went down, or he decided to season his valor with a little discretion."

"It was loud—everybody firing in a confined space. I had powder all over me from their shots hitting the wall behind us. I want to say we traded bullets for about five minutes, but it was what? Half that?"

"Less. A minute."

"And . . . "

"Our guest arrived."

"At first—at first it was like, I couldn't figure out what I was seeing. I'm trying to line up the guy who's directly across from me—all I need is for him to stick up his head again—and all of a sudden, there's a shadow in the way. That was my first thought: *It's a shadow.* Only, who's casting it? And why is it hanging in the air like that? And why is it fucking eight feet tall?"

"None of us understood what was in front of us. I thought it was a woman in a burka, someone I'd missed when we'd entered the courtyard. As you say, though, you don't meet a lot of eight-foot-tall women, in or out of Iraq."

"Next thing . . . no, that isn't what happened."

"What?"

"I was going to say the thing—the Shadow—was in among the hostiles, which is true, it went for them first, but before it did, there was a moment . . . "

"You saw something—something else."

"Yeah," Davis said. "This pain shot straight through my head. We're talking instant migraine, so intense I practically puked. That wasn't all: this chill . . . I was freezing, colder than I've ever been, like you read about in Polar expeditions. I couldn't—the courtyard—"

"What?"

"The courtyard wasn't—I was somewhere high, like, a hundred miles high, so far up I could see the curve of the Earth below me. Clouds, continents, the ocean: what you see in the pictures they take from orbit. Stars, space, all around me. Directly, overhead, a little farther away than you are from me, there was this thing. I don't know what the fuck it was. Big—long, maybe long as a house. It bulged in the middle, tapered at the ends. The surface was dark, shiny—does that make any sense? The thing was covered in—it looked like some kind of lacquer. Maybe it was made out of the lacquer.

"Anyway, one moment, my head's about to crack open, my teeth are chattering and my skin's blue, and I'm in outer space. The next, all of that's gone, I'm back in the courtyard, and the Shadow—the thing is ripping the hostiles to shreds."

"And then," the Lieutenant said, "it was our turn."

V

November 11, 2004, 11:13 AM
In the six hundred twenty-five days since that afternoon in the hospital, how many times had Davis recited the order of events in the courtyard, whether with the Lieutenant, or with Lee once his meds had been stabilized, or with Han once he'd regained the ability to speak (though not especially well)? At some point a couple of months on, he'd realized he'd been keeping count— *That's the thirty-eighth time; that's the forty-third*—and then, a couple of months after that, he'd realized that he'd lost track. The narrative of their encounter with what Davis continued to think of as the Shadow had become daily catechism, to be reviewed morning, noon, and night, and whenever else he happened to think of it.

None of them had even tried to run, which there were times Davis judged a sign of courage, and times he deemed an index of their collective shock at the speed and ferocity of the thing's assault on the insurgents. Heads, arms, legs were separated from bodies as if by a pair of razored blades, and wherever a wound opened red, there was the thing's splintered maw, drinking the blood like a kid stooping to a water fountain. The smells of blood, piss, and shit mixed with those of gunpowder and hot metal. While Davis knew they had been the next course on the Shadow's menu, he found it difficult not to wonder how the situation might have played out had Lee—followed immediately by Lugo and Weymouth—not opened up on the thing. Of course, the instant that narrow head with its spotlight eyes, its scarlet mouth, turned in their direction, everyone else's guns erupted, and the scene concluded the way it had to. But if Lee had been able to restrain himself . . .

Lugo was first to die. In a single leap, the Shadow closed the distance between them and drove one of its sharpened hands into his throat, venting his carotid over Davis, whom it caught with its other hand and flung into one of the side walls with such force his spine and ribs lit up like the Fourth of July. As he was dropping onto his back, turtling on his pack, the thing was raising its head from Lugo's neck, spearing Petit through his armor and hauling him towards it. Remsnyder ran at it from behind; the thing's hand lashed out and struck his head from his shoulders. It was done with Petit in time to catch Remsnyder's body on the fall and jam its mouth onto the bubbling neck. It had shoved Petit's body against the Lieutenant, whose feet tangled with Petit's and sent the pair of them down. This put him out of the way of Manfred and Weymouth, who screamed for everyone to get clear and fired full automatic. Impossible as it seemed, they missed, and for their troubles, the Shadow lopped Manfred's right arm off at the elbow and opened

Weymouth like a Christmas present. From the ground, the Lieutenant shot at it; the thing sliced through his weapon and the leg underneath it. Now Bay, Han, and Lee tried full auto, which brought the thing to Bay, whose face it bit off. It swatted Han to the ground, but Lee somehow ducked the swipe it aimed at him and tagged it at close range. The Shadow threw Bay's body across the courtyard, yanked Lee's rifle from his hands, and swung it against his head like a ballplayer aiming for the stands. He crumpled, the thing reaching out for him, and Han leapt up, his bayonet ridiculously small in his hand. He drove it into the thing's side—what would be the floating ribs on a man—to the hilt. The Shadow, whose only sound thus far had been its feeding, opened its jaws and shrieked, a high scream more like the cry of a bat, or a hawk, than anything human. It caught Han with an elbow to the temple that tumbled him to the dirt, set its foot on his head, and pressed down. Han's scream competed with the sound of his skull cracking in multiple spots. Davis was certain the thing meant to grind Han's head to paste, but it staggered off him, one claw reaching for the weapon buried in its skin. Blood so dark it was purple was oozing around the hilt. The Shadow spread its arms, its wings cracked open, and it was gone, fled into the blue sky that Davis would spend the next quarter-hour staring at, as the Lieutenant called for help and tried to tourniquet first his leg then Manfred's arm.

Davis had stared at the sky before—who has not?—but, helpless on his back, his spine a length of molten steel, his ears full of Manfred whimpering that he was gonna die, oh sweet Jesus, he was gonna fucking die, the Lieutenant talking over him, insisting no he wasn't, he was gonna be fine, it was just a little paper cut, the washed blue bowl overhead seemed less sheltering canopy and more endless depth, a gullet over which he had the sickening sensation of dangling. As Manfred's cries diminished and the Lieutenant told—ordered him to stay with him, Davis flailed his arms at the ground to either side of him in an effort to grip onto an anchor, something that would keep him from hurtling into that blue abyss.

The weeks and months to come would bring the inevitable nightmares, the majority of them the Shadow's attack replayed at half-, full-, or double-speed, with a gruesome fate for himself edited in. Sometimes repeating the events on his own or with a combination of the others led to a less-disturbed sleep; sometimes it did not. There was one dream, though, that no amount of discussion could help, and that was the one in which Davis was plummeting through the sky, lost in an appetite that would never be sated.

VI

12:26 AM
Once he was done setting the next log on the fire, Davis leaned back and said, "I figure it's some kind of stun effect."

"How so?" Lee said.

"The thing lands in between two groups of heavily-armed men: it has to do something to even the odds. It hits us with a psychic blast, shorts out our brains so that we're easier prey."

"Didn't seem to do much to Lee," the Lieutenant said.

"No brain!" Han shouted.

"Ha-fucking-ha," Lee said.

"Maybe there were too many of us," Davis said. "Maybe it miscalculated. Maybe Lee's a mutant and this is his special gift. Had the thing zigged instead of zagged, gone for us instead of the insurgents, I don't think any of us would be sitting here, regardless of our super powers."

"Speak for yourself," Lee said.

"For a theory," the Lieutenant said, "it's not bad. But there's a sizable hole in it. You," he pointed at Davis, "saw the thing's coffin or whatever. Lee," a nod to him, "was privy to a bat's-eye view of the thing's approach to one of its hunts in—did we ever decide if it was Laos or Cambodia?"

"No sir," Lee said. "It looked an awful lot like some of the scenery from the first *Tomb Raider* movie, which I'm pretty sure was filmed in Cambodia, but I'm not positive."

"You didn't see Angelina Jolie running around?" Davis said.

"If only," Lee said.

"So with Lee, we're in Southeast Asia," the Lieutenant said, "with or without the lovely Ms. Jolie. From what Han's been able to tell me, he was standing on the moon or someplace very similar to it. I don't believe he could see the Earth from where he was, but I'm not enough of an astronomer to know what that means.

"As for myself, I had a confused glimpse of the thing tearing its way through the interior of an airplane—what I'm reasonably certain was a B-17, probably during the Second World War.

"You see what I mean? None of us witnessed the same scene—none of us witnessed the same time, which you would imagine we would have if we'd been subject to a deliberate attack. You would expect the thing to hit us all with the same image. It's more efficient."

"Maybe that isn't how this works," Davis said. "Suppose what it does is more like a cluster bomb, a host of memories it packs around a psychic charge? If each of us thinks he's someplace different from everybody else, doesn't that maximize confusion, create optimal conditions for an attack?"

The Lieutenant frowned. Lee said, "What's your theory, sir?"

"I don't have one," the Lieutenant said. "Regardless of its intent, the thing got in our heads."

"And stayed there," Lee said.

"Stuck," Han said, tapping his right temple.

"Yes," the Lieutenant said. "Whatever their precise function, our exposure to the thing's memories appears to have established a link between us and it."

Davis said, "Which is what's going to bring it right here."

VII

2004-2005

When Davis was on board the plane to Germany, he could permit himself to
hope that he was, however temporarily, out of immediate danger of death—not
from the injury to his back, which, though painful in the extreme, he had
known from the start would not claim his life, but from the reappearance of
the Shadow. Until their backup arrived in a hurry of bootsteps and rattle of
armor, he had been waiting for the sky to vomit the figure it had swallowed
minutes (moments?) prior, for his blood to leap into the thing's jagged mouth.
The mature course of action had seemed to prepare for his imminent end,
which he had attempted, only to find the effort beyond him. Whenever word
of some acquaintance's failure to return from the latest patrol had prompted
Davis to picture his final seconds, he had envisioned his face growing calm,
even peaceful, his lips shaping the syllables of a heartfelt Act of Contrition.
However, between the channel of fire that had replaced his spine and the
vertiginous sensation that he might plunge into the sky—not to mention, the
Lieutenant's continuing monologue to Manfred, the pungence of gunpowder
mixed with the bloody reek of meat, the low moans coming from Han—Davis
was unable to concentrate. Rather than any gesture of reconciliation towards
the God with Whom he had not been concerned since his discovery of what lay
beneath his prom date's panties junior year, Davis's attention had been snarled
in the sound of the Shadow's claws puncturing Lugo's neck, the fountain of
Weymouth's blood over its arm and chest, the wet slap of his entrails hitting
the ground, the stretch of the thing's mouth as it released its scream. Despite
his back, which had drawn his vocal chords taut, once the reinforcements had
arrived and a red-faced medic peppered him with questions while performing a
quick assessment of him, Davis had strained to warn them of their danger. But
all his insistence that they had to watch the sky had brought him was a sedative
that pulled him into a vague, gray place.

   Nor had his time at the Battalion Aid Station, then some larger facility
(Camp Victory? with whatever they gave him, most of the details a variety
of medical staff poured into his ears sluiced right back out again) caused
him to feel any more secure. As the gray place loosened its hold on him and
he stared up at the canvas roof of the BAS, Davis had wanted to demand
what the fuck everyone was thinking. Didn't they know the Shadow could
slice through this material like it was cling film? Didn't they understand
it was waiting to descend on them right now, this very fucking minute?
It would rip them to shreds; it would drink their fucking *blood*. At the
presence of a corpsman beside him, he'd realized he was shouting—or
as close to shouting as his voice could manage—but he'd been unable to
restrain himself, which had led to calming banalities and more vague
grayness. He had returned to something like consciousness inside a larger
space in the CSH, where the sight of the nearest wall trembling from the

wind had drawn his stomach tight and sped a fresh round of protests from his mouth. When he struggled up out of the shot that outburst occasioned, Davis had found himself in a dim cavern whose curving sides rang with the din of enormous engines. His momentary impression that he was dead and this some unexpected, bare-bones afterlife was replaced by the recognition that he was on a transport out of Iraq—who knew to where? It didn't matter. A flood of tears had rolled from his eyes as the dread coiling his guts had, if not fled, at least calmed.

At Landstuhl, in a solidly-built hospital with drab but sturdy walls and a firm ceiling, Davis was calmer. (As long as he did not dwell on the way the Shadow's claws had split Petit's armor, sliced the Lieutenant's rifle in two.) That, and the surgeries required to relieve the pressure on his spine left him, to quote a song he'd never liked that much, comfortably numb.

Not until he was back in America, though, reclining in the late-Medieval luxury of Walter Reed, the width of an ocean and a continent separating him from Fallujah, did Davis feel anything like a sense of security. Even after his first round of conversations with the Lieutenant had offered him the dubious reassurance that, if he were delusional, he was in good company, a cold comfort made chillier still by Lee, his meds approaching the proper levels, corroborating their narrative, Davis found it less difficult than he would have anticipated to persuade himself that Remsnyder's head leaping from his body on a jet of blood was seven thousand miles away. And while his pulse still quickened whenever his vision strayed to the rectangle of sky framed by the room's lone window, he could almost pretend that this was a different sky. After all, hadn't that been the subtext of all the stories he'd heard from other vets about earlier wars? Weird shit happened, yes—sometimes, very bad weird shit happened—but it took place over there, In Country, in another place where things didn't work the same way they did in the good old U.S. of A. If you could keep that in mind, Davis judged, front-and-center in your consciousness, you might be able to live with the impossible.

Everything went—you couldn't call it swimmingly—it went, anyway, until Davis began his rehabilitation, which consisted of: a) learning how to walk again and b) strength training for his newly-(re)educated legs. Of course, he had been in pain after the initial injury—though shock and fear had kept the hurt from overwhelming him—and his nerves had flared throughout his hospital stay—especially following his surgery—though a pharmacopeia had damped those sensations down to smoldering. Rehab was different. Rehab was a long, low-ceilinged room that smelled of sweat and industrial antiseptic, one end of which grazed a small herd of the kind of exercise machines you saw faded celebrities hawking on late-night TV, the center of which held a trio of parallel bars set too low, and the near end of which was home to a series of overlapping blue mats whose extensive cracks suggested an aerial view of a river basin. Rehab was slow stretches on the mats, then gripping onto the parallel bars while you tried to coax your right leg into moving forward; once you could lurch along the bars and back, rehab was time on one of the exercise machines, flat on your back, your legs bent, your feet pressed against a pair of pedals connected to a series of weights you raised by extending your legs. Rehab was about confronting pain, inviting it in, asking it to sit down and have a beer so the two of you could talk for a while. Rehab was not leaning on the heavy-duty opiates and their synthetic friends; it was remaining content with the over-the-counter options and ice-packs. It was the promise of a walk outside—an enticement that made Davis's palms sweat and his mouth go dry.

When the surgeon had told Davis the operation had been a success, there appeared to be no permanent damage to his spinal cord, Davis had imagined himself, freed of his cast and its coterie of pulleys and counterweights, sitting up on his own and strolling out the front door. Actually, he'd been running in his fantasy. The reality, he quickly discovered, was that merely raising himself to a sitting position was an enterprise far more involved than he ever had appreciated, as was a range of action so automatic it existed below his being able to admit he'd never given it much thought. He supposed the therapists here were as good as you were going to find, but that didn't make the routines they subjected him to—he subjected himself to—any easier or less painful.

It was during one of these sessions, his back feeling as if it had been scraped raw and the exposed tissue generously salted, that Davis had his first inkling that Fallujah was not a self-contained narrative, a short, grisly tale; rather, it was the opening chapter of a novel, one of those eight-hundred-page, Stephen-King specials. Lucy, Davis's primary therapist, had him on what he had christened the Rack. His target was twenty leg presses; in a fit of bravado, he had promised her thirty. No doubt, Davis had known instances of greater pain, but those had been spikes on the graph. Though set at a lower level, this hurt was constant, and while Lucy had assured him that he would become used to it, so far, he hadn't. The pain glared like the sun flaring off a window; it flooded his mind white, made focusing on anything else impossible. That Lucy was encouraging him, he knew from the tone of her voice, but he could not distinguish individual words. Already, his vision was blurred from the sweat streaming out of him, so when the blur fractured, became a kaleidoscope-jumble of color and geometry, he thought little of it, and raised his fingers to clear his eyes.

According to Lucy, Davis removed his hand from his face, paused, then fell off the machine on his right side, trembling and jerking. For what she called his seizure's duration, which she clocked at three minutes fifteen seconds, Davis uttered no sound except for a gulping noise that made his therapist fear he was about to swallow his tongue.

To the Lieutenant, then to Lee and eventually Han, Davis would compare what he saw when the rehab room went far away to a wide-screen movie, one of those panoramic deals that was supposed to impart the sensation of flying over the Rockies, or holding on for dear life as a roller coaster whipped up and down its course. A surplus of detail crowded his vision. He was in the middle of a sandy street bordered by short buildings whose walls appeared to consist of sheets of long, dried grass framed with slender sticks. A dozen, two dozen women and children dressed in pastel robes and turbans ran frantically from one side of the street to the other as men wearing dark brown shirts and pants aimed Kalashnikovs at them. Some of the men were riding brown and white horses; some were stalking the street; some were emerging from alleys between the buildings, several of whose walls were releasing thick smoke. Davis estimated ten men. The sounds—it was as if the soundtrack to this film had been set to record the slightest vibration of air, which it played back at twice the normal level. Screams raked his eardrums. Sandals scraped the ground. Guns cracked; bullets thudded into skin. Horses whickered. Fire snapped. An immense thirst, worse than any he had known, possessed him. His throat was not dry; it was arid, as if it—as if he were composed of dust from which the last eyedropper of moisture had long been squeezed.

One of the men—not the nearest, who was walking the opposite direction from Davis's position, but the next closest, whose horse had shied from the flames sprouting from a grass wall and so turned its rider in Davis's direction—caught sight of Davis, his face contracting in confusion at what he saw. The man, who might have been in his early twenties, started to raise his rifle, and everything sped up, the movie fast-forwarded. There was—his vision wavered, and the man's gun dipped, his eyes widening. Davis was next to him—he had half-scaled the horse and speared the hollow of the man's throat with his right hand, whose fingers, he saw, were twice as long as they had been, tapered to a set of blades. He felt the man's tissue part, the ends of his fingers (talons?) scrape bone. Blood washed over his palm, his wrist, and the sensation jolted him. His talons flicked to the left, and the man's head tipped back like a tree falling away from its base. Blood misted the air, and before he realized what was happening, his mouth was clamped to the wound, full of hot, copper liquid. The taste was rain falling in the desert; in three mighty gulps, he had emptied the corpse and was springing over its fellows, into the midst of the brightly-robed women and children.

The immediate result of Davis's three-minute hallucination was the suspension of his physical therapy and an MRI of his brain. Asked by Lucy what he recalled of the experience, Davis had shaken his head and answered, "Nothing." It was the same response he gave to the new doctor who stopped into his room a week later and, without identifying himself as a psychiatrist, told Davis he was interested in the nightmares that had brought him screaming out of sleep six of the last seven nights. This was a rather substantial change in his nightly routine; taken together with his recent seizure, it seemed like cause for concern. Perhaps Davis could relate what he remembered of his nightmares?

How to tell this doctor that closing his eyes—an act he resisted for as long as could each night—brought him to that yellow-brown street; the lime, saffron, and orange cloth stretching as mothers hauled their children behind them; the dull muzzles of the Kalashnikovs coughing fire? How to describe the sensations that still lived in his skin, his muscles: the tearing of skin for his too-long fingers; the bounce of a heart in his hand the instant before he tore it from its setting; the eggshell crunch of bone between his jaws? Most of all, how to convey to this doctor, this shrink who was either an unskilled actor or not trying very hard, the concentrate of pleasure that was the rush of blood into his mouth, down his throat, the satisfaction of his terrific thirst so momentary it made the thirst that much worse? Although Davis had repeated his earlier disavowal and maintained it in the face of the doctor's extended—and, to be fair, sympathetic—questions until the man left, a week's worth of poor sleep made the wisdom of his decision appear less a foregone conclusion. What he had seen—what he had been part of the other week was too similar to the vision he'd had in the courtyard not to be related; the question was, how? Were Davis to summarize his personal horror ride to the psychiatrist—he would have to tell him about Fallujah first, of course—might the doctor have more success at understanding the connections between his driver's-seat views of the Shadow's activities?

Sure, Davis thought, *right after he's had you fitted for your straightjacket.* The ironic thing was, how often had he argued the benefits of the Army's psychiatric care with Lugo? It had been their running gag. Lugo would return from reading his e-mail with news of some guy stateside who'd lost it, shot his wife, himself, which would prompt Davis to say that it was a shame the guy hadn't gotten help before it came to that. Help, Lugo would say, from who? The Army? Man, you must be joking. The Army don't want nothing to do with no grunt can't keep his shit together. No, no, Davis would say, sure, they still had a ways to go, but the Army was changing. The kinds of combat-induced pathologies it used to pretend didn't exist were much more likely to be treated early and effectively. (If Lee and Han were present, and/or Remsnyder, they'd ooh and aah over Davis's vocabulary.) Oh yeah, Lugo would reply, if they don't discharge your ass right outta here, they'll stick you at some bullshit post where you won't hurt anyone. No, no, Davis would say, that was a rumor. Oh yeah, Lugo would say, like the rumor about the guys who went to the doctor for help with their PTSD and were told they were suffering from a fucking pre-existing condition, so it wasn't the Army's problem? No, no, Davis would say, that was a few bad guys. Oh yeah, Lugo would say.

Before he and the Lieutenant—who had been abducted by a platoon of siblings, their spouses, and their kids for ten days in Florida—discussed the matter, Davis passed his nightly struggles to stay awake wondering if the psychiatric ward was the worst place he might wind up. His only images of such places came from films like *One Flew Over the Cuckoo's Nest*, *Awakenings*, and *K-PAX*, but based on those examples, he could expect to spend his days robed and slippered, possibly medicated, free to read what he wanted except during individual and group therapy sessions. If it wasn't quite the career as a psychologist he'd envisioned, he'd at least be in some kind of proximity to the mental health field. Sure, it would be a scam, but didn't the taxpayers of the U.S. of A. owe him recompense for shipping him to a place where the Shadow could just drop in and shred his life? The windows would be barred or meshed, the doors reinforced—you could almost fool yourself such a location would be safe.

However, with his second episode, it became clear that safe was one of those words that had been bayoneted, its meaning spilled on the floor. Davis had been approved to resume therapy with Lucy, who had been honestly happy to see him again. It was late in the day; what with the complete breakdown in his sleeping patterns, he wasn't in optimal condition for another go-around on the Rack, but after so much time stuck in his head, terrified at what was in there with him, the prospect of a vigorous workout was something he was actually looking forward to. As before, gentle stretching preceded the main event, which Lucy told Davis he didn't have to do but for which he had cavalierly assured her he was, if not completely able, at least ready and willing. With the second push of his feet against the pedals, pain ignited up his back, and his lack of sleep did not aid in his tolerating it. Each subsequent retraction and extension of his legs ratcheted the hurt up one more degree, until he was lying on a bed of fire.

This time.

VIII

2:15 AM

"My vision didn't blur—it cracked, as if my knees levering up and down were an image on a TV screen and something smacked the glass. Everything spiderwebbed and fell away. What replaced it was movement—I was moving up, my arms beating down; there was this feeling that they were bigger, much bigger, that when I swept them down, they were gathering the air and piling it beneath them. I looked below me, and there were bodies— parts of bodies, organs—all over the place. There was less blood than there should have been. Seeing them scattered across the ground—it was like having a bird's- eye view of some kind of bizarre design. Most of them were men, twenties and thirties; although there were two women and a couple-three kids. Almost everybody was wearing jeans and workboots, sweatshirts, baseball caps, except for a pair of guys dressed in khaki and I'm pretty sure cowboy hats."

"What the fuck?" Lee said.

"Cowboys," Han said.

"Texas Border Patrol," the Lieutenant said.

"So those other people were like, illegal immigrants?" Lee said.

The Lieutenant nodded.

Davis said, "I've never been to Texas, but the spot looked like what you see on TV. Sandy, full of rocks, some scrub brush and short trees. There was a muddy stream—you might call it a river, I guess, if that was what you were used to—in the near distance, and a group of hills further off. The sun was perched on top of the hills, setting, and that red ball made me beat me arms again and again, shrinking the scene below, raising me higher into the sky. There was—I felt full—more than full, gorged, but thirsty, still thirsty, that same, overpowering dryness I'd experienced the previous . . . time. The thirst was so strong, so compelling, I was a little surprised when I kept climbing. My flight was connected to the sun balanced on that hill, a kind of—not panic, exactly: it was more like urgency. I was moving, now. The air was thinning; my arms stretched even larger to scoop enough of it to keep me moving. The temperature had dropped—was dropping, plunging down. Something happened—my mouth was already closed, but it was as if it sealed somehow. Same thing with my nostrils; I mean, they closed themselves off. My eyes misted, then cleared. I pumped my arms harder than I had before. This time, I didn't lose speed; I kept moving forward.

"Ahead, I saw the thing I'd seen in the courtyard—a huge shape, big as a house. Pointed at the ends, fat in the middle. Dark—maybe dark purple, maybe not—and shiny. The moment it came into view, this surge of . . . I don't know what to call it. Honestly, I want to say it was a cross between the way you feel when you put your bag down on your old bed and, 'Mommy,' that little kid feeling, except that neither of those is completely right. My arms were condensing, growing substantial. I was heading towards the middle. As I drew closer, its surface rippled, like water moving out from where a stone strikes it. At the center of the ripple, a kind of pucker opened into the thing. That was my destination."

"And?" Lee said.

"Lucy emptied her Gatorade on me and brought me out of it."

"You have got to be fucking kidding me," Lee said.

"Afraid not," Davis said.

"How long was this one?" the Lieutenant asked.

"Almost five minutes."

"It took her that long to toss her Gatorade on you?" Lee said.

"There was some kind of commotion at the same time, a couple of guys got into a fight. She tried to find help; when she couldn't, she doused me."

Lee shook his head.

"And you have since confirmed the existence of this object," the Lieutenant said.

"Yes, sir," Davis said. "It took some doing. The thing's damned near impossible to see, and while no one would come out and say so to me, I'm pretty sure it doesn't show up on radar, either. The couple of pictures we got were more dumb luck than anything."

"'We'?" Lee said.

"I . . . "

The Lieutenant said, "I put Mr. Davis in touch with a friend of mine in Intelligence."

"Oh," Lee said. "Wait—shit: you mean the CIA's involved?"

"Relax," Davis said.

"Because I swear to God," Lee said, "those stupid motherfuckers would fuck up getting toast out of the toaster and blame us for their burned fingers."

"It's under control," the Lieutenant said. "This is our party. No one else has been invited."

"Doesn't mean they won't show up," Lee said. "Stupid assholes with their fucking sunglasses and their, 'We're so scary.' Oooh." He turned his head and spat.

Davis stole a look at the sky. Stars were winking out and in as something passed in front of them. His heart jumped, his hand was on his stake before he identified the shape as some kind of bird. The Lieutenant had noticed his movement; his hand over his stake, he said, "Everything all right, Davis?"

"Fine," Davis said. "Bird."

"What?" Lee said.

"Bird," Han said.

"Oh," Lee said. "So. I have a question."

"Go ahead," the Lieutenant said.

"The whole daylight thing," Lee said, "the having to be back in its coffin before sunset—what's up with that?"

"It does seem . . . atypical, doesn't it?" the Lieutenant said. "Vampires are traditionally creatures of the night."

"Actually, sir," Lee said, "that's not exactly true. The original Dracula—you know, in the book—he could go out in daylight; he just lost his powers."

"Lee," the Lieutenant said, "you are a font of information. Is this what our monster is trying to avoid?"

"I don't know," Lee said. "Could be."

"I don't think so," Davis said. "It's not as if daylight makes its teeth any sharper."

"Then what is it?" Lee said.

"Beats me," Davis said. "Don't we need daylight to make Vitamin D? Maybe it's the same, uses the sun to manufacture some kind of vital substance."

"Not bad," the Lieutenant said.

"For something you pulled out of your ass," Lee said.

"Hey—you asked," Davis said.

"Perhaps it's time for some review," the Lieutenant said. "Can we agree on that? Good.

"We have this thing—this vampire," holding up a hand to Davis, "that spends its nights in an orbiting coffin. At dawn or thereabouts, it departs said refuge in search of blood, which it apparently obtains from a single source."

"Us," Han said.

"Us," the Lieutenant said. "It glides down into the atmosphere on the lookout for likely victims—of likely groups of victims, since it prefers to feed on large numbers of people at the same time. Possibly, it burns through its food quickly."

"It's always thirsty," Davis said. "No matter how much it drinks, it's never enough."

"Yeah," Lee said, "I felt it, too."

"So did we all," the Lieutenant said. "It looks to satisfy its thirst at locations where its actions will draw little to no attention. These include remote areas such as the U.S.-Mexico border, the Sahara and Gobi, and the Andes. It also likes conflict zones, whether Iraq, Darfur, or the Congo. How it locates these sites is unknown. We estimate that it visits between four and seven of them per day. That we have been able to determine, there does not appear to be an underlying pattern to its selection of either target areas or individuals within those areas. The vampire's exact level of intelligence is another unknown. It possesses considerable abilities as a predator, not least of them its speed, reaction time, and strength. Nor should we forget its teeth and," a rap of the artificial leg, "claws."

"Not to mention that mind thing," Lee said.

"Yes," the Lieutenant said. "Whether by accident or design, the vampire's appearance is accompanied by a telepathic jolt that momentarily disorients its intended victims, rendering them easier prey. For those who survive the meeting," a nod at them, "a link remains that may be activated by persistent, pronounced stress, whether physical or mental. The result of this activation is a period of clairvoyance, during which the lucky individual rides along for the vampire's current activities. Whether the vampire usually has equal access to our perceptions during this time is unclear; our combined accounts suggest it does not.

"However, there are exceptions."

IX

2005

"I know how we can kill it," Davis said. "At least, I think I do—how we can get it to come to a place where we can kill it."

Lee put his Big Mac on his tray and looked out the restaurant window. The Lieutenant paused in the act of dipping his fries into a tub of barbecue sauce. Han continued chewing his McNugget but nodded twice.

"The other day—two days ago, Wednesday—I got to it."

"What do you mean?" the Lieutenant said.

"It was coming in for a landing, and I made it mess up."

"Bullshit," Lee said. He did not shift his gaze from the window. His face was flushed.

"How?" the Lieutenant said.

"I was having a bad day, worse than the usual bad day. Things at Home Depot—the manager's okay, but the assistant manager's a raging asshole. Anyway, I decided a workout might help. I'd bought these Kung Fu DVDs—"

"Kung Fu," the Lieutenant said.

Davis shrugged. "Seemed more interesting than running a treadmill."

Through a mouthful of McNugget, Han said, "Bruce Lee."

"Yeah," Davis said. "I put the first disc on. To start with, everything's fine. I'm taking it easy, staying well below the danger level. My back's starting to ache, the way it always does, but that's okay, I can live with it. As long as I keep the situation in low gear, I can continue with my tiger style."

"Did it help?" the Lieutenant asked.

"My worse-than-bad day? Not really. But it was something to do, you know?"

The Lieutenant nodded. Lee stared at the traffic edging up the road in front of the McDonald's. Han bit another McNugget.

"This time, there was no warning. My back's feeling like someone's stitching it with a hot needle, then I'm dropping out of heavy cloud cover. Below, a squat hill pushes up from dense jungle. A group of men are sitting around the top of the hill. They're wearing fatigues, carrying Kalashnikovs. I think I'm somewhere in South America: maybe these guys are FARQ; maybe they're some of Chavez's boys.

"I've been through the drill enough to know what's on the way: a ringside seat for blood and carnage. It's reached the point, when one of these incidents overtakes me, I don't freak out. The emotion that grips me is dread, sickness at what's coming. But this happens so fast, there isn't time for any of that. Instead, anger—the anger that usually shows up a couple of hours later, when I'm still trying to get the taste of blood out of my mouth, still trying to convince myself that I'm not the one who's so thirsty—for once, that anger arrives on time and loaded for bear. It's like the fire that's crackling on my back finds its way into my veins and ignites me.

"What's funny is, the anger makes my connection to the thing even more intense. The wind is pressing my face, rushing over my arms—my wings—I'm aware of currents in the air, places where it's thicker, thinner, and I twitch my nerves to adjust for it. There's one guy standing off from the rest, closer to the treeline, though not so much I—the thing won't be able to take him. I can practically see the route to him, a steep dive with a sharp turn at the very end that'll let the thing knife through him. He's sporting a bush hat, which he's pushed back on his head. His shirt's open, T-shirt dark with sweat. He's holding his weapon self-consciously, trying to looking like a badass, and it's this, more than the smoothness of his skin, the couple of whiskers on his chin, that makes it clear he isn't even eighteen. It—I—we jackknife into the dive, and thirsty, Christ, thirsty isn't the word: this is dryness that reaches right through to your fucking soul. I've never understood what makes the thing tick—what *drives* it—so well.

"At the same time, the anger's still there. The closer we draw to the kid, the hotter it burns. We've reached the bottom of the dive and pulled up; we're streaking over the underbrush. The kid's completely oblivious to the fact that his bloody dismemberment is fifty feet away and closing fast. I'm so close to the thing, I can feel the way its fangs push against one another as they jut from its mouth. We're on top of the kid; the thing's preparing to retract its wings, slice him open, and drive its face into him. The kid is dead; he's dead and he just doesn't know it, yet.

"Only, it's like—I'm like—I don't even think, *No*, or, *Stop*, or *Pull up*. It's more . . . I push; I shove against the thing I'm inside and its arms move. Its fucking arms jerk up as if someone's passed a current through them. Someone has—I have. I'm the current. The motion throws off the thing's strike, sends it wide. It flails at the kid as it flies past him, but he's out of reach. I can sense—the thing's completely confused. There's a clump of bushes straight ahead—*wham*."

The Lieutenant had adopted his best you'd-better-not-be-bullshitting-me stare. He said, "I take it that severed the connection."

Davis shook his head. "No, sir. You would expect that—it's what would have happened in the past—but this time, it was like, I was so close to the thing, it was going to take something more to shake me loose."

"And?" the Lieutenant said.

Lee shoved his tray back, toppling his super-sized Dr Pepper, whose lid popped off, splashing a wave of soda and ice cubes across the table. While Davis and the Lieutenant grabbed napkins, Lee stood and said, "What the fuck, Davis?"

"What?" Davis said.

"I said: What the fuck, asshole," Lee said. Several diners at nearby tables turned their heads toward him.

"Inside voices," the Lieutenant said. "Sit down."

"I don't think so," Lee said. "I don't have to listen to this shit." With that, he stalked away from the table, through the men and women swiftly returning their attentions to the meals in front of them, and out the side door.

"What the fuck?" Davis said, dropping his wad of soggy napkins on Lee's tray.

"That seems to be the question of the moment," the Lieutenant said.

"Sir—"

"Our friend and fellow is not having the best of months," the Lieutenant said. "In fact, he is not having the best of years. You remember the snafus with his disability checks."

"I thought that was taken care of."

"It was, but it was accompanied by the departure of Lee's wife and their two-year-old. Compared to what he was, Lee is vastly improved. In terms of the nuances of his emotional health, however, he has miles to go. The shit with his disability did not help; nor did spending all day home with a toddler who didn't recognize his father."

"He didn't—"

"No, but I gather it was a close thing. A generous percentage of the wedding flatware paid the price for Lee's inability to manage himself. In short order, the situation became too much for Shari, who called her father to come for her and Douglas."

"Bitch," Han said.

"Since then," the Lieutenant said, "Lee's situation has not improved. A visit to the local bar for a night of drinking alone ended with him in the drunk tank. Shari's been talking separation, possibly divorce, and while Lee tends to be a bit paranoid about the matter, there may be someone else involved, an old boyfriend. Those members of Lee's family who've visited him, called him, he has rebuffed in a fairly direct way. To top it all off, he's been subject to the same, intermittent feast of blood as the rest of us."

"Oh," Davis said. "I had no—Lee doesn't talk to me—"

"Never mind. Finish your story."

"It's not a story."

"Sorry. Poor choice of words. Go on, please."

"All right," Davis said. "Okay. You have to understand, I was as surprised by all of this as—well, as anyone. I couldn't believe I'd affected the thing. If it hadn't been so real, so like all the other times, I would have thought I was hallucinating, on some kind of wish-fulfillment trip. As it was, there I was as the thing picked itself up from the jungle floor. The anger—my anger—I guess it was still there, but . . . on hold.

"The second the thing was upright, someone shouted and the air was hot with bullets. Most of them shredded leaves, chipped bark, but a few of them tagged the thing's arm, its shoulder. Something was wrong—mixing in with its confusion, there was another emotion, something down the block from fear. I wasn't doing anything: I was still stunned by what I'd made happen. The thing jumped, and someone—maybe a couple of guys—tracked it, headed it off, hit it in I can't tell you how many places—it felt as the thing had been punched a dozen times at once. It spun off course, slapped a tree, and went down, snapping branches on its way.

"Now it was pissed. Even before it picked itself up, the place it landed was being subject to intensive defoliation. A shot tore its ear. Its anger—if what I felt was fire, this was lava, thicker, slower-moving, hotter. It retreated, scuttled half a dozen trees deeper into the jungle. Whoever those guys were, they were professionals. They advanced on the spot where the thing fell and, when they saw it wasn't there anymore, they didn't rush in after it. Instead, they fell back to a defensive posture while one of them put in a call—for air support, I'm guessing.

"The thing was angry and hurt and the thirst—" Davis shook his head. He sipped his Coke. "What came next—I'm not sure I can describe it. There was this surge in my head—not the thing's head, this was my brain I'm talking about—and the thing was looking out of my eyes."

"It turned the tables on you," the Lieutenant said.

"Not exactly," Davis said. "I continued watching the soldiers maybe seventy-five feet in front of me, but I was . . . aware of the thing staring at the DVD still playing on the TV. It was as if the scene was on a screen just out of view." He shook his head. "I'm not describing it right.

"Anyway, that was when the connection broke."

Davis watched the Lieutenant evade an immediate response by taking a generous bite of his Double Quarter Pounder with Cheese and chewing it with great care. Han swallowed and said, "Soldiers."

"What?"

"Soldiers," Han said.

Through his mouthful of burger, the Lieutenant said, "He wants to know what happened to the soldiers. Right?"

Han nodded.

"Beats the shit out of me," Davis said. "Maybe their air support showed up and bombed the fucker to hell. Maybe they evac'd out of there."

"But that isn't what you think," the Lieutenant said. "You think it got them."

"Yes sir," Davis said. "The minute it was free of me, I think it had those poor bastards for lunch."

"It seems a bit much to hope otherwise, doesn't it?"

"Yes sir, it does."

When the Lieutenant opted for another bite of his sandwich, Davis said, "Well?"

The Lieutenant answered by lifting his eyebrows. Han switched from McNuggets to fries.

"As I see it," Davis began. He stopped, paused, started again. "We know that the thing fucked with us in Fallujah, linked up with us. So far, this situation has only worked to our disadvantage: whenever one of us is in sufficient discomfort, the connection activates and dumps us behind the thing's eyes for somewhere in the vicinity of three to five minutes. With all due respect to Lee, this has not been beneficial to anyone's mental health.

"But what if—suppose we could duplicate what happened to me? Not just once, but over and over—even if only for ten or fifteen seconds at a time—interfere with whatever it's doing, seriously fuck with it."

"Then what?" the Lieutenant said. "We're a thorn in its side. So?"

"Sir," Davis said, "those soldiers hit it. Okay, yes, their fire wasn't any more effective than ours was, but I'm willing to bet their percentages were significantly higher. That's what me being on board in an—enhanced way did to the thing. We wouldn't be a thorn—we'd be the goddamned bayonet Han jammed in its ribs.

"Not that we should wait for someone else to take it down. I'm proposing something more ambitious."

"All right."

"If we can disrupt the thing's routine—especially if we cut into its feeding—it won't take very long for it to want to find us. Assuming the second part of my experience—the thing has a look through our eyes—if that happens again, we can arrange it so that we let it know where we're going to be. We pick a location with a clearing where the thing can land and surrounding tree cover where we can wait to ambush it. Before any of us goes to ruin the thing's day, he puts pictures, maps, satellite photos of the spot on display, so that when the thing's staring out of his eyes, that's what it sees. If the same images keep showing up in front of it, it should get the point."

The Lieutenant took the rest of his meal to reply. Han offered no comment. When the Lieutenant had settled into his chair after tilting his tray into the garbage and stacking it on top of the can, he said, "I don't know, Davis. There are an awful lot more ifs than I prefer to hear in a plan. *If* we can access the thing the same way you did; *if* that wasn't a fluke. *If* the thing does the reverse-vision stuff; *if* it understands what we're showing it. *If* we can find a way to kill it." He shook his head.

"Granted," Davis said, "there's a lot we'd have to figure out, not least how to put it down and keep it down. I have some ideas about that, but nothing developed. It would be nice if we could control our connection to the thing, too. I'm wondering if what activates the jump is some chemical our bodies are releasing when they're under stress—maybe adrenaline. If we had access to a supply of adrenaline, we could experiment with doses—"

"You're really serious about this."

"What's the alternative?" Davis said. "Lee isn't the only one whose life is fucked, is he? How many more operations are you scheduled for, Han? Four? Five?"

"Four," Han said.

"And how're things in the meantime?"

Han did not answer.

"What about you, sir?" Davis said. "Oh sure, your wife and kids stuck around, but how do they act after you've had one of your fits, or spells, or whatever the fuck you call them? Do they rush right up to give Daddy a hug, or do they keep away from you, in case you might do something even worse? Weren't you coaching your son's soccer team? How's that working out for you? I bet it's a lot of fun every time the ref makes a lousy call."

"Enough, Davis."

"It isn't as if I'm in any better shape. I have to make sure I remember to swallow a couple of tranquilizers before I go to work so I don't collapse in the middle of trying to help some customer load his fertilizer into his car. Okay,

Rochelle had dumped me while I was away, but let me tell you how the dating scene is for a vet who's prone to seizures should things get a little too exciting. As for returning to college, earning my BS—maybe if I could have stopped worrying about how goddamned exposed I was walking from building to building, I could've focused on some of what the professors were saying and not fucking had to withdraw.

"This isn't the magic bullet," Davis said. "It isn't going to make all the bad things go away. It's . . . it is what it fucking is."

"All right," the Lieutenant said. "I'm listening. Han—you listening?"

"Listening," Han said.

X

4:11 AM

"So where do you think it came from?" Lee said.

"What do you mean?" Davis said. "We know where it comes from."

"No," Lee said, "I mean, before."

"Its secret origin," the Lieutenant said.

"Yeah," Lee said.

"How should I know?" Davis said.

"You're the man with the plan," Lee said. "Mr. Idea."

The Lieutenant said, "I take it you have a theory, Lee."

Lee glanced at the heap of coals that had been the fire. "Nah, not really."

"That sounds like a yes to me," the Lieutenant said.

"Yeah," Han said.

"Come on," Davis said. "What do you think?"

"Well," Lee said, then broke off, laughing. "No, no."

"Talk!" Davis said.

"You tell us your theory," the Lieutenant said, "I'll tell you mine."

"Okay, okay," Lee said, laughing. "All right. The way I see it, this vampire is like, the advance for an invasion. It flies around in its pod, looking for suitable planets, and when it finds one, it parks itself above the surface, calls its buddies, and waits for them to arrive."

"Not bad," the Lieutenant said.

"Hang on," Davis said. "What does it do for blood while it's Boldly Going Where No Vampire Has Gone Before?"

"I don't know," Lee said. "Maybe it has some stored in its coffin."

"That's an awful lot of blood," Davis said.

"Even in MRE form," the Lieutenant said.

"Maybe it has something in the coffin that makes blood for it."

"Then why would it leave to go hunting?" Davis said.

"It's in suspended animation," Lee said. "That's it. It doesn't wake up till it's arrived at a habitable planet."

"How does it know it's located one?" Davis said.

"Obviously," the Lieutenant said, "the coffin's equipped with some sophisticated tech."

"Thank you, sir," Lee said.

"Not at all," the Lieutenant said.

"I don't know," Davis said.

"What do you know?" Lee said.

"I told you—"

"Be real," Lee said. "You're telling me you haven't given five minutes to wondering how the vampire got to where it is?"

"I—"

"Yeah," Han said.

"I'm more concerned with the thing's future than I am with its past," Davis said, "but yes, I have wondered about where it came from. There's a lot of science I don't know, but I'm not sure about an alien being able to survive on human blood—about an alien needing human blood. It could be, I guess; it just seems a bit of a stretch."

"You're saying it came from here," the Lieutenant said.

"That's bullshit," Lee said.

"Why shouldn't it?" Davis said. "There's been life on Earth for something like three point seven *billion* years. Are you telling me this couldn't have developed?"

"Your logic's shaky," the Lieutenant said. "Just because something hasn't been disproved doesn't mean it's true."

"All I'm saying is, we don't know everything that's ever been alive on the planet."

"Point taken," the Lieutenant said, "but this thing lives above—well above the surface of the planet. How do you explain that?"

"Some kind of escape pod," Davis said. "I mean, you guys know about the asteroid, right? The one that's supposed to have wiped out the dinosaurs? Suppose this guy and his friends—suppose their city was directly in this asteroid's path? Maybe our thing was the only one who made it to the rockets on time? Or maybe it built this itself."

"Like Superman," Lee said, "only, he's a vampire, and he doesn't leave Krypton, he just floats around it so he can snack on the other survivors."

"Sun," Han said.

"What?" Lee said.

"Yellow sun," Han said.

Davis said, "He means Superman needs a yellow sun for his powers. Krypton had a red sun, so he wouldn't have been able to do much snacking."

"Yeah, well, we have a yellow sun," Lee said, "so what's the problem?"

"Never mind."

"Or maybe you've figured out the real reason the dinosaurs went extinct," Lee said. "Vampires got them all."

"That's clever," Davis said. "You're very clever, Lee."

"What about you, sir?" Lee said.

"Me?" the Lieutenant said. "I'm afraid the scenario I've invented is much more lurid than either of yours. I incline to the view that the vampire is here as a punishment."

"For what?" Davis said.

"I haven't the faintest clue," the Lieutenant said. "What kind of crime does a monster commit? Maybe it stole someone else's victims. Maybe it killed another vampire. Whatever it did, it was placed in that coffin and sent out into space. Whether its fellows intended us as its final destination, or planned for it to drift endlessly, I can't say. But I wonder if its blood-drinking—that craving—might not be part of its punishment."

"How?" Lee said.

"Say the vampire's used to feeding on a substance like blood, only better, more nutritious, more satisfying. Part of the reason for sending it here is that all that will be available to it is this poor substitute that leaves it perpetually thirsty. Not only does it have to cross significant distances, expose itself to potential harm to feed, the best it can do will never be good enough."

"That," Lee said, "is fucked up."

"There's a reason they made me an officer," the Lieutenant said. He turned to Han. "What about you, Han? Any thoughts concerning the nature of our imminent guest?"

"Devil," Han said.

"Ah," the Lieutenant said.

"Which?" Lee asked. "A devil, or the Devil?"

Han shrugged.

XI

2005-2006

To start with, the Lieutenant called once a week, on a Saturday night. Davis could not help reflecting on what this said about the state of the man's life, his marriage, that he spent the peak hours of his weekend in a long-distance conversation with a former subordinate—as well as the commentary their calls offered on his own state of affairs, that not only was he always in his apartment for the Lieutenant's call, but that starting late Thursday, up to a day earlier if his week was especially shitty, he looked forward to it.

There was a rhythm, almost a ritual, to each call. The Lieutenant asked Davis how he'd been; he answered, "Fine, sir," and offered a précis of the last seven days at Home Depot, which tended to consist of a summary of his assistant manager's most egregious offenses. If he'd steered clear of Adams, he might list the titles of whatever movies he'd rented, along with one- or two-sentence reviews of each. Occasionally, he would narrate his latest failed date, recasting stilted frustration as comic misadventure. At the conclusion of his recitation, Davis would swat the Lieutenant's question back to him. The Lieutenant would answer, "Can't complain," and follow with a distillation of his week that focused on his dissatisfaction with his position at Stillwater, a defense contractor who had promised him a career as exciting as the one he'd left but delivered little more than lunches, dinners, and cocktail parties at which the Lieutenant was trotted out, he said, so everyone could admire his goddamned plastic leg and congratulate his employers on hiring him. At least the money was decent, and Barbara enjoyed the opportunity to dress up and go out to nicer places than he'd ever been able to afford. The Lieutenant did not speak about his children; although if asked, he would say that they were hanging in there. From time to time, he shared news of Lee, whom he called on Sunday and whose situation never seemed to improve that much, and Han, whose sister he e-mailed every Monday and who reported that her brother was making progress with his injuries; in fact, Han was starting to e-mail the Lieutenant, himself.

This portion of their conversation, which Davis thought of as the Prelude, over, the real reason for the call—what Davis thought of as the SITREP—ensued. The Lieutenant, whose sentences hitherto had been loose, lazy, tightened his syntax as he quizzed Davis about the status of the Plan. In response, Davis kept his replies short, to the point. Have we settled on a location? The Lieutenant would ask. Yes sir, Davis would say, Thompson's Grove. That was the spot in the Catskills, the Lieutenant would say, south slope of Winger Mountain, about a half mile east of the principle trail to the summit. Exactly, sir, Davis would say. Research indicates the Mountain itself is among the least visited in the Catskill Preserve, and Thompson's Grove about the most obscure spot on it. The location is sufficiently removed from civilian populations not to place them in immediate jeopardy, yet still readily accessible by us. Good, good, the Lieutenant would say. I'll notify Lee and Han.

The SITREP finished, Davis and the Lieutenant would move to Coming Attractions: review their priorities for the week ahead, wish one another well, and hang up. As the months slid by and the Plan's more elaborate elements came into play—especially once Davis commenced his experiments dosing himself with adrenaline—the Lieutenant began adding the odd Wednesday night to his call schedule. After Davis had determined the proper amount for inducing a look through the Shadow's eyes—and after he'd succeeded in affecting the thing a second time, causing it to release its hold on a man Davis was reasonably sure was a Somali pirate—the Wednesday exchanges became part of their routine. Certainly, they helped Davis and the Lieutenant to coordinate their experiences interrupting the Shadow's routine with the reports coming in from Lee and Han, which arrived with increasing frequency once Lee and Han had found their adrenaline doses and were mastering the trick of interfering with the Shadow. However, in the moment immediately preceding their setting their respective phones down, Davis would be struck by the impression that the Lieutenant and he were on the verge of saying something else, something more—he couldn't say what, exactly, only that it would be significant in a way—in a different way from their usual conversation. It was how he'd felt in the days leading up to Fallujah, as if, with such momentous events roiling on the horizon, he should be speaking about important matters, meaningful things.

Twice, they came close to such an exchange. The first time followed a discussion of the armaments the Lieutenant had purchased at a recent gun show across the border in Pennsylvania. "God love the NRA," he'd said and listed the four Glock 21s's, sixteen extra clips, ten boxes of .45 ammunition, four AR-15's, sixteen extra high-capacity magazines for them, thirty boxes of 223 Remington ammo, and four USGI M7 bayonets.

"Jesus, sir," Davis had said when the Lieutenant was done. "That's a shitload of ordnance."

"I stopped at the grenade launcher," the Lieutenant said. "It seemed excessive."

"You do remember how much effect our guns had on the thing the last time . . . "

"Think of this as a supplement to the Plan. Even with one of us on board, once the thing shows up, it's going to be a threat. We know it's easier to hit when someone's messing with its controls, so let's exploit that. The more we can tag it, the more we can slow it down, improve our chances of using your secret weapon on it."

"Fair enough."

"Good. I'm glad you agree."

Davis was opening his mouth to suggest possible positions the four of them might take around the clearing when the Lieutenant said, "Davis."

"Sir?"

"Would you say you've had a good life? Scratch that—would you say you've had a satisfactory life?"

"I . . . I don't know. I guess so."

"I've been thinking about my father these past few days. It's the anniversary of his death, twenty-one years ago this Monday. He came here from Mexico City when he was sixteen, worked as a fruit picker for a couple of years, then fell into a job at a diner. He started busing tables, talked his way into the kitchen, and became the principle cook for the night shift. That was how he met my mother: she was a waitress there. She was from Mexico, too, although the country—apparently, she thought my old man was some kind of city-slicker, not to be trusted by a virtuous girl. I guess she was right, because my older brother was born seven months after their wedding. But I came along two years after that, so I don't think that was the only reason for them tying the knot.

"He died when I was five, my father. An embolism burst in his brain. He was at work, just getting into the swing of things. The coroner said he was dead before he reached the floor. He was twenty-seven. What I wonder is, when he looked at his life, at everything he'd done, was it what he wanted? Even if it was different, was it enough?

"How many people do you suppose exit this world satisfied with what they've managed to accomplish in it, Davis? How many of our fellows slipped their mortal coils content with what their eighteen or twenty-one or twenty-seven years had meant?"

"There was the Mission," Davis said. "Ask them in public, and they'd laugh, offer some smartass remark, but talk to them one-on-one, and they'd tell you they believed in what we were doing, even if things could get pretty fucked-up. I'm not sure if that would've been enough for Lugo, or Manfred—for anyone—but it would've counted for something."

"True," the Lieutenant said. "The question is, will something do?"

"I guess it has to."

Their second such conversation came two weeks before the weekend the four of them were scheduled to travel to Upstate New York. They were reviewing the final draft of the Plan, which Davis thought must be something like the Plan version 22.0—although little had changed in the way of the principles since they'd finalized them a month earlier. Ten minutes before dawn, they would take up their positions in the trees around the clearing. If north was twelve o'clock, then Lee and Han would be at twelve—necessary because Han would be injecting himself at t-minus one minute and would require protection—the Lieutenant would take two, and Davis three. The woods were reasonably thick: if they positioned themselves about ten feet in, then the Shadow would be unable to come in on top of them. If it wanted them, it would have to land, shift to foot, and that would be the cue for the three of them aiming their AR-15's to fire. In the meantime, Han would have snuck on board the Shadow and be preparing to jam it. As soon as he saw the opportunity, he would do his utmost to take the thing's legs out from under it, a maneuver he had been rehearsing for several weeks and become reasonably proficient at. The average time Han guesstimated he'd been able to knock the Shadow's legs out was fifteen seconds, though he had reached the vicinity of thirty once. This would be their window: the instant the thing's legs crumpled, two of them had to be up and on it, probably Davis and Lee since the Lieutenant wasn't placing any bets on his sprinter's start. One of them would draw the Shadow's notice, the other hit it with the secret weapon. If for any reason the first attacker failed, the second could engage if he saw the opportunity; otherwise, he would have to return to the woods, because Han's hold on the thing would be wearing off. Once the Lieutenant observed this, he would inject himself and they would begin round two. Round two was the same as round one except for the presumed lack of one man, just as round three counted on two of them being gone. Round four, the Lieutenant said, was him eating a bullet. By that point, there might not be anything he could do to stop the ugly son of a bitch drinking his blood, but that didn't mean he had to stay around for the event.

Davis knew they would recite the Plan again on Saturday, and then next

Wednesday, and then the Saturday after that, and then the Wednesday two weeks from now. At the Quality Inn in Kingston, they would recite the Plan, and again as they drove into the Catskills, and yet again as they hiked up Winger Mountain. "Preparation" the Lieutenant had said in Iraq, "is what ensures you will fuck up only eighty percent of what you are trying to do." If the exact numbers sounded overly optimistic to Davis, he agreed with the general sentiment.

Without preamble, the Lieutenant said, "You know, Davis, when my older brother was twenty-four, he left his girlfriend for a married Russian émigré six years his senior—whom he had met, ironically enough, through his ex, who had been tutoring Margarita, her husband, Sergei, and their four year old, Stasu, in English."

"No sir," Davis said, "I'm pretty sure you never told me this."

"You have to understand," the Lieutenant went on, "until this point, my brother, Alberto, had led a reasonably sedate and unimpressive life. Prior to this, the most daring thing he'd done was go out with Alexandra, the tutor, who was Jewish, which made our very Catholic mother very nervous. Yet here he was, packing his clothes and his books, emptying his meager bank account, and driving out of town with Margarita in the passenger's seat and Stasu in the back with all the stuff they couldn't squeeze in the trunk. They headed west, first to St. Louis for a couple of months, next to New Mexico for three years, and finally to Portland—actually, it's just outside Portland, but I can never remember the name of the town.

"She was a veterinarian, Margarita. With Alberto's help, she succeeded in having her credentials transferred over here. Has her own practice, these days, treats horses, cows, farm animals. Alberto helps her; he's her assistant and office manager. Sergei gave them custody of Stasu; they have two more kids, girls, Helena and Catherine. Beautiful kids, my nieces.

"You have any brothers or sisters, Davis?"

"A younger brother, sir. He wants to be a priest."

"Really?"

"Yes, sir."

"Isn't that funny."

XII

5:53 AM

Lying on the ground he'd swept clear of rocks and branches, his rifle propped on a small log, the sky a red bowl overhead, Davis experienced a moment of complete and utter doubt. Not only did the course of action on which they had set out appear wildly implausible, but everything from the courtyard in Fallujah on acquired the sheen of the unreal, the delusional. An eight-foot-tall space vampire? Visions of soaring through the sky, of savaging scores of men, women, and children around the globe? Injecting himself with adrenaline, for Christ's sake? What was any of this but the world's biggest symptom, a massive fantasy his mind had conjured to escape a reality it couldn't bear? What had happened— what scene was the Shadow substituting for? Had they in fact found a trap in the courtyard, an IED that had shredded them in its fiery teeth? Was he lying in a hospital bed somewhere, his body ruined, his mind hopelessly crippled?

When the Shadow was standing in the clearing, swinging its narrow head from side to side, Davis felt something like relief. If this dark thing and its depravities were a hallucination, he could be true to it. The Shadow parted its fangs as if tasting the dawn. Davis tensed, prepared to find himself someplace else, subject to a clip from the thing's history, but the worst he felt was a sudden buzzing in his skull that reminded him of nothing so much as the old fuse box in his parents' basement. He adjusted his rifle and squeezed the trigger.

The air rang with gunfire. Davis thought his first burst caught the thing in the belly: he saw it step back, though that might have been due to either Lee or the Lieutenant, who had fired along with him. Almost too fast to follow, the Shadow jumped, a black scribble against the sky, but someone anticipated its leap and aimed ahead of it. At least one of the bullets connected; Davis saw the Shadow's right eye pucker. Stick-arms jerking, it fell at the edge of the treeline, ten feet in front of him. He shot at its head, its shoulders. Geysers of dirt marked his misses. The Shadow threw itself backwards, but collapsed where it landed.

"NOW!" the Lieutenant screamed.

Davis grabbed for his stake with his left hand as he dropped the rifle from his right. Almost before his fingers had closed on the weapon, he was on his feet and rushing into the clearing. To the right, Lee burst out of the trees, his stake held overhead in both hands, his mouth open in a bellow. In front of them, the Shadow was thrashing from side to side like the world's largest insect pinned through the middle. Its claws scythed grass, bushes. Davis saw that its right eye had indeed been hit, and partially collapsed. Lee was not slowing his charge. Davis sprinted to reach the Shadow at the same time.

Although the thing's legs were motionless, its claws were fast as ever. As Davis came abreast of it, jabbing at its head, its arm snapped in his direction. Pain razored up his left arm. Blood spattered the grass, the Shadow's head jerked towards him, and the momentary distraction this offered was, perhaps, what allowed Lee to tumble into a forward roll that dropped him under the Shadow's other claw and up again to drive his stake down into the base of its throat. Reaching for the cell phone in his shirt pocket, Davis backpedaled. The thing's maw gaped as Lee held on to shove the weapon as far as it would go. The Shadow twisted and thrust its claws into Lee's collarbone and ribs. His eyes bulged and he released the stake. Davis had the cell phone in his hand. The Shadow tore its claw from Lee's chest and ripped him open. Davis pressed the three and hit SEND.

In the woods, there was a white flash and the CRUMP of explosives detonating. A cloud of debris rushed between the trunks. The Shadow jolted as if a bolt of lightning had speared it.

"SHIT!" the Lieutenant was screaming. "SHIT!"

The Shadow was on its feet, Lee dangling from its left claw like a child's bedraggled plaything. Davis backpedaled. With its right claw, the Shadow reached for the stake jutting from its throat. Davis pressed the two and SEND.

He was knocked from his feet by the force of the blast, which shoved the air from his lungs and pushed sight and sound away from him. He was aware of the ground pressing against his back, a fine rain of particles pattering his skin, but his body was contracted around his chest, which could not bring in any air. Suffocating, he was suffocating. He tried to move his hands, his feet, but his extremities did not appear to be receiving his brain's instructions. Perhaps his hand-crafted bomb had accomplished what the Shadow could not.

What he could feel of the world was bleeding away.

XIII

2006

Although Lee wanted to wait for sunset, if not total darkness, a preference Davis shared, the Lieutenant insisted they shoulder their packs and start the trail up Winger Mountain while the sun would be broadcasting its light for another couple of hours. At the expressions on Lee and Davis's faces, he said, "Relax. The thing sweeps the Grove first thing in the morning. It's long gone, off feeding someplace."

The trail was not unpleasant. Had they been so inclined, its lower reaches were wide enough that they could have walked them two abreast. (They opted for single file, Lee taking point, Han next, the Lieutenant third, and Davis bringing up the rear. It spread the targets out.) The ground was matted with the leaves of the trees that flanked the trail and stationed the gradual slopes to either side. (While he had never been any good at keeping the names of such things straight, Davis had an idea the trees were a mix of maple and oak, the occasional white one a birch.) With their crowns full of leaves, the trees almost obscured the sky's blue emptiness. (All the same, Davis didn't look up any more than he could help.)

They reached the path to Thompson's Grove sooner than Davis had anticipated. A piece of wood weathered gray and nailed to a tree chest-high pointed right, to a narrower route that appeared overgrown a hundred yards or so in the distance. Lee withdrew the machete he had sheathed on his belt and struck the sign once, twice, until it flew off the tree into the forest.

"Hey," Davis said, "that's vandalism."

"Sue me," Lee said.

Once they were well into the greenery, the mosquitoes, which had ventured only the occasional scout so long as they kept to the trail, descended in clouds. "Damnit!" the Lieutenant said, slapping his cheek. "I used bug spray."

"Probably tastes like dessert topping to them, sir," Lee called. "Although, damn! at this rate, there won't be any blood left in us for Count Dracula."

Thompson's Grove was an irregular circle, forty feet across. Grass stood thigh-high. A few bushes punctuated the terrain. Davis could feel the sky hungry above them. Lee and Han walked the perimeter while he and the Lieutenant stayed near the trees. All of their rifles were out. Lee and Han declared the area secure, but the four of them waited until the sun was finally down to clear the center of the Grove and build their fire.

Lee had been, Davis supposed the word was *off*, since they'd met in Kingston that morning. His eyes shone in his face, whose flesh seemed drawn around the bones. When Davis embraced him in the lobby of the Quality Inn, it had been like putting his arms around one of the support cables on a suspension bridge, something bracing an enormous weight. It might be the prospect of their upcoming encounter, although Davis suspected there was more to it. The Lieutenant's most recent report had been that Lee was continuing to struggle: Shari had won custody of Douglas, with whom Lee was permitted supervised visits every other Saturday. He'd enrolled at his local community college, but stopped attending classes after the first week. The Lieutenant wasn't sure he'd go so far as to call Lee an alcoholic, but there was no doubt the man liked his beer a good deal more than was healthy. After the wood was gathered and stacked, the fire kindled, the sandwiches Davis had prepared distributed, Lee cleared his throat and said, "I know the Lieutenant has an order he wants us to follow, but there's something I need to know about."

"All right," the Lieutenant said through a mouthful of turkey on rye, "ask away."

"It's the connection we have to the thing," Lee said. "Okay, so: we've got a direct line into its central nervous system. The right amount of adrenaline, and we can hijack it. Problem is, the link works both ways. At least, we know that, when the thing's angry, it can look out of our eyes. What if it can do more? What if it can do to us what we've done to it, take us over?"

"There's been no evidence of that," Davis said. "Don't you think, if it could do that, it would have by now?"

"Not necessarily," Lee said.

"Oh? Why not?"

"Why would it need to? We're trying to get its attention; it doesn't need to do anything to get ours."

"It's an unknown," the Lieutenant said. "It's conceivable the thing could assume control of whoever's hooked up to it and try to use him for support. I have to say, though, that even if it could possess one of us, I have a hard time imagining it doing so while the rest of us are trying to shorten its lifespan. To tell you the truth, should we succeed in killing it, I'd be more worried about it using the connection as a means of escape."

"Escape?" Davis said.

Lee said, "The Lieutenant means it leaves its body behind for one of ours."

"Could it do that?"

"I don't know," the Lieutenant said, "I only mention it as a worst-case scenario. Our ability to share its perceptions, to affect its actions, seems to suggest some degree of congruity between the thing and us. On the other hand, it is a considerable leap from there to its being able to inhabit us."

"Maybe that's how it makes more of itself," Lee said. "One dies, one's born."

"Phoenix," Han said.

"This is all pretty speculative," Davis said.

"Yes it is," the Lieutenant said. "Should the thing seize any of us, however, it will have been speculation well-spent."

"What do you propose, then, sir?" Davis said.

"Assuming any of us survives the morning," the Lieutenant said, "we will have to proceed with great caution." He held up his pistol.

XIV

6:42 AM

Davis opened his eyes to a hole in the sky. Round, black—for a moment, he had the impression the earth had gained a strange new satellite, or that some unimaginable catastrophe had blown an opening in the atmosphere, and then his vision adjusted and he realized that he was looking up into the barrel of the Lieutenant's Glock. The man himself half-crouched beside Davis, his eyes narrowed. His lips moved, and Davis struggled to pick his words out of the white noise ringing in his ears.

"Davis," he said. "You there?"

"Yeah," Davis said. Something was burning; a charcoal reek stung his nostrils. His mouth tasted like ashes. He pushed himself up on his elbows. "Is it—"

"Whoa," the Lieutenant said, holding his free hand up like a traffic cop. "Take it easy, soldier. That was some blast."

"Did we—"

"We did."

"Yeah?"

"We blew it to Kingdom Come," the Lieutenant said. "No doubt, there are pieces of it scattered here and there, but the majority of it is so much dust."

"Lee—"

"You saw what the thing did to him—although, stupid motherfucker, it serves him right, grabbing the wrong Goddamned stake. Of all the stupid fucking . . . "

Davis swallowed. "Han?"

The Lieutenant shook his head.

Davis lay back. "Fuck."

"Never mind," the Lieutenant said. His pistol had not moved. "Shit happens. The question before us now is, Did it work? Are we well and truly rid of that thing, that fucking blood-drinking monster, or are we fooling ourselves? What do you say, Davis?"

"I . . . " His throat was dry. "Lee grabbed the wrong one?"

"He did."

"How is that possible?" "I don't know," the Lieutenant said. "I do not fucking know."

"I specifically gave each of us—"

"I know; I watched you. In the excitement of the moment, Lee and Han must have mixed them up."

"Mixed . . . " Davis raised his hands to his forehead. Behind the Lieutenant, the sky was a blue chasm.

"Or could be, the confusion was deliberate."

"What?"

"Maybe they switched stakes on purpose."

"No."

"I don't think so, either, but we all know it wasn't much of a life for Han."

"That doesn't mean—"

"It doesn't."

"Jesus." Davis sat up.

The Lieutenant steadied his gun. "So?"

"I take it you're fine."

"As far as I've been able to determine, yes."

"Could the thing have had something to do with it?"

"The mix-up?"

"Made Han switch the stakes or something?"

"That presumes it knew what they were, which supposes it had been spying on us through Han's eyes for not a few hours, which assumes it comprehended us—our language, our technology—in excess of prior evidence."

"Yeah," Davis said. "Still."

"It was an accident," the Lieutenant said. "Let it go."

"What makes you so sure you're all right?"

"I've had no indications to the contrary. I appear in control of my own thoughts and actions. I'm aware of no alien presence crowding my mind. While I am thirsty, I have to desire to quench that thirst from one of your arteries."

"Would you be, though? Aware of the thing hiding in you?"

The Lieutenant shrugged. "Possibly not. You're taking a long time to answer my question; you know that."

"I don't know how I am," Davis said. "No, I can't feel the thing either, and no, I don't want to drink your blood. Is that enough?"

"Davis," the Lieutenant said, "I will do this. You need to understand that. You are as close to me as anyone, these days, and I will shoot you in the head if I deem it necessary. If I believed the thing were in me, I would turn this gun on myself without a second thought. Am I making myself clear? Let me know it's over, or let me finish it."

The Lieutenant's face was flushed. "All right," Davis said. He closed his eyes. "All right." He took a deep breath. Another.

When he opened his eyes, he said, "It's gone."

"You're positive."

"Yes, sir."

"You cannot be lying to me."

"I know. I'm not."

The end of the pistol wavered, and for a moment, Davis was certain that the Lieutenant was unconvinced, that he was going to squeeze the trigger, anyway. He wondered if he'd see the muzzle flash.

Then the pistol lowered and the Lieutenant said, "Good man." He holstered the gun and extended his hand. "Come on. There's a lot we have to do."

Davis caught the Lieutenant's hand and hauled himself to his feet. Behind the Lieutenant, he saw the charred place that had been the Shadow, Lee's torn and blackened form to one side of it. Further back, smoke continued to drift out of the spot in the trees where Han had lain. The Lieutenant turned and started walking towards the trees. He did not ask, and Davis did not tell him, what he had seen with his eyes closed. He wasn't sure how he could have said that the image behind his eyelids was the same as the image in front of them: the unending sky, blue, ravenous.

John Langan *is the author of novel* House of Windows *(2009) and collection* Mr. Gaunt and Other Uneasy Encounters *(2008). He lives in Upstate New York with his wife, son, two cats, and a small pond of frogs.*

Some horror enthusiasts rail that the vampire is no longer a monster, that the icon has been turned primarily into a desirable anti-hero rather than the dreaded blood-drinking undead fiend, or that the trope suffers from the "same old story too often retold" syndrome. Langan in this novella, however, gives us a handsomely crafted, highly effective, thoroughly relevant, completely twenty-first century vampire story.

CERTAIN DEATH FOR A KNOWN PERSON

STEVE DUFFY

On the whole my life has been pleasant, but unexceptional. Honestly, you wouldn't pay to read my autobiography, apart from a couple of odd occurrences; or actually just the one occurrence, the beginning of a chain of events which seems, twenty-three years on, still to be working itself out. The rest of it—school, university, work—is everybody's story, and I shan't bore you with it. As for the incident in question, this is what happened:

It was my first term at the University of Exeter, where I shared a room with a bloke called Dave Masters. We're good friends still, and meet up every year or so if it's possible. Both of us were West Country boys: I was from Weston-super-Mare, and he was from a small village to the north of Dartmoor called Inwardleigh ("Really?" I asked him when we first met, and made him show me in the road atlas). He used to go back home for the weekend with a big bag of laundry under his arm—both his and mine, God love him—and leave me the digs to myself. He had a girlfriend at home, and they were both anxious to make sure the relationship didn't fizzle out. They've been married twenty years now, Dave and Cathy, so I suppose it was worth the effort.

One weekend towards the end of the first term, Dave suggested I come back with him: it was Cathy's birthday, and there was a party at her house. *Why not?* I thought. So come Friday we took the bus from Exeter to Okehampton, then walked the couple of miles to Inwardleigh, where Dave's folks lived. We stopped for tea (dropping off our washing in the process—students, eh?) and then Dave's dad drove us the twelve miles or so to High Thornhays, Cathy's parents' place up on Dartmoor.

It was a big old house that stood on its own on a shoulder of the high moorland. Inside, it was a real rabbit warren, all corridors and staircases, the sort of place it takes a week to find your way around. They needed a big place: besides Monica and Tom, Cathy's mum and dad, there were four Headley children, all daughters. Cathy was the eldest at eighteen, then there was Emily, then Fiona, then Trish. They filled up that crossword puzzle of a house between them: I remember there always being laughter round each corner, as I tried to find my way from one room to another. I liked it very much; I liked the Headleys, too.

At first sight it all might have been a bit intimidating, but the warmth of the Headleys' welcome put me completely at my ease. While I was still trying to get everybody's name right, they were already treating me like an old friend, showing me where I'd be sleeping and asking me if I'd eaten yet. It helped me get over the other stumbling blocks, to do with class and money and my ingrained inferiority complex concerning both those things. I'd never been the guest of anyone as well off as the Headleys, nor of anyone who lived in a house like High Thornhays. It was all a learning curve for me, and it was all good.

That first evening Monica and Tom went out, so Dave and the girls and I had the house to ourselves. I remember us all listening to records in one of the many odd rooms in High Thornhays—I mean, one of the rooms whose original purpose it was hard to guess. You came across them all through the house; half-a-dozen steps, a narrow corridor, then a strange little space like an architect's afterthought, largely unclassifiable. I did ask at first, but the answers I got—"Oh, it was the muniment room," or "This used to be the back receiving parlour"—only left me more confused. I forget the name of the room we were in, but it was long and narrow, and the girls used it as a sort of downstairs den. There was a TV and a stereo, and all along one wall mullioned windows looking out over the moor. There were curtains to the windows, but nobody drew them shut. I remember thinking at some point in the evening how we must have looked to anybody outside in the dark and the cold and the constant wind, how enviably comfy and cosy. But of course, there was no one outside. There were no casual passers-by at High Thornhays. If you were out on the moor at that time of night and you were anywhere near the house, then you probably had business with the Headleys; in which case, you wouldn't waste your time hanging around outside the windows, would you? That whole curtains thing was just a hang-up I had. It came, I suppose, from spending my formative years feeling the glare of constant observation back in our suburban semi in Weston-super-Mare.

So there we were in the long room, Dave and I already making inroads into the booze meant for tomorrow's party. I remember being quite witty, and surprising myself in the process, though I expect this had more to do with the good nature of our hosts than with any latent charisma I might have possessed. They were so perfectly apt to be charmed, even the Elephant Man might have made a good impression.

Really, they were terrific, the Headley girls. Just looking at them made you feel slightly sub-standard in comparison. Do you know what I mean? Those well-bred, well-educated, well-to-do young ladies who just seem so . . . wholesome? Cathy, for instance, all honey and rose-hips and coltishly long in the bone: I could have gone seriously stupid over Cathy, but of course she was Dave's girlfriend, so no way. Even little Trish, at thirteen the youngest of the pack, was so playfully vivacious, an absolute stunner-in-waiting—though obviously she was even farther out of bounds than her eldest sister, before you get the wrong idea. Fiona, the second youngest, was adorably earnest; she wore specs, and was hugely bookish, so we hit it off straight away. I might as well admit it, I even fancied Monica, their mother. (Later on that first evening, after the girls had gone to bed, I caused Dave to snort beer down his nose when I drunkenly described Monica as a—wait for it—as a "mumsy vixen.")

And then there was Emily, a year-and-a-half younger than Cathy: Emily, for whom it was impossible not to fall, if you were the falling kind. I remember asking Dave how old she was, and thinking *Sixteen isn't that young. Not really.* Like that wasn't a clue right there.

It was all in her smile. When she smiled, you felt personally singled out for commendation, as if someone had leaned down from the gods and trained a spotlight on you. One glance and your whole being was illuminated, you felt the glow of her friendliness all toasty on your face. Your flushed, inebriated face, you understand—your half-wit's phizog, with its stupid goonish leer.

Did Emily notice that she was being ogled by a cretin? I hoped not: if she had, it would have been scaldingly embarrassing. Looking at it objectively, with the benefit of hindsight, I doubt whether my gruesome fixation even registered on her radar. Why should it have? I was nineteen and . . . shall we be kind, and say unpolished? Whereas she was sixteen-and-a-half, improbably, cartoonishly enthused still by everything she lit upon, thrilled by the vividness of her own response. She wanted for nothing, everybody loved her, and she had the natural grace not to let it ruin her. Life had thrown no setbacks into her path, so far, everything had been good, and nothing had hurt. She was in a magic bubble, and it was slightly heartbreaking to think that one day it would have to break, because none of us gets through wholly unscathed, do we? Nobody gets a clear run at it.

Over breakfast the next morning, scratchy and hungover, I remember squinting through bloodshot eyes at Emily rough-and-tumbling with Jess, the family Labrador, and feeling old for the first time in my life. Not just old*er*, you understand, as in a mere two-and-a-half years older, but actually *old*; that feeling I know only too well now on the long slope down to the big five-oh. Creaky, rusting in the chassis, fundamentally unserviceable. I felt it first in the kitchens at High Thornhays, gazing at Emily as she straightened up from playing with the dog and shook her strawberry blond hair off her face. "Have you looked outside?" she wanted to know. "It's just begun to snow!"

Which it had: big fat flakes that soon gave way to a thick and steady whiteout. Bad news for that evening's party, of course, but what with snowballs and snowmen and all the rest of it, there were compensations. Nothing like a snowball in the face to tackle that hangover. All through the afternoon, people who'd been invited to Cathy's eighteenth were phoning up with apologies: *Sorry, can't risk it if it stays like this.* Everyone thereabouts knew better than to take a car out in that sort of weather. Naturally enough, Cathy was a bit upset, and Dave took her up to her room, trying to cheer her up. Meanwhile, I helped Tom bring more logs in from the stable block, and we got all the fireplaces banked up and roaring, just in case.

Around dusk, when the snow had stopped falling and all of Dartmoor lay under several feet of drift, I was looking out of the diamond-leaded windows in the long room round the side of the house. The wind had driven a gap in the clouds, and the snow looked quite blue beneath the hard and brittle stars. Around the windows the lamplight from inside shone out through the stained glass, coloring the closest of the snow banks a cheerful harlequin pattern. Away beyond that, the slopes of the high tors looked picturesque, yet forbidding. I shivered, and wandered back through to the kitchens, the warm hospitable heart of the house.

There, Monica and the girls were getting on with the arrangements for the party despite everything. You never know, said Monica, more in hope than expectation, and sure enough a handful of people braved the conditions— local folk, mostly, people from Chagford and Gidleigh and Lettaford. Nobody from further afield than Okehampton was risking it.

Cathy was great: she smiled and made the best of things, and I was more than a little envious of Dave as I watched them both chatting to the neighbours. You had to be, because they were so clearly made for each other. (It took me the best part of twenty years to find a Cathy of my own; they don't grow on trees.) Inwardly I sighed, and went to look for Emily. Just for a chat.

Annoyingly, she'd found someone her own age to talk to: a girl from school, Pippa or something, all gosh-and-golly, and they were deep in conversation about boys and pony club and stuff I can't even imagine. "Hiya, Mike," Emily said brightly, seeing me loitering by the door to the hallway, glass in hand. "You all right? Hey, I think Fiona was looking for you just now!"

"You setting him up, Em?" the other girl wanted to know. They giggled, and I joined in the laughter, just so they'd know it was all a perfectly splendid joke but I was totally in on it, yeah. Ha-ha, yeah, right. Fiona. *Don't push it, girly*, I thought.

Tipsily aware of the need for dignity and poise in all things, I strolled through to the front parlour, where Fiona wanted to know which I preferred, Alan Garner or Tolkien. Well, this is the thing about being a bookworm. When romantic expectations fizzle out, you can always spend a good couple of hours debating the merits of Middle-Earth over Elidor. By the time we'd decided that Jenny Agutter should be the girl if they ever made *The Owl Service* into a film, most of the other guests had gone home, and I was into my ninth or tenth pint, and feeling no pain.

Soon after midnight Tom and Monica went upstairs, leaving us young folk to it. "Don't burn the house down," said Tom. He may have been looking at me; I may have been one or two over my limit by then. I didn't take it personally. Then again, I may not have fully understood what he was saying at the time. Conversation was getting difficult, mostly because of the seven-second delay newly developed between my brain and my organs of speech. But it was okay. It was fine. I remember all of us sitting in the long room where the record player was, the funny long room, and I was saying how this was a funny room, because it was all long, and we all laughed, because that was funny in itself . . . and then I remember there being no electric lights on any more, only the firelight all flickering and magical, and someone was reaching around me, tucking a tartan car blanket around my shoulders . . .

"Emily?"

"All right, Mike?" she said, her voice kindly as ever. "How you doing? You were nodding off then." I was sprawled back into a corner of the sofa, and she was leaning over me with that heart-melting smile of hers. Very close; close enough to kiss, if I dared go for it. Solicitously she removed the pint glass from my unresisting hand. "Just put that down there, out of the way. Are you going to be okay here, then? Or shall we try and get you up to bed?"

"Fine here," I assured her. Suave to the core, I was going to point out there was plenty of room for two if she cared to join me, but by the time I'd figured out which order the words should go in, she was gone; and very shortly after that I was gone as well.

I don't know what time it was when the ferocity of my own snoring brought me round. I'm not even sure that I came round all the way, so strictly speaking I don't know whether what I'm about to tell you actually happened, or whether it took place only in some abnormally detailed dream-version of reality. I know what I believe to be true, but you'll judge that for yourselves. This is what I remember:

It was night outside, but the fire in the grate was still in, banked down to a glowing bed of embers. That helped me realize where I was; that and the starlight, reflected off the snow outside and streaming through the still uncurtained windows. The room was dark but not inky black. You could make out shapes, and even a measure of detail; you could probably have found a book, but you wouldn't have been able to read it, not without turning on a light.

I wanted no light. I wanted only about another twelve hours or so of sleep, and the soothing hand of a beautiful woman on my brow, and possibly a cup of tea, if there was one going. I was thinking in an aimless way about getting back off again, when I realized I wasn't alone in the room.

Someone was sitting in one of the armchairs over by the windows. I could see a head, silhouetted against the gleam of the snowfields outside, but no features, none of the detail; the firelight was too low for that. I must have caught my breath in surprise, or grunted or something, because the figure raised a hand in silent acknowledgement.

Who was it? I assumed it was somebody else sleeping over for the night, one of the neighbors who'd maybe had one over the eight. Had I been introduced? Well, that was anyone's guess. I yawned and said, "All right?"

"Fine, thank you. Nice of you to ask." A man. I didn't recognise the voice—no, that's not it, exactly. I *thought* I did; I just couldn't put a name to it. He spoke a cultured RP English with just the slightest edge; that cool sardonic humor that comes with the assumption of unbounded and perpetual pre-eminence. The sort of voice that built the Empire, and left half the world wishing we'd stayed at home instead.

"What time is it?" I would have told him how *I* was, but he hadn't asked.

The other—the guest—shifted a little in his seat and glanced over his shoulder through the window. I still couldn't see his face, but I thought I saw a glint of something red as he turned his head. He may have been wearing glasses, and they may have caught the firelight. "It's very late. Or very early still, depending on which way you look at it."

Well, that was helpful. "Have you got a watch on?"

"I don't have any *use* for watches," admitted the guest, politely amused at the notion. "I'm always on time, you see, wherever I arrive." And modest with it. Clearly, a prince among men.

"No? Well, doesn't matter." I was quite prepared to leave it at that. I was very, very tired, remember, and a bit drunk still, I dare say; not in the mood for late-night conversation. I was settling back on the sofa, when the guest spoke again.

"Nice party." Not inflected one way or the other; an open-ended statement, or a polite enquiry.

"Yeah. Yeah, it was great." Had I said anything? Had I done anything? Spilled my drink over him? Come on to his wife? I couldn't remember.

"All the young people enjoying themselves." Again without discernible inflection. A pause, then: "*You* were certainly having a ball."

Oh Christ. I had done something. What?

"Talking to Emily, I mean." Friendly on the surface; but no further. Underneath that? You wouldn't want to look.

"They're great . . . all the girls." I so didn't want to be having this conversation. "Really nice family. Nice people."

"Yes, but Emily is your favorite, isn't she?"

Oh, no way. No way had I made it that obvious. "I wouldn't say—"

"That's because you think this is an ordinary conversation."

Could there be anything more calculated to make you throw your brakes on? In the end I just didn't know what else to say. "Isn't it?"

"No,' said the guest, so categorically that it seemed to leave no space for an answer. After a little while, during which time I'd almost decided that the whole thing was actually just an extremely weird dream, he resumed. "No, it isn't. Encounters such as this, they don't happen every day, you see, Mike."

That sounded ominous. Was it a sex thing? You heard about these posh people. Aloud I said, "Encounter?"

"Rendezvous. *Rencontre.* Whatever." He waved a hand, as if granting me the freedom to fill in the synonym of my choice. "You see, my role here tonight—my purpose—was primarily to observe. Nothing more for now. And then when I saw that we were both *observing* the same thing . . . Well, it seemed only polite to consult, so to speak. One aficionado to another."

Sometimes when he spoke there was the slightest pause before the noun, as if there were other names for everything—secret names some of them—and he had to be careful which names he used. Careful, because his choice would determine how much he might reveal of his true intent—of his true nature, maybe.

"What do you mean?" It was hypnotic, the dance of the language, but treacherous as well. A snake will dance and weave before it strikes.

The guest sighed, and leaned forwards. Clasping his hands, he rested the point of his chin on the extended tips of his index fingers. Still his face was indistinguishable in the dark. "The matter of Emily," he said, and a shudder passed through the room, passed all the way through me. I swear it did.

"Little Emily." Savoring the words. "So special—but you saw that straight away, didn't you? I noticed you noticing. Such a lovely girl. So . . . vivacious."

I wanted to stop him right there, before he went any further. Our parents' generation had a phrase—it sounds absurdly dated now, but it expressed exactly what I felt—*I don't like the tone of your voice.* But he was speaking still:

"*Vivacious.* I wonder, is that exactly the word I was looking for—I mean, in terms of its etymology? Ah, though, I was forgetting: I doubt that sort of thing is covered in college any more. Lively, tenacious of life; long lived." He tutted, like a Sunday painter who'd selected the wrong color. "What do you think?"

"I know what vivacious means," I said sullenly. I wished I knew the word that would get him to piss off, though politely.

"But is it appropriate to the matter at hand? Is it apposite? Is it correct?" With that last word, a hard flinty quality came into his speech: the *k* sounds practically knapped sparks off the edges of the air.

"Eh? What are you getting at?" For the first time since my arrival at High Thornhays I was on the defensive. Old habits born of inadequacy coming to the fore: truculence, sullenness . . . and just the beginnings of fear. The man with no face there in the armchair: I was already afraid of him. Not nearly as afraid as I ought to have been, not yet. But soon; very soon.

Already I had that sick black-hole sensation of sliding towards something awful, the kind of feeling we associate only with bad dreams, because we're conditioned to believe that such things never happen in real life. Then why do they seem so familiar in our dreams? And why did I feel as though I knew this man, when I'd never to the best of my recollection met him? Why could I already sense what he was going to say, when I asked him "What do you mean?"

"I mean, she *looks* healthy enough," began the guest; and there it was. It was that odd dreamy foreknowledge of his answer that made me panic, as much as what he said. "She *looks* healthy enough, I grant you that. But how could you know, just from looking? How could you possibly be sure?" He spread his hands wide. "How could you know what's inside?" The word fell very heavily in the darkened room. Absurd as it sounds, I was already thinking, *Yes, exactly, how* can *you know*?

"I mean, what about leukemia?" said the guest, pronouncing that tricky first syllable to a nicety. "Hyperplasic transformation of leucopoietic tissue. Half of all cancers in teenage children. Or meningitis: presents as a headache and irritability. Well." He tittered. "Irritability, in teenagers? How could you even guess, until it was far too late? So many forms; so many causes. Viruses, fungi, bacteria, carcinomas . . . " A languid flourish of his hand, sketching out a process of infinite regression.

"Carcinomas? What do you mean?" There was a tremor in my voice I didn't like. "Nobody's got cancer."

"Ah, well, cancer." He might have been describing an old bad penny of a friend, a mischievous roué impossible to dislike. "I suppose there's always that moment, isn't there, when the first cell divides in a slightly different way? And you don't know it, but inside you something is already changing—the traitor cell, the Judas tissue? And it starts like *that*—at the snap of a finger." A dry clicking of cold bones.

"Cancer. Limbs of the crab. And there are so many places it can hide. Have you ever stopped to consider this? The body is infinitely tolerant in this respect, Mike, infinitely welcoming. All the major organs, of course—but the big toe? The humble hallux, this-little-piggy-went-to-market? Cancer in your big toe? Look it up in the textbooks. And while you're there, try cancer of the rectum. Cancer of the womb. Cancer of the tongue—even cancer of the *eyeball*. Imagine that, Mike!"

How could I not? I wonder: did he know that anything to do with eyes terrified me, ever since that playground fight when I'd nearly lost the sight in my right eye? I think he probably did. I don't think there was much he didn't know. He wanted me terrified, you see. He wanted me to panic. And there was no stopping him, he was off again.

"Or the neurodegenerative diseases! It's a list as long as your arm, all the Herr Doktors jostling for immortality in the medical texts. Sandhoff, Spielmeyer, Kreutzfeld-Jakob, Pelizaeus-Merzbacher, Schilder and Pick. Body dementia. Corticobasal degeneration. Spinocerebellar ataxia. All of it lying in wait as you grow old, and you never know. Neurons deteriorating, connections broken all across the cortex, until all of a sudden you're sitting in the day ward in incontinence pants, crying because you've dropped your sippy-cup. It could happen to anyone. To Emily, even—why not?"

"Are you a doctor?" It was all I could think of to say. I hoped it might distract him.

He chuckled, softly and disagreeably. "A doctor? Let me see. What would be the *opposite* of doctor, do you think? A doctor; no. No, I'm afraid not, Mike—but I could have a look at it for you, if you like?" Again that creepy chuckle, hardly aspirated, pent up jealously in his throat. "Isn't that how the old joke goes?"

"I don't understand—"

"In the context of Emily? Why not? Why not, Mike? Just because you're besotted with her after what—a day?—that won't save her. She can't be sheltered from the world indefinitely, you know! Nothing protects a person forever. All the love in the world weighs less than a new strain of flu—remember that. The love of the poets may be constant and unchanging, but viruses mutate. Viruses win in the end." I knew he was smiling; I knew how hideous that smile would be. "You're smitten; how sweet. But that won't save her. Bear that in mind, while you consider all the possibilities."

How desperately I wanted this filth to stop; this madness, this indecency. Suppose I simply left the room, got up and walked out? Either the dream would be over and I'd wake up, or I'd be out in the hallway at least, and hopefully he wouldn't come after me. But before I could shift a muscle he said, "No, wait," as casually as that, almost absentmindedly, the way you'd invite someone to take a seat . . .

. . . and there I was, pinned against the cushions. I couldn't move. I tried, but found myself rooted in the chair. Again, it was that feeling we get in dreams, when we're trapped in the grip of the monster, unable to escape. That was the point at which I lost it, in retrospect, the point at which I came to believe that the shape in the armchair was something other than a commonplace pervert or sadist, something other than conventionally wicked, or conventionally insane. The fear was racking up inside me, mounting in an exponential clamor, as he spoke again:

"I mean, accidents! We haven't even mentioned accidents yet, have we? That road down to Tawton, for instance. Monica takes it far too fast, you know, that sharp right-hander near the junction with the A30. She drives Emily and Trish down to pony club each Sunday. Trish goes in the passenger seat, but Emily's in the back, without a seatbelt. Now, what if one fine day in . . . May, shall we say? May the twenty-third, next year? Just for the sake of argument. Now, suppose on that bright May morning, something were to be coming the other way along that lane. A Land Rover, say—or better still, a tractor. A big Massey Ferguson, with a tank full of silage behind it. Both going a bit too fast, neither of them concentrating . . . and poor Emily in the back, without a seatbelt, remember? No protection; no chance. Massive head trauma, a grievous insult to the brain—that's what the doctors would say at the post-mortem. It could happen. *I could make it happen.*"

So calm, so matter-of-fact, but such a terrible depth of malice and psychosis behind every word he spoke. Such a wicked joy in destruction. I was so scared now; so scared, you wouldn't believe it. Dream or not, I knew I was trapped in the presence of a very bad thing, maybe the worst thing of all, and I didn't dare imagine what it wanted with me.

"Or suicide." I must have tried to say something, because he raised his voice insistently. "Yes. Suicide. It would take longer, quite a while longer, but in the end there is nothing more sure. You see, deep in every human heart there is a place with no way out—you might not believe it, Mike, but it's true, it's true, it's so terribly true. And I could find that place. I could take her by the hand and lead her there, and then vanish with a puff of smoke—like that!"

He raised his closed fist to his mouth, blew it open to show nothing. And behind his spread fingers, the nothing where his face should have been.

"Why are you *saying* this?" I was almost sobbing. I'd tried to get up again, tried to run away like a child, but I couldn't. I was rooted to the chair. He had me fast. "Why are you telling me these things? What do you *want*?"

"What do I want?" He sounded positively jovial. "Well, Mike, I want to ask your opinion on something. I'd like you to make a choice."

Somehow, I'd known he was going to say it; feared that he would. Aloud I said, "I don't understand," but I'd known before he even spoke, the way you do in dreams. And of course he was having none of it.

"Yes you do. Don't play the innocent, Mike; don't waste my time. You're a part of this now. Look it up in your Schrödinger: the presence of an observer necessarily affects that which is observed." He emphasized each beat with a tap of his finger on the chair arm, like an impatient lecturer pointing out the relevant passage in a textbook. "You stuck your nose in at a critical juncture. Don't complain now when you get it nipped."

I heard his teeth click together as he suited the action to the word. It was a silly thing to do, a childish thing, beneath his dignity really, but it scared me more than I can ever hope to tell you. From then on, the notion of his teeth simply paralyzed me with fear. I was terrified of how they might look, if I could only see them. How long; how sharp . . . how many.

"This is the very essence of free will." He was back in control now, any momentary irritation suppressed. He knew he had me where he wanted me, after all. "A God-given gift, the measure of man. You ought to be glad of the chance to use it—I mean really slam it on the table for once, that existential joker. Isn't it exciting? Isn't it . . . stimulating?

"Look! Here's our little Emily, tripping through the maze, tra-la. The paths fork ahead of her, and at the end of each path lies death. Those are the rules. This path is long and meandering, with primroses growing in the borders and bluebirds singing. *This* path is the shortest of short cuts." A chop of the hand; final. "And at the fork, we stand together, you and I. Our job is to send her this way, or that. So, again: I would like you to choose. How shall it be? How shall it happen? Which path? What will come to pass?"

"You can't do this," I said, sobbing almost; but he didn't even dignify that with an answer. He *could* do it: of course he could. That was his job, and I was co-opted. I knew it, and he knew I knew.

There followed a gap—I have no way of judging how long it lasted. It seemed like hours, and I couldn't say anything. The fear was so complete, like a ball of molten glass blown all around me, leaving me perfectly, hermetically trapped. In the space of a few minutes I'd been subtracted from the world of chance and accident and scraping through, and thrown screaming into the awful arena of first causes. Five minutes' conversation in the dark. It had the skewed and brutal logic of a nightmare, the worst you could ever have. It might even have *been* a nightmare, except for the wetness of the tears on my face. The tears at least felt real.

And all the time he waited, the guest with only shadow for a face. He sat with steepled fingers and waited for me to betray myself. Eventually he leant forward. "Poor Mike. It isn't easy, is it? But I'm afraid I'm going to have to press you, you know. Time's a-wasting, and we haven't got all night."

Hanging there between us was a threat—a threat every bit as real as a drunken skid on the motorway or a sharpened razor's edge; the crumbling edge of a precipice without a bottom, the ground giving way beneath your feet. Again he spoke:

"So?"

I knew I had to say something. "Not her," I managed, just. "Not her."

"Not her?" Such disappointment in his voice; such contemptuousness. "Is that it? Is that the sum and aggregate of your deliberations? *Not her*? T'ch. I think someone isn't trying."

"Do it to someone else." It was all I could think of to say.

"Michael! But we were supposed to decide!" Almost petulant. "The garden of forking paths, remember?"

"Do it to somebody else." I was actually sobbing now; my face was absolutely drenched with tears. "It doesn't have to be her."

"Really?" the guest asked, as if this was an aspect of it that had never struck him until now. "You think not?"

"No! Do it to someone else! Anyone!"

"Anyone?" He sounded shocked. "Oh, not to anyone, Mike. Those aren't the rules at all. We aren't the agents of blind chance, you know. Don't think that for a moment. No, if it were to happen—I only say *if*, mind—then it would have to be someone else further down the line. One of the other branches of the path, you understand. That's the only way it could happen. The repercussions otherwise . . . " He spread his hands, sketching an immensity of disruption.

"Do it to someone else, then," I begged. It was the only way out that I could see.

"You're sure?" He seemed disappointed. It was horrible. "You're absolutely sure?"

"Yes," I said unhesitatingly.

"Oh, very well,' he said. "If you insist. Now, who?"

"*Who*? I don't know!"

"It has to be somebody, Mike. Not just anybody." He was explaining the rules of the game, very patiently, to an idiot. "You are choosing certain death for a known person, not just throwing a coin off the top of the Empire State Building. I have to have a name."

"I—I—I don't know . . . " He'd blocked off my escape. Again, I could feel myself sliding down into total, suffocating horror.

"Do you want me to help?" Kindly, yet at the same time inexorable. "Is that it? Shall I narrow it down for you?"

I couldn't speak. I just nodded, and he inclined his own head. "After all," he said, "I suppose I have the advantage in some respects. When you can see a little further along the forks, then you have the ability to make an aesthetically pleasing choice—and that is important, Mike. It's important to have standards.

"Goodness!" He sighed. "Let me think. Something equivalent, something . . . something fitting. There is a balance in all things, Mike, though it may not be immediately apparent. Interconnections, synchronicities. One woman wakes up well, and half a world away another feels the lump in her breast and tries to decide whether to bother the doctor with it.

"I'm prevaricating. A name, a name. How about . . . oh! How about *Alethea Kakoulis*? I don't think you know her, do you?"

The name meant nothing to me, nothing whatsoever, so of course I seized upon it, like a man in a shipwreck grabbing a lifebelt out of the hands of another survivor. "Her! Yes! Whatever you said. Do it to her. Do it to—"

Without warning the room exploded into light, sharp bright searing white, and I threw up my hands to guard my eyes. "Do what?" said a voice at my elbow. "Christ, Mike, you all right? You sounded like you were having a right go at someone, there."

It was Dave, come down to check on me. The armchair over by the window was empty. There was no one else in the room.

He said he'd heard a voice from out in the hallway, so he'd come in and switched the light on, thinking I was already awake, that there was someone in there with me. But I was on my own. Clearly, I'd been talking in my sleep. "You'd better not make a habit of that," he told me, "or else I'll be putting in for a new roommate. Jesus, Mike, you were screaming like your throat had been cut!"

Quite. Anyway, Dave fetched me a glass of water and led me upstairs to my bedroom, but even there I couldn't shake the feeling it was all still happening, that I hadn't woken up at all—or that I'd never been asleep. I remember sitting propped up against the pillows with my arms around my knees, bedside lamp switched on, thinking no, it couldn't have been a dream, it couldn't . . .

. . . and then, the next thing I knew, it was Sunday morning, and High Thornhays was coming to life once more. The rumble of Victorian plumbing, the clattering of feet on wooden floorboards, the high clear laughter of the girls through all the passageways. Nothing drives away your fears quite like the rising sun over gleaming snowfields. It's white magic, proof against all the terrors of night.

Going down to breakfast I was already well on the way to sublimating all my memories of the long room: a bad dream, nothing more. I couldn't look

Emily in the face over the breakfast table, though, not quite. That much at least had changed. But nobody noticed—and hey, I was entitled to be a little quiet that morning, after my drunken-eejit stumblings of the night before. By mid-morning we'd dug out the driveway, and the snowplow was laboring up the main road to meet us, and by teatime Tom Headley was driving us back to Exeter in the car.

First of all, let me set your mind at rest, and tell you Emily got through all right—she survived, she's alive to this day. She and her husband live in Poole, where they run a gallery. As for myself, I visited High Thornhays on several more occasions during my time at college, but nothing extraordinary ever happened. I never bagged myself a Headley gal, and I never met anyone worse than myself, as the old saying goes. I made a special point of inviting myself up to Dartmoor the following spring, on May the twenty-third—I took my dream, or whatever it was, that seriously, at least—but as luck would have it, Emily had knocked pony club on the head by then. In fact, she'd started going out with a boy from Newton Abbot, and we saw very little of her that weekend. She was there to wave me off on the evening of my departure, as cheerful as ever.

Once that particular date had passed, and the charm had been broken, I rarely if ever thought about the man in the armchair again. Life has a way of filling in the empty places, if you let it. I'm one of those people who hardly ever remember their dreams, and those I do remember haven't featured the party guest, not for a long time now. Life settled into its everyday groove, which was fine by me. I wasn't looking for anything deeper. As Bertolt Brecht said, in a poem I once knew off by heart, but seem to have forgotten most of now, nothing could be harder than the quest for fun.

In 1984 the quest took me from Exeter up to London, where I made good use of my 2.2 in English lit playing roadie for a shambling indie band called the Stellar Gibbons. Off the back of that I got a job in a rehearsal studios near Clink Wharf, and within ten years I was running the place—not bad for someone with my essentially adolescent approach to career-building. It was there I first met Lee Oliveira.

Lee came highly recommended from the temping agency, and even though I'd already filled the vacancy, her interview lasted twice as long as the woman's who actually got the job. She was interested in music, and I was interested in her; one thing led to another, and we've been together the best part of a decade now. We have our own place in Islington, and Lee's expecting at last. All those years of sperm tests and fertility clinics, and then everything fell into place a month or two ago quite naturally. We were knocked out. Lee's folks came over from their retirement pad on the Algarve, my mum and dad drove up from Weston, and there was a get-together. It was nice.

Lee's second scan was on the morning of July the seventh. I'd been up all night in the studio with a band getting ready for their first big national tour, but there was no way I was missing that appointment. I met her in the doctor's waiting room at half eight; I held her hand while they moved the sensor across her belly and we watched the magic images on the screen. Afterwards, she went into work and I caught the bus home.

The doctor's was in Munster Square, near Regent's Park. I walked as far as Euston and jumped on a number 30. No sooner had I sat down than I was fishing my copy of the scan out of its manila envelope. The woman next to me saw me holding it up to the light (*Now, which bit is the head again?*) and smiled before popping the buds of her Walkman into her ears. I fished out my iPod and followed suit, thinking to listen through some live-in-studio rehearsals from the night before. The first track opened on amplifier hum and the plugging-in of jacks. But then instead of the drummer's count-in there came a voice:

"A significant proportion of birth defects don't necessarily show up on scans, Mike. The really nasty ones, too. Should they do an amniocentesis, be particularly sure to ask—"

That was all I heard. I'd already ripped off my headphones and lurched up out of my seat. The gray daylight of a mild July morning in London was overlaid with a flashbulb burst of white, and for the first time in over twenty-three years I remembered the fleeting impression, that blood-red retinal afterimage that I'd blinked away, that night in the long room at High Thornhays when Dave turned on the light. The man in the armchair, the flicker of glowing coals in his eyes, the terrible tiger's smile . . .

The bus was just pulling up at the next stop, and without thinking I barged my way off. I couldn't stay in that confined space, not now the panic had sunk its hooks so deep into my crawling skin. My iPod—an engraved present from Lee—was still on the seat, along with the ultrasound scan of our unborn baby. The police returned them to me later, when they allowed me to leave the scene. Because this was exactly nine forty-five AM on Thursday the seventh of July, 2005, near the junction of Tavistock Square and Upper Woburn Place, and not two minutes after I'd got off the bus an eighteen-year-old on the top deck, Hasib Hussain from Leeds, set off the explosive device in his rucksack, killing thirteen of my fellow passengers. Across London, more bombs were already being detonated.

The rest of that morning was a blur, really, the bad news filtering through from across the capital while we waited behind police cordons to be told what to do. Mobile phone networks were all down, and we had to make do with rumors and Chinese whispers and whatever the coppers would let on, which wasn't much at first, and all the time we were smelling it on the air: Death, in a leafy London square. The simplest things—buses, tube trains—stood revealed as agents of potential chaos. Everything had the capacity to harm you. Everything you thought you knew.

I wasn't scared for me, not really; only for Lee, and the baby. She, of course, was horrified, and there was a lot of crying and pledging of love that evening, when I finally got home. As we lay in bed hugging each other, I remember her saying, "This feels like such a turning point for us, Mike; it's like a second chance. Like we've been spared. We've been so *lucky*—first the baby, and now you getting off that bus at exactly the right time." Of course, I hadn't told her *why* I'd got off the bus. How could I? "I just feel"—she wiped her nose on a tissue and squeezed my arm—" I just feel as though it's time to do all the things we've ever wanted to do—do them *now*. There's no point in putting anything off any more—don't you feel that way? We should just go for it, full-on, live each day as if it's going to be our last. Don't you think?'

I agreed with her, and squeezed her back and told her I loved her. I believe I also told her everything was going to be all right, which is a thing we all do, I suppose, a lie we all tell. In times of crisis we crave parental reassurance, an order of protection unavailable in the grown-up world. Somehow or other we got off to sleep, and the panic went away for the space of a few hours. No dreams—not that I remember—but on waking it was his words that were running through my head, the voice that had cut through my headphones on the bus. Without thinking I reached across and laid a hand across Lee's stomach.

It wasn't until teatime that next day that Lee told me the first of the things she was planning to do, the one big thing she'd been putting off for God knows how long. It was so important to her now, she said, now that she was going to have a child of her own. I was uneasy even before she told me, and afterwards . . . this was when the panic kicked in, for real this time; and it's never gone away, not once, in all the days and weeks since.

Lee was adopted, you see; she never knew her birth parents. The Oliveiras had shortened her birth name to Lee, and when she'd asked what the full version had been her parents had told her, "Never you mind." Now, she did mind; she felt it was a necessary step towards self-knowledge. She didn't want to involve her folks, so instead she was going to get hold of her adoption file from the council. Already she'd been in touch with the General Register Office, and they'd told her what to do, who to see, what forms to fill out. She told me all this over dinner that Friday evening, and ever since then I've been waiting in a kind of daze for the axe to fall.

It's August now, a hot brassy afternoon heavy with the threat of thunderstorms and downpour. I've been home from work since lunchtime; I had a feeling it would have arrived, and of course it had, punctual as any bad news and as impossible to ignore. It was waiting on the doormat with the flyers and the junk mail, a big white envelope with the council's logo on it, for the personal attention of "Lee Oliveira." I haven't opened it; it's lying in front of me on the kitchen table. I know what it'll say. I know the name inside—I never forgot it. Lee for Alethea; seems all too obvious. Poor Mrs. Kakoulis; though I doubt she was a Mrs., somehow. Did he visit her as well, the uninvited party guest, the bad man in the dark? Which of the forking paths did he push her down, to which dizzy cliff-edge?

And now, as the clock ticks on against the wreck of the day and the last assurances of rationality fall behind like flotsam on a sea deceptively calm for the time being, I sit at the kitchen table with no protection from my nightmares and wait for Lee to come home. Our baby, too—our gorgeous, impossible baby girl—nestled inside her and growing, getting bigger every day. In my head there's the ringing of static, the numbing feedback whine of blank horror and tireless malevolence. I don't know what I'll say to her, when she opens the envelope and tells me what's inside. I don't know what I can say. There is only one question I have, and I can't ask it of any living being, Lee least of all:

Will it be before the birth, or afterwards? When will it happen? When?

Steve Duffy's *stories have appeared in numerous magazines and anthologies in Europe and North America. His third collection of short supernatural fiction,* Tragic Life Stories, *was launched in Brighton, England, at the World Horror Convention 2010; his fourth,* The Moment of Panic *is due to appear in 2011, and will include the International Horror Guild award-winning short story,* "The Rag-and-Bone Men." *Steve lives in North Wales.*

"Certain Death For A Known Person" began as a phrase jotted in a notebook some time in the late 1980s, and became a story some twenty years later. It was written in a rented cottage in the Welsh countryside, one cold week in the deep midwinter; the author would like to thank his sister, Kathy Hubbard, for being as generous with her encouragement and advice during its writing as she is in so many other ways. Thanks are also due to editors Michael Kelly (who published the story in his anthology Apparitions*), and Barbara Roden (who oversaw its inclusion into* Tragic Life Stories*), for helping to present this nasty little tale in the best possible light.*

"Frost Mountain Picnic Massacre" offered us the horror of having no choice. The narrator of Steve Duffy's "Certain Death For a Known Person" is forced to make a choice, and is warned there will be repercussions. We suspect— since this is a story, of course—young Mike will have to confront them in a personal and painful manner. Unless, of course, he—and we—can deny, without doubt, that there "is a balance in all things . . . though it may not be immediately apparent. Interconnections, synchronicities."

Well—can you?

THE ONES WHO GOT AWAY

STEPHEN GRAHAM JONES

Later we would learn that the guy kept a machete close to his front door. That he kept it there specifically for people like us. For the chance of people like us. That he'd been waiting.

I was fifteen.

It was supposed to be a simple thing we were doing.

In a way, I guess it was. Just not the way Mark had told us it would be.

If you're wondering, this is the story of why I'm not a criminal. And also why I pick my pizza up instead of having it delivered. It starts with us getting tighter and tighter with Mark, letting him spot us a bag here, a case there, a ride in-between, until we owe him enough that it's easier to just do this thing for him than try to scrounge up the cash.

What you need to know about Mark is that he's twenty-five, twenty-six, and smart enough not to be in jail yet but stupid enough to be selling out the front door of his apartment.

Like we were geniuses ourselves, yeah.

As these things go, what started out as a custody dispute took a complicated turn, and whoever Mark was in the hole with came to him for a serious favor, the kind he couldn't really say no to. The less he knew, the better.

What he did know, or at least what he told us, was that somebody needed to have the fear of God placed in them.

This was what he'd been told.

In his smoky living room, I'd looked to Tim and he was already pulling his eyes away, focusing on, I don't know. Something besides me.

"The fear of God," though.

I was stupid enough to ask just what, specifically, that might be. Mark narrowed his eyes in thought, as if considering the many answers. By ten, when I knew it was time to be home already, what the three of us finally hit on as the real and true proper fear of God was to think you're going to die, to be sure this is the end, and then live.

We thought we were helping Mark with his dilemma.

Sitting across from us, he crushed out cigarette after cigarette, squinched his face up as if trying to stay awake. Every few minutes he'd lean his head back and rub the bridge of his nose.

The trick of this operation was that there couldn't be any bruises or cuts, nothing that would show in court.

Of all the things we'd thought of, the knives and guns and nails and fire and acid and, for some reason, a whole series of things involving the tongue and pieces of wire, the only thing that left a mark on just the mind, not the body, was tape. Duct tape. A dollar and change at the convenience store.

This is how you plan a kidnapping.

Mark's suggestion that it should be us instead of him in the van came down to his knowledge of the law: we were minors. Even if we got caught, it'd get kicked when we turned eighteen.

To prove this, he told us his own story: at sixteen, he'd killed his stepdad with a hammer because of a bad scene involving a sister, and then just had to spend two years in lock-up.

Our objection—mine—was that this was all different, wasn't it? It's not like we were going to kill anybody.

So, yeah, I was the first one of us that said it: we.

If Tim heard it, he didn't look over.

The second part of Mark's argument was What could we really be charged with anyway? Rolling some suit into a van for a joyride?

The third, more reluctant part had to do with a tally he had in his head of bags we'd taken on credit, cases we'd helped top off, rides we'd bummed.

Not counting tonight, of course, he added. Because we were his friends.

The rest of it, the next eighteen hours, was nothing big. Looking back, I know my heart should have been hammering the whole time, that I shouldn't have been able to talk to my parents in the kitchen, shouldn't have been able to hold food down, shouldn't have been able to stop fidgeting long enough to concentrate on any shows.

The truth of it is that there were long stretches in there where I didn't even think about what we were doing that night.

It was just going to be a thing, a favor, nothing. Then we'd have a clean tab with Mark, and Mark would have a clean tab with whoever he owed, and maybe it even went farther up than that.

Nicholas, of course—it was his parent's front door we were already aimed at—he was probably doing all the little kid things he was supposed to be doing for those eighteen hours: cartoons, cereal, remote control cars. Baseball in the yard with the old man, who, then anyway, was still just a dad. Just catching bad throws, trying to coach them better.

At five after six, Tim called me.

Mark had just called him, from a payphone.

We had a pizza to deliver.

On the pockmarked coffee table in Mark's apartment was all we were going to need: two rolls of duct tape, two pairs of gloves, and an old pizza bag from a place that had shut its doors back when Tim and me'd been in junior high.

The gloves were because tape was great for prints, Mark told us.

What that said to us was that he wasn't setting us up. That he really would be doing this himself, if he didn't want to help us out.

Like I said, we were fifteen.

Tim still is.

The van Mark had for us was primer black, no chrome, so obviously stolen that my first impulse was to cruise the bowling alley, nod to Sherry and the rest of the girls, then just keep driving.

If the van were on a car lot in some comedy sketch, where there's car lots that cater to bad guys, the salesmen would look back to the van a few times for the jittery, ski-masked kidnappers, and keep shaking his head, telling them they didn't want that one, no. That one was only for serious kidnappers. Cargo space like that? Current tags? Thin hotel mattresses inside, to muffle sound?

No, no, the one they wanted, it was this hot little number he'd just gotten in yesterday.

Then, when the kidnappers fell in with him, to see this hot little number, one would stay behind, his ski-mask eyes still locked on the van.

The reason he's wearing a ski mask, of course, is that he's me.

What I was thinking was that this could work, that we could really do this.

Instead of giving us a map or note, Mark followed us out to the curb, his head ducked into his shoulders the way it did anytime he was outside, like he knew God was watching, or he had a bad history with birds. He told Tim the address, then told Tim to say it back.

2243 Hickory.

It was up on the hill, a rich place.

"Sure about this?" Mark asked as we were climbing into the van.

I smiled a criminal smile, the kind where just one side of your mouth goes up, and didn't answer him.

2243 Hickory. A lawyer's house, probably.

We were supposed to take whoever answered the door. Nothing about it that wasn't going to be easy.

To make it more real, we stopped for a pizza to put in the pizza bag. It took all the money we had on us, but this was serious business. Another way to look at it was we were paying twelve dollars for all the weed and beer and gas Mark had burned on our undeserving selves.

In which case it was a bargain.

The smell of pizza filled the van.

On the inside of his forearm, Tim had written the address. Instead of "Hickory," though, he'd just put "H." All he'd have to do would be lick it a couple of times and it'd be gone.

Like *2243H* meant anything anyway.

Then, I mean.

Now I drive past that house at least once a month.

We finally decided it should be Tim who went to the door. Because he already had a windbreaker on, like pizza guys maybe wore once upon a time. And because he had an assistant manager haircut. And because I said that I would do all the taping and sit on the guy in the back while we drove around.

How I was going to get the tape started with my gloved fingers, who knew?

How I was going to stop crying down my throat was just as much a mystery.

In the van, Tim walking up the curved sidewalk to the front door, I was making deals with anybody who would listen.

They weren't listening, though.

Or, they didn't hear that I was including Tim in the deals as well.

Or that I meant to, anyway.

As for the actual house we went to, it was 2234 Hickory, not 2243 like it should have been. Just a couple of numbers flipped. Tim would probably say that they were all the same house anyway, right? Up there on the hill? If he could still say.

As to what happened with whatever custody case we supposed to be helping with, I never knew, and don't have any idea how to find out. But I do know that the name associated with the property records for 2243 Hickory wasn't a lawyer like we thought, but a family court judge.

We were supposed to have grabbed his wife, his daughter, his beagle.

I've seen them through their front window on Thanksgiving eight times now.

They're happy, happy enough, and I'm happy for them.

All this happiness.

When I finally made it back to Mark's the week after, somebody else answered the door. He had all different furniture behind him, like the girl at the portrait studio had rolled down a different background.

What I did was nod, wave an apology, then spin on my heel—very cool, very criminal—walk away.

What I would be wearing when I did that was a suit, for Tim. Or, for his family, really, who had no idea I'd been there that night.

Anything I could have said to them, it wouldn't have helped.

This is the part of the story where I tell about meeting Tim in the third grade, I know. And all our forts and adventures and girlfriends, and how we were family for each other when our families weren't.

But that's not part of this.

I owe him that much.

We should have cruised the bowling alley on the way up the hill that night, though. One last time. We should have coasted past the glass doors in slow-motion, our teeth set, our hands out the open window, palms to the outsides of the van doors as if holding them shut.

The girls we never married would still be talking about us. We'd be the standard they measure their husbands against now. The ones who got away.

But now I'm just not wanting to tell the rest.

It happens anyway, I guess.

Nicholas answers the door in his sock feet, and Tim holds the pizza up in perfect imitation of a thousand deliveries, says some made-up amount of dollars.

Then, when Nicholas leans over to see the pizza sign on the van, Tim does it, just as Mark played it out for us fifty times: spins the pizza into the house like a frisbee, so everybody'll be looking at it, instead of him and who he's dragging through the front door.

On top of the pizza, stuck there with a toothpick, is the envelope Mark said we had to leave.

Putting it inside the box was our idea.

It was licked shut, but we knew what it said: if you want whoever we've got back, then do this, that, or whatever.

As the pizza floated through the door, I saw me in the back of the van with Nicholas, playing games until midnight. Making friends. Tim driving and driving.

We were doing him a favor, really, Nicholas. Giving him a story for school.

But then the pizza hit, slid to its stop down the tiled hall of that house.

Mark was twelve miles away, maybe more.

I was only just then realizing that.

The way some things happen is like dominoes falling. Which I know I should be able to say something better, but that's really all it was. Nothing fancy.

Domino one: the pizza lands.

Domino two: Nicholas, who'd turned to track the pizza, turns back to Tim, like to see if this is a joke, only stops with his head halfway around, like he's seeing somebody else now.

Domino three: Tim leans forward, to hug Nicholas close to him, start running back to the van.

Domino four: what I used to think was the contoured leg of a kitchen table, but now know to be one of those fancy wooden pepper grinders (my wife brought one home from the crafts superstore; I threw up, left the room), it comes fast and level around the frame of the door, connects with Tim's face, his head popping back from it.

Domino five, the last domino: Tim, maybe—hopefully—unconscious, being dragged into the house by Nicholas's father, who looks long at the van before closing the door.

The reason I can tell myself that Tim was unconscious is the simple fact that Nicholas's father didn't come out for me too. Which is a question he would had to have asked, a question Tim wouldn't have been able to lie about, even if he tried: whether he was alone.

So what I do now is convince myself he was knocked out. That he didn't have to feel what happened to him over the next forty-five minutes, like Nicholas did. Or saw, anyway. Maybe was even forced to see.

In the newspapers, it was why Nicholas's mom left Nicholas's dad: because what he did to the drugged-up kid who broke into their home, he did while Nicholas watched, transfixed, his fingertips to the pear wallpaper so he wouldn't fall down.

It involved a kitchen chair, some tape, a hammer. Pliers for the teeth, which he pushed into Tim's earholes and nostrils and tear ducts, just making it up as he went.

How long I was in the truck was forty-eight minutes.

It's better if Tim was knocked out the whole time.

What people say now—it's still the worst thing to have ever happened—what they say now is that they understand Nicholas's dad. That they would have done the same thing. That, once a person crosses the threshold into your house, where you family is, that he's giving up every right to life he ever had.

This is what you do if you're a traitor and in the same break room with people saying that: nod.

This is what you do if you hate yourself and can't sleep and have your hands balled into fists under the sheets all night every night: agree with them for real. That, if anybody tries to come in your door one night, then all bets are off.

And then you're a traitor.

Nevermind that, a few months before Nicholas's harmless juvenile delinquency bloomed into a five-year stretch with no parole, you went to his apartment, to buy a bag. He was Mark all over, right down to how he narrowed his eyes as he pulled on his cigarette, right down to how he ducked his head into his shoulders like his neck was still remembering long hair. And you didn't use anymore then, hadn't since the night before your wedding, would even stop at the grocery store on the way home, to flush the bag over and over, until the assistant manager knocked on the door, asked if there was a problem.

Yes, there was.

It was a funny question, really.

The problem was that one time while your friend's head was floating across a lawn, a machete glinting real casual in the doorway behind it, a thing happened that you didn't understand for years: the life meant for Nicholas, you got. And he got yours.

That's not the funny part, though.

The funny part, the reason the assistant manager finally has to get the police involved in removing you from the bathroom, is that you can still smell the pizza from that night. And that sometimes, driving home to your family after a normal day, you think it was all worth it. That things happen for a reason.

It's not the kind of thing Nicholas would understand, though.

Nevermind Tim.

Stephen Graham Jones *is the author of novels* The Fast Red Road: A Plainsong *(2000),* All the Beautiful Sinners *(2003),* The Bird Is Gone: A Manifesto *(2003),* Demon Theory *(2006),* The Long Trial of Nolan Dugatti, *and* Ledfeather *(both 2008).* It Came from Del Rio, *a bunnyhead zombie book set in South Texas, was published in October 2010. Two more novels,* Flushboy *and* Not for Nothing *are forthcoming. His numerous works of short fiction have appeared in many diverse publications. His first collection,* Bleed into Me: A Book of Stories, *was published in 2005. A second,* The Ones That Got Away, *will be published in late 2010. He was the recipient of Texas Institute of Letters Jesse Jones Award for Fiction (2005) and a National Endowment for the Arts Fellowship in Literature: Fiction (2001). His day job is Professor of English, University of Colorado at Boulder.*

I never watch the news on television. But one evening recently one of the local news shows came on while I was talking to my son. I started to turn it off. But the offspring, an education major, said, "Wait. Listen to this. I heard about it on the radio." It was an all-too-true story of unthinkably cruel child abuse. We wondered what life would be like for the children who had been taken away from their monstrous parents. Would they overcome what they had been through? What would be the whole story ultimately be?

Stephen Graham Jones tells us a story we might hear or read of as "news." But "the news" tells only a part of it. He tells us the *whole* story . . . and we are unlikely to ever forget it.

LENG

MARC LAIDLAW

Expeditionary Notes of the Second Mycological Survey of the Leng Plateau Region

Aug. 3

No adventurer has ever followed lightly in the footsteps of a missing survey team, and today's encounter in the Amari Café did little to relieve my anxiety. Having arrived in Thangyal in the midst of the Summer Grass Festival, which celebrates the harvest of *Cordyceps sinensis*, the prized caterpillar fungus, we first sought a reasonably hygienic hotel in which to stow our gear. Lodging accomplished, Phupten led me several blocks to the café—and what a walk it was! Sidewalks covered with cordyceps! Thousands of them laid out to dry on tarps and blankets, the withered little *hyphae*-riddled worms with their dark fungal stalks outthrust like black mono-antennae, capped with tiny spores (*asci*). Everywhere we stepped, an exotic specimen cried out for inspection. Never have I seen so many mushrooms in one place, let alone the rare cordyceps; never have I visited a culture where mushrooms were of such great ethnic and economic importance. It is no wonder the fungi are beloved and appreciated, and that the cheerful little urchins who incessantly spit in the street possess at their tongue-tips (along with sunflower hulls) the practical field lore of a trained mycologist; for these withered larvae and plump *Tricholoma matsutake* and aromatic *Boletus edulis* have brought revivifying amounts of income to the previously cash-starved locals. For myself, a mere mushroom enthusiast, it was an intoxicating stroll. I can hardly imagine what it must have been like for my predecessors, treading these same cracked sidewalks ten months ago.

Phupten assured me that every Westerner in Thangyal ends up in the cramped café presided over by the rosy-cheeked Mr. Zhang, and this was the main reason for our choice of eatery. Mr. Zhang, formerly of Lhasa, proved to be a thin, jolly restaurateur in a shabby suit jacket, his cuffs protected from sputtering grease by colorful sleeve protectors cut from what appeared to be the legs of a child's pajamas. At first, while we poured ourselves tea and ate

various yak-fraught Tibetan versions of American standards,
enough. Mr. Zhang required only occasional interpretive
Phupten, and my comment on his excellent command of
led him to the subject of his previous tutors—namely, the
of the Schurr-Perry expedition.

Here, at a moment that could have been interpreted as inau.,
those inclined to read supernatural meaning into random events, the lignus
dimmed and the power went out completely—a common event in Thangyal,
Phupten stressed, as if he thought me susceptible to influence by such
auspices. Although the cafe darkened, Mr. Zhang's chapped cheeks burned
brighter, kindling my own excitement as he lit into a firsthand account of the
last known days of Danielle Schurr and her husband, Heinrich Perry.

According to Mr. Zhang, Danielle and Heinrich spent several weeks in
Thangyal last October-November, preparing to penetrate the Plateau of Leng
[so-called, in fanciful old accounts, the "Forbidden Plateau" *Journals of the
Eldwythe Expedition* (1903)] (which I mistakenly thought I had packed, damn
it). Thangyal still has no airstrip of its own, and like me they had relied on
Land Rover and local drivers to reach it. Upon arrival, they encountered great
difficulty in arranging for guides and packhorses to carry their belongings
beyond vehicular routes, and had been obliged to wait while all manner of
supplies were shipped in and travel arrangements made. During this wait,
Heinrich had schooled our host in English, while Danielle had broadened his
American cuisine repertoire. (I have her to thank for the banana pancakes
that warm me even now.)

The jovial restaurateur tried many times to talk them out of their foray—and
not merely because of winter's onset. Were there political considerations?
I asked. For while the Chinese government has relaxed travel restrictions
through some border zones of the Tibetan Autonomous Region, stringent
regulations are still in effect for Westerners who wish to press into the interior.
Many of these stipulations (as I know firsthand) exist mainly to divert tourist
lucre into the prefecture's treasury by way of costly travel permits. But in the
case of Leng, there seem to be less obvious motives for the restrictions. Despite
assurances that I would never repeat his words to any official, Mr. Zhang
refused to elaborate on what sort of benefit the Chinese government derived
from restricting access. Leng is hardly a mineral rich region; there has been
little or no military development there, which indicates it is strategically useless;
and recent human rights reports declare it devoid of prisons or other political
installations. It remains an area almost completely bypassed by civilizing
influences, an astonishing anachronism as China pushes development into
every last quarter of Tibet. As a zone set apart from the usual depredations,
such resource conservation seems distinctly odd; but perhaps they have other
plans for its exploitation. Mr. Zhang's warnings were sufficiently vague that I
could easily picture my predecessors brushing them aside. Once he realized
that it was my intent to follow them, he directed the same warnings at me. Any

. for permission to enter the plateau region would be met with refusal, .id; thus confirming my decision to file no such requests, but depend on ʋ remoteness of the region to lend me anonymity.

When he saw it was my fixed purpose to follow the Schurr-Perry trail, Mr. Zhang got up and shuffled back into the kitchen—now lit solely by a gas stovetop. He returned with a dog-eared ledger and said something in Tibetan which Phupten interpreted as, "Guestbook."

Mr. Zhang opened the ledger, spread it flat on the checkered tablecloth, and guided us backward through the entries—past colorful doodles and excitable notes from the Amari's many international diners—notes in English and German and French. Here were mountaineers bragging of climbs they had just made or climbs just ahead of them, penniless wanderers hoping someone might forward a few million yuan, laments of narrowly missed rendezvous.

Mr. Zhang stopped flipping pages and directed our attention to a ragged strip where one sheet had been ripped from the book.

"Here," he said. "Heinrich and Danielle? They write thank you Mr. Zhang. They say, we go Leng. Bu Gompa. Anyone follow, they read this note, say wait for them in spring. But . . . no come back."

I speak no Tibetan, but I recognized a few words I have heard many times recently, albeit in different context. The locals are always making pilgrimages to their various *gompas*, by which they mean a temple or monastery. And *bu* I know from *Yartse gunbu*, the local name for the caterpillar fungus. Its precise meaning is "summer grass, winter worm," which is a colorful (if backwards) way of describing the metamorphosis of the cordyceps-inoculated caterpillar, which overwinters as a worm, only to sprout a grasslike fungal stalk, the fruiting body or *stroma*, in early summer (once the fungus has entirely consumed it from within).

I clumsily translated the name as, "Temple of the Worm?"

Mr. Zhang said something urgently to Phupten, who listened, nodded, and turned to translate.

"Yes, monastery. Bu Gompa sits in the pass above Leng Plateau. Very old temple, from old religion, pre-Buddhist."

"A Bon temple, you mean?"

"Not Bon-po. Very much older. Bu Gompa for all that time, gateway to Leng. Priests are now Buddhist, but they still guard plateau."

Mr. Zhang was not done with his guest book. "This page, when my friends not return, two men come. Say they look for Heinrich and Danielle. Look for news of expedition."

"This was when?"

"In . . . January? Before they supposed come back. No one worried yet. Tibetan men, say Heinrich friend, ask see guest book. I very busy, many people in restaurant. Think no problem, they look for friends. I go in kitchen, very busy. I come out, they gone. Oh well. Book still here. Later I see page gone!"

"The one Heinrich and Danielle wrote in, you mean? Saying where they were going?"

"Yes."

"These men were Tibetan, you say?"

"Yes. I not see them in Thangyal before, but so many in town. Not only Yartse Festival. Many travelers. I worry they take page, get money from Heinrich and Danielle family."

"Blackmail," said Phupten.

I assured Mr. Zhang that we had heard of no such attempts. I explained that I had followed Heinrich and Danielle's trail after reading a series of letters and articles published in the *Journal of the Mycological Society* in advance of their departure. But all of Mr. Zhang's information was new to me; and that regarding the gompa was particularly interesting, as it suggested where I might next seek news of their whereabouts.

At about this time, the power was restored and a fresh flood of festival attendees pushed into the café. Thinking it right to clear the table for new customers, we bid farewell to Mr. Zhang, thanked him for his kindness, and stepped back out onto a sidewalk now almost completely covered with fungi. I stopped to watch some old gentlemen playing mahjongg on a table they'd set up on the sidewalk, and was hardly surprised to discover that in place of cash or poker chips, they were betting with *Yartse gunbu*.

Aug. 6

This morning, having finally reached the end of the tortuously stony road beyond Thangyal, we climbed from the Land Rovers and found an entire village sitting out in the sun to await our arrival. Our ponies should have been waiting for us, but apparently the drivers had expected us a week ago and turned them loose to graze in the high meadows. Even so, you might have thought the whole village had sat on the streetside, patiently waiting out the week, as if our arrival were the highpoint of the season and well worth any delay. To mark the moment with a bit of ceremony, I passed around biscuits and let the assemblage pore through my mushroom atlas, which was handed about with amazement and appreciation by the entire community. They pointed out various rare species, giving me the impression that many could be found in the region—however, Phupten was too busy remedying the horse situation to interpret, and I soon reached the limits of my ability to communicate with any subtlety.

Phupten eventually signaled me that immediate arrangements had been made, and that we could set off without further ado. The horses would follow once they had been retrieved and laden with supplies offloaded from the vehicles. With a camp-following of dogs and children, we plunged onto a muddy footpath among the houses. As we passed to the limits of the village, we encountered a number of mushroom hunters returning from their morning labors with plastic grocery bags, wicker baskets, or nylon backpacks bulging with *shamu*—the local term for mushrooms of all varieties. Phupten helped me interview the collectors, making quick inventories of local names, edibility, and market prices they earn from the buyers who scour these remote villages for delicacies. One cannot underestimate the value of mushrooms to these people. Species that grow abundantly here are prized in Japan and Korea, where they absolutely resist cultivation. Although the villagers receive a pittance compared to supermarket prices in Tokyo and Seoul, the influx of cash has completely transformed this previously impoverished land. The mud houses are freshly painted in bright acrylics; solar panels and satellite dishes spring up plentiful as sunflowers. The young men dash about on motorcycles as colorful as their temples. Since a study of mushroom economics had been the announced purpose of the Schurr-Perry expedition (although I suspected the unstated motive force was more likely a desire to discover and name some new species found only in Leng), I decided to see if this might be a path already taken. I showed each collector a photograph of Heinrich and Danielle, copied from the dust jacket of their landmark *Fungi of Yunnan*, to see what memories the image might jog loose. One group of giggling youths remembered them well; the adults were harder to pin down. I found reassurance, however, in the innocent recognition of the children, and now feel I am definitely on the right trail—although the chance of losing it remains tremendous in the narrow defiles of the only land route into Leng.

Beyond the village, we crossed a river by way of a swaying cable bridge. Keeping close to the west bank, working our way upriver, we spent the morning traversing damp meadows further dampened by frequent cloudbursts. Our gear, now swaying awkwardly on the backs of four ponies, caught up with us in the early afternoon. Not long after, we crossed back to the east bank, on a much older bridge that put me in mind of a stockade. The blackened timbers were topped with protective shapes that again served as reminders of the mushroom's ancient significance. The more stylized carvings were clearly meant to represent shelf fungi, tree ears, king boletes. The bridge also marked the point at which I felt we had crossed a divide in time. I saw no more hazardous electric lines strung between fencepost and rooftop; no dish antennae were in evidence. The mudbrick walls were topped with mats of cut sod, which made them wide enough that small dogs could run along the heights, barking down at us. Children followed us through streets that ran like muddy streams. Eventually, at the edge of a walled field, we left them all behind, flashing peace signs and shouting after us, "*Shamu-pa! Shamu-pa!*" Phutpen laughed and said, "They call you 'Mushroom Man,'" which sat very well with me. Our guides grinned and set the horses on at greater speed.

After that, all other habitations were simpler and more temporary affairs. Phupten brought us to the black felt tent of a yak herder, where an elderly nomad woman cut squeaking slices of a hard rubbery cheese and sprinkled it with brown sugar; I was grateful for the butter tea that washed it down. But it was the large basket of matsutake that held my interest, each little bud wrapped in an origami packet of rhododendron leaves.

Regretfully, as we ascend we are bound to leave such woodland curiosities behind. The higher elevations are more secretive with their treasures. Consider the elusive cordyceps—notoriously hard to spy, with its one thin filament lost among so many blades of real grass.

Late in the day, we came in sight of the massif that guards the pass into Leng. The late afternoon light made the barrier appear unnaturally close, sharp and serrated as a knife held to my eyes. Such was the clarity of the air that for a moment I felt a kind of horizontal vertigo. I imagined myself in danger of falling forward and stumbling over the rim of the mountains into a deep blue void. When a violet translucence flared above the range, it edged the snowy crests as if auroral lights were spilling up from the plateau hidden beyond them. I suppose this strange, brief atmospheric phenomenon may be akin to the green flash of the equatorial latitudes, but it also made me more aware than ever of the imminent onset of altitude sickness, and the ominous tinge of an incipient migraine. I was grateful when our guides, immediately after this, announced it was time to make camp.

We spread our tents in a wide meadow between two rivers. The rush of rapids was almost deafening. One of our guides, doubling as cook, filled pots and a kettle from one of the streams and soon had tea and soup underway. From a bloody plastic grocery bag, he produced rich chunks of yak and hacked them up along with fresh herbs and wild garlic he had gathered along the trail. I offered several prize boletes of my own finding. We ate and ate well in the shadow of a tall white stupa, also in the shape of a mushroom, adorned with a Buddha's eyes, and I was reminded of another interest of Heinrich's and Danielle's. They had read conjecture in *The Journal of Ethnopharmacology* that the words Amanita and Amrita had their nomenclatural similarity rooted in a single sacred practice. Amrita is the Buddhist equivalent of ambrosia, or the Sanskrit *soma*, a sacred foodstuff; and it has been suggested that certain Buddhist practices may have been inspired, or at least augmented, by visions following ingestion of the highly psychoactive *Amanita muscaria*. The Schurr-Perrys had stated a desire to be the discoverers (and namers) of *Amanita lengensis*, should such exist. In this way the mycological world resembles the quantum world, in being a realm so rich and various that simply searching for new forms seems to call them into creation; where labels may predate and even prophesy the things to which they are eventually applied; in which scientists now chart out the psychic territory known as *Apprehension*.

When I asked which species we might find beyond the pass, I was surprised to learn from Phupten that our guides had only visited Bu Gompa once or twice in their lifetimes, and had never actually set foot in Leng. Such pilgrimages are not undertaken lightly. Leng is held in such reverence and awe, as a place of supernal power, that they believe it unwise to venture there too often.

Sharing our interest in all things mycological, the horsemen related a tale of a stupa-shaped mushroom that had bloated to enormous size and died away to puddled slime in the course of one growing season. This had occurred in their childhoods, but pilgrims still visited the spot in hopes the *Guru Shamu* might reappear. With what in retrospect seems arrogant pedantry, I found myself explaining that the fruiting body they saw, impressive as it might have seemed, was still only a comparatively tiny eruption from a much vaster fungus, the *real* guru, growing unseen and unmeasured beneath the soil. They looked at me with disappointment, as if I had just declared them retarded. In other words, this was hardly news to them. I eventually succeeded, through Phupten, in apologizing. I explained that in the West, extensive knowledge of mushrooms is considered bizarre at worst, the mark of an enthusiast at best. We shared a good laugh. At last I am among kindred spirits. So much about our lives is different, but in our passion for mushrooms we are of one mind.

Aug. 8

A day of astonishment—of revelation. Almost too much to encompass as I sit here typing by the light of my laptop, wrapped up in my sleeping bag as if under the stars, but with my gear pitched instead in a chilly stone cell. I should sleep, I know. I am exhausted and the laptop battery needs charging; but I fear losing track of any detail. I must write while this is all fresh.

After yesterday's slow progress and mounting disappointments, we were relieved to sight the Leng Pass by late morning. We had ascended to such an altitude that even now, in midsummer, snow comes down to the level of the trail in numerous places. Blue deer capered on the steep ragged scree above us, lammergeier were our constant observers, and once we startled a flock of white-eared pheasant, large as turkeys, that hopped rather than flew away through the boulders. The occasional stinkhorn, fancifully obscene, was still to be found among the thinly scattered pine needles, but my desire to forage had receded with the elevation. Grateful to have woken with a clear head, and not at all eager to trigger another migraine, I resolved to conserve my strength. But it was hard to slow down once I saw my view of the sky steadily broadening, with no further mountains moving into the notch above.

We passed cairns of engraved stones and desiccated offerings that seemed neither plant nor animal but something in between, and entered a long flat valley, sinuously curved to match the river flowing through it. The valley floor was high marshland, studded with the medicinal rhubarb we have seen everywhere. This was all picturesque enough, but above it on a slope of the pass, just at the highest point where snow laced the scree, was the most wonderful sight of the journey. Its prayer flags flying against the clouds seemed triumphant banners set out for our welcome. We had reached Bu Gompa, which straddles and guards the entrance to Leng.

Thunder rumbled; rain fell in gray ribbons. Phupten said the monks were bound to read this as an auspicious sign, coupled with our arrival. Our horsemen quickened their steps, and even the ponies hurried as if the object of their own private pilgrimage were in sight. The monastery loomed over us. Above it, among shelves of rock on the steeper slopes, I saw the pockmarks of clustered caves like the openings of beehives. Then we were through a painted gate and the place had consumed us. Happily lost among tall sod-draped walls, I breathed in the musty atmosphere of woodsmoke, rancid butter and human waste that I have come to associate with all such picturesque scenes in this country.

Several boys, young monks, were first to greet us, laughing and ducking out of sight, then running ahead to alert their elders. We climbed switchback streets, perpetually urged and beckoned to the height of the pass. At last we entered a walled courtyard. A wide flight of steps soared to a pair of immense doors, presumably the entrance to the main temple. As Phupten conversed with a small contingent of monks, I tried these doors and found them locked. It seemed propitious to leave an offering of ten dollars to show our good intentions and dispose the monks toward our cause. Meanwhile, our horsemen laid themselves repeatedly on the flags of the courtyard, in prayerful prostrations, aligned along some faded tracework of symbols so ancient I could detect no underlying pattern. Although the walls were bright with fresh paint, this monastery seemed remote enough to have escaped destruction during the Cultural Revolution.

I retreated down the steps to find Phupten perplexed. The monks, he said, had been expecting us. They led us around the side of the building, skirting the huge locked doors, and entered the main hall by a small curtained passage.

We had seen many fantastically colorful temples along our route, lurid to the point of being DayGlo. This one impressed by its warm burnished hues. Rich russets, silvery grays, pallid ivories. Everywhere were exquisite *thangkas*, hand-painted hangings in colors so subdued they evoked a world of perpetual dusk. There was light in these paintings that seemed to emanate from within and could hardly be fully explained by the shifting glow of the numerous butter lamps. Bodhisattvas floated among sharp mountains, hovering cross-legged above vast emerald seas from which radiated gilt filaments painted with such skill that they seemed to vibrate on the optic nerve, creating the illusion of swaying like strands of golden grass. Most of the traditional Buddhas and Bodhisattvas had grown familiar to me after so many recent temple visits but Phupten pointed out one figure new to me, and quite unusual, which made numerous appearances throughout the room. Pre-Buddhist, and predating even the ancient Bon-po religion of Tibet, Phupten thought this to be the patron of those original priests of Leng. Where Buddhist iconography was highly schematic, drawn according to regular geometric formulae, this figure harkened back to an older style, one unconcerned with distinct form and completely innocent of the rules of perspective: amorphous, eyeless, mouthless, but not completely faceless. Having noticed it once, I began to spy it everywhere, lurking within nearly all the *thangkas*, a ubiquitous shadow beneath every emerald expanse.

I noticed our horsemen moving about the room in clockwise fashion, lighting incense and butter lamps, leaving offerings of currency at several of the shrines. Having taken up this practice myself, as a matter of courtesy rather than devotion, I began to follow their example; but Phupten took my arm and for the first time in our journey, told me to hang back. When I asked why, he pulled me into a corner of the room and whispered, with curious urgency, "If you look, you see no pictures of His Holiness."

It was true enough, and remarkable, given the common appearance of the Dalai Lama in every temple we had visited across the eastern fringe of Tibet.

"Not good. Old disagreement. They do practice here, very old, from Leng. His Holiness say very bad. Three years ago, the priests of Leng, they speak out against Dalai Lama, that he is suppressing their religion. He says, their protector deity is like a demon—"

"I thought all the old Bon spirits were demons once."

"Yes, but this one never enlightened. False wisdom. So, a very big fight, and even a man who try to kill his Holiness in Dharamsala. They said it was Chinese assassin behind it, but many believe it was ordered by monks of Leng."

"So . . . no offerings," I finished.

"Yes."

"But what about our guides? Don't they know?"

Before he could answer, our inspection of the temple was interrupted by the arrival of several more monks. Two were elders, dignified men, strong but gentle seeming. The third was younger, with strongly Caucasian features. In his monastic garb, with head shaved, and given the fact I had only seen him as a lecturer, at a distance, at one or two mycological conferences, I suppose I can be forgiven for not having recognized him until he came up to me, put out his hand, and said, "You don't recognize me, do you? Heinrich Perry!"

Ten minutes later, we were seated in the courtyard enjoying a sun break, sipping tea and chewing dumplings of tea-moistened *tsampa*. It seemed that all the monks of Bu Gompa had turned out to get a look at me. They laughed and posed for photographs, until their various duties took them off again, for meditation or debate. Heinrich said news of our coming had preceded us up the passes; he had been expecting us since our visit to Mr. Zhang, although he was surprised anyone would have followed in his footsteps. The Schurr-Perry expedition was anything but lost. He had already found more than he ever expected to find, without even crossing into Leng. His wife had ventured onto the plateau and made discoveries of her own, but Heinrich had not set foot across the threshold.

"And where is Ms. Schurr?" I asked.

Heinrich gestured airily in the direction of the surrounding slopes. "She is in retreat." Leaving me to infer some transcendental meaning in this statement, he must have seen my glazed expression, for he laughed and elaborated: "Above the monastery are many old caves used for meditation. She has been there since her return from the plateau." He leaned forward and said confidentially, "She has been recognized as a superior practitioner, while I scrub pots and chop wood!"

So our predecessors, far from lost, had simply gone native. And their mycological survey? Their dreams of discovering new species in Leng? It was hard to believe they had given up on their passion.

Heinrich said, "Not at all. I would say we have embraced it. The Leng Plateau is a treasure chest of rarities, previously unknown. Once you attain the plateau, it is impossible to describe the wealth of discovery that awaits. But . . . once I reached this spot, such things lost their importance. Danielle has never been one to hold back, but I . . . I feel fulfilled as a porter at the gate. All Leng lies before me, but I know myself not yet ready for what it has to offer."

This seemed like a shame, and I said as much, for Perry's reports had always been received eagerly by mycological society. In a profession which had yearly become more and more the domain of geneticists, more partitioned into microscopic domains, Perry and Schurr had been unafraid of bold strokes and sweeping statements. Their papers, while thoroughly grounded in empirical observation, never shied from leaning out over the thrilling edge of speculation. Their gift of synthesis was to couple personal reportage with ecological insight; their reports, while botanically rigorous, did not neglect the social and economic implications of their finds. Yet apparently the line between devout ethnomycology and monastic assimilation had been porous. I considered it a shame, but then felt awkward and ashamed of myself for harboring critical thoughts of this pair, whom I knew not at all. If they had found personal fulfillment in casting aside purely academic concerns and embracing the spiritual, then who was I to judge them? If anything, I felt a keen resolve to work even harder in order to compensate for the loss of Schurr-Perry's ongoing contributions to the field. The success of my foray into Leng seems more crucial than ever.

By now it was early evening, and we walked out to stand on a temple balcony, looking out across the very threshold of Leng. The serried peaks opened before us like a curtain of violet ice pulled back to reveal a sea of rolling green that broke against the misty edges of infinity. The most evocative passages of the literature of Leng came rushing back to me—from the lush descriptions of Gallardo's *Folk and Lore of the Forbidden Plateaux* (1860) to the spare journal entries of the tragic Eldwythe misadventure of 1903, made all the more macabre and ironic by its innocence of the repercussions it would inevitably have on British and Russian relations.

" . . . lost land of unnameable mysteries . . . beauty beyond reach and beyond utterance . . . effulgent as the evenstar's radiance alight on the breast of earth, enflaming the mind and senses . . . " Although I had always thought such descriptions must have been flights of fancy, my first sight of Leng simply made me sympathetic to the self-avowed descriptive failings of all previous writers.

It was no wonder Perry had stopped here, I thought, for to descend into that remote wilderness was to risk stripping it of the intense mystery that gave rise to its fantastic beauty. While I knew that on the morrow we would put one foot before the other and gradually make our way down to that strange green plain, I regretted the thought of taking any action that would lessen Leng's magic while heightening its reality. It struck me as a dreamland, suspended in its own hallucination of itself, impervious to the senses. And yet such bubbles—how readily they burst. I feared this was a delusion of the evening, of the twilight air, doomed by the threat of morning. But there was nothing for it. I tried to hold on to a sense of anticipation, reminding myself of what Perry had hinted: That new discoveries awaited us below.

Horns resounded deep within the monastery, amid the clanging of cymbals and bells, and several boys came to fetch us back. Just before we turned away, the first stars appeared above the misty plains, and I sent up a fervent wish that I would never forget the feelings that had accompanied their arrival. Needless to say, these impressions will make no appearance in my published survey notes. In fact, I hope I can word my reports in such a way that none of my colleagues feel compelled to follow my trail and impinge upon this mystic land. It is such a strange feeling, as if I have been entrusted with a secret rare and exquisite, one that seems to blow up from the plateau on scented winds. I feel it would be wrong, shameful, to blunt it with too many perceivers. I am of course committed to sharing the knowledge I find here, and in no danger of falling into the trap that claimed the Schurr-Perry party. But I find myself certain that those Tibetans who visited Mr. Zhang and tore the entry from his guestbook must have been sent at Heinrich Perry's request, in an understandable attempt to cover up his trail.

During dinner, we spoke only of plans for the journey ahead. Phupten dined with the drivers, so I relied on Perry for interpretation. It seemed strange to me that they would have embraced him as a lama when his only real expertise, to my knowledge, was in the area of mycology. Likewise, how had Danielle managed to distinguish herself so swiftly among this group of lifelong spiritual practitioners? It was one thing to rush ahead fearlessly, as Heinrich had suggested was her wont—and quite another to convert that mortal zeal into an act of transcendence.

These questions were hard to frame while my hosts plied me with such a remarkable meal. Knowing my interest in local mushrooms, the monk chefs contrived a meal of savories that grew within range of the temple, prime among them a delectable red fly agaric, or chicken egg mushroom—*Amanita hemibapha* [once incorrectly known as Caesar's mushroom (or, I would imagine, "Gesar's mushroom" in these lands), viz., *Amanita caesarea*, but delightful whatever its name]. In my tea I found a special additive—a wrinkled grub, perhaps three inches long, like a sodden medicinal root. Heinrich confirmed my suspicion that it was nothing less than cordyceps, and a most prized variety, being collected along the edges of the grasslands that blanket the plateau. Like the worm in a bottle of tequila, it bobbed against my lips as I drank. In tropical climes, where insects are rife, the invasive cordyceps comes in many forms, to encompass the wild variety of insect hosts; but in these high cold climes, its hosts are few and unprepossessing. Whatever traits might have distinguished *Cordyceps lengensis* from the more common variety were not at all obvious to my eye; in fact, soaked and swimming in tea, it looked more like a shred of ginseng than anything else. Heinrich said the monks called it *phowa bu*, which I hesitate to translate. "Death Worm" gives the wrong impression altogether and "Transcendence Worm" is not much better. Phowa is a ritual done at the moment of death, intended to launch its practitioner cleanly into the Pure Lands through his crown—to be more precise, through the fontanelle at the top of the skull. Heinrich claims that in true practitioners of phowa, a blood blister forms at the top of one's head, and a hole opens there. This channel is just wide and deep enough to hold a single stalk of grass—and in fact, this is the traditional test used by lamas to gauge an initiate's readiness. With its single grasslike stalk, the shriveled cordyceps serves as a humble reminder of the sacred practice.

I asked Heinrich if I might see fresh specimens of *Cordyceps lengensis* before my departure, but he demurred—and there I caught a glimpse of the old academic, cagey and wary with his findings. "Of course," I quipped, "you have yet to publish!" And was gratified to hear him laugh. I'd struck truth! For all his monastic garb, he is still a mushroom hunter through and through--protective of his private foraging grounds!

Although the sun had barely set, I found the cumulative exertions of the last few days, and the effects of the altitude, had overcome me. The cordyceps infusion seems to have some medicinal properties, for tonight as I lay down to make these entries, I found my breathing easy. Normally these past few nights, I have felt a crushing weight on my chest, exaggerated when I recline, and I wake many times before dawn, gasping for breath. Something tells me that tonight I will sleep well.

Stray thought—Heinrich's research re Amanita/Amrita. Must ask in the morning. Where that led him; what he found, if anything. Cordyceps aplenty, but no sign of *Amanita lengensis*. I'd like to charge the laptop before I go, but I couldn't ask them to run the generator all night. Low on power.

Undated Entry

Phupten is dead. Or worse.

I believe our guides may have met a similar fate—I cannot call it an end, although it might be that. I will do my best to explain while I still have power, in hopes this laptop may be found by someone who may benefit by my warnings. I cannot flee back across the pass. The only other path is a trackless one, forward across the plateau. Leng. There are good reasons not know it any better than I do already.

Two nights ago? Three? Phupten woke me in the dark monastic cell, with a flashlight in my eyes and fear in his voice. He said we were at risk of losing our guides to the gompa. Whether they had planned it from the start, or merely found themselves seduced by the monastic order upon arrival, he was unsure. They had mentioned childhood vows that needed renewing, but apparently things had gone too far.

I was already dressed inside my sleeping bag, so I scrambled out and followed him along dark halls, taking nothing but the few valuables in my backpack. We passed under timbered passages and starry gaps, and eventually came to the side door of the great hall. Inside, the monks sat chanting in row upon row with our guides now among them. Phupten held me back, as if I would have plunged among them—but I was not inclined to interrupt that ceremony.

Both guides stood at the head of the temple, close to the central altar. Incense fumes shrouded them, as if they were being fumigated, purified in sacred smoke. The smoke rose from a fat gray mass, as large as a man's torso, that smoldered but did not seem to burn. A lama stood near the men, his face hidden behind a richly embroidered veil of yellow cloth shot through with gold and red. He held a long wooden wand, possibly a yarrow stalk, which he used to softly prod and poke at the lump, stirring up thick billowing clouds of the odorless incense with each touch. I realized I was seeing a tangible version of the icon featured in so many *thangkas*—the local protector deity made manifest, squatting in the place that should have been occupied by a Buddha or Bodhisattva.

Sensing our arrival, the lama laid down his wand and walked toward us, stripping off his veil as if it were a surgeon's mask. I was much surprised to find Heinrich leading a ceremony of such obvious importance. Without a word, he took me by the arm and steered me toward the side door. I looked around and discovered that Phupten had already crept away.

"Your guides have elected to stay," he said.

"If they wish to take monastic vows it's no business of mine," I said. "But they should first fulfill their obligation to the survey. You know the importance of our work, Heinrich. Once you were as devoted to mycology as anyone on earth. Can't you ask them to postpone this sudden bout of spirituality for a few weeks? I'll be happy to leave them with you on my return from the plateau."

Rather than argue, Heinrich led me away with a gentleness that later seemed more forceful than sympathetic.

"I understand your point of view, but there is another," he said patiently.

"When Dani and I first arrived here, our survey seemed more pressing than anything on earth. I remember my eagerness to catalog the contents of Leng. But there is a faster way to that knowledge. A richer and deeper kind of knowing."

We were moving up the mountainside along a rough path. The hollow eye sockets of caves peered down without seeing us. The cloistered buildings fell below.

"Speak with Danielle," Heinrich said. "She can explain better than I."

Starshine through the frayed clouds was all the light we had, but on the snowy flanks of the mountains it was almost dazzling. Heinrich brought me to a black throat of darkness. Small icons sculpted of butter and barley flour were arranged at its mouth; there were shapes like spindles, bulbs, ears. We stepped inside. My first impression was of choking dryness and dust. I saw a gray knot, far back in the cave, bobbing in the guttering light of a single butter lamp that burned on the ground before it. I could make out a figure wrapped in robes, with head bowed slightly forward. All was gray—the face, the long hair cleanly parted down the middle. I supposed it was a woman, but she did not speak, nor stir to greet us.

"This is Danielle," Heinrich said. "She has answers to all your questions."

I was not sure what to ask, but I swore I heard her answering already. Deeper into the cave I went, stooping as the ceiling lowered, until my ears were very near her mouth. The sound of speech was louder now but still indecipherable, like mumbles inside which something was gnawing. Thinking it might help to match mouth to syllable, I watched her face until I was certain her mouth never moved. When I stepped back, a faint gray filament stirred in the breeze I'd made. It jutted from her scalp like a stalk of straw. The mark of the *phowa* adept. It seemed incredible she could have attained such a transcendent state in so little time. Was this why they had decided to remain? Could the monks of Bu Gompa offer a short path to enlightenment? Was there something about Leng itself, something in the rarified air, in the snowy mountains and the rolling misty grasslands, that provoked insight? I thought of how I had felt looking out over the fields—as if perpetually on the verge of understanding, of merging with a mystery that underlay all existence. But I had hesitated then and I hesitated now, even as I teetered on the brink. Doubt assailed me, and I have been trained to rely on doubt. Was enlightenment invariably good and wise? Was it possible that some forms of enlightenment, more abrupt than others, might be more than a weak mind could encompass? Were there not perhaps monks who, at the moment of insight, simply went mad? Or in a sense shattered?

Heinrich had been joined by others. Dark shapes clustered outside the cave, with the stars beyond them looking infinitely farther than stars had ever looked to me before. There was some aspect of menace in the silent arrival of the monks, and I suddenly felt myself the victim of a fraud. Doubt drove me entirely now. In a last bid to assert my rationality, to make all this as real as I felt it needed to be, I turned back to Danielle Schurr. It was time to end all deception. My fingers closed on the blade that jutted from her crown. Far from a dry grassy stalk, it proved to be pliable, rubbery, tough. I thought of the lure of a benthic anglerfish—something that belonged far deeper than this cave extended. As I pulled it from her scalp, or tried to, the top half of her head tore away in my hand, hanging from the end of the stalk in shreds, like a wet paper bag. The rest of her, what was left of her, exploded like a damp tissue balloon packed with gray dust. If you have ever kicked a puffball fungus, you might have some idea of the swirling clouds of spores that poured like scentless incense from the soft gray body—in such quantity that the dry husk was instantly emptied and lay slumped across the floor, inseparable from its robes.

I knew I must not breathe till I was far from the cave, but of course I already had gasped. Thus the shock of terror plays a critical role in the inoculation. I backed away, expecting to be caught by Heinrich and his cohorts. But no one stopped me. All stood aside.

My descent was a desperate and precarious one, especially once I abandoned the trail and cut off along the only available route—the pass leading down into Leng. The thought that I might accidentally blunder back into the monastery filled me with terror. By starlight, and some miracle, I found my way off the treacherous rocks and onto a stable path. An enormous clanking shape lurched toward me, matching my wild imaginings of some shaggy supernatural guardian that had descended to track me down. It proved to be one of the pack horses, bearing an ungainly bundle quickly assembled from our belongings, and led by none other than Phupten. He was as startled to see me as I was to meet him, for he had understandably thought only of saving himself. He said the path in the other direction had been gated off, the far side of the monastery impassable; so he'd had no choice but to flee toward Leng.

Behind us came the drone of horns, and I half expected the baying of hounds in pursuit. But though cymbals clashed and bells clanged and chanting rose up to the stars, nothing but sound pursued us down through the pass toward the unknown plateau of Leng, which became less unknown with each step. We fled through icy mountain fogs so luminous that I thought several times the sun must be rising, but each time found myself deceived.

At last, in exhaustion, Phupten pegged the ponies and dragged down blankets, and built a fire among the roots of a tree to give us some shelter against a miserable rain. We made plans for the morning, plans that have since evaporated. We debated whether we should wait till the following night to try and sneak back the way we had come. I dreaded the thought of returning to the monastery; it seemed impossible that we could ever creep unseen through the narrow maze of lanes; and who knew what the monks would do if they apprehended us? But Phupten insisted this was the only way back. For ages, it had been the one route into and out of Leng. There in the cold night, knowing that Leng was close, I regretted ever seeking it out. I wanted nothing more than to have remained ignorant of its mystery.

We slept there fitfully, shivering, and I dreamt fearful dreams of something wary and watchful toward which we fled. Small white buds were stirring among the roots of the tree, growing swiftly like *plasmodium* in a stop-motion film; they bulged from the soil and then opened, staring at me, a cluster of bloodshot eyes.

I jerked awake in a frozen dawn, hearing Phupten calling my name. But he was nowhere to be seen. The ponies waited where he had tethered them, so I thought he must have gone off for water or more wood.

I waited there all morning.

The mist veiled the mountains as if urging me to forget them. In the other direction, endless rolling hills of grass emerged. Alluring terrain, yet the notion of venturing there seemed madder than going to sea without a compass or the slightest knowledge of celestial navigation. I clung to the misty margin and watched the grasslands through much of the day, noting the way the light shifted and phantom sprites sometimes moved through the air above the rippling strands, auroral presences like the vaporous dreams of things hidden below the soil. I wondered if the Chinese suspected what dreamed there—if they hoped to harness it somehow, to tame or oppress it. Or had it managed to hide itself from them—from all controlling powers? Was it not itself an agent of utter control? Maddening insights flowered perpetually within me, the merest of them impervious to transcription. I wondered if there were degrees of immersion . . . or infection. Danielle had rushed out to meet the powers of the plateau . . . I continued to hold back . . . I felt on the verge of exploding with insight; as my mind quickened, I felt it ever more incumbent upon me to hold very still. A horrid wisdom took hold. These thoughts were only technically my own. Something else had planted them. In me, they would come to fruit.

I realized my eyes had closed, rolling back in my skull to point at a hidden horizon. With an effort of recall that felt like lurching disappointment, I disgorged a memory of Danielle Schurr's final, meditative posture. This drove me to my feet. I stamped about, remembering how to walk. I felt emptied out. Cored. I foraged among the packs for food, hoping nourishment would abate my unaccustomed sense of lightness. Altitude still explained a great deal, I told myself. But something else was wrong. Almost everything.

In the afternoon I finally saw Phupten, far out on the sea of grass. He would not come close enough for me to read his features, nor did I dare walk out to greet him. Maybe he had been there all along. He stood with his face turned in my direction, and I began to hear mumbling like that which had filled the space in Danielle's cave. I could not resolve words. The tone was plaintive, pleading, then insistent. Phupten walked off some distance, sat down, and grew very still. I believe night came again, although it might have been a different kind of darkness falling. My head swarmed—swarms—with dreams not my own. Leng stretches out forever, and beneath its thin skin of grass and soil waits a presence vast and ancient but hardly unconscious. It watches with Phupten's eyes, while he still has them. I dreamt it spoke to me, promising I would understand all. It would hold back nothing. I would *become* the mystery—the far-off allure of things just beyond the horizon. The twilight hour, the gate of dreams. All these would be all that is left of me, for all these things are Leng of the violet light. I felt myself spread to great immensity. Only the smallest leap was needed—only the softest touch and form would no longer contain me.

I woke to find myself walking out onto the plateau. Onto the endless green where Phupten waited. I crossed the threshold. The veil parted. I beheld Leng.

The plateau spread to infinity before me, but it was bare and horrible, a squirming ocean beneath a gravelled skin, with splintered bones that tore up through the hide, rending the fleshy softness that heaved in a semblance of life. A trillion tendrils stirred upon its surface, antennae generating the illusion that protected it, *configuring the veil.* This was Leng. *Is!* A name and a place and a thing. Leng is what dreams at the roof of the world and sends its relentless imaginings to cover the planet. The light that shines here is not the violet and orange of twilight or dusk. It is the gray of a suffocating mist, a cloud of obscuring putrefaction, full of blind motes that cannot be called living yet swarm like flies and infest every pore with grasping hunger. A vastness starving and all-consuming that throws up ragged shadows like clots of tar to flap overhead in the form of the faceless winged creatures that wheel away from the plateau to snatch whatever hapless souls they find beyond the gates of nightmare and carry them back here, toward a pale gray haze of shriveled peaks so lofty that even though they rise at an infinite distance, still they dwarf everything. And having glimpsed the impossible temple upon those improbable peaks, I know I can never return. Even though I took but the one step across the threshold and then fell back, I cannot unsee what I have seen. There is no unknowing. The veil is forever rent. I cannot wake. And though I write these words because I am compelled, because Leng's spell is such that others will read this and be drawn to it, I pray for an end to wakefulness and sleep. I cannot stop my ears or eyes or mind from knowing what waits. Leng's vision for Earth is a blind and senseless cloud that spreads and infects and feeds only to spread, infect and feed. And its unearthly beauty—we are drawn to it like any lure. I pray you have not touched me. I pray the power has

Marc Laidlaw *is the author of six novels, including the International Horror Guild Award winner,* The 37th Mandala. *His short stories have appeared in numerous magazines and anthologies since the 1970s. In 1997, he joined Valve Software as a writer and creator of* Half-Life, *which has become one of the most popular videogame series of all time. He lives in Washington State with his wife and two daughters, and continues to writes occasional short fiction between playing too many videogames.*

Written as one of twenty-four tales for Ellen Datlow's *Lovecraft Unbound,*
Laidlaw's "Leng" draws on both research—he's written on Tibetan themes and
settings before, most notably in his novel *Neon Lotus* (1988)—and experience
(he visited Tibet in 2007). As for Lovecraft's core principles, as Laidlaw writes,
" . . . we may eschew arbitrary tentacles and embrace his passion for the role of
amateur in science . . . and remember that as he beat the twilit byways of New
England, looking for insights which must remain nameless and ineffable, to be
spied just beyond the limits of our capacity for knowledge, he found not only
horror but beauty."

TORN AWAY

JOE R. LANSDALE

He was a young man in an old black car, parked out by the railroad tracks near an oil well that still pumped, pulling up that East Texas crude. I got word of the car from Mrs. Roark, who lived on the far side of the tracks. She called my office and told me that car and man had been sitting there since late afternoon, and from her kitchen window she had seen the driver get out of the car once, while it was still light, and walk to the other side, probably to relieve himself. She said he was dressed in black and wore a black hat, and just the outfit spooked her.

Now, at midnight, the car was still there, though she hadn't seen him in a quite a while, and she was worried about going to sleep, him being just across the tracks, and she wondered if I'd take a look and make sure he wasn't a robber or killer or worse.

Being Chief of Police of a small town in East Texas can be more interesting than you might think. But, not my town. It had a population of about three hundred and was a lazy sort of place where the big news was someone putting a dead armadillo in the high school principal's mailbox.

I had one deputy, and his was the night shift, but he had called in sick for a couple of days, and I knew good and well he was just spending a little extra time at home with his new bride. I didn't tell him I knew, because I didn't care. I had been married once, and happily, until my wife died suddenly in childbirth, losing the baby in the process.

Frankly, I've never gotten over it. The house seemed too large and the rooms too empty. Sometimes, late at night, I looked at her photograph and cried. Fact was, I preferred the night shift. I didn't sleep much.

So, when Mrs. Roark called and told me about the car, I drove out there, and sure enough, the car was still there, and when I hit my lights on high, I saw that it looked like it had seen a lot of road. It was caked in dust, and the tires looked thin. I bumped the siren once, and saw someone sit up in the seat and position his hands on the steering wheel.

I left the light on to keep him a little blinded, got out, and went over and tapped on the glass. The driver rolled it down.

"Hello, sir," I said. "May I see your license?"

He turned his face into my flashlight and blinked, and took out his wallet and pushed his license out to me. It said his name was Judah Wilson. The license was invalid by a couple of months, and the photo on it looked somewhat like him but it was faded and not reliable. I told him so.

"Oh," he said. "I should have noticed it was out of date."

"This is your picture, here?" I asked.

He nodded.

I thought about giving him a ticket for the problem with the license and sending him on his way, but there was something about him that made me suspicious; the photo not being quite right. I said, "I tell you what, Mr. Wilson. You follow me to the station and we can talk there."

"Is that necessary?" he said.

"I'm afraid so," I said.

At the station, I found myself a little nervous, because the man was over six feet tall and well built and looked as if he could be trouble. His hat and suit were a bit worn, and out of style, but had at one time been of good quality. His shoes needed a shine. But so did mine. I had him seat himself in front of my desk and I went around to my chair and, without thinking about it, unfastened my holster flap where he couldn't see me do it. I studied the photo. I said, "This looks like you, but . . . not quite."

"It's me," he said. "I'm older by a few years. A few years can make a difference."

"I just need to make a call," I said. I wasn't able to go somewhere private and call, since I was the only one there, and yet I was not in a position where I felt comfortable locking him up. I made the call and he listened, and when I finished, I said, "I guess you heard that?"

"The owner of the license is dead?"

"That's right. That means you have another man's out-of-date license."

He sighed. "Well, it wasn't out of date when I first got it and it's not another man. Exactly. It's just that I can't duplicate another person completely, and some less than others, and this man was one of the hard ones. I don't know what the difference is with one and then another, but there's sometimes a difference. Like you buy a knockoff product that has the same general appearance, but on closer inspection you can tell it's not the real deal."

"I'm not sure I understand," I said, "but I'm going to ask you to stand up and walk over to the wall there, and put your hands on it, spread your legs for a pat down. I got reason to hold you."

He did what I asked, sighing as he did. I gave him his Miranda rights. He listened and said he understood. I marched him to one of the two cages we had in the back. I put him in one and locked the door.

"You really ought not do this," he said.

"Is that a threat?"

"No, it's a warning."

"You're behind bars, sir, not me."

"I know," he said, and went and sat on the bunk and looked at a space between his shoes.

I was about to walk away, when he said, "Watch this."

I turned, and his body shifted, as if there was something inside him trying to get out, and then his face popped and crawled, and I let out a gasp. He lifted his chin and looked up. Inside his black suit, under his black hat, he looked almost exactly like me.

I felt weak in the knees and grabbed the bars for support. He said, "Don't worry, I can shift the way I look because I do not have a core, but I can't turn to smoke and flow through the bars. You've got me. And that ought to worry you."

There was a bench on the outside of the bars for visitors to sit and talk to their friends or loved ones on the other side, and I sat down there and tried to get my breath. I kept staring at him, seeing my face under that black hat. It wasn't quite right. There was something missing in the face, same as the one he had before, but it was close enough.

A long moment passed before he spoke. "Now watch."

He closed his eyes and tightened his mouth, shifted back, and looked the way he had before, like Wilson. Or almost like Wilson.

"It's best you let me out," he said.

I shook my head.

He sighed. "I'm not like anyone you've dealt with before."

"I don't doubt that," I said, and took my pistol out of its holster and laid it on my knee. He was behind bars, but the whole thing with his face, the way his body shifted under his suit, I couldn't help but think I might have to shoot him. I thought I ought to call my deputy and have him come in, but I wasn't sure what he could do. I wanted to call someone, but I couldn't think of anyone to call. I felt as if every thought I had ever possessed was jumbled up inside my head, knotted up and as confused as Alexander's Gordian knot.

I made myself breathe slowly and deeply.

He took off his hat and placed it on the bunk beside him and stared at me.

I said, "Tell me who you really are. What you are. Why you're here."

"You wouldn't understand."

"Try me."

"It wouldn't make any difference," he said, and smiled at me. The smile had about as much warmth as a hotel ice machine.

"Are you . . . are you from somewhere else?"

"You mean am I from Mars? From somewhere out there?" He pointed up to give his words emphasis.

"Yes."

"No. I'm not. I'm from right here on earth, and I am a human being. Or at least I once was."

I bent forward, overwhelmed, feeling light-headed and strange.

"What I can tell you is there is something coming, and when it gets here, you won't like it. Let me out."

"I can't do that."

"Because I'm not who I say I am?"

I nodded. "And because the man you look like is dead."

"Don't worry. I didn't kill him. He died and I took his identity. It was simple, really. I was in the hospital, for a badly sprained wrist; had to have a kind of support cast. Accident. Silly, really. I fell off a ladder working in a bookstore. But I was there, and Wilson died because of a car accident. It was time for me to move on anyway. I can't stay anywhere very long, because it'll find me."

"It?"

"Just listen. His family was in his room, and when they left out to do what was needed to be done about having the body dismissed, I went in and found his pants and looked through his pockets and took his wallet. I pulled back the sheet and studied his face. I became him. It was okay until tonight, long as I kept on the move and didn't have trouble with the law. But tonight, me being tired and you checking me out . . . It's come to an end."

"You could be me if you wanted to?"

"I could. If I killed you and hid the body, I could go right on being you. But not here. I wouldn't know your ways, your mannerisms, your experiences, but I could use the face and body and move on; become you somewhere else. Or use the face and not the name. There's all kinds of ways to play it. But I'm behind bars and you're out there, so you've got no worries. Besides, I don't kill. I'm not a murderer. Thing is, none of it matters now; I've lost time and I've lost ground. It's coming and I need to put enough miles between me and it to give myself time to truly rest."

"You're crazy."

"You saw me change."

"I saw something."

"You know what you saw."

I nodded. "Yeah. Yeah, I do." I got up and slipped the gun into its holster and took hold of the bars and said, "Tell me about yourself. Tell me now."

"If I do, will you let me out?"

For a moment I didn't know what to say to that. Finally I said, "Maybe."

"Ha. You're pulling my leg. You're the law. You're dedicated."

"I don't know if the law covers this," I said. "I don't know what I might do. I know this: what you got is a story, and I got a gun and you behind bars, and you say something's coming, so it seems the problem is yours."

"Something is coming all right, and if you're in the way, it could bother you. It could do more than just bother. Look here. Listen up." He stood up and spread his arms and stood under the light on the ceiling.

"What do you see?"

"A man."

"Yes. But what is missing? What do you not see?"

I shook my head.

"Look at the floor where you stand. What do you see?"

I looked. I saw nothing, and said as much.

"No. You see something all right. Think about it . . . Here. Listen. Move to your right."

I stepped to my right.

"What moved with you?" he asked.

"Nothing moved with me."

"Look at me."

I looked. He stepped right. "Look on the ground. What do you see?"

"Nothing."

"Correct. Now follow me when I step left."

He stepped left. "What do you see now?"

"Still nothing."

He nodded. "Look at your feet again. Step left."

I did.

"Step right."

I did . . . and then I got it. I had a shadow and it moved with me. I jerked my head toward him and saw that where he had stood there was nothing. No shadow.

He stepped right, then left. He spun about like a top.

"My husk is empty," he said. "I am without shadow."

I took hold of the bars again, stood there trembling. I said, "Tell me."

"Will it matter? Will you help me out?"

"Perhaps. Tell me."

He sat down on the bunk again. "All right," he said. "I will."

"My troubles began during the War Between the States. For me that was a year or two after the war started. Eighteen sixty-two."

"The Civil War?"

"That's what I said."

"You're a time traveler?"

"In a way we all are time travelers. We travel from our date of birth until our date of death. We travel through time as it happens. Not around it, but through it. I am like that, same as you. But I have traveled farther and longer. I was born in 1840. I fought in the Civil War. I was killed in 1864."

"Killed?" I said.

"I was struck by a musket ball, during . . . Never mind. The where and how of it is unimportant. But I was struck dead and laid down in a shallow grave, and I was uncovered by wild dogs who meant to tear at my flesh. I know this because she told me."

I took my seat on the bench again. I didn't know what to think. What to feel.

"An old woman chased the dogs away and finished digging me up and took me home and I came alive again on her kitchen table, stretched out there naked as the day I was born, my chest and legs covered in designs made in chicken blood. Standing by the table with a big fruit jar full of something dark was the old woman. And she told me then I was hers. She was a witch. A real witch. She had rescued me from death and brought me to life with a spell, but she had kept my shadow; had torn it away from me with her enchantments. If I had it back, she said, after being brought back from the dead, I would die as others die, and I would not have the powers that I have now."

"The shape changing?" I said.

Wilson, for I knew no other name by which to call him, nodded. "That, and my ability to live on and on and on."

"And the jar of shadow?"

"She kept it on a shelf. My shadow was small at first, minuscule, like a piece of folded cloth. As time went on, it swelled and filled the jar. The jar could only hold my shadow for so long, and when it swelled enough, the jar would break, unless moved to some larger container, but once it was free, it could never be contained again. Even then, as long as I stayed away from it, I would remain ageless, be able to change my shape. But, if it found me, it would take me and I would age the way I should have aged; all the years that had passed would collect inside me, turn me inside out."

"Why didn't the witch use the spell on herself, to keep from aging?"

"Because you had to be young for it to work, or so she told me. But perhaps it was because she knew that eventually, no matter what it was contained within, it would get out. You had to worry about it forever pursing you, forever fleeing.

"As time went on, my shadow grew, and the old woman placed the jar in a crock, and one day we heard the jar crack inside the crock, and we knew the shadow was growing. During the day I did her bidding. I chopped and gathered wood. I worked her garden. I cooked her meals and washed her clothes. At night I lay on the floor in the thin clothes she had given me, shivering or sweating, according to the weather, unable to move because of the magic marks the old witch had made on my body. And my shadow, I could hear it moving around inside the crock, like insects in a hive.

"Then, one morning I awoke and nothing held me. The spell was broken. In the night the old woman had died. I buried the crock deep in the ground inside the floorless cabin and I set the place on fire and burned it and the old woman's body up. I went away then, walking as fast and as far as I could go.

"All I could think about was my shadow. When I lay down at night I felt as if I could hear it swell inside that crock, under the ground, and that it was breaking free, and coming up through the earth, taking to the wind, moving deliberately after me. I knew this as surely as if I could see it. I knew this because it was part of me and it was missing. I knew it traveled only at night, and found dark places during the day, for it had lost its host, and without me, it couldn't stand the light of day. I knew all of this instinctively, the way a chicken knows to set a nest, the way a fish knows to swim or a dog knows to bark.

"I moved across the land, year after year, ahead of my shadow, moving when it moved, at night, sleeping during the days, sometimes, but often driving day and night until exhaustion took me. The decades ticked by. I grew weary. That's why I was in the car during the night when I should have been moving. I slept the day and planned to move on when night came. Kept telling myself, You're too tired to drive. Just a few more minutes. A half hour. And then you can go. It's only just dark. Thoughts like that; the kind of thoughts an exhausted man thinks. I had been that way before, all tuckered out, and it had almost caught me. I was down with some disease or another. Down for three days, and I awoke, some kind of internal clock ticking louder and louder, and I knew it was near. This was over a hundred years ago, that near catch, and I still remember it sharp as a moment ago. The air turned cold in the dead of summer, and the world felt strange and out of whack, as if something had tilted. I took a horse and rode out. As I rode, I looked back, and there it was, a dark swirl of gloom tumbling toward me, dead as a distant star.

"I whipped that horse and rode it until it keeled over. I whipped it to its feet, rode it until it fell over dead. I ran on foot and found a barn and stole another horse, rode it for miles. I caught a train and just kept going. But it had been close. I had felt it coming, and that had saved me. I feel that way now. In this damn cell I'll meet my Waterloo, and there you'll stand, watching it happen."

I stood there for a long moment, and then I got the cell key and opened the door. I said, "Not if you run."

Wilson stood up and adjusted his hat and came out of the cell, showed me a thin smile. "Bless you . . . By the way. The real name, it's Elton Bloodline. Thank you, thank you."

"Go!"

I followed as Bloodline moved swiftly to the door, opened it, and stepped out. The wind was chill and Bloodline stopped as if something wet had crawled up his spine; he went white under the overhanging light. He turned his head and looked, and I looked too.

Way down the street, the darkness pulsed and moved toward us on the breeze; it twisted and balled and sometimes resembled a giant dark and faceless man, running.

"It's found me." Bloodline seemed frozen to the spot. "Torn away, and now it's coming back."

I grabbed his arm. "Come. Come with me. Now!"

He came alert then. We darted to the police car. He got in and I got behind the wheel and started up the engine and drove away in a roar and a squeal of tires.

I glanced in the rearview. And there it was, a shadow man, maybe ten feet high, passing under streetlights, pulling their glow into its ebony self. It ran swiftly on what looked like long, wide, black, paper-wobbly legs, and then its legs fluttered out from under it and it was a writhing wraith, a tumbleweed of darkness.

I put my foot to the floor and the car jumped and we put space between us and it, and then I hit something in the road, a pothole maybe, but whatever it was it was a big bad bump and the right front tire blew. The car swerved and the back end spun to where the front should have been. As it did, through the windshield I saw that the shadow looked like an inkblot, then I saw lights from the streetlamps, and then the car flipped and bounced and I didn't see much of anything for a while.

I couldn't have been out longer than a few seconds. When I awoke, I discovered that I was hanging upside down. Through habit, I had fastened my seat belt. Bloodline, in his haste and fear, had not; he was wadded up on the ceiling of the car and he was starting to move. I unfastened my belt and managed not to drop too hard or too fast by bracing my hands on the ceiling of the car and twisting my feet around to catch myself. I glanced about. The front and back glass were still intact. The glass on the driver's side was knocked out and the passenger's side was cracked in such a way that you couldn't see out of it.

Bloodline sat up, shook his head, and looked at me. I saw the hope drain out of him and he began to shake. "You tried," he said, and then the car was flung upright and we crashed together, and then I heard glass break, and a big dark hand jutted through the shattered windshield. It grabbed at Bloodline. He tried to slide backward, but it stretched and followed and got him around the waist. I grabbed his legs and tugged, but the thing was strong. It pulled him through the glass, cutting him with jagged shards stuck together by the windshield's safety goo, and then it pulled so hard that he was snatched from my grasp.

I wiggled through the busted-out driver's window, and on my hands and knees I crawled along the street, glass sticking into my hands, the reek of spilled fuel in the air. I got to one knee and looked; I saw that Bloodline's shadow was completely in the shape of a large man. It had grown from only moments ago, standing now twenty feet high and four feet wide. It lifted Bloodline high into the air, tilted its head back, and carefully swallowed him.

The shadow swelled and vibrated. There was a pause, and then it throbbed even more. With a sound like metal being torn, it grew smaller, rapidly. Smaller and smaller, and then, there it stood, a shadow the shape and size of a man. It looked at me, or would have had it had it eyes. The darkness it was made of began to whirl in upon itself. The shape grew pale, and finally it was Bloodline standing there, the way I'd seen him before, but nude, his suit and hat and shoes all gone; his nude body shivering in the wind. He looked at me and a strange expression ran across his face, the kind you might have when someone points a loaded gun at you and you know he is going to pull the trigger. He turned his head and looked to his left, and there, poking out from him, framed by the street-lights behind him, was his shadow.

Then he withered. He bent and he bowed and his skin creaked and his bones cracked, and his flesh began to fall in strips off his broken skeleton. The strips fell into the street and the bones came down like dominoes dropped, rattled on the concrete; the skull rolled between my feet. When I looked down at it, it was grinning, and shadows moved behind the sockets, and then even they were gone and the darkness that replaced them was thin. The skull collapsed. I stepped back, let out an involuntary cry.

Then all of it, the skull, the bones, and the strips of flesh, were caught up on the chill wind, and then they were dust, and then they were gone, and then the air warmed up and the night brightened, and the lights all along the street seemed clearer and I was left standing there, all alone.

Joe R. Lansdale *is the author of over thirty novels and numerous short stories. His novella,* Bubba Hotep, *was made into an award-winning film of the same name, as was* Incident On and Off a Mountain Road. *Both were directed by Don Coscarelli. His works have received numerous recognitions, including the Edgar, seven Bram Stoker awards, the Grinizani Prize for Literature, American Mystery Award, the International Horror Award, British Fantasy Award, and many others.*

As you probably know, Joe R. Lansdale is a noted spinner of yarns. In "Torn Away" he is specifically writing—as was Kelly Armstrong's story—for a *Twilight Zone* tribute anthology. Teleplays for that profoundly influential series often wound up reminding us there were shadows that might devour us, or that no one can escape Fate, even with the help of an East Texas cop. There's another interesting aspect to "Torn Away" that makes it, to me, more up-to-date than nostalgic: Mr. Bloodline is the ultimate "identity thief" who is, eventually, robbed of all identity.

THE NOWHERE MAN

SARAH PINBOROUGH

―✦―

"I've had enough. I'm getting out of here, I swear to God I am." Amy had been sitting cross-legged on the end of Ben's bed wearing the same jeans, T-shirt and trainers she would disappear in later that night, when she whispered the words to herself, or to him or the pitch black outside. Ben wasn't sure which, or even whether she'd meant to say the words aloud at all. He just sat silently in the dark and listened. From somewhere down the corridor of the small single-story house he was sure he could hear Mum's rattling breath ticking away the hours. Or maybe it was just his imagination and straining ears playing tricks on him. Maybe Amy's mood was catching. She was fifteen, and it seemed to Ben that she'd been saying a lot of crazy stuff since she'd got so close to adulthood. And also since Mum had started spending most of her time in bed or in the chair on the porch, displaying her cancer to everyone who passed.

Getting out of here.

At twelve, it seemed that he saw the world much more clearly than his sister. Dad was long gone, only a vague memory of dark curls and sweet beery breath. Mum was sick—*No. Dying, Mum was dying, no get out of jail free card for her*—and they were just kids, and this was their home and where they went to school and where there were people to look after them. To smother them with kindness and kisses that stank of guilt and the invisible burden of responsibility that they were all so eagerly waiting to ditch.

Yes, he thought as they both sat there gazing out of his paint-chipped window, sometimes it would be easier for Amy, for both of them, if she would just let things take their course without fighting all the time. There was no getting out of here. Not for a while yet.

Ben never told the police those words she'd said in the days after she disappeared. He didn't see the point. Amy hadn't run away, no matter what she might have said she was going to do. He knew this for a fact because he knew his sister. And he knew that she would never, ever have left him behind on his own with Mum. Uh-uh, no way.

And it wasn't as if the police needed any more encouragement to think that she'd just up and left Bracknell, heading for one of the big cities and a new life. He could see it on their faces. After all, what teenage girl wouldn't want to get away from this tiny, dusty barely-town and the pressures of looking after a dying woman? And a pretty girl like Amy Kremmer? Who could blame her for escaping?

For a while they'd buzzed uniformly around in the early summer heat of the house until eventually they disappeared, drifting away one by one, all agreeing that Amy had just taken flight. It was easier to believe than the alternative, and with only three hundred or so houses to search it hadn't taken long to ascertain that Amy wasn't locked away or buried in someone's cellar or back yard. Maybe she was out there hidden in the drying farmlands and pastures on the other side of the highway, but there'd been a stream of police and local pick-ups trekking out to the horizon searching for any hint of her in the first days after she vanished, and they all came back without a trace. And anyway. People didn't do that kind of thing in a little town like Bracknell. People here *cared*.

Behind the dry handkerchief on her too-pale face, Mum had loved the whole sorry trauma although no one but Ben could see it. She'd loved that all that health and vitality had gone before she had. She didn't think that Amy had gone off to the city either. Not a chance. Because despite the cancer eating her lungs, his mother was a bitch. Always had been, always would be, and the only people that seemed to remember that were Ben, Amy and their mother herself. Since she'd got sick and saintly she'd hidden it better from the rest of the world, but she still knew that Amy wouldn't have left Ben behind. Not if there had been any choice in the matter.

Mum had cried a lot in the first days after Amy went, sucking the sympathy out of people as if it could keep her alive longer, and soon Amy's name turned dirty and muddy. The selfish girl who ran away and left her mother dying. What kind of a girl would do that? *Probably a slut. Probably pregnant. Probably a whore by now.* Slowly people stopped talking and got back to living, but Amy's memory was tainted and that made her mother happy.

Ben didn't cry. He couldn't bring himself to. Sometimes, his stomach icy in the dry heat of the afternoon, he would go into the dusty stale air of Amy's bedroom and look at the things that she would never have left behind. Her favorite jacket still hung on the back of the door, her wallet in the pocket. Her lipstick and the other stuff girls used were still in the tatty pink bag on the dresser.

In the small heart-shaped box by her bed was the shoelace necklace Trav had given her before he went off to college at the end of the previous summer. There was a rumor that he'd found himself a new girlfriend and Ben figured it was true, but Amy still loved him. If she'd run away she would have worn that necklace to give her strength, like an amulet against the world. She believed in all that shit. And maybe if you believed in it, then it worked. That necklace was the most precious thing she owned. He knew that because she never talked about and rarely wore it, but sometimes at the end of a bad day with Mum she would take it out of the box and just sit and hold it, a faraway look in her eyes.

Holding the metal pendant in his own sweaty palm he would wish Amy had worn it anyway. And then he wouldn't have known for certain that she was dead. That someone had done something very bad to her and that her cold, damaged body lay in a lonely undiscovered place and there was nothing he could do to help.

Sometimes when his mother was dozing, he would watch her and the greedy monster that was eating her up from the inside out. And he would think of Amy decomposing wherever *her* monster had left her, feeling the knowledge of her death like a heavy tumor in his own heart. Maybe they were all rotting in their own way. Turning from something they had once been into something entirely new and far less pleasant.

By the time the summer was at its height and the tiny local school had locked its doors for the long holiday, no one talked about Amy any more. She was forgotten by pretty much everyone but Ben. Miss Bellew, the teacher at school, had looked sadly at him from time to time, but he never knew whether that was because of Amy, or because Mum now had to use the oxygen tank pretty much all the time and a care nurse had moved into the spare room, which surely must mean that she was finally losing a fight with someone. And this time she was going to lose to herself. The irony of that thought made Ben smile, a private, angry twist on his face. But sometimes in the dark of the night it would make him cry hot tears, though he could never understand why.

He stayed out of the house as much as he could in those weeks. The nurse—Mrs. Cooper, a thin tall woman with the beginnings of a moustache that he couldn't help stare at—bustled about the house, her presence leaving a sterile bleached scent behind her. She fed his almost-no-longer mother cocktails of drugs or bowls of thin soup and washed her stained and sweaty sheets, tutting quietly under her breath as if his dying mother should know better than to soil her sheets at her age. Watching her, Ben knew when he was in the way. With a woman like Mrs. Cooper a twelve-year-old boy would *always* be in the way. And so the weeks after Amy vanished, a time in which he didn't feel much like playing at all, were forced into a time of outdoors, fresh air, hanging around with kids with too many hours and too little to do with them.

The school playing field lay behind the small building that served to educate all the children in Bracknell aged from four to fourteen, which at last count amounted to thirty-seven young and fragile souls. It was a vast sports area for such a small school, but out here where there was way too much land for people to ever fill the irregularity went unnoticed. And in the long, hot days of summer, so did the field itself.

By the afternoon that Ben, Cath, and Wrighty sat in the middle of the wicket talking about everything and nothing in that way that only kids can, the ground beneath them was hard and cracked, the green that had covered it not that many weeks before already forgotten.

It was Wrighty who saw him first, a dark shadow out by the boundary.

"Who the hell is that?" His voice was soft, just the hint of mild alarm. Wrighty was a whole year older than Ben and nearly a foot taller, as blond and tanned as Ben was pale and dark. Ben figured that pretty soon the two of them wouldn't be hanging out together, but he hoped the friendship would last the final year before Wrighty started getting the bus into the bigger school at Launceston. There was only so much someone could lose in one summer.

Absently pulling loose tufts of dead brown grass out from the wrinkled earth and tossing them into the still air, the three of them squinted in the sunshine that refused to duck behind the thin wisps of cloud, their bodies slowly stiffening.

A man stood very still just beyond the faded white chalk line one hundred-and-fifty yards away, staring directly towards them. The sunlight glared down right behind him, making it difficult to see more than a blur of a shape.

"Is that Scratcher?" Cath's braces had been fitted less than a week before, and the spray of saliva that came out with her words was the closest to watering the desperate grass had experienced in the two weeks since school had closed. Ben glanced at her sadly. If anything was going to force Wrighty away from him, it was Cath. Image began to matter at thirteen and Cath was never going to have the easy style of their older friend. And that was going to start counting big time to Damien Wright. Ben had seen it happen with Amy and her friends a couple of years earlier. That crazy teenage stuff took hold and real things didn't matter any more.

"Nah." Wrighty, still their friend for now, shook his head. "Why would Scratcher be out here in the holidays? He'll be in a bar somewhere in Launceston getting wasted." Scratcher was the school caretaker and groundsman, so nick-named because of the flaking eczema on his face and arms that he worried at constantly. "And anyway, isn't that guy wearing a suit?" His head tilted slightly as he stared across the wasteland.

Ben raised himself up on the knees of his battered Levis, green eyes focused. Had the man taken a step forward? It sure seemed that way, the image clearer than it had been only moments previously as if the stranger had moved into a patch of shadow. Yeah, he was wearing a suit, black or navy blue, Ben couldn't decide from this distance. But he could see the shirt and tie within the exposed V at the top of the blazer. His breath caught in his throat with curiosity. No one, but no one in Bracknell wore a suit unless they were going to a funeral, and even then not always.

His heart juddered.

Mum.

Maybe something had happened at home. For a moment bright lights sparkled with darkness at the corners of his eyes, his mouth opening as the breath trapped in his healthy lungs forced itself out with the shock. Aaaahhh.

He could hear it buzzing in his ears like when he'd finally realized that Amy wasn't coming home.

It was the flash of light at the man's side that set the blood rushing to his brain. Something was glinting in his hand as it hung downwards. What was that? He glanced over at Cath and Wrighty and noticed that the gangly girl had taken hold of the older boy's sleeve, tucking her body closer to his. *Yeah right, Cath. Any excuse. Like that's ever going to happen.* Hating his own cruel thought and the truth that was in it, he looked back. "What's he holding?"

"Dunno. Can't quite make it out," Wrighty said.

They sat frozen like meercats staring out over the African plains for five minutes or more, and the man stared back.

Cath tugged at Damien. "I don't like it. I don't like him. This is weird."

It was only when the stranger started coming towards them that they pulled themselves upright, shaking the dust from their knees and the pins and needles from their ankles and feet. He was coming right at them. And he wasn't walking or strolling. He was striding. Big long steps full of determination. Like the Terminator, the second one, coming out of the fl ames. Ben's heart was pounding now, his eyes once again drawn back to the thing that shone as it swung to and fro by the man's side, getting too close to them, far too quickly. His pupils widened and then contracted back in on themselves in real fear.

"He's got a knife," he said, his face burning in the sun. "Jesus."

"That's not a knife. That's a fucking machete." Damien's voice was low and Cath had pulled herself behind both boys now, the situation no longer just an opportunity to give her crush on Wrighty free rein. Ben could almost feel her trembling, as if the slight juddering of her body was causing the air to shake.

The man was only forty or so feet away from them now, his head tilted downwards so they couldn't make out his face. But Ben could see the silver streaks that ran through dark head of hair and the way that the suit didn't fit him quite right, the legs stopping two or three inches from the ankle to reveal pale skin where there should have been socks. Dust from the playing field had risen like a tide, clinging to the sharp black polish on his lace-up shoes, and for a moment the three children stood hypnotized as they watched the man getting closer and closer.

Afterwards Ben couldn't remember if anyone had actually yelled out to start running. Probably. All he knew was that one minute they were standing, and the next he had turned and his legs were pumping like crazy, the hot air steaming in his lungs as it ripped and tore its way in and out, the sudden exertion shocking his system. Cath sprinted in front of him, her thin freckly legs stretching out beneath the loose edges of her canvas shorts, her awkwardness suddenly vanished and her body comfortable with itself for once as her trainers pounded the thirsty ground. Just behind her was Wrighty, his running less elegant but equally as efficient. Ben focused on them as he pushed himself forward, fighting the urge to look back, sure that he would see the stranger almost touching the thin sweaty cotton of his T-shirt.

Within moments they tumbled around the edge of the school building, leaning sweaty bodies against the cool bricks, head and eyes throbbing with excited blood.

"We gotta . . . we gotta . . . " Cath was leaning over, holding her knees. "We gotta tell someone." Straightening up, she hopped from one foot to the other. "Come on."

Ben peered round the edge of the building. The man in the suit hadn't chased after them, but was still walking at the same swift pace across the field. Whereas when they'd run they'd veered left aiming for the protection of the school house, the stranger continued on the same path, a straight line, through the wicket and heading to the other side of the boundary.

"Hey." Ben voice was hoarse, his lungs raw. *Was this what it was like for Mum? All the time?* "Hey." He glanced back round at the other two. "I don't think he's following us. He's not coming this way. Look."

Despite Cath tugging him back, Wrighty cautiously looked round the edge of the building. He wiped his nose with the back of his hand, the sprint having made it run. "We still got to tell someone. He's dangerous. Who knows where he's going?"

"Come on!" Cath was almost in tears, not sharing their confidence that the man wasn't heading in their direction.

Wrighty stepped back. The stranger was almost level with where they stood and Ben pulled himself in against the wall. He thought of the machete. And then thought of Amy. *I'm getting out of here. I swear to God I am.* A trickle of sweat ran down the back of his neck. He didn't look round to the other two.

"You guys go. I'm going to follow him."

"What? Don't be stupid!" Wrighty shook his arm. "We're all going. Now come on!"

Ben shook his head, glaring into his friend's face. "No." Damien's eyes shook with controlled panic, but Ben knew that his own gaze was firm. "I have to follow him. You go with Cath. I'll be fine. I'll be careful."

From the corner of his eye he could see the dark shape come into view as it passed. It was enough to send the other two running down the side of the building and disappearing round to the front, Wrighty cursing under his breath.

Knowing they were gone, Ben relaxed slightly as he watched the back of the moving suit. He had maybe ten minutes before the others came back armed with adults. Ten minutes to keep him in sight. A stranger with a knife. Amy.

Stepping back out into the sunshine, he trotted across to the middle of the field so that he was directly in line about thirty yards or so behind the stranger. Matching the brisk pace, Ben could feel his legs shaking, his whole body weak, not from the exertion of the run—he was twelve, he could run that over and over before tiredness would catch him—but from the tingling of anticipation and terror running down his spine, stealing his energy. *What if the man turned around? What would he do then? What if the man was Amy's* killer? *What if he decided to do to Ben whatever it was he'd done to his sister?* *What if? What if?* None of it mattered. All Ben could see was the man and the knife, and the possibility of an answer for Amy. For him. For the witch that was dying at home.

Picking up his pace, he followed the stranger on his too-straight path out of the field and into the play area for the younger kids. The man in the suit didn't look around once, as if as soon as the three children had run from him, he'd forgotten they had ever been there. Surely he could sense Ben following him? Didn't everybody get that funny prickly feeling on their soft exposed skin when they could feel someone walking just that bit too purposefully behind them? Maybe he did. Maybe he knew Ben was there. Maybe that was all part of the plan. It made Ben shiver but didn't slow him down.

Silently, in single file, Ben a little closer now, they strode past the swings and roundabout that had lived there since he and Amy had been toddlers and all around him were Amy's ghosts. *Amy at seven helping him on the slide, Amy at ten picking him up and dusting him off when he fell off the climbing frame* . . . All the Amys that had ever been were urging him onwards to finish this, to see this through, to *find* her.

He focused on the mystery in front of him, blurring everything else out. The man's suit was black, but it had pinstripes of yellow or faded white running through it, the lines not quite straight but coming down through the outfit at a slight diagonal as if made from reject material. On the shoulders was a fine coating of dust or dandruff, and Ben could see the angle of bones protruding through the jacket as the arms swung. The man was skeletally thin. He stored these images safely in his mind for when the man had gone. When the police had taken him. He saved them because of Amy.

When the figure in front stopped suddenly at the base of the oak tree Ben almost stumbled into him, his stomach leaping sickly into his mouth. But still the man didn't glance behind to the sweating scruffy boy only a few feet away. Instead, he looked intently at the ground at the base of the gnarled trunk and then, satisfied with whatever he saw there, up into its dense leaves. He placed the machete between his teeth and started to climb. The thick branches rustled and cracked as he nimbly worked his way through them, his body disappearing. Eventually, the tree fell silent as its occupant found a perch and all Ben could see was one leg from the knee down, hanging out of the foliage, swinging slightly. The kneecap pointed through the worn suit that frayed at the hem, and above that shiny shoe he could make out one black mole against the too-pale skin.

Ben watched that leg swing for what seemed like forever, but which was probably only three or four minutes, confusion and frustration making tears prick at the back of his eyes. What was he doing up there? What was he waiting for? Did he wait for Amy here? And if he was just waiting for a kid to kill then why hadn't he spotted Ben? He must be able to see him from up there.

Looking back, he could just make out the some running figures in the distance. Wrighty and a couple of people behind him. Not Cath. Two men. Time trembled.

He started back up at the swinging leg, his heart exploding with weeks of grief.

"Where's Amy?" He yelled up to the shoe, to the ankle, to the weird suit. "What did you do to my sister? I need to know!"

Heat buzzed through him, burning him from the toes up, eating its way through his limbs until it erupted in scalding tears from his eyes.

The leg froze.

"I need to know!"

He could hear Wrighty calling him now and he knew they'd be here in seconds. "I need to know before they get here." His words seemed drained of echo, no energy left to travel to the tree. "I need to know for myself."

The leg disappeared into the branches, its owner pulling it up to safety and out of sight. Ben howled. He was still shouting Amy's name when Wrighty grabbed him.

The men, Wrighty's dad one of them, didn't find anything in the tree. They called up at first, and then despite Ben trying to stop them, the other farmer, Bill Anderson, climbed it while Wrighty's old man kept his shotgun firmly fixed into the green and brown of its limbs. A few seconds later Mr. Anderson re-emerged, his weather-battered face unamused. "Nothing. There's no one up there." They stared at Ben as if he could give them an explanation. And then at Wrighty.

"If this is you kids' idea of a joke then I'm going to give you the hiding of your life." That was aimed at Damien alone. Ben didn't have a dad to beat him, and the mothers of the town felt sad for him about that. Beating and bonding. In Bracknell the two often went hand in hand with the men and their sons.

Ben shook his head, rapidly. Too rapidly. "No! There was a man with a knife and a suit and he had a mole on his ankle and he was on the field and . . . "

"Okay, son." The hardness went out of Mr. Wright's eyes. "It's okay. Calm down. Maybe there was someone." He looked around at the emptiness of the deserted school grounds and then back up at the tree. "But they're not here now." The anger may have faded, but Ben could see the man's disbelief like a halo shining out from him.

"Now, let's get back. Me and Bill have got some more harvesting to get in before finishing for the day. We can talk about this some more later." He flashed Damien a look that said he'd definitely be hearing more from his old man on this one, and then the two men walked off ahead, leaving the boys to trail behind.

"Jesus, Ben, all you had to do was follow him." The disgust was all too clear in Wrighty's voice.

"I didn't lose him, Wrighty. He was in the tree. I swear it. He was just sat up in the tree."

"Maybe he came down the other side when you were yelling."

"I didn't lose him. He was in the tree." His sadness threatened to overwhelm him. It was hopeless and he knew it. Listening carefully, deep inside, he could hear the delicate invisible strands that bonded their friendship snapping with each step they took.

Wrighty spat into the ground and neither of them spoke another word on the long walk home.

He wasn't sleeping. He didn't think he was ever going to sleep again. Neither Cath nor Wrighty had come to see him that day, although Cath's mum had come and had a whispered conversation with Mrs. Cooper, as if because her job was to keep Mum alive this gave her parental rights over Ben. She'd made a lot of humming noises as she listened and when Cath's mum left Mrs. Cooper let out a long world-weary sigh and shot him a withering glance. And that was that. No conversation. No care. He'd thought about talking to Mum about it, that's how desperate he'd got. But she had started to smell funny and was nearly always asleep or pretending to be asleep. And when she did open her eyes sometimes as he leaned in, breath held to kiss her goodnight, he could still see the meanness there gripping onto life. Maybe that was all that kept her going.

The warm night breeze teased him through the open window, tickling his legs where the covers were kicked off. He stared at the ceiling, and at the shapes that seemed to dance in the film that covered his eyes. He was dead inside. He was sure of it. He could feel his organs settling heavy in his back.

"Psst!"

The hand reached in through the window and shook his calf. Ben jumped, his organs retaking their positions, and then he smiled, feeling the life flooding back to him. Wrighty! He'd snuck out to come and see him and sort things out. Eagerly sitting up, the smile froze on his face.

It wasn't Wrighty at the window. The face that stared through it was flaky like Scratcher's, the skin too tight over the bones under that mop of black and silvery hair. The dark eyes twinkled and Ben thought he could see universes of stars in them. The scream desperate to escape his throat fought with his lungs' urge to breathe in, and although his mouth was open, nothing seemed to be happening. Eventually the breathing won, sucking the air in deep gasps. He hugged his knees to his chest, eyes flicking to the closed door. *The man was back, the man was back, he'd vanished, he couldn't be here, he couldn't know where he lived, he couldn't . . . he couldn't.* Bringing his eyes back to what was so solidly in front of him, Ben tried to focus. To calm himself down. The man had *vanished*, and now he was here. And there was nothing Ben could do about it apart from *see it through.*

The man at the window raised one finger to his lips. The nail on it was bitten to the quick, ragged tags of skin hanging down the outside edge. He stayed like that for a moment, and then lowered it slowly.

"You said Amy. You were looking for Amy." He sounded curious. Why would he be curious?

Ben nodded, his head incredibly heavy and his bladder screamed in panic at him with the movement.

"You are Ben." There was a lilt in the whispered words and Ben couldn't make out the accent. Scottish maybe? Who knew? He'd never been out of Bracknell and the only accents he'd heard were on the TV. The stranger was foreign though. He nodded again. Somewhere in his dry throat he tested his words.

"Did you kill Amy? Are you going to kill me?" He didn't sound like himself, his tongue heavy with a terror that seemed to be intensifying as the rest of him calmed. Maybe he could make it to the door and Mrs. Cooper down the hall. Maybe he could live through the night. Maybe someone would believe him this time. Maybe, maybe, maybe. All plausible possibilities. But he knew, deep in the hidden place where the body clock ticks almost unheard, that if this man wanted to kill him then he would. He was dead. Tonight or tomorrow, window open or shut . . . the eventuality would be the same.

The man's head tilted and Ben could see a small shower of dead skin fall to his shoulders from his scalp. Some came from his cheek too. He stared, transfixed. Whatever was wrong with this man, it wasn't eczema like Scratcher's. This was something else. He thought of the cancer eating mum's lungs. Maybe cancer was eating the stranger's face.

"Amy. Yes. I can take you there. But there's not much time." Again the strange accent. "You are Ben?"

Ben nodded again.

The dark eyes continued to twinkle and he smiled. The teeth there were perfect white but his gums were receding, bright flecks of red blood appearing in the crescents between his canines. "Good. Good. Then come with me." He raised his finger again and curled it, the move practiced, as if he were speaking to someone who didn't understand and needed the physical clue.

Amy. The man knew where Amy was. Ben stared for a second at the strange face and then kicked back the covers and reached for his jeans, pulling them over his underpants, tugged on his T-shirt and squeezed his feet into his trainers.

His stomach in his mouth, he leaned forward to open the window further to climb out when he paused. "Can I bring something to give to Amy?"

The idea seemed to amuse the man, who licked a trickle of blood from his front teeth. "Certainly. You can try. No harm. But be quick."

Unsure of whether he was dreaming or not, the surreal reality of the vanished man too much to really think about, Ben crept out of his room and across the dark corridor. Guiding himself by memory and habit, he stole into his sister's abandoned bedroom and grabbed the heart shaped box from beside her bed. He ripped the pendant out, enjoying the coolness of it against his skin.

Opening his own door, he feared and hoped that the man had vanished again, expecting to see only the night looking back at him from the window. How would he feel? Relieved? Disappointed?

But the grinning face was still there, framed by the familiarity of his bedroom, and Ben held the pendant up. "Will I be able to give this to her?"

The man shrugged. "Don't know if it'll get there. We'll see." The grin stretched. "Now come." He held up the machete. "Time, time, time."

Ben stared at the sharp metal; long, wide and fierce. How could he have forgotten about the knife? *That's not a knife. It's a fucking machete.* He swallowed hard. As yet, the man hadn't tried to hurt him. But so far, ever since he'd appeared on the edge of the field, nothing about this man had seemed normal. "You go ahead. I'll follow you."

Pausing on the windowsill, he smelt the dried wood and faded paint and felt the rush of twelve years of existence flooding over him. *I've had enough. I'm getting out of here.* Maybe this was it. The end. Maybe he'd never come back. Maybe by the next day he'd be rotting somewhere with Amy, lost and soon forgotten. He let the thought play in his head for a moment and then thought of Bracknell, Mum, and Mrs. Cooper, and he realized that he didn't much care either way. But he did care about Amy. He needed to know about her. Swinging his legs over the side, for the second time that day he followed the man that strode ahead of him.

This time it was different. Every so often the man with the knife would turn around and grin, checking Ben was following, and Ben would raise a hand and wave and they would continue in silence, cutting their way through the silent town. It wasn't long before they were crossing the field in the exact same line the man had taken and Ben wondered if the ghosts of he, Cath, and Wrighty of the afternoon were somewhere ahead of him, sprinting in panic, stuck in the afternoon heat, no cool of the night for them.

He strode on, the flash of white from the man's legs and the shine of the metal in the moonlight his only torch. He knew every inch of the ground of this town, had lived it, fallen and fought in the dust of it for all his life, and his feet carried him confidently at the swift pace the man was setting.

Before long they came to stop at the base of the tree, this time Ben standing side by side with the man. What would happen now? Would the man vanish again? The real and the unreal, the seen and the unseen blurred in his head.

The man was still grinning as he pointed into the branches with the machete. His gums were rivers of blood now, some escaping into the creases by his mouth, looking like a parody of an old woman with too much lipstick on. It didn't seem to bother him though. *Was he dying? Were they all just dying?*

"You climb first."

Ben stared at him, the question in his head tumbling out before he could check it. "Are you sick? Do you have cancer?"

The breeze lifted the thick hair that was more silver than it had been at Ben's window. "I'll be better when we get there."

Ben looked up at the tree, knowing he was going to climb it whatever the man said or did. And knowing that when he got up there, he would vanish. One way or another. Just like the man had this afternoon. He ran his fingers over the rough bark feeling its life singing in his soul. "What do you need the knife for?" His finger dug in, finding a tentative hold.

"To open the door. To get us there."

One foot gripping the tree, he pulled himself upwards, enjoying the way the ancient tree felt as he gripped it. "And where is 'there' exactly?" He looked down at the man who carefully pushed him up with his free hand, full of strength despite his appearance. Ben disappeared into the branches but the man's response was clear.

"Nowhere."

Finding a seat on the largest branch, the sweet smell of leaves and wood almost smothering him, he looked down confused. "Nowhere? How can we go nowhere? Nowhere isn't a place."

The machete was between the man's teeth again and as he pulled himself up, wrapping himself round a thick branch opposite, Ben could see where it had sliced into the corners of his mouth. When he took it out he laughed, a coppery sound, real and true and yet so very different from anything Ben had ever heard.

"Yes. The Nowhere." He glanced around at the leaves that caressed him. "This is The Somewhere. *There* is The Nowhere. It's the same but very different. You'll see. Sometimes things from The Somewhere find themselves in The Nowhere. Car keys, toys, people." He laughed more gently this time. "Sometimes we bring them. Like you."

Nothing and everything was making sense. The world was stumbling for its feet in his head. "And Amy's there?"

The Nowhere man nodded. "She talks about you all the time. She wants to see you. She came in a dream and she couldn't get back." He was twitching slightly and Ben could see that whatever was going to happen, wherever they were going, the stranger was eager to get there. He needed to get there. The skin and the blood told Ben that.

The familiar smell of the night, of his sleeping home filled his nostrils. "Will I be able to come back?" *Wrighty. Cath.*

An almost invisible shrug. "Some can. Some can't. Who knows?"

Mum. Ben thought of her mean eyes, wheezing breath and the oxygen tank and Mrs. Cooper. He thought of two vanished children, two empty bedrooms and her dying alone. "Will she still be here when I get back?" He didn't need to say who. He had a feeling that the Nowhere man knew a lot more than he was letting on.

"She'll still be here. Maybe not the same, but still here. *If* you get back." Lifting the machete the Nowhere man stopped grinning. "Are you ready?"

Shutting his eyes, Ben took a deep breath, gripped the necklace, and nodded.

For a moment the silence of the night was disturbed by the rustling in the tree. From somewhere in its branches a pendant tumbled and hit the ground, and then the old life settled, the balance restored, to sleep until morning.

Sarah Pinborough *is the author of six horror novels and her first thriller,* A Matter of Blood, *was released by Gollancz (U.K.) in March 2010, and is the first of The Dog-Faced Gods trilogy. Her first YA novel,* The Double-Edged Sword, *will be out under the name Sarah Silverwood later this year. Pinborough was the 2009 winner of the British Fantasy Award for Best Short Story, and has three times been short-listed for Best Novel. She has also been short-listed for a World Fantasy Award and her novella* The Language of Dying *was nominated for the 2009 Shirley Jackson Award.*

The Nowhere Man was the seed of Pinborough's YA trilogy The Nowhere Chronicles. Written under the name Sarah Silverwood, the first book, The Double-Edged Sword, *was published in September 2010.*

Pinborough presents us with a fine example of "disquieting" fiction. A boy whose sister has gone missing and whose dying mother is more monstrous than maternal teeters on the brink of adolescence with full knowledge he will soon lose his last meaningful connections. Ben is as alone as any lost explorer of the unknown. Being Somewhere can mean you are really Nowhere.

THE BONE'S PRAYER

CAITLÍN R. KIERNAN

The sea pronounces something, over and over, in a hoarse whisper;
I cannot quite make it out. ~ Annie Dillard

1.

She has been walking the beach all afternoon, which isn't unusual for days when she cannot write. And there have been several dry days now in a row, one following wordlessly after the next. A mute procession of empty hours, or, worse still, a procession of hours spent carefully composing sentences and paragraphs that briefly deceive her into thinking that the drought has finally passed. But then she reads back over the pages, and the prose thuds and clangs artlessly against itself, or it leads off somewhere she has not the time or the skill or the inclination to follow. She has deadlines, and bills, and the expectations of readers, and all these things must be factored into the question of whether a productive hour is, indeed, productive.

It becomes intolerable, the mute procession and the false starts, the cigarettes and coffee and all those books silently watching her from their places on the shelves that line her office. And, so, she eventually, inevitably, goes to the beach, which is not so very far away, hardly an hour's drive south from the city. She goes to the beach, and she tries very hard not to think of what isn't getting written. She tries only to hear the waves, the gulls and cormorants, the wind, tries to take in so much of the sand and the sky and the blue-green sea that there is no room remaining for her anxieties.

And sometimes it even works.

Today is a Saturday near the end of winter, and there are violent gusts off the sound that bite straight through her gloves and her long wool coat. Gusts that have twice now almost managed to dislodge the fleece-lined cap with flaps to keep her ears warm. Thick clouds the color of Wedgwood china hide the sun and threaten snow. But, thanks to the inclement weather, she has the beach all to herself, and that more than makes up for the discomfort. This solitude, like the breathy rhythm of the surf, and the smell of the incoming tide, is a balm. She begins at Moonstone Beach and walks the mile or so south and west to the scatter of abandoned summer cottages at Greenhill Point. Then she walks back, following the narrow strip of beach stretching between Block Island Sound and the low dunes dividing the beach from Trustom Pond.

The estuary is frozen solid, and when she climbs the dunes and stares out across the ice, there are flocks of mallards there, and Canadian geese, and a few swans wandering disconsolately about, looking lost. In the summer, the land around the salt pond is a verdant tangle of dog roses, poison ivy, greenbriers, and goldenrod. But now it is ringed by a homogenous brown snarl, and the only sign of green anywhere in this landscape are a few spruce trees and red cedars, dotting the southern edge of the forest to the north.

She turns back towards the sea and the cobble-strewn sand. It doesn't seem to her that the sea changes its hues with the season. Today, it wears the same restless shade of celadon that it wears in June, quickly darkening to a Persian blue where the water begins to grow deep, only a little ways out from shore. Ever shifting, never still, it is her only constant, nonetheless. It is her comfort, the sight of the sea, even in a month as bleak and dead as this.

She begins gathering a handful of pebbles, meaning to carry them back towards the dunes and find a dry place to sit, hopefully somewhere out of the worst of the wind. This beach is somewhat famous for the pebbles that fetch up here from submerged outcroppings of igneous stone, earth that was the molten-hot core of a mountain range millions of years before the coming of the dinosaurs. Here and there among the polished lumps of granite are the milky white moonstones that give the beach its name. She used to collect them, until she had a hundred or so, and they lost their novelty. There are also strands of kelp and bladderwrack, the claws and carapaces and jointed legs of dismembered crabs and lobsters, an occasional mermaid's purse—all the usual detritus. In the summer months, there would be added to this an assortment of human jetsam—water bottles, beer cans, stray flip flops, Styrofoam cups, and all manner of plastic refuse—the thoughtless filth that people leave behind. And this is another reason that she prefers the beach in winter.

She has selected six pebbles, and is looking for a seventh (having decided she would choose seven and only seven), when she spots a small, peculiar stone. It's shaped like a teardrop, and is the color of pea soup. The stone glistens wetly in the dim afternoon light, and she can clearly see that there are markings etched deeply into its smooth surface. One of them looks a bit like a left-facing swastika, and another reminds her of a Greek *ichthus*. For a moment, the stone strikes her as something repulsive, like coming upon a rotting fish or a discarded prophylactic, and she draws her hand back. But that first impression quickly passes, and soon she's at a loss even to account for it. It is some manner of remarkable artifact, whether very old or newly crafted, and she adds it to the six pebbles in her hand before turning once more towards the frozen expanse of Trustom Pond.

2.

It's Friday evening, two days after her trip from Providence to the beach. Usually, she looks forward to Friday's, because on Friday nights Sammie almost always stops by after work. Sammie is the closest thing she has to a close friend, and, from time to time, they've been lovers, as well. The writer, whose name is Edith (though that isn't the name that appears on the covers of her novels), is not an outgoing person. Crowds make her nervous, and she avoids bars and nightclubs, and even dreads trips to the market. She orders everything she can off the Internet—clothing, books, CDs, DVDs, electronics—because she hates malls and shopping centers. She hates the thought of being seen. To her knowledge, psychiatrists have yet to coin a term for people who have a morbid fear of being looked at, but she figures *antisocial* is accurate enough. However, most times, she enjoys having Sammie around, and Sammie never gets angry when Edith needs to be left alone for a week or two.

They've been mistaken for sisters, despite the fact that they really don't look very much alike. Sammie is two or three inches taller and has striking jet-black hair just beginning to show strands of gray. Edith's hair is an unremarkable dishwater blond. Sammie's eyes are a bright hazel green, and Edith's are a dull brown. Sammie has delicate hands and the long, tapered fingers of a pianist, and Edith's hands are thick, her fingers stubby. She keeps her nails chewed down to the quick, and there are nicotine stains on her skin. Sammie quit smoking years ago, before they met.

"Well, it was just lying there on the sand," Edith says. "And it really doesn't look all that old."

"It's a rock," Sammie replies, still peering at the peculiar greenish stone, holding it up to the lamp on the table next to Edith's bed. "What do you mean, it doesn't look old? All rocks look old to me."

"The carving, I mean," Edith replies, trying to decide if she really wants another of the stale madeleines that Sammie brought with her; they taste faintly of lemon extract, and are shaped like scallop shells. "I mean the carving in the rock looks fresh. If it had been rolling around in the ocean for any time at all the edges would be worn smooth by now."

"I think it's soapstone," Sammie says, and turns the pebble over and over, examining the marks on it. "But I don't think you find soapstone around here."

"Like I was saying, I figure someone bought it in a shop somewhere and lost it. Maybe it was their lucky charm. Or maybe it didn't mean anything to them."

"It feels funny," Sammie says, and before Edith can ask her to explain what she means, Sammie adds. "Slippery. Oily. Slick. You know?"

"I haven't noticed that," Edith says, although she has. The lie surprises her, and she can't imagine why she didn't just admit that she's also noticed the slithery sensation she gets whenever she holds the stone for more than a minute or two.

"You should show it to someone. A geologist or an archeologist or someone who knows about this stuff."

"I honestly don't think it's very old," Edith replies, and decides against a fourth madeleine. Instead, she lights a cigarette and thinks about going to the kitchen for a beer. "If I took it to an archeologist, they'd probably tell me the thing was bought for five bucks in a souvenir shop in Misquamicut."

"I really don't like the way it feels," Sammie says.

"Then put it down."

"Is that supposed to be a Jesus fish?" Sammie asks, pointing to the symbol that reminded Edith of an *ichthus*.

"Sort of looks like one," Edith replies.

"And *this* one, this one right here," Sammie says and taps the nail of her index finger against the stone. "That looks like astrology, the symbol for Neptune."

"I thought it was a trident, or a pitchfork," Edith sighs, wishing Sammie would put the stone away so they could talk about something else, almost anything else at all. The stone makes her uneasy, and three times in two days she's almost thrown it into the trash, so she wouldn't have to think about it or look at it anymore. "Can we please talk about something else for a while? You've been gawking at that awful thing for half an hour now."

Sammie turns her head, looking away from the stone, looking over her left shoulder at Edith. She's frowning slightly, and her neatly waxed eyebrows are furrowed.

"You *asked* me what I thought of it," she says, sounding more defensive than annoyed, more confused than angry. "*You're* the one who started this."

"It's not like I *meant* to find it, you know."

"It's not like you had to bring it home, either."

Sammie watches her a moment or two longer, then turns back to the tear-shaped stone.

"This one is a sun cross," she says, indicating another of the symbols. "Here, the cross held inside a circle. It's something else you see in astrology, the sign for the earth."

"I never knew you were into horoscopes," Edith says, and she takes a long drag on her cigarette and holds the smoke in her lungs until she begins to feel dizzy. Then she exhales through her nostrils.

"Why does it bother you?" Sammie asks.

"I never said it did."

"You just called it 'that awful thing,' didn't you?"

"I'm going to get a beer," Edith tells her. "Do you want one, as long as I'm up?"

"Sure," Sammie says and nods, not looking away from the stone. "I'd love a beer, as long as you're up."

Edith stands and pulls her bathrobe closed, tugging roughly at the terrycloth belt. The robe is a buttery yellow, and has small blue ducks printed on it. "You can have it if want it," she tells Sammie, who frowns softly, then sets the stone down on the bedside table.

"No," she replies. "It's yours. You found it, so you should keep it. Besides, it's a hell of a lot more interesting than most of the junk you haul back from the shore. At least this time the house doesn't smell like dead fish and seaweed. But I still say you should find an archeologist to take a look at it. Might turn out to be something rare."

"Perhaps," Edith says. "But I was thinking, just now, maybe it wasn't lost. Maybe someone got rid of it on purpose."

"Anything's possible."

"I'm afraid all I have is Heineken," Edith says, nodding towards the kitchen.

"Heineken's fine by me. Moochers can't be choosers."

"I meant to get something else, because I know you don't like Heineken. But I haven't been to the store in a few days."

"The Heineken's fine, really. I promise."

Edith manages the ghost of a smile, then goes to the kitchen, leaving Sammie (whose birth name is Samantha, but everyone knows better than to call her that) alone in the bedroom with the peculiar greenish stone. Neither of them mentions it again that night, and later, for the first time in almost three weeks, they make love.

3.

"Well, first off, continents don't just *sink*," Edith says, and she's beginning to suspect that she might only be dreaming. She's sitting on the closed toilet lid in her tiny bathroom, and Sammie is standing up in the claw-foot tub. Sammie was the one who started talking about Atlantis, and then Mu, and Madame Blavatsky's Lemuria.

"And I read about another one," she says. "When I was a kid, I found a book in the library, *Mysteries of the Sea*, or something like that. Maybe one of those *Time-Life* series. One of the stories was about a ship finding an uncharted island somewhere in the South Pacific, back in the twenties, I think. They found an island, complete with the ruins of a gigantic city, but then the whole thing sank in an earthquake. Islands can sink, right?" she asks.

"Not overnight," Edith says, more interested in watching Sammie bathe than all this nonsense about lost worlds.

"What about Krakatoa? Or Santorini?"

"Those were both volcanic eruptions. And the islands didn't sink, they exploded. *Boom*," and Edith makes a violent motion in the air with her right hand. "For that matter, neither was completely submerged."

"Sometimes you talk like a scientist," Sammie says, and she stares down at the water in the cast-iron tub.

"Are you saying I'm pedantic?"

"No, I'm not saying that. It's kind of sexy, actually. Big brains get me wet."

There's a sudden fluttering noise in the hallway, and Edith looks in that direction. The bathroom door is standing half open, but the hallway's too dark to see whatever might have made the sound.

"Okay," Sammie continues, "so maybe, instead, there have been cities that never sank, because the things that built them never lived on land. Or maybe they lived on land a long time ago, but then returned to the water. You know, like whales and dolphins."

Edith frowns and turns back to the tub. "You're sort of just making this up as you go along, aren't you?"

"Does that matter?" Sammie asks her.

"Whales don't build cities," Edith says, and there's a finality in her voice that *should* have been sufficient to steer the conversation in another direction. But when Sammie's been drinking and gets something in her head, she can go on about it for hours.

"Whales sing songs," she says. "And maybe if we were able to understand those songs, we'd know about whoever built the cities."

Edith frowns at her, trying not to think about the fluttering noise from the hall. "If we could understand those songs," she says, "I suspect we'd mostly hear about horny whales, or which sort of krill tastes the best."

"Maybe," Sammie replies, and then she shrugs her narrow shoulders. "But the whales *would* know about the cities. Especially sperm whales, because they dive so deep and all."

"You're still working from an *a priori* assumption that the cities have ever existed. You're trying to find evidence to solve an imaginary problem."

Sammie holds up the greenish stone from the beach, then, as if it offers some refutation, or maybe she thinks Edith has forgotten it. In the light from the fluorescent bulb above the sink, the stone looks greasy. Sammie's fingers look greasy, too, as if something has seeped out of the rock and stained her hands.

I really don't like the way it feels.

"It's just something one of the summer people dropped," Edith says, wondering why Sammie didn't leave the stone lying on the table beside the bed, why she's in the tub with it. "The thing was probably made on an Indian Reservation in Arizona, or in China. It's just a piece of junk."

"Can't you hear it?" Sammie asks her. "If you listen very closely, it's singing. Not the same song that whales sing, but it's singing, all the same."

"Stones don't sing," Edith says, "no matter what's carved on them. I don't hear anything at all."

Sammie looks mildly disappointed, and she shrugs again. "Well, I hear it. I've been hearing it all night. It's almost a lamentation. A dirge. And I don't just hear it, Edith, I can *feel* it. In my bones, I can feel it."

"Really, I don't know what you mean," Edith says, and before she can add, *and I don't care, either,* Sammie is already talking again.

"My body hears the song. Every *cell* in my body hears the song, and it's like they want to answer. It's a song the ocean sings, that the ocean has always *been* singing. But, suddenly, my body remembers it, from a very, very long time ago, I think. Back when there were still only fish, maybe, and nothing had crawled out to live on the land."

"You were making more sense with Atlantis and the theosophists," Edith sighs. She sits there on the toilet, staring at the greasy-looking stone in Sammie's greasy-looking hands. The rock's surface is iridescent, and it shimmers with a riot of colors, a rainbow film on an oil-slick mud puddle, or the nacreous lining of an abalone shell. Sammie's hands have become iridescent, as well, and she's saying something about inherited memories, the collective unconscious, somatic and genetic recollection, and Edith wants to ask her, *Now who sounds like a scientist?* But she doesn't.

"We don't know what's down there," Sammie says. "Not really. I read somewhere that we know more about the surface of the moon than about the deep sea. Did you even know that? Do you know about the Marianas Trench? It's so deep, Edith, that if you were to set Mount Everest at the bottom, there would still be more than a mile of water covering the mountaintop."

"Yes, I know a little about the Marianas Trench," Edith replies, trying to be patient without trying to *sound* like she's having to try to be patient. And that's when Sammie stops rolling the tear-shaped stone between her fingers and quickly slips it down to the clean-shaven space between her legs and into her vagina. There's no time for Edith to try to stop her.

"Do you think that was such a good idea?" Edith asks. Sammie only smiles back, a furtive sort of smile, and doesn't answer the question. But she finally sits down in the tub, and Edith sees that where only a few moments before the water was clear and clean, now it has become murky, and dark strands of kelp float on the surface. There's a sharp crust of tiny barnacles clinging to the white enamel, and she opens her mouth to tell Sammie to be careful, that they're sharp, and she could cut herself. But then the fluttering noise comes from the hallway again, louder than before, and, hearing it, she's afraid to say anything at all.

"It's a message in a bottle," Sammie whispers. "Or those golden phonograph records they sent off on the *Voyager* probes. Messages like that, no one ever expects to get an answer, but we keep sending them off, anyway."

"I don't hear anything," Edith lies.

"Then I suggest you should try listening more closely. It's the most beautiful song I've ever heard. And it's taken so terribly long to get here."

Edith shuts her eyes and smells the ocean, and she smells an evaporating tide pool trapped between rime-scarred boulders, and a salt-marsh mudflat, and all the soft, pale creatures that live in the briny ooze, and, last of all, the sweet hint of pink dog roses in the air. She keeps her eyes shut tightly, straining not to hear the strange, unpleasant commotion in the hallway, which sound nothing at all like any music she's ever heard. And, for a hopeful moment, Edith begins to believe she's waking up, before the dream abruptly drops away beneath her feet, the dream and the tile floor of the bathroom, and she understands that the water's only getting deeper.

4.

There are dreams that stack in tiers, like a gaily frosted birthday cake, and, too, there are dreams that sit nested snuggly one within the other, the way that Russian matryoshka dolls may be opened to reveal a dizzying regression of inner dolls. Edith cannot say if *this* dream is falling into itself, or merely progressing from tier to tier, whether up or down. She is sitting on the sand among the cobbles at Moonstone Beach, listening to the surf. Above her, the sky is low and looks like curdled milk. In her right hand, she's holding a stick that the retreating tide left stranded, and all about her, she's traced the designs from the peculiar greenish stone. They form a sort of mandala, and she sits at its center. If asked, she could not say whether the circle is meant to contain her, or to protect her. Possibly, it's meant to do both. Possibly, it is insufficient for either task.

The wind is the half-heard voice of the beach, or the voice of the sea. Behind her, it rattles the dry reeds at the edge of Trustom Pond, and before her, it whips the crests of the breakers into a fine spray.

There is something else there with her, tucked in amongst the sand and the cobbles and the symbols she's traced on the shore. Something that desperately needs to be seen, and that would have her gaze upon nothing else. But Edith doesn't look at it, not yet. She will *not* look at it until she can no longer bear the pain that comes from averting her eyes.

Only a few moments ago, Sammie was standing somewhere behind her, standing very near, and talking about the January thirteen winters before, when a tank barge and a tug ran aground here. The barge spilled more than eight hundred thousand gallons of toxic heating oil into the sea and onto the beach. The name of the barge was *North Cape*, and the tug was named *Scandia*, and, during a storm, they'd run afoul of the rocks in the shallows just offshore. Both Trustom and Card ponds were contaminated by the spill, and the beach was littered with the corpses of tens of millions of poisoned sea birds, lobsters, surf clams, and starfish.

"It was a massacre," Sammie said, before she stopped talking. There was an unmistakable trace of bitterness in her voice, Edith thought. "She doesn't forget these things. Maybe people do. Maybe the birds come back and the lobsters come back, and no one tells tourists what happened here, but the *sea* remembers."

Edith asked her if that was why the song from the stone is a dirge, if it laments all the creatures killed in the oil spill. But Sammie said no, that the stone was made to keep the memory of a far more appalling day, one that predated the coming of man and was now otherwise lost to the mind of the world.

"Why are we here?" Edith asked.

"Because you would not hear the song," Sammie replied. She said nothing else after that, and Edith assumes she's alone now, sitting here alone on Moonstone Beach, buffeted by the icy wind and doing her best not to see the thing half buried in the sand only a foot or so away. She understands perfectly well that she's fighting a losing battle.

I will close my eyes, she thinks. *I can't see anything with my eyes shut. I'll close my eyes, and keep them closed until I wake up.*

But shutting her eyes only releases the next doll in the stack, so to speak, and Edith finds herself adrift in an all-but-impenetrable blackness, a blackness that is almost absolute. She recalls, clearly, standing and walking out into Block Island Sound, recalls the freezing saltwater lapping at her ankles, and then her knees, recalls it rushing up her nostrils and down her throat, searing her lungs as she sank. But she was *not* drowned, and maybe that was the magic of the carved stone at work, and maybe it was some other magic, entirely. The currents carried her away from land and into the Atlantic, ferrying her north and east past Cape Cod, and at last she'd left the sheer bluffs of the continental shelf behind. Far below her, hidden in veils of perpetual night, lie flat abyssal plains of clay and silt and diatomaceous slime. She is suspended above them, unable to fall any farther, and yet incapable of ever again rising to the surface.

All around her—over and below and on every side—indistinct shapes come and go. Some are very small, a parade of eyeless fish and curious squid, jellies and other bathypelagic creatures that she knows no names for. Others, though, move by like enormous, half-glimpsed phantoms, and she can only guess at their identity. Some are surely whales, and probably also enormous deepwater sharks and cephalopods. But others are indescribable, and plainly much too vast to be any manner of cetacean or squid. Occasionally, she reaches out a hand, and her fingers glide over that alien flesh as it rushes by in the gloom. Sometimes, it seems smooth as any silk, and other times, rough as sandpaper. The haunted, endless night is *filled* with phantoms, and *I am just one more, she thinks. They must wonder at me, too, at what I am, at where so strange a beast could have come from.*

And the next leviathan glares back at her with a bulging ebony eye the size of a dinner plate. There's no pupil in that eye, nor evidence of an iris, nothing to mar such an unfathomable countenance. And then the eye is gone, replaced by a flank adorned with huge photophores, each one glowing with a gentle pale-blue light. The sight delights her, and she extends a hand to stroke the thing as it moves past. And Edith clearly sees the thin, translucent webbing that's grown between her own fingers, and the long hooked claws that have replaced the nails she chews to nubs. In the muted blue light cast by the bioluminescent creature, she sees that there are fine scales dappling the backs of both her hands, and they shimmer dully, reminding her of the oily, prismatic stone.

Edith opens her eyes, and she is once more merely sitting within the mandala that she's drawn on Moonstone Beach, thirteen years after the wreck of the *North Cape*. She's still clutching the piece of driftwood and shivering in the wind. She looks over her shoulder, hoping to find Sammie there, but sees at once that she's still alone.

"Sam, I don't *know* what I'm *meant* to listening for," she says, almost shouting to hear herself over the wind. "I don't *know* what it is, but I *am* listening."

When there's no reply, she isn't disappointed or surprised, because she understood well enough that she *wouldn't* be answered. Any answer she needs is right here before her, held within a crab-gnawed and gull-pecked anatomy, that misshapen mound of rotting flesh coughed up by whatever indifferent gods or goddesses or genderless deities call the globe's ocean their domain.

In the sand before her is a slit, and at first she thinks it is no more than some depression fashioned with her own busy fingers. She leans towards it, and now the wind is speaking, though she cannot say that the words are meant for her ears. She cannot say they are meant for any ears, at all:

There are stories that have no proper beginning. Stories for which no convenient, familiar "Once upon a time . . . " praeambulum exists. They may, for instance, be contained within larger stories, interwoven with the finest of gradations, and so setting them apart is a necessarily arbitrary undertaking. Let us say, then, that this story is of that species. Where it truly began is not where we will start its telling, for to attempt such a thing would require a patience and the requisite time for infinite regression. I may say that the sea had a daughter, though she has spent every day of her life on dry land. At once, the tumult of a hundred questions about how such a thing ever came to be will spring to mind. What is the nature of the sea's womb? With what or whom did she or he have congress to find himself or herself with child? What of the midwife? What is the gestation time of all the oceans of the world, or its sperm count, when considered as a single being? And, while we're at it, which being, and from which pantheon, do I mean when I say "the sea"? Am I speaking of the incestuous union of Oceanus and his sister Tethys? Do I mean to say Poseidon, or Neptune, Ægir and Rán, or Susanoo of the Shinto, or Arnapkapfaaluk of the Inuit?

I mean only to say the sea.

The sea had a daughter, but she was orphaned. She grew up in a city of men, a city at the mouths of two rivers that flowed down into a wide bay, fed by other rivers and dotted by more than thirty rocky, weathered islands. Here she was a child, and then a young woman. Here, she thought, she would grow to be an old woman. She'd never desired to travel, and had never ventured very far inland. She had seen photographs of mountain ranges, and read descriptions of the world's great deserts, and that was sufficient.

Edith places the tip of one index finger into the nearer end the slit in the sand. Except it is not merely sand, though there is something of quartz granules and mica flakes and dark specks of feldspar in its composition. *It is flesh* crafted *from sand*, she thinks, *or sand painstakingly crafted from flesh.*

The gross physiology is self evident now, the *labia magora* and *labia minor*, the *glans clitoris* and clitoral hood. It weeps, or simply secretes, something not so different from sea foam. And lying within it is the teardrop-shaped stone that Sammie slipped inside herself while standing in the tub.

Do you think that was such a good idea?

It's a message in a bottle. Messages like that, no one ever expects to get an answer, but we keep sending them off, anyway.

And Edith removes the stone from the slit in the sand, which then immediately closes, leaving behind no trace that it was ever actually there. She stares at the spot for a moment, comprehending, and then she flings the stone into the sea. There's no splash; the waves take it back without any sound and without so much as a ripple.

The circuit has been closed, she thinks, though the metaphor strikes her as not entirely appropriate.

She looks to the sky, and sees birds wheeling against the curdled clouds. The dream pushes her back into wakefulness, then, and, for a while, Edith lies still, squinting at the half-light of dawn and listening to a woman sobbing softly somewhere in the room.

5.

When Edith was seven years old, she saw a mermaid. One summer's day, she'd gone on a picnic with the aunt and uncle who raised her (after the death of her parents), to the rocky shore below Beavertail Lighthouse on Conanicut Island. There are tidal pools there, deep and gaping clefts opened between tilted beds of slate and phyllite, and in one of them she saw the mermaid. It rose, suddenly, towards the surface, as if lunging towards her. What most surprised her child's mind was how little it resembled any of the mermaids she'd seen in movies and storybooks, in that it was not a pretty girl with the tail of a fish. Still, she recognized it at once for what it was, if only because there was nothing else it could have been. Also, she was surprised that it seemed so hungry. The mermaid never broke the surface of the pool, but floated just beneath that turbulent, glistening membrane dividing one world from the other.

I may say that the sea had a daughter, though she has spent every day of her life on dry land.

The mermaid watched her for a while, and Edith watched the mermaid. It had black eyes, eyes like holes poked into the night sky, and did not seem to have eyelids of any sort. At least, Edith never saw it blink. And then, as abruptly as it had risen, the mermaid sank back into the deep cleft in the rock, leaving behind nothing for a seven-year-old girl to stare at but the sloshing surface of the pool. Later, she told her aunt and uncle what she'd seen, and they both smiled and laughed (though not unkindly) and explained that it had only been a harbor seal, *not* a mermaid.

When they got back home that evening, her uncle even showed her a color picture of a harbor seal in one of his encyclopedias. It made Edith think of a fat dog that had learned to live in the ocean, and looked nothing whatsoever like the mermaid that had watched her. But she didn't say this to her uncle, because she'd begun to suspect that it was somehow *wrong* to see mermaids, and that any time you saw one, you were expected to agree that what you'd really seen was a harbor seal, instead. Which is what she did. Her aunt and uncle surely had enough trouble without her seeing mermaids that she shouldn't see.

A week later, they had her baptized again.

Her uncle nailed her bedroom window shut.

Her aunt made her say the Lord's Prayer every night before bed, and also sewed sprigs of dried wormwood into her clothes.

And they never went back down to the rocky place below the lighthouse at Beavertail, and always thereafter had their picnics far from the sea.

6.

Edith does not doubt that she's now awake, any more than, a moment before she opened her eyes, she doubted that she was still dreaming. This is not the next tier, nor merely the next painted wooden doll in the matryoshka's stack. This is the world of her waking, conscious mind, and this time she will not deny that for the sake of sanity or convenience. There has always been too much of lies about her, too much pretend. When her eyes have grown accustomed to the early morning light, she sits up in bed. Sammie is still crying, somewhere in the room, somewhere very close by, and as soon as Edith sits up, she sees her crouching naked on the hardwood floor near the foot of the bed. All around her, the floor is wet. She has her back turned to Edith, and her head is bowed so that her black hair hangs down to the pine floorboards. Edith glances immediately to the little table beside the bed, but the peculiar tear-shaped pebble from Moonstone Beach is gone. She knew that it would be, but she looked anyway. The air in the room smells like a fish market.

Sammie, or the thing that now occupies the place in this universe where Sammie used to be, has stopped sobbing and has begun a ragged sort of trilling chant in no language that Edith knows or thinks she's ever heard. It sounds much more like the winter wind, and like waves rolling against sand, and the screech of herring gulls, than it sounds like human speech. Edith opens her mouth and almost calls out to Sammie, but then she stops herself. The thing on the floor probably wouldn't answer to that name, anyway. And she'd rather not use any of the names to which it might respond.

Its skin is the same murky pea green as the vanished stone, and bears all the same marks that were carved into the stone. All the same wounds, each pregnant with significance and connotations that Edith has only just begun to grasp. There is a pentacle—or something almost like a pentacle—cut deeply into each of Sammie's shoulders, and a vertical line of left-facing swastikas decorates the length of her spine. Wherever this new flesh has been sliced open, it leaks a greasy black substance that must be blood. Below the swastikas, there is the symbol that reminded them both of a Greek *ichthus*, centered just above Sammie's ass. Edith cannot help but wonder if Sammie was reborn with these wounds already in place, like birthmarks, or if they came later, not so differently than the stigmata of Catholic saints. Or if maybe they're self-inflicted, and Edith remembers her own hands in the dream, the sharp claws where her nails had been. In the end, it hardly matters how the marks came to be; the meaning is the same, either way.

Do you think that was such a good idea?

It's a message in a bottle. No one ever expects to get an answer, but we keep sending them off . . .

"When you're ready," Edith says, almost whispering, "I'll be right here. There's no hurry. I know how long you've been waiting." Then she lies back down, and turns to face the wall.

Caitlín R. Kiernan *has published eight novels, including* Daughter of Hounds *and* The Red Tree. *She is a prolific author of short fiction, and her stories have been collected in* Tales of Pain and Wonder; From Weird and Distant Shores; Alabaster; To Charles Fort, With Love; A is for Alien; *and, most recently,* The Ammonite Violin & Others. *Since 2004, she has also published the monthly ezine,* Sirenia Digest, *which features her erotica. Caitlín is currently working on her next novel,* The Wolf Who Cried Girl. *She lives in Providence, Rhode Island, with her partner Kathryn and two cats.*

Kiernan's writing has been eliciting admiration for more than a decade. Jeff VanderMeer's recent desciption fits it as well as anyone's: "Her unabashedly adult, lush prose recalls some unholy mix of H.P. Lovecraft and Angela Carter." Although you'll find Kiernan's short work in most of the "award-winning-quality" genre anthologies and various periodicals, she also publishes *Sirenia Digest*, the ezine mentioned above, each month. The PDF journal is packed with vignettes and short stories, and she occasionally slips in an original story that hasn't been published elsewhere. That's where I discovered the haunting "The Bone's Prayer."

And, after reading it, I shall forevermore be cautious about what stones I pick up on beaches.

THE WATER TOWER

JOHN MANTOOTH

"There's an alien in the water tower."

Jeremy Posey stood at the front door of Heather's trailer, dressed in camouflage fatigues, glasses crooked on his sunburned nose. Above him, the sun passed its zenith and hung lazily in the western sky. His dirty-blond hair caught the light and filtered it towards Heather in soft hues.

"Clyde found it, yesterday, floating right in the tank. I overheard him talking to Ronnie Pearson about it. You know the rooms in our house are thin as paper. He said it was light blue, the color of a vein. Tiny, but a big head. Ronnie said that made sense cause aliens are smarter than us, but if you ask me, it's pretty dumb to end up dead inside a water tower."

Heather waited, wondering where all this was going. With Jeremy, you never knew. He took the special ed classes in school, but it wasn't so much that he wasn't smart or couldn't learn, it was more that he was just Jeremy. He would never fit in anywhere in life. His older brother Clyde just let him tag along because Jeremy would do his dirty work, like stealing whiskey from their father or sneaking up to Jenny Willoughby's window to take pictures of her. Heather was Jeremy's one friend, and even she could only take him in small doses.

"Anyway," he said, after he caught his breath. "I thought you might like to see it."

"So let me get this straight," Heather said. "You want me to walk all the way through the woods, clear out to the train tracks to see something dead in a water tower?"

Jeremy smiled. He had a good one, and when he did it at just the right time, Heather always liked him, always wanted to root for him. "I got a feeling about this," he said. "This could be big. But we've got to beat Ronnie and Clyde out there. Summer school lets out in like an hour. They'll go to Clyde's house to drink for awhile." He glanced at the sky. "I'd say we've got until dark." Reaching into the pocket of his shorts, he pulled out a slim, silver camera. "Digital. If this is what I think it is, I'm going to have pictures to prove it."

"And what do you think it is, Jeremy?"

His grin widened. "An alien, of course."

Heather laughed. Not at him exactly. No, his enthusiasm was revved too high for that. She laughed because she wanted to go, well she wanted to get out from under the same roof where she had spent the better part of a long, hot summer trying to avoid her mother and especially the men that came over in the afternoon.

She looked at Jeremy, his big smile still plastered across his face. Someone had given him a bad haircut. Probably Jeremy himself, considering he barely had enough money most of the time to get a roast beef sandwich at Hardees, and his dad didn't believe in personal grooming. Despite all this, something was right about Jeremy. It was hard to say what, exactly, but it was there. She knew it.

"Okay," she said. "I'll go. But I want my name on any pictures you take. It would be nice to beat the Barrows to the punch."

"Barrows?"

"Ronnie and Clyde." Jeremy frowned like he sometimes did in class when he didn't understand. "Never mind," she said. "Let's get out of here."

Heather had no sooner said the words when an old blue truck spun its tires out on the road and turned down the worn gravel drive leading to her trailer.

Heather's mother appeared framed behind the kitchen window, a silent face next to the smudged glass. Heather saw her take a drag of her cigarette and watch the truck roll toward the house. She did not look in Heather's direction.

At a certain point, somewhere past the junkyard, out beyond the little pond that, over the years, had been used to dump the things even the junkyard didn't want, the woods changed. But not just the woods. The things in the woods changed as well. Artifacts from a different world slowly began to appear: remnants of a car buried under kudzu vines; a pile of beer bottles so old the labels had faded into obscurity, bled white by the long sun; a pair of trousers, half buried in the mud. A plow had lain too long in the sun and turned a fleshy white so it appeared to Heather like a skeleton, wooden arms stiff and outstretched, grasping for something just out of reach.

"There's a whole world back here," Heather said.

"Yeah, my dad told me about it once. The water tower, these ruins, all of it was once a town. I forget the name."

"What happened?"

Jeremy shrugged. "Don't know. I guess folks went in for trailer parks and electricity. No power out here. But it's got something else." He looked around. "Soul. Yeah. It's got soul."

Heather smiled.

"What? You know what I mean. You've been to places before that suck the soul right out of you before, right? Like the trailer park where you live. No soul. Soul sucking, but no soul. Except when it rains. Everyplace has got soul then."

Heather grinned. Jeremy was right. This place did have soul. On their left, a creek weaved between the trees. A wooden fence leaned precariously over the water, one of its poles dangling free and occasionally dipping into the slight current. A snapping turtle lay sunning itself on a moss covered rock, and overhead the tall pines swayed mysteriously, giving Heather a pleasing touch of vertigo each time she looked up.

She saw how this might have been a community. The structures, little more than vine-covered ruins, were sinking deeper into the earth with each passing year. The homes had been burned, the walls inside black and raw. Inside the least damaged, Heather found bedding and clothes and some dirty magazines.

"This is where David Masters and Jessica McKissick used to come," Jeremy said. "Me and Ronnie used to climb that tree—" He pointed at a tall, leaning oak. "—and watch them. They put on a hell of a show. At least until she got pregnant."

"Jessica McKissick? I didn't know she was pregnant."

"She was. Then she wasn't." Jeremy leaned over close to Heather and whispered, "I think she had an abortion, or maybe just got rid of it."

"Did her parents know?"

Jeremy shrugged. "I doubt it. Ronnie and me and David, of course. We might have been the only ones. I could tell because she started wearing big sweaters and jackets and stuff. Anyway, once that happened, the show stopped."

"It's just hard to believe. How she could get pregnant and hide the whole thing from her parents," Heather said. She was intrigued, especially by how a girl could get pregnant, have the baby, and her parents never be the wiser. "So, she got rid of it?"

Jeremy shrugged. "She doesn't have a baby anymore. My brother saw her a few weeks ago. He said she definitely wasn't pregnant."

Heather thought of her mother, perpetual drink in one hand, half-smoked cigarette in the other. Thought of her mother's long face, always so blank and uncurious, always ready to speak without thinking, to criticize without understanding who she criticized.

Heather tried to picture herself pregnant. Tried to think of how it would feel to have a life growing inside her, kicking and turning and needing. Would her mom notice? Possibly not. Weeks might go by without interaction between them. If Heather put a little more effort into it, she could go forever without her mother seeing her.

The last time Heather saw her father was two years ago, at the end of sixth grade. Because her mother wouldn't take her, Heather had saved the money for cab fare and traveled down to the VA where her father lived full time. He'd been in the Gulf War and had come back with shrapnel embedded in the back of his neck and spine, but that wasn't why he was off.

According to her mother, it was just his crazy gene kicking in.

"What happened to him," her mother had said shortly after he was committed, "will happen to you one day, too."

Heather, only eleven, wanted to know why.

"DNA."

"Huh?"

"The stuff in your blood that makes you, you. You're a Watson, Heather. You've got the same genes as your father. I should have known when I married him, his elevator would eventually get stuck." She breathed out a long column of smoke, watching it drift lazily across the room. "Just like his father and his father before him."

Heather didn't see her father as crazy. In fact, she considered him—had considered him—the sanest person she knew time. Sure there had been moments when he seemed different, at odds with the world, but that was what made him special to Heather. They were alike in that way.

When she was nine, he'd taken her to Disney World, just the two of them. He told her she was a princess, just like the real ones.

"Real ones?" she'd said.

"Cinderella, Snow White, Sleeping Beauty. All of them. You're a princess too."

"But they're not real, Daddy."

He smiled, surveyed the park, as if to spot one in order to prove his point. At that moment, the park seemed deserted, forlorn almost, in the twilight of the late afternoon. His smile dissipated, turned to a look of confusion. He touched her shoulder.

"You're going and going until one day you find there's no where to go."

She waited, her nine-year-old mind, spinning, trying to make connections that were not there.

"You look in the mirror. You realize the person looking back is you. That's when it falls apart."

Heather said nothing. His smile came back. "Hey," he said, "a princess."

Heather followed his gaze, but she saw only the long shadows of the sun falling across the park.

The last time she'd seen him, at the VA, he had said nothing at all. He looked past her, his gaze fixed on the wall behind her, where a dark, mud-colored stain, possibly blood, had resisted all efforts to clean it. Her father's lips moved soundlessly. He might have been praying. Or cataloguing all the ways such a stain might have ended up on the wall. He might have been reading some secret language in that stain, some otherworldly alphabet only he knew. Maybe, Heather would know it too, one day. This was what she liked to think when she thought about her father. He wasn't crazy. Instead, he had uncovered the secrets of the world, lifting the veil over them and finding himself stunned to silence by what he had found.

⊰⊱

A house appeared, shimmering in the distance, its eaves dripping with Spanish moss, its front door stripped bare of paint, the color of flesh. The yard, if you could call it that, was a mess of trash and weeds, all tangled together with the undergrowth, which to Heather seemed to creep forth from the trees like sentient fingers searching for something to touch.

The smell was of man, not trees.

"Better steer clear," Heather whispered. She knew there were meth labs out here. And crack houses. And other places that stopped being anything except dead ends. Dying places.

Too late. Jeremy had already seen something that held him mesmerized. Heather followed his gaze to the makeshift porch, where an old rocking chair creaked in the wind.

"That's my dad's hat," he said.

A red hat lay in the seat of the chair.

A shadow moved inside the house past a window and was gone.

"Let's keep going," Heather said. But her heart wasn't in the words. If she'd been in Jeremy's shoes, she would want to investigate too. There was something about your parents, Heather thought: Whatever they did, they pulled you along too. Even out here in the woods, in the middle of a place that might as well not exist. You were always part of them, even when they stopped being part of you.

"Is this where he goes?" Jeremy said. "Don't tell me this is where he goes." His voice was angry but weak. A tear ran down his cheek.

"Maybe it would be better—"

"No. I'm going in."

Heather followed him.

The door swung open soundlessly, revealing a darkened room. A naked woman lay on a couch, smoking something that did not look like a cigarette. She was old, her body wrinkled and crushed by gravity. She brushed long gray-black bangs from her eyes and exhaled a stream of smoke.

"Who are you?"

"Where's my dad?"

"Your dad?"

"His hat is on the porch."

The woman sat up, making no effort to cover herself. Her breasts, once large, now hung down her chest like empty bags.

"What's your name?"

"Jeremy Reddin."

She nodded. "He never told me."

"That he had kids?"

"That he had any other than the one that died."

Jeremy looked at his feet. "There's me and my older brother."

The woman took another toke. "And little Sam."

"He only lived for an hour."

The woman leaned back on the couch and closed her eyes. Her knees opened, revealing a dark bed of hair between her thighs. Heather looked away.

"Yeah, but I hear it was a good hour," she said, her eyes still closed, a look of complete relaxation on her face.

"Where is he?"

Without opening her eyes, the woman pointed to the back of the house. "Out where the graves are." She took another drag.

Heather followed Jeremy down a short hallway and into a bedroom covered with clothes and trash and a smell Heather recognized as menstrual blood. A door on the other side of the room, swayed in a slight breeze.

Passing through the door was like passing into another world, or at least another time. The trees swallowed up the sun back here, forming a perfect canopy of dark green, like pictures Heather had seen of tropical jungles. It made Heather think of hiding under the covers with her father when she'd been a kid.

Jeremy sucked in a deep breath. Stood still. Looked at the clearing where a man lay on the ground, his arms wrapped around something, his broad back turned to them.

"Dad?" Jeremy said.

The man did not move.

Jeremy took a step closer. Heather waited, tense. Unsure how to stand. What to do other than watch.

"Dad?"

There was no response, and for an instant, Heather thought he might be dead.

Jeremy crouched next to the man. Heather heard the woman's voice behind them.

"He's in the mud," she said dreamily.

Jeremy turned and grimaced at the woman before reaching for his father. He grabbed his shoulders and rolled him over on his back. The man moved his head and mumbled something. But Jeremy wasn't listening. His attention had turned to what his father had been holding—a rock, a crude marker. He knelt and read the inscription in silence.

The woman stood beside Heather now. She had a needle in her hand. The sharp point dripped with a fluid the color of honey. Heather watched as the woman plunged it into her own arm, squeezing the syringe, as her face went from serene to ecstatic to unknowing.

Once drained, the syringe fell from her fingers, and she stumbled past Heather. When she fell on top of Jeremy's father, he barely seemed to notice. They lay together like that, still. Everything was still except for the tall pines agitated by the wind.

Jeremy stepped around them, his face wet with tears. He paused on the other side of their bodies, looking at them. The woman said something to him, but Heather couldn't make it out. Whatever it was made Jeremy break.

His shoulders drooped. His face twisted into a mask of agony. His thick glasses slid off his nose and landed in the grass.

He cursed loudly and reached for them, but came up empty. Heather started forward to help him, but before she could get there, in his blindness, he managed to crush them underfoot.

They'd been walking for nearly two hours when the rain began. The journey turned to a slow crawl, as Heather lost her way several times, and had to backtrack through the muck to regain her bearings. Jeremy was little help without his glasses, and the deeper they traveled into the woods, the more Heather seemed to lose her grip on the world she knew. The trailer park seemed far away, and more than that, it seemed unimportant, like a relic from the past.

As they walked, Heather thought little about the alien or the water tower. At this point she expected to find neither. Instead, her thoughts returned to snippets of sounds and images from the house they'd visited earlier. She kept seeing Jeremy's father prone on the ground, arms flung around the gravestone, as if he might pull it into himself, and somehow embrace all of his might-have-beens. She saw him turn over, dead-eyed, and not recognize his own son. She heard the woman's cigarette-stained voice.

He's in the mud.

Heather knew mud was a name for heroin. She'd learned that in health last year. And if she had to guess, based on the way the woman and Jeremy's father acted, they were using heroin. The woman's statement seemed to go beyond slang to describe where the man really was, as if he were trying to find his traction, trying to climb out of a pit where solid ground no longer existed, where one slip led to the next, until he was wallowing in it, drowning instead of moving.

This is what she was thinking when the trees parted at last to reveal a dark sky. The rain had turned to a fine mist, and a pale sliver of moon hung above the sunset. The water tower loomed in the distance on the other side of a wet meadow.

Like everything out here, rust held sway. The actual tank was roofless, whether from a storm or the hands of man, Heather could only guess. The corrugated tin had turned to a burnished red beneath all the rust. Four stilts held it off the ground, nudging the lip of the tank in line with some of the nearby treetops. Railroad trestles, eaten by time and weather, formed a half-realized path to the tower before disappearing in the high weeds.

"I see it," Heather said.

Jeremy said nothing, but he quickened his pace. Heather knew the water tower had become like a totem to him now, a goal he had fixed in his mind. It mattered little what was actually there—most likely a dead bird, stripped of its feathers or a poor raccoon who drowned inside the murky silt.

Underneath the tower, water dripped from the slats overhead and landed on their upturned faces. On the other side, they found a badly mangled ladder.

Several steps were broken or missing, but Jeremy felt around for one of the solid ones and began to climb.

Heather followed, pulling herself over the open spaces where the steps were missing, willing herself to the top where she joined Jeremy on the wooden catwalk. She peered over the lip of the tank.

Inside, past endless rivulets of corrugated tin, a shallow pool looked back at her. A foreign smell came up from the tank, causing Heather to hold her breath. She saw no alien. She saw nothing in the dark.

The tank shuddered as Jeremy grabbed the rim and shook. The water, dark and shiny as oil, lapped against the sides, but nothing surfaced.

He gave the tank another shake. "It can't be too deep."

"Maybe the Barrows were just bullshitting," Heather said.

"No. There's something here." He pulled himself up. "I'm going in."

Before Heather could stop him, a sound came from the logging road. She turned and saw a truck rumbling toward them from the east.

"Hurry," she said. "I think your brother's here."

A thud welled up from inside the tank, followed by a groan of pain. "I'm in," Jeremy said.

As Heather pulled herself over the rim, she looked at the moon. A gleaming silver arc, carrying the stars in the same way a mother carries her children, rocking them to sleep, singing the day shut, opening the night. As she fell, she told herself she would keep the moon in sight, a constant to guide her where all other markers had failed.

She hit the water and then the bottom, first with her feet and then when they couldn't sustain the impact she crumpled to her knees, cracking them hard against the tank. Rolling over in the shallow water, she found the crescent moon, cradling the stars. The pain in her legs begged for her to scream out, but the moon calmed her like any good mother would.

"I think I messed my up my ankle," Jeremy said.

"Don't talk," Heather said. "Look at the moon."

"What?"

"It'll calm you."

Jeremy turned his face up to the moon, its slivered shine opening his face up, glinting in the tiny space of his squinted eyes. Despite the pain, despite the smell, despite the terror she felt at being ridiculed by Ronnie and Clyde, this image of Jeremy was too much. He looked smaller somehow down here, but more defined, more in focus. The shadows hid his faults, the moonglow highlighted everything good about him and Heather could see now there was a lot good about Jeremy. Seeing him like this, now, in this other world made her feel like a part of something mysterious and grand, but also sad. A great, silent secret. She shivered.

Two doors slammed outside the tower. Voices boomed.

"You're buying me a twelve-pack if there's nothing here, Clyde."

"How about you buy me a case if there is?" Clyde said. He sounded confident. Heather looked around the tank, but it had grown even darker now and she could barely make out Jeremy, much less an alien.

"If I see an alien, I'm going to extract the bastard and sell him on eBay."

"Well get ready to extract. Here. Take a flashlight."

Heather heard them struggling up the ladder, cursing as they came to the missing steps. She had no idea what to do. In seconds, the flashlights would shine down here, exposing them.

She looked back at the moon, as if an answer might come from there. There was none. In fact, the moon had slipped away, obscured by the clouds. She thought of her father. Maybe that's what happened to him too. Maybe the clouds had simply rolled in.

This thought made Heather angry, even while she found it soothing. If clouds rolled in, they could roll away. It made sense. But why had it happened at all? And why was she here in this water tank waiting to be humiliated? Heather felt the urge to hit something, to strike out.

Backing into the curved wall of the tank, she kicked it twice with her heels as hard as she could.

"Was that you, Ronnie?"

The voices were above them now.

"From down there."

Heather knocked again, this time with her fists.

"Oh shit."

"You didn't tell me the fucker was alive."

"It wasn't."

A series of furious knockings came from the other side of the tank as Jeremy began to hit the walls. Heather joined him and together they made the tower wobble on its wooden legs. Soon she was throwing her body against the walls as the water sloshed around her knees. The sky was completely dark now and the stars seemed to list from side to side as they rocked the tank. At thirteen, Heather had never been drunk, though she imagined this was what it must feel like. The sky appeared to spin above her, to come loose from its fragile place. She had no idea how long this lasted. It seemed like forever.

When they stopped, Heather was soaked and exhilarated. There was little doubt the Barrows had split. To be sure, she calmed her breathing and listened. Outside, an engine turned over and tires scattered gravel.

"Awesome," Heather said. Her words echoed in the dark tank, plinking off the tin walls, falling soundless into the water.

Jeremy said nothing. She heard him breathing nearby.

"Jeremy?"

She reached for him in the darkness. He was there, beside her. Taking her shoulders, he turned her gently. At first, she thought he was about to kiss her, but rather than lifting her face up to his, he tilted her head down.

"There's something touching my leg."

The clouds around the moon dissolved. Moonlight played over the water, making the smallest ripples shine like silk. It was there, bathed in moonshine, near Heather's feet. It had been there all along; she'd probably brushed against it without even knowing, unaware of the deadness against her legs. She felt a sudden urge to wipe them clean.

Jeremy spoke the question, even as it formed inside her mind. "What is it?"

Heather knelt for a better look. Blue and bloated, almost fishlike in the murky water. Hands splayed apart as if the creature had been pleading. Both knees bent, the creature's feet in the air. Heather counted the toes. Ten. Ten fingers. She lifted her gaze to the head. Proportionally, too large for its body. The mouth hung open in a toothless scream. Its eyes were open in an expression Heather recognized, though for a time she could not place it. She bent closer, trying to read the eyes. What did they say? Where had she seen them before? Then the moon shifted or the clouds did, but whatever happened made the shadows creep away, and she saw her own reflection in the water staring up at her as if she were a different person, an underwater person, sharing the same body and personality and memories as her normal self. This underwater person, though knew all the secrets. And finally she knew where she recognized the eyes. They belonged to the girl staring back at her. The look, she understood now, was simple confusion and fear. Nothing so confusing and frightening as being born into death.

An arm fell around her shoulders. Jeremy knelt beside her, pulling her close. Together they gazed down at the creature.

"Is it an alien?" he said at last.

"Yeah," Heather said, seeing them all in the water now, the baby, Jeremy, and herself. "It is."

=======

John Mantooth's *short fiction has appeared in numerous online and print publications including* Fantasy Magazine, Thuglit, On Spec, Shimmer, *and* The Haunted Legends *anthology. He also received the Barksdale-Maynard award for his short story "Slide." He confesses that he has never actually climbed a water tower himself.*

=======

I wonder if Heather and Jeremy get out of that water tank. I worry about Jeremy getting his glasses replaced. Point is, by the end of this story, I cared enough about the characters to consider their futures. I hope they escape the water tower as well as the horrors of their families and the place in which they live. They will thrive because Heather will understand how special she is and Jeremy will learn he's not institutionally "special" after all.

Or maybe, like the "alien," they never get out.

IN THE PORCHES OF MY EARS

NORMAN PRENTISS

Helen and I should have paid more attention to the couple we followed into the movie theater: his stiff, halting walk, and the way the woman clung to him, arm around his waist and her body pressed tight to his side. I read love into their close posture, an older couple exchanging long-held decorum for the sort of public display more common among today's younger people. I felt embarrassed for them and looked away. I regret that neither my wife nor I noticed a crucial detail in time, but real life doesn't always inspire the interpretative urgency of images projected on a screen, and it's not as if a prop department provided the obvious clues: sunglasses worn indoors, or a thin white cane tapping the ground, sweeping the air.

Helen went ahead to get us seats, while I stood in line at concessions to buy bottled waters. We disliked popcorn for its metallic, fake butter smell and, more importantly, because we chose not to contribute to the surrounding crunch—a sound like feet stomping through dead leaves, intruding over a film's quieter moments. For similar reasons, we avoided candy, with its noisome wrappers, and the worst abomination of recent years, the plastic tray of corn chips and hot cheese dip. Fortunately, the Midtowne Cinema didn't serve the latter, making it one of our preferred neighborhood theaters. That, and the slightly older clientele who behaved according to that lost era, back before people trained themselves to shout over rented movies in their living rooms.

The Midtowne wasn't quite an art house, rarely showing films with subtitles or excessive nudity. Instead, it tended towards Shakespeare or Dickens or E.M. Forster adaptations, the big-screen, bigger-budget equivalents to television's *Masterpiece Theatre*, which I tended to prefer; or, closer to Helen's taste, romantic comedies more palatably delivered through British accents.

Helen had chosen the afternoon's entertainment, so we'd once again see that short, slightly goofy actor who survived an embarrassing sex scandal a few years back and still, *still* managed onscreen to charm the sandy-haired, long-legged actress (who was actually American-born, but approximated the preferred accent well enough for most, and smiled brightly enough to provoke the rest to forgive her). I brought the water bottles into the auditorium—two dollars each, unfortunately, but we broke even by saving as much on matinee admission—and searched for Helen in the flickering dark.

We were later than I expected. Previews had already started, and the semi-dark auditorium was mostly full. I knew Helen's preference for an aisle seat, on the right side of the main section, but the crowd had forced her to sit farther back than usual. I walked past her before a whispered "Psst, Steve," called me to the correct row.

She turned sideways, legs in the aisle so I could scoot past easily. I handed her a water bottle before I sat down.

"Is this okay?" she asked.

"Fine." I responded without really thinking. It was her movie choice, so it wouldn't bother me to sit too far back from the picture.

Helen gestured toward the man in front of me, then forked her middle- and forefinger to point at her eyes. I recognized the man from the couple I'd half-noticed on the way inside. He sat tall in his seat: his shoulders and gangly gray-fuzzed head, from my vantage, cut a dark notch into the bottom of the screen like the interlocking edge of a missing jigsaw piece. His companion was a good bit shorter, granting my wife a clear view of the film.

I knew Helen felt guilty because she liked the aisle, actually thought she needed it because she typically left to use the restroom at least twice during a ninety-minute film. The water bottle didn't help, obviously.

Music swelled from the preview's soundtrack, and a glossy country manor montage shimmered onscreen. Like a sequel to *Age of Innocence*, or maybe *A Room with a Different View*. "I can see fine," I assured her. Besides, the slight obstruction was better than having Helen climb over my legs several times once the film was in progress. "As long as there's no subtitles," I joked.

Helen pointed to her eyes again, and her fingertips nearly touched the lenses of her glasses. I could tell she wanted to say more, but she stopped herself.

"What is it?"

I spoke normally, just loud enough so she'd hear over the trailer's quoted blurb from *The New Yorker*, but from Helen's expression you would think I'd shouted "Fire!"

"Never mind," she said, especially quiet, but her message clear.

Then the man in front of me turned his head. It was a quick motion, almost like a muscle spasm, and he held the angle for a long, awkward profile. His shoulder pressed into the chair cushion, and he twisted his head further around toward me. From a trick of the projection light, I assumed, his eyes appeared fogged, the irises lined like veined gray marble.

His companion tapped him. "The movie's about to start." As if she'd activated a button on the man's shoulder, his head snapped quickly around, face front.

"Strange," I said, barely audible, but still Helen winced. I couldn't understand her agitation. In our shared interpretation of moviegoer etiquette, it was perfectly acceptable to speak quietly during the "coming attractions" portion of the show.

The exit lights dimmed completely, and the studio logo appeared on the screen. Then before the credits, a pan over Trafalgar Square, then Big Ben, then a red double-decker bus. Quick establishing shots so any idiot would know—

"We're in England."

The woman in front of us spoke with a conspirator's whisper, a quiet, urgent tone far less musical than the lover's lilt she'd expressed earlier when she tapped his shoulder.

Jeez. Thanks for stating the obvious, lady.

The credits began, yellow lettering over a long shot of the Thames river and the London skyline. The two main actors' names appeared first, then the film title.

In that same strident whisper, the woman read aloud to her companion. The stars, the co-stars, the "Special Appearance by Sir James So-and-so." The screenwriter, editor, for-God's-sake the music composer, and finally the director.

He can see for himself, I thought. He's not . . .

But of course, he was, and I'd been a fool for not realizing sooner. For a moment I held out a glimmer of hope that the man was simply illiterate. Once the credits ended, she'd grow silent and they'd watch the movie in peace. Wishful thinking, however, because I recalled how she'd held him close coming inside the building. Guiding him.

And I knew she'd be talking over the entire movie.

If we'd figured it out sooner, we could have moved. Dark as it was, I barely distinguished a few unoccupied seats scattered around the theater—including an empty to my left—but no pairs together. Helen and I always had to sit together. If the movie ended up being ruined for us, at least it would be a shared experience.

The commentary began in earnest. "She's trying to lock the door, but she's got too much in her arms. A purse, an accordion briefcase, a grocery sack, and a Styrofoam coffee cup. The lid's loose on the coffee."

Onscreen, the Emma- or Judi- or Gwyneth-person—possibly I've conflated the actor's name with the character's—juggled the coffee cup, the lid flew up and the liquid slipped out and over her work clothes. "Damn, damn, damn," she said in a delightful accent, and the audience roared with laughter.

"She spilled it," the man's companion told him. "A huge coffee stain on her blouse."

I hadn't laughed. The woman's commentary—I assumed she was the blind man's wife—had telegraphed the spill. Had the lid really been loose? Enough for any of us to see the clue?

"I can't believe this," I whispered to Helen, and she half-winced again. Finally, I realized the source of her tension: the commonplace wisdom that a person lacking in one physical sense gained extra ability in another—in this case, hearing.

Sure. His loudmouth wife can ruin the whole film for us, but God forbid we whisper anything that might hurt the guy's feelings.

Helen risked a quick whisper of her own: "I'm sorry."

It wasn't her fault, of course—not really. But we'd been married almost fifteen years, and familiar intimacy brought its own yardstick for blame. The woman, her husband, the situation itself created the problem, and we could share disapproval of the couple's imposition, or shake fists skyward in synchronized dismay at Fates who brought us together at the same showing. And yet, Helen had eaten her lunch slowly this afternoon, had misremembered the show's start time, which in turn limited her seating options (and she must have the aisle seat, and must see these British comedies the first weekend of their release). So I blamed her a bit, then—the type of blame saved for those you love deeply, blame you savored as you indulged a spouse's habits and peculiar tastes.

Helen did the same for me. When she disliked one of my film choices—the somber violence of the latest *King Lear* adaptation, or any Thomas Hardy depression-fest other than *Under the Greenwood Tree*—I could sense her unspoken discomfort beside me, all while the film flickered toward an inevitable, tragic end. In an odd way, her discomfort often improved the experience for me, magnifying the tension of the film. Making it more authentic.

The tension was all wrong here, though, since nothing spoiled a comedy like an explanation. As the Rupert- or Ian- or Trevor-character blustered through confident proclamations, and Emma/Judi/Gwyneth mugged a sour expression, the blind man's wife stated the obvious: "His arrogance offends her. He's so self-centered, he doesn't yet realize he's in love with her."

Oh, really? Do tell.

It was easy enough to infer the same conclusions from the dialogue. I could have closed my eyes and done fine without the woman's incessant whispers. Score myself a hundred on the quiz. Besides, these romantic comedies all followed the same formula: the guy would Darcy her for a bit, she'd come around just when it seemed too late, there'd be a misunderstanding on one or both sides, until a ridiculous coincidence threw them awkwardly and then blissfully together, the end.

"Now she puts her Chinese take-out cartons in the trash, aware she's eaten too much, but also aware it doesn't matter, because she's alone."

A slight bit of interpretation there, against the whimsical Supremes song hurrying love on the soundtrack, but probably accurate. At that moment, I wondered exactly how many others in the theater could hear the woman's commentary. The people in front of them, surely, were in the same position as Helen and I: close enough to overhear, but too close to make a show of offense. Nobody else seemed to react to the voice: no grunts of disapproval, no agitated shiftings in the seats. There wasn't that ripple of cold scorn that chills the orchestra seats when a cell phone goes off during the first aria. Perhaps her whisper was one of those trained, directed voices, sharp in proximity but dropping off quickly with distance—as if an invisible bubble cushioned the sound into a tight circumference.

Lucky us.

I actually tried to control my indignation, for Helen's sake. We were both hypersensitive to extraneous chatter during a film, but this was her type of movie (though not, as was already evident, the pinnacle of the art form), and I was determined not to spoil her experience further by huffing my disapproval throughout. Instead, I touched the top of Helen's hand on our shared armrest. Our secret signal in the dark: three quick taps, for *I-love-you.*

It was a slight film, stupidly titled *Casting a Romance*: a reference to the Darcy character's job as a casting director for movies, then a pun on casting a *fishing* line, since he joins the girl and her father at a summer cottage, only to lose his stuffy demeanor amid hooks and slipping into lakes, and her getting a massive rainbow trout next to his emasculating tadpole. Somewhere along the way—about halfway between Helen's first and second trips to the Ladies' Room—I'd settled into the film, and into the commentary. I grudgingly appreciated it after a while—the woman's skill at selecting the right details, firing the narration rapidly into her husband's hungry ear. To keep myself amused, I played around a bit, closing my eyes for short stretches and letting the woman's words weave images around the dialogue. When Helen returned from the restroom, I didn't have the burden of summarizing what she missed: the woman's commentary easily filled the gaps.

After a while, I didn't mind being in the bubble with them. The shape of the blind man's head became familiar to me, atop his thin neck and leaning perpetually to one side to catch his wife's every word. That sharp underlying whisper became part of the film, like the experts' comments during a televised sporting event. I half-toyed with the idea she was an expert herself. For example, she whispered how the man left his jacket draped over the chair, and she warned, correctly, that the plane tickets would spill out. She also predicted the moment when he realized his embarrassing connection to the heroine's brother—the cad who'd tried to blackmail him into an acting job during the first reel. Her delivery was so good, that I suspected she'd seen the film before—perhaps even practiced with a notepad and a stopwatch, to pinpoint the precise moments to whisper crucial details or hiss clues that inattentive viewers might miss.

So, I'd grudgingly grown to admire her skill, almost to rely on it for my full appreciation of the movie. And then she did that malicious thing during the final scene.

She changed the ending. It was almost elegant how she did it, an interplay between the silences and the openness of the characters' final words. Onscreen, the man said "I still love you," and there was a faint rise in his voice, maybe the actor's insecurity rather than the character's, but the woman twisted a question mark over his declaration.

"They say they are in love," she whispered, "but they don't mean it. He reaches out to hug her—" and on the screen they are hugging, "but she pulls away. It is too little, too late."

I realized, then, how precarious this type of movie was: a teasing, near-romance, suspended over ninety brittle minutes. The main characters' re-lationship is simultaneously inevitable and fragile—a happy ending endlessly deferred, the threat of ruin always beneath the comic surface.

The actress laughed onscreen, a clear display of relief and joy, and the woman said: "She's bitter. It is a dry, empty laugh. Her face is full of scorn."

I reached again for Helen's hand beside me. We didn't speak; our touch expressed the outrage well enough. This horrible woman at once betrayed the movie, and her blind husband.

I felt certain now that she'd rehearsed the commentary. How else could she best deliver her poison into his ear—at what time, and at how strong a dose—certain no additional dialogue would provide an antidote?

Thinking back, I realized something more sinister. The woman's descriptions of the lead actor had made him taller than the visual reality, gave him a thin neck and wobbled head that tilted awkwardly to the side, very much like . . . the head in front of me, a shadow rising above the seat to darken the bottom edge of the movie frame. She'd transformed the hero into a younger version of her husband, making the character fit how the blind man—for lack of a better word—*saw* himself. For him, the disappointed ending would be particularly cruel.

The camera pulled back from the onscreen couple's happy, final embrace, and a song blared from the soundtrack. The song was allegedly a cheerful choice, with an upbeat tempo and optimistic lyrics. Most people in the audience probably tried not to dwell on how the lead singer died of a drug overdose, just as the group verged on the brink of stardom.

The blind man's shoulders shook in uneven rhythm. His head, formerly tilted toward his wife, now drooped forward. I couldn't hear over the joyful soundtrack, but clearly, the man was crying.

Still, neither Helen nor I said anything—to them, or to each other. The woman had done an awful, unforgivable thing to her husband, but we decided it wasn't our place to comment. An overheard whisper is sacred, like the bond of a confessional. We needn't involve ourselves in another couples' private drama—even if its language had been forced upon us, even if (and I knew Helen felt this more than I did) the whispered words had spoiled our afternoon's entertainment.

My wife and I didn't need to voice this decision. It was communicated though a strange telepathy, refined over many years in darkened movie houses: a released breath after an exciting chase scene; an imperceptible shift in posture to convey boredom; a barely audible sigh at a beautifully framed landscape. We felt from each other what we couldn't hear or see. Helen's soft gasp had told me, "It's not worth it." I tapped my foot on the floor, as if to say, "You're right. I'll let it go."

Like many patrons of the Midtowne Cinema, we were "credit sitters." We wouldn't stay to the very end, necessarily—even the greatest film buff has little interest in what stylist coiffed the extras' hair, or who catered lunches for the crew—but it was always worth sitting through the list of characters, to recognize an actor's name and think, "Ah, I thought I'd seen him before. Wasn't he the one in . . . ?"

But the blind man and his companion began to leave right away. The woman seemed to lift him from his seat. Together, they moved slowly into the aisle. Instead of guiding him, as she had upon entering the theater, it now seemed more like she was carrying him out, her arm around his back and supporting slumped, defeated shoulders. The house lights were raised slightly to help people exit, and I'd caught a brief glimpse of his sad expression. I wished his wife had given him more time to collect himself, before exposing his raw emotions to the bright, sighted world of the lobby.

In a bizarre, random thought, I wondered if she'd purposely ushered him out before the rapid scroll of names and obscure job titles made a mockery of her remarkable skill. She would have short-circuited trying to keep up, like an early computer instructed to divide by zero.

Helen and I waited through the rest of the cast list, maintaining our silence even as the real-life names of "Florist" and "Waiter #4" floated toward the ceiling. About a third of the seats were still occupied when we stood to leave. After we pushed through the double doors into the lobby, my wife took a detour to the side: another trip to the ladies' room.

I dropped our empty water bottles into the recycle bin, then stood aside near the front doors. A line stretched outside, people buying tickets for the next show, and a steady trickle emerged from the auditorium doors on either side of the concessions counter. They blinked their eyes against fresh light, and all of them had pleasant expressions on their faces. Some people, at least, had been allowed to enjoy the film.

Beside an archway to the side hallway, I spotted the blind man. He stood by himself, slouched slightly against the wall. His head bobbled indecisively on the thin neck, as if longing to lean toward his wife's voice.

The opportunity presented itself. Despite what Helen and I tacitly agreed to, I moved toward him, my tennis shoes soundless—to me, at least—over the lobby's worn beige carpet.

"Excuse me," I said, but before I got the words out, his face turned toward me. He looked older than I'd imagined, overhead lamps etching shadows under the wrinkles in his skin. Although he was dressed in casual clothes—a light blue short-sleeve shirt and twill pants—he stiffened into a formal posture which, sadly, made him seem more foolish than dignified. His eyes were expectant and vacant and puffy red.

"Excuse me," I repeated, stalling for time even as I feared one of our wives would return from the ladies' room. My voice was loud, but I couldn't control it—as if I needed to pierce the fog of his blank stare. "I just, um, I just wanted to say . . . "

"Yes." It was the first time I'd heard him speak. His voice sounded weakened by his bout of tears, with barely strength to encourage me to continue.

People walked past us, oblivious. I squinted down the hallway toward the rest rooms. No sign yet of Helen, or the awful, whispering woman.

"The movie didn't end the way she described it to you." I blurted out the rest, before I lost my nerve. "The couple was happy at the end. Still in love. I thought you should know."

The blind man didn't react at first. Then I saw something like relief: his body relaxing, the tight line of his mouth loosening as if he sought permission to smile.

He swung his left arm to the side with a flourish, cupped his right arm over his stomach and bent his torso forward in a deep, exaggerated bow. He straightened, then spoke with a firmness I hadn't expected: "Oh, thank you. Thank you *so* much. I don't know what I would have done without your help."

It was a parody of gratefulness. The sarcasm settled into his face, an expression of scorn that immediately dismissed me from his presence.

Luckily, I spotted Helen approaching. I crossed to meet her in the archway, and I steered her across the lobby, keeping her distant from the blind man. As we reached the sidewalk outside, before the theater door swung shut with a rusty squeak, I thought I heard the blind man thank me again.

At dinner, we didn't discuss the film as we normally would. No revisiting favorite lines of dialogue, seeking subtleties in the script; no ranking of the performances or nuanced comparisons to films of similar type. Instead, we tore small pieces off store-bought rolls or rearranged silk flowers, their petals dusty in a white ceramic vase. We took turns saying we were hungry, wondering aloud when the minestrone soup would arrive.

Finally, Helen broached the subject. "I don't know what I was thinking. I wish I hadn't sat there."

"No need to blame yourself," I said. "I hadn't even noticed the guy was blind. And who'd ever expect his wife to describe the whole film for him?"

"I wish I hadn't sat there," Helen repeated.

That was pretty much all we needed to say about the matter. After the main course, though, when we decided not to stay for dessert or coffee, the waitress took too long to bring our check. In the awkward silence, I weakened and decided to confess. I told her about my curious encounter with the blind man in the lobby.

Helen shivered, like it was the most frightening story she'd ever heard.

Let me tell you about a different movie. It's another romantic comedy, this time about a long-married couple who stop everything so they can take a month to travel the world together. The man is reluctant at first, afraid to fall behind on his work accounts, and it's not their anniversary or either of their birthdays, and he's never been that spontaneous anyway. But she convinces him, and she's already booked the flights, the hotels, the cruise ship, and she's bought books and brochures and printed off pages and pages of advice from travel Web sites: little restaurants tourists didn't visit; special tours given only Sunday afternoons, if you know who to ask; "must see" lists for each city, itineraries to fill each day.

Before they leave, she surprises him with a wrapped package, and it's a digital camera with lots of storage space, so they can take as many pictures as they want. He'd never believed in photographs, thought taking them distracted from the experience of travel. On previous trips, other tourists were a nuisance with cameras, blocking his view or popping a flash to interrupt the soft calm of natural light. But it's a thoughtful gift, and he finds out he enjoys it: framing a waterfall or mountain or monument, with her in the foreground, and the fun of checking through the pictures that night in the hotel.

He had agreed to the trip just to please her, but soon her enthusiasm wins him over, and he ends up loving it. To be a better comedy, though, things need to go wrong: missed connections, bungled hotel reservations; a random "I'll have that" finger pointed at a menu, and lamb brains arrive at the table, or a five-pound exotic fish with bubble eyes staring up from the plate; or ill-pronounced words to a French street juggler—*fou* instead of *feu*, for instance, ("You called him crazy, m'sieu!")—and hilarious misunderstandings ensue.

But there's none of that. Similar things occur, but not often, nothing major. A forgotten toothbrush, rather than a lost passport. She's a fantastic tour guide, and he loves her more than ever. The trip is unforgettable, revitalizing. Okay, it's not that great a film: no conflict, no complications. But it's sweet.

After the trip, he has the memories, and the pictures. The woman smiles in all of them—leaning against the ship rail during their Hawaii cruise, the Nepali coast in the background; tiny in one corner, hair windswept, with the Grand Canyon vast behind her; at a table outside a Venice cafe, a glass of local vintage raised for the camera, and for him.

He's printed all the photos, hundreds of them. He fans a stack, like a cartoon flip-book, and the world rushes behind his wife's constant, smiling image. The heavy paper stock creates a gust of air, almost like a whisper.

Bladder cancer, it says. *Inoperable.*

Everything had seemed like one of Helen's fluffy, happy-ending movies. She kept it that way as long as she could.

The specialists call it bladder cancer, if that's where the tumor originates, even if the disease spreads to other parts of the body. Helen's frequent visits to the bathroom were a symptom, but the change happened gradually, and neither of us had noticed. By the time she got the diagnosis, things had progressed too far. Even with radical treatment, the prognosis wasn't good. When she found out, she decided not to tell me. Instead, she announced, "Let's take a trip!"

If this were really a movie, that omission makes for a more significant story. We were always a happy couple, but *I* was especially happy during that month-long vacation. I was happy. I can only imagine what really went on in Helen's mind, despite those ever-present smiles. Thoughts of aggressive therapy when she returned home; dread of long hospital days, pain still sharp through medicated fog. If she was lucky, maybe, a swift decline.

The trip wasn't for her benefit, but for mine. A beautiful, poignant farewell gift. And always, beneath the sweet surface of her romantic comedy, an awful, unnarrated tragedy.

I hate myself for not noticing it. Helen spared me the knowledge, as long as she could.

One day near the end, from the intensive care bed that she'd dreaded in silence, she revealed something very strange. I almost wish she hadn't told me—though I can understand why she needed to. Something else happened that day at the theater, after we sat behind the blind man and his talkative companion. In the ladies' room, when the film was over, Helen heard that whispered voice again, from the adjoining stall. The voice was clear and directed; Helen knew she was the only one who could hear it. The whisper began at the precise moment when my wife strained and began to empty her bladder. Helen remembered exactly what the voice had said: "It doesn't hurt. It's just a minor inconvenience, so you put it off. By the time you get to a doctor, it will be too late." As she repeated the words, Helen's voice, weakened by the cancer and the treatments, achieved a perfect, uncanny duplication of the woman's urgent whisper.

The hospital seemed instantly more sterile and hopeless and cold. Helen passed away that night, while I was home asleep.

And now, all my movies are sad. I go to them alone. I want to feel Helen's presence in the empty seat next to me, embrace those half-conscious signals we always shared in the dark. I want to tap the top of her hand gently, three times.

Instead, I lean my head slightly to the side. A whispered voice distorts the context of the film, makes the story all about me and my loss. It changes the ending, twists it into something horrible.

Norman Prentiss *recently won the Bram Stoker Award for Superior Achievement in Short Fiction for the story reprinted in this volume. His first book,* Invisible Fences, *was published in May 2010. Other fiction has appeared in* Tales from the Gorezone, Damned Nation, Postscripts, *the Shivers anthology series, and at the* Horror Drive-In *Web site. His poetry is forthcoming in* A Sea of Alone: Poems for Alfred Hitchcock *and has appeared in* Writer Online, Southern Poetry Review, *and Baltimore's* City Paper. *Essays on gothic and sensation literature have been published in* Victorian Poetry, Colby Quarterly, *and* The Thomas Hardy Review.

Another slice of life story but, unlike O'Nan's, "In the Porches of My Ears" has a whisper of the uncanny: the blind man's wife in the ladies' room. Does that make it fantasy? Or was it merely an odd coincidence? There's no atmosphere of dread, just a numbing sadness and subtle realization of the darkness lurking in any life. The title, by the way, comes from a well-known tale of horror:

> Upon my secure hour thy uncle stole,
> With juice of cursed hebenon in a vial,
> And in the porches of my ears did pour
> The leperous distilment; whose effect
> Holds such an enmity with blood of man
> That swift as quicksilver it courses through
> The natural gates and alleys of the body,
> And with a sudden vigour doth posset
> And curd, like eager droppings into milk,
> The thin and wholesome blood . . .
> —William Shakespeare, *Hamlet*, Act 1, Scene V

THE CINDERELLA GAME

KELLY LINK

One day Peter would have his own secret hideaway just like this one, his stepfather's forbidden room, up in the finished attic: leather couches, stereo system with speakers the size of school lockers, flat screen television, and so many horror movies you'd be able to watch a different one every night of the year. The movie Peter picked turned out to be in a foreign language, but it was still pretty scary and there were werewolves in it.

"What are you doing?" someone said. Peter spilled popcorn all over the couch.

His new stepsister Darcy stood in the door that went down to the second floor. Her hair was black and knotted and stringy, and, no surprise, she was wearing one of her dozens of princess dresses. This one had been pink and spangled at one point. Now it looked like something a zombie would wear to a fancy dress party.

"What are you doing up here?" Peter saw, with fascinated horror, the greasy smears left behind on the leather as he chased popcorn back into the bowl. "Go away. Why aren't you asleep?"

His stepsister said, "Dad says I'm not allowed to watch scary movies." She'd holstered a fairy wand in the pocket of her princess gown. The battered tiara on her head was missing most of its rhinestones.

You are *a scary movie*, Peter thought. "How long have you been standing here?"

"Not long. Since the werewolf bit the other lady. You were picking your nose."

It got better and better. "If you're not allowed to watch scary movies, then what are you doing up here?"

"What are *you* doing up here?" Darcy said. "We're not supposed to watch television up here without an adult. Why aren't you in bed? Where's Mrs. Daly?"

"She had to go home. Somebody called and said her husband was in the hospital. Mom hasn't come back yet," Peter said. "So I'm in charge until they get home. She and your dad are still out on their we-won't-go-on-a-honeymoon-we'll just-have-a-mini-honeymoon-every-Monday-night-for-the-rest-of-our-lives special date. Apparently there was a wait at the restaurant, blah blah blah, and so they're going to a later movie. They called and I said that Mrs. Daly was in the bathroom. So just go back to bed, okay?"

"You're not my babysitter," his stepsister said. "You're only three years older than me."

"Four and a half years older," he said. "So you have to do what I say. If I told you to go jump in a fire then you'd have to jump. Got it?"

"I'm not a baby," Darcy said. But she was. She was only eight.

One of the movie werewolves was roaming through a house, playing hide and seek. There were puddles of blood everywhere. It came into a room where there was a parrot, reached up with a human-like paw, and opened the door of the cage. Peter and Darcy both watched for a minute, and then Peter said, "You *are* a baby. You have over a hundred stuffed animals. You know all the words to all the songs from *The Little Mermaid*. My mom told me you still wet the bed."

"Why are you so mean?" She said it like she was actually curious.

Peter addressed the werewolves. "How can I explain this so that someone your age will understand? I'm not mean. I'm just honest. It's not like I'm your real brother. We just happen to live in the same house because your father needed someone to do his taxes, and my mother is a certified accountant. The rest of it I don't even pretend to understand." Although he did. Her father was rich. His mother wasn't. "Okay? Now go to bed."

"No." Darcy did a little dance, as if to demonstrate that she could do whatever she wanted.

"Fine," he said. "Stay here and watch the werewolf movie then."

"I don't want to."

"Then go play princess or whatever it is you're always doing." Darcy had a closet with just princess dresses in it. And tiaras. And fairy wands. And fairy wings.

"You play with me," she said. "Or I'll tell everyone you pick your nose."

"Who cares," Peter said. "Go away."

"I'll pay you."

"How much?" he said, just out of curiosity.

"Ten dollars."

He thought for a minute. Her grandparents had given her a check for her birthday. Little kids never knew what to do with money and as far as he could tell, her father bought her everything she wanted anyway. And she got an allowance. Peter got one now too, of course, but he'd knocked a glass of orange juice over on his laptop and his mom said she was only going to pay for half of what a new one would cost. "Make it fifty."

"Twenty," Darcy said. She came over and sat on the couch beside him. She smelled awful. A rank, feral smell, like something that lived in a cave. He'd heard his stepfather tell his mother that half the time Darcy only ran the water and then splashed it around with her hands behind a locked door.

Make-believe baths, which was funny when you thought about how much she worshipped Ariel from *The Little Mermaid*. When Darcy really took a bath she left a ring of grime around the tub. He'd seen it with his own eyes.

Peter said, "What does this involve, exactly?"

"We could play Three Little Pigs. Or Cinderella. You be the evil stepsister."

Like everything was already decided. Just to annoy her, Peter said, "For a lousy twenty bucks I get to be whoever I want. I'm Cinderella. You can be the evil stepsister."

"You can't be Cinderella!"

"Why not?"

"Because you're a boy."

"So what?"

Darcy seemed to have no answer to this. She examined the hem of her princess dress. Pulled a few remaining sequins off, as if they were scabs. Finally she said, "My dad says I have to be nice to you. Because this is really my house, and you're a guest, even though I didn't invite you to come live here and now you're going to live here all the time and never go away unless you die or get sent away to military school or something."

"Don't count on it," Peter said, feeling really annoyed now. So that was his stepfather's plan. Or maybe it was his mother, still working out the details of her new, perfect life, worrying that Peter was going to mess things up now that she'd gotten it. He'd gone in and out of three schools in the last two years. It was easy enough to get thrown out of school if you wanted to be. If they sent him away, he'd come right back. "Maybe I like it here."

Darcy looked at him suspiciously. It wasn't like she was problem free, either. She went to see a therapist every Tuesday to deal with some "abandonment issues" which were apparently due to the fact that her real mother now lived in Hawaii.

Peter said, "I'm Cinderella. Deal with it."

His stepsister shrugged. She said, "If I'm the evil stepsister then I get to tell you what to do. First you have to go put the toilet seat down in the bathroom. And I get to hold the remote and you have to go to bed first. And you have to cry a lot. And sing. And make me a peanut butter sandwich with no crusts. And a bowl of chocolate ice cream. And I get your Playstation, because Cinderella doesn't get to have any toys."

"I've changed my mind," Peter said, when she seemed to have finished. He grinned at her. *My what big teeth I have.* "I'm going to be the *evil* Cinderella."

She bared her teeth right back at him. "Wrong. Cinderella isn't evil. She gets to go to the ball and wear a princess dress. And mice like her."

"Cinderella might be evil," Peter said, thinking it through, remembering how it went in the Disney movie. Everybody treated Cinderella like she was a pushover. Didn't she sleep in a fireplace? "If her evil stepsister keeps making fun of her and taking away her Playstation, she might burn down the house with everyone in it."

"That isn't how the story goes. This is stupid," Darcy said. She was beginning to sound less sure of herself, however.

"This is the new, improved version. No fairy godmother. No prince. No glass slipper. No happy ending. Better run away, Darcy. Because evil Cinderella is coming to get you." Peter stood up. Loomed over Darcy in what he hoped was a menacing way. The werewolves were howling on the TV.

Darcy shrank back into the couch. Held up her fairy wand as if it would keep her safe. "No, wait! You have to count to one hundred first. And I'll go hide."

Peter grabbed the stupid, cheap wand. Pointed it at Darcy's throat. Tapped it on her chest and when she looked down, bounced it off her nose. "I'll count to ten. Unless you want to pay me another ten bucks. Then I'll count higher."

"I only have five more dollars!" Darcy protested.

"You got fifty bucks from your grandparents last weekend."

"Your mom made me put half of it into a savings account."

"Okay. I'll count to twenty-three." He put the werewolf movie on pause. "One."

He went into all the bedrooms on the second floor, flicking the light switches on and off. She wasn't under any of the beds. Or in the closets. Or behind the shower curtain in the show-off master bathroom. Or in either of the other two bathrooms on the second floor. He couldn't believe how many bathrooms there were in this house. Back in the dark hallway again he saw something and paused. It was a mirror and he was in it. He paused to look at himself. No Cinderella here. Something dangerous. Something out of place. He felt a low, wild, wolfish delight rise up in him. His mother looked at him sometimes as if she wasn't sure who he was. He wasn't sure, either. He had to look away from what he saw in the face in the mirror.

Wasn't there some other fairy tale? *I'll huff and I'll puff and I'll blow your house down.* He'd like to blow this house down. The first time his mother had brought him over for dinner, she'd said, "Well, what do you think?" In the car, as they came up the driveway. What he'd thought was that it was like television. He'd never seen a house like it except on TV. There had been two forks at dinner and a white cloth napkin he was afraid to use in case he got it dirty. Some kind of vegetable that he didn't even recognize, and macaroni and cheese that didn't taste right. He'd chewed with his mouth open on purpose, and the little girl across the table watched him the whole time.

Everyone was always watching him. Waiting for him to mess up. Even his friends at his last school had acted sometimes like they thought was crazy. Egged him on and then went silent when he didn't punk out. No friends yet at this new school. No bad influences, his mother said. A new start. But she was the one who had changed. Said things like, "I always wanted a little girl and now I've got one!" And, "It will be good for you, having a little sister. You're a role model now, Peter, believe it or not, so try to act like one."

Peter's mother let Darcy climb into bed with her and her new husband. Lay on the floor of the living room with her head in her new husband's lap. Darcy curled up beside them. Pretending to be a family, but he knew better. He could see the way Darcy wrinkled her nose when his mother hugged her. As if she smelled something bad, which was ironic, considering.

Peter went down the stairs two at a time. That black tide of miserable joy rose higher still, the way it always did when he knew he was doing exactly the wrong thing. As if he were going to die of it, whatever it was that he was becoming.

Darcy wasn't in the laundry room. Or the dining room. Peter went into the kitchen next, and knew immediately that she was here. Could feel her here, somewhere, holding her breath, squeezing her eyes shut, picking at her sequins. He thought of the babysitter, Mrs. Daly, and how afraid she'd looked when she left. Almost wished that she hadn't left, or that his mother and stepfather had skipped the movie, come home when they were supposed to. Wished that he'd told them about Mrs. Daly, except that his mother had sounded as if she were having a good time. As if she were happy.

He kicked a chair at the kitchen table and almost jumped out of his skin to hear it crash on the floor. Stomped around, throwing open the cabinet doors. Howling tunelessly, just for effect, except that it wasn't just for effect. He was enjoying himself. For a moment he didn't really even want to find his stepsister. Maybe no one would ever see her again.

She was folded up under the kitchen sink. Scrambled out when the door was flung open, and slapped his leg when he tried to grab her. Then scooted away on her hands and knees across the floor. There was a sort of sting in his calf now and he looked down and saw a fork was sticking out of him. It looked funny there. The tines hadn't gone far in, but still there were four little holes in the fabric of his jeans. Around the four little holes the black jeans turned blacker. Now it hurt.

"You stabbed me!" Peter said. He almost laughed. "With a fork!"

"I'm the evil stepsister," his stepsister said, glaring at him. "Of course I stabbed you. I'll stab you again if you don't do what I say."

"With what, a spoon?" he said. "You are going to be in so much trouble."

"I don't care," Darcy said. "Evil stepsisters don't care about getting in trouble." She stood up and straightened her princess dress. Then she walked over and gave him a little furious shove. Not such a little shove. He staggered back and then lurched forward again. Swung out for balance, and hit her across her middle with the back of one hand. Maybe he did it on purpose, but he didn't *think* he'd meant to do it. Either way the result was terrible. Blow your house down. Darcy was flung back across the room like she was just a piece of paper.

Now I've done it, he thought. Now they really will send me away. Felt a howling rage so enormous and hurtful that he gasped out loud. He darted after her, bent over her, and grabbed a shoulder. Shook it hard. Darcy's head flopped back and hit the refrigerator door and she made a little noise. "You made me," he said. "Not my fault. If you tell them—"

And stopped. "My mother is going to—" he said, and then had to stop again. He let go of Darcy. He couldn't imagine what his mother would do.

He knelt down. Saw his own blood smeared on the tiles. Not much. His leg felt warm. Darcy looked up at him, her ratty hair all in her face. She had her pajama bottoms on under that stupid dress. She was holding one arm with the other, like maybe he'd broken it. She didn't cry or yell at him and her eyes were enormous and black. Probably she had a concussion. Maybe they'd run into Mrs. Daly and her husband when they went to the hospital. He felt like throwing up.

"I don't know what I'm supposed to do!" he said. It came out in a roar. He didn't even know what he meant. "I don't know what I'm doing here! Tell me what I'm doing here."

Darcy stared at him. She seemed astonished. "You're Peter," she said. "You're being my stepbrother."

"Your evil stepbrother," he said and forced out a laugh, trying to make it a joke. But it was a wild, evil laugh.

Darcy got up, rubbing her head. She swung her other arm in a way that suggested it wasn't broken after all. He tried to feel relieved about this, but instead he just felt guiltier. He could think of no way to make things better and so he did nothing. He watched while Darcy went over and picked up the fork where he'd dropped it, carried it over to the sink, and then stood on the footstool to rinse it off. She looked over at him. Said, with a shrug, "They're home."

Car lights bounced against the windows.

His stepsister got down off the stool. She had a wet sponge in her hand. Calmly she crouched down and scrubbed at the bloody tiles. Swiped once at the blood on his jeans, and then gave up. Went back to the sink, stopping to pick up and straighten the chair he'd knocked over, and ran the water again to get the blood out of the sponge while he just sat and watched.

His mother came in first. She was laughing, probably at something his stepfather had said. His stepfather was always making jokes. It was one of the things Peter hated most about his stepfather, how he could make his mother laugh so easily. And how quickly her face would change from laughter, when she talked to Peter, or like now, when she looked over and saw Darcy at the sink, Peter on the floor. His stepfather came in right behind her, still saying something funny, his mouth invisible behind that bearish, bluish-blackish beard. He was holding a doggy bag.

"Peter," his mother said, knowing right away, the way she always did. "What's going on?"

He opened up his mouth to explain everything, but Darcy got there first. She ran over and hugged his mother around the legs. Lucky for his mother she wasn't holding a fork. And now here it came, the end of everything.

"Mommy," Darcy said, and Peter could see the magical effect this one word had, even on accountants. How his mother grew rigid with surprise, then lovingly pliant, as if Darcy had injected her with some kind of muscle relaxant.

Darcy turned her head, still holding his mother in that monstrously loving hold, and gave Peter a look he didn't understand until she began to speak in a rush. "Mommy, it was Cinderella because I couldn't sleep and Mrs. Daly had to go home and I woke up and we were waiting for you to come home and I got scared. Don't be angry. Peter and I were just playing a game. I was the evil stepsister." Again she looked at Peter.

"And I was Cinderella," Peter said. The leg of his pants was stiff with blood, but he could come up with an explanation tomorrow if only Darcy continued to keep his mother distracted. He had to get upstairs before anyone else. Get changed into his pajamas. Put things away in the forbidden room, where the werewolves waited patiently in the dark for their story to begin again. To begin the game again. No one could see what was in Darcy's face right now but him. He wished she would look away. He saw that she still had a smear of his blood on her hand, from the sponge and she glanced down and saw it too. Slowly, still looking at Peter, she wiped her hand against the princess dress until there was nothing left to see.

Kelly Link is the author of three collections of short stories, Stranger Things Happen, Magic for Beginners, *and* Pretty Monsters. *Her short stories have won three Nebulas, a Hugo, and a World Fantasy Award. Link and her family live in Northampton, Massachusetts, where she and her husband, Gavin J. Grant, run Small Beer Press, and play ping-pong. Since 1996 they have published the occasional zine* Lady Churchill's Rosebud Wristlet.

Blood, the realization that Peter has just discovered something horrible, and the sure knowledge that—somehow—there's not going to be a "happy ever after" for anyone in that fictional kitchen but then do any of these characters deserve to be so rewarded?

Do any of us ever truly live happily ever after?

That's the thing about Kelly Link's stories: Even when writing what seems to be a straightforward story for younger readers, there's a complexity that make you think.

Thinking. That's a scary thought.

THE JACARANDA SMILE

GEMMA FILES

Saw a dead bird in the fountain I eat my lunch by yesterday, eddying stickily to and fro: Bound loosely together with its own decay in a graceful/awful parody of flight, pre-skeletal wings unraveling on a feed-jet tide while its eyeless head cocked back and forth and up and down by turns, like it was listening for . . . something, whatever. No metaphor immediately suggested itself.

Which is why, after staring at it fixedly for a minute, I eventually just noted it all down—fountain, bird, my own vaguely queasy response—and tucked it away, neatly, for further reference.

Afterwards, I came home late, hot and exhausted, to find an email from Dad waiting in my in-box. It said the hospital had finally agreed to turn the penultimate switch on his "significant other," Aoife. Since the funeral would be held Saturday, in Australia, he didn't expect me to get there in time, and would prefer I not waste my money trying.

Three spare sentences, maybe four. The first I'd heard from him in . . . months?

Yes: Two, almost exactly.

I sat there at my computer, frowning slightly; looked at the REPLY icon, without hitting it. And as I read the message on my screen once more, cursor flashing aimlessly in the corner of my eye like an incipient migraine tic, I couldn't help but replay that moment when they first told him the extent of Aoife's damage; how he'd hugged me tight, trembling slightly, while I'd just looked straight down at his sandals, to avoid having to look anywhere else. Because it was somehow less intimate, less embarrassing, to count the sunspots on my estranged father's feet (with their crepe-like skin and overlong old man's nails) than to think directly about what was happening. What *had* happened, already. What was going to happen now.

These miles between us always left open, like unhealed lacunae. There's still half a world of distance between Canada and Australia: Toronto vs. Melbourne, daughter vs. father, writer vs. writer—my life vs. his life, give or take the few small instances where our very separate histories inform each other. His version, vs. my version.

I closed out, shut down my system. Then made more notes, almost reflexively—followed my own unholy instinct to rape and plunder my every experience for enough grit to make a bright new pearl; to *use* it, before sheer psychological self-preservation drives me to forget those little details that make a story *really* snap, crackle and pop. What else is life for, after all, if not to provide that sort of wonderfully fecund raw feed? God knows, given its usual content, it'd be a pretty unbearable trip if we couldn't at least aspire to make it into something else.

I went to bed. I didn't dream. In the morning, I got up again, and went back to work. Sat at my desk, did my duty. Ate lunch by the same fountain, in almost exactly the same place.

The bird, what was left of it, was still there.

All stories have to start somewhere: It's a law, like gravity. But when writers say that, what we really mean is that all our stories have to start somewhere, usually with another story. And I am no exception to this rule.

So: Once upon a time . . .

. . . a little girl saw her parents' battles finally end when her father packed up and fled the North American continent entirely, leaving both his lost love and the child who reminded him of her far behind. Neither of them were bad people, but they weren't meant to be married—not to each other, anyhow. That's how I used to console myself, before I figured out doing so meant acknowledging how much better off everybody involved would be, if only I didn't exist.

Dad went, I stayed. Eventually, he invoked his due visitation rights. Mom didn't contest. And thus I ferried myself back and forth between two hemispheres each Christmas as an "unaccompanied minor," trading day for night, night for day. Went down to Van Diemen's Land, where Outback and Bush alike are clogged with red dirt and empty roads, flora and fauna nothing but a carnival showcase for evolutionary dead ends. Australia, where winter is summer and fall spring, and when you uncork the plug, the water spins the wrong way down the drain.

Since I don't interact with my dad on a regular basis, it's become fairly easy for him to rest out of sight and mind for me, most days; same as me for him, I'm sure. Whenever we do think of each other, meanwhile, it's probably less as ourselves than as a matched pair of long-distance fantasy versions. For me, it's him when I was nine. For him, it's me when *I* was nine.

Too bad, for both of us, that I'm not nine anymore.

So yes, I have a life, and yes, he plays little part in it; I've spent the last thirty years going through things Dad had nothing to do with, all of which have shaped the adult I am today far more than any genetic component he and I may still share. Oh, he thinks he "thinks" of me, but does he *think* of me? Do I "think" of him? Not like he'd like, and not like I'd like. And if my aunt had nuts she'd be my uncle, and if things weren't the same they'd be different . . .

Nostalgia means "our pain," in Latin. That's memory for you, in a big honking nutshell. It's a curse, osmotically infectious, a shared hallucination, the madness of crowds, the haunted and the haunting. Another country, half the whole wide world away, populated by nothing . . .

. . . but ghosts.

The first time my mom read "The Jacaranda Smile," she looked up at me with her eyebrows knit and her eyes ever-so-slightly narrowed—not mad, simply quizzical.

"That's not how it happened," she said.

"Which part?"

"Any of it."

So she didn't like it, which was a pity. But I gave up on getting my mother's approval long ago, right about the same time I made it clear that—whether I wrote "what [I] know" or not—nothing I hammered together out of my own highly subjective life experience was ever going to get me onto Oprah Winfrey's Book Club list.

Here's how it works: I'm a writer, which means I lie for a living—take things I think I remember happening and spin tales from them, then sell what's left behind. I fabricate until I move from what might have happened to what never did, which is where I finally gain control over my own material, to shape it as I will.

"They're giving you a prize for this?"

"Three hundred dollars U.S., publication in their anthology. Plus a trip to Melbourne."

"Will there be a dinner?"

"Formal, yes. Got any fashion tips?"

Another look, like she wasn't sure if I was joking, or whether I actually meant it. Or both.

"If you're thinking about patterns, try a vertical one," she said, finally. "It'll make you look slimmer, from a distance."

After Dad left, Mom got a job at Wintario. We moved from Hocken Avenue to Wychwood, further west along St. Clair, where just being in the front yard made me nervous. A certain tree grew there, dead center. When winter came, it shed its leaves to reveal a horrible secret—a stunted branch that thrust itself from the main trunk and raised fistfuls of twigs to a pewter sky, howling. This, to my child's mind, was the "witch" in Wychwood. It watched me slouch off to school every morning, then hesitate at the corner every night, trying to get up the courage to scuttle past it towards safety.

I got sick a lot. Early one morning of Year One, I woke with a splitting headache, turned over, and vomited into my own bed. My mother held me over the toilet until the sun came up. It was stomach flu, but I thought I was going to die. Every headache was a brain tumor. At Hillcrest Elementary,

which was under repairs, I shared a portable classroom with twenty or so
other children. They found me sullen, strange and arrogant. I found them
hideously stupid.

Our teacher, Mrs. Rudnick, told us that if Ronald Reagan were elected
President that year, the world would end. He was. At night I lay awake,
wondering what it would be like: Would somebody, somewhere, simply flick
a switch, and make everything I knew disappear? And even worse—

—what then?

It's hard, sometimes, to remember just how passionately I used to love
my dad and how deeply I felt his absence, after he went back to Australia
for good—an intimate hurt, one that left no visible scar. I set up an altar to
him in my closet, where I'd write little notes on the backs of old scripts and
burn them in what used to be his ashtray, when he still smoked. I'd watch the
smoke spiral upward, hoping it might translate itself to the other side of the
world and crack that aching silence wide enough for him to suddenly "know"
what I wanted him to do or say, without my ever having to *ask* at all. Make
him *want* to, without question or regret, as naturally as though he'd thought
of it himself.

Magic: At bottom it's all just nursery-school science. Every magician is
nothing but a kid in a tantrum writ large, who draws dirty pictures of their
enemies in wax, or cloth, or sand, and then rips them limb from limb.

When I was a child, I used to cut pieces out of things, as small as I could
manage, and then hide them where they wouldn't be found until later, if
at all: Cushions, plants, photographs. After I turned nine—the year of the
divorce—my acting out became shaped by my increasing addiction to books
on Witchcraft Made Easy. One time, I saved my menstrual blood in a bottle,
kept it until it turned black and stinking, then dropped it down a dusty grate
in Dad and Aoife's bedroom with its stopper pulled out, right before I got on
the plane back to Canada. Took them a week to figure out where all those ants
were coming from, and why.

Aoife and I had our problems, right from the start; the usual first-marriage
kid/step-whatever bullshit. "You're not my mother!" "I wouldn't want to be!"
All that.

But the last time I saw her, before "The Jacaranda Smile"—saw them—
things were fine. We were all adults. Did the guided tour, hit the old, familiar
places . . . and that was a bit weird, actually. Because wherever we went, I saw
each place with the past overlaid upon it like some peeling decal, tinting it
retroactively: *Ah, here's where I felt sad, where I felt bad, where I felt mad.
Where I wanted to kill—*

(myself, him, you)

But it was okay overall, and I was glad I'd come. I had a good time, took a
lot of notes, went home. And then, eventually, the way I always do . . .

. . . I used them as mulch, kindling, classic grist. And I wrote myself a
story.

The house at Wychwood was dry, stinking of Vaseline Intensive Care and mold. I spent my weekends in the enclosed "airlock" between our outside and inside doors, reading Tintin books and dreaming about the day when Dad would come back. I tried to tell myself stories, but I hadn't quite gotten the knack of it yet. Images possessed me, there in the fading light—so real, so immediate, that to negotiate them through a mundane gauntlet of things like spelling or punctuation seemed superfluous at best.

At school, I read everything I could get my hands on (aside from the assigned texts). One day, I discovered *Wuthering Heights*: Heathcliff chasing Cathy's ghost down the moors, freezing to death on her grave. That night, I couldn't sleep, paralyzed by the horrid idea of mortality made palpable. The next night was the same, only worse.

Mom brought in a radio, which lulled me to the brink, where I'd shut my eyes—and the ghosts would rear up again as a wave of dread, all around me.

Another yell, more comforting: Mom held my hand, told me to visualize a bright green world, take it from lava-lump to fresh new continents, let it suck me in. When it wore off, so did her patience: "Count your blessings, for a change," she snapped, and stomped off to her own bed. I lay awake until my heartbeat drowned me at last, forcing me down in a spray of purest terror.

The best thing about my childhood is that I didn't know any better; it certainly made it easier to forgive, if not forget. The worst thing about my childhood is that my parents didn't know any better, either . . . not her, not him. Though Mom at least knew enough to be there.

So I learned to keep my mouth shut at night, slowly memorizing the angles of my ceiling. Taking Mom's advice, I *made* myself think of something else.

And "something else" became, at last, a story.

One story, then another, then another. None of them were bedtime material. I told them at school—not to my friends, since I had none. To everybody else. They didn't get me love, but then again, I didn't want any. What they got me was left the hell alone, which was more than good enough, at the time.

Still is.

"The Jacaranda Smile" takes place in Dad and Aoife's home, an edifice as far from Wychwood as humanly imaginable: A 1920s Art Deco building located in the middle of Melbourne's South Yarra neighborhood, with a jacaranda tree in its yard so large that if you glanced out the front windows, you'd find yourself staring straight into a haze of bright lavender-blue, harebell-shaped flower clusters. Dad told me when they shed they all fell at once like confetti, leaving the snaky branches bare. Granted, I was never around for that, but if I screw my mental eyes up in just the right way, I think I can conjure a pretty good idea of what it looked like. Benefits of a vivid imagination.

The roof was all brick-colored tiles, humped to provide guttering. Inside, the rooms stood high-ceilinged, shrouded from the glare of the Australian sky by thick, white, all-but-impenetrable curtains. The dark wood paneling was banded like a coffin's, and a deliberate crack had been left at the top of every wall, to allow for expansion (or shrinkage) of the plaster under seasonal shifts of heat and cold.

Much of the original interior design had been preserved intact, detailing so impressively specific I can still reel off bits of it: A frosted glass window incised with the figure of a peacock half-rampant, next to the living-room fireplace; a dining room with sliding doors, like the galley of some long-sunk ocean liner; a "sun room" bulging straight out from the front of the building, overhanging the main doors, which viewed the tree on one side and looked back into the master bedroom on the other. Heated towel-racks in the bathroom, built-in shoe racks in the bedroom closets . . . all the "everyday" amenities of a very different age, as though you'd rented space in some unregistered hotel. My first impulse, most mornings, was to check my pillow for mints.

On the landing, coming up to take the initial tour, we passed a glass light fixture built to look like some frosted Cubist rose that hung heavy with dust, its base stacked with 365 days' worth of dried-out bug-corpses. I can still remember the first time I saw Dad turn it on—how it sparked, and smoked; stank, too. Like—

(something dead)

As I already said, Aoife and I had been getting along. Which is probably why she told me a secret she'd been carrying around with her since the previous Christmas: Though he'd checked into the hospital after telling everyone he had pneumonia, Dad had actually been there for triple bypass surgery.

"Look, Ellie," she explained, sheepish yet defensive, "I know it sounds barking, but it's the Industry—they've got this collective allergy to wrinklies. Look old, you're out of it for life."

(What Aoife and Dad did for a living, back then, was produce industrial films, which is not even a quarter as glamorous as you might expect something involving the words "produce" and "films" to be. But reasonably lucrative, when the going was good.)

For an otherwise tiny adventure in cardiac attack, Dad's "episode" was still fairly traumatic: Chest pains at the gym led to blackout, then a quick trip to emergency. He kept telling Aoife it was just acid reflux . . . right up until his doctor burst back in, sonograms in hand, to inform him that his arteries were already so plaque-clogged his heart had begun pumping its necessary daily dose of blood *backwards* throughout his body, just to compensate.

After which, hey presto: Crack your breastbone open, do a scrape, sew you back up and Bob's your uncle.

I remember Aoife topping this up with an equally disquieting anecdote about them almost immediately having to go visit an older male friend who'd just had a similar operation—Dad pretending to be awake, sympathetic, amusing, "normal," a mere week after having exited a different wing of the same ward himself. Laughing, as she did so: *No, but really—got to admit, it's pretty bloody funny. Don't you?*

For me, though, the truly relevant part was how I'd to hear all this from her, rather than from him . . . and how completely normal that seemed, at the time.

But back to the story.

"The Jacaranda Smile" begins with Dad and Aoife—their fictional analogues "Graham" and "Eve," rather—dealing with much the same situation: A shocking near-miss with death followed by recovery in a vacuum, aggravated by "necessary" secrecy about "Eve's" true condition (I decided to give her the bypass, not him, thus pretending I wasn't telling tales out of school). Lard in some exposition stressing the hidden financial pressures behind their move, the deadly serious truths behind this whole ridiculous charade . . . and the real action begins.

Immediately after moving in, "Eve" begins to see and hear things. She finds a word (CONCEPTION) written at the very top of a closet while she's cleaning it, and can't figure out how someone might have reached high enough to be able to write it there. She has a persistent feeling of being watched, especially while reading in the sunroom. Waking in the middle of the night because her scar itches, she gets up to put Vitamin E cream on it, and feels a deliberate, cold finger being laid along the rucked tissue, skimming it slowly, horridly gentle. Like when you caress your lover's zipper, just before pulling it down.

As all this is going on, "Ally" (my avatar) arrives from Canada to stay with them while looking for a part-time job and registering with the Victoria Cinematic Academy, preparing for her Screenwriting Program entrance interview. She's seldom there, and when she is, she sure isn't thinking about what might or might not be going on with Graham and Eve. Of course, Eve being who she is, she hasn't told anybody what's happening, either; she's busy being sensible, fighting unreasonable fear with logic and silence. And it never really changes, not even after a celebratory Ally-welcoming dinner out ends with Eve feeling her throat contract, which sends her back to hospital.

But then, Ally begins to see stuff too.

A girl—maybe nine years old, her features blurred by distance—sits in the heart of the jacaranda tree, perfectly placed to stare into the sunroom window. She wears unseasonable polyester clothing and has limp, bleached hair. The girl hunches over a book, only glancing up when she senses Ally looking; a predatory profile gives way to three-quarters of a secretive smile, as if she recognizes Ally—but Ally doesn't recognize her. A neighbor kid, a trespasser? A truly elaborate trick of the Antipodean light? And then . . .

. . . she's gone.

So we speed on, tension mounting quietly, exacerbated by the occasional flare-up between Graham and Ally, or Eve and Ally, or Graham, Eve, and Ally. The girl hangs over it all carrion crow-style, a constant background presence, human embodiment of Ally's continual underlying melancholy over her own past actions. All the stuff she wishes she could deny or dispense of, knowing she *must* take responsibility for what she did, even if her dad will never do the same—

Until: A day when Graham's off doing something, leaving Eve and Ally alone in the apartment together: Ally in the sunroom, Eve in the kitchen. Suddenly, Ally feels "the stare" Eve's told her about, and turns her head to see the kid from the tree looking back at her from *inside* the master bedroom— hidden behind its drawn curtain, visible to Ally, but not to whoever might enter the room. Not smiling, for once, just . . . empty-looking. And for some reason, this makes Ally desperately afraid, especially so because she can hear Eve's hand on the bedroom doorknob . . .

She runs, pausing in the doorway. Eve's over by the closet, right next to the window, and Ally can see the girl's humped shadow lurking behind the curtain. Eve looks up at Ally's entrance, surprised. Behind her, the curtain slips away and the girl steps forward. She lays one hand lightly between Eve's shoulder blades—just behind where Eve's heart would be, were their positions reversed. She looks at Ally over Eve's shoulder, smiles—and disappears, as Graham's key rattles in the lock downstairs.

Eve crumples, has another heart attack, dies between them in the ambulance. And when Ally comes back to the apartment, she discovers the jacaranda tree has shed completely, leaving its limbs naked and empty.

A week later, just before she leaves—all plans for Australian higher education abandoned—Ally finds a recent photo of Eve (taken at the welcome-back dinner), its face carefully cut out, buried under the sofa cushions. Not wanting to upset Graham further, Ally hides it in her suitcase. And a month after that, at home in Canada, when she and her mom are cleaning out closets, they find a shoebox—dating to the 1970s—full of similarly mutilated snaps of Graham, Eve, Ally. Plus one picture of Ally alone, from the same period: Up in a tree in Australia, wearing her usual unseasonal polyester Canadian clothes, scowling down at the lens over a book about witchcraft.

Because that's what the "ghost" has been all along, of course: Ally's bile and rage from her child-becoming-teenager years, concentrated into some sort of fetch—a doppelganger boomerang arcing back around, long after she's forgotten she threw it in the first place. All those evil spells she once worked against Aoife—

("Eve," I mean)

—finally brought to term when Ally doesn't even remember exactly why she wanted any of it done anymore, let alone with such passionate, single-minded, lizard-brain intensity. Ignorant art, aimless craft, but working still, even now she's no longer angry—not at Eve, anyway. Not at anything much, but herself.

The writing on the wall: CONCEPTION. A malign birth, out of one world and into another. As you conceive it, so it occurs. *As I will, so mote it be.*

Magic.

<hr />

It took years for me to understand what I'd done to myself at Wychwood, all in the name of not being "weak." Eventually, I was sent to my first psychiatrist; these days, I think I'm about as "cured" as I'm ever going to get. But I haven't really been afraid since Wychwood, not in the same innocent way. I bred it out of myself, along with a lot of other things—things like sorrow, empathy. The recognition (for a very long time) that anyone besides me was capable of feeling pain, as well as inflicting it.

Though people liked "The Jacaranda Smile," almost universally, I certainly never expected it to take me back to Australia that last time. Naturally, I stayed with Dad and Aoife until the Terror Incognita awards dinner. Dad didn't say much about the story overall, aside from the predictable *well done, good luck, good on ya'*; Aoife was positively gushing, which surprised me just a tad, given the context.

So I wore my vertically patterned dress and I got my plaque: A bunyip rampant, BEST NEW FICTION OF 2008, with my name inscribed beneath. I told Dad and Aoife thanks for the inspiration, no hard feelings, goodbye. I got ready to go home.

And the very same day I was finally all set to leave, Dad found Aoife lying on their bedroom floor, eyes wide open, the left pupil dilated and unresponsive.

I went back to Wychwood again, once. I was two years into my therapy then, walking up to Dr. Spring's office past the St. Clair West subway station, the same Loblaw's Mom and I used to shop at, the little park where I once went skating with no gloves on, and watched my hands slowly turn white. The tree was still there. I stood at its foot and looked up into its halo of leaves, so like any one of the trees I'd sat in over a lifetime, here or in Australia.

It was the height of summer, smell of fresh-cut grass filtering over from and adjacent lawn. In the distance, through an open window, somebody was playing early Gary Numan at full blast: *Down in the park where the mech-men meet the machines and play kill by numbers/Down in the park with a friend named Five . . .*

There, under deceptive cover of green, the witch leered impassively back down at me. I felt light-headed, oddly naked from the eyes up, as though my thoughts had suddenly become big enough for any random passer-by to read them in an uncensored wave: all that guilt, and rage, and hatred. Everything a nine-year-old whose parents have just broken up can never express, especially out loud.

Everything so ugly it can't be voiced, for fear of making the only person you have left turn away and leave you alone in the dark, with only the ghost of your own dead self for company.

The doctors said it was a stroke, brought on by a blood-clot; yes, Aoife'd been on the usual so-now-you're-past-fifty! thinners, gone to all her regular check-ups, ate right, exercised. But things change. Stuff just . . . happens.

I'd like, if only for the sake of closure, to tell you that Dad eventually got drunk one night, called up and accused me of somehow stage-managing Aoife's death—not least because then I could tell you how I told him, calmly: *But that's just crazy-talk, Grayson.*

He never did, though—mostly because it *would* be crazy-talk, and he's never liked looking crazy.

But man, that would've really been something, huh? *I* would've really been something, then . . . to touch him like that, so deeply, so directly. Like that apocryphal story about the old Jewish guy who supposedly read *Mein Kampf* whenever he got depressed, because it always cheered him up to be told just how powerful he actually was.

There's only one place I have that kind of power: On paper. On my home computer's screen, between cursor-blinks, for the mere microsecond it takes to lay a synaptic mine into the dead space between pixels. If I can write, I'm the most powerful person alive; if I can't write, I waver. And if nobody reads what I write, after enough time goes by . . .

. . . I disappear completely.

And so we return to the bird in the fountain, that dancing toy of dust-in-progress. A cheap image, like most of the ones I cobble my tales together from: The Underneath risen up, as it always will—the dark in every crack, the bone under every stone.

If word is bond and in the beginning was the word, then the word really is the deed, after all; I sinned in my heart, and now it's come home to roost—all my pretty chickens, in one fell swoop. My unremembered musings made karma.

But there are no jacaranda trees in Canada, that I know of.

Let's put it like this, then: Back when, on some level, my Dad killed my heart . . . but two months ago, on some whole other level, I "killed" his. Which probably—at long last—makes us even.

And I want to run from that idea, even as it forms. I want to run half the whole wide world away, in the other direction, as far from Toronto as from Melbourne—and stay there, forever. Never come back.

I consider all my uncaught thoughts, my misplaced impulses, my unspoken hatreds flocking like crows, swarming, sent out beyond recall. All the many times, over the years, I wished death on my mother, my lovers, my bosses, myself.

And I think: *I'll see that girl again, sometime.*

Thinking, at the same dislocated moment: *But I see her already, every day.*

In the mirror, in old photos, out the window, in the passing crowd. Down the block, around the corner, at the very outer edge of where my eyes don't see. Everywhere.

Thinking how ridiculous it is to be almost forty years old and still care so very much about something which happened oh so long ago, something I had absolutely nothing to do with. Something I'll never be able to change, no matter how many stories I write.

I wanted Aoife dead, and she is.

I wanted Dad dead, and he will be. Soon enough.

I wanted to die myself, more times than once; don't anymore, of course. Not for years.

And now—

Now I sit here, waiting. Writing. What else can I do? There's a story, buried, under all these bits and pieces. If I can find it, I can tell it—control it. Sell it.

Make sure there's something left of me for people to read, and remember, after.

Gemma Files *won the 1999 International Horror Guild Best Short Fiction award for her story "The Emperor's Old Bones." She is the author of two collections* (Kissing Carrion *and* The Worm in Every Heart) *and two chapbooks of poetry. "The Jacaranda Smile" was nominated for a 2009 Shirley Jackson Award in the short fiction category; her story "each thing I show you is a piece of my death," co-written with her husband Stephen J. Barringer and originally published in* Clockwork Phoenix 2 *(edited by Mike Allan) was nominated as best novellette. Her first novel,* A Book of Tongues: Volume One of the Hexslinger Series, *was published in 2010. It will be followed by a sequel,* A Rope of Thorns, *in 2011.*

In general, I think most editors (and readers) tend not to care for stories about writers writing stories about writers writing stories. But Gemma Files proves an exception to generalities with "The Jacaranda Tree." Perhaps one reason her story is exceptional is because it's objective rather than introspective. Her narrator discovers more than she expects about herself by observation rather than looking inward. As for the rest, well, the Underneath does rise up, and it always will, to become "the dark in every crack, the bone under every stone."

THE OTHER BOX

GERARD HOUARNER

Samarra discovered the box on the foyer floor when she came home from the boutique.

Rectangular, wrapped in crinkled, off-white paper, secured with rough twine, the box was about the size of a human head.

Samarra froze. Cold dread chased the day's hectic rush of customers and sales rep pitches for the new season from her mind. The box. The house took a spin around her. Someone whispered in her ear, "Farewell," and she whirled around to face the open doorway. No, that voice was a memory, like the warm breath that had carried the word. No, no, imagination.

The box. That was a transgression. It shouldn't have been inside waiting for her. They'd all left the house together this morning. The floor had been empty.

She dropped her purse and shoulder bag, putting both hands over her belly, where an ache had awakened.

She started as the alarm system's rhythmic beeping signaled ~~for~~ her to punch in the security code. Between the piercing pulses, she thought she heard voices crying, like newborn kittens mewling for milk.

Samarra backed out, checked the house number on the door and glanced at the azalea in the front yard. Of course, she was home. She took out the cell phone with a trembling hand.

No. Stop. The system hadn't gone off. No one had broken in. There was no real danger.

Dread knotted into terror. Guts twitched and bubbled. But she gritted her teeth, breathed deeply, steadily. She had to deal with this. The kids were coming home soon. With the alarm still beeping, she re-entered the foyer, reached slowly down, palms suddenly moist, hands shaking, breath short, knees weak and legs drained of blood.

Something whimpered in a far corner. Or was that her breathing? What was going on?

Samarra nearly fell backwards when her hands shot up: the package was light as a balloon, as if even the cardboard, paper, and twine between her fingertips weighed nothing. She squeezed the box, almost expecting her fingers to pass through, but the sides were firm, unyielding.

Real. Not dangerous. A trick, that was all.

The house settled into a reality she understood. Yes, the faint trace of her own perfume, which Justine had dabbed on herself this morning when she thought her mother wasn't looking, couldn't smell it. Mirabel's spilled milk. Rey's sweaty scent, punctuated by craft glue.

The ache in her belly dwindled into a brief spasm, then was gone.

She laughed, with relief as much as delight, and quickly shut off the alarm. It really was time for a vacation, she thought, when she started taking life's little mysteries too seriously. In the space between what she'd done, had yet to do, and what she'd feared had happened, a garden of ideas blossomed, like flowers after a desert rain.

Maybe one of her children had answered an ad for air from the Himalayas.

Her youngest at four, Rey, always wanted to do things like that: taste the bread he'd seen freshly baked on a five-year-old PBS cooking show; wear the costume and headdress of Navajo kachina or Apache spirit dancer dolls from his uncle Reynaldo's collection; sing a duet with the tenor of an Italian opera playing on the classical music radio station.

He always wanted something he couldn't have, which made birthdays and holidays difficult, even at his age.

Or perhaps one of her girls had left a message.

Mirabel, the middle one, a precocious six, was in that phase, pretending to be an angel and leaving cryptic crayon scrawls on random walls, somehow managing to mark even the cathedral living room ceiling. Her husband, Allan, had to use a ladder to reach it so he could wipe away the signs she'd left. Flying deeper into her private garden, Samarra imagined Mirabel in full angel fantasy, writing a poem on the box's inside, sparking a metamorphoses in her mind that had changed common cardboard into gossamer angel wings.

Transfiguration seemed to be the first real goal Mirabel had found for herself in her brief life, and neither Samarra nor Allan knew what to do to get her to move on to more realistic wishes. If the box's illusion of weightlessness was her work, there'd be no stopping Mirabel trying to achieve the same effect on everything else she could write on.

Justine, the eldest of their children at a stately nine, had given up most of her childish habits and become more involved in the real world, the world of school and other children and games and phones and computers. But she still dreamed, though, as she liked to say, not all dreams come true, or even promise success.

"Dreams lie," she'd recently pronounced, picking at her bowl of cereal as if it had been poisoned with broccoli. "Not everyone from the tribe comes back from a night on the mountaintop with a secret name, not every hunter brings home meat for the village. Sometimes something else's dreams come true instead of yours. The mountain and the sky and the storm and the hunger hold on to a name. Or the animal spirit gets away. Or," she'd said, dropping the spoon on the floor, "it's the bad dreams that come true."

Samarra didn't know where the girl had found those words, and had felt sad that her eldest's innocence was fading so soon. She'd checked Justine's clothes and her skin, carefully interviewed teachers, and watched her closely on play dates, to be certain the loss was part of her daughter's natural evolution and not the consequence of unwanted attention.

Maybe the box was one of Justine's dreams come true. Or perhaps the whole day was her daughter's dream that had slipped into Samarra's mind while she lay sleeping. Maybe the day hadn't even started yet, but she'd gone through it all in a dream just to reach this moment, this gift from her oldest daughter. What could the box contain: a million dollar check? Free passes to Heaven? A lifetime fifty percent discount coupon for all purchases made by household members under the age of eighteen?

Samarra laughed again as she put the box down on the dining room table and pinched herself. Pain shot dutifully to her brain, reminding her she was also tired from work, and hungry. She recalled the day with the clarity of the waking and not the fuzzy logic of dream, which was good because she needed the day's receipts in the checking account.

Like Allan said, she was far too involved in the children's fantasy worlds. It wasn't hard to see which side of the orchard fence their fruit had fallen on. But if she also had the head to run a successful business, then so did their kids, so everything would turn about fine. Eventually.

Which left her with the problem of the box, quite real, though not entirely logical.

Aside from its apparent solidity and weightlessness, there was no mailing label or postmark, no explanation of how the box had gotten into the house when she'd been the last to leave, setting the alarm and locking the door. Allan was still at work, Rey at daycare, and the girls were at their Tuesday dance class.

The reality was that no one had been home to accept the package, or take it off the porch and into the house.

There was only one possibility: Allan had taken time off from work and planted the box for her.

Anniversary? Birthday? Had she, in bouncing back and forth between real and unreal worlds, forgotten an important date? Hurriedly, she checked through her electronic calendar, found nothing.

Maybe he'd made arrangements for a surprise vacation. She frowned slightly, thinking of the trouble she'd have making sure the store was covered during the day on short notice. And the kids: was Rey supposed to come along while the others stayed at Reynaldo's or one of their friends' houses so they wouldn't miss school?

Allan liked surprises, and even found most of the rest of the family's fantastic digressions amusing, but he also had his feet firmly planted on

Earth. He wouldn't do anything to upset important routines. So maybe the trip was for next summer.

Or perhaps, the surprise was something else entirely.

With the tiniest sliver of apprehension that the box might contain a notice of divorce, Samarra took it up to the bedroom, dropped it on the dresser, and changed. Before leaving to pick up Rey, she put her ear against the wrapping and gave the box a jiggle. There was no rustle or rattle, though a wave of nausea passed through her, as if she'd been the one shaken. She put the box down, called Meg at the boutique, as much to check in on the late store traffic as to make sure her new sales clerk hadn't closed early, and went out.

She picked up Rey first, secured him in his carseat, then drove on to the dance school to get Mirabel and Justine. While she waited for the girls to come out of the little strip mall studio, she ordered dinner from a Thai restaurant next door. By the time she had her brown paper bag of food, Mirabel was sitting in the backseat next to Rey, writing furiously in her notebook while Rey demanded she show him what she'd learned in dance class. Samarra put the bag between them and asked, "Where's Justine?"

"She was picked up," Mirabel answered, snatching the food and putting the bag on her lap. She began covering the bag with illegible signs.

Samarra started home, calling Allan on her cell phone. Fun was fun, but he really should have called her if he was going to leave work early and pick up one of the kids. When he didn't answer, she checked to see if she had any messages, found none. So whatever was going on involved a conspiracy between father and oldest daughter. Samarra smiled through her irritation, wondering what kind of dream they were trying to make real, together.

Allan came home at his usual time, after Rey and Mirabel had eaten. The children were upstairs, quiet, lost in the little words inside their rooms. Samarra sat on the too-soft sofa, her attention bouncing off of the television screen, the noise of the evening news washing over her like a tide of sewage.

"Where's Justine?" she asked, when Allan sat down next to her, alone.

Nerves already brittle from the long wait, the absence of any surprise at his arrival, and the residue of a whisper from the earlier twist of reality, Samarra cracked when he frowned and asked, "How should I know?"

There was a moment of silence, the tip of an iceberg tearing below reality's water line into Samarra's heart.

She hit Allan with the tray of remotes as she screamed, pummeled him with fists and knees as he tried to restrain her, and howled at Mirabel, who had emerged from the room she shared with Justine to stand at the head of the stairs. Both of the little girl's empty hands twitched. Rey wailed in his room.

Justine. Her scent made Samarra light-headed when she ran up to the girls' room and crushed her daughter's pillow against her face. She curled up in Justine's bed and refused to move, violently resisting Allan's pull and ignoring Mirabel's tearful pleas for her to be Mommy again.

Mirabel picked up her pad and pen before Allan led her to Rey's room.

The police arrived within the half hour. Allan had already checked with Reynaldo, the neighbors, and tried reaching the school. A police detective checked again, following up with family friends and neighbors up and down the block, as well as school officials.

The dance studio was closed. Mirabel insisted she'd never said their daddy had picked Justine up, only that her sister had been picked up. When the detective asked by who, she answered: "An angel."

Mirabel couldn't describe the angel and withdrew deeper into her drawing. She only started screaming with blind, wide-eyed terror when the detective took her pen away, leaving her nothing with which to write. An ambulance was called when she tried scratching symbols into her forearm with her fingernail, even after the detective tried giving back the pen.

Rey demanded to know how angels flew.

The detective studied the picture Mirabel had been drawing and shook his head at the abstract pattern of swirling lines, a weather map of conflicting currents smashing into one another, and fragments of what might be a fairy tale about a war between men and fairies, or maybe angels and men. He asked Samarra and Allan if any of it meant something to them, studying their faces carefully as they denied finding any hidden significance. With a grunt, he tossed the paper aside.

Samarra dragged herself out of Justine's bed. She couldn't meet Allan's gaze as she explained her rationale for thinking he'd picked her up. It had all started with the box she'd found in the foyer.

"What box?" Allan asked.

So did the detective, who offered them all a ride to the hospital behind Mirabel's ambulance. He waited for Samarra to bring the box down.

Rey wanted to hold it, but the detective didn't think that was a good idea.

While Mirabel was safely in the emergency room, the detective and a partner who had just arrived withdrew to the hospital security office to open the box. Allan kept Rey in the waiting room while Samarra stayed with Mirabel as her wounded arm was dressed, but had to leave when a social worker came to interview her daughter. The social worker also had questions for Samarra, and later for Allan and Rey.

Face reddened with rage and shame, Samarra understood. They were only looking out for her children. She'd done the same. She was that kind of mother.

While they waited for doctors and detectives to sift through their lives and the hospital held both Mirabel and Rey for observation, Allan told his wife what the detectives had let him know about what had happened with the box.

"The thing fell apart. Self-destructed. They cut the string, pulled away the wrapping, and all they found underneath was a heavy stock paper box, almost like origami, all trick folds sticking together and turning back on themselves—until the cop tapped the side and it fell apart."

"No ransom note?"

"No. They had a man there to take fingerprints, but he didn't find anything, either. They took the paper away to see if it can be traced to a store."

Samarra stared at him until he added, "They checked surveillance tapes from nearby businesses, but they didn't have the right angles to show the kids walking from the van to the school. Nothing else suspicious showed up.

She looked away, her gaze falling on a silent television screen in the waiting room displaying a cable news show. She became momentarily lost in a clip showing soldiers drifting across rough, rocky ground, weapons poised for firing, and then a line of them on a mountainside. Allan waited for her to say something, but she was out of air and words. He took her hand in both of his and said, "I'm sorry I didn't leave it there for you as a surprise."

"I lost Justine."

"Rey must have made it. Saw some kind of origami show and left it for us when we went out this morning. Bet he was the last one out before you locked up. You just didn't catch it before you closed the door. Probably playing with the girls in their dream world."

"I don't remember."

"You don't have to."

She shivered from the barest sting of condemnation in the phrase.

The next day, with Mirabel and Rey returned to their custody, the detective came by to report that the dance studio owners had been interviewed. They denied Justine ever came to school, though their van driver confirmed he'd picked up both girls up after school along with the other students.

The studio owner said they'd tried to call Justine's parents to find out what happened, and had left messages on their cell phones. They'd assumed Justine had another appointment, as often happened with their students, which was why they still charged for lessons if the parents didn't cancel their child's lesson.

Samarra and Allan checked their phones again, this time found the messages. Phone records confirmed they'd been sent at the beginning of Justine's class. It had just taken time for the calls to come through the system and reach them.

Samarra threw her phone at a wall and screamed. Allan held her in a tight embrace, containing her rage rather than comforting her. His breath smelled of mint. She quieted only when Rey picked up the broken cell phone and began speaking into it. She snatched the phone away. Rey cried, saying he'd been speaking to Justine and she'd been telling him not to be sad.

The detective checked the phone, shook his head.

School officials confirmed Justine had been in class, left on time with Mirabel on the shuttle van. The driver denied seeing anything unusual as he'd watched his charges go inside the studio, though he couldn't confirm for certain that he'd seen Justine go inside. "The count was good as when they got on," he said, "and I checked the seats after they went inside. Nobody was left. And no one was hanging around outside the school, either."

The other children confirmed Justine had been on the van, though a few couldn't remember if she'd been in the locker room changing with them, and no one could recall seeing her in class. The ones who'd thought about her while in the studio assumed she was in the back or left early. She'd never been a popular child.

Mirabel couldn't say when the angel had come to pick up her sister.

Justine had vanished from the shuttle pack without a trace between the curb and the front door.

More questions would be asked, the detective assured Samarra. Background checks would be done, and the area canvassed for witnesses.

Word reached Samarra through the detective's partner that Allan's mother and father had volunteered to take the other two children, and Allan, with them, and warned that Samarra was not quite right, that she had funny ideas and encouraged the children to think odd things, and they'd never favored the marriage, and the police should investigate Samara's equally bizarre brother, Reynaldo, and perhaps check to see where the rest of her family was, and if they'd made any sudden trips to the area.

Samarra couldn't speak through the ruins of her broken heart when the partner asked how she felt about what the family said. Her own mother and father were no longer around to defend her, and the rest of the family never followed them out of the old country to make a life in the new world. She knew them only as blurry faces from old photographs taken in stark, empty places.

That night, Samarra read to her children from *1001 Arabian Nights*, as if she could keep them with her through the power of simple storytelling. By the time she was done with "Ali Baba and the Forty Thieves," with its magical door to treasures, Rey and Maribel were both asleep. She kept reading to herself through the night, in the girls' room, with Rey now in Justine's bed. Sleep seemed more distant than the magic of djinn, on the other side of a door she could not open.

Allan's parents rented a suite at a nearby hotel. He'd heard what they'd said and refused to let them stay in the guest room. They argued during a visit to the house, with Allan standing up to their demands to take the children out of the house. The plainclothes officer assigned to the family during the investigation threatened to report them all to child protection services.

"It wasn't Samarra's fault," Allan said, pleading for belief.

"The angel was beautiful," Mirabel said once, but no more about angels after her grandmother told her to stop. She drew disconnected lines on the bandage covering the wound on her arm, as if completing the picture she'd started on her skin, and mumbled stories Samarra recognized from bedtime readings.

"Where's the box?" Rey asked his mother

"Baby, did you make it? Please, be honest with Mommy. Did you?"

"No. I want to make one. I have to see it."

"Sorry, baby. It's gone."

The last word rang like a bell inside her chest. She grabbed the boy and held him close to make the hollow ringing inside her go away, until he fidgeted and wormed his way free.

The detective focused on Mirabel as the only witness to what had really happened. He talked about her as the sole survivor of a traumatic incident, and he had a police department child psychologist conduct an interview to see if anything might come of tests performed with pictures and words and games with dolls.

When they came home from the interviews, Samarra said to them, "We'll get Justine back." She squeezed their hands as she took them past the police guard and said, "I won't let anything happen to you. Not a thing."

The children didn't ask about their sister, what had happened to her, when they'd go back to school, why people were watching the house. They went to their rooms and their own worlds, as if they were only waiting for what they knew was going to happen next.

Samarra clung desperately to what she thought was their certainty that Justine would be back.

Three days after Justine's disappearance, and after a long talk with the lead detective, Allan relented and let his mother have Mirabel for an overnight visit, balancing his concern for both families by asking Reynaldo to pick up Rey.

"The police don't think our families are a threat," Allan said, slowly, carefully, as if still trying to understand everything he'd been told. "They hope a change of scenery might shake something lose for the kids. Maybe they'll open up to someone besides us and cops. According to that psychologist, it hasn't quite sunk in for them that Justine is gone."

Samarra felt the hole through which Justine had fallen grow wider. "I want them here. With me."

"Just for the night," Allan said, almost touching her hand, but not quite. "There'll be cops posted. They'll be safe. They need to get away from the craziness here. And you need the rest."

In response to Samarra's shivering silence, he added, "Anything to get Justine back."

As the weight of the house's emptiness settled over them that night, Allan suggested they take a drive through the neighborhood, just in case. The subtle growl of the car's engine and the wind's gentle keening at the windows filled the quiet space between them. Allan drove with his fists clenched around the steering wheel, eyes red, lips pursed. Samarra studied the shadows and alleys, and had Allan stop at every Dumpster so she could look in. Just in case.

Later, after they'd come home, Samarra sat in the living room alone in darkness, as she'd done every night since Justine was gone. This time, there was no officer sitting in the kitchen, no security car outside. She couldn't watch her sleeping children from the doorway to their rooms. She listened as always to the latest string of condolences, offers for help, tips, Meg's update on the boutique, instead of trying to sleep. She heard Rey screaming with laughter in the background when Reynaldo called to say her son was negotiating with the spirits. Mirabel called, whispered, "Don't be scared, Mommy," as if she was doing something her grandmother had forbidden. Allan's father later left a message to say everything was fine and they were watching a movie with animated penguins.

"No," Samarra said, "let her tell you a story."

The litany of sadness weathered Samarra's resolve until there was nothing left for her to feel except the raw truth: Justine was gone. Her little girl was all alone, somewhere, with someone who shouldn't have her. Crying for her mother. Or worse.

Samarra hungered for one of Justine's good, truthful dreams. Or a sacred scribble from Mirabel. Even an impossible need from Rey to fulfill. A real and present taste of the miracle that were her children. Her belly and back ached with their missing weight.

Maybe just Allan holding her for a little while, as a friend, as the father of their children, as the man she loved, would be enough.

But she couldn't bring herself to go to him. She had to save herself for her children. Even if she'd let one of them slip away.

Allan hadn't come down to her these past nights, perhaps for one of those same reasons. He left her alone this night, as well. She eventually went to bed but couldn't feel Allan next to her, as if they'd been imprisoned in separate cells of shock and grief.

The next morning, the detective's partner came calling to say they were needed at the station.

Samarra wept for the entire ride, knowing from the official silence that she was going to hear that Justine was dead.

In a small, badly lit room that smelled faintly like a men's locker room, the lead detective announced in a small, dead voice that Mirabel had disappeared from the hotel suite Allan's parents had rented.

Samarra screamed and for a moment could see or feel nothing, only hear her voice like the alien sound of a demon rising through her to answer for her against the unspeakable.

When she'd regained her senses, two female police officers were holding her down in a chair. An emergency worker tended to Allan's bloody face. She babbled, mixing questions with threats and pleas, as if by the force of her words she could change what had been said in the room, or maybe just bring Mirabel back.

The detective was gone, replaced by a man in a darker, crisper suit who introduced himself with aggressive self-confidence as a federal agent. He assured them Rey had already been picked up from his uncle and was under protective custody. He was being transferred to a safe house used for special federal witnesses, and as soon arrangements were in place they'd be taken there to see the boy. As he spoke, fear drained Samarra's determination to create another, far more sane, reality.

There was no escaping a world in which two of her children were gone.

The agent's voice droned on, asking blunt questions about friends, family, enemies, that they'd already answered. She didn't get angry when he asked if Allan was really Mirabel's or Justine's father. The DNA tests had already been ordered.

She occupied herself with the calculus of loss, assessing whether or not both she and Allan were now each responsible for the disappearance of one of their children and if this somehow resolved the equation of their lives together.

Allan didn't look like himself with all the bandages covering his face.

After running through his inventory of questions, the agent informed them that the hotel security cameras had not revealed Mirabel leaving her grandparents' suite or the hotel. The police officer on duty downstairs had not seen anything unusual. The hotel staff was being interviewed and background checks were being performed, but so far, no leads had turned up. All the calls to the house would be reviewed, again.

He presented them with a plastic bin of Mirabel's effects: the clothes she'd worn that day, the change of clothes Samarra had packed for tomorrow, a stack of writing and drawings, on tissues, paper, cups and plates, bed sheets and pillow cases, taken from Mirabel's room.

Holding her daughter's old clothes to her face, she smelled the ink, still fresh, from Mirabel's signs and stories, mingled with her daughter's scent. Samarra wanted to crawl into the lines Mirabel had left behind to see if they might lead her to where her daughter might be hiding.

"Once upon a time," Samarra whispered, as if beginning a story to entertain her children, "I had daughters."

Neither she nor Allan found anything that might lead the agent to their other missing daughter.

"Is it that hard to find a six-year-old girl wandering around in her pajamas?" Samarra asked.

When they were released, Allan asked to be dropped off at the hospital where his mother had been taken after she discovered Mirabel missing. Samarra went home. Someone would come by later to take them to the safe house to visit Rey.

When she walked into the still house, everything inside of her twisted, as if a hand had closed around her guts and organs to rip them out.

Allan never came home. Samarra didn't care. She sat on the floor of the girls' room under the blankets from their beds, as if they might crawl out from the folds and rejoin her. The police officer who came to pick her up to visit Rey said her husband had decided to stay with his father, in a different hotel. They'd already visited Rey in the safe house. It was her turn.

She asked if Reynaldo could come along, and they picked him up on the way. She needed the strength of her own blood to get through so much emptiness.

And in the company of her older brother, she could remember what it felt like to be a little girl, and in that resonance be close to her daughters, again.

"That Fed thinks Allan's family got something to do with all this," Reynaldo whispered in the back of the car. He'd already shaken a small, straw figure smelling of sage in the air, "To ward of the electronics," he'd assured her.

"Good," Samarra said. She sat forward, already thinking of things she could tell the agent about the way she'd been treated, about how that family could very well have had the children kidnapped to get them away from her. Could Allan be on it? A bitter drip of tears burned her eyes.

"You know that's not right."

"Why? How would you know?"

"You don't remember," he said with sadness weighing down his words so they fell like anchors through a sea without currents.

"What?"

"Our brothers and sisters."

"We don't have any." Her brother was not just older, but near enough in age to be a real father to her. He'd always been a little crazy, though fiercely protective and generous. Now eccentricity was apparently slipping into dementia. She should have been paying closer attention; she'd missed this development.

Another loss. In the depths of her solitude, Samarra felt chilled to the bone. Only Rey was left.

"I told you I never wanted kids," Reynaldo said.

Letting the boy stay with his uncle had been a terrible mistake. She was lucky Rey hadn't been taken in the night along with Mirabel.

"I knew something like this would happen."

The boy didn't need any more crazy ideas filling his head. He needed to hang on to the real world. Both of them did. Reynaldo's spirit dolls and wild stories weren't going to protect them.

"Every war has its cost," Reynaldo said. "Look at what happened to our family. Look at us."

Samarra spoke to the officer driving the car. He gave her a sharp glance, spoke quietly into a radio and listened to the scratchy reply, then drove Reynaldo back home.

"You're making a mistake," Reynaldo said, leaning into the back seat while holding the door open.

Samarra laughed at the echo of her own thoughts and shut the door.

The blinders the driver had made Samarra put on were removed after the car stopped in front of a small wooden cottage at the end of a dirt road. The sea's salt tang was sharp in the air, but the surrounding pines hid any trace of a world beyond the silent wall of their shadows.

Rey was inside sitting at a card table in the middle of the living room, boosted by a couple of phone books so he could examine a pile of electronic parts. A woman sat with him in jeans and a blouse, badge at her hip, displaying a metal component with wires dangling like the arms of a dead squid while explaining its function in surveillance to Rey. The boy stared at each place her finger touched, as if absorbing secrets encoded in the matte black finish. Samarra had to call his name twice before he noticed her.

"I can make this," he said, after Samarra finally let him go. He pointed to the kitchen table, where the two other guardian agents sat drinking coffee in front of a few laptops with screens filled with live video feeds and quivering sensor lines. All three agents laughed.

She stayed longer than her time limit, and sang songs with the boy she'd usually sing with Justine or Mirabel. She told him the stories from his favorite books while sketching the pictures that normally accompanied, as if channeling Mirabel. Then she made one up, about two or seven or twelve brothers and sisters in a far-off land, born to a great destiny, blessed with magical powers, yet lost, waiting for the moment of their purpose. Even the guards looked puzzled as she leapt from one part of the tale to the other, bending and twisting the story until she thought Justine was speaking through her from one of her dreams.

Samarra gave up, to Rey's exaggerated relief, and had dinner with him and the guards, and afterwards they watched a cartoon about penguins while she held him on her lap until the driver finally said she needed to go home.

Reynaldo's message lay waiting for her on the answering machine: "We were too young to be soldiers," he said, his voice quavering. "Now we're too old."

She hit the delete button.

Sleep was a country to which she couldn't travel. She expected the phone to ring any moment. When it finally did, she couldn't pick up. A voice on the other end barked through the speaker between rings, telling her something that made her belly convulse again. The phone continued to ring, insisting. She couldn't tell if it was the police or someone else offering condolences. Then the doorbell rang.

In the first light of dawn, the agent who'd promised her son's safety stood in her doorway, pale, visibly shaken, and said Rey was gone.

So was Reynaldo. His front door had been left open. His keys and wallet were still in the apartment. The lights had been left on. The detective on the scene thought he might have gone out in his slippers.

She was brought to an office in a glass office building and questioned, coaxed, comforted, threatened. She answered every question she could, speaking through her tight fists squeezed against her mouth to keep from cursing and lashing out. But she couldn't tell the agents where Reynaldo might have gone or who would have taken her children. She didn't know. They asked her why he'd called her before vanishing. Her brother's final, mad message were the family's private shame and had no bearing on her lost children. She told them they'd talked about their own parents and the harsh life they'd had in the old country.

The agents could not explain how their protection had failed Rey.

The agents kept her through the day and into the night, but nothing they said reached through the fog of loss that had cut her off from the world. She couldn't trust herself, her husband, or the authorities. There was no one left to help her. No one left, at all.

In the night, she was released and taken home.

Allan called. She let the machine take messages. He rambled, exhausted the time limit, called back again and again, leaving snippets of his guilt and anger on the digital machine. He'd spent the day with the agents, as well. He was being followed. Everyone he knew had been questioned. He felt humiliated. Missed the kids. Couldn't go home. Not to the empty house. Where should he go to look for them, he kept asking. Who took them, he repeated, like another agent sent to besiege her. Why?

Samarra nearly picked up the phone to tell him the house was not empty. But as her hand settled on the receiver, the lie poisoned her tongue and her fingers slipped from the plastic handset.

She lay in the dark, heart jumping at every passing car in the street, every creak and knock in the house. She pleaded with the shadows to take her, the bed to swallow her, the walls or floor or closet to open and reveal that secret passage her children and brother had not been able to resist entering, perhaps knowing or hoping she'd be follow.

When morning came, she was still in her sweat-soaked bed, cold and alone. When she saw herself reflected in the dresser mirror, she closed the drapes and covered every mirror in the house, never wanting to look into her own eyes, again.

Days passed like shadows marching across the depths of a deep and narrow valley, brief flickers of light carving tall prison walls from darkness. Agents watched from their cars, just close enough for her to notice. Reporters thrust microphones and cameras at her when she left the house, recorded every move she made as she went to the police, to the government agents, private detectives. There were many questions, but she only knew one answer: I don't know.

Allan remained reclusive. She only knew he was still in the world because federal agents asked her to corroborate what he'd told them, and twice, left them waiting together in a motel room. He watched television both times. She napped on the first visit, read the book she'd brought with her the second.

Her lawyer reviewed offers for interviews, books, movies, and handled the store receipts while pointing out that Meg could only hold down the boutique for so long. Morose friends sat beside her as she waited for news, their expressions blurs lacking anchorage in hope, their brittle words of comfort shattering against her despair.

A distant cousin called to say she'd heard about Samarra's terrible ordeal, was very sorry and had the funeral arrangements been made.

Samarra waited, night after night, to disappear and join her children and brother wherever they'd gone. The faces of strangers haunted her dreams, reminding her of magazine pictures of the widows of men, mothers of children, lost in a war or a cleansing or some other form of terror, alone in their homes or gathered in protest at a square or in front of a government building.

Their eyes, she recalled, had stared through the photographer's lens and the flat simulacrum of the page. The detachment in the collective isolation of their gaze had shaken her loose from the heavenly comfort of her life's nest, the beating heart of her own, still living family. Even then, she'd understood that if she'd been in the same room with any one of those poor souls, they'd never see her. They would always be looking beyond the moment, searching for the road that might lead them to what had gone missing from their lives.

She took down the sheet covering the dresser mirror. Her face was a stranger's, but this time she recognized the eyes. Samarra released her reflections, needing the cold comfort of their company.

Days flowed into weeks, then months. The family's story was optioned selectively and lingered in the electronic air, in library stacks and on the covers of bundled magazines left out for recycling. Videos and pictures from the tragic story circulated on the Internet. A quickly made family cable movie hinted at family troubles and runaway children. Blogs and message boards fed the mystery for a while, but comments and discussion threads faded into silence. The telephone stopped ringing, even late at night. The agents sifted through the resurgence of responses, tracked down suspects identified by profiling, but found nothing.

She still flinched at the blame placed on her for losing the children.

The seasons changed, a new school year started. Rey had been eager to start kindergarten, having tasted only enough of the world's wonders in pre-school to know he was hungry for more. Mirabel would have been reluctant to go back to the mild teasing her odd behavior sometimes inspired from even her kindred in class. But she'd looked forward to assuming the role of Rey's older protective sister in school, as if she could hide what she was under a burden of responsibility. Justine had been racing ahead with her studies, poised to skip grades and looking forward with a mix of dread and predatory joy to being placed with older children in another school after the coming year. Already, she'd been dropping her few friends and preparing herself for a terrible dislocation. Samarra was certain Justine would have brought up, once a day, for this entire semester, a neighbor's comment that she should pretend to be stupid so she could stay with her friends and meet boys her own age.

When the leaves changed and her children still weren't home, Samarra thought of another way to share their fate. Preparing the fresh roast she kept in the refrigerator in case they returned, she stared at the boning knife in her hand. She held it close to her wrist, letting blood drip on her skin. Curious, she let the blade hover at her throat.

Thoughts crowded her mind, slipping out of reach whenever she focused on them. A few broke free, flew on wings beating to the rhythm of her racing heart. They promised blood, and flashed visions of monsters and fire consuming her children. She choked on a cry as her hands trembled, her knees buckled.

Then a promise caressed her fingers, slowed and soothed the tumult of thoughts. Pushed the knife closer.

A sliver of comfort pierced her terrors. Her babies had crossed over to someplace else. If she stopped being here, she could follow and be with them, there.

Like the knife and the blood, the thought didn't feel like a part of her. But it seemed like a simple truth. The smell of raw meat gave the idea the weight of reality. A single, simple cut, and she'd be with them. Wherever there was. The logic was inescapable.

Relieved that she'd found a way back to the children, Samarra pushed the blade's edge against her throat.

The touch of cold metal against her skin sent a shock through her body, as if she'd connected not with Rey, Justine, and Mirabel, but the barbed fencing of the prison cage which kept them from her. She dropped the knife in horror. It landed on the kitchen tile with a hollow clatter.

Sammara broke down and wept at the edge of what she'd almost done.

They weren't dead. She wasn't crazy. She was a better mother than the one who almost killed herself. Not good enough to keep her babies, but not so bad as to run away when they needed her.

Something had slipped through her despair, led her to the brink of self-destruction. Intangible, invisible, yet all around. Capable of anything.

Certainly a thing able to make her babies disappear.

If she'd been a better mother, she could have heard that vast and terrible thing laughing at her from the empty corners of the house.

That night, Mirabel flew on ephemeral wings. Rey forged his own reality from the world's raw foundations. Justine saw far, dreamed further. They felt warm in her arms as she kissed them all goodnight before she woke.

The next day, she refused to believe she'd nearly cut herself, laughed at the memory of an invisible entity in the house. She certainly wasn't going crazy.

Allan informed her by postcard that he was living at his parents' house. He wasn't talking to anyone. His family's lawyer contacted hers and they quickly reached a divorce settlement. She refused to give up the house, fearing the children would come back someday and she wouldn't be there for them. Her lawyer referred her to a therapist. Meg finally bought the boutique.

Snow returned, and the house weighed on her with the solemnity of a marble mausoleum. She heard footsteps running up and down the stairs. Echoes of giggles. Singing. But there were no snow angels in the backyard, or sled tracks, or forts stocked with snowballs. No sinister laugh of monsters.

Her bed was sometimes warm from the heat of a missing lover.

She bought frames by the case, filling walls and flat surfaces with pictures. The faces of her children stared at her from every space and angle. Memories replaced the life she wanted back.

She lasted through the winter by sitting into the early morning hours at a seat by the door waiting for the bell to ring. She listened for a surreptitious raising of windows and the sound of bare feet tip-toeing on wood flooring upstairs, since the children might very well try to surprise her in the morning and pretend they'd been home all the time. It was a lie she understood she would have believed.

But when the days slowly stretched out on longer beds of light, when the snow melted and buds appeared on ice slick branches, cracks of doubt shot through her determination to hold on.

With the help of answers to her therapist's questions she didn't divulge in sessions, Samarra concluded that whatever else had happened to Justine, Mirabel, and Rey, they were far from the life they'd shared together. New experiences had shaped, and scarred, them. Maybe her babies couldn't come back to the graveyard of their past. Home might not be a real place for them, anymore. Mommy and Daddy, empty words. Perhaps they had other plans, or the road they traveled on was taking them to another place they needed to be.

The thing on the other side of the boning knife may have shown her a piece of the truth.

Something else had to be done. She couldn't sit in the big house and wait. She had to go out, hunt them down, transform herself into a mother they'd recognize and need to hold them in her arms, again.

She could be that kind of mother.

The seeds of a plan dug its roots in her mind. Hope gave her the strength to begin the transformation while keeping how and why to herself.

The house was sold by mid-spring, a year after the children had vanished. With a gym bag full of her share of real estate and media money bundled in cash, Samarra drove off in a used car to follow them, and in her way, disappeared.

She bought a cottage in the country, far from the closest town, under an identity she'd purchased from a reliable source. The silence of shadows beneath the pines lived with her. Water came from a well, food was scheduled for regular delivery, in exchange for the large denomination bill in its hiding place, once a month at the head of the winding dirt path between the pocked road and her front door. The car was parked in a ditch. She took down the mail box, let the path grow invisible from the road. Chopping wood for cool nights and long, cold winters provided exercise.

There was enough cash to stay on the road of her children's disappearance for decades.

Samarra spent the first night of her journey invisible in the wilderness, surrounded by the boxes containing everything she'd ever need from her old life. In her dreams, she heard children laughing, running footsteps, the rustling of paper and the clink of small tools, as they explored their new home.

The next morning, the smell of ink and glue, and the scent of the last perfume she'd bought for herself which she'd let Justine try, haunted the cabin's musty air. She looked out the door expecting to see Mirabel and Rey running down the path, with Justine lagging behind in case one of them fell, to pick them up and take them safely back to their mother.

The path was empty. Birds sang and chirped in the distance. Insects trilled and clicked. Sunlight skimmed the tree tops.

"Oh, Justine, you were the one I could always talk to," Samarra said to the dust and dander and spider silk dancing in the night-scrubbed air, "more than with Allan, Reynaldo, anybody else. Even when you scared me." Acid dew tears beaded in the corners of her eyes.

"Are you sending me your dreams, or am I remembering my own these days? You take care of Rey and Mirabel. Remember me. Remember, I love you. No matter what. Don't forget that, whatever happens, whatever they do to you. No matter what you do. I'll always love you all. Nothing can take that away.

"I'm coming for you. Watch for me, please. Let me help. Please, my baby, please let's all come home together."

The peace that followed her plea gave Samarra a certainty as hard as the surrounding hills' stone foundations that she'd catch up to the children in this place.

She went back inside to work her way out from the roots of her plan. Breaking open the boxes she'd brought, Samarra built three altars, one for each wall of the cottage. Justine's she built around the fireplace, Mirabel's and Rey's, over the boarded up windows. They looked like memorials to her missing children, dense with framed pictures, clay models and finger paintings, baby shoes, packs of favored candies and cakes, soda bottles, well-worn stuffed animals, threadbare safety blankets, hair clippings, report cards, rickety toys, homemade Halloween costumes and masks.

But in her mind the altars were only sketches of her living children, abstract representations requiring reality's fine details to open the way wide to wherever they'd gone, whoever they'd become. Crude lighthouses signaling the way home for her babies.

Samarra had only a mother's love. More was needed to reach them, sparks thrown off by their gifts to raise a more powerful light, a touch of her children's divine nature to fuel the fire.

Justine's presence lingered in Samarra's dreams, her scent on the pillow, echoes of her whispers in the dusk. She held on to the signs, desperate for proof that she wasn't simply a mad woman fighting off grief's reality. She'd picked up the trail, tuned into a signal. That was what was happening. Her plan had found the right soil in which to grow.

She wrote down her visions in the leftover pages of old school notebooks and sketched images that stayed with her after she woke: stark black mountains against a red sky, plains filled with hordes of golden figures, worms rising from the ashen soil of blackened forests, and things that were lines and angles instead of limbs and torsos, shifting and disappearing into one another. She stuck the pages in layers around Justine's altar, until the floor, walls, and ceiling were coated with a savage collage of words and pictures mined from another world.

They made no sense, told her nothing of what her daughter was doing or where she was. Samarra's tears made the ink run, and she found more comfort in what was left.

The scents and whispers faded, dreams drained into the daylight hours. She wakened from a black pit of sleep to the habit of already scrawling, first on the remaining blank paper, then across the walls surrounding Mirabel's altar, and on the floor and ceiling, using ink, pencil, chalk, paint, charcoal. It was Mirabel's turn to be channeled, and Samarra left herself open to inspiration every moment of the day and night, forgetting to eat or change out of soiled clothes as she wrote whatever came into her mind. Mirabel's favorite books flowed easily from her hand, perfectly reproduced to the last comma, then bedtime stories Samarra had spun for her of forest witches and mermaids, ghosts, and warrior women; and then imaginary letters from Mirabel, not to her mother, father, siblings or classmates, but to strangers, friends she hadn't made, yet, and lovers, and children to be born. Secret coded messages emerged, maps and plans and designs

When writing materials ran out, Samarra carved into the space reserved for Mirabel inside the cabin with a knife, and when she ran out of space, the deluge spilled out over the outside of the cabin, the roof, nearby trees, until she awoke weak and filthy, her hands aching, vision blurry, lost in the woods.

She followed the trail of Mirabel's angel scrawls back to the cabin and recovered her strength in the gift of quiet granted by her daughter. As soon as she could, Samarra went out and followed the trail she'd made back through the woods, hoping she'd been given a direction in which to pursue her children. But the trail beyond the last carving ended over a cliff, into the sea churning and rolling below. Samarra built a small altar to her middle child at the last tree she'd carved, burying writings and a hair clip and a few tin toys among the roots, encasing others in a small, wooden chest she'd found in the cabin and leaving it suspended on a low branch.

It was when she was securing the box with string that she felt an urge to build. A vision for a construction, both simple and complex, stormed her mind: corners, flat surfaces, depths, imbued with the lightness of air, the solidity of earthly matter. Rey had come to her, wanting to rebuild the box she'd found so long ago, the day her children began disappearing.

The terror unleashed by the task numbed her fingers, and for days she wouldn't leave the bed.

But as plans for the object filled her mind with possible measurements, textures and angles, Samarra couldn't deny her youngest's obsession. She let herself approach the obligation to face her fear, to confront the first symbol of everything terrible that had happened to her. The young had their needs. The language of mystery, its logic. The road they'd taken was there for her to follow. She was that kind of mother.

She used leaves, at first, and sticks, not wanting to disturb the materials she'd already used for the girls. Small to large, she fashioned crude models, seeking proper proportions, folds and corners, filling the space around Rey's altar with a range of pyramidal mountains. By the time the paper and craft supplies she'd requested through the store that dropped off her provisions had arrived, she'd established the fundamental proportions of the box she'd found in the foyer.

She began building in earnest. From memory and what Allan had told her, she concluded an origami structure of folded paper had been used to build the original box. She worked through daylight hours and by candlelight, laboring to build on simple crafting skills she'd learned in workshops with her children, experimenting, failing, adding slowly to the mountains she'd already built only the models in which she thought she'd achieved a small measure of perfection.

Rebuilding the box would not be easy. She wrestled with the problems of weight and size and texture until she ended each day in screams of despair, more than once racing to the cliff's edge through the night woods, determined to throw herself over rather than face another day of imperfections. She'd come so far, but not far enough.

So far, the sea crashing to shore in the night made her realize, in this world. Justine, Mirabel, and Rey had brought her to this edge of everything. They weren't on this side. They were showing her something. The sea. A barrier. A wall.

A wall had doors. And a box, a lid or flaps for opening.

So the end she'd reached was not a final one. Justine, Mirabel, and Rey were beyond the sea, the air she breathed, the land she stood on. They were on the other side of the box. Waiting.

Samarra cried out with joy. She ran out into midnight woods as if she'd heard her children coming, again. She tripped and fell, then waited, listening to rustling underbrush, grunts, trilling, snuffling, catching eyes shining with starlight, raising her cheeks to the kiss of moth wings, feeling that she was close. So close.

The seasons passed, and the boxes she built slowly approached the perfection for which Rey always strived, working on wrapping and string and bow to complete the replication. She took her final products out along the trail she'd blazed, past the last carving, until the line of boxes reached the cliff, where she tossed them into the water and watched as they were consumed by the churning froth below.

When the boxes stopped decomposing along the path, when they survived the sea and bobbed in the backwash and tidal currents until they were swept to open water; when the boxes felt like air in her hands with the substance of their content, she knew she'd found the gate to where she needed to go, at last.

Her children could tell her no more.

Opening the gate was her task, alone.

There was only one more thing she could copy. She positioned boxes one at a time for months inside the cabin at the same distance from the front door as the one she'd found in her old home. Each morning she opened a box, carefully examining the surfaces for changes or messages. Breathing deeply from the air inside the box, it seemed like a trick of changing atmospheric pressure sucked the air out of her lungs. After whispering, then screaming, into the boxes for Justine, Mirabel, and Rey, their names sounded like words spoken in a foreign language.

The boxes piled high around her, like offerings to the living altar to her children she'd become. There were so many, she couldn't be certain she'd made them all. It seemed they were appearing on their own, relentless, like an incessant knocking at the door, demanding attention. Accusing. She searched through them all again, day after day, in case one had been changed for her.

The day came when she knew something more was needed.

She left notes in the boxes, asking for instructions, pleading for guidance. They appeared to remain unread. She stuffed the boxes with the contents of the altars for her children. Built stick-figure totems representing each child, attaching hair clippings, swatches of clothing, and after kissing each one, whispered for them to let her through, and placed them into boxes.

When this tactic failed, Samarra sat in the cabin in despair. There was nothing more for her to do. She could only wait, like a beggar at a palace door, and plead to the sky and sea and earth for entry.

In the cold nights, when she didn't bother lighting candles, stove or fireplace, she imagined her babies sitting in the darkness, waiting for her, and to pass the time she told the stories she'd given them when they were much younger, a long time ago. They needed her, and she'd failed them, so she had to give them something. Because that was the kind of mother she was.

And in the old stories, as fresh now in her telling as when she'd first passed them along, as clear in her mind as when she'd set them down on paper and carved them into wood, she recognized Justine, Mirabel, Rey, herself, their story, in the adventures of heroes and the unwinding threads of fatal fairy tales.

Not everything was as it seemed, she heard herself say, time and again. Witches could be beautiful. Even the strongest had flaws by which they fell. Changelings passed between worlds, forever out of place, looking for the way home.

Sacrifices were demanded.

She'd given everything, she told the darkness. There was nothing left.

But, of course, she knew there was always something left.

In the morning, she chose a box as perfect as any other she'd made and opened herself to it with a long cut across her wrist. Blood dribbled to stain its walls and pool on the bottom. Then she closed the box, wrapped it in paper and twine, and waited to bury it at her doorstep in the heart of the night. When she was done, the woods were quiet, and no eyes caught the moonlight coming down through the trees.

She waited as many nights as it took for her to lose her family, and then dug out the hole at her doorstep.

The box was gone. But the things she found in the hole wrenched her stomach and made her heave and gasp for air.

Keeping her head turned away, she quickly threw dirt back to cover what kicked and writhed and stared at her with wide, innocent eyes. Faint mewling rose through the loose soil. She slid a nearby stone over the broken ground to keep what was in it from rising. Closed the door. Collapsed to her knees, shivering, surprised to find she was crying cold tears when she pressed the palm of her hand to her face to feel something warm and alive against her skin.

Samarra's belly ached. She bled from between her legs, where muscle and tissue throbbed and burned and pulsed with the pain of violation. Or perhaps, deliverance.

Fairy tale equations circled through her mind. Maybe she should have kept what had been left for her. Cared for and raised them. If only to see what they would become. Maybe they were a part of the equation, a crucial proof of something she did not want to know, but which would resolve the mystery of her own children.

Perhaps, they were her real babies, returned to her as they'd been taken, preserved for her to nourish and care for when she'd done what was needed for another's brood.

Or they might have been an answer to her knocking on the gate to a place in which she was not welcome. A warning.

A desire she couldn't name, could never fulfill, fluttered in her heart, and for that moment she experienced what Rey must have felt when he wanted to taste the bread baked on a television show or sing opera at a recording session taped long ago; what Mirabel sought to express with her restless hand; what Justine listened for in her dreams. Samarra also wanted to capture something that always seemed just beyond her reach.

Standing at the gate she could not cross, a hope rose in her that at least Rey had finally seized the secret machinery he'd been chasing since he was born, and Mirabel's angel scrawl had broken her story out of its mundane boundaries, and dreams had, at last, delivered Justine's secret name. They didn't have to be changelings. They could be angels, risen now to their appointed place, with Samarra left behind to atone for an act she couldn't remember.

Or they could all be something else entirely. Even, only, human.

The knock on the door woke her.

She lay against the door. Her sleep had been as black as the night embracing her cabin. Confused, she moaned and tasted old blood in her mouth.

"You shouldn't have come," her brother Reynaldo said, from the other said. "We're too old."

Samarra opened the door.

In the first slivers of dawn, she didn't find Reynaldo. Only another box, on the stone covering the hole she'd dug.

The paper wrapping was stained, the twine string rougher than the first she'd found long ago, and wet. A stream of dark, thick liquid crept slowly out from under the box, across the stone, toward her. The sides bulged out unevenly.

Truths found or lost since her children left suddenly didn't matter, Samarra realized, because the moment's truth told her there were always deeper mysteries to solve.

She stepped forward, reaching for the other box. It had all the weight and mass the first one lacked.

Samarra opened the other box.

And didn't have time to scream.

Gerard Houarner *is a product of the NYC public school system, attended the then-free City College of New York, taking writing workshops under Joseph Heller and Joel Oppenheimer while sneaking into William Burroughs' hallucinogenic classes. He later attained a couple of Masters degrees in psychology from Teachers College, Columbia University, so he could make a living in the pre-gentrified Lower East Side and Hell's Kitchen, and near the still ungentrified birthplace of hip-hop in the Bronx. He currently works in a state psychiatric facility by day. For the past and whatever may come in the future for writing, visit www. gerardhouarner.com.*

"The Other Box" is a good example of why I love dark stories so much more than most "horror" films. If you were pitching this as a movie, the first thing they'd ask would be: "Well, what *was* in the other box?" They'd also want you to come up with an explanation of where the children went. "So, let's say they lived on this ancient Indian burial ground . . . " or "We need a scene with, like, demons that . . . " or "It was the uncle, right?" Et cetera. And whatever flick eventually was made would have nothing of what this tale has in spades: questions answerable only by your own imagination. And *you* are scary. (So am I.)

WHITE CHARLES

SARAH MONETTE

The crate arrived at the Parrington on a Wednesday, but it was Friday before anyone mentioned it to me. Anything addressed from Miss Griselda Parrington, the younger of Samuel Mather Parrington's two daughters, was automatically routed to Dr. Starkweather's office, regardless of whose name she had written on it. I was, in truth, intensely grateful for this policy, for Miss Parrington most often addressed her parcels to me. She felt that we were "kindred spirits"; she considered me the only employee of the museum with the sensitivity and intelligence to appreciate her finds. Considering that she had inherited all of her father's magpie-like attraction to the outré and none of his discernment, her opinion was less flattering than one might think. I endured some teasing on the subject, though not nearly as much as I might have; in general, the curators' attitude was one of "there but for the grace of God." They were even, I think, rather grateful, if not *to me* precisely, then at least for my existence.

Miss Parrington's packages were inevitably accompanied by letters, sometimes quite lengthy, explaining what she persisted in referring to as the provenance, although it was no such thing. "I found this in a lovely antique shop in Belgravia that Mimi showed me," conveyed no useful information at all, since nine times out of ten she neglected to provide any further clues to Mimi's identity, and on the tenth time, when we managed to determine that "Mimi" was Sarah Brandon-Forbes, wife of the eminent diplomat, a polite letter would elicit the response that Lady Brandon-Forbes had never been in any antique shop in Belgravia in her life. The bulk of Miss Parrington's letters described, lavishly, what she *believed* the provenance to be, flights of fancy more suited to a romantic novelist than to even an amateur historian. But the letters had to be read and answered; Dr. Starkweather had been emphatic on the subject: they were addressed to me, therefore it was my responsibility to answer them.

It was perhaps the part of my job I hated most.

That Friday, when I found the letter in my pigeonhole, I recognized Miss Parrington's handwriting and flinched from it. My first instinct was to lose the letter by any means necessary, but no matter how tempting, it was not a viable solution. Dr. Starkweather saw through me as if I were a pane of glass; he would not be fooled by such an obvious lie. There was, therefore, neither sense nor benefit in putting off the task, unpleasant though it was. I opened the envelope then and there, and read the letter on the way back to my office.

It was a superbly representative specimen, running to three pages, close-written front and back, and containing absolutely no useful information of any kind. She had been at an estate sale—and of course she neglected to mention whose estate—she had recognized the name Carolus Albinus as someone in whom her father had been interested, and thus she had bid on and purchased a job lot of fire-damaged books, along with a picture she was quite sure would prove when cleaned to be an original Vermeer. She had not so much as opened the crate in which the books were packed, knowing—she said coyly—that I would prefer to make all the discoveries myself. But I would see that she was right about the Vermeer.

I propped my throbbing head on my hand and wrote back, thanking her for thinking of the museum and disclaiming all knowledge of seventeenth-century Dutch painters. I posted the letter, dry-swallowed an aspirin, and returned to the round of my usual duties. I gladly forgot about Miss Parrington's crate.

I should have known better.

On the next Tuesday, I was standing in Dr. Starkweather's office, helplessly watching him and Mr. Browne tear strips off each other over a *casus belli* they had both already forgotten, when we were startled by a shriek from the direction of the mail room. Dr. Starkweather raced to investigate, Mr. Browne and myself close behind, and we found Mr. Ferrick, one of the junior-most of the junior curators, sitting on the floor beside an open crate, his spectacles askew and one hand pressed to his chest.

"What on *Earth?*" said Dr. Starkweather.

Mr. Ferrick yelped and shot to his feet in a welter of apologetic half-sentences.

"Are you all right?" said Mr. Browne. "What happened?"

"I don't know," said Mr. Ferrick. "I was opening the crate and something—it flew into my face—I thought—" He glanced at Dr. Starkweather's fulminating expression and sensibly did not explain what he had thought.

A closer look at the crate caused my heart to sink, in rather the same way that reading the *Oedipus Tyrannos* did. "Is that, er, the crate from Miss Parrington?"

"Yes," said Mr. Ferrick, puzzled.

"Oh good God," said Dr. Starkweather in tones of utmost loathing, probably prompted equally by Miss Parrington and me.

"She said she, er . . . that is, she didn't open the crate. So it probably—"

"A bit of straw," Dr. Starkweather said, seizing a piece from the floor and brandishing it at us. "You've heard of the boy who cried wolf, Mr. Ferrick?"

"Yes, Dr. Starkweather," Mr. Ferrick said, blushing.

"Good God," Dr. Starkweather said again, more generally, and stormed out, Mr Browne at his heels already girding himself to re-enter the fray.

I saw an opportunity to let Dr. Starkweather forget about me, and stayed where I was. Mr. Ferrick edged over to the crate as if he expected something else to leap out at him; it was with visible reluctance that he reached inside.

"What did you think it was?" I said.

"Beg pardon?"

"The, er, whatever it was that flew into your face. What did you think it was?"

"Oh. I've been spending too much time in Entomology," he said with a grimace. I waited while he lifted out a book so blackened with smoke that it was impossible to say what color the binding had originally been. "It looked like a spider," he said finally, tightly. "An enormous white spider. But Dr. Starkweather was right. It was just straw."

"Make out an inventory," I said, "and, er, bring it to me when you're done." And I left him to his straw.

Mr. Ferrick's inventory included several works by Carolus Albinus, one by the alchemist Johann de Winter, three by the pseudonymous and frequently untruthful Rose Mundy, and a leather-bound commonplace book evidently compiled by the owner of the library—a deduction which would have been more satisfying if he had signed his name to it anywhere. One of the Carolus Albinus books was rare enough to be valuable even in its damaged condition: the 1588 Prague edition of the *De Spiritu et Morte* with the Vermeulen woodcuts said to have driven the printer mad. The rest of them were merely good practice for the junior archivists. I heard from Mr. Lucent, who was friends with Mr. Browne's second in command Mr. Etheredge, that the "Vermeer" was no such thing and was sadly unsurprised. The crate and straw were both reused—I believe in packing a set of canopic jars to be shipped to San Francisco—and that was that. Another of Miss Parrington's well-meaning disasters dealt with.

Except that the night watchmen, a pair of stalwarts named Fiske and Hobden, began to complain of rats.

"Rats?" said Dr. Starkweather. "What nonsense!"

The rest of us could not afford to be so cavalier, and even Dr. Starkweather had to rethink his position when Miss Chatteris came to him on behalf of the docents and announced that the first time one of them saw so much as a whisker of a rat, they were all quitting.

"But there have never been rats!" protested Mr. Tilley, the oldest of the curators. "Never!"

Hobden and Fiske, stolid and walrus-mustached and as identical as twins, said they could not speak to that, but Mr. Tilley was welcome to tell them what else the scuttling noises might be.

Mr. Lucent rather wistfully suggested getting a museum cat and was promptly shouted down.

Dr. Starkweather grudgingly authorized the purchase of rat-traps, which were baited and set and caught no rats.

Mr. Browne was denied permission to purchase a quantity of arsenic sufficient—said Miss Coburn, who did the calculations—to poison the entire staff.

Frantic and paranoid inventory-taking revealed no damage that could be ascribed to rats, although Decorative Arts suffered a species of palace coup over an infestation of moths in one of their storerooms and our Orientalist, Mr. Denton, pitched a public and monumental temper tantrum over what he claimed was water damage to a suit of bamboo armor. Mr. Browne took advantage of the opportunity to start a campaign to have the main building re-roofed. Dr. Starkweather chose, with some justification, to take this as fomenting insurrection, and the rats were forgotten entirely in the resultant carnage.

Except by Hobden and Fiske—and by me, although that was my own fault for staying in the museum after dark. I was writing an article which required the consultation of (it seemed in my more despondent moods) no less than half the contents of my office. Thus working on it at home was futile, and working on it during the day was proving impossible, as the inventories were bringing to light unidentifiables overlooked in the *last* inventory, and everyone was bringing them to me. The puzzles and mysteries were welcome, but I had promised this article to the editor of *American Antiquities* nearly six months ago, and I was beginning to despair of finishing it. Being insomniac by nature, I found the practice of working at night more congenial than otherwise, and the Parrington was blessedly quiet. Fiske and Hobden's rounds were metronomically regular, and they did not disturb me.

And then there was the scuttling.

It was a ghastly noise, dry and rasping and somehow slithery, and it was weirdly omnidirectional, so that while I was sure it was not in the office with me, I could never tell where in fact it was. It was horribly intermittent, too, the sound of something scrabbling, and stopping, and then scrabbling again. As if it were searching for the best vantage point from which to observe me, and the night I had that thought, I went out to the front entrance and asked the watchman if they had had any luck at ridding the museum of rats.

He gave me a long, steady look and then said, "No, sir. Have some tea."

I accepted the mug he offered; the tea was hot and sweet and very strong. He watched, and when I had met whatever his criteria were, he said, "Me and Hob, we reckon maybe it ain't rats."

This was Fiske, then; I was relieved not to have to ask. "No?"

"No, sir. Y'see, Hob has a dog what is a champion ratter. Very well known, is Mingus. And me and Hob brought Mingus in, sir, quiet-like, feeling that what His Nibs don't know, he won't lose sleep over . . . "

"Quite," I said, perceiving that Fiske would not continue until he had been reassured on that point.

"Thank you, sir. So Hob brought Mingus in, and the dog, sir, did not rat."

"He didn't?"

"No, sir. We took him all over the museum, and not a peep out of him. And before you ask, sir, that dratted scratching noise seemed like it was following us about. Mingus heard it, sure enough, but he wouldn't go after it. Just whined and kind of cringed when Hob tried him. So we figured, Hob and myself, that it ain't rats."

"What do, er, you and Mr. Hobden think it is?"

Mr. Fiske looked at me solemnly and said, "As to that, sir, we ain't got the least idea."

Two nights later, I saw it, entirely by accident—and not "accident" meaning happenstance or coincidence, but "accident" quite literally: I fell on the stairs from the mailroom to the west storage rooms. The stairs were of the sort that consist only of treads—no risers—and when I opened my eyes from my involuntary flinch, I was staring down into the triangular space beneath the stairs and watching something scuttling out of sight. I saw it for less than a second, but I saw that it was white, and it was not a rat. And I all too easily recognized the sound.

For a moment, I was petrified, my body as heavy and cold and unresponsive as marble, and then I scrambled frantically up the stairs, banging my already bruised knees, smacking my raw palms as I fumbled with the door. It was more luck than anything else that I got the door open, and I locked it behind me with shaking fingers, then slumped against it, panting painfully for breath. And then I heard that dry, rasping, scuttling sound from somewhere ahead of me in the storage room, and with the dreadful epiphantic clarity of a lightning bolt, I knew and whispered aloud because it was too terrible a thing to have pent and unvoiced in my skull, "It's in the walls." Even that was not the truth of my horror, for in fact that was no more than a banality. What made my chest seem too small for the panicked beating of my heart was not that it was *in* the walls, but that it was *using* the walls, as a subway train uses its tunnels.

Subway trains, unlike rats, have drivers.

And then I was running, my mind full of a dry, rustling panic. Later, I would reason with myself, would point out that it had not harmed anyone, or even any*thing*, that there was not the slightest shred of proof that its intentions were malicious, or indeed that it had any intentions at all. But nothing I came up with, no reasoned argument, no rational observation, could withstand the instinctive visceral loathing I had felt for that white scuttling shape. I remembered that Hobden's dog, a champion ratter, would not go after this thing. I remembered Mr. Ferrick, shaken and embarrassed, describing the "enormous white spider" that had flung itself in his face. And I wondered that night, pacing from room to sleepless room of my apartment, just what else Miss Parrington had bought in that job lot of worthless books.

Was it a sign of insanity that I assumed from the moment I saw it that it was not natural? I do not know. I do know that discovering it to be a gigantic albino tarantula would have been an overpowering relief, and by the very magnitude of that imagined relief, I knew it was no such thing.

The next morning, I prevailed on Mr. Lucent to ask a favor of one of his friends in Entomology, and the two of them met me in the mailroom. I brought a flashlight. Mr. Lucent's friend was Mr. Vanderhoef, a shy young man who wore thick horn-rimmed spectacles and was an expert on African termites. Everyone in the museum, of course, knew about Mr. Ferrick's spider, and I explained that I thought I had seen it the night before. Mr. Vanderhoef looked dubious, but not reluctant, and contorted himself quite cheerfully into the awkward space beneath the stairs. I passed him the flashlight.

"A big piece of plaster is missing," he reported after a moment. "That must be how—oh! There is . . . something has been nesting here."

"Nesting?" Mr. Lucent said unhappily. "You mean it *is* rats?"

"No," said Mr. Vanderhoef, rather absently. "There aren't droppings, and it doesn't look . . . In truth, I'm not sure what it *does* look like."

"What do you mean?" I said. Mr. Lucent and I were now both peering between the treads of the stairs, but all we could see was Mr. Vanderhoef's shock of blond hair.

"There are no droppings, no caches of food, no eggs—nor viviparous offspring for that matter . . . "

"It couldn't be a, er, trap?"

"How do you mean?"

"Well, er, like a . . . like a spider's web."

"Ah. No."

"So, what is it using to nest in?" Mr. Lucent asked before I could find a way to get Mr. Vanderhoef to expand. "It isn't as if we've got a lot of twigs and whatnot in the museum."

"No, no," said Mr. Vanderhoef. "Paper. Newspaper, mostly, although I think I see the remains of one of Dr. Starkweather's memoranda."

"Paper," I said.

"Mr. Booth?" said Mr. Lucent, apparently not liking the sound of my voice.

"You're quite sure it couldn't be a spider?"

"That isn't what I said. This is not a *web*. There are spiders that don't build webs, but arachnids are not my specialty, and I cannot say for certain—"

"Is there anyone in the museum who would know?"

"Dr. Phillips is our arachnid expert, but he's on an expedition in Brazil until Christmas."

"Thank you," I said, because it was important to remember to be courteous, "you've been very kind."

"Mr. Booth!"

I stopped at the top of the stairs. "Yes, Mr. Lucent?"

"Did you . . . what were you . . . where are you going?"

"Paper," I said. "Will you ask Major Galbraith to get the plaster repaired?"

Mr. Lucent sputtered; I made good my escape and went to do what I should have done weeks ago and examine the commonplace book from Mr. Ferrick's inventory.

Mr. Ferrick was not happy to see me, though I could not tell if it was a guilty conscience—an affliction which seemed to be frequently visited on the junior curators in my presence—or simply that I irritated him. In either case, he stared at me as blankly as if I had asked about the second book of Aristotle's *Poetics*.

"The commonplace book," I said. "From, er, Miss Parrington's crate."

I noted that he had not been at the Parrington long enough for her name to have its full effect; we all winced reflexively, even Dr. Starkweather, but Mr. Ferrick merely frowned and said, "Is that the crate with the damaged books?"

"And the enormous white spider," I said before I could stop myself.

He gave me a look of mingled shock and reproach and said, "Oh! *That* commonplace book. I gave it to Mr. Lucent because it was holograph. Was that wrong?"

It was now obvious that he did not like me. I was glad he was a naturalist by training; once he had finished his probationary period, I was unlikely to have to deal with him again.

"No," I said. "That's fine." I was as pleased to leave as he was to have me go.

I spent the rest of the morning in a treasure hunt that was simultaneously ridiculous and nightmarish, pursuing the trail of the commonplace book from Mr. Ferrick to Mr. Lucent; from Mr. Lucent—who was miffed at me, he said, for rushing away in the middle of things and leaving him "holding the baby," although whether he meant by that the hole in the plaster, or Mr. Vanderhoef, or possibly Major Galbraith, I could not determine and did not like to ask—to Mr. Roxham; from Mr. Roxham, after a protracted and egregiously dusty search, to Miss Atterbury; from Miss Atterbury to Mr. Vine; and finally from Mr. Vine to Mr. Horton, who said, "Oh, I haven't gotten to it yet," and reached unerringly into the middle of one of the stacks of books waiting to be catalogued that surrounded his desk.

I retreated to my office with my prize and locked the door. The first few pages of the commonplace book told me that its owner was strongly antiquarian in his tastes, largely self-educated, and with an unhealthy penchant for the occult. Judging by the authors he quoted, he must have had quite the collection; the coup of the 1588 Albinus paled in comparison.

I flipped steadily through the pages, trying not to inhale too deeply, for the book reeked of smoke and secondarily of tobacco, and there was another scent, too faint for me to identify but sharply unpleasant. I was looking for quotes from Carolus Albinus or one of the other books that had been in the crate, and I found them starting about three-quarters of the way through. Albinus; Mundy; a lengthy passage from de Winter on golems; a passage from an even more unpleasant author on the abomination called a Hand of Glory, although I had never seen these particular virtues ascribed to it before; and then the quotes began to be interspersed with dated entries such as one might find in a diary. These were written in a highly elliptical style, using an idiosyncratic set of abbreviations, and I could make neither heads nor tails of them, except for repeated references to "cllg"—"calling"?—someone or something called White Charles—the literal translation, of course, of Carolus Albinus, but the referent was decidedly not a book. And I did recognize the diagram drawn painstakingly on one verso page.

He had summoned something he called White Charles—presumably because he was using Carolus Albinus as his principal text, which ought to mean I could use my own knowledge of Carolus Albinus at least to make a guess at what he had been trying to do and what that white scuttling thing was.

So. He had summoned something, following—or improvising on—the rites of Carolus Albinus. Albinus had been a necromancer who dabbled in alchemy; White Charles was probably a revenant of some kind. The passage about the Hand of Glory suggested several further hypotheses; I was selfishly, squeamishly grateful that he had not discussed *that* matter in any greater detail. He had wanted power, no doubt, imagining it was something one could acquire like a new umbrella.

Whatever he had summoned, its actions indicated clearly that it had self-volition, unlike what very little I knew of golems. It had preserved itself from the fire, stowed away with the books—*its* books? I wondered. Did it know that those particular books were relevant to its existence, or was it mere coincidence? On reaching the museum, it had acted to preserve itself again, scavenged paper, made a nest. It had not, so far as I knew, harmed anyone, although it had greatly perturbed Fiske and Hobden—and Mingus—and had scared the lights and liver out of me. I certainly did not like the idea of a necromantic spider scuttling around the museum, but I could not immediately see any way of either catching or destroying it, and I quailed from the thought of explaining my theory to Dr. Starkweather—or even Mr. Lucent.

I would watch, I told myself. Probably before long, the thing would die or de-animate or whatever the correct term was, and it would not be necessary to take any action at all.

But over the next week, it became apparent that if I had decided to watch White Charles, White Charles had also decided to watch me. Any time I was in the museum after dark, the scuttling dogged my footsteps, and I could sit in my office and track the thing's loathsome progress from wall to ceiling and back to wall. The plaster under the mail room stairs had been patched, but that clearly hadn't caused White Charles more than a momentary inconvenience.

It unnerved me, but it still was not doing any harm, and surely it would disintegrate soon. Surely I would not have to . . . to hunt it down, or any of the other melodramatic imaginings that plagued me when I tried to sleep. I wanted desperately to avoid seeing it again, and most especially to avoid seeing it more clearly. This way, at least I could *pretend* I believed it was some sort of albino spider.

I was very carefully not thinking about Hands of Glory.

It was a Wednesday night when I finally finished my article for *American Antiquities*. I tidied the manuscript into an envelope and started for the mailroom to leave it in the box for Miss Rivers the typist, but as I turned into the hallway leading to the mail room, I stopped so abruptly I nearly stumbled over my own feet. There was someone standing in the middle of the hall, a strange slouched figure who was certainly neither Hobden nor Fiske.

I had thought I was the only person left in the building save the watchmen. "Wh-who's there?" I said, my voice wobbling and squeaking embarrassingly, and groped toward the light switch.

"*Noli facere.*"

It was not a human voice; it crackled and shirred like paper. And it spoke in Latin. I think I knew then, although I did not want to.

"Who are you? How did you get in here?"

"*In a box,*" it said, in Latin. It understood English, even if it would not, or could not, speak it. "*Full of smoke and straw and lies.*" It took a step toward me, rustling and crackling. I took a step back.

"What are you?" I said, although I did not expect an answer. I only wanted to distract it while I gathered myself to run for the front entrance and Fiske and Hobden.

But even as I began to turn, shifting my weight, it said, "*I am the ghost of a Hand of Glory.*" This time I did fall, sprawling my full ungainly length on the marble; before I could pick myself up, before I could even roll over, it was on top of me, paper scratching and scuffling, pinning me flat, holding my wrists in the small of my back. It should not have been able to hold me—even at the time I knew that, but I could not move, could not free myself.

"*He called me* White Charles," it said, the English words gratingly incongruous, and though it spoke in my ear, there was no breath, only the rustling and sighing of paper. "*But he did not know me to name me truly. You do.*"

"No, I don't!" I said vehemently.

"*You lie,*" it said, and I shuddered and cringed into the floor, because it should not have known that, no matter how closely it had observed me.

And what served it for eyes? Had it fashioned those out of paper, too?

"What do you want?" I asked.

It pressed even closer. I had often wondered morbidly what it would be like to be buried under one of the teetering stacks of paper that rose in my office like the topless towers of Ilium; now I knew that I did not want to know. It said, in the soft susurration of paper, "*I want freedom.*"

I tried to scream, but there was paper blocking my mouth. I heaved desperately against the—truly, almost negligible—weight on my back, bucking like a wild horse in a dime novel. I could not dislodge it; it seemed to have molded itself to me and merely waited until I was lying still again.

"*It must be you,*" it said. "*No one else knows what I am.*"

No one else was a threat to it, it meant, but dear God, neither was I! I had no idea how to banish it or to bind it—I did not even know how that foolish antiquarian had managed to summon it. Carolus Albinus alone could never have given him the idea of making a golem from a Hand of Glory, and I could not begin to imagine what mishmash of experiment and tradition and insanity he must ultimately have used.

The paper crinkled as the thing settled lower. I strained away from the paper covering my mouth and now also my nose, and realized that I did know one thing. The antiquarian had tried to fight his creature by burning his books; he had failed, but he had hurt it. It had taken White Charles several weeks in the museum to reach the point where it could be a danger to anyone. Moreover, it had stayed with the books when that was surely the most inconvenient and dangerous course of action. And although it said he had not known it, perhaps there was nevertheless a reason he had called it White Charles.

It was the ghost of a Hand of Glory, it said, yet it clothed itself first in paper.

Perhaps it was merely panic and lack of oxygen that made me so certain I was correct, but I twisted my head, freeing my mouth, and said, "White Charles," as loudly and clearly as I could. I felt the thing flinch.

"That *is* your name," I said. "Your name and your nature, and you cannot escape it."

Its hold on me loosened; I lunged free, crawled a few awkward paces, then got my feet under me and ran. I did not look back. The single sheets of paper that flew around me and slid under my feet were evidence enough. I had hurt it; worse than that, I had guessed its secret. It would not confront me directly again if it could help it.

I was not foolish enough to believe that that meant I was safe.

In the front entrance, behind the long curving counter that separated the coat check from the rotunda with its Foucault's Pendulum ceaselessly swinging, Mr. Fiske and Mr. Hobden came to their feet in alarm as I burst through the doors.

"I need your help," I said between heaving, panting breaths.

"All right, sir," said one, after exchanging an unfathomable look with the other. "What is it you need?"

"The furnace is going, isn't it?"

A stupid question, but they took it in good part. "Yes, sir," one of them said, taking a step forward. "First of October, just like clockwork. Takes a powerful amount of heating, the museum does."

"And you have the, er, the keys? To the boiler room?"

"I do."

"Then please, if you'd, er . . . That is, there's something I need to burn."

"All right," he said equitably, as if he had received stranger requests. Given how long the two of them had worked for the museum, I supposed it was possible that he had.

"What is it you're wanting to burn, Mr. Booth?" said the other, and I was appalled by my own inability to remember which of them was Fiske and which was Hobden.

"Ah," I said. "As to that, I, um . . . "

"Fiske, sir," he said, without any trace of surprise or resentment. I wondered in miserable distracted panic how many times he had faced that blank look from men who saw him every day.

"Fiske, yes. I, er, I'm going to need your help. I need to get into Dr. Starkweather's office."

"Oh," said Fiske. "Oh dear."

Most of the books from Miss Parrington's crate were readily accessible to me. The commonplace book was still in my office; the others were languishing in the communal office of the junior archivists. But the valuable one, Carolus Albinus' *De Spiritu et Morte*, Prague 1588, was immured in Dr. Starkweather's office against the alleged depredations of Mr. Browne and the Department of Restoration and Repairs.

Mr. Fiske had the key to Dr. Starkweather's office, of course, but he balked at letting me in to appropriate something I had already confessed I intended to burn. His position was entirely reasonable and understandable, and it made me so frustrated that I wanted to sit down and howl at the ceiling. Finally, in desperation, I said, "This will get rid of the, er, the rats that aren't rats."

Fiske's eyebrows rose. But he said, "Well, nothing else has, true enough. All right. But when he asks, I don't know anything about it."

"Absolutely. I'll tell him I picked the lock."

"*Can* you?"

"No, but I doubt Dr. Starkweather will, er, ask for a demonstration."

"Fair enough," Fiske said, and he escorted me—and my increasingly unwieldy stack of books—to Dr. Starkweather's office. It took me only a moment to find the *De Spiritu et Morte*, for unlike my own, Dr. Starkweather's office was immaculately tidy and oppressively well-organized. Fiske watched from the doorway, and he locked the door again when I came out.

"That it?" he said.

"Yes. This is all of them." I thought it likely that the only book it was necessary to destroy was the *De Spiritu et Morte*, but I was not prepared to gamble.

Hobden was waiting in the doorway of the boiler room, and he was not alone. For a moment, in bad light and panic, I thought the other person was White Charles, but then he shifted a little, and I realized it was Achitophel Bates, the colored man who maintained the boilers and other machinery of the museum's infrastructure. I had thought—assumed—hoped—that he had already gone home.

"Good evening, Mr. Booth," he said. He was Southern by birth, and spoke with a slow unhurriable dignity even to Dr. Starkweather.

"Er . . . good evening. I . . . that is . . . " I looked at Hobden, who merely shook his head.

"Mr. Hobden says you're wanting to burn some books." Achitophel Bates was a tall, thin man, as tall as I, and when he looked into my eyes, he did not have to crane to do so. "Seems like a funny thing for an archivist like yourself to want, Mr. Booth."

I was unaccustomed to have anyone identify my profession correctly, much less a colored mechanic, and my surprise must have shown, for he said, "Not all colored men are ignoramuses, Mr. Booth. Some of us can even read."

"I . . . I didn't mean . . . " But I could not take back words I had not said, words I would never have said aloud.

Achitophel Bates waved the matter aside with one long hand. "But tell me, why are you burning books at this time of night?"

I did think of lying, but it was hopeless. Even if I had had any gift for deception, I had no story I could tell. I had nothing but the truth, and so that was what I told Achitophel Bates and the listening Hobden and Fiske. Achitophel Bates' eyebrows climbed higher and higher as I spoke, and when I had finished—or, at least, had run out of words—there was a long silence. In it I could see Achitophel Bates trying to decide if this was some sort of elaborate and cruel hoax. Certainly, it was a more plausible explanation than my lame and faltering truth.

"You remember the trouble we had with Mingus," said Hobden or Fiske.

"I do," said Achitophel Bates, and he looked thoughtfully from me to the watchmen and back again. "You think this is part of that same trouble, Hob?"

"Mr. Booth thinks so," said the watchman, and therefore he was Hobden and surely I could remember that if I tried. "And he's a learned man."

Achitophel Bates snorted. "*Learned* men. Haven't you been working here long enough to know about *learned* men, Hob?"

"Mr. Booth ain't like Dr. Starkweather," said Fiske mildly. "Or like that crazy man—what was his name?—who came down here and tried to get you to sabotage the boilers."

"Mr. Clarence Clyde Blessington," Achitophel Bates said, rolling the name out with a certain degree of relish.

"Oh dear," I said involuntarily. "Mr. Blessington is, er . . . "

"A committed Marxist and a card-carrying member of the Communist Party," Achitophel Bates finished. "Yes, I know. He told me. He showed me the card, even, when he was trying to persuade me that he knew what being oppressed by the bourgeoisie was like better than I did. Tell you the truth, I prefer Mr. Vanderhoef. He won't admit I exist, but at least he doesn't try to *improve* me." His sigh was a mixture of exasperation and contempt. "So just because he's a learned man, Fiske, doesn't mean a goddamn thing."

"I . . . I wouldn't . . . " But what was it, exactly, that I would not do? I settled on, "I wouldn't tell a lie like that," even though that was not, exactly, the point at issue.

"I admit," said Achitophel Bates, "that I would expect a liar to have a better story—and to tell it better, too. And I *do* remember the trouble you had with your dog, Hob, and that's not behavior I've ever seen out of a ratter. So, all right. Let's say it's true. Let's say there's some sort of monster wandering around the museum. I still don't see why you need to burn those books."

"I told you," I said despairingly. Had he not understood? "It's the only way I can think of to destroy it."

"And destroying it has to be the answer?"

"It tried to kill me!"

"Well, what choice did it have?" Achitophel Bates said reasonably, and I stared at him, abruptly and utterly bereft of words. "It doesn't want to be your slave."

"I don't want—"

"I know. And I believe you. For one thing, I figure if that's what you wanted, you could manage it for yourself, you being a learned man and all." And I winced at the derision in his voice. "But how is White Charles supposed to know that?"

And when I floundered, he pressed his point: "You'll forgive me if I have some sympathy for a slave who wants to be free."

He was not old enough to have been a slave—but of course, I realized, flushing hot with my own failure to think the matter through, his parents would have been.

"I . . . I don't want to enslave anyone. But I also don't want to be killed so that White Charles can be free of the slavery I'm not trying to . . . that is . . ." I became hopelessly muddled in my own syntax and fell silent.

"That's a reasonable position," Achitophel Bates said, so gravely that I suspected he was mocking me. "So what you need isn't to burn it. You need to talk to it."

"You, er, you are assuming that it is an entity with whom one can have a reasoned conversation."

"*You* said it had self-volition. And that it spoke to you. So what other conclusion should I draw?"

"And if you're wrong?" I said and hated how near to sullen I sounded.

"Then I'll throw the damn books in the furnace myself. But I'm not wrong. The only question is, how do you convince it to talk to you?"

"*It is not necessary,*" said a new voice, and even if it had not spoken in Latin, I would have known it to be White Charles, for it was a *new* voice in the most fundamental sense of the word, harsh and dull and not in the slightest human. It had spoken from inside the boiler room; Achitophel Bates turned and pushed the door all the way open and I saw why.

White Charles had abandoned its first body and built itself a second one out of newspaper and scrap lumber and an assortment of Achitophel Bates' tools. Where I had gathered only impressions of that first body, I saw this one all too clearly, slumped and strange, as if it could not quite remember what a human body felt like. Its hands were enormous, with screwdrivers and socket wrenches for fingers, its head no more than a suggestion, a lump between the hulking shoulders.

I thought, distantly and quite calmly, that if it did intend evil, we were all doomed.

But, "Audivi," it said. *I heard. "You do not wish to command me?"*

"No," I said. And then I realized that by speaking in English, the language in which White Charles had been given the name it hated, I was belying myself. I groped after my Latin; I read it fluently, but had not had to attempt composition since I graduated from Brockstone School. "I do not," I said finally, haltingly— although at least in these circumstances I had an excuse for my habitual hesitations and stammers. "I want no one to be hurt." Clumsy, but my meaning should be clear.

There was a silence long enough that I began to believe that self-assessment had been rankest hubris, but then White Charles said, "*I do not want to hurt.*"

I thought, suddenly and painfully, of the creature in Mary Shelley's novel, which had not done evil until it was taught that evil was all it could expect, and which had yet been so horrible of aspect and origin that it was never offered anything else. Certainly, White Charles was horrible—*the ghost of a Hand of Glory*—but that horribleness was not the fault of the intelligence which animated its scavenged bodies. Like Frankenstein's creature, it had not asked for the parody of life it had been given, and although, whatever my sins, I was not Victor Frankenstein, I had an obligation not to perpetuate evil for its own sake.

"What do you want?" I asked it, as I had asked it before, but this time I asked in awkward Latin, and this time White Charles stood and answered me, if not face to face—for indeed it did not exactly have a face—openly. "*I want freedom.*" It made a strange gesture with the massive armatures of its hands and said, "*I want freedom from this.*" *Iste.* This itself, and very emphatically.

"The body?" I said, guessing both at its meaning and at the right word.

"*It is not correct,*" said White Charles.

"I don't understand."

"*That a ghost of a Hand of Glory should exist. It is not correct. It is not right. I do not want to be this thing.*"

"What is it saying?" Achitophel Bates said in an undertone.

"It says it wants to be free of being what it is," I said, which was a syntactic nightmare but—I thought—substantially accurate.

"It wants you to kill it? That's awfully convenient."

The irony and skepticism in his voice made me flinch, but I swallowed hard and said, "It understands English. If I were lying, it would know." And I looked, rather desperately, to White Charles.

"*Verax,*" it said. And then slowly, and as if it were actually painful to it, "*Truthful.*"

"But how can you want that?" Achitophel Bates demanded, almost angrily. "How can you want to die?"

"*I was not meant to live,*" White Charles said in Latin, and I translated. "*I am not a living thing enslaved, but a dead thing . . .*" Another of its strange gestures, which I thought perhaps meant it could not find a word to express its meaning. "*A dead thing called into life to be a slave. It is not the same.*"

"Frankenstein's creature was a new life created out of death," I said, half to myself, "but that's a poet's conceit."

"*Sum mors vetus,*" said White Charles. *I am old death.* "*I am death that was never alive.*"

"The ghost of a Hand of Glory," I said. "Not even the ghost of the man whose hand was cut off."

"*You understand,*" said White Charles.

"The ghost of a book," I said, and only then realized that I was still carrying the entire unwieldy stack of books from Miss Parrington's crate.

"So that means we're burning the books after all?" Fiske said doubtfully.

"No," I said, purely on instinct, and was echoed by White Charles' clamorous voice. There was silence for a moment, as Fiske and Hobden carefully did not ask the next obvious question, and Achitophel Bates stood with his arms folded, waiting to see what I would do.

"He brought you out of the book," I said, thinking of that paper body, of the name the creature bore and hated. Then I remembered something else and fell into English because I could not think of the Latin words quickly enough. "No. He called you out of the book. Called you and bound you and feared you so greatly that no binding could ever be enough."

"*He bound me to murder at his command,*" said White Charles, "*and he was not wrong to fear what I would do if the binding failed.*"

I did not, I decided, want to know anything more about the antiquarian or his death. I found my Latin again and said, "*If you were called out of the book, you must go back into the book.*"

White Charles said again, "*You understand,*" and although its voice was not expressive, I thought the emotion in it was relief.

Achitophel Bates was still angry, although I could not tell whether his anger was directed at me or at White Charles or at something else entirely. But he came with us to the rotunda, as did Fiske and Hobden, and watched disapprovingly as I opened the antiquarian's books and used them to lay out a rough circle, with the Carolus Albinus in the center. White Charles also watched, its low-slung head turning minutely to follow my progress.

My circle was somewhat cramped because of the Foucault's pendulum, but this was the largest open space in the museum that did not also contain a host of valuable objects. It would have to do.

Abruptly, Achitophel Bates blocked my path. "Do you know what you're doing?"

"More or less," I said. "Education is, er, not without value."

"I never said it was. But my experience has been that the *value* is in the man, not in what he knows."

I was assailed by examples confirming his contention. Learned men—learned persons, I corrected myself, thinking of my colleague Miss Coburn—were just as prone to be selfish, short-sighted, and stupid as anyone else. Or even more so, as the evidence of White Charles itself suggested. It took a learned man to make such a terrible and complicated mistake.

" . . . I do know what I'm doing. And I, er . . . that is, it's the right thing to do."

"*I want freedom*," White Charles said thunderously from the other side of the circle, and Achitophel Bates raised his hands in a gesture of surrender.

"That word it keeps using. *Libertas*. Is that liberty?"

"Yes."

"All right," said Achitophel Bates. "I guess from where he's standing, liberty and death are the same thing. Not like Patrick Henry."

"It, er, *is* dead. The state it's in . . . there isn't a word for it, but it isn't alive. 'Awake' is closer. Maybe."

Achitophel Bates was frowning, but it seemed more concentration than anger. "Well, I can't argue a creature has free will and then argue it can't choose for itself. As long as you're sure what you're doing is going to do what it wants."

"As sure as I can be," I said.

He looked at me searchingly, but seemed to accept that I was telling the truth. "All right," he said and stepped aside.

I picked up the de Winter and closed it to create a door in the circle and said in Latin, "Step inside."

White Charles did not hesitate. Its groaning, grinding body shambled past me to stand over the book in the center of the circle. I stepped into the circle myself, then opened the de Winter again and put it back in its place. I knelt in front of White Charles and opened the Albinus at random. It fell open, as books will, to a page that had been often consulted, adorned in this instance with a Vermeulen woodcut of a grave-robber—not inappropriate in a ghoulish Sortes Vergilianae fashion. I reminded myself not to wonder how the antiquarian had come by his materials.

I looked up at White Charles. It was still horrific in aspect, a crude approximation of the human form built by something that did not wish to be human, but I was no longer frightened of it. Achitophel Bates was right. When given the chance, it did not choose evil.

The longest part of my preparations had been working out the Latin; while awkwardness did not matter, imprecision might matter a great deal, and the consequences of using the wrong word could be rather worse than fatal. My words were inelegant, but I knew their meaning was correct.

"You were called from this book," I said in simple, careful Latin, "and now I call you back to it. Relinquish this unnatural existence. Rest." And, although even now I cringed from touching the creature, I reached out and guided one of its screwdriver-fingers to touch the page.

Around the circle, one by one, the books snapped shut.

The edifice that was White Charles was perfectly still for a moment; I saw—or thought I saw—something depart from it, and it went from being a constructed body to being simply an amalgamation of metal and wood. It swayed and sagged, and at the same time I realized what was going to happen, the entire thing came down on my head.

I regained consciousness on the sofa in the Curators' Lounge with the doubled bulldog visages of Hobden and Fiske staring down at me.

"You all right there, Mr. Booth?" said one. And I still could not tell one from the other.

"I, er . . . did it work?"

"As best any of us can tell," said the other.

Everything hurt. My right wrist was made of broken glass. My head was pounding; I felt that if I could observe it from the outside, I would see my temples pulsing like the gills of a fish. "Oh God, the books!"

I started to get up, but sagged and failed halfway.

"D'you reckon you ought to have a doctor, Mr. Booth? You've got a lump on your forehead like a goose-egg, and you're not a good color."

"I'm never a good color," I said. "But we can't leave the books in the rotunda—not to mention the, er, the tools and whatnot. It must be nearly dawn."

"Just past it," said one of them. "But don't worry. We took care of that part. Although Bates said he'd have a word with you later about his tools."

"I put the books back where you found them," said the other, who therefore had to be Fiske. "Including the fancy one in His Nibs' office. I may have got some of the others wrong."

"It doesn't matter," I said. I could not bear it any longer; I reached out with my left hand, caught the material of his sleeve. "Are you Fiske?"

"Yessir," he said, though he and Hobden exchanged alarmed glances.

I squinted to focus, first on his face, then on Hobden's. They were not identical lead soldiers, after all; they were men. And when finally, reluctantly, I met their eyes, first one and then the other, both frowning and worried, at last I saw. Fiske's eyes were brown. Hobden's eyes were blue. And around those eyes, dark and pale, their faces resolved. Nothing changed, for indeed there was nothing in them that needed changing, but I saw them.

But I looked away quickly, before they could see me in return.

Sarah Monette *grew up in Oak Ridge, Tennessee, one of the three secret cities of the Manhattan Project, and now lives in a 104-year-old house in the Upper Midwest with a great many books, four cats, and one husband. Her Ph.D. diploma (English Literature, 2004) hangs in the kitchen. Her first four novels were published by Ace Books. Her short stories have appeared in* Strange Horizons, Weird Tales, *and* Lady Churchill's Rosebud Wristlet, *among other venues, and have been reprinted in several "year's best" anthologies; a short story collection,* The Bone Key, *was published in 2007. She has written one novel (*A Companion to Wolves, *2007) and three short stories with Elizabeth Bear, and hopes to write more. Her next novel,* The Goblin Emperor, *will be published under the name Katherine Addison. Visit Monette online at www.sarahmonette.com.*

The narrator of "White Charles," Kyle Murchison Booth, appears in a number of "necromantic mystery" stories by Sarah Monette—ten of which are collected in *The Bone Key*. As the author wrote in her introduction to the book, the "more I read [M.R.] James and [H.P.] Lovecraft, the more I found myself wanting to take their stories apart and put them back together with a fifth gear, as it were: the psychological and psychosexual focus of that other James. *The Turn of the Screw* is, after all, also a magnificent work of horror." I, for one, am glad she did and rejoice to again encounter the "neurotic, erudite, insomniac" museum archivist who inadvertently became a magnet for the supernatural.

EVERYTHING DIES, BABY

NADIA BULKIN

It was the middle of a high-wind, full-sun summer Sunday when the Wagners heard a big bang from the backyard and looked out the kitchen window to see a dead man. He was in a closed and broken oak coffin, a lot better looking than Joe's had been, and one foot with a black shoe was kicking out of the bottom end. At first Beth stalled, just like her black Camaro had a habit of doing on the way to work, but then the baby pulled on her hair to kick start her and she went outside with a rolling pin.

Beth circled the smoking, broken coffin in the rising dust of their dry backyard. The lock had broken off. She would have run to get a tarp and call the police if she hadn't heard a faint human moan coming from inside.

She leaned down closer and heard it again: a long and muffled "oh." Boys from the high school, she concluded. Their fathers never gave them enough work. She didn't know why those cow-tippers chose this house, given she was no waitress at Chickpea, but she'd stopped wondering why things happened since Joe died.

"Yeah, have a good time in there, you little freak," she said.

Beth and the baby stayed away from the kitchen until dinnertime. Then the evening news from Omaha switched from coverage of a plane crash near the Sandhills to pale and sickly complaining about drug prices, the baby pinched her nose and whined for food, and Beth went to reheat chicken from the night before. While she waited she looked out the window. There was only a half-moon, but she thought she saw the coffin lid thrown open. Good, she thought, they've gone.

Except someone then knocked at the door. All rational thoughts fell out of Beth's head and she stood there in the kitchen with her back to the noise, trying to breathe, until the baby shouted, "Mommy! There's somebody!"

*Some*body. A no-name. A stranger, a vagrant, a criminal. A convict from the penitentiary down the road. She grabbed her rolling pin and pulled the door open with a hard twist and a snarl—but on the other side was a much less imposing creature. A slight man in a gray suit stood on her stoop under the flickering porch light, swarmed by moths. He looked sick and powdered and foreign. Beth clenched the rolling pin.

"Yes?"

"Hello," he said, but it was barely recognizable as a human voice. He cleared his throat and tried again. "Hello." That time it came out better. "Can I use your phone?"

Beth narrowed her eyes. "Why?"

"Because . . . I'm . . . trying to figure out how I got here." The stranger scratched at the suit like it itched, like it wasn't his. "I'm sorry, I know this must seem strange to you. I'm, uh . . . I'm unarmed."

Joe had said something very similar when he first met her. She was stranded in her Camaro as usual and when he stopped his jeep behind her she immediately rolled up her windows. "Miss, I'm unarmed!" Joe had shouted from the other side of the glass, waving his empty hands. Just as she had then, Beth opened the door another few inches. Silently, she let the stranger in.

He smelled musty, like an unclean lab, and dragged himself down the hallway with stiff jerks that looked painful. When Beth handed him the phone he nearly dropped it, and after he dragged himself to the kitchen for privacy he could not seem to make his fingers work with the buttons. He kept muttering. He kept starting over.

The baby looked at her mother as if she'd let in a coyote.

"He just needs to use the phone, Janelle."

In a minute the man came back into the living room, holding the phone in his hand like a dead raccoon. "My brother didn't answer," he muttered, "and my mother hung up on me." He wheezed for a while in contemplation and then looked at Beth. "Where are we?"

"Bermuda," said the baby. The man looked shocked. His bloodshot eyes swung back to Beth for confirmation. "In McKinley County, Nebraska," the baby finished, resting her plump chin on her plump fist and raising her eyebrows at the stranger. "In America," she added, when his eyes didn't get any calmer.

"Where did you think you were?" Beth asked.

"I live in Denver."

"How did you get here?"

"I don't know."

Paranoia climbed up her spine, demanding she expel this stranger from her territory, but he looked like such a deer in headlights. She'd run over her share of those—her dodgy Camaro liked the taste of blood. He had their gentle brown eyes, soft as a newborn's. People didn't have eyes like that these days. People didn't knock on strangers' doors. Beth chewed her nail. If she shooed him away he'd either knock on McCormick's door and get his head shot through, or knock on the Samsons' door and get arrested—and by the looks of him the cops would assume he was either a terrorist or a mobster without bothering to notice what a deer in headlights he was. No, she was going to save this one.

"Well, maybe you'll remember later," said Beth, taking her thumb out from between her lips. The microwave started beeping. "We were just gonna have dinner, do you want some?"

The man looked even more bewildered. "You're very kind, Mrs. . . . "

"Beth. Wagner."

"My name is Hamzah al-Faraj."

Beth managed a smile.

Weeds with tender white and yellow flowers curled up and over the coffin as if to bind it to the earth. For years this was a yard nothing grew in, but all at once insects with metallic exoskeletons were walking floral vines like tight rope; all of a sudden, the soil was moist. Eventually a green tide would turn the broken coffin into a hill.

On his first day with the Wagners, Hamzah spent hours extracting the splinters he got pounding his way out of the coffin. He was in a hurry to forget it. Waking up inside that tiny dark death trap with the worst body ache of his life hadn't been pleasant, and besides, all he really wanted to do at first was eat. Even the stuff he didn't like, even the stuff he knew was unholy. He took out goods the Wagners had forgotten they had: jars of fermenting preservatives, take-out from chain restaurants that had closed and moved away, cookies in aluminum foil from many Christmases past, vegetables growing colonies in the bottom drawer. He ate it all, expiration date be damned. He never got sick, so he ate more, and his dead exterior sloughed off like snakeskin. The ache faded. He ran laps. Bermuda was a strange place to discover *joie de vivre*.

And because of this he did wonder if the baby was onto something when she asked him how dying was. The neighbors were not angelic, but sometimes at dusk rings of light did crown them.

"I think you're our present," said Janelle. She was sitting on Beth's lap and staring at Hamzah with the eyes of an old judge in the rich dark quiet of the night. "To make up for Daddy. Mommy, you remember, like when you took the broken toaster back to the store and came back with a new one."

Later, on the staircase, Beth apologized to Hamzah for Janelle's presumptuousness. She also wanted to ask him why he wasn't trying to hitch a ride back to Denver, but she was afraid of giving him ideas. She went to sleep holding her breath, waiting for the big wind to knock down their house of cards.

And as the living slept, voices gathered on the roof. Like squirrels they pawed at the shingles and scrambled from corner to corner, hissing to each other and searching the roof for weak spots. They pressed their proto-lips against the asphalt rectangles and whispered, "He belongs to us!" Beth mistook them for the radio, and when she heard their demands, she just hit the buttons next to her bed. At last one voice fell through a tiny hole in the roof onto the cold pillow next to hers, crying, "Give him back!" so up close and personal that Beth did sit up and shout into the dark: "Joe!"

But it was not Joe who'd come back, and this she remembered in the morning when she saw Hamzah in the kitchen, pouring juice for Janelle. This she remembered every time she heard her gap-toothed baby laugh. Sometimes she did need to put her hands on the man's face to realize that this was not Joe—this was the deer in headlights.

"Joe," she said in the bathroom, looking up at the crack in the ceiling, "I love you. I hope you are all right with this. I hope this was your doing." She thought about what Joe said in the hospital near the end—*Be good to yourself, Beth*—and nodded bravely. "I know this was your doing. Goodbye. I love you." And then she went back out and had breakfast with Hamzah and Janelle.

It was only when Hamzah moved to the upstairs bedroom that the voices on the roof found him. Then he'd wake up tossing in the sheets, asking Beth for mosquito repellent.

Whenever anyone knocked at the door, Beth closed her eyes and felt Chinook winds rock her knees. There it was: reality, Joe's gravestone, the dentist's office, the dying Camaro, the crass combine harvester world that ripped the seeds off the stalk and left behind mannequins of straw. She could try to ignore it, yes, but it would stand out there through seasons of sleet and fire with hunched shoulders, knocking.

She had let the world take Joe. She would not knuckle under like that again, so she always made Hamzah hide upstairs before answering the door.

One Saturday it was McCormick, red and sweating with his hands on his hips and his Colt .44 Magnum dangling. "Say Beth," he said, "you heard about that plane crash in the Sandhills? The plane goin' to Milwaukee?"

She chewed her lip.

"There's this huge chunk of metal in my backyard and I can't figure out where the hell it came from. It almost looks like it came off a plane. You wanna see it?"

It was a reminder she did not need. Hamzah's mother lived in Milwaukee and Beth knew this by now. She could slam the door in McCormick's face and the backyard could consume the coffin whole but the wind was picking up. The cards were shuddering like her bones.

Hamzah found her sitting at the table. "Beth?"

"There was a plane crash east of here," Beth said. She pulled out an old newspaper, the one she'd saved. "It was going to Milwaukee. Everybody died. Including you."

He pinched his hand. It hurt; that was a good sign. "I didn't go on any plane," he murmured.

"My neighbor has something that looks like a piece of a plane in his yard, okay? You must have fallen out while it was going down!"

She'd gotten very loud by then. Beth wiped the wetness off her face and pointed at the front page.

Hamzah looked at the smoking black wreckage and the helicopters circling it like scavengers. It had been a 737 once. The cranes would come back from Canada and wonder why the hell there were human bits in their nests.

"I didn't get on any plane," he said, "and I woke up in that thing out there, remember, not some airplane seat." He cautiously put his hand on Beth's shoulder. "I wasn't on that plane. I didn't die."

Beth looked up, wiping her nose. He was trying to smile and when he squeezed her weak bones, her heartbeat slowed. His other hand folded up the newspaper and she buried that ugly air crash under the bills and credit card offers and other unwelcome guests.

But they both knew that he'd been dead. Even Janelle dropped a road-killed squirrel in their backyard, hoping to bring it back to life. It stayed dead and smashed, and in the wake of Janelle's disappointment they buried the poor thing in the moist dark soil. From its body sprouted an even denser wilderness of weeds and insect eyes.

The Wagners spent their days in the jungle they had grown and went to sleep listening to cicadae. It was just as well, even if they got eaten up by chiggers, because the ghosts were getting out of control.

They had begun by manifesting in mirrors, as well as in doorways and around corners—but then as rotating shadows only, tricks of the light. Then one night Janelle woke up in the middle of the night to see dark pillars of smog bent over her, voices begging her to "give him back to us." Janelle ran to her mother's bed, but they were only too happy to follow her there, leaving burn-marks on the carpet.

Hamzah suggested they move. He didn't say back to Denver but Beth suspected it was what he had in mind. That only made the hauntings worse: the day after he made the suggestion they started growing bodies.

It was life as a perpetual wake. They came in all forms, from all places—some old and some very young, in cotton sweats and business suits. From the ceiling and the floor they watched the living eat dinner. When their billowing faces got too close Beth would swat them away. But before they floated away they would breathe hot cobwebs down Hamzah's neck, and when they grew stubby burned hands they would press those to his skin too.

Their touch scalded, but only for a moment. Beth touched his arm when he jolted for the tenth time. "Just leave it," she murmured. "They'll go away on their own."

But they stayed, all the way through primetime television. They crowded round Hamzah and piled their hands on him, and though he shook them all off like mayflies they began to leave behind a dull ache, a stiffness.

"Are you okay?" asked Janelle. "You look sick."

Hamzah turned his head to answer her and his eyes suddenly swung up toward the ceiling, then down to the floor. He stumbled and grabbed the arms of the chair.

"Hamzah?" Beth stood up, but he could not meet her eyes. Instead he leaned his head down between his knees and squeezed his neck until something seemed to rattle his spine, making him seize up with a cry. Janelle shrieked along with him and covered her ears.

Beth tried to grab onto his limbs to steady him, but even if she put all her weight into it she could not stop the awful contortions of his face. "Hamzah, what is it? *What?*"

In a moment his body slowed down, and his facial muscles drooped. He opened his eyes, and he was the deer in headlights again—panicked and stuck. Beth gave him her sweetest smile, trying to reassure him that she was no semi-truck.

"What is it?" she asked again, not above a whisper.

"I felt my bones breaking. I smell . . . " He took a deep breath. All she smelled was the ghosts' charcoal. "Asphalt and metal. And blood. My blood. God, it's *strong*, Beth."

"What's strong?"

"The car that hit me."

Beth's jaw dropped and she took a hesitant step back, through a cloud of ghosts. "A car hit you?"

One of the ghosts put its hands over his eyes. Beth jumped at it, screaming at it to get away from him, but Hamzah had already seen the headlights of the Chrysler come charging out of downtown Denver, the first in a stream of traffic. A golden demon—an angel? Drivers had trouble at dusk. So did pedestrians. The half-light deceived them all. He shouldn't have stepped onto the street. But he didn't think the car was so close. Then all of a sudden the car was right there, up against his legs with the force of three hundred horses. His body flopping like a fish.

"Yes, and I . . . " Hamzah winced. "I didn't get up. Beth, I'm dead, I died."

Beth immediately shook her head. Her fingers kept catching in the knots in her hair. "But we knew . . . " she whispered. "We know . . . you came back, Hamzah."

He was looking at the ghosts. Some were missing noses, others eyes. Some wore dangling oxygen masks like yokes. They smoldered, he realized, because they were still in the fires of the 737. He stood up, sweeping past Beth and her protests, and started stumbling toward them. "Why are you here?" he asked.

Some of them looked away, suddenly shy, revealing bloody ears. He reached out his hand for them and they faded. "Please," he said.

Finally a few of them on the other side of the room murmured through null mouths, "Come back, passenger. Come away with us." And then the others joined, kneeling at Hamzah's feet like lepers in the rain: "You, the one who fell. The man in the cargohold. The missing."

"The cargohold," Hamzah muttered, putting his hand to his suddenly sweaty forehead. The room was swinging again—the carpet seemed miles away, and it seemed to be crawling with the bodies of the dead.

"Don't listen to them!" Beth's voice interrupted. "Hamzah, it doesn't matter! It doesn't matter what happened then! What matters is you're alive *now*!" She was fighting through the ghosts—they were getting thicker all the time. Janelle was curled up like a snail, an isolated little bundle of pink and blond lying low under the passing storm. Her mother tried shoving one of the ghosts into the television, but her hands just went right through.

"If my coffin was in the cargohold . . . " He cupped his mouth, feeling motion-sick. "I'm part of that flight."

"Come away with us . . . " the ghosts warbled, pawing at his clothes, making his knees pulse with undead pain. "We can go together. We can leave the fire together."

"No!" Beth shouted, but he could see that she was drowning. Their funereal smoke was making her eyes water. "I am not going to let you take him too!"

Hamzah outstretched his hand to her, open and empty as it had been from the very beginning. His hand shot through the ghosts and Beth grabbed hold of it. For a second she stopped screaming. He was still whole. Something was still whole.

"Let's talk," said Hamzah. "Come on."

They went to the bedroom and talked. The ghosts thought Beth was preparing to kill him, and except for a lingering old man ghost trying to hide in the grains of the wooden closet, they wanted to give them privacy.

"They're still in the fire," he whispered. "They won't leave without me. Beth, they'll never leave you two alone."

"I'll take it. What about you."

He sighed, knowing what she would say. "What about me."

"What if you came back for us?" She lifted her head and stared at him with her mouth open, as if it was what she had wanted to say all summer. He touched the corner of her mouth and her chapped lips tried to smile. "Maybe Janelle was right."

"As a present for you," said Hamzah, effortlessly returning the smile. "Right, maybe that's right. But maybe it's been long enough."

Beth covered her eyes. "But we still . . . "

"Everything dies, Beth."

She looked at him. His hands were in her hair; his eyes were bright but tired. She kissed him.

In a few hours Beth gathered the strength to go to the medicine cabinet. She passed the congregation of ghosts without word, and this time they courteously seeped out of her way. Then she returned to the bedroom and softly closed the door. Softly was the way the world would end.

By the time the man from the National Transportation Safety Bureau arrived at their rickety house on Coolidge Street, Hamzah was back in the coffin he'd come in. The yard was still blooming, and the NTSB investigator looked shocked to be wading through high grass when the house itself looked so tame. He looked back at Beth, holding out his clipboard like a wing.

"Aren't any snakes, are there?"

Beth shrugged in her bare legs. "They're probably not poisonous."

The investigator resumed goose-stepping toward the exposed coffin. "And you say it fell out of the sky the day of the crash?" She nodded. "There was something wrong with the cargo door, you see, ma'am. Caused the whole damn crash." He shook his head as Beth listened to the wind. "Must not be nice having a coffin in your backyard."

Beth shrugged. "He was good company."

The investigator laughed and Beth took a deep, lung-searing breath. She could smell fall coming from over the Rocky Mountains. Black birds like boomerangs crossed overhead, and the trees were the color of fire.

Nadia Bulkin watches Air Crash Investigation *before traveling by plane. It makes her feel better. She has a B.A. in Political Science from Barnard College and hopes to attend graduate school soon. Her stories have been published in* Strange Horizons, Fantasy Magazine, ChiZine, *and elsewhere. Her story, "Intertropical Convergence Zone," was nominated for a Shirley Jackson Award. She lives in suburban Nebraska. At 6 PM in her Nebraskan hometown it is 6 AM in her other hometown of Jakarta, Indonesia. For more about her, visit nadiabulkin. wordpress.com or intertribal.livejournal.com*

Bulkin's title is taken from Bruce Springsteen's song, "Atlantic City": "Everything dies, baby, that's a fact, but maybe everything that dies someday comes back." (It is highly doubtful the author was born when *Nebraska*, the album that tune is on, was first released—which may truly prove some things never die.) But if you think the true darkness in this surreal little tale has anything to do with a dead man coming back to life or ghosts, then you need to read it again.

BRUISE FOR BRUISE

ROBERT DAVIES

Joss Coffington came to Promise to find the girl with God on her back.

He had heard many rumors about the strange town before, and had passed along a few he had made up when he was on his sixth or seventh beer, but it wasn't until he heard that particular rumor, that of the bruised girl, that he finally took to walking. He wasn't alone on those dusty back roads, either, and most of them that crowded Joss on the road were going to see the girl, too, going to the town of Promise, where monsters were born.

Some said it was contaminated well water or rainbow glinting oils that shimmered on the creek, drowned ill spirits or chemicals that spurred the blood to strange, unseen designs. Others claimed it was unseen radiation pulsing from the new power lines that snaked across the sky, trailing alongside the highway between here and there. Still others said it was simply divine will made flesh, a harsh judgment made upon a town founded by sinners when the country was being born. Perhaps it was without any reason at all, but each passing year saw strange folk filling the small houses and narrow roads of Promise, united only by their differences, untouched by the world beyond.

The birth rate in Promise was low—snake-belly low to be precise. Whether the fault lay in the seed or in the womb, none could say; but, in those jackpot moments when life found root, the town of Promise could be sure of one thing: after nine months of morning sickness and sibilant prayer, something never seen before would be spilled screaming into the world, or silent as the case may be.

Sometimes there would be something of the mother in the child, and sometimes something of the father; there was always something of the town. Leathery wings sprouted oftentimes, as common as fingers. Fur of every hue. Horns and scales were plentiful, too. Lots of feathers and thorns and glass and steel. Beneath the apple trees and the pine, anatomy was negotiable. Anything was probable. Every now and then, though, the tired wet nurses, long inured to the strange fecundity of flesh, would whistle in awe as they lifted a newborn from the amniotic slime.

Something truly special would be seen.

The Eddington triplets were each born with an extra mouth on their foreheads; the better to sing His praises, Father Quine had said, smiling. Justice Peck arrived, took two deep breaths, and burst into silent blue flame. The great-granddaughter of Old Khoas was born flower-faced and her every breath was a yellow cloud of pollen. Jirrup the Younger emerged limbless and scaled, and like the original beast his eyes were eyes of gold. The blind watchmaker's daughter Undulia grew monstrously fat and fetid as she approached her blessed day. She spilled her blue-eyed daughter in a ruinous, thick tide. To the shock of all, this newborn daughter, grunting and wailing, then gave birth to another smaller girl the size of a fist, swollen with child. This last tiny daughter, still nameless, still shivering with the chill outside the womb, stood shakily and birthed a finger-sized son whose wormy penis dragged on the floor.

Ruth's twin brothers, Luke and Persistence, came into the world in a crimson flood, the jagged steel knives growing out of their fingers and cruelly hooked thumbs must have sorely treated their mother's insides. She had survived, though it had been doubtful considering the blood that had come that December morning, and it was this improbable survival that made her someone of consequence in the town, with handsome Father Quine singling her out as a model of right living and righteous prayer.

Ruth Mingleton, however, seemed plainer than milk when she came two years later. Excitement and congratulations for a healthy girl quickly gave way to uneasy smiles and averted eyes, until soon the townsfolk were crossing the street to avoid the Mingletons and their enigmatic child. Ruth was one of the untouched, it seemed—a curiosity in a town of curiosities.

Ruth's father was let go from the sawmill; later that week, he was let down from the wobbling rafters of their ancient barn, his pants filled and his throat maroon. Her two brothers, her mother and Ruth kept to themselves then, the pale blue curtains drawn, the doors bolted. They seldom ventured into the town save for the Sunday sermons of Father Quine, though they sat at the very back, and for the necessary staples of whisky, gossip, and salt. They helped keep the glass smith in business, so it seemed, as their windows were often shattered by stones; the perilous, unkempt lawn in front of their house came to glitter in the moonlight.

They lived like that for years until Luke and Persistence snuck away one night and got themselves hitched to the passing Carnival of Blood and Thunder, which was keen on upgrading its freak show. But too much cheap whisky, an aversion to cayenne, and too many fistfights over the insatiable and mercurial Lobster Girl finally got them fired on the outskirts of Biloxi in a thunderstorm, and they came back to the town, heartbroken, penniless, and sullen as ever.

And so the story has it that it came in the darkest part of night, with a hammer and with nails and with hands that wielded them with a feral mastery. Down through the ceiling, or up through the floor, one could not rightly say. It came upon Ruth on the eve of her thirteenth birthday and made her anew. It found the bruises beneath her skin and made of them a poetry. It found the songs in her bones and made them break. It found the angel she saw on the tain and ruined its pale and perfect skin.

Ruth Mingleton didn't even cry.

She awoke to find bluish yellow smears spread across her skin—an image of a thorn on her cheek, a suggestion of velvet wings on her stomach, a golden hint of the lip-stained Grail on her inner thigh. The bones beneath her skin only accentuated the designs: her breathing would give flight to a seabird on her right shoulder; the shift of her jaw would rock the ark on her throat.

It was Ruth's mother who brought the bruises to the attention of Father Quine.

Dressed in the perfect fuligin of faith, Meticulous Quine sported great, snowy wings, just like ancient Uriel of the Scarred Palms. His black eyes glinted, and his voice was honey. He saw something in the bruises that most others did not. Ruth's mother saw it, too. They prayed together.

The townsfolk quickly took interest in Ruth then, began to murmur that she had finally revealed the gift of her birth. Of course, many claimed they had known all along that Ruth was special, revealing the hidden bits of wisdom they had hoarded for years, awaiting this day of revelation. Others, mostly those left-handed it must be said, still expressed doubt, but they were quickly silenced by the knowing frowns of Father Quine or the squinting glare of Ruth's mother. Ruth's brothers would shake their glinting fingers and make them ring.

The excitement in the town waned rather quickly, what with the coming of the harvest and the promise of another deep, implacable winter.

It was then that the breathtaking bruise of the thrice-nailed Christ across her back appeared. While the lesser transgressions on Ruth's arms and legs quickly healed, the Christ refused to fade. Indeed, He seemed to gain solidity with every passing day, and the stony dust of Golgotha circling her waist sprouted pale yellow flowers that glistened when she sweat.

The townsfolk crowded the narrow lane to the Mingleton's house from sunrise to dark, pleading for a chance to see, perhaps to touch, whispering and pointing out those that had thrown stones or foolishly spoken ill words before.

The pilgrims came soon after.

They came first from the outlying tobacco farms and cornfields, and then neighboring towns and fishing villages, and then from those distant states where truth can be a crime. Some carried the heavy riches they had acquired, eager to lay them before Ruth; others came with only scraps of cloth wrapping their bloody feet and foreign tongues in their mouths. One and all they came for the daughter of bruises and the stories on her skin.

Father Quine and the town elders ordered a scaffold and stage of rough-hewn wood to be erected on the Common, on the very spot where a meteorite fell in the time before trees. Blood-red tents quickly sprung up around the scaffold, followed by hawkers' tables and kiosks and craft-laden blankets until the entire common resembled a harvest fair. Meaty smoke rose from hissing, snapping cooking fires. Brightly colored pennons snapped. They built the ticket booth on the distant edge of the Common. To lessen the taint of commerce around such a profound miracle, Father Quine had said. Great lengths of yellow rope were strung up to form an orderly queue, snaking back and forth across the trampled grass.

Luke and Persistence collected the golden tickets at the foot of the stairs at the side of the stage, spearing them with their jagged fingers. At the ticket booth, Ruth's mother counted the money, each coin like a rosary bead in her calloused hands. Father Quine passed through the crowds nibbling on sugared insects, looking about with unconcealed pride, his wings stirring the warm, summer air.

Ruth sat on a stool at the center of the stage, a flask of warm water by her feet. She wore denim shorts and a thin white shirt that barely covered her tiny breasts. It was ripped open in the back, the better to reveal the bruised face and chest of the crucified Christ.

Nobody ever asked, but the bruises did hurt her. Each new one ached to the very heart of the bone. Sometimes Ruth awoke with a cracked rib, her breath piercing like a knife. Sometimes she awoke only to faint away from the nauseous pain writhing beneath her skin. Still, she would sit patiently on her stool as the sunburned pilgrims bought their tickets, formed a line, and ascended the stairs to examine her flesh. Lesser, smaller bruises appeared daily on her wrists and throat, her feet and her belly, her breasts, but the pilgrims hardly noticed these scenes from forgotten pages of the Bible and those other books.

They had come only for the Christ.

At the end of the day, Ruth's mother would climb the stairs and lead her back home, Luke and Persistence following a few steps back. Ruth always trembled as she walked, her legs grown stiff, her stomach empty. A few of the more pious pilgrims would trail behind the Mingletons and gather in small groups outside their house; some took to picking up the shards of glass that still littered the lawn, placing them on the tongue and swallowing them. But all the curtains were drawn tight, and in time the darkness and the silence would urge the pilgrims to move on.

Her mother examined Ruth every evening, her calloused hands flexing as she traced the fading lines of bruises and injured flesh. She marked which bruises were fading, and which were still visible. When she was done, truly done, she sent Ruth to stumble onto her mattress. Ruth slept, but she never dreamed.

After two weeks on the stage, Ruth hardly saw the pilgrims anymore as they passed before her. The pain of her new bruises and splintered bone paled beneath the simple, dull ache of sitting there, pilgrim by pilgrim, hour upon hour, sunrise until sunset. The sun burned her skin. Insects bit her eyelids and buzzed in her ears. Through it all, her bruises shone with vitality, in strange, curious shapes that beguiled the eye.

So, of course, Ruth did not notice when Joss Coffington stopped before her, and she did not hear when he stifled a cry. Only after several moments did she realize he stood there at all, his shadow shielding her from the blinding sun. He did not look at her wounds; he was looking at her face, at her.

"I love you," he said. He stood there, unmoving. Ruth looked up and caught a glimpse of his face before he was ushered off the stage by the stern-faced Father Quine.

Ruth was not so complacent after that. She started to look at the pilgrims as they came to see her, looking into their faces for something, making some uncomfortable, making some regret. Father Quine suggested a hood, and her mother agreed; but a few days later a crown of thorny bruises circled Ruth's brow, with glinting red berries of blood, and the hood was forgotten and the ticket price was raised.

Joss Coffington returned, day after day, ignoring the dark looks of Father Quine and Ruth's mother, ignoring the increasing cost as they tried to dissuade him. He paid whatever they asked and climbed the stair to stand before her, shielding her from the hot sun, if only for a moment. Most days he said nothing. On others, he again professed his love for her. Sometimes he smiled, but it seemed quite difficult for him to do. He always stood until he was forced off the platform by Father Quine or one of Ruth's brothers.

So it came to pass that on one of those August days that made you curse the sun, Ruth waited on the stool, ignoring the countless pilgrims that passed by her and their pleas for healing or riches or prophecy. She was blind with agony, sweating. A large bruise on her right leg showed the epic Fall of Jericho; the whisper of angels casting down that ancient wall had nearly broken the femur in three places, so fierce was the reckoning of their angelic fury.

It was late in the day, and he had not yet come. She feared they had finally scared him off. Her mouth was dry but she did not care any longer. She almost let herself slip from the stool, let herself slip from her skin.

Father Quine's voice broke the silence, and a scuffle broke out in the line. Ruth turned to see Joss Coffington push Quine and a few pilgrims aside and dart up the stairs.

He ran to her and put his hand on her shoulder.

"You don't have to stay here," he said.

He reached down and pulled her arm, but she was immovable, inviolate in her agony. A statue would have moved more readily; but where a statue would be cool stone, she was fevered, damp flesh. She looked into his eyes.

"Go," she said. "Go, before it is too late."

Footsteps rattled the scaffold. Persistence and Luke moved forward as one. Father Quine urged them on. Persistence grabbed Joss Coffington by the collar and pulled him down, his fingers slicing into Coffington's shoulders. Luke slammed his right knee into Coffington's face with a wet crack, again and again. Persistence kicked his spine and slashed at his side. Coffington fell limp.

The crowd barely reacted. If anything, they regarded the entire event as an inconvenience, something that kept them from the momentary miracle of standing before Ruth and seeing her bruises and her pain. They had all come so far to see her. They had waited so long.

Ruth saw Joss Coffington lying on the scaffold. She sat still. Her hands opened and closed.

A silence fell on the crowd.

Ruth seemed to whisper to herself, looking down.

"What is it, child?" said Father Quine.

She whispered again.

Father Quine moved to her side, leaning down to hear.

Striking like a cobra, Ruth grabbed Father Quine's arm and he dropped to his knees. The memory of her every wound passed through her fingertips and burned into his mind. His skin grew damp and darkened with Biblical scenes. Bone snapped and feathers smoked. Reddish spittle fell from his mouth, followed by a scream. Father Quine slumped forward, his wings aflame.

Ruth stood and looked toward her brothers. "Stand back," she said, her fingertips smoldering. "I have ages within me."

Persistence and Luke stood still, shocked by her feral eyes. But their surprise gave way and as one they smiled and slowly circled her like hungry wolves. Their mother shouted from the chaotic crowd. People pushed and shoved to get out of the way, their eyes fixated on the strange tableau upon the stage. Those wise to the danger of crowds drifted away from the stage, forking their fingers and spitting twice.

The brothers lunged, but they were thrown back

Thrown back not by force, but by a look, a casual gesture. Each jerked upright, like fish upon the line, held in place by unseen chains. Dark, bruised lines slipped across their faces, across the skin of their throats; the painful lines formed angels, magi, and flibbertigibbets by the dozen. Reptilian in their speed, they shifted so quickly that it seemed the figures danced. The skin split in their wake, bleeding. The lines slowed and dissipated, leaving the brothers' sweat-sheeted skin red. Spent, they dropped to the platform, one atop the other.

Ruth's dripping hands were ruined now, tattered and charred.

She knelt beside Joss Coffington and touched his face. She listened at his mouth for breath. Her shattered fingers trailed across his chest and found no heartbeat.

She turned to face the crowd, and her eyes held only vengeance. Not the petty vengeance of rage or jealousy, but that primordial ire that ignited the stars. Ruth found her mother and pointed directly at her, freezing her in place. Ruth's gaze took in the entire crowd, each one a celebrant, each one an idolater. Ruth shouted a word heard only in the quiet days before the caul dried on the world, and she tore her throat to shreds.

Everyone in the town felt it, though none would ever agree what had happened.

Some said it was a simple feather or the passing of warm wind over a cloudy dandelion; others said it was the touch of a lover, of a mother, of a glass-eyed stranger. Some said it felt like grass growing. Others mentioned razors, warm oil, and the cracking of a knuckle. Old Khoas said it was rust, and he was right. A few said nothing at all, but it was there in their eyes. It entered them, unfurled itself, and never left.

She opened Joss Coffington's shirt and pressed her smoldering hand against his chest. The blood spilling from her mouth sizzled when it hit her fingers. She leaned against him, putting all her weight against that hand. Her shirt fell away, and her bruises were lambent.

There was that strange wind again and Ruth stood, her eyes wild.

Joss Coffington sat up and winced. He looked up and took Ruth's waiting hand.

The mark of her hand on his chest had swollen already, the skin shiny and red. What she did to the townsfolk that day, she did to him, too, only different. Everything they were, the secrets of their blood and memories, was now in him, coiled like so many serpents, all clenched at the base of his skull like a writhing fist. He was legion.

She put an arm around him and they walked off the stage and down the stairs, heedless of the crowds around them. A few of the townsfolk knelt, reaching out to touch them as they passed. One brushed a finger against the gaping wound at Coffington's side, pulling it away with awe.

They walked out of the town, and they walked until their feet bled, and then they walked until the stars filled the sky. Those that followed after Joss and Ruth lost them in the darkness in a matter of hours. None saw them after that.

Behind them, in Promise, it took several weeks for the stories and rumors to die down. The townsfolk tried to carry on as they had before, but something was amiss. Old Khoas was the first to notice, but he said nothing. The wooden platform fell during a bad nor'easter and the town was suffocated in white. The frightened elders called a meeting on the town common and patiently waited as everyone came. The blue moonlight blackening their faces, the townsfolk listened as the wingless Quine began to speak, but his words were unnecessary. It had become increasingly clear that the wet nurses had nothing to do, and most in the town were certain they never would again. Other elders took their turns to speak, but most townsfolk had stopped listening, and alone or in small groups they drifted off into the darkness, until, at long last, there was only the bruised whiteness of the empty Common beneath the cold winter moon.

Robert Davies *writes stories about voracious babies, eidolons, and exploding suns. Mimetic fiction is for wimps. Raised on a steady diet of weird paperbacks,*

Infocom games, and comic books, Rob has always wanted to be a writer. (Well, actually, he first wanted to be a dinosaur, but that didn't work out so well.) His stories have sold to Weird Tales, Interzone, Shroud Magazine, *and* Murky Depths. *His novella,* Hiram Grange and the Digital Eucharist, *was recently released. His is working on his first novel,* The Bitter Taste of the World Snake's Tail. *Rob lives in Somerville, Massachusetts, with his high school sweetheart Sara and two cats, Lilith and Tiamat. He thinks Brian Wilson is God.*

Hey, you *really* expect me to comment on this story? Okay: It's a love story. A weird love story.

RESPECTS

RAMSEY CAMPBELL

By the time Dorothy finished hobbling downstairs, somebody had rung three times and knocked several more. Charmaine Bullough and some of her children were blocking the short garden path under a nondescript November sky. "What did you see?" Charmaine demanded at once.

"Why, nothing to bother about." Dorothy had glimpsed six-year-old Brad kicking the door, but tried to believe he'd simply wanted to help his mother. "Shouldn't you be at school?" she asked him.

Brad jerked a thumb at eight-year-old J-Bu. "She's not," he shouted.

Perhaps his absent siblings were, but not barely teenage Angelina, who was brandishing a bunch of flowers. "Are those for me?" Dorothy suggested out of pleasantness rather than because it seemed remotely likely, then saw the extent of her mistake. "Sorry," she murmured.

Half a dozen bouquets and as many wreaths were tied to the lamp-standard on the corner of the main road, beyond her gate. Charmaine's scowl seemed to tug the roots of her black hair paler. "What do you mean, it's not worth bothering about?"

"I didn't realise you meant last week," Dorothy said with the kind of patience she'd had to use on children and parents too when she was teaching.

"You saw the police drive our Keanu off the road, didn't you?"

"I'm afraid I can't say I did."

At once, despite their assortment of fathers, the children resembled their mother more than ever. Their aggressive defensiveness turned resentful in a moment, accentuating their features, which were already as sharp as smashed glass. "Can't or won't?" Charmaine said.

"I only heard the crash."

Dorothy had heard the cause as well—the wild screech of tyres as the fifteen-year-old had attempted to swerve the stolen Punto into her road apparently at eighty miles an hour, only to ram a van parked opposite her house—but she didn't want to upset the children, although Brad's attention seemed to have lapsed. "Wanna wee," he announced and made to push past her, the soles of his trainers lighting up at every step.

As Dorothy raised a hand to detain him, J-Bu shook a fist that set bracelets clacking on her thin arm. "Don't you touch my brother. We can get you put in prison."

"You shouldn't just walk into someone else's house," Dorothy said and did her best to smile. "You don't want to end up—"

"Like who?" Angelina interrupted, her eyes and the studs in her nose glinting. "Like Keanu? You saying he was in your house?"

Dorothy might have. The day before the crash she'd come home to find him gazing out of her front room. He hadn't moved until she managed to fumble her key into the lock, at which point he'd let himself out of the back door. Apart from her peace of mind he'd stolen only an old handbag that contained an empty purse, and so she hadn't hurried to report him to the overworked police. If she had, might they have given him no chance to steal the car? As Dorothy refrained from saying any of this, Charmaine dragged Brad back. "Come out of there. We don't want anyone else making trouble for us."

"I'm sorry not to be more help," Dorothy felt bound to say. "I do know how you feel."

Angelina peered so closely at her that Dorothy smelled some kind of smoke on the girl's breath. "How?"

"I lost my husband just about a year ago."

"Was he as old as you?" J-Bu said.

"Even older," said Dorothy, managing to laugh.

"Then it's not the same," Angelina objected. "It was time he went."

"Old people take the money we could have," said J-Bu.

"It's ours for all the things we need," Brad said.

"Never mind that now," said Charmaine and fixed Dorothy with her scowl. "So you're not going to be a witness."

"To what, forgive me?"

"To how they killed my son. I'll be taking them to court. The social worker says I'm entitled."

"They'll have to pay for Keanu," said Brad.

Dorothy took time over drawing a breath. "I don't think I've anything to offer except sympathy."

"That won't put shoes on their feet. Come on, all of you. Let's see Keanu has some fresh flowers. He deserves the best," Charmaine added louder still.

Brad ran to the streetlamp and snatched off a bouquet. About to throw them over Dorothy's wall, he saw her watching and flung them in the road. As Angelina substituted her flowers, Dorothy seemed to hear a noise closer to the house. She might have thought a rose was scratching at the window, but the flower was inches distant. In any case, the noise had sounded muffled by the glass. She picked up a beer can and a hamburger's polystyrene shell from her garden and carried them into the house.

When she and Harry had moved in she'd been able to run through it without pausing for breath. She could easily outdistance him to the bedroom, which had been part of their fun. Now she tried not to breathe, since the flimsy shell harboured the chewed remains of its contents. She hadn't reached the kitchen when she had to gasp, but any unwelcome smell was blotted out by the scents of flowers in vases in every downstairs room.

She dumped the rubbish in the backyard bin and locked the back door. The putty was still soft around the pane Mr Thorpe had replaced. Though he'd assured her it was safe, she was testing the glass with her knuckles when something sprawled into the hall. It was the free weekly newspaper, and Keanu's death occupied the front page. **LOCAL TEENAGER DIES IN POLICE CHASE.**

She still had to decide whether to remember Harry in the paper. She took it into the dining-room, where a vaseful of chrysanthemums held up their dense yellow heads towards the false sun of a Chinese paper globe, and spread the obituary pages across the table. Keanu was in them too. Which of the remembrances were meant to be witty or even intended as a joke? "Kee brought excitement into everyone's life"? "He was a rogue like children are supposed to be"? "There wasn't a day he didn't come up with some new trick"? "He raced through life like he knew he had to take it while he could"? "Even us that was his family couldn't keep up with his speed"? Quite a few of them took it, Dorothy suspected, along with other drugs. "When he was little his feet lit up when he walked, now they do because he's God's new angel." She dabbed at her eyes, which had grown so blurred that the shadows of stalks drooping out of the vase appeared to grope at the newsprint. She could do with a walk herself.

She buttoned up her winter overcoat, which felt heavier than last year, and collected her library books from the front room. Trying to read herself to sleep only reminded her that she was alone in bed, but even downstairs she hadn't finished any of them—the deaths in the detective stories seemed insultingly trivial, and the comic novels left her cold now that she couldn't share the jokes. She lingered for a sniff at the multicoloured polyanthuses in the vase on her mother's old sideboard before loading her scruffiest handbag with the books. The sadder a bag looked, the less likely it was to be snatched.

The street was relatively quiet beneath the vague grey sky, with just a few houses pounding like nightclubs. The riots in Keanu's memory—children smashing shop windows and pelting police cars with bricks—had petered out, and in any case they hadn't started until nightfall. Most of the children weren't home from school or wherever else they were. Stringy teenagers were loitering near the house with the reinforced front door, presumably waiting for the owner of the silver Jaguar to deal with them. At the far end of the street from Dorothy's house the library was a long low blotchy concrete building, easily mistaken for a new church.

She was greeted by the clacking of computer keyboards. Some of the users had piled books on the tables, but only to hide the screens from the library staff. As she headed for the shelves Dorothy glimpsed instructions for making a bomb and caught sight of a film that might have shown an equestrian busy with the tackle of her horse if it had been wearing any. On an impulse Dorothy selected guides to various Mediterranean holiday resorts. Perhaps one or more of her widowed friends might like to join her next year. She couldn't imagine travelling by herself.

She had to slow before she reached her gate. A low glare of sunlight cast the shadow of a rosebush on the front window before being extinguished by clouds, leaving her the impression that a thin silhouette had reared up and then crouched out of sight beyond the glass. She rummaged nervously in her handbag and unlocked the door. It had moved just a few inches when it encountered an obstruction that scraped across the carpet. Someone had strewn Michaelmas daisies along the hall.

Were they from her garden? So far the vandals had left her flowers alone, no doubt from indifference. As her eyes adjusted to the dimness she saw that the plants were scattered the length of the hall, beyond which she could hear a succession of dull impacts as sluggish as a faltering heart. Water was dripping off the kitchen table from the overturned vase, where the trail of flowers ended. She flustered to the back door, but it was locked and intact, and there was no other sign of intrusion. She had to conclude that she'd knocked the vase over and, still without noticing unless she'd forgotten, tracked the flowers through the house.

The idea made her feel more alone and, in a new way, more nervous. She was also disconcerted by how dead the flowers were, though she'd picked them yesterday; the stalks were close to crumbling in her hands, and she had to sweep the withered petals into a dustpan. She binned it all and replenished the vase with Harry's cyclamen before sitting on the worn stairs while she rang Helena to confirm Wednesday lunch. They always met midweek, but she wanted to talk to someone. Once she realised that Helena's grandchildren were visiting she brought the call to an end.

The house was big enough for children, except that she and Harry couldn't have any, and now it kept feeling too big. Perhaps they should have moved, but she couldn't face doing so on her own. She cooked vegetables to accompany the rest of yesterday's casserole, and ate in the dining-room to the sound of superannuated pop songs on the radio, and leafed through her library books in the front room before watching a musical that would have made Harry restless. She could hear gangs roving the streets, and was afraid her lit window might attract them. Once she'd checked the doors and downstairs windows she plodded up to bed.

Girls were awaiting customers on the main road. As Dorothy left the curtains open a finger's width she saw Winona Bullough negotiate with a driver and climb into his car. Was the girl even sixteen? Dorothy was close to asking Harry, but it felt too much like talking to herself, not a habit she was anxious to acquire. She climbed into her side of the bed and hugged Harry's pillow as she reached with her free hand for the light-cord.

The night was a medley of shouts, some of which were merely conversations, and smashed glass. Eventually she slept, to be wakened by light in the room.

As she blinked, the thin shaft coasted along the bedroom wall. She heard the taxi turn out of the road, leaving her unsure whether she had glimpsed a silhouette that reminded her of stalks. Perhaps the headlamps had sent a shadow from her garden, though wasn't the angle wrong? She stared at the dark and tried not to imagine that it was staring back at her. "There's nobody," she whispered, hugging the pillow.

She needed to be more active, that was all. She had to occupy her mind and tire her body out to woo a night's unbroken sleep. She spent as much of Saturday in weeding the front garden as the pangs of her spine would allow. By late afternoon she wasn't even half finished, and almost forgot to buy a wreath. She might have taken Harry some of his own flowers, but she liked to support the florist's on the main road, especially since it had been damaged by the riots. At least the window had been replaced. Though the florist was about to close, he offered Dorothy a cup of tea while his assistant plaited flowers in a ring. Some good folk hadn't been driven out yet, Dorothy told them both, sounding her age.

She draped the wreath over the phone in her hall and felt as if she was saying goodbye to any calls, an idea too silly to consider. After dinner she read about far places that might have changed since she and Harry had visited them, and watched a love story in tears that would have embarrassed him. She was in bed by the time the Saturday-night uproar began. Once she was wakened by a metallic clack that sounded closer than outside, but when she stumbled to the landing the hall was empty. Perhaps a wind had snapped the letterbox. As she huddled under the quilt she wondered if she ought to have noticed something about the hall, but the impression was too faint to keep her awake. It was on her mind when church bells roused her, and as soon as she reached the stairs she saw what was troubling her. There was no sign of the wreath.

She grabbed the banister so as not to fall. She was hastening to reassure herself that the flowers were under the hall table, but they weren't. Had she forgotten taking them somewhere? They were in none of the ground-floor rooms, nor the bathroom, her bedroom, the other one that could have been a nursery but had all too seldom even done duty as a guest room. She was returning downstairs when she saw a single flower on the carpet inches from the front door.

Could a thief have dragged the wreath through the letterbox? She'd heard that criminals used rods to fish property from inside houses. She heaved the bolts out of their sockets and flung the door open, but there was no evidence on the path. It didn't seem worth reporting the theft to the police. She would have to take Harry flowers from the garden. She dressed in her oldest clothes and brought tools from the shed, and was stooping to uproot a weed that appeared to have sprouted overnight when she happened to glance over the wall. She straightened up and gasped, not only with the twinge in her back. One of the tributes to Keanu looked far too familiar.

She clutched at her back as she hobbled to the streetlamp. There was the wreath she'd seen made up at the florist's. It was the only item to lack a written tag. "Earned yourself some wings, Kee" and "Give them hell up there" and "Get the angels singing along with your iPod" were among the messages. The wreath was hung on the corner of a bouquet's wrapping. Dorothy glared about as she retrieved it, daring anyone to object. As she slammed the front door she thought she heard small feet running away.

She had no reason to feel guilty, and was furious to find she did. She locked away the tools and changed into the dark suit that Harry used to like her to wear whenever they dined out. A bus from the shattered shelter on the main road took her to the churchyard, past houses twice the size of hers. All the trees in their gardens were bare now. She and Harry had been fond of telling each other that they would see them blossom next year. The trees in the graveyard were monotonously evergreen, but she never knew what that was meant to imply. She cleared last week's flowers away from Harry's stone and replaced them with the wreath, murmuring a few sentences that were starting to feel formulaic. She dropped the stale flowers in the wire bin outside the concrete wedge of a church on her way to the bus.

As it passed her road she saw the Bulloughs on her path. Charmaine and her offspring strode to meet her at the lamp. "Brad says you lifted our Keanu's flowers."

"Then I'm afraid he's mistaken. I'm afraid—"

"You should be," said Arnie, the biggest and presumably the eldest of the brood. "Don't talk to my mam like that, you old twat."

Dorothy had begun to shake—not visibly, she hoped—but stood her ground. "I don't think I'm being offensive."

"You're doing it now," Arnie said, and his face twisted with loathing. "Talking like a teacher."

"Leave it, Arn," his mother said more indulgently than reprovingly, and stared harder at Dorothy. "What were you doing touching Keanu's things?"

"As I was trying to explain, they weren't his. I'm not accusing anybody, but someone took a wreath I'd bought and put it here."

"Why didn't you?" demanded Angelina.

"Because they were for my husband."

"When are you going to get Kee some?" J-Bu said at once.

"She's not," Charmaine said, saving Dorothy the task of being more polite. "Where were these ones you took supposed to be?"

"They were in my house."

"Someone broke in, did they? Show us where."

"There's no sign of how they did it, but—"

"Know what I think? You're mad."

"Should be locked up," said Angelina.

"And never mind expecting us to pay for it," Arnie said.

"I'm warning you in front of witnesses," said their mother. "Don't you ever touch anything that belongs to this family again."

"You keep your dirty hands off," J-Bu translated.

"Mad old bitch," added Brad.

Dorothy still had her dignity, which she bore into the house without responding further. Once the door was closed she gave in to shivering. She stood in the hall until the bout was over, then peeked around the doorway of the front room. She didn't know how long she had to loiter before an angry glance showed that the pavement was deserted. "Go on, say I'm a coward," she murmured. "Maybe it isn't wise to be too brave when you're on your own."

Who was she talking to? She'd always found the notion that Harry might have stayed with her too delicate to put to any test. Perhaps she felt a little less alone for having spoken; certainly while weeding the garden she felt watched. She had an intermittent sense of it during her meal, not that she had much appetite, and as she tried to read and to quell her thoughts with television. It followed her to bed, where she wakened in the middle of the night to see a gliding strip of light display part of a skinny silhouette. Or had the crouching shape as thin as twigs scuttled across the band of light? Blinking showed her only the light on the wall, and she let the scent of flowers lull her to sleep.

It took daylight to remind her there were no flowers in the room. There seemed to be more of a scent around her bed than the flowers in the house accounted for. Were her senses letting her down? She was glad of an excuse to go out. Now that they'd closed the post office around the corner the nearest was over a mile away, and she meant to enjoy the walk.

She had to step into the road to avoid vehicles parked on the pavement, which was also perilous with cyclists taking time off school. Before she reached the post office her aching skull felt brittle with the sirens of police cars and ambulances in a hurry to be elsewhere, not to mention the battering clatter of road drills. As she shuffled to the counter she was disconcerted by how much pleasure she took in complaining about all this to her fellow pensioners. Was she turning into just another old curmudgeon weighed down by weary grievances? Once she'd thanked the postmaster several times for her pension she headed for the bus stop. One walk was enough after all.

Although nobody was waiting outside her house, something was amiss. She stepped gingerly down from the bus and limped through gaps in the traffic. What had changed about her garden? She was at the corner of the road when she realised she couldn't see a single flower.

Every one had been trampled flat. Most of the stalks were snapped and the blossoms trodden into the earth, which displayed the prints of small trainers. Dorothy held onto the gatepost while she told herself that the flowers would grow again and she would live to see them, and then she walked stiff as a puppet into the house to call the police.

While it wasn't an emergency, she didn't expect to wait nearly four unsettled hours for a constable less than half her age to show up. By this time a downpour had practically erased the footprints, which he regarded as too common to be traceable. "Have you any idea who's responsible?" he hoped if not the opposite, and pushed his cap higher on his prematurely furrowed forehead.

"The family of the boy you were trying to catch last week."

"Did you see them?"

"I'm certain someone must have. Mrs Thorpe opposite hardly ever leaves the house. Too worried that clan or someone like them will break in."

"I'll make enquiries." As Dorothy started to follow him he said "I'll let you know the outcome."

He was gone long enough to have visited several of her neighbours. She hurried to admit him when the doorbell rang, but he looked embarrassed, perhaps by her eagerness. "Unfortunately I haven't been able to take any statements."

"You mean nobody will say what they saw," Dorothy protested in disbelief.

"I'm not at liberty to report their comments."

As soon as he drove away she crossed the road. Mrs Thorpe saw her coming and made to retreat from the window, then adopted a sympathetic wistful smile and spread her arms in a generalised embrace while shaking her head. Dorothy tried the next house, where the less elderly but equally frail of the unmarried sisters answered the door. "I'm sorry," she said, and Dorothy saw that she shouldn't expect any witness to risk more on her behalf. She was trudging home when she caught sight of an intruder in her front room.

Or was it a distorted reflection of Keanu's memorial, thinned by the glare of sunlight on the window? At first she thought she was seeing worse than unkempt hair above an erased face, and then she realised it was a tangle of flowers perched like a makeshift crown or halo on the head, even if they looked as though they were sprouting from a dismayingly misshapen cranium. As she ventured a faltering step the silhouette crouched before sidling out of view. She didn't think a reflection could do that, and she shook her keys at the house on her way to the door.

A scent of flowers greeted her in the hall. Perhaps her senses were on edge, but the smell was overpowering—sickly and thick. It reminded her how much perfume someone significantly older might wear to disguise the staleness of their flesh. Shadows hunched behind the furniture as she searched the rooms, clothes stirred in her wardrobe when she flung it open, hangers jangled at her pounce in the guest room, but she had already established that the back door and windows were locked. She halted on the stairs, waving her hands to waft away the relentless scent. "I saw you," she panted.

But had she? Dorothy kept having to glance around while she cooked her dinner and did her best to eat it, though the taste seemed to have been invaded by a floral scent, and later as she tried to read and then to watch television. She was distracted by fancying there was an extra shadow in the room, impossible to locate unless it was behind her. She almost said "Stay out of here" as she took refuge in bed. She mouthed the words at the dark and immediately regretted advertising her nervousness.

She had to imagine Harry would protect her before she was able to sleep. She dreamed he was stroking her face, and in the depths of the night she thought he was. Certainly something like a caress was tracing her upturned face. As she groped for the cord, the sensation slipped down her cheek. The light gave her time to glimpse the insect that had crawled off her face, waving its mocking antennae. It might have been a centipede or millipede—she had no chance to count its many legs as it scurried under the bed.

She spent the rest of the interminable night sitting against the headboard, the bedclothes wrapped tight around her drawn-up legs. She felt surrounded, not only by an oppressive blend of perfume that suggested somebody had brought her flowers—on what occasion, she preferred not to think. As soon as daylight paled Keanu's streetlamp she grabbed clothes and shook them above the stairs on her way to the bathroom.

She found a can of insect spray in the kitchen. When she made herself kneel, stiff with apprehension as much as with rheumatism, she saw dozens of flowers under her bed. They were from the garden—trampled, every one of them. Which was worse: that an intruder had hidden them in her room or that she'd unknowingly done so? She fetched a brush and dustpan and shuddered as she swept the debris up, but no insects were lurking. Once she'd emptied the dustpan and vacuumed the carpet she dressed for gardening. She wanted to clear up the mess out there, and not to think.

She was loading a second bin-liner with crushed muddy flowers when she heard Charmaine Bullough and her youngest children outdoing the traffic for noise on the main road. Dorothy managed not to speak while they lingered by the memorial, but Brad came to her gate to smirk at her labours. "I wonder who could have done this," she said.

"Don't you go saying it was them," Charmaine shouted. "That's defamation. We'll have you in court."

"I was simply wondering who would have had a motive."

"Never mind sounding like the police either. Why'd anybody need one?"

"Shouldn't have touched our Kee's flowers," J-Bu said.

Her mother aimed a vicious backhand swipe at her head, but a sojourn in the pub had diminished her skills. As Charmaine regained her balance Dorothy blurted "I don't think he would mind."

"Who says?" demanded Brad.

"Maybe he would if he could." Dorothy almost left it at that, but she'd been alone with the idea long enough. "I think he was in my house."

"You say one more word about him and you won't like what you get," Charmaine deafened her by promising. "He never went anywhere he wasn't wanted."

Then that should be Charmaine's house, Dorothy reflected, and at once she saw how to be rid of him. She didn't speak while the Bulloughs stared at her, although it looked as if she was heeding Charmaine's warning. When they straggled towards their house she packed away her tools and headed for the florist's. "Visiting again?" the assistant said, and it was easiest to tell her yes, though Dorothy had learned to stay clear of the churchyard during the week, when it tended to be occupied by drunks and other addicts. She wouldn't be sending a remembrance to the paper either. She didn't want to put Harry in the same place as Keanu, even if she wished she'd had the boy to teach.

Waiting for nightfall made her feel uncomfortably like a criminal. Of course that was silly, and tomorrow she could discuss next year's holiday with Helena over lunch. She could have imagined that her unjustified guilt was raising the scents of the wreath. It must be the smell of the house, though she had the notion that it masked some less welcome odour. At last the dwindling day released her, but witnesses were loitering on both sides of the road.

She would be committing no crime—more like the opposite. As she tried to believe they were too preoccupied with their needs to notice or at least to identify her, a police car cruised into the road. In seconds the pavements were deserted, and Dorothy followed the car, hoping for once that it wouldn't stop at the Bullough house.

It didn't, but she did. She limped up the garden path as swiftly as her legs would work, past a motor bicycle that the younger Bulloughs had tired of riding up and down the street, and posted the wreath through the massively brass-hinged mahogany door of the pebbledashed terrace house. She heard Charmaine and an indeterminate number of her children screaming at one another, and wondered whether they would sound any different if they had a more than unexpected visitor. "Go home to your mother," she murmured.

The police were out of sight. Customers were reappearing from the alleys between the houses. She did her best not to hurry, though she wasn't anxious to be nearby when any of the Bulloughs found the wreath. She was several houses distant from her own when she glimpsed movement outside her gate.

The flowers tied to the lamp-standard were soaked in orange light. Most of them were blackened by it, looking rotten. Though the concrete post was no wider than her hand, a shape was using it for cover. As she took a not entirely willing step a bunch of flowers nodded around the post and dodged back. She thought the skulker was using them to hide whatever was left of its face. She wouldn't be scared away from her own house. She stamped towards it, making all the noise she could, and the remnant of a body sidled around the post, keeping it between them. She avoided it as much as she was able on the way to her gate. As she unlocked the door she heard a scuttling of less than feet behind her. It was receding, and she managed not to look while it grew inaudible somewhere across the road.

The house still smelled rather too intensely floral. In the morning she could tone that down before she went for lunch. She made up for the dinner she'd found unappetising last night, and bookmarked pages in the travel guide to show Helena, and even found reasons to giggle at a comedy on television. After all that and the rest of the day she felt ready for bed.

She stooped to peer under it, but the carpet was bare, though a faint scent lingered in the room. It seemed unthreatening as she lay in bed. Could the flowers have been intended as some kind of peace offering? In a way she'd been the last person to speak to Keanu. The idea fell short of keeping her awake, but the smell of flowers roused her. It was stronger and more suggestive of rot, and most of all it was closer. The flowers were in bed with her. There were insects as well, which didn't entirely explain the jerky movements of the mass of stalks that nestled against her. She was able to believe they were only stalks until their head, decorated or masked or overgrown with shrivelled flowers, lolled against her face.

The Oxford Companion to English Literature *describes* **Ramsey Campbell** *as "Britain's most respected living horror writer." He has been given more awards than any other writer in the field, including the Grand Master Award of the World Horror Convention, the Lifetime Achievement Award of the Horror Writers Association and the Living Legend Award of the International Horror Guild. Among his novels are* The Face That Must Die, Incarnate, Midnight Sun, The Count of Eleven, Silent Children, The Darkest Part of the Woods, The Overnight, Secret Story, The Grin of the Dark, Thieving Fear, *and* Creatures of the Pool. *Forthcoming are* The Seven Days of Cain *and* Ghosts Know. *His collections include* Waking Nightmares, Alone with the Horrors, Ghosts and Grisly Things, Told by the Dead, *and* Just Behind You, *and his non-fiction is collected as* Ramsey Campbell, Probably. *His novels* The Nameless *and* Pact of the Fathers *have been filmed in Spain. His regular columns appear in* Prism, All Hallows, Dead Reckonings, *and* Video Watchdog. *He is the President of the British Fantasy Society and of the Society of Fantastic Films.*

Ramsey Campbell lives on Merseyside with his wife Jenny. His pleasures include classical music, good food and wine, and whatever's in that pipe. His Web site is at www.ramseycampbell.com.

When first published, Mr. Campbell wrote of "Respects" that it "owes its existence to the present trend of treating young criminals as folk heroes. Not long before I wrote it a young car thief was eulogised in the obituary pages of the local free newspaper at least as sentimentally as the miscreant in my tale. As far as I can see, there's one less thief to bother the rest of us. Since I wrote the story, shopkeepers in an entire suburb were terrorized into shutting their premises out of a show of respect for a gang member who was gunned down. It seems as if the kind of family I wrote about in *The One Safe Place* has begun to rule our streets. Time for another novel, perhaps, if I don't get stomped to death first for remonstrating with their kind."

We can only hope Mr. Campbell is not stomped and does write the novel.

DIAMOND SHELL

DEBORAH BIANCOTTI

People without walls learn to avert their eyes.

1. Last Day: Shel

The phone was ringing and that wasn't right. She squinted at the clock. It seemed to say 0280, and that couldn't be right either.

She fumbled for the handset, for the light, for the edge of the bedside table so she could navigate her way around the glass of water to where the phone—

She had it.

"Hello?" she croaked.

"Shel?" said the voice. "Did I wake you?"

It sounded querulous, uncertain, more a whisper than a full noise. She hadn't been able to make out the caller ID.

"Of course you fucking woke me," she said. "It's . . . " She checked the clock again. "After two."

There was a pause and then the tone went flat. Had they hung up?

Christ.

They'd hung up.

She fumbled for the lamp. The weak blue light of the phone screen wasn't enough in the middle of the night. Too blurry for her eyes to make out. Seriously, the middle of the night—she should just ignore it. Probably a wrong number anyhow.

She flipped over to the received calls and read the most recent one. It said Mish.

"Shit," she said.

She hit the call button. Engaged. She flipped the phone closed, opened it, hit the call button again. Engaged. Well, who the hell was Mish calling now? Two o'clock in the morning, for god's sake. It took eight minutes to get through. By then she was awake.

"Yeah?"

"Mish, shit, did you just call? Are you okay? You sound terrible. What's up?"

Her voice was still thick with sleep. So was her head. Something wasn't adding up, and it wasn't just that Mish wasn't the kind of person to call—

"It's not Mish," said the voice. A tremulous catch on the last syllable. "It's Ace."

Oh, great.

"Ace? Fuck," she said. "What are *you* doing with Mishi's phone? Where is she?"

Ace took a breath, or gave a sigh, or did whatever deadbeat junkie losers did when they didn't have a good answer.

"She's gone," he said. "She's . . . gone."

Shel was already cold, sitting up out of the bedsheets, back against the bedhead, free hand rubbing at her scalp, trying to force some wakefulness out of her skull, or into it. She was already cold, but that made her shiver.

What the hell Mish had ever seen in this no-good—

"Gone," she said carefully, "where?"

"Just gone. All her stuff's here, but—"

"Where's here? Where are you?"

"Mishi's place."

"Stay the fuck there," she said, "I'm coming over."

The cabbie knew dick about Pyrmont. Not a surprise. Pyrmont only figured on a cabbie's radar when there was a casino pick-up to be had. Nowadays Pyrmont was a backwater. Boatloads of migrants had passed through here in the fifties, arriving in Sydney with hope and glad hearts. Now hope was limited to what you could afford to drop into a slot machine. Or couldn't.

An anachronistic village on the arse of Sydney's only casino. A shag on a rock.

She gave the cabbie directions to Mish's apartment complex and handed him a twenty.

"Keep the change."

To his credit, he could at least follow instructions.

They pulled up on the corner opposite the cluster of high-rise apartments. On the street was an old man in a three-piece, skin pink all over his head, no discernible hair anywhere else on his body. Casino refuse, Shel figured. It took her a moment to realize he was urinating unselfconsciously into the gutter, the stub of his pink penis wrapped in both hands.

"You right?" she said, allowing a sneer into her voice.

His suit shone at knees and elbows. A dribble of piss escaped him and he turned to Shel, his lower lip sagging and his eyes like uncooked egg whites.

He nodded dumbly.

"Then stop pissing in the street," she suggested.

He muttered something that was lost in a thick accent and a drunken mumble. But he accompanied the noise by releasing one of his hands to give her the finger.

"Charming!"

She buzzed the number for Mish's apartment, buzzed and buzzed and muttered "C'mon Ace" under her breath until the door finally clicked open. She shoved through into the too-bright, tiled foyer, and out the other side into a dark courtyard. There were five high rises in this complex. Mish's was the next one on the right.

2. Two Days Earlier: Mishi

Mish had moved to Sydney to be anonymous. Moved from a small sugar-farming town in North Queensland. Moved because in Halifax—her home town—there was no such thing as your business and my business. Everything was everyone's business.

Here the city's noise and bustle kept everyone else preoccupied. There were more people, but there was more privacy too. She could lie down in the middle of the road and no one would do anything except politely look away.

She liked it like that.

"I'm sorry," said Mishi, "what?"

"I was talking about being invisible," said Shel.

"Right."

They were outside eating lunch in the gray of a city weekday, concrete and cement bookending the space where they sat with their salads on wide white plates.

Mishi wondered how anything could retain its whiteness in the leaden city air. She'd been starving before. Now she toyed with her food, smearing it around the plate. She hated eating here, outside with the thoroughfares on two sides, but it was one of the few places left where Shel could smoke. Another thing Mishi didn't like.

Shel was hard-edged, lost inside herself, calloused from hard living. But calloused in a good way, so she said. Calloused like a musician's hands. Toughened enough that she could produce something beautiful. That was Shel's spin on things.

"It's one of the drawbacks of a growing population," Shel said. "So many people wind up feeling, you know. Invisible."

She punctuated the statement with a plume of gray smoke and a wave of her cigarette.

"I like it," said Mishi.

Shel laughed. "Only you would *like* being invisible!"

Mishi didn't reply, so Shel added, "Do you know the percentage of women in the population of Sydney? Fifty-eight! Fifty-eight percent of all inhabitants are women. And single women outnumber married ones. So our odds are—"

"By how much?"

Shel hesitated. "Which bit?"

"Single to married. How much?"

"Oh," she waved her cigarette again. "I can't recall. What's it matter? The outcome's the same. Our odds are bad, Mish baby."

Mishi pushed salad around her plate with an oversized fork. There was no point arguing with Shel. It wasn't about the statistics or the difficulty or the inevitability of everyone else's failure. For Shel it was about the preciousness of her own imminent success.

"You're never short of a date, anyhow," Mishi said, supplying exactly the phrase she knew Shel was looking for.

Shel rewarded her with a smile. "Ha! Thanks, doll."

Mishi left most of her lunch uneaten, so afterwards she paused to pick up a sandwich in a convenience store. The label on the egg-and-lettuce promised "made daily," and then noted an expiry date. She took it to the checkout and raised it towards the smiling man behind the security screen.

"This expired yesterday," she said. "Do you give a discount?"

Steel security wires separated the man from his customers. Wide enough to let convenience products through, but not so wide that crazies could launch themselves at the till. She passed the sandwich through the wires so he could check the date.

"I can't sell you this," he said. "I'm so sorry."

He kept smiling while he said it, inserting the sandwich into some hidden space under the bench.

"I don't mind," said Mish. "I'll pay full price."

"Dan will fetch you another," said the man.

"There weren't any other egg sandwiches," she explained.

"I'm so sorry."

Dan was a skinny teenager with long arms, his elbows the widest part of his body. He returned holding a new Made Daily. Mishi took it without looking at it, paid full price, and carried it home still snug in its plastic skin.

Only when she was home, cross-legged on the floorboards did she pull the sandwich out. Chicken marinated in sweet chili. She didn't like chili.

She took a few bites anyway and stared out the French doors to the city beyond.

She liked the city best this way. Under glass.

Shel called her an anathema. She lived in the inner city, but so high up she felt out of reach of it. She could be anywhere in the world, hanging high above the accents. There was a sameness to cities like this one, but you had to be inside them to find it.

The casino squatted to the right of her field of vision like a black beetle on the water, its vibrant neon lights describing a wave along its roof. Part of the developers' plan to fit the casino into its environs. Symbolic of the harbor or some other cliché. That's how it'd been sold to the local residents anyway.

Mishi didn't mind the building. It was this kind of incongruity that gave the city its character.

She liked everything about the city. Liked its walls and its protective layer of noise.

3. Last Day: Shel

Upstairs on the twelfth floor, Ace was crying. Shel fought the urge to tell him to snap out of it. She was always fighting that urge.

One day she'd lose the fight and start shouting *snap out of it* until the world exploded.

He was sitting on the floor by the French doors of Mish's apartment, caught in a pool of pale glow from the city outside. The apartment was small, like a bunker, the view from the balcony its only selling point.

Shel crossed to where Ace sat. Beside him were Mish's phone, handbag, keys.

"What's going on, Ace?"

He lay against the wall like a crumpled doll, one knee up, hands loose in his lap. He whimpered but didn't answer in any verbal way she understood.

Shel backtracked, checked the bedroom, checked the bathroom. Both rooms empty, both painted in neutral white and beige. Both barely big enough for the furniture in them.

She swore for several seconds, then rounded on Ace again.

"What's going on?"

He turned to look out to the sky.

"She's not coming back, not this time."

She fought that urge again.

"You gotta help me, Ace. Help Mish."

She put one hand on the wall to steady herself, or stop herself from hitting him clean across the face. The wall was warm.

"How long since you seen her?" Ace asked.

"Uh," said Shel, "three days, maybe. We had lunch."

She brushed her palm along the wall, looking for the source of the heat. There wasn't anything that could heat an apartment from the walls. She knew that. She was a fan of architecture. Just like she was a fan of art and innovation and financial management and survival. Modern living made her a fan of all these things. She had to be, just to keep up. Just to get by.

"What about you?" she asked. "When did you last see her?"

"Not for weeks." He looked up at her. In the light from the casino she could see his eyes were puffy and pink.

She should probably feel sorry for him.

Ace was a weedy, overgrown kid who still dressed in skateboarding gear and hadn't yet acknowledged his receding hairline. He moved through jobs faster than Shel moved through men, and—just like Shel—he liked a certain type. He liked jobs in the entertainment industry. What most surprised Shel was that he kept getting them.

"Why are you here tonight, Ace?" she asked.

He shrugged, head lolling against the wall.

"How'd you get in?" she snapped.

"I never gave her keys back," he said.

Shel hesitated.

"Can you feel how warm it is in here?"

"Sure," he choked.

He pressed a palm to his eyes and sobbed. Crying for himself, Shel decided. Crying because he was too useless to know what to do except call someone who'd never liked him in the middle of the night to sob to about his missing ex-girlfriend.

"I'm calling the police," she said. "You got anything you want to tell me first?"

Behind his hand, he shook his head and sobbed.

The cops, when they arrived, were detached. Kind, but unpanicked. They'd seen stranger things, they assured her, and would be more than willing to list Mish as one of the city's missing. But beyond that they had nothing to offer. There was, after all, no evidence of a crime. No theft, no marks of violence, no goodbye note and most importantly, no body.

"You could take him in for questioning," Shel suggested.

She indicated Ace with a jerk of her chin. He was sitting on the lounge beside the other officer, torso almost concave in the soft upholstery.

"We could do that," the cop confirmed, "if we had reason."

"You could check security footage, right? See if she left any time recently, without her purse."

The cop was patient. "We could," he said. "If we had cause."

Shel, for once, had nothing to say. She was tired, confused, and the sun was still a couple hours off.

"Some people," said the cop *sotto voce*, "fake their own disappearance." He paused to let that sink in. "She maybe have something going on in her life that would cause her to consider that?"

Who doesn't? Shel thought. The deadbeat ex-boyfriend, the married man she was sleeping with, the no-hope job, the inflated mortgage for the apartment with no ventilation and the expensive view outside its French doors.

"No," said Shel. "I can't imagine."

4. Two Days Earlier: Mishi

Mishi had a set of cards. Long, narrow cards with meditative reminders on them. "Harmony" said one card. "Peace." "Worth." "Light." She shuffled them and drew out three to meditate on. Three was a random number. Meditation allowed room for the random.

This day she drew out "Adventure." "Surrender." "Serenity."

She lined the cards up on the floor and stared until her vision blurred to gray grit. She tried to find the way to inner peace. The escape, the surrender. The serenity.

5. Last Day: Shel

"I'll keep the keys, then," Shel said.

The cops looked to Ace, and she looked to Ace, and Ace looked back between them and shrugged.

"I'll need your name," one of the cops said.

They let her scour the apartment for a suicide note, searching all the drawers and the bedroom cupboard where most of Mish's stuff was crammed in fragile towers.

"Let me know if she comes back," Ace said as they ushered him out.

If. Not when.

They caught the lift together, uncomfortably cramped in a space that only just met building regulations.

"You need a lift someplace?" one cop asked.

"No," said Shel. "But he does."

Ace gave her a nonplussed look.

"Thanks," he said.

She waved goodbye outside the building and pretended to walk away. Once they'd left she crept back to the apartment complex, pacing it out, looking down sidestreets and going so far as to walk to the corners, scouring the spaces beside the parked cars and the insides of the cars themselves.

She didn't know what she was looking for. Mish, of course. Or some sign of her. A shoe, a bracelet, a hairpin, for god's sake. Anything.

There was nothing to be found, or if there was, she couldn't tell who it belonged to anyhow.

She circled back to the front of the apartment complex.

"Got any change, love?"

Shel was so intent on the ground she nearly walked right past him. It was his feet she saw first. They were bare but so covered in grime she figured at first he was wearing brown socks. He was homeless, she realized. Coat ripped at every seam, trousers so full of muck they could stand upright on their own.

"No," she said out of habit. "Wait, sorry."

She fished some coins from her pocket.

The man held out a hand. His palm, like the rest of him, was dirty.

"Thanks," he said. "Decent of you."

His voice was too loud, and he punctuated his polite statements with a bob of his shoulders. Like he was reciting something he'd learned a long time ago. He had a wiry beard and hair that stood up on end. He looked fifty but probably wasn't.

She went to move away but a loud exclamation from the man stopped her. Tourette's, she realized, noting the involuntary roll of his head and the click-click-clicking sound of his tongue.

"Not mine," he said, "not mine, not-mine."

"Sorry?" Shel said.

He was trying to hand her something, plucking it from the palm where she'd laid her change.

"Not mine," he said again, and his posture relaxed. "You gave me your key accidentally."

"What? No, I didn't."

Shel took the key and turned it over between her fingers. She felt in the pocket where it had ostensibly been, but found no imprint, no supernatural sign that the thing had ever rested there.

"I don't think it's mine," she murmured.

It was small and bright, like the key from a little girl's journal. It took her back. Afternoons on a window seat, rain outside, adults in other rooms. It was a long time since she'd felt like that. Hidden, secretive, lost in her own world.

The homeless guy shrugged and turned away.

"Tell me," she called, "you around here much?"

She moved towards him.

"Sure," he said. "Sometimes. More down by the casino. People going in, they sometimes think it's lucky to give money to a bum."

With a laugh.

Shel pointed back to the apartment complex.

"You seen a woman here recently, come out of the building?"

The homeless guy looked at her like she might be crazy.

"In the last two days," she persisted. "Short. Long dark hair. Wears trousers with oversized shoes and, and shirts with high collars. Even in summer."

Recognition was streamlining the man's face, smoothing out his premature wrinkles.

"You a friend?" he asked.

"Yeah, I'm a friend. You've seen her, right?"

"Maybe."

"Where'd you see her?"

He shrugged, looked to his dirty feet, looked away.

"You're not in trouble, I just need to know where she is."

The man shook his head and then his neck dissolved in a series of ticks and jerks. His hand fisted around the coins she'd given him. She waited silently, pretending more patience than she had.

When his attack subsided, he said, "I can't explain it."

"Sure you can."

"I can show you," he said. "But only because you've got the key."

"The—right. I've got the key."

She held it up so he could see it.

"Show me then," she prompted.

He turned and walked along the dark street, and she followed.

They walked the perimeter of the apartment complex, signified by a smooth eight-foot fence. Faux cast iron poles every half-foot, the tops bent inwards to make climbing impossible. With a rope you could drag yourself to the top, but you couldn't easily get over to the other side. And you sure couldn't get back out.

The homeless guy banked where the fencing parted from the sidewalk. He followed it around through a full tropical planting of tall ferns and an uneven groundcover.

Shel kept following. Nearly rolled her ankle a couple times, but managed to keep up. Just. The figure in front of her disappeared behind hanging palm leaves. She had to duck to avoid their recoil. She kept one hand on the fence while she followed, trailing her fingers along it. Tried not to imagine snakes and other monsters in the plants with her. Tried not to think about what it would be like to be dragged through here, or pushed or kidnapped.

Tried not to think about the fact she was following some stranger into the dark. The city, with its instant access to all parts of humanity, had made her nonchalant. Her mother would be horrified to see her here like this, alone but for a man she didn't know and the congestive anonymity of the dark.

Her ankle rolled again and she let out her breath in a hiss. In front of her the homeless guy didn't even slow.

"Hey, what's your name?" she called.

He didn't answer.

She stumbled to keep up and almost bumped into him when he stopped.

There was no noise except for the faint heartbeat of traffic and the more immediate sound of the wind. From here the dense foliage obscured even the power of the city lights. She could see the eastern edge of the apartment complex, the edge that fell away into the ocean. She could feel the ocean winds on her skin and smell salt and tropical plants. It felt wrong, to be perched on the edge of a city and feel like you were in the middle of a jungle.

The wind ripped around them, through the trees, pulling at Shel's jacket. She folded her arms against it. In the moonlight she could just make out the dirty arm of the homeless man pointing.

"Your friend," he said, "that her apartment?"

Shel followed his hand.

"Which one do you mean?" she asked to be sure.

The man twitched as he counted.

"Third one down."

"Which building? Which side?"

He explained. She had to concede he was right. That was Mish's apartment.

But from here there was barely anything to be seen. Only the tops of the French doors were visible over the brick balcony. A rectangle of Mish's ceiling, the light fixture on the balcony. She stood on her toes to be sure.

"Did you see something there?" she asked.

He nodded.

"When?"

"Two nights back."

When he failed to continue, she prompted him.

"And what the fuck," she asked, "did you see?"

"No need for the language," he said.

He gave her a hurt look. But in the sweep of shadow and wind it only served to deepen the darkness under his brow and exaggerate the curl of his lip.

"Sorry, sorry," she said quickly. "Sorry. Listen! Tell me what you saw."

He nodded, obliged.

"The woman in the apartment. The woman with long thin arms and small shoulders and hair that was straight and black and—"

"Yes," said Shel. "What was she doing, when you saw her?"

He chewed like he had a mouthful of cud.

"Opening a door."

A pause. Nothing but the wind and the night to fill it.

"Is that it?" she asked.

He nodded.

"She went through it," he said. "And she never came back.'

Shel fought the urge to run back to the apartment. It couldn't be true, her adult brain knew that. She'd looked in every room and the cupboard, too. It wasn't like the apartment afforded many places to hide. There weren't that many doors. The front door, the bedroom, the bathroom, that was it. Maybe the cupboard doors counted, but as small as Mish was, Shel doubted she was curled up in a cupboard somewhere.

Still, when she thought of it her heart leapt into her throat. What if, against all sense, Mish was curled like a shell in a cupboard in the kitchen. What if she was rolled, foetal-like and calcified, rocking in a grave behind the—

She pushed the images aside.

"I figure," said the man, "the door took her into the center."

Shel couldn't help herself.

"Of . . . ?"

He twitched.

"The heart of things. The center of this place."

"What in god's name," said Shel, "are you talking about?"

"She found a way out," he said. He added thoughtfully, "Or a way in."

Shel was about to give him a piece of her mind when he hushed her. Held a finger against his lips and whispered around it.

"Can't you feel it?"

"Feel what?"

"You have to be quiet," he said.

Apart from the exasperated scream in her head, she was quiet. Her hair caught in the wind and she had to pull it off her face and hold it in a fist at the back of her head.

"You have to be *really* quiet," said the homeless guy. "Inside and out. Like you're meditating."

"Meditating?" she said. "The fuck?"

It was a knack she figured she didn't have. But since nothing else was forthcoming, she silenced herself and waited, watching the homeless guy. If it wasn't for Mish, she wouldn't be out here, standing in the midst of this, this damned darkness, this craziness.

If it wasn't for Mish, she wouldn't have tried. And maybe that was true of a lot of things. Mish made her feel anything was possible. That's why they were friends.

She stood and shut her eyes, trying for stillness.

"It's all about what you're prepared to witness," said her companion. "See?"

No.

She focused on the glint of city lights on the water, the echo of traffic. She focused on the meniscus of light where the night sky bled out over the lumps of buildings and bridge and light and light.

She was quiet enough and still enough for long enough to finally understand what he meant. Perched out here above the ocean, she could feel it. Something ancient and lost, something whole but with a missing piece at its heart. She felt the dread rise from the earth beneath her feet and crawl up her legs, making hollows in her skin.

She thought she was going to be sick.

Shel turned and stumbled from the space, falling more than once to her knees. Something was eating the space behind her. She had to pull herself along the fence to stop from being dragged backwards. She kept moving, the stink of squashed leaves and ground beneath her. It smelled wrong.

When she broke into the light of the street she stumbled, nearly into the path of a white minibus. She tripped backwards and fell, landing hard on the gutter.

"Stupid bitch!"

There were shouts and jeers from inside the bus as the rest of the dozen occupants joined in. Their echo added to the reassuring perfume of fuel fumes.

Shel got to her feet uncertainly. Her hip ached where she'd landed on it in the gutter. Her knees were scraped and raw. She was shaking all over, so hard her teeth were chattering.

She kept her back to the road and faced the dark space where the homeless man had led her. There was no sign of him. He was probably watching her from the dark. He would probably always be watching her.

She thought she would never be free of his eyes ever again. He had seen right into her. And the city with its mega-watt load of noise and energy and its million babbling examples of humanity had climbed right into his gaze after her and drilled into her core.

He'd been right. She could feel it. The whole fragile sugar castle of the city, with nothing for its foundations but two hundred years of loss.

6. Two Days Earlier: Mishi

Mishi had thrown away the other half of the sandwich. It was one AM. She couldn't sleep and the meditation wasn't helping. She couldn't clear her mind. How desirable was that, anyhow? She'd spent a lifetime cultivating this mind. Clearing it was the last thing she wanted.

She roamed the narrow edges of the apartment. Looking for something, looking for—

The lights on the roof of the casino pulsed reassuringly. Always made her feel like there was life nearby. Something going on. People, if she needed them. Sometimes she went and sat in one of the bars, taking in the noise. She never stayed long.

But not tonight.

She sat back on the floor by the doors and wrapped her arms around her waist. To hold herself together. Figured she'd ride out the evening, wait for morning.

It was cold, with the night air dribbling off the harbor into her apartment. She leaned forward so her elbows covered her knees. For warmth, she told herself. A posture of obeisance to the world outside her window.

Strange.

Before her in the floorboards, a small key was caught. Angled into the gap in the wood point-first with only one round edge protruded.

She dug at it with a thumbnail, working it out of the wood. A small plain key, bright and practically weightless. She turned it over and over in her hand.

"Never seen you before," she murmured. "Where'd you come from?"

In the buzz of distant noise her voice felt wrong. She kept it to herself after that.

The key was light. She could feel neither its temperature nor weight. Was it metal? She tapped it against her forehead, trying to get a sense of it.

Nothing.

She bent her nails against it, trying to prove it was real.

The key defied her.

She dropped it on the floor, listening to the *ding* it made against the wood. Pushed it back and forth on the boards beside her meditative cards.

She wanted to feel something.

Adventure, she thought. *Surrender. Serenity. Like the cards said.*

She squeezed her eyes tight and tipped forward, bowing her head. She tipped and tipped over the key, bending at the waist, anticipating the smooth, cool floor on her forehead. Surrender. It was an escape, a release, stomach on her thighs, forearms over her head, face towards floor.

Serenity.

She tipped forward with a sense the floor would catch her.

When it didn't, there wasn't even time for surprise. Only a pure static feeling like emotional white noise.

She spiraled through the floor and out of reality like she was falling through a trapdoor. In one swooping gesture she was released to live free between the bones of the city.

Deborah Biancotti *is a writer based in inner-city Sydney, Australia. Her first short story collection,* A Book of Endings, *was shortlisted in 2010 for the William L. Crawford Award for Best First Fantasy Book. Her short stories have appeared in* Clockwork Phoenix, Ideomancer, Eidolon 1, Borderlands, *and* Infinity Plus, *and anthologies including* The Year's Best Australian SF & Fantasy *and* Australian Dark Fantasy and Horror. *She has upcoming fiction in* Baggage, *a novella for three-author anthology* Ishtar, *and a non-fiction essay in* Twenty-First Century Gothic. *Biancotti is now working on her first novel (working title:* Broken*) and planning her second (*Body*). You can find her online at deborahbiancotti.net.*

When someone opens a door in a story and never comes back through it, one is left to wonder: Rather than being the end of the story—is this really just the beginning?

NUB HUT

KURT DINAN

—————

Four of us surround the hole in the ice, each lying with an arm submerged deep in the water. This is nothing like I pictured. In my mind I saw smaller, individual holes and a sense of transformation. Instead, the hole is one large opening maybe ten feet across, and all I feel is the great freeze as we wait under the Alaskan moon, the snow twinkling down like millions of tiny flash bulbs.

Hannah wears only jeans and a Gamecocks sweatshirt. She hasn't moved or said a word since we began, but her frozen breath still occasionally drifts up. Beside her, Nigel Nine Toes is pants-less. His argument that his missing toe should make him an automatic for the Nub Hut ended with the admission that he lost it to a lawnmower when he was sixteen. The Nub Hut, Sheila proclaimed, must have standards.

The smart money is on Gillian. She's built like a lumberjack, even wearing flannel shirts and boots like she's off to chop down sequoias. Gillian's worked the slime line at the cannery for years. She'll be radiating fish stink the rest of her life, however long that is.

Me, I'm in true winter wear—thermals, rubber-soled boots, an Arctic jacket—and am resting on a blanket I swiped from the bunkhouse. Using a gutting knife, I cut off a coat sleeve so nothing would come between my bare arm and the water. All four of us are alike in that respect. That and the mandatory rope, of course, one end tied around an ankle and the other spiked through the ice.

We wait in the glow of the Nub Hut. What once housed two snowcats and the back-up generator now sits thirty yards away onshore. The windows are covered with thick black plastic, but orange firelight seeps through the slats. A spray painted NUB HUT streaks down the door. Muffled music plays inside, evidence someone scavenged a battery.

"Think you can guess how long it's been, Alan?"

Nigel Nine Toes speaks through chattering teeth. He may be thirty, he may be fifty; it's hard to tell. Alaska weathers a man, and that's just what he wants. "To be reduced to my base animal" is how Nigel puts it. He stalks around camp spouting about the chaotic beauty of the tundra while making sure we're all aware of his Che Guevara shirt. To most of us though, he's just the guy who complains that his recreations of famous paintings infused with aborted fetuses are kept out of galleries due to an elaborate conspiracy.

"Come on," Nigel says. "Take a guess. How long?"

I can't turn his way because my ear is frozen to the ice. "An hour?"

"Forty minutes. And that's why you won't make it. Your mind is weak. Only the primal can survive. All humanity must be whittled away until all that remains is a god, a creator, an explosion, and implosion of raw energy."

So that's Nigel.

This is the first conversation in some time. All of us shouted in solidarity when we first plunged our arms in, but the camaraderie wore off fast. This isn't about friendship; this is about the Nub Hut. Tell four people only two will be chosen and inevitably this is what happens.

"I'm having a hard time breathing," Gillian says. "Can't catch any air."

"Arm feels like it's in a vice," I tell her.

"I can't keep my thoughts straight."

"I'm seeing double."

And on and on.

The first few minutes of submersion were the worst. Nothing but burn. The icy water collapsed around my arm squeezing out the blood. Only through sheer will power was I able to keep it in the hole. But you want willpower? Sheila's nothing more than a torso now. There's talk she'll do her ears soon. None of us doubt it.

The door to the Nub Hut opens and music pours into the night. Nigel Nine Toes says it's Neil Young but Gillian says it's America and now they're arguing over who sang "A Horse with No Name."

For a brief moment I see inside—firelight, shadows, maybe a table—then someone steps out and shuts the door before anyone can see. Whatever happens inside the Nub Hut is a mystery, but it must be wonderful.

At the sound of boots crunching snow, I tear my ear off the ice, leaving behind a pulp of skin. Warm blood trickles down my neck, dotting the ice. As the silhouette draws closer, the outline becomes clear and Gillian says, "MilaGino."

Between them, Mila and Gino have been married separately five times. Sheila presided over their sixth attempt last week in the Nub Hut. They spent their wedding night holding hands under water. Afterward, Mila sacrificed her right arm, Gino his left. Now they're sewn together at the shoulder.

They take a knee and I feel stale breath on my face. MilaGino speak as one, both mouths repeating the words a moment apart, creating a strange echo.

"How are you holding up?"

I attempt to respond, but my tongue is a balled-up sock.

"It's okay, Alan," they say putting a hand on my shoulder. "We understand."

But they can't understand. Maybe they could when they wandered camp as lonely hearts before the takeover. Or maybe they could have understood in the days after the revolt when we were all unified, everyone joyous in having a place to call our own, a place where we belonged. But they can't understand anymore. Now they're muscle for Sheila. Now they belong to the Nub Hut.

While the wind chips at my face, MilaGino survey the others. Everyone smiles through frozen lips. Hannah and Nigel push their arms deeper into the water. We're all dogs hoping to go home from the pound.

MilaGino draw out the choice, discussing us privately, their faces inches apart. But it's all show. Everyone knows who makes the final call. They nod simultaneously then say, "Hannah, come join us in the Nub Hut." And my arm burns all over again.

Just one look at Hannah, with her hangdog face and saddle bags making it appear that she's carrying hundreds of pennies in her pockets, and you can understand how it's a thinly disguised pity pick. Every society needs a target. And who's easier than the woman who spends her free time talking of Renaissance festivals and reading her silly backward comics? I might feel sorry for Hannah if I didn't hate her so much right now.

Hannah's sweatshirt clings to the ice as MilaGino help her up. With a jerk, her hoodie tears away, leaving white university letters behind. MilaGino lose their footing for a moment, slipping on the ice and tumbling sideways before regaining balance. As they guide Hannah up the path, her feet barely touch the snowy ground.

"There's gotta be some sort of mistake," Nigel says.

"That it wasn't you?" Gillian says. "Let's see, Nigel. Sweet Hannah without an offensive bone in her body, or you with your pseudo-intellectual bullshit and babies playing poker."

"They're fetuses. It's symbolic."

"What it is is asinine."

"I have a hundred dollars that says you played softball in college, Gillian."

"Asshole."

"Dyke."

It's like that.

My lips twitch as if electrified and now I've lost all sensation in my feet. My eyes are closed before I realize it.

This is how it happens. No matter what you try, you never take root. It's years of no luck with work, no luck with women, no luck at all. You're on an endless search without a clear destination. You tell yourself it's in the next city or the next town, but everywhere you go you're a cipher. On the outside you look like everyone else, but inside you're ash and isolation. Then on the Discovery Channel you see Alaska's promise of endless possibilities as the last frontier. And if you're twenty-nine and have traveled nothing but dead-end roads, you'll follow whichever star lights the way. It's only when you get here that you realize the entire state is filled with mirror images of yourself waiting for further directions.

Cheers erupting inside the Nub Hut shake me from my haze. We crane our necks for any sign. Hannah must be submitting to the blade. She belongs to them now. As the ovation dies down, we all crumble back onto the ice. No one has to mention the resentment surging through each of us.

Minutes later, Gillian whispers, "Alan?" A thin layer of frost covers her face. Her lips are white in the moonlight, but it's her eyes, wide and bottomless, that frighten me.

"It's so strange," she says, "I'm not even cold anymore."

Gripping the hole's edge with her free arm, Gillian pulls herself into the water. She drifts downward like a snowflake before disappearing altogether. The rope around her feet snakes behind her until going taut. Someone will reel her in later.

I'm too cold to move, too cold to respond. I just stare into the abyss. Maybe in the daylight I could see her, but in the darkness the black water reveals nothing.

Nigel begins laughing and can't stop choking on his words. Finally he roars, "Ophelia of the Arctic," and pounds the ice with his free hand until I think bones might break.

In the beginning, only two others joined Sheila in the Nub Hut. Lorna iced her toes, Trevor his hand. After that, everyone flocked to the hole for a chance at metamorphosis. Now supposedly there's a pile of severed nipples on a table. Gillian said the Asian from Toledo sliced off his lips. Rumor is some are talking castration next. No one can touch Sheila though. She sacrificed both legs the day after removing her arms. Even God's terrified of Sheila at this point.

"Why don't you take a swim too, Alan?" Nigel says. "Join your friend. This is beyond you. Your core self isn't—"

Even with Nigel's yammering and the wind howling across the Chukchi Sea, I hear the party in the Nub Hut. Harriet must've finished the sawing by now. She used to go through three hundred fish an hour, so it makes sense that she commands the knife. Once done, Marco does a fishing line suture, closing the wound in a crisscross of railroad tracks. Sometimes though the soldering gun is necessary.

There's no burn anymore, no freezing, not even any pressure. I even have to double check to make sure my arm's still in the water. Gillian watches me through the ice. She stares wide-eyed, our faces separated by inches. Free from the confines of her hat, red hair swims around her face. With her eyes, she blinks out Morse code messages I can't decipher.

In the weeks leading up to the revolution there were grumblings throughout camp as if Alaska had reneged on her promise. Then one day Sheila pulled the conveyor belt's emergency shutdown and Milo sledgehammered the control panel announcing, "This belongs to us now." There wasn't much thinking after that, just years of frustration pouring out in busted jaws and smashed machinery while Sheila smiled surveying the chaos. Outnumbered, and with no help for hundreds of miles, management evacuated in the buses. Two days later, Sheila birthed the Nub Hut.

"They won't take you." Nigel's voice creaks like a rusty hinge. "You don't belong here. You never have."

I want to tell him how there isn't anywhere else. How he'll never get up because his bare legs are welded to the ice. But what comes out instead is, "Sherrshingfel" before my tongue freezes and my vision fails.

I'm not sure how long I'm out. I'm dreaming of roads clogged with hitchhikers heading north to the Nub Hut when plastic sliding across the ice snaps me back. With my free hand I paw at my face, chipping away the frost sealing my eyes. The noise grows louder until it is right in front of me. Nigel bays with excitement. When I can finally see again, I am staring at four rubber-soled boots. MilaGino.

Trailing behind, pulled in her red disk sled, sits a triumphant Sheila ready to announce her final selection. She is propped on a pillow, little more than a face peeking out from the blanket bundled around her. MilaGino scoops her from the sled, holding her high like a newborn.

Sheila's teeth, now filed to sharp points, gleam in the moonlight. No one mentions the scar anymore, zigzagging across her face, that in the old world kept her working alone in backrooms away from the public. Now Sheila is beautiful. Now Sheila is someone. Now Sheila rules the Nub Hut.

"After tonight, we will be complete," she says. "There is only room for one more. The Nub Hut is not for everyone."

It's Nigel. Sheila doesn't have to say anymore for me to know. I can instinctively recognize defeat. The decision radiates from Sheila's eyes, from her aura, even from the air.

Nigel Nine Toes must sense it too because he kicks spastically, contorting his body in anticipation. For the briefest of moments, his arm leaves the water. The withered limb is nothing but a shriveled birch twig. He thrusts it back in, his eyes wide. When he speaks, each word is a tiny earthquake.

"I'm sorry, Sheila," he says. "Please."

She surveys Nigel Nine Toes like a saddened parent, then gives a private shake of her head. She whispers to MilaGino who reverently places her back on the disc before turning to Nigel.

Despite the thrashing and screaming, it only takes a moment for MilaGino to cut the rope around Nigel's ankle. At first I think he will refuse to move, but Nigel gets to his feet wailing endlessly. His bare legs are nothing but charcoal down the front. The crying doesn't stop even as he stumbles away from the hole, away from the camp, away from the Nub Hut. He disappears across the ice into the darkness until he is nothing but a beast howling in the distance.

MilaGino reaches under my armpits and lifts me, careful not to touch the dead limb. My entire left side hangs slack. Dynamite detonates throughout my body.

"Welcome," Sheila says finally. She smiles from atop her cushioned throne. Sheila the sacrificer. Sheila the leader. Sheila of the Nub Hut.

But the smile can't disguise her disappointment. This wasn't the plan.

She wanted Nigel. To her, I'm the also-ran, now substituted as a last-minute replacement for the Nub Hut.

"We need to set you down for a minute, Alan, so we can get Sheila back," MilaGino says, lowering me. "After we get her inside, we'll—"

They slip like before, teetering on the hole's edge, but this time there's no quick recovery. Their arms flail, and there's a moment where I know I can reach with my good hand to steady them. Instead, I let MilaGino tumble into the hole. The splash is a muted explosion. They scream in harmony before the water immobilizes their bodies and drags them under.

Moments pass before Sheila finally says, "Take me back inside, Alex." She wants to sound commanding, but her voice waivers. She can't keep my eye. Sheila can't even get my name right.

But I couldn't care less. Because now I am engulfed in the transformation of the Nub Hut. The change is nothing physical; it's more a clarity of purpose. Is this what Sheila felt when she first conceived the Nub Hut? Is this what surges through her when she selects new citizens? Maybe. It doesn't matter anymore.

I watch the water until its surface is a glass-topped table. Sheila begs for help, but whether it's the wind or the music drowning out her cries, no one appears. When she finally quiets, her change is also complete. No longer is she Sheila of the Nub Hut—she's simply Sheila with the scar-carved face.

I pull her towards me, then use my head to bump the sled the remainder of the way to the hole. Then I begin the long crawl home. Up ahead the Nub Hut awaits.

Kurt Dinan's *stories have twice appeared in* ChiZine *(once winning the 2007 short story contest), and in the anthologies* Horror Library III *and* IV, Dark Faith, *and* Darkness on the Edge: Stories Inspired by the Songs of Bruce Springsteen. *He lives in Cincinnati with his wife and three sons.*

On first reaction, you might think of this as a pretty bizarre story. But is it? A culture has been created here, an exclusive group created within it. Humans have a primal need to be part of a group. For our ancestors, survival meant acceptance into a group. Beyond survival: whatever defined "success" or "power" could usually be won only by belonging to an elite circle or gaining its favor. We still want to know and to be known and accepted. What we are willing to do—the ways we enact our desire to belong, the rituals and rule we accept—differs according to the culture. Some people play golf. Others have cosmetic surgery. These people . . . well, they do something else.

THE CABINET CHILD

STEVE RASNIC TEM

⟨⬥⟩

Around the beginning of the last century, near a small southwest Virginia town which no longer exists, a childless woman named Alma lived with her gentleman farmer husband in a large house on a ridge on the outskirts of this soon-to-be-forgotten town. The woman was not childless because of any medical condition—her husband simply felt that children were "ill-advised" in their circumstances, that there was no space for children in the twenty-or-so rooms of what he called their modest home.

Not being of a demonstrative inclination, his wife kept her disappointment largely to herself, but it could not have been more obvious if she had screamed it from their many-gabled roof. Sometimes, in fact, she muttered it in dialog with whoever should pass, and when no one was looking, she pretended to scream. Over the years despair worked its way into her eyes and drifted down into her cheeks, and the weight of her grief kept her bent and shuffling.

Although her husband Jacob was an insensitive man he was not in-observant. After enduring a number of years of his wife's sad display he apparently decided it gave an inappropriate impression of his household's tenor to the outside world and became determined to do something about it. He did not share his thinking with her directly, of course, but after an equal number of years enduring his maddening obstinacy his wife was well acquainted with his opinions and attitudes. Without so much as a knock he came into her bedroom one afternoon as she sat staring out her window and said, "I have decided you need something to cheer yourself up, my dear. John Hand will be bringing his wagon around soon and you may choose anything on it. Let us call it an early Christmas present, why don't we?"

She looked up at him curiously. After having prayed aloud for some sign of his attention, for so many nights, she could scarcely believe her ears. Was this some trick? As little as it was, still he had never offered her such a prize before. She thought at first that somehow he had hurt his face, then realized what she had taken for a wound was simply a strained and unaccustomed smile. He carried that awkward smile out the door with him, thank God. She did not think she could bear it if such a thing were running around loose in her private quarters.

John Hand was known throughout the region as a fine furniture craftsman who hauled his pieces around in a large gray wagon as roughly made as his furniture was exquisitely constructed. And yet this wagon had not fallen apart in over twenty years of travels up and down wild hollows and over worn mountain ridges with no paved roads. She had not perused his inventory herself, but people both in town and on the outlying farms claimed he carried goods to suit every taste and had a knack for finding the very thing that would please you, that is, if you had any capacity for being pleased at all, which some folk clearly did not.

Alma had twenty rooms full of furniture, the vast majority of it handed down from various branches of Jacob's family. Alma had never known her husband to be very close to his relations, but any time one of them died and there were goods to be divided he was one of the first to call with his respects. And although he was hardly liked by any of those grieving relatives he always seemed able to talk them into letting him leave with some item he did not rightly deserve.

Sometimes at night she would catch him with his new acquisitions, stroking and talking to them as if they had replaced the family he no longer much cared for. She could not understand what had come over her that she would have married such a greedy man.

Although she needed no furniture, without question Alma was sorely in need of being pleased, which was why she was at the front gate with an apron pocket full of Jacob's money the next time John Hand came trundling down the road in that horse-drawn wagon full of his wares.

Even though she waved almost frantically Hand did not appear to acknowledge her, but then stopped abruptly in front of their grand gate. She had seen him in town before but never paid him much attention. When Hand suddenly jumped down and stood peering up at her she was somewhat alarmed by the smallness of the man—he was thin as a pin and painfully bent, the top of his head not even reaching to her shoulders, and she was not a particularly tall woman. The wagon loomed like a great ocean liner behind him, and she could not imagine how this crooked little man had filled it with all this furniture, pieces so jammed together it looked like a puzzle successfully completed.

Then Mr. Hand turned his head rather sideways and presented her with a beatific smile, and, completely charmed, she felt prepared to go with anything the little man cared to suggest.

"A present from the husband, no?"

"Well, yes, he said I could choose anything."

"But not the present madam most wished for." He said it as if it were undeniable fact, and she did not correct him. Surely he had simply guessed, based on some clues in her appearance?

He gazed at her well past the point of discomfort, then clambered up the side of the wagon, monkey-like and with surprising speed. The next thing she knew he had landed in front of her, holding a small, polished wood cabinet supported by his disproportionately large palm and the cabinet's four unusually long and thin, spiderish legs. "I must confess it has had a previous owner," he said with a mock sad expression. "She was like you, wanting a child so very much. This was to be in the nursery, to hold its dainty little clothes."

Alma was alarmed for a number of reasons, not the least of which that she'd never told the little man that she had wanted a child. Then she quickly realized what a hurtful insult this was on his part—to give someone never to have children a cabinet to hold its clothes? She turned and made for the gate, averting her head so the vicious little man would not see her streaming tears.

"Wait! Please," he said, and a certain softness in his voice stopped her more firmly than a hand on her shoulder ever could. She turned just as he shoved the small cabinet into her open arms. "You will not be—unfulfilled by this gift, I assure you." And with a quick turn he had leapt back onto the seat and the tired-looking horses were pulling him away. She stood awkwardly, unable to speak, the cabinet clutched to her breast like a stricken child.

In her bedroom she carried the beautifully polished cabinet with the long, delicate legs to a shadowed corner away from the window, the door, and any other furniture. She did not understand this impulse exactly; she just felt the need to isolate the cabinet, to protect it from any other element in her previous life in this house. Because somehow she already knew that her life after the arrival of this delicate assemblage of different shades of wood would be a very different affair.

Once she had the cabinet positioned as seemed appropriate—based on some criteria whose source was completely mysterious to her—she sat on the edge of her bed and watched it until it was time to go downstairs and prepare dinner for her husband. Afterwards she came back and sat in the same position, gazing, singing softly to herself for two, three, four hours at least. Until the sounds in the rest of the house had faded. Until the soft amber glow of the new day appeared in one corner of her window. And until the stirrings inside the cabinet became loud enough for her to hear.

She came unsteadily to her feet and walked across the rug with her heart racing, blood rushing loudly into her ears. She held her breath, and when the small voice flowered on the other side of the shiny cabinet wall, she opened its tiny door.

Twenty years after his wife's death Jacob entered her bedroom for the third and final time. The first time had been the afternoon he had strode in to announce his well-meant but inadequate gift to her. The second time had been to find her lifeless body sprawled on the rug when she had failed to come down for supper. And now this third visit, for reasons he did not fully understand, except that he had been overcome with a terrible sadness and sense of dislocation these past few weeks, and this dusty bed chamber was the one place he knew he needed to be.

He would have come before—he would have come a thousand times before—if he had not been so afraid he could never make himself leave.

He had left the room exactly as it had been on Alma's last day: the covers pulled back neatly, as if she planned an early return to bed, a robe draped across the back of a cream-upholstered settee, a vanity table bare of cosmetics but displaying an antique brush and comb, a half-dozen leather-bound books on a shelf mounted on the wall by her window. In her closet he knew he would find no more than a few changes of clothes. He didn't bother to look because he knew they betrayed nothing of who she had been. She had lived in this room as he imagined nuns must live, their spare possessions a few bare strokes to portray who they had been.

It pained him that it was with her as it had been with everyone else in his life—some scattered sticks of furniture all he had left to remember them by—where they had sat, what they had touched, what they had held and cared for. He had always made sure that when some member of the family died he got something, any small thing, they had handled and loved, to take back here to watch and listen to. And yet none was haunted, not even by a whisper. He knew—he had watched and listened for those departed loved ones most of his adult life.

His family hadn't wanted him to marry her. No good can come, they said, of a union with one so strange. And though he had loved his family he had separated from them, aligning himself with her in this grand house away from the staring eyes of the town. It had not been a conventional marriage—she could not abide being touched and permitted him to see her only at certain times of the day, and even then he might not even be present as far as she was concerned, so intent was she on her conversation with the people and things he could not see.

His family virtually abandoned him over his choice, but as a grown man it was his choice to make. He was never sure if his beloved Alma had such choices. Alma had been driven, apparently, by whatever stray winds entered her brain.

The gift she had chosen in lieu of a child (for how could he give his child such a mother, or give his wife such a tender thing to care for?) still sat in its corner in shadow, appearing to lean his way on its insubstantial legs. He perceived a narrow crack in the front surface of the small cabinet, which drew him closer to inspect the damage, but it was only that the small door was ajar, inviting him to secure it further, or to peek inside.

Jacob led himself into the corner with his lantern held before him, and grasping the miniature knob with two trembling fingers pulled it away from the frame, and seeing that the door had a twin, unclasped the other side and spread both doors like wings that might fly away with this beautiful box. He stepped closer then, moving the light across the cabinet's interior like a blazing eye.

The inside was furnished like some doll's house, and it saddened him to see this late evidence of the state of Alma's thinking. Here and there were actual pieces of doll furniture, perhaps kept from her girlhood or "borrowed" from some neighbor child. Then there were pieces—a settee very like the one in this room, a high-backed Queen Anne chair—carved, apparently, from soap, now discolored and furred by years of clinging dust and lint.

Other furniture had been assembled from spools and emery boards, clothespins, a small jewelry box, then what appeared to be half a broken drinking cup cleverly upholstered with a woman's faded black evening glove.

He was surprised to find in one corner a small portrait of himself, finely painted in delicate strokes, and one of Alma set beside it. And underneath, in tiny, almost unreadable script, two words, which he was sure he could not read correctly, but which might have said "Father," "Mother."

He decided he had been hearing the breathing for some time—he just hadn't been sure of its nature, or its source. The past few years he had suffered from a series of respiratory ailments, and had become accustomed to hearing a soft, secondary wheeze, or leak, with each inhalation and exhalation of breath. That could easily have been the origin of the sounds he was hearing.

But he suspected not. With shaking hand he reached into the far corner of the box, where a variety of handkerchiefs and lacy napkins lay piled. He peeled them off slowly, until finally he reached that faint outline beneath a swatch of dress lace, a short thing curled onto itself, faintly moving with a labored rasp.

He could have stopped then, and thought he should, but his hand was moving again with so little direction, and just nudged that bit of cloth, which dropped down a bare quarter inch.

Nothing there, really, except the tiny eyes. Tissue worn to transparency, flesh vanished into the dusty air, and the child's breathing so slight, a parenthesis, a comma. Jacob stared down solemnly at this kind afterthought, shadow of a shadow, a ghost of a chance. Those eyes so innocent, and yet so old, and desperately tired, an intelligence with no reason to be. Dissolving. The weary breathing stopped.

In the family plot, what little family there might be, there by Alma's grave he erected a small stone: "C. Child" in bold but fine lettering. There he buried the cabinet and all it had contained, because what else had there been to bury? Two years later he joined them there, on the other side.

Steve Rasnic Tem *is a past winner of the Bram Stoker, International Horror Guild, British Fantasy, and World Fantasy Awards. His most recent book is a collection of short story collaborations with wife Melanie Tem,* In Concert. *Steve's audio collection* Invisible *was recently published by* Speaking Volumes *(speakingvolumes.us) in CD and MP3 download. Also available is an ebook of the Tems' fantasy novel* Daughters *(macabreink.com/store/). You may visit the Tem home on the Web at www.m-s-tem.com.*

Two human hearts, the subjectivity of truth, the uncertainty of factual accuracy, and a step from what is usually recognized as reality into some other realm. But if truth is subjective and fact uncertain, then who is to say what is real and what is not? In "The Cabinet Child," Steve Rasnic Tem has given us a poignant story that moves one to ask such questions while really not caring if they are answered.

CHERRYSTONE
AND SHARDS OF ICE

EKATERINA SEDIA

—◆—

I sat with my face in my hands; not due to inebriation, which was greater than what my finances allowed, but less than what I wanted it to be. My distress was caused by a combination of events that involved the crooked militia, a slick merchant, and a deceitful woman. As a result, my financial and moral state left much to be desired; so I drank on credit.

Just as the world was starting to soften around the edges, a shadow fell across the stained tablecloth of the restaurant table. I did not look up. While I was not a man to avoid the inevitable, I still did not relish the sight of my doom's portends. I wanted to see neither goons, nor the ungrateful bitches.

"Excuse me," said a male voice directly above and far, far from my bowed head. "Messer Lonagan?"

The address was polite enough to make me raise my gaze. Two thugs in the uniforms of the Areti clan grinned at me with as much sincere joy as a shark that spotted a flounder.

"Yes," I said, too smart and too experienced to lie. "What can I do for you?"

"Venerable Mistress Areti desires to see you."

I sighed and took another sip of my wine. "I'd rather stay where I am. I had the most wretched day, and surely the Venerable Mistress can find someone better qualified than I." Not that I liked turning down a paycheck, but Areti's gold to a businessman was like a millstone to a swimmer.

One of the thugs grabbed my right wrist, pressing it against the table where it rested. The other goon opened his jacket, extracting a pistol with a heavy handle, flipped it in his hand with a rehearsed motion, and brought it down across my fingers—lightly, but with enough force to give me an idea of how much it would hurt when he did it in earnest. His eyes glinted with a malicious promise.

"Please don't break my hand." I felt tired rather than scared. "I need it."

"Will you come then?"

What was a man to do? I followed them out of the restaurant, into the streets filled with silvery mist highlighted by an occasional hazy sphere of a gas lamp. On our way, we took a shortcut and skimmed along the edge of the deaders' town, where ghostly dead man's birches shone through the droplets of moisture in the air, their branches studded with tiny green flickers, the condensation weeping silently down their trunks.

We walked across a wooden bridge that creaked and resonated under our feet. I smelled something musty, and a moment later spotted a dead beggar, who sat in the middle of the bridge, reclining by the guardrail. His eyes bulged out of his swollen dark face, and his thick purple tongue protruded where his lower jaw used to be, but was now gone, lost forever. He would not walk around for long, and seemed to know it—his white eyes were turned upwards, greeting the stars as they sprinkled across the darkened sky.

"Filthy rat," said on of my guides. "He probably died a beggar."

"Likely," I agreed, and couldn't look away.

The other guide spat, propelling a gob of saliva and phlegm that landed with a satisfying smack onto the beggar's left eye. "I can't believe it. They are everywhere nowadays—their part of town just keeps on spreading."

"That doesn't require a great deal of faith, to believe that," I said. "The dead will always outnumber the living."

"How's that?"

"You live, you die. Everyone who's now alive will end up in the deaders' town. Even you, so be nice to them."

The guards huffed, but their gazes slid off the beggar and turned downward, to the slats under our feet. One could live in this place and be carefree only if he did not think of his inevitable demise, the inexplicable one-way traffic. I couldn't ignore this silent but constant shuffling from one side of the town to the other; I couldn't forget that the deader city swelled with every passing year, encroaching onto the town of the living. Soon, the alivers' town would be but a fleck in the sea of rotting flesh. I was never carefree.

I shook my head and stepped off the bridge onto the quartz pavement, where the gaslights were installed with regularity, and the trees emitted no deathly glow, but cast deep, cool shadows, soft as crushed silk. A light perfume of jasmine scented the night, and soft singing came from nearby—the sort of thing the alivers enjoy.

The Areti manor squatted squarely on the hillside, its windows shuttered, but a soft glow of lamplight seeped around the edges, beckoning. The three of us entered the hallway. Darkness pooled in the rounded recesses of the walls, and my soft-soled shoes seemed too loud. There didn't seem to be any people here, just echoes. There were no doors either—just curtains that billowed in the entryways, blown about by the dusty winds that skipped around the manor, unchallenged.

"In here," one of the goons said, and pulled open a curtain decorated with a beaded dragon. Its eyes glinted in the firelight that reached from within.

I entered a vast hall drenched in shadows. "Venerable Mistress?"

"Right this way, Lonagan." She reclined on a chaise made of solid oak, and still it creaked under her weight. The fireplace cast a semicircle of orange light, and I stepped closer.

Her face was oval and pretty, with large doe eyes and a prim, full-lipped mouth. Her long auburn hair curled and cascaded, descending onto her shoulders and chest, playing like waterfalls across the vast terrain that was her body. She was a landscape, not a woman—hills and valleys of flesh stretched before me in every direction, barely contained on the gigantic chaise. Only her face and hands seemed human.

I bowed. "What can I do for you, Venerable Mistress Areti?"

She smiled, and for a moment I forgot about her distended body, and looked into her ink-blue, almost black eyes. "I hear that you can find things."

I inclined my head. "That is indeed the case. What would you like me to find?"

Her smile grew colder, tighter. "I thought you could figure that out."

"No," I said with rising irritation. "I'm not a magician. I'm just a thorough man."

She undulated with laughter, sending slow, hypnotic waves through her flesh. "All right then. I lost a gemstone—or rather, it was stolen from me. By the deaders."

"Are you sure?" The deaders were not known for crime—that was the province of the still-living.

"Oh, quite sure. You see, they are recent deaders, and I fear that my men were somehow responsible for their transition."

It still sounded strange to me, but I nodded. Who was I to judge? Perhaps they had the stone on them while they transitioned; perhaps their passions were slower to die than was common. "What is this stone like?"

"It's a cherrystone." She lifted a delicate, fine hand, and spread her index finger and thumb half an inch apart. "Small, pink. You'll know it when you see it."

I was certain of that. Even though I've never held anything as valuable as a cherrystone in my hands, I heard enough about them and their powers to know how rare they were. Especially pink ones—chances were, it was the only one in town.

"What about those who took it?"

She shrugged. "Ask my guardsmen for a description."

"Do you know their names?"

"I would imagine they've shed their names by now, so they would be useless to you."

So it was longer than a week since they were dead. Yet, I couldn't imagine why she would wait a week to start looking for her cherrystone. The only conclusion that made sense was the one that didn't make sense—that they were dead while committing the theft.

"Be discreet," she said, just as I was about to leave. "You understand how precarious my situation is."

"Of course, Venerable Mistress. I won't say a word."

I left the crackling of the fire and the oaken chaise behind, and walked along the corridor, back to the entrance. This place did not fill me with trepidation any longer—the air of lonely neglect made me feel sorry for her, despite the Areti's bloody reputation. I liked to think that my sympathy was not contaminated by the promise of a paycheck.

One had to be careful in the deaders' town, and I watched my step, even though I had connections there. The inhabitants were not violent by nature, but protective of what little lives they had. I prepared myself for the stench by putting a generous dollop of wintergreen ointment under my nose, and stowed the can in my pocket. Abiding the old habits, I waited for the nightfall, to sneak in under the cover of darkness.

The moment my foot touched the soft moss that grew through the cracks in wooden pavements, I realized that I was foolish—deaders did not sleep, and night made no difference. I heard the ice merchants calling in high voices, and the scraping of their trunks full of green translucent chunks of ice as they pulled them by the ropes.

I kept close to the buildings, and hid my face in the collar of my jacket. A few passersby did not seem to notice me, as they shambled along. Jas, the deader I was going to see lived well away from the border of the alivers; it wasn't the first time that I visited him, but the gravity of my task made me feel ill at ease.

I saw his house, recognizable because of the brick-red shutters, and sped up my steps. The houses seemed superfluous—if it wasn't for the need to contain the cold, the deaders could've just as easily lived outside, shambled along whatever streets, forests or valleys they chose. But they kept to the town, nestled inside in the protective cocoon of ice, trying to slow their decay. Couldn't say I blamed them.

I passed a white house, with a small courtyard and a garden in front of it, and paused. One did not see decorations in these parts too often. And I also saw a young girl in the yard. Unaware that anyone was watching, she hummed to herself, and practiced her dance steps. She must've died just recently—her skin was pale but whole, and her downy hair blew about her thin face as she twirled with her arms raised. I didn't know exactly what happens after death, but I noticed that it affected coordination; the girl stumbled, and almost fell over. Stubbornly, she steadied herself, and started on sidesteps.

She noticed me watching, and gasped. In her fright, she bolted away, running straight into a gatepost. It would've been comical if the impact wasn't so great—it threw her backwards, and she landed on her rump.

I swung the gates open, and helped her up. "I'm so sorry," I said. "I didn't mean to scare you. I just stopped to watch—you dance very prettily."

She sniffed. "Do I have a bruise?"

I nodded. An angry purple spot was spreading across her white forehead.

She gave a little cry and whimpered. Dead didn't weep, but there was a phlegmy rattle deep in her chest.

"I'm sorry," I said. "It's just a bruise."

Her mouth curled downwards. "You don't understand. It'll never heal."

I knew that she was right, and felt wretched. I didn't mean to shorten her time, I didn't want to speed up her decay.

She finally looked at me. "It's not your fault. It was an accident."

I nodded. "Thank you."

"You're an aliver. What are you doing here?"

"I came to see your neighbor," I said. "The one who lives in that house."

"I know him. I think. A tall young man, right?"

"Yes, that's the one. I guess I'd best be going."

"Why do you want to see him?" I was certain now that she hadn't been among the dead for long—she asked too many questions. The deaders were usually more reserved, less curious.

Of course I wasn't going to tell her the exact truth; but I wasn't going to lie either, not after I hurt her. "He's my brother," I said. "Used to be, I mean."

Her mouth opened in awe. "And you still see him?"

"Why not?"

"No one else does."

She was right, of course. I opened the gate, all the while feeling her curious stare at the back of my neck. Before I stepped into the street, I turned to face her again. "I know. The alivers prefer not to think about the folks here. And I can't stop thinking about them . . . you."

I knocked on the dingy, peeling door of the house with red shutters. It gave under my knuckles, and I stepped inside. My teeth started chattering as soon as I crossed the threshold.

"It's you," Jas said.

"It's me. How are you?"

He sat slouching on the floor, his back propped against an ice chest. It was half-full of dirty water and pellucid ice shards. He had changed little since last I saw him—perhaps a bit more decay darkening the skin around his eyes and on his temples, perhaps more sinking around his mouth; but he was still in good shape—as good as one can expect after ten years of death. "All right, I suppose. You?"

"Same." I sat by the door, the warmest spot of this one-room house. "Want me to fetch an ice merchant for you?"

"Nah. What do you want?"

I gave a laugh that sounded unconvincing even to me. "Do I need a reason to see you?"

He coughed, and it sounded like something came loose in his chest with a sickening tear of wet tissue. "Nah. But you usually have one. I'm not as dull as you think."

"I don't think you're dull. You're right; I do have a question. I'm looking for two deaders—new ones. One is tall and dark, has only one hand. The other is medium height, light hair, no beard. Young."

The ruin that was my brother nodded. "I know them. Still, it wouldn't kill you to come and just visit."

"I didn't think you wanted me to. Every time I come you act like you don't want me here."

"I don't want. I can't; I'd like to, but I can't. And I forget a lot, y'know?" His tongue turned awkwardly in his mouth, scraping against blackened teeth. "When you come, you remind me. And I don't want to forget. So please come. To remind me."

"Jas . . . "

"Lemme finish. Other deaders, they don't remember squat. Who they were, and they tell me, they tell, 'How do you know you even have a brother? Who can know such a thing? You can't remember about the alivers.' But I do, because of you. I'm lucky—everyone else, they're alone. But not me, not me."

"All right, Jas." My voice shook a bit, but I didn't think he'd noticed. "I'll come more often. But now I need to know about those men."

"Why?"

I hesitated; not that mistrusted Jas, but the deaders had loyalty to their own kind, not to the alivers—even if they were kin. "They might know something that is of interest to me."

Jas shook his head. "You're still dealing in secrets. Dangerous trade."

"I know. I almost had my hand broken the other day."

Jas sat up. "Like the man you're looking for."

I felt a chill, and it didn't come from the icebox. "I thought his hand was missing."

"They broke it first, then cut it off, then slit his throat." Jas spoke with relish. I noticed it before; the deaders seemed to enjoy the details of death.

"Who?"

Jas shrugged. "The Areti goons, who else? I sure hope they don't want anything from you; they and the deaders have been fighting for no one remembers how long."

"You know why?"

He nodded. "Every deader knows. It's about a curse, and a cherrystone."

"Areti's cherrystone?"

His lungs whistled a bit—the sound that signified laughter. "Is that what she'd been telling you? No, that's ours. It's our curse, see, and we're keeping it, Areti or not." Jas stood. "C'mon. There's someone I want you to meet."

I stepped toward the door, but Jas shook his head. "It's too warm out. We'll go the other way."

He creaked and groaned, but bent down enough to touch the earthen floor. He groped around in the dirt.

"Can I give you a hand?"

"Sure." He pointed out a bronze ring mounted on a wooden trapdoor, hidden under a layer of dirt. I never noticed that it was there.

I pulled on the ring, and as the dust and grime cloud settled, I saw a rickety ladder leading downwards. "Where does it go?"

"To other houses . . . everywhere. It's nicer to travel underground, cooler."

That explained the scant traffic on the surface. I let Jas descend, and followed him. It wasn't nearly as dark as I had expected—strange fluorescent creatures darted to and fro among the weakly glowing walls of the tunnel, and sick, gangly dead man's birches illuminated the way with their dead light.

There were ladders everywhere, and the deaders too—the underground seemed a much more animated place than the surface. I mimicked Jas' shambling gait, eager not to attract attention. "Should I even be here?" I asked Jas.

He stopped and mulled it over for a moment. "Don't see why not. You'll move here, sooner or later. As long as you don't hurt the deaders, you're all right."

I was moved that he never even considered the possibility of my betrayal; then again, perhaps it was one of the deaders' limitations. Just as they forgot their relatives, so perhaps they lost their understanding of the ways of the living.

He led me deeper into the labyrinth. The passersby grew less frequent, and the light—weaker. I could not discern the direction, but guessed that we were close to the river once I noticed drops of moisture seeping along the support beams through the earthen walls.

He stopped and looked around, as if getting his bearings. Then, he sat down on the earthen floor.

"What now?"

"Now we wait," he said.

We didn't wait for long. I did suspect before that the deaders could communicate with each other through some unfathomable means. Soon, four deaders showed up, then three more. All of the newcomers sat down on the floor and remained quiet, as more of them kept arriving.

There were all kinds of them there—young and old, and even one child. Some were dead long enough to lose most of their skin and flesh—at least two hundred years; others were quite fresh. Even the girl I met earlier showed up; I noticed with a pang of guilt that the purple bruise on her forehead was spreading. Despite my repeated application of the wintergreen ointment, the air grew putrid with their smell, and my heart was uneasy. There I was, underground, surrounded by a throng of deaders. If they turned on me, I would never be able to fight through them—or find my way back to the surface. The trust I attributed to Jas was actually mine.

Underground, I had lost the sense of time, and only knew that it was passing—slowly, like water weeping from the walls. The sounds of soft, dry voices of the deaders mingled with the dripping of water; while the monotony of it was somewhat lulling, the content was certainly not.

I learned that the cherrystone in question was cursed. A traveling warlock passed through our town, many years ago. When the Areti came to the warlock, demanding that he lend his talent to them, they were met with a refusal. They sent their thugs to make him pay for their humiliation, but the thugs were never heard from again. The warlock was nonetheless angry with the Areti. Before he left, he hid the cherrystone somewhere in town, and told them that as long as the cursed stone was within the town walls, our dead would walk the land.

When his prediction came true, the Areti looked for it. They looked everywhere—on the bottom of the river, under every rock, even in the catacombs under the deaders' town. After a few years they stopped looking—old legends are easy to forget. The cherrystone was left be, until the present Mistress of the Areti clan realized her mortality. The search for the cherrystone had become an obsession, and she sent her goons and hirelings to look for it. It took her awhile, but she had learned that it was in deaders' town.

"Why does she want it?" I said.

"To end the curse," said one of the oldest deaders.

I nodded. I could understand that desire, and yet I wasn't sure why the Areti were so concerned about it.

"It's their family's curse, or so they see it. It's the matter of honor for them," said the child. "They don't care what will happen to us. They only know that they don't want to become us."

There was no good way to ask this question, but I asked anyway. "Do you . . . do you like being like this?"

They whistled and chortled, their laughter akin to scratching of nails.

"You'll see when you're in my shoes," Jas said. "It's more life, even though you might not see it as such. See, I don't relish being what I am, but I still prefer it to lying still in the ground, being eaten by worms."

"Do you know where that cherrystone is?"

The crowd grew silent, and I felt their eyes on me, judging, weighing. "'Course we do," Jas said. "That's the first thing you learn as a deader—it's important, see. And we tell it to each other every day, so that we don't forget—about the Areti, about their snooping goons . . . "

The appearance of two more deaders interrupted him. One was tall and dark, one-handed. The other, a teenager, seemed young enough to be his son, but his light hair belied this conclusion. His nostrils were torn open, and a slow trickle of pus trekked across his pale lips and down his chin.

"You came to kill us," the youngster said.

Once again, I grew aware of precariousness of my situation, and protested my innocence with as much sincerity as I could muster.

"The Areti sent you," his companion said. "Just like they sent us."

I shrugged. "So? I find things; I never killed anyone."

Jas' heavy hand lay on my shoulder. I could feel through my jacket how cold and clammy it was. "He wouldn't do something like that," he said to the gathering. "He knows better."

I nodded. "I do. Only others don't. You think people across the river would listen to me? Or to you, for that matter. Far as everyone's concerned, if the stone is gone, so much the better. The Areti won't leave you alone. Not with the present Mistress."

Everyone nodded in agreement.

"She won't stop," the bruised girl said. "Not until she's one of us." She gave me a meaningful look. "Will you help us?"

"Whoa," I said. "You're not asking me to kill her, are you?"

They murmured that it wouldn't be a bad idea, and after all, it wouldn't be all bad for her. The deaders' town was a nice place.

"I'm not a murderer," I said. "But I think I can help you. The stone needs to stay in town, right? Doesn't matter where?"

"No," Jas said. "But she won't stop looking."

"I think I know a good place for it," I said. "Just give me the stone, and don't worry about a thing. She'll never find it."

Their silence was unnatural—not even a sound of breathing broke it. Dozens of dead eyes look at me, expressionless, weighing my proposal in their oozing, ruined skulls. I asked a lot of them—to put their very existence into the hands of an aliver, a being as alien to them as they were to me.

If I were in his shoes, I doubt I would've done what Jas had done: he pointed at the girl with the purple bruise. "Give it to him," he said.

The girl stepped back, away from me, and I reached out, afraid that she would stumble and fall again. She remained on her feet—I supposed she was getting a hang of her new limitations. "Why do you think he'll help us?" she asked Jas, but her hand was already reaching for her chest.

"He's my brother," Jas said.

Her fingers pushed away a flimsy shawl that cradled her slender shoulders, and I gasped at the sight of a deep wound, left by a dagger. That was what killed her—an angry father, a jealous husband, a sullen stranger. She reached deep into the wound, pulling out a small round object, covered with congealed gore. I tried not to flinch as the bloodied cherrystone lay in my palm.

"Be careful with it," the one-handed man told me. "It's a powerful thing."

"What can it do?" I said, rolling it on my palm gingerly. It left a trail, but didn't seem very powerful.

"Whatever it has to do," Jas said.

<hr>

The sight of the moonlit Areti manor greeted me from afar. It was deep night, and not a window shone in the darkness. The bulk of the building sat immobile but sinister, as a stone gargoyle ready to come to life and rip out the heart of the next victim. I heaved a sigh and slowed my steps; no doubt, the manor would be guarded, and I was disinclined to reveal my presence just yet. Fortunately, in my line of business I had learned a thing or two about surreptitious visits.

I avoided the front door, where the two goons of my recent acquaintance sat on the steps, trading monosyllabic talk. My soft-soled shoes made no sound on the grass as I edged around the corner and along the wall, looking for a different point of entry. There was a backdoor, as I had expected, latched shut from the inside. Worse, the door was cased in iron, and a slightest manipulation would surely reverberate through the building.

In the pale moonlight, I let my fingers run along the edges of the door, looking for a gap. The door was quite well fitted, and I procured a short knife with thin blade from my pocket, and forced it between the door and the wall that surrounded it, trying to feel the latch inside. The scraping of metal against metal tore the still air. I jerked my hand away, and fell into a crouch by the wall. I waited for a long while, but nobody appeared.

I explored the perimeter of the manor again, in hopes of finding a ground level window or another door. None were forthcoming, and I returned to the back entrance guarded by iron. I wondered if the cherrystone could be of use, and took it out of my pocket. It glowed softly, and I touched it to the door. Nothing happened.

"Come on," I whispered to it. "Do you want to be found and destroyed?"

The stone did not answer.

I felt foolish, carrying on a conversation with an inanimate object, but persisted. I sat down, my back against the cold wall, cradling the stone's tiny light in my open palms. "See," I told it, "it's like this. I could just give you up, take my money, and go home. But it's bigger than me or her or even you . . ."

My voice caught in my throat as my own words reached me. There was no doubt that the Areti would kill me—break my fingers, cut off my hand, perhaps rip my nostrils open, just like they did to the dead boy. But I also realized that it would be better to die now and have a place to go than eke out another few years and succumb to the black nothingness to which people from other places went. We lived with the deaders for so long that we saw them as a nuisance; we didn't realize how lucky we were to have them—to become them. And this stone made it all possible. I closed my hand around it, protecting it, protecting all of us.

The stone grew warmer in my hand, and soon it burned it. It shone brighter too, and narrow white beams of light squeezed between my fingers—my fist looked like a star. When I touched it to the door, the metal sang, barely audible, and the door swung open. I entered the dark dusty hallway, my way illuminated by the cherrystone.

I followed it to the dark recesses of the sleeping manor, to the kitchen. There, a massive brick stove towered against the far wall. The light beams cut through the stone as if it was butter, forming a long, narrow tunnel behind the stove, just spacious enough to let my hand through.

I released the cherrystone, and let it roll into its new hiding place. As it cooled and darkened, what was left of its power sealed the passage, returning it to the normal appearance of the brickwork of the stove and stone of the walls.

As quietly as I entered, I left. I crossed the river as the sun was rising above the rooftops. I listened to the crowing of roosters and to the first banging of shutters, inhaled the sweet aroma of baking bread, basked in the first sunrays alighting on my shoulders. I was heading back to my favorite restaurant, where I intended to drink until the Areti thugs found me.

I thought about what would be my last trip to the deaders' town—how I would shamble along, until I arrived to Jas' house. I would have to tell him right away that I was his brother, before I forget and lose the tentative connection between us, and ask him to remind me. Then I would settle next to the ice chest, and we would talk, in loopy, halting sentences. And we would remind each other every day, so that we don't forget, keeping the memory of our shared blood alive.

⎯◆⎯

Ekaterina Sedia *resides in the Pinelands of New Jersey. Her critically acclaimed novels,* The Secret History of Moscow *and* The Alchemy of Stone *were published, respectively, in 2007 and 2008. Her next novel,* The House of Discarded Dreams, *is coming out in late 2010. Her short stories have sold to* Analog, Baen's Universe, Dark Wisdom, *and* Clarkesworld, *as well as numerous anthologies, including* Haunted Legends *and* Magic in the Mirrorstone. *She is also the editor of anthologies* Running with the Pack *(2010) and the World Fantasy Award-winning* Paper Cities *(2008). Visit her at www.ekaterinasedia.com.*

⎯◆⎯

Sedia often offers a "different" viewpoint in her fiction, which means the reader makes interesting new discoveries. Here, in this universe, death means black nothingness—except to the inhabitants of this enchanted town. So "to eke out another few years" as a "deader" seems preferable. As the narrator says: "The deaders' town was a nice place . . . we didn't realize how lucky we were to have them—to become them."

THE CREVASSE

DALE BAILEY & NATHAN BALLINGRUD

What he loved was the silence, the pristine clarity of the ice shelf: the purposeful breathing of the dogs straining against their traces, the hiss of the runners, the opalescent arc of the sky. Garner peered through shifting veils of snow at the endless sweep of glacial terrain before him, the wind gnawing at him, forcing him to reach up periodically and scrape at the thin crust of ice that clung to the edges of his facemask, the dry rasp of the fabric against his face reminding him that he was alive.

There were fourteen of them. Four men, one of them, Faber, strapped to the back of Garner's sledge, mostly unconscious, but occasionally surfacing out of the morphine depths to moan. Ten dogs, big Greenland huskies, gray and white. Two sledges. And the silence, scouring him of memory and desire, hollowing him out inside. It was what he'd come to Antarctica for.

And then, abruptly, the silence split open like a wound:

A thunderous crack, loud as lightning cleaving stone, shivered the ice, and the dogs of the lead sledge, maybe twenty-five yards ahead of Garner, erupted into panicky cries. Garner saw it happen: the lead sledge sloughed over—hurling Connelly into the snow—and plunged nose first through the ice, as though an enormous hand had reached up through the earth to snatch it under. Startled, he watched an instant longer. The wrecked sledge, jutting out of the earth like a broken stone, hurtled at him, closer, closer. Then time stuttered, leaping forward. Garner flung one of the brakes out behind him. The hook skittered over the ice. Garner felt the jolt in his spine when it caught. Rope sang out behind him, arresting his momentum. But it wouldn't be enough.

Garner flung out a second brake, then another. The hooks snagged, jerking the sledge around and up on a single runner. For a moment Garner thought that it was going to roll, dragging the dogs along behind it. Then the airborne runner slammed back to earth and the sledge skidded to a stop in a glittering spray of ice.

Dogs boiled back into its shadow, howling and snapping. Ignoring them, Garner clambered free. He glanced back at Faber, still miraculously strapped to the travois, his face ashen, and then he pelted toward the wrecked sledge, dodging a minefield of spilled cargo: food and tents, cooking gear, his medical bag, disgorging a bright freight of tools and the few precious ampules of morphine McReady had been willing to spare, like a fan of scattered diamonds.

The wrecked sledge hung precariously, canted on a lip of ice above a black crevasse. As Garner stood there, it slipped an inch, and then another, dragged down by the weight of the dogs. He could hear them whining, claws scrabbling as they strained against harnesses drawn taut by the weight of Atka, the lead dog, dangling out of sight beyond the edge of the abyss.

Garner visualized him—thrashing against his tack in a black well as the jagged circle of grayish light above shrank away, inch by lurching inch—and he felt the pull of night inside himself, the age-old gravity of the dark. Then a hand closed around his ankle.

Bishop, clinging to the ice, a hand-slip away from tumbling into the crevasse himself: face blanched, eyes red rimmed inside his goggles.

"Shit," Garner said. "Here—"

He reached down, locked his hand around Bishop's wrist, and hauled him up, boots slipping. Momentum carried him over backwards, floundering in the snow as Bishop curled fetal beside him.

"You okay?"

"My ankle," he said through gritted teeth.

"Here, let me see."

"Not now. Connelly. What happened to Connelly?"

"He fell off—"

With a metallic screech, the sledge broke loose. It slid a foot, a foot and a half, and then it hung up. The dogs screamed. Garner had never heard a dog make a noise like that—he didn't know dogs *could* make a noise like that—and for a moment their blind, inarticulate terror swam through him. He thought again of Atka, dangling there, turning, feet clawing at the darkness, and he felt something stir inside him once again—

"Steady, man," Bishop said.

Garner drew in a long breath, icy air lacerating his lungs.

"You gotta be steady now, Doc," Bishop said. "You gotta go cut him loose."

"No—"

"We're gonna lose the sledge. And the rest of the team. That happens, we're all gonna die out here, okay? I'm busted up right now, I need you to do this thing—"

"What about Connell—?"

"Not now, Doc. Listen to me. We don't have time. Okay?"

Bishop held his gaze. Garner tried to look away, could not. The other man's eyes fixed him.

"Okay," he said.

Garner stood and stumbled away. Went to his knees to dig through the wreckage. Flung aside a sack of rice, frozen in clumps, wrenched open a crate of flares—useless—shoved it aside, and dragged another one toward him. This time he was lucky: he dug out a coil of rope, a hammer, a handful of pitons. The sledge lurched on its lip of ice, the rear end swinging, setting off another round of whimpering.

"Hurry," Bishop said.

Garner drove the pitons deep into the permafrost and threaded the rope through their eyes, his hands stiff inside his gloves. Lashing the other end around his waist, he edged back onto the broken ice shelf. It shifted underneath him, creaking. The sledge shuddered, but held. Below him, beyond the moiling clump of dogs, he could see the leather trace leads, stretched taut across the jagged rim of the abyss.

He dropped back, letting rope out as he descended. The world fell away above him. Down and down, and then he was on his knees at the very edge of the shelf, the hot, rank stink of the dogs enveloping him. He used his teeth to loosen one glove. Working quickly against the icy assault of the elements, he fumbled his knife out of its sheath and pressed the blade to the first of the traces. He sawed at it until the leather separated with a snap.

Atka's weight shifted in the darkness below him, and the dog howled mournfully. Garner set to work on the second trace, felt it let go, everything—the sledge, the terrified dogs—slipping toward darkness. For a moment he thought the whole thing would go. But it held. He went to work on the third trace, gone loose now by some trick of tension. It too separated beneath his blade, and he once again felt Atka's weight shift in the well of darkness beneath him.

Garner peered into the blackness. He could see the dim blur of the dog, could feel its dumb terror welling up around him, and as he brought the blade to the final trace, a painstakingly erected dike gave way in his mind. Memory flooded through him: the feel of mangled flesh beneath his fingers, the distant *whump* of artillery, Elizabeth's drawn and somber face.

His fingers faltered. Tears blinded him. The sledge shifted above him as Atka thrashed in his harness. Still he hesitated.

The rope creaked under the strain of additional weight. Ice rained down around him. Garner looked up to see Connelly working his way hand over hand down the rope.

"Do it," Connelly grunted, his eyes like chips of flint. "Cut him loose."

Garner's fingers loosened around the hilt of the blade. He felt the tug of the dark at his feet, Atka whining.

"Give me the goddamn knife," Connelly said, wrenching it away, and together they clung there on the single narrow thread of gray rope, two men and one knife and the enormous gulf of the sky overhead as Connelly sawed savagely at the last of the traces. It held for a moment, and then, abruptly, it gave, loose ends curling back and away from the blade.

Atka fell howling into darkness.

———※———

They made camp.

The traces of the lead sledge had to be untangled and repaired, the dogs tended to, the weight redistributed to account for Atka's loss. While Connelly busied himself with these chores, Garner stabilized Faber—the blood had frozen to a black crust inside the makeshift splint Garner had applied yesterday, after the accident—and wrapped Bishop's ankle. These were automatic actions. Serving in France he'd learned the trick of letting his body work while his mind traveled to other places; it had been crucial to keeping his sanity during the war, when the people brought to him for treatment had been butchered by German submachine guns or burned and blistered by mustard gas. He worked to save those men, though it was hopeless work. Mankind had acquired an appetite for dying; doctors had become shepherds to the process. Surrounded by screams and spilled blood, he'd anchored himself to memories of his wife, Elizabeth: the warmth of her kitchen back home in Boston, and the warmth of her body too.

But all that was gone.

Now, when he let his mind wander, it went to dark places, and he found himself concentrating instead on the minutiae of these rote tasks like a first-year medical student. He cut a length of bandage and applied a compression wrap to Bishop's exposed ankle, covering both ankle and foot in careful figure-eights. He kept his mind in the moment, listening to the harsh labor of their lungs in the frigid air, to Connelly's chained fury as he worked at the traces, and to the muffled sounds of the dogs as they burrowed into the snow to rest.

And he listened, too, to Atka's distant cries, leaking from the crevasse like blood.

"Can't believe that dog's still alive," Bishop said, testing his ankle against his weight. He grimaced and sat down on a crate. "He's a tough old bastard."

Garner imagined Elizabeth's face, drawn tight with pain and determination, while he fought a war on the far side of the ocean. Was she afraid too, suspended over her own dark hollow? Did she cry out for him?

"Help me with this tent," Garner said.

They'd broken off from the main body of the expedition to bring Faber back to one of the supply depots on the Ross Ice Shelf, where Garner could care for him. They would wait there for the remainder of the expedition, which suited Garner just fine, but troubled both Bishop and Connelly, who had higher aspirations for their time here.

Nightfall was still a month away, but if they were going to camp here while they made repairs, they would need the tents to harvest warmth. Connelly approached as they drove pegs into the permafrost, his eyes impassive as they swept over Faber, still tied down to the travois, locked inside a morphine dream. He regarded Bishop's ankle and asked him how it was.

"It'll do," Bishop said. "It'll have to. How are the dogs?"

"We need to start figuring what we can do without," Connelly said. "We're gonna have to leave some stuff behind."

"We're only down one dog," Bishop said. "It shouldn't be too hard to compensate."

"We're down two. One of the swing dogs snapped her foreleg." He opened one of the bags lashed to the rear sledge, removing an Army-issue revolver. "So go ahead and figure what we don't need. I gotta tend to her." He tossed a contemptuous glance at Garner. "Don't worry, I won't ask *you* to do it."

Garner watched as Connelly approached the injured dog, lying away from the others in the snow. She licked obsessively at her broken leg. As Connelly approached she looked up at him and her tail wagged weakly. Connelly aimed the pistol and fired a bullet through her head. The shot made a flat, inconsequential sound, swallowed up by the vastness of the open plain.

Garner turned away, emotion surging through him with a surprising, disorienting energy. Bishop met his gaze and offered a rueful smile.

"Bad day," he said.

Still, Atka whimpered.

Garner lay wakeful, staring at the canvas, taut and smooth as the interior of an egg above him. Faber moaned, calling out after some fever phantom. Garner almost envied the man. Not the injury—a nasty compound fracture of the femur, the product of a bad step on the ice when he'd stepped outside the circle of tents to piss—but the sweet oblivion of the morphine doze.

In France, in the war, he'd known plenty of doctors who'd used the stuff to chase away the night haunts. He'd also seen the fevered agony of withdrawal. He had no wish to experience that, but he felt the opiate lure all the same. He'd felt it then, when he'd had thoughts of Elizabeth to sustain him. And he felt it now—stronger still—when he didn't.

Elizabeth had fallen victim to the greatest cosmic prank of all time, the flu that had swept across the world in the spring and summer of 1918, as if the bloody abattoir in the trenches hadn't been evidence enough of humanity's divine disfavor. That's what Elizabeth had called it in the last letter he'd ever had from her: God's judgment on a world gone mad. Garner had given up on God by then: he'd packed away the Bible Elizabeth had pressed upon him after a week in the field hospital, knowing that its paltry lies could bring him no comfort in the face of such horror, and it hadn't. Not then, and not later, when he'd come home to face Elizabeth's mute and barren grave. Garner had taken McReady's offer to accompany the expedition soon after, and though he'd stowed the Bible in his gear before he left, he hadn't opened it since and he wouldn't open it here, either, lying sleepless beside a man who might yet die because he'd had to take a piss—yet another grand cosmic joke—in a place so hellish and forsaken that even Elizabeth's God could find no purchase here.

There could be no God in such a place.

Just the relentless shriek of the wind tearing at the flimsy canvas, and the death-howl agony of the dog. Just emptiness, and the unyielding porcelain dome of the polar sky.

Garner sat up, breathing heavily.

Faber muttered under his breath. Garner leaned over the injured man, the stench of fever hot in his nostrils. He smoothed Faber's hair back from his forehead and studied the leg, swollen tight as a sausage inside the sealskin legging. Garner didn't like to think what he might see if he slit open that sausage to reveal the leg underneath: the viscous pit of the wound itself, crimson lines of sepsis twining around Faber's thigh like a malevolent vine as they climbed inexorably toward his heart.

Atka howled, a long rising cry that broke into pitiful yelps, died away, and renewed itself, like the shriek of sirens on the French front.

"Jesus," Garner whispered.

He fished a flask out of his pack and allowed himself a single swallow of whiskey. Then he sat in the dark, listening to the mournful lament of the dog, his mind filling with hospital images: the red splash of tissue in a steel tray, the enflamed wound of an amputation, the hand folding itself into an outraged fist as the arm fell away. He thought of Elizabeth, too, Elizabeth most all, buried months before Garner had gotten back from Europe. And he thought of Connelly, that aggrieved look as he turned away to deal with the injured swing dog.

Don't worry, I won't ask you to do it.

Crouching in the low tent, Garner dressed. He shoved a flashlight into his jacket, shouldered aside the tent flap, and leaned into the wind tearing across the waste. The crevasse lay before him, rope still trailing through the pitons to dangle into the pit below.

Garner felt the pull of darkness. And Atka, screaming.

"Okay," he muttered. "All right, I'm coming."

Once again he lashed the rope around his waist. This time he didn't hesitate as he backed out onto the ledge of creaking ice. Hand over hand he went, backward and down, boots scuffing until he stepped into space and hung suspended in a well of shadow.

Panic seized him, the black certainty that nothing lay beneath him. The crevasse yawned under his feet, like a wedge of vacuum driven into the heart of the planet. Then, below him—ten feet? twenty?—Atka mewled, piteous as a freshly whelped pup, eyes squeezed shut against the light. Garner thought of the dog, curled in agony upon some shelf of subterranean ice, and began to lower himself into the pit, darkness rising to envelop him.

One heartbeat, then another and another and another, his breath diaphanous in the gloom, his boots scrabbling for solid ground. Scrabbling and finding it. Garner clung to the rope, testing the surface with his weight.

It held.

Garner took the flashlight from his jacket, and switched it on. Atka peered up at him, brown eyes iridescent with pain. The dog's legs twisted underneath it, and its tail wagged feebly. Blood glistened at its muzzle. As he moved closer, Garner saw that a dagger of bone had pierced its torso, unveiling the slick yellow gleam of subcutaneous fat and deeper still, half visible through tufts of coarse fur, the bloody pulse of viscera. And it had shat itself—Garner could smell it—a thin gruel congealing on the dank stone.

"Okay," he said. "Okay, Atka."

Kneeling, Garner caressed the dog. It growled and subsided, surrendering to his ministrations.

"Good boy, Atka," he whispered. "Settle down, boy."

Garner slid his knife free of its sheath, bent forward, and brought the blade to the dog's throat. Atka whimpered—"Shhh," Garner whispered—as he bore down with the edge, steeling himself against the thing he was about to do—

Something moved in the darkness beneath him: a leathery rasp, the echoing clatter of stone on stone, of loose pebbles tumbling into darkness. Atka whimpered again, legs twitching as he tried to shove himself back against the wall. Garner, startled, shoved the blade forward. Atka's neck unseamed itself in a welter of black arterial blood. The dog stiffened, shuddered once, and died—Garner watched its eyes dim in the space of a single heartbeat—and once again something shifted in the darkness at Garner's back. Garner scuttled backward, slamming his shoulders into the wall by Atka's corpse. He froze there, probing the darkness.

Then, when nothing came—had he imagined it? He must have imagined it—Garner aimed the flashlight light into the gloom. His breath caught in his throat. He shoved himself erect in amazement, the rope pooling at his feet.

Vast.

The place was vast: walls of naked stone climbing in cathedral arcs to the undersurface of the polar plain and a floor worn smooth as glass over long ages, stretching out before him until it dropped away into an abyss of darkness. Struck dumb with terror—or was it wonder?—Garner stumbled forward, the rope unspooling behind him until he drew up at the precipice, pointed the light into the shadows before him, and saw what it was that he had discovered.

A stairwell, cut seamlessly into the stone itself, and no human stairwell either: each riser fell away three feet or more, the stair itself winding endlessly into fathomless depths of earth, down and down and down until it curved away beyond the reach of his frail human light, and further still toward some awful destination he scarcely dared imagine. Garner felt the lure and hunger of the place singing in his bones. Something deep inside him, some mute inarticulate longing, cried out in response, and before he knew it he found himself scrambling down the first riser and then another, the flashlight carving slices out of the darkness to reveal a bas relief of inhuman creatures lunging at him in glimpses: taloned feet and clawed hands and sinuous Medusa coils that seemed to writhe about one another in the fitful and imperfect glare. And through it all the terrible summons of the place, drawing him down into the dark.

"Elizabeth—" he gasped, stumbling down another riser and another, until the rope, forgotten, jerked taut about his waist. He looked up at the pale circle of Connelly's face far above him.

"What the hell are you doing down there, Doc," Connelly shouted, his voice thick with rage, and then, almost against his will, Garner found himself ascending once again into the light.

No sooner had he gained his footing than Connelly grabbed him by the collar and swung him to the ground. Garner scrabbled for purchase in the snow but Connelly kicked him back down again, his blond, bearded face contorted in rage.

"You stupid son of a bitch! Do you care if we all die out here?"

"Get off me!"

"For a dog? For a goddamned *dog*?" Connelly tried to kick him again, but Garner grabbed his foot and rolled, bringing the other man down on top of him. The two of them grappled in the snow, their heavy coats and gloves making any real damage all but impossible.

The flaps to one of the tents opened and Bishop limped out, his face a caricature of alarm. He was buttoning his coat even as he approached. "Stop! *Stop it right now!*"

Garner clambered to his feet, staggering backward a few steps. Connelly rose to one knee, leaning over and panting. He pointed at Garner. "I found him in the crevasse! He went down alone!"

Garner leaned against one of the packed sledges. He could feel Bishop watching him as tugged free a glove to poke at a tender spot on his face, but he didn't look up.

"Is this true?"

"Of course it's true!" Connelly said, but Bishop waved him into silence.

Garner looked up at him, breath heaving in his lungs. "You've got to see it," he said. "My God, Bishop."

Bishop turned his gaze to the crevasse, where he saw the pitons and the rope spilling into the darkness. "Oh, Doc," he said quietly.

"It's not a crevasse, Bishop. It's a stairwell."

Connelly strode toward Garner, jabbing his finger at him. "What? You lost your goddamned mind."

"Look for yourself!"

Bishop interposed himself between the two men. "*Enough!*" He turned to face Connelly. "Back off."

"But—"

"I said back off!"

Connelly peeled his lips back, then turned and stalked back toward the crevasse. He knelt by its edge and started hauling up the rope.

Bishop turned to Garner. "Explain yourself."

All at once, Garner's passion drained from him. He felt a wash of exhaustion. His muscles ached. How could he explain this to him? He could he explain this so that they'd understand? "Atka," he said simply, imploringly. "I could hear him."

A look of deep regret fell over Bishop's face. "Doc . . . Atka was a just a dog. We have to get Faber to the depot."

"I could still hear him."

"You have to pull yourself together. There are real lives at stake here, do you get that? Me and Connelly, we aren't doctors. Faber needs *you*."

"But—"

"Do you get that?"

"I . . . yeah. Yeah, I know."

"When you go down into places like that, especially by yourself, you're putting us all at risk. What are we gonna do without Doc, huh?"

This was not an argument Garner would win. Not this way. So he grabbed Bishop by the arm and led him toward the crevasse. "Look," he said.

Bishop wrenched his arm free, his face darkening. Connelly straightened, watching this exchange. "Don't put your hands on me, Doc," Bishop said.

Garner released him. "Bishop," he said. "Please."

Bishop paused a moment, then walked toward the opening. "All right."

Connelly exploded. "Oh for Christ's sake!"

"We're not going inside it," Bishop said, looking at them both. "I'm going to look, okay Doc? That's all you get."

Garner nodded. "Okay," he said. "Okay."

The two of them approached the edge of the crevasse. Closer, Garner felt it like a hook in his liver, tugging him down. It took an act of will to stop at the edge, to remain still and unshaken and look at these other two men as if his whole life did not hinge upon this moment.

"It's a stairwell," he said. His voice did not shake. His body did not move. "It's carved into the rock. It's got . . . designs of some kind."

Bishop peered down into the darkness for a long moment. "I don't see anything," he said at last.

"I'm telling you, it's *there*!" Garner stopped and gathered himself. He tried another tack. "This, this could be the scientific discovery of the century. You want to stick it to McReady? Let him plant his little flag. This is evidence of, of . . ." He trailed off. He didn't know what it was evidence of.

"We'll mark the location," Bishop said. "We'll come back. If what you say is true it's not going anywhere."

Garner switched on his flashlight. "Look," he said, and he threw it down.

The flashlight arced end over end, its white beam slicing through the darkness with a scalpel's clean efficiency, illuminating flashes of hewn rock and what might have been carvings or just natural irregularities. It clattered to a landing beside the corpse of the dog, casting in bright relief its open jaw and lolling tongue, and the black pool of blood beneath it.

Bishop looked for a moment, and shook his head. "God damn it, Doc," he said. "You're really straining my patience. Come on."

Bishop was about to turn away when Atka's body jerked once—Garner saw it—and then again, almost imperceptibly. Reaching out, Garner seized Bishop's sleeve. "What now, for Christ's—" the other man started to say, his voice harsh with annoyance. Then the body was yanked into the surrounding darkness so quickly it seemed as though it had vanished into thin air. Only its blood, a smeared trail into shadow, testified to its ever having been there at all. That, and the jostled flashlight, which rolled in a lazy half circle, its unobstructed light spearing first into empty darkness and then into smooth cold stone before settling at last on what might have been a carven, clawed foot. The beam flickered and went out.

"What the fuck . . ." Bishop said.

A scream erupted from the tent behind them.

Faber.

Garner broke into a clumsy run, high-stepping through the piled snow. The other men shouted behind him but their words were lost in the wind and in his own hard breathing. His body was moving according to its training but his mind was pinned like a writhing insect in the hole behind him, in the stark, burning image of what he had just seen. He was transported by fear and adrenaline and by something else, by some other emotion he had not felt in many years or perhaps ever in his life, some heart-filling glorious exaltation that threatened to snuff him out like a dying cinder.

Faber was sitting upright in the tent—it stank of sweat and urine and kerosene, eye-watering and sharp—his thick hair a dark corona around his head, his skin as pale as a cavefish. He was still trying to scream, but his voice had broken, and his utmost effort could now produce only a long, cracked wheeze, which seemed forced through his throat like steel wool. His leg stuck out of the blanket, still grossly swollen.

The warmth from the Nansen cooker was almost oppressive.

Garner dropped to his knees beside him and tried to ease him back down into his sleeping bag, but Faber resisted. He fixed his eyes on Garner, his painful wheeze trailing into silence. Hooking his fingers in Garner's collar, he pulled him close, so close that Garner could smell the sour taint of his breath.

"Faber, relax, relax!"

"It—" Faber's voice locked. He swallowed and tried again. "It laid an egg in me."

Bishop and Connelly crowded through the tent flap, and Garner felt suddenly hemmed in, overwhelmed by the heat and the stink and the steam rising in wisps from their clothes as they pushed closer, staring down at Faber.

"What's going on?" Bishop asked. "Is he all right?"

Faber eyed them wildly. Ignoring them, Garner placed his hands on Faber's cheeks and turned his head toward him. "Look at me, Faber. Look at me. What do you mean?"

Faber found a way to smile. "In my dream. It put my head inside its body, and it laid an egg in me."

Connelly said, "He's delirious. See what happens when you leave him alone?"

Garner fished an ampule of morphine out of his bag. Faber saw what he was doing and his body bucked.

"No!" he screamed, summoning his voice again. "No!" His leg thrashed out, knocking over the Nansen cooker. Cursing, Connelly dove at the overturned stove, but it was already too late. Kerosene splashed over the blankets and supplies, engulfing the tent in flames. The men moved in a sudden tangle of panic. Bishop stumbled back out of the tent and Connelly shoved Garner aside—Garner rolled over on his back and came to rest there—as he lunged for Faber's legs, dragging him backward. Screaming, Faber clutched at the ground to resist, but Connelly was too strong. A moment later, Faber was gone, dragging a smoldering rucksack with him.

Still inside the tent, Garner lay back, watching as the fire spread hungrily along the roof, dropping tongues of flame onto the ground, onto his own body. Garner closed his eyes as the heat gathered him up like a furnace-hearted lover.

What he felt, though, was not the fire's heat, but the cool breath of underground earth, the silence of the deep tomb buried beneath the ice shelf. The stairs descended before him, and at the bottom he heard a noise again: A woman's voice, calling for him. Wondering where he was.

Elizabeth, he called, his voice echoing off the stone. Are you there?

If only he'd gotten to see her, he thought. If only he'd gotten to bury her. To fill those beautiful eyes with dirt. To cover her in darkness.

Elizabeth, can you hear me?

Then Connelly's big arms enveloped him, and he felt the heat again, searing bands of pain around his legs and chest. It was like being wrapped in a star. "I ought to let you burn, you stupid son of a bitch," Connelly hissed, but he didn't. He lugged Garner outside—Garner opened his eyes in time to see the canvas part in front of him, like fiery curtains—and dumped him in the snow instead. The pain went away, briefly, and Garner mourned its passing. He rolled over and lifted his head. Connelly stood over him, his face twisted in disgust. Behind him the tent flickered and burned like a dropped torch.

Faber's quavering voice hung over it all, rising and falling like the wind.

Connelly tossed an ampule and a syringe onto the ground by Garner. "Faber's leg's opened up again," he said. "Go and do your job."

Garner climbed slowly to his feet, feeling the skin on his chest and legs tighten. He'd been burned; he'd have to wait until he'd tended to Faber to find out how badly.

"And then help us pack up," Bishop called as he led the dogs to their harnesses, his voice harsh and strained. "We're getting the hell out of here."

⊷

By the time they reached the depot, Faber was dead. Connelly spat into the snow and turned away to unhitch the dogs, while Garner and Bishop went inside and started a fire. Bishop started water boiling for coffee. Garner unpacked their bedclothes and dressed the cots, moving gingerly. Once the place was warm enough he undressed and surveyed the burn damage. It would leave scars.

The next morning they wrapped Faber's body and packed it in an ice locker.

After that they settled in to wait.

The ship would not return for a month yet, and though McReady's expedition was due back before then, the vagaries of Antarctic experience made that a tenuous proposition at best. In any case, they were stuck with each other for some time yet, and not even the generous stocks of the depot—a relative wealth of food and medical supplies, playing cards and books—could fully distract them from their grievances.

In the days that followed, Connelly managed to bank his anger at Garner, but it would not take much to set it off again; so Garner tried to keep a low profile. As with the trenches in France, corpses were easy to explain in Antarctica.

A couple of weeks into that empty expanse of time, while Connelly dozed on his cot and Bishop read through an old natural history magazine, Garner decided to risk broaching the subject of what had happened in the crevasse.

"You saw it," he said, quietly, so as not to wake Connelly.

Bishop took a moment to acknowledge that he'd heard him. Finally he tilted the magazine away, and sighed. "Saw what," he said.

"You know what."

Bishop shook his head. "No," he said. "I don't. I don't know what you're talking about."

"Something was there."

Bishop said nothing. He lifted the magazine again, but his eyes were still.

"Something was down there," Garner said.

"No there wasn't."

"It pulled Atka. I know you saw it."

Bishop refused to look at him. "This is an empty place," he said, after a long silence. "There's nothing here." He blinked, and turned a page in the magazine. "Nothing."

Garner leaned back onto his cot, looking at the ceiling.

Although the long Antarctic day had not yet finished, it was shading into dusk, the sun hovering over the horizon like a great boiling eye. It cast long shadows, and the lamp Bishop had lit to read by set them dancing. Garner watched them caper across the ceiling. Some time later, Bishop snuffed out the lamp and dragged the curtains over the windows, consigning them all to darkness. With it, Garner felt something like peace stir inside him. He let it move through him in waves, he felt it ebb and flow with each slow pulse of his heart.

A gust of wind scattered fine crystals of snow against the window, and he found himself wondering what the night would be like in this cold country. He imagined the sky dissolving to reveal the hard vault of stars, the galaxy turning above him like a cog in a vast, unknowable engine. And behind it all, the emptiness into which men hurled their prayers. It occurred to him that he could leave now, walk out into the long twilight and keep going until the earth opened beneath him and he found himself descending strange stairs, while the world around him broke silently into snow, and into night.

Garner closed his eyes.

Dale Bailey *lives in North Carolina with his family and has published three novels,* The Fallen, House of Bones, *and* Sleeping Policemen *(with Jack Slay, Jr.). A fourth novel,* The Clearing, *is in the works. His short fiction, available in* The Resurrection Man's Legacy and Other Stories, *won the International Horror Guild Award, and has been twice nominated for the Nebula Award.*

Nathan Ballingrud *lives with his daughter in Asheville, NC. His stories have appeared in several places, including* Inferno: New Tales of Terror and the Supernatural, The Del Rey Book of Science Fiction and Fantasy, *and a number of year's best anthologies. He won the Shirley Jackson Award for his short story* "The Monsters of Heaven."

We visited the Arctic with Barbara Roden in a story inspired by Poe. Now, we've journeyed to the Antarctic in a tale that is a tribute to H.P. Lovecraft. But since we are visiting places that can't be scribed on any map nor fathomed by the human mind. I assume, dear reader, you are realizing what a long strange—but I do hope worthwhile—trip we're on here?

VIC

MAURA McHUGH

Vic's room was small and awkward, just like him.

When Father built the extension above the garage the narrow asymmetrical space was intended as a storage closet for chemicals, equipment, and spare parts, not for toys, books, and a boy. Its best feature was a large double window that spied across the fenced-in overgrown back yard, and offered Vic a slice of the street and the houses beyond. The sash only opened a little, but the breaths of air that slipped in spoke of wet grass and freedom, and masked the workshop stench from next door.

The branches of a close-planted sycamore shattered Vic's view into hundreds of puzzle pieces. On windy nights, after Mom turned off the TV—wedged in at the bottom of his cramped bed—he lay and watched the shadows cast by the trashing tree roil across the ceiling and crash against the walls. He invented stories about the chaotic shapes, which usually involved knights or spacemen who quested and conquered. It helped him fall sleep when the aches and pains were troublesome.

Sometimes, when it was stormy, the branches groaned and the twigs scraped the glass, and their jabbering profiles told darker stories where heroes failed and monsters triumphed. Then he would pull the covers up to the bottom of his crooked nose, turn the TV on low, curl his back to the window, and watch the screen sideways.

He could never bear to draw the blinds.

The stitches itched.

Vic sat cross-legged on his bed in the shifting afternoon light, and busied his hands with the *Big Book of Butterflies* Father checked out of the library for him.

Twap: the sound of a basketball bouncing off paving echoed through the inch of open window. Vic laid the book down on the pillow carefully, and gripped the headboard so he could climb up on the mattress. Unfurling sycamore buds waved in a spring breeze, and Vic had to crick his neck to get a good view of his neighbor's neat garden, which had a pond in which red fish swam. The movement triggered a resentful throb, but he ignored it.

A boy, a little taller than Vic, bounced a basketball in between the fragile Cherry tree and squat statues. His lips moved as if he narrated his circuits around the tidy obstacles. On a couple of previous occasions Vic had seen him slip aside a board in the garden's slatted back fence, squeeze through the gap, and bounce his ball down the street to an unknown destination. The boy always returned, but his absences never raised an alarm. Vic knew because on each occasion he waited by the window until the boy returned home safely.

A scattershot of rain pelted the glass in an offbeat tempo. Vic placed his lopsided fingers over his chest and tapped along to his heart's erratic rhythm, the one Mom called Take Five. "You're a little out of step," she said whenever she pressed her ear to his chest. After she lifted her face, and revealed the scars that rucked her cheek, she'd add, "Keep beating kiddo."

Vic trampled over the bedcovers to gaze at the bus stop across the street. In the mornings the kids stood there and jostled each other as they waited for their ride to school, supervised by vigilant parents. Now, it was deserted.

Vic hesitated, sidestepped to the bottom of the bed, and stretched for a peek at Rain's bedroom window. Vic didn't know her real name, but she reminded him of the changeable nature of rain: how it freshened up a summer's day, hammered leaves into the ground, or softened the world behind a veil of mystery. Today she worked on her homework at a desk by the window. She chewed on a florescent yellow pen, and frowned. Vic was sure she was smart, so it had to be a tough question.

The front door slammed. Vic dropped down on his mattress, and pulled the book over his lap. The slow, heavy tread on the carpeted stairs confirmed Father's return. Vic watched the tongue of light under the door. A shadow hesitated outside. Anxiety and excitement soured his stomach. The footfalls continued, and keys jangled. Father entered his workroom, and Vic turned back to the book on his lap.

"Egg, larva, chrysalis, imago," he read as he traced the circular chart that mapped the butterfly's life cycle. He flipped the yellowed pages so the musty library-smell drifted upwards.

A memory rose in Vic's mind like an air bubble drawn to the surface of water: a cheerful elderly librarian with steel eyeglasses and blue hair handed him a plastic-coated book. Vic squeezed his eyes shut and tried to capture the details, but they melted under scrutiny. Sometimes strangers' faces haunted him with uneasy familiarity.

Vic opened the front page. Old dates were pressed on the paper higgledy-piggledy. He tried to figure out how often the book had been borrowed and for how long. A rash of loans clustered around the same period every year, probably for a school project.

He imagined Rain's hands on the pages as she researched her paper, bit her pen, and wrote about the Nymphalidae species and their spectacular colors. His fingers slid across the glossy image of Blue Morpho, with its iridescent turquoise and aquamarine wings.

Drip.

A black splotch covered the image.

A machine hummed into life next door.

The stitches were barbed wire strangling his throat, but Vic focused on the book. He couldn't let the page stain. Not on Rain's favourite butterfly. His hands shook as he daubed at the paper with a corner of his cotton bed sheet; it turned navy, as if dipped in ink. *Morpho menelaus* recovered intact.

"What are you doing, Victor?"—Mom's voice from the doorway. He spun in surprise. Alarm remapped the scars on her face into livid lines of fear.

Vic rushed to reassure her. "It's all right, I got to it in time."

Her voice spiked. "Your neck!"

His fingers touched the bandages, and felt the damp.

She almost screamed, "Father!"

A *thump* from next door, like a hammer dropped on the floor.

Mom lurched towards Vic, and knocked into the corner of the television on her blind side.

Just as her hand brushed his arm the pain became a saw ripping through his neck. He fell backwards into twilight, the book clasped to his chest.

His mattress became a cloud of multi-hued butterflies, and Vic burst through them, falling into darkness, until they swooped and bore him up into a blinding white sky on wings that pounded a five/four beat.

Vic woke to Mom's touch on his forehead and a pressure on his throat. He blinked crust out of his eyes, and opened his mouth to speak, but she shook her head. "No talking for a while." Pain was cottonballed and distant.

His father slouched in the doorway, a silhouette of unease against the light in the hall. Despite the distance he reeked of Marlboros and sweat. Mom's good eye was red, puffy, but she smiled. "You need to rest." She levered herself from the bed with her cane, but held onto his hand. "Tomorrow, when you're feeling better, we'll watch a movie downstairs on the big television. All of us together." Vic clutched her hand to indicate his delight at the treat.

Father shifted and stuck his hands into the pockets of his trousers, "It's not wise, Mary. The boy needs rest."

Mom dropped Vic's hand, and swiveled sharply using her cane. "He needs a diversion!" The pitch of her voice skidded upward abruptly, and its intensity startled Vic. "Being pent up like this isn't healthy!"

"It's for his own good," Father said in his coaxing voice.

Mom's hand tightened around the handle of her walking stick. "It's suffocating. Unnatural." The anger slipped from her voice as quickly as it appeared, but a sloped resignation remained in her shoulders. Father opened up his arm to help her shuffle through the narrow space to the doorway.

"I'll check on you soon," she said, and closed the door quietly.

Vic sat up in bed, and touched the bandages that swaddled the length of his neck. New wrappings bound his wrists. He pulled back his sheets. Virgin strips encased his ankles. Under his crumpled teddy-bear pyjama top a new dressing twisted upwards from his bellybutton. He drew the material back, and followed the trail that criss-crossed older wounds. It terminated above his heart, from where all the other marks radiated.

Shadows moved under the door.

He eased out of bed. Dizziness threatened to topple him, but he leaned against a wall until the crashing in his head abated. He walked to the door, and laid his ear against the smooth grain.

Father's voice, low and stubborn: "It's not working." Mom's angry response was muffled. Father's response contained frigid resolve. "No. There's no point. I won't do it again."

"You promised!" so loud it shocked Vic back from the door, but he could still hear the sobbed entreaties of his mother, and the *shh*ing noises of his father.

Barely audible: "We could begin over."

Vic stumbled back and sat on the bed hard. Pain shot up his spine and shook his heart. He shouldn't listen to private conversations, he'd been told so before. Just as it was wrong to explore the house. Bad things happened when he disobeyed.

Memories, tightly barred, threatened to tear open. Behind it images strained: *a small limp foot jutted over the edge of a metal table; a scarlet toenail dripped red; and a clear plastic mask descended towards Vic's face.*

Vic's clenched fists lay on his lap: one dark, one pale. His chest constricted, but not from the wound.

Tap tap tap. The tree clattered for Vic's attention. He scooted around, and gazed out the window. The late evening light slanted into the neighbour's pond so the fish glowed. The boy wore a hoodie emblazoned with the word Mavericks, and dribbled his basketball around imaginary players. He spun, halted, stared at his house, and back at the fence. Vic's breath caught as the boy weighed his options.

A short sprint; the board pushed aside; and an empty garden. The fish circled the pool.

Vic dragged himself upright using the windowsill, and shuffled to the end of the bed. Rain and her younger sister, dressed in party clothes, danced in front of a tall mirror and mouthed words to a song he couldn't hear, their bodies graceful with freedom. His world was a coffin-sized room while theirs was limitless.

We could begin over.

He didn't know why his heart struggled to beat when it hurt so much.

The unhindered light under the door offered a chance. He stood, and tested the knob. It turned.

Vic put on jeans, T-shirt, and sneakers. He didn't own a jacket, so he pulled on two sweaters. It would be cold. Underneath the dull heartbreak exhilaration and fear warred.

Out. He was going out.

A sob of lonely hurt hitched his chest. He squashed it. Soon he'd be gone.

No longer a bother, a source of tears and fights, or secrets behind locked doors. Without him, they could start over.

He opened the door.

It proved surprisingly simple to escape the house. Father clanked about in the workroom as Vic crept down the stairs. The television blared in the den. In the kitchen the key stuck out of the backdoor lock. A *click*, and he was outside, smelling the breeze, brisk and heavy with the scent of damp earth.

He looked up at the darkening sky, stars and crescent moon ghost imprints on the purple-navy expanse, and for a moment the world tipped forwards and back. The noises of the neighbourhood flooded him: cars rolled past, feet slapped the sidewalk as a pair of children dashed past the house, and dogs barked sulky reminders about their evening walk.

He was out.

Vic propelled forward on clumsy legs, anxious to flee the shadow of the house in case the panic submerged by the wonder would surface and drown him. He lumbered through the long grass to the wooden fence. Vic had long ago spotted the broken board that the local cats used to stalk through the garden. He kicked it out of place, sucked in his stom and wiggled through on his side.

He stood up quickly, trembling, and checked to see if anyone noticed his exit. There were few people about. The smell of cooking food wafted from the houses. Families gathered to eat at this time. Vic knew because he'd watched them.

A man in an overcoat strode past. Across the street a young woman with a stroller glanced at him, smiled, and kept going.

He was part of the world. Accepted by it.

Across the street Rain's house loomed. For a stomach-plunging instant Vic considered ringing the doorbell. He dismissed the idea. Vic didn't know what to say, and . . . Rain might not like him. The plummet in his gut returned. His feet hurried away from the emotion and followed the same course the boy next door had taken.

Orange streetlights flickered on as he passed, and soon he was at the top of the street, at an intersection. New territory. Across the street a playground guarded the entrance to a park. Colorful tubular towers sprouted from the ground, connected by passageways, and accessed by ladders, ropes, and ramps. Slides and swings dotted the spaces in between. In his rush to reach it he ignored the lights. Brakes screeched and a horn blared as a van skidded to avoid him.

The area was deserted. The glow of the nearby lights slicked the smooth surfaces of the playground equipment. Vic climbed a metal ladder, crawled into the top of a round tower, and looked out of the arched window at the passing people. The wind thrummed through the empty spaces. He found a broken lumpy crayon, and wrote "Vic" on a wooden strut in the roof. He wondered if he could live there at night, and emerge to play with the children during the day.

Twap: the sound of a basketball. He switched to the opposite window and saw his neighbour throw a ball at a hoop.

Vic whooshed down the yellow slide, and approached the boy. He stopped on the edge of the dimly lit court, and waited. After a couple of moments the boy dribbled his ball towards Vic. "Hey," he said.

"Hi," Vic grinned.

"You play?"

Vic shook his head. The boy raised an eyebrow at that. "What, never?"

Vic noticed the suspicious tone. "I've been sick."

The boy bounced the ball a couple of times and nodded, as if this information made perfect sense. "Wanna learn?"

Vic bobbed his head, afraid to speak in case he messed up an unknown code of conduct.

"I'm Don," the boy added, and bounced the ball at Vic, who huffed when he caught it.

"I'm Vic," he responded, and threw it back at Don.

The boy tucked the ball under his arm, and cocked his hip. "First, I'll explain the basics."

Half an hour later Vic's breath rasped from effort. His legs throbbed with the malicious promise of a later reckoning, but he couldn't stop smiling. He'd scored his first point. As soon as his hand touched the ball it was as if the memory of the game was hard-wired in his body, despite its slowness. He had to stop for a breather several times, but Don hadn't complained, and used the breaks to describe tactics, or demonstrate a couple of special moves.

Vic wanted to play basketball with him forever.

Don paused, his cheeks glowing, and his breath visible. "You sure you haven't played before?" Vic shook his head. Don jerked his chin at Vic's hands. "Were you burned?" Fear rendered Vic mute; the bandages and his mis-matched hands were clearly visible. "My uncle's a firefighter," a swell of pride, "so I know about skin grafts."

Vic yanked the sleeves of his sweater over his wrists, and dipped his head.

"You home-schooled?" Another nod. Don laughed. "You escape for a night?" Vic's eyes widened, and the boy bounced the ball harder. "Know the feeling." He paused and checked a chunky watch on his wrist. "I gotta go soon. Even my mom'll notice I'm missing."

"Vic?"

Don's stance stiffened, and his gaze flicked to behind Vic's shoulder. Vic turned. His mother hobbled from the direction of the shadowed park, bundled up in a long coat, scarf, and hat. Behind her, the darker blot of Father's presence. Her cane tapped like the rattle of twigs against a windowpane. "I was so worried," she gasped.

"I'm fine," he said, and wrapped his happiness tight about him, desperate to keep it. He stepped back from her. "Just shooting hoops with Don." He loved the normalcy of the new words on his tongue.

She paused about ten feet from Vic. "Don?" she said, and her voice glitched in a funny way.

Father took a step forward. "Don't." She half-swivelled, and Vic couldn't see the expression on her face, but Father didn't move or say anything else.

Don fidgeted, and glanced over at the playground and the streetlights beyond. "Well, see ya, Vic."

"Wait, Don is it?" her voice smoothed out, and became the sound of a beautiful, caring, Mother. Someone you trusted with your life.

Don stopped, and a hungering need rose in pupils wide from the lack of light. "Yes, ma'am."

"Do you like drinking chocolate?" She glided closer to the boy without a trace of a limp.

"I sure do."

"Why don't I fix you some, as thanks for being such good friends with my boy?" Mom held out a hand, and Vic noticed for the first time that her fingernails were long and sharp.

A memory erupted: *Vic approached the sleeping boy on the table, hoping to wake him so they could play together.*

Don took a step towards Mom.

A puddle of blood glued the sheet to the boy's leg.

Don's hand rose dreamily upwards.

The cloth slid a little as Vic touched the boy, and exposed the . . .

Vic jumped between them and shoved Don so hard the boy almost fell backwards. "Like I want this loser coming to my house!" Vic yelled.

The enchantment broke, and bitter rejection replaced it. "Screw you Vic," Don bellowed, and he ran with fast angry steps towards the light, and safety.

For a while there was only the sound of traffic and the crack of Mom's knuckles as she clenched and unclenched her fingers. She sighed, a long release of irritation, and hobbled to Vic. "I do it to make you better, Vic." She touched the curve of his neck. Dampness bloomed against his skin, and the discomfort hidden by activity sharpened. Her voice caught, broke. "I *can't* lose you."

Vic stared down at his sneakers, scuffed for the first time. "Promise you'll leave Don alone."

Her silence offered no assurances.

Exhaustion settled on Vic with the weight of sorrow. He staggered, but Father caught and lifted Vic. "He taught me to layup," Vic said, and closed his eyes as the pain returned with the fury of the repressed. Father kissed Vic's forehead, and in surprise Vic opened his eyes and looked directly at his father for the first time he could remember. "Don't begin over," Vic whispered, too low for Mom to hear.

His father froze, and guilt tightened the smudged circles under his eyes. He bent his head and gripped Vic tight. Vic buried his face in his father's raincoat, inhaled the smell of cigarettes and formaldehyde, and cried.

Father hugged Vic close to his chest as they walked home. Mom held onto the crook of Father's arm. As they left the playground Rain and her sister bounced by, giggling and chattering, on either side of their mother. A blue enamel butterfly glittered among Rain's curls. She smiled briefly at Vic, and he imagined how she saw them: a father carrying a son tuckered out from activity, his wife by his side; a family.

Later that night the shadows of the sycamore combed the walls and ceiling of Vic's room with urgent movements. He lay under mom's hand-stitched quilt and groggily watched the shapes become tall lean basketball players who tossed a ball to each other, dodged, dribbled, and dunked. Thousands of shadow hands applauded the game.

The injection Father gave Vic softened the world, and dragged his eyes closed.

Vic remembered Rain dancing, loose-limbed and radiant, and Don's frowned concentration as he leaped with the ball. Their beauty suffused him and his heartbeat lurched.

Mom stroked his forehead and Vic cracked open heavy eyelids. She smelled of soap and tears. The bed creaked when she settled beside him. She placed her hand on his chest, and her fingers echoed the stuttering rhythm.

It was hard to breathe.

Father sat on the bottom of the mattress, and placed his hands on Vic's feet. He nodded.

Vic closed his eyes.

Mom kissed his cheek. "You're a little out of step," she said.

Vic kept beating for as long as he could.

Maura McHugh *was born in the U.S.A. but transplanted to Ireland when she was too young to protest. Her short stories and poetry have appeared in publications such as* Fantasy, Shroud, Paradox, Goblin Fruit, *and* M-Brane SF. *A script she wrote for a short film was shot and premiered in 2009, and she has written a graphic novel,* Róisín Dubh, *which is due out from at the end of 2010. Earlier this year she co-edited/juried The Campaign for Real Fear horror fiction contest with Christopher Fowler, and the winning stories were published in* Black Static *and podcast by Action Audio. She lives in Galway, Ireland and when she's not writing she works as a blogger, newsletter editor and Web content manager for the Irish Playwrights and Screenwriters Guild. Her Web site is splinister.com*

This subtle story is not one you can rush through. Since I was reading a lot of stories, I admit to, initially, getting to the end and realizing I needed to go back and read more slowly to fully appreciate it. I did . . . Then I was too stunned to read another story for quite a while.

HALLOWEEN TOWN

LUCIUS SHEPARD

This is the story of Clyde Ormoloo and the willow wan, but it's also the story of Halloween, the spindly, skinny town that lies along the bottom of the Shilkonic Gorge, a meandering crack in the earth so narrow that on a clear day the sky appears to those hundreds of feet below as a crooked seam of blue mineral running through dark stone. Spanning the gorge is a forest with a canopy so dense that a grown man, if he steps carefully, can walk across it; thus many who live in Halloween must travel for more than a mile along the river (the Mossbach) that divides their town should they wish to see daylight. The precipitous granite walls are concave, forming a great vaulted roof overhead, and this concavity becomes exaggerated near the apex of the gorge, where the serpentine roots of oak and hawthorn and elm burst through thin shelves of rock, braiding their undersides like enormous varicose veins.

Though a young boy can toss a stone from one bank to the other, the Mossbach is held to be quite a broad river by the citizenry, and this is scarcely surprising, considering their narrow perspective. Space is at a premium and the houses of the town, lacking all foundation, must be bolted to the walls of the gorge. Their rooms, rarely more than ten feet deep, are stacked one atop another, like the uneven, teetering columns of blocks erected by a toddler, and are ascended to by means of external ladders or rickety stairs or platforms raised by pulleys (a situation that has proved a boon to fitness). A small house may reach a height of forty feet and larger ones, double stacks topped off by ornamental peaked roofs, often tower more than eighty feet above the Mossbach. When families grow close, rooms may be added that connect two or more houses, thereby creating a pattern of square shapes across the granite redolent of an enormous crossword puzzle; when feuds occur, these connecting rooms may be demolished. Public venues like O'Malloy's Inn and the Downlow have expanded by carving out rooms from the rock, but for much of its length, with its purplish days and quirky architecture and night mists, Halloween seems a habitation suited for a society of intelligent pigeons . . . though on occasion a purely human note is sounded. Sandy shingles notch the granite shore and piers of age-blackened wood extend out over the water, illumined by gas lamps or a single dangling bulb, assisting the passage of the flat-bottomed skiffs that constitute the river's sole traffic. Frequently you will see a moon-pale girl (or a dark-skinned girl with a peculiar pallor) sitting at the end of such a pier beneath a fan of radiance, watching elusive, luminous silver fish appearing and disappearing beneath the surface with the intermittency of fireflies, waiting for her lover to come poling his skiff out of the sempiternal gloom.

At forty-one, Clyde Ormoloo had the lean, muscular body of a construction worker (which, in fact, he had been) and the bleak disposition of a French philosopher plagued by doubts concerning the substantive worth of existence (which, in essence, he had become). His seamed face, surmounted by a scalp upon which was raised a crop of black stubble, was surpassingly ugly, yet ugly in such a way that appealed to women who prize men for their brutishness and use them as a setting to show off the diamond of their beauty. These women did not stay for long, put off by Clyde's unrelenting and perhaps unnatural scrutiny. Three years previously, while working a construction site in Beaver Falls, Pennsylvania (his home and the birthplace of Joe Namath, the former NFL quarterback), he had been struck a glancing blow to the head by a rivet dropped from the floor above and, as a result, he had begun to see too deeply into people. The injury was not a broken spine (he was in the hospital one night for observation), yet it paralyzed Clyde. Whereas before the accident he had been a beer guzzler, an ass-grabber, a blue-collar bon vivant, now when he looked into a woman's eyes (or a man's, for that matter), he saw a terrible incoherence, flashes of greed, lust, and fear exploding into a shrapnel of thought that somehow succeeded in contriving a human likeness. His friends seemed unfamiliar—he understood that he had not known them, merely recognized the shapes of their madness. He asked questions that made them uncomfortable and made comments that they failed to grasp and took for insults. Increasingly, women told their friends they didn't know him anymore and turned away when he drew near. Men rejected him less subtly and formed new friendships with those whose madnesses complemented their own.

"Sooner or later," said one of his doctors, "almost everyone arrives at the conclusion that people are chaotic skinbags driven by the basest of motives. You'll adjust."

None of the doctors could explain Clyde's sudden increase in intelligence and they were bemused by his contention that this increase was a byproduct of improved vision. In Clyde's view, his new capacity to analyze and break down the images conveyed by light lay at the root of his problem—the rivet had struck his skull above the site of the visual cortex, had it not? At the movies, in rock clubs, in any poorly lit circumstance, he felt almost normal, though most movies—themselves creations of light—seemed designed to inspire Pavlovian responses in idiots, and thus Clyde began attending the local arthouse, hiding his face beneath a golf cap so as not to be recognized.

"Try sunglasses," suggested a specialist.

Sunglasses helped, but Clyde felt like a pretentious ass wearing them day in, day out during the gray inclemency of a Beaver Falls winter. He considered moving to Florida, but knew this would be no more than a stopgap. The sole passion he clung to from his old, happy life (never mind that it had been an illusion) was his love of football, and for a while he thought football might save him. He spent hours each night watching ESPN Classic and the NFL Network. Football was the perfect metaphor, he thought, for contemporary man's frustration with the limitations of the social order, and therein rested its appeal. Whenever the officials (who in the main were professional men, lawyers, accountants, insurance executives, and the like, apt instruments of repression) threw their yellow flags and blew their silver whistles, preventing a three-hundred-pound mesomorph from ripping out a young quarterback's throat, they were in effect reminding the millions tuning in that they could expect no more than a partial fulfillment of their desires . . . and yet they did this with the rabid participation of the masses, who dressed in appropriate colors, rooting for the home team or the visitors, but acknowledging by the sameness of their dress that there was only one side, the side that sold them jerseys and caps. Thus football had evolved into a training tool of the corporate oligarchy, posing a dreary object lesson that conditioned proles to accept their cancer-ridden, consumerist fates enthusiastically. Having thought these things, the game lost much of its appeal for Clyde. And so, plagued by light, alone in a world where solitude is frowned upon, if not perceived as the symptom of a deviant pathology, he petitioned the town of Halloween to grant him citizenship.

The population of Halloween fluctuates between three thousand and thirty-eight hundred, and is sustained at those levels by the Town Council. At the time Clyde put in his application, the population hovered around thirty-two hundred, so breaching the upper limit would not be a problem. To his surprise, the decision to reject or approve him would not be rendered by the council in full session, but by a committee of three men named Brad, Carmine, and Spooz, and the meeting was held at the Sub-Café, an establishment that had been excavated out of the granite; a neon sign was bracketed to the rock above the entrance, indigo letters flashing on and off, producing eerie reflections in the water, and the interior looked a little like Brownie's back in Beaver Falls, with digital beer signs and some meager Christmas decorations and piped-in music (the Pogues were playing when he entered), TVs mounted here and there, maple paneling and subdued lighting, photographs of former patrons on the walls, tables, a horseshoe-shaped bar and waitresses wearing indigo Sub-Café T-shirts. A comforting mutter arose from the crowd at the bar, and two of the committee were seated at a back table.

Carmine and Spooz, it turned out, were cousins who did not share a family resemblance. Spooz was a genial, round-cheeked man in his mid-thirties, already going bald, and Carmine was five or six years younger, lean and sallow, with a vulpine face, given to toothpick-chewing and lip-curling. Brad, who had to be called away from a group gathered around a punchboard, was a black guy with baby dreads, a real beanpole, maybe six-six or six-seven. He brought a beer over for Clyde and gave him a grin as he pulled a chair up to the table. They drank and talked small and Clyde, gesturing at the TVs, asked if they had cable.

"Shit, no," said Carmine, and Spooz said, "The cable and the satellite company are having a turf war, so nobody can get either one."

"Cable wouldn't work down here, anyway," said Carmine. "Satellite, neither."

"How come?" Clyde asked.

"We got a service that burns stuff for us," Spooz said. "They send DVDs down the next day."

"Ormoloo," said Brad. "That's French, isn't it? Doesn't it have something to do with gilding?"

"Beats me." Clyde drained his glass and signaled the waitress to bring another round. "My dad was this big old guy who founded a hippie commune out in Oregon. He changed his name legally to Elephant Ormoloo. When my mom married him, she changed hers to Tijuana Ormoloo. When she divorced him, she changed it back to Marian Bleier. She told me I could choose between Bleier and Ormoloo. I was ten years old and pissed at her for leaving my dad, even though he'd been screwing around on her, so I chose Ormoloo. Anyway . . . " Cliff resettled in his chair. "I don't think my dad even realized it sounded French. He used to buy these Hindu posters from a head shop. You know, the ones with blue goddesses and guys with elephant heads and all that. He loved those damn posters. I think he was trying for a Hindu effect with the name."

After a silence during which the PA system began piping in the Pretenders, Carmine shifted his toothpick from one side of his mouth to the other with his tongue and said, "Too much information, guy."

Irritated, Clyde said, "I thought you wanted to know shit about me."

"Take it easy, man," said Brad, and Spooz, with an apologetic look, said, "We want to get to know you, okay? But we got a lot of ground to cover here."

Clyde hadn't noticed any particular rush on the part of the committee, but kept his mouth shut.

Spooz unfolded a wrinked sheet of paper and spread it on the table. To make it stay flat, he put empties on it top and bottom. The paper was Clyde's application.

"So, Cliff," Spooz said. "Seems like you've got a very excellent reason for wanting to move here."

"That's Clyde, not Cliff," said Clyde,

Spooz peered at the paper. "Oh . . . right."

The waitress delivered their beers and plunked herself down in the chair next to Clyde. She was a big sexy girl, a strawberry blonde with a big butt, big thighs, big everything, kind of an R. Crumb woman, albeit with a less ferocious smile.

"You going to sit in, Joanie?" Brad asked.

"Might as well." She winked at Clyde. "I ain't making no money."

"I thought you guys were going to decide," said Clyde, feeling that things were becoming a bit arbitrary. "Can just anybody get in on this?"

"That's how democracy works," said Carmine. "They do it different where you come from?"

"Maybe he doesn't like girls." Joanie did a movie star-quality pout.

"I like girls fine. I . . . It's . . . " Clyde drew a breath and let it run out. "This is important to me, and I don't think you're taking it seriously. You don't know my name, you're not asking questions. My application looks like it's been in the wastebasket. I'm getting the idea this is all a big joke to you people."

"You want me to fuck off, I will," Joanie said.

"I don't want anybody to fuck off. Okay? All I want is for this to be a real interview."

Carmine gave him the fisheye. "You don't think this is a real interview?"

"We're in a freaking bar, for Christ's sakes. Not the town hall."

"So what're you saying? The interview's not real unless it's in a building with a dome?" Carmine spat on the floor, and Joanie punched him in the arm and said, "You going to clean that up?"

"This is the town hall," Carmine said.

"Uh-huh. Sure it is," said Clyde.

Brad tapped him on the arm in order to break up the stare-down he was having with Carmine. "It's the truth, dude. Anywhere the committee meets, it's the town hall."

Carmine popped a knuckle. "I suppose where you come from, they do that different, too."

"Yeah, matter of fact." Clyde fixed him with a death stare. "One thing, they don't let sour little fucks decide anything important."

"All right, all right," Spooz said. "Let's everybody calm down. The man wants some questions. Anyone have a question?"

Carmine said meanly, "I got nothing," and Brad appeared to be mulling it over.

"What sort of work you do?" Joanie asked.

Clyde started to point out that the question had been answered on his application; but he was grateful for this much semblance of order and said, "Construction. I'm qualified to operate most types of heavy machinery. I do carpentry, masonry, roofing. I've done some wiring, but just basic stuff. Pretty much you name it." He glanced at Carmine and added, "Too much information?"

Carmine held out a hand palm down and waggled it, as if to say that Clyde was right on the edge of overcommunicating.

Brad said, "I don't believe we've got any construction going, but he could start out down at the Dots."

Spooz agreed and Clyde was about to ask what were the Dots, when Joanie cut in and asked if he had a girlfriend.

"How about we keep it serious?" said Spooz.

"I am serious!" she said.

"Naw," said Clyde. "No girlfriend. But I'm accepting applications."

Joanie took a pretend-swat at him with a menu.

Brad followed with a question about his expertise in furniture building, and then Spooz and Joanie had questions about his long-term goals (indefinite), his police record (nothing heavy-duty since he was kid), and his health concerns (none as far as he knew). They had other questions, too, which Clyde answered honestly. He began to relax, to think that he was making an overall good impression—Brad and Joanie were in his corner for sure, and though Spooz was Carmine's cousin, Clyde had the idea that they weren't close, so he figured as long as he didn't blow it, he was in.

The atmosphere grew convivial, they had a few more beers, and at last Spooz said to his colleagues, "Well, I guess we know enough, huh?"

Joanie and Brad concurred, and Clyde asked if they wanted him to go away so they could talk things over. Not necessary, they told him, and then Carmine said, "Here's a question for you. How do you feel about the Cowboys?"

At a loss, Clyde said, "You talking about the Dallas Cowboys?"

Carmine nodded, and Clyde, assuming that this didn't require a legitimate answer, said, "Screw 'em. I'm a Steelers fan."

Brad, who had been resting his elbows on the table, sat back in his chair. Joanie was frozen for a second and then busied herself in bussing the table. Spooz lowered his eyes as if deeply saddened. Carmine smiled thinly and inspected his fingernails.

"Are you fucking kidding me?" Clyde said. "That was a serious question?"

Brad asked what time it was, and Spooz checked his watch and said it was six-thirty.

"Hey," said Clyde. "You need me to be a Cowboys fan, I'll be a Cowboys fan. I don't give a good goddamn about football, really."

That seemed to horrify them.

"What do you want from me? You want I should paint myself silver and blue every Sunday? Come on!"

"Monday," said Brad. "We don't get the games until Monday."

Spooz's stern expression dissolved into a grin. "I can't keep this up. Congratulations, man."

Baffled for the moment, Clyde said, "What are you talking?"

"You've been jumped in. This was like your initiation. The council accepted you last week."

"You'll be on probationary status for six months," Joanie said. "But it's more-or-less a done deal."

Brad and Spooz both shook his hand, and Joanie gave him a hug and a kiss with a little extra on it, and people came over from the bar to congratulate him. Clyde kept saying happily, "I can't believe you guys were just busting my chops. You fuckers had me going there!"

Carmine, who apparently had taken a real dislike to him, waited until the crowd around Clyde had dissipated to offer a limp handshake. "Don't get giddy," he said, putting his mouth close beside Clyde's cheek. "Things might not work out for you here."

Walnuts are Halloween's chief export, its only source of income (apart from the occasional tourist and the post office, which does a bang-up business once a year, stamping cards and letters) and are prized by connoisseurs in the upper world for their rich, fruity flavor, a flavor derived from steeping in the ponds south of town known as the Dots—three of them, round as periods, they create an elision interrupting the erratic black sentence of the Mossbach. Recently there have been complaints that the walnuts are no longer up to standard. The mulberries and plants that, dissolved into a residue, suffuse the walnuts, imbuing them with their distinct taste, no longer fall from the sky crack in profusion; and neither do the walnuts fall so thickly as they once they did, plop-plopping into the water like a sort of wooden hail. Nowadays the townspeople are not above importing mulberries and certain weeds and even walnuts, and dumping them into the ponds, a practice decried by connoisseurs; yet they continue to pay the exorbitant prices.

Each morning Clyde would pole his skiff (something more difficult to do than it would appear) from the north end of town, where he had found temporary living quarters, to the Dots. He recalled how it had been going to work in Beaver Falls, steering his pickup past strip malls with gray snow banked out front, his seat littered with half-crushed cans and fast food garbage, pieces of bun, greasy paper, a fragment of tomato, a dead French fry, the heater cooking it all into a rotten smell, while the idiot voices of drive-time America yammered and puffy-faced, sullen, half-asleep drivers drank bitter coffee, listening to Howard Stern and Mancow Muller, trying to remember the gross bits with which to amuse their friends . . . and he contrasted that with the uncanny peace of going to work now, gliding downstream beneath the still-darkened seam of sky, the only sound that of his pole lifting and planting, inhaling the cool, damp smell of the river mixed with fleeting odors of fish death and breakfasts cooking and limeflowers (a species with velvety greenish-white blooms peculiar to Halloween, sprouting from the dirt and birdlime that accumulated on the ledges), and occasionally another skiff coming toward him, the boatman saluting, and his thoughts glided, too, never stressed or scattered, just taking in the sights, past the simple, linear houses spread out across the rock walls like anagrams and scrambles, the blurred letters of the neon signs flickering softly in the mist, the lights at the end of spidery docks glowing witchily, haloed by glittering white particles, and once he reached the Dots, shallow circles of crystalline water illuminated in a such a way as to reveal their walnut-covered bottoms (yet not enough light to trouble him), he would put on waders and grab a long rake and turn the walnuts so as to ensure they received the benefits of immersion on all sides equally.

Between fifty and sixty men and women joined him on the morning shift and he became friendly with several, and friends with one: Dell Weimer, a blond, overweight transplant from Lake Parsippany, New Jersey, where he had managed a convenience store. Dell had recently finished a short stretch in the Tubes, the geological formation that served as Halloween's main punitive device, and would say nothing about it other than that it was " . . . some evil shit." He was forthcoming, however, about the rest of the town in which he had lived for six years.

One morning Dell straightened from his labors and, as he was wont to do, clutched his back and began grousing about the job. "Fuck a bunch of walnuts," he said on this occasion. "Here we are breaking our butts for nothing!"

Clyde asked him to explain, because he had been led to believe the town depended on the walnuts, and Dell said, "Ever hear of Pet Nylund?"

"Sounds familiar."

"You know. The rock star guy."

"Yeah . . . yeah! My ex used to liked his stuff. Real morbid crap."

"He's born and raised in Halloween."

"You're kidding?"

"Yeah, he lives here when he's not in L.A. I'll show you his place. He bought up all the land around the gorge—he must own a fucking million acres. He invested heavy in energy and bioengineering stocks about thirty years ago and the stock went through the roof."

"Bioengineering. Tinkering with genes and all that?"

"Right. He had his own company come down in here . . . Mutagenics, I think their name was. They were doing experiments south of the Dots, flushing shit into the river. Don't eat nothing come out of that river, son, 'less you want to grow gills." Dell paused to work out a kink. "Like I was saying, they flushed their chemicals so they washed away underground. The Mossbach goes subta— . . . you know."

"Subterranean."

"Yeah, right. God only knows what's growing down there. The Mutagenics people couldn't leave fast enough, so you know some bad shit happened. But even though the water here's okay, the fishies got that poison in 'em and there is some weird-looking stuff in that river. Anyhow, Pet's worth billions, so he endows the town. Now the town's a billionaire, too. Nobody's got to work, except for Nylund struck a deal with the council. In return for the endowment, people have to live like always until after he dies. He doesn't want to watch the place change and he knows the money's bound to change it. After he's gone, he don't give a damn about what happens, but for now we got to bust our behinds." Dell winced and rubbed his back again. "If he shows his face around here, I might do us all a favor and off the son-of-a-bitch."

That night in the Sub-Café, Clyde asked Joanie, with whom he was having a thing, if the Pet Nylund story was true.

"Who told you? Dell, I bet," she said. "That lazy bastard's going to wind up back in the Tubes."

She told the bartender that she was going on break and hustled Clyde out onto the pier that fronted the bar. The mist was thick and, although he heard people laughing out on the water, he couldn't see past the end of the pier. Eight or nine skiffs were tied up to the pilings; the current made them appear to nudge against each other with ungainly eagerness, like pigs at a trough.

"You're not supposed to know any of that stuff until you're off probation," Joanie said.

"Why not?"

"Because knowing about it might make you unmotivated."

"There's no reason to think it'll make me less unmotivated five months from now."

Joanie cast about to see if anyone were within earshot. "It's all about the benefits, see. They kick in once you're a citizen. Retirement, full medical . . . and I mean full. They'll even pay for a tummy tuck, anything you want. Nylund thinks if the probationers knew, they wouldn't get into the spirit of the town. They'd just be faking it."

The water slurped against the pilings, as if a big something had given them a lick.

"Dell mentioned this company, Mutagenics."

"You don't want to be talking about that," said Joanie, affecting a sober expression. "And don't you even think about going south of the Dots. We got this one idiot who goes south a lot, but one day she's going to turn up missing. Happens eventually to everybody who pokes their nose down there."

"So what's up with that?"

"If I could tell you, I'd probably be missing. I don't go there. Ever. But don't talk about it, okay? With Dell or anyone . . . except with me. I don't want you getting in trouble. With me . . . " She threw a stiff punch to the point of his shoulder. "You're already in trouble."

"Ow! Jesus!" He grabbed her and pulled her against him. He squeezed and her breath came out in a trebly *oof*. Her eyes half-closed and she ground her hips against him. The mists swirled and thickened, sealing them off from the Sub-Café, until only a vague purplish flickering remained of the sign.

"Ouch," Joannie said.

Ms. Helene Kmiec, the widow of Stan Kmiec, former head of the town council, was (at thirty-six) a relatively young woman to have endured such a tragedy, and this perhaps explained her emotional resilience. Since her husband's death eight months ago in a boating accident south of the Dots, she had taken a succession of lovers and started a new business involving the use of a webcam and bondage gear (this according to Dell, who further stated that Ms. Kmiec, a petite blonde with, in his words, "trophy-sized balloons," could give him a spanking any old time she wanted). She also took in boarders. The remainder of her time was devoted to the care and feeding of the town's sole surviving cat, a Turkish angora named Prince Shalimar who had survived for five and a half years, considerably longer, it was believed, than any other cat in Halloween's shadowy history.

"Something around here likes cats a leetle too much," she said to Clyde on the occasion of their first meeting. "People claim to have seen it, but this is all they've come up with."

She handed Clyde a photocopied poster with an artist's rendering of a raggedy Rorschach inkblot looming over a cat and underneath it the words:

REWARD!!!
For Information Leading to the Capture of
Halloween's Cat Killer

Beneath that was Ms. Kmiec's contact information.

"It's not much to go on," Clyde said, and tried to hand back the poster. Ms. Kmiec told him to hang onto it—she had plenty more.

"The damn thing's fast," she said. "Fast and sneaky. Hard to get a handle on its particulars. At least that gives you a general idea of its size." She studied the picture. "It's nailed damn near every cat in town for the past forty years, but it's not getting Princey."

"You think it's the same one's been doing it all that time?"

"Doesn't matter," she said. "It comes around here, I got something for it. One or many, old or young, that sucker's going down."

"Why don't you get a dog?"

"Dogs get taken by things in the river. Cats have the good sense to stay clear of the water."

They were sitting together on a sofa in her cramped, fourth-floor living room, a ten-by-eight foot space with a door that connected to a corridor leading to the house next door. Its cadmium yellow walls were dense with framed photographs, many of them shots of Ms. Kmiec in various states of undress, and the largest depicting her arm-in-arm with the late Mr. Kmiec, a pudgy, white-haired gent whose frown lines and frozen smile implied that such an expression did not come easily to his face. In this photograph she wore an ankle-length skirt, a cardigan, and a prim, gone-to-Jesus expression, leaving the impression that she had stepped away from the sexual arena before her time, an error since corrected. The skirt and the cardigan had been replaced that day with a gold dressing gown loosely belted over a skimpy black latex costume.

"There's one thing we should get straight before you move in," she said. "For the record, I did not kill my husband. You may hear talk that I did . . ."

"I'm not big on gossip," Clyde said, avoiding looking at her for fear he might see the truth of her statement—the light in the room was brighter than he would have liked.

" . . . but I didn't. Stan was a chore and we didn't always get along. There's times now I still resent him, but he was a good guy at heart. He was always helping me with my projects. Matter of fact, he was helping me out the day he died. We were down south looking for the cat killer and something snaked over the side of the skiff and took him under. Wasn't a thing I could have done. People say if I'd loved Stan, I would have gone in after him. Maybe there's some truth to that. I did love him, but Stan was twenty-six years older than me. Maybe I didn't love him enough."

She inched forward on the sofa, reached out her hand and touched Mr. Kmiec's image on the wall opposite. She seemed to be having a moment and Cliff waited until she had leaned back to ask what she had meant by "something snaked over the side."

"South of the Dots there's a lot of strange flora and fauna," she said. "We don't know half what's there. Don't you be going down that way until you get acclimated." She patted his knee. "We wouldn't want to lose you."

A masculine wail of distress floated up from below and Ms. Kmiec jumped to her feet. "Oh, damn! I forgot about him! Here I am chattering away and . . . I don't know what I'm thinking about!" She fingered out a key from the pocket of her robe and passed it to Clyde. "I have to take care of something. Can you show yourself up? It's the eighth floor."

Clyde said, "Sure," and scrunched in his knees so she could get past.

"Now I put you right above the Prince's room," she said as she stood in the open door, a section of the gorge's granite wall visible behind her. "I know you're bound to have company, and I don't care about that. But I made certain the bed in that room is extra stable, because the Prince hates sharp noises. So if the headboard comes loose and starts banging, or whatever, do your best to fix it temporarily and I'll get someone in to do repairs ASAP. All right?"

She shrugged out of her robe and tossed it onto the arm of the sofa and started down the ladder, seeding Cliff's brain with an afterimage of pale, shapely legs and swelling breasts restrained by narrow, shiny strips of rubber. A second later her head popped back into view.

"If you want, look in on the Prince. He loves new people." Her brow furrowed, as if trying to recall some further instruction; then she brightened and said, "Welcome to Kasa Kmiec!"

The eighth floor was a room with a half-bath added on. Within a ten-by-twelve space, it contained a captain's bed with shelves in the bottom, a wicker chair, bookshelves and a TV niche built into the walls, a stove and sink, and small refrigerator. It was as cunningly crafted as a ship's cabin, with every inch of space utilized. Initially Clyde felt he might break something whenever he moved, but he adapted to his new quarters and soon, when lying on the bed, he began to have a sense of spaciousness.

He enjoyed sitting in the wicker chair after work with the lamp dialed low, vegetating until his energy returned, and then he would turn the light on full. He had discovered that he liked being smart when alone, liked the solitary richness of his mind, and he would sketch plans for the house he intended to build after he got off probation; he would read and speculate on subjects of which he had been unaware prior to the accident (Indian influences on Byzantine architecture, the effects of globalization upon Lhasa and environs, et al.); but always his thoughts returned to the town where he had sought refuge, whose origins no one appeared to know or question, whose very existence seemed as mysterious as the nation of Myanmar or the migratory impulses of sea turtles. He had supposed—unrealistically, perhaps—that the people of Halloween would have a clearer perspective on life than did the people in Beaver Falls; but they had similar gaps in their worldview and ignored these gaps as if they were insignificant, as if by not including them in the picture, everything made sense, everything was fine. He had hoped the town would be a solution, but now he suspected it was simply another sort of problem, more exotic and perhaps more complex, one that he would have to leave the light on a great deal in order to resolve if he hoped to get to the bottom of it.

When he heard the winch complain, the chain slithering through the pulley, signs that Joanie was on her way up in the elevator that operated above the fifth floor, he would dim the lamp so he would be unable to perceive the telltales that betrayed the base workings of her mind and the fabrication of her personality. She understood why he did this—at least he had explained his troubles—but it played into her appreciation of herself as an entry-level girlfriend, and she often asked if she wasn't pretty enough for him, if that was why he lowered the lights. He told her that she was more than pretty enough, but she grew increasingly morose and would say she knew they were a short-term thing and that he would someday soon find someone who made him happy, as would she, and it was better this way—this way, when the inevitable happened they would stay friends because they had been honest with each other and hadn't gotten all deluded, and until then, well, they'd have some fun, wouldn't they? Even in the half-dark, he realized it was a self-fulfilling prophecy, that her low self-esteem foredoomed the relationship. Understanding this about her, having so much apperception of the human ritual, dismayed him and he would try to boost her spirits by telling her stories about his life topside (the citizens of Halloween referred to other parts of America as "topside" or "the republic") or by mocking Mrs. Kmiec's cat.

Beside the bed was a trapdoor that had once permitted egress to the floor below, but now was blocked by a sheet of two-inch Plexiglas—a plastic cube had been constructed within the old wooden room for the protection of its sole inhabitant, a fluffy white blob with a face and feet. When Clyde first opened the trapdoor, Prince Shalimar had freaked out, climbing the walls, throwing himself at the inner door; now, grown accustomed to Clyde and Joanie peering at him, he never glanced in their direction. The place was a cat paradise filled with mazes upon which to climb, scratching posts, dangling toys, and catnip mice. Infrequently the Prince would swat at one or another of the toys; now and then he would chew on a catnip mouse; but a vast majority of his time was spent sleeping in a pillowed basket close to his litter box.

"It's not even a cat anymore," Joanie said one evening as they looked down on the Prince, snoozing on his pillow. "It's like some kind of mutant."

"Ms. Kmiec gives him enemas," said Clyde.

"You're kidding!"

"Swear to God. I looked down there one time and she had a plastic tube up his butt."

"Did she see you?"

"Yeah. She waved and went on with her business."

"Wasn't the cat pissed?"

"She was wearing work gloves and holding him down, but by the time I looked, he seemed to have quit struggling and was just lying there."

Joanie shook her head in wonderment. "Helene is very, very weird."

"Do you know her?"

"Not so much. She used to come to the bar with Stan. She's always been weird. My big sister was the same year in school as with her—she says Helene was already into the dominatrix stuff when she was a kid. She quit doing it for Stan."

"Maybe she didn't quit. Maybe Stan was her only client for a while."

"Maybe."

Joanie leaned against him and Clyde draped an arm over her shoulder; the edge of his hand nudged her breast. They watched as the Prince gave a mighty fishlike heave and managed to flop onto his back.

"He doesn't even have the energy to miaow anymore," Clyde said. "He makes this sound instead. 'Mrap, mrap.' It's like half a miaow. A shorthand miaow."

Joanie caught his hand and placed it full on her breast. "Something happens to Helene, the poor bastard won't stand a fighting chance. Nobody else is going to do for him the way she does. He'll be like a bonbon for that fucking thing."

They made loud, sweaty love with no regard for Prince's sensibilities, banging the headboard against the wall, and afterward, with Joanie snoring gently beside him, Clyde was unable to rid himself of the image and lay thinking that they were all bonbons, soft white things in their flimsy protective shells, helplessly awaiting the emergence of some black maw or circumstance.

Seven weeks after his arrival in Halloween, Clyde was working with a group of twenty or twenty-five in the central Dot, when he heard from Mary Alonso, a sinewy, brown-skinned gay woman in her early thirties, that Dell had been banished.

"'Banished'?" he said, and laughed. "You can't banish people, not since the Middle Ages."

"Tell that to Dell." Mary leaned against the rocky wall, a pose that stretched her T-shirt across her diminutive breasts, making them look like lumps of muscle. "They sent him up to the republic and he can't come back. He'd been to the Tubes nine times. The tenth time and you're gone."

"Is that some kind of rule? Nobody told me."

"When you're through probation you get a book with the town laws. There aren't many of them. Don't kill anybody, don't rape anybody, don't screw up constantly. I guess they got Dell on the 'don't screw up constantly.'"

"What the hell? Don't you have people believe in the Constitution down here?"

"The Constitution's not what it used to be," Mary said. "Guess you didn't notice."

"Well, how's about Helene Kmeic?"

"Huh?"

"Helene Kmeic. Chances are she killed her husband. The way Joanie tells it, they didn't hardly investigate."

"I wouldn't know about that." Mary started raking again.

"Is Dell still around? Are they holding him somewhere?"

"Once they decide you're gone, you're gone. Only reason I know about it, I was at home and Tom Mihalic come around saying I had to work Dell's shift."

Distraught, Clyde threw aside his rake and went splashing away from the ranks of toiling men and women, stomping down hard, trying to crush as many walnuts as he could. He didn't slow his pace until he had gone halfway along the narrow channel between the second and third Dot, and then only because he noticed the light had paled.

Unlike the other two Dots, the third and largest (some ninety feet in diameter) lay at the bottom of a hole that appeared to have been punched through from the surface—probably an old sinkhole—and was open to the weather. At present it was raining straight down, raining hard (a fact that wasn't apparent back in the second Dot, where the walls of the Shilkonic all but sealed them off from the sky), and the pond was empty of laborers. The effect was of a pillar of rain resembling one of those transporter beams used in science fiction movies, except this was much bigger, a ninety-foot-wide column of excited gray particles preparing to zap a giant up from the bowels of an ashen planet, making a seething sound as it did, and amplifying the omnipresent damp smell of the gorge. Staring at it, Clyde's anger planed away into despondency. He and Dell hadn't been that close. They had gone out drinking three or four times, and he'd visited Dell's place to watch DVDs, and they hung out during their lunch breaks, and that was it. But their relationship had the imprimatur of friendship. Dell's breezy, profane irreverence reminded him of his friends back in Beaver Falls. People gossiped about each other a lot in Halloween, yet he recognized that they shied away from certain people and subjects: Pet Nylund and why there was no cable

TV and what had happened to Helene Kmiec's husband, to name three. Dell had talked freely about these and other taboos, though most of his talk was BS (perhaps that explained why he'd been banished), and while Clyde had been reluctant to respond in kind, due to his probationary status, neither had he discouraged Dell. A fly's worth of guilt traipsed across his brain and he brushed it aside, telling himself that Dell was his own man and he, Clyde, wasn't about to make this into a soap opera of recriminations and what-ifs.

By the time he reached the pond, the rain had stopped. Under ordinary circumstances, he kept clear of the third Dot (Spooz, as a representative of the council, had written a note excusing him from work there because of his sensitivity to light), yet Clyde felt he needed every jot of intellect in order to deal with his emotions and he moved out into the pond, glancing anxiously at the turbulent sky and the gaping crack of the gorge across the way—less than two months in town and he had already become an agoraphobe. To his left, a section of the granite wall evolved into a ledge. He boosted himself onto it and sat with his legs dangling. Twenty feet farther to the left lay a beach of sand and dirt and rubble, where grew several low bushes surrounding a stunted willow, the sole tree in all of Halloween. Clyde considered the complicated patterns of the bare twigs, thinking this was something the supporters of intelligent design, mistaking (as they frequently did) mere intricacy for skillful engineering, might point to in order to demonstrate the infinite forethought that had gone into God's universal blueprint. Hell, he could do a better job himself, given the right tools. For starters, he'd outfit everyone with male and female genitalia so they wouldn't be constantly trying to fuck one another over, and once they had experienced the joys of childbirth, they would likely stop trying to fuck themselves over, recognizing that survival was overrated, and would abandon procreation to the lesser orders and become a species of bonbon who placidly waited for extinction, recognizing this to be the summit of human aspiration. That question settled, he turned his attention to the matter at hand. He had been wrong in trying to banish Dell from mind, basically duplicating the action of the town. Not that he cared to hold onto guilt or any other emotion where Dell was concerned, but he needed to think about why he had been banished and how this might apply to him. He began to whistle—Clyde was an accomplished whistler and had gotten in the habit of accompanying himself while thinking. Whistling orchestrated his thoughts into a calm and orderly pattern, preferable to their usual agitated run. The sinkhole responded with a hint of reverb, adding a mellifluous quality to his tone, distracting him, and it was then he spotted a woman with pale skin and shoulder-length auburn hair peering at him through the willow twigs.

"Jesus!" said Clyde, for she had given him a start.

The twigs sectioned her face like the separations of a jigsaw puzzle, causing her to appear, as she turned her head, like a stained glass image come to life. She stepped out of cover, hopped up onto the far end of the ledge, scowled and said, "Get out of my way."

She was slender and tall, and had on a white sundress that, being a little damp, clung to her body. She wore kneepads and elbow pads, and on her feet were a pair of brown sports shoes.

"Aren't you cold?" Clyde asked.

She pulled a pair of thin gloves from the pocket of her skirt and put them on. In a town where pale women predominated, her pallor was abnormal, like chalk. Her mouth was so wide, its corners seemed to carry out the lines of her slanted cheekbones, and was perfectly molded, the lips neither too full nor too thin, lending her an air of confidence and serenity; her eyes, too, were wide, teardrop-shaped, almost azure in color. She let the scowl lapse into a mask of hostile diffidence, but her face was an open book to Clyde. Her confidence was not based on her beauty (in truth, he didn't perceive her as beautiful, merely attractive—she was too skinny for his tastes), but spoke to the fact that she had little regard for beauty . . . and not much regard for anything or anyone, if he read her right. She told him once again to move it so she could pass, and Clyde, irritated by her peremptory manner, pointed at the water and said, "Go around."

"I don't want to get wet," she said.

"Yeah, I just bet you don't. That would be icky."

She affected a delighted expression and laughed: two notes, sharply struck, from the treble end of a keyboard. "You're being clever, aren't you? Now let me by."

Clyde was tempted to make her squeeze past, and perhaps he would have done so once upon a time, but he was fascinated by the way her face changed with the movement of eyes and mouth, with every shift in attitude, one moment having an Asian cast, the next seeming entirely Caucasian, and the next expressing an alien quality . . . and this grounded the charge of his anger. Wondering how old she was (he would not have been surprised to learn she was forty or twenty-five), he eased off the ledge and into the water.

As she walked past him on long, muscular legs, he tried to make nice, saying, "My name's Clyde."

"How appropriate," she said.

When she reached the end of the ledge, she grabbed a miniscule projection of stone, placed the toe of one shoe in an equally imperceptible notch, and then went spidering across the granite face, making the traverse with such speed and precision, it was as if she were wearing sucker pads on her fingers and toes. Within seconds she had disappeared into the channel that led back to the second Dot.

"Whoa!" said Clyde.

He told no one about having seen the woman. He did not tell Joanie because he knew she would leap to the conclusion that his interest was more than casual (which it wasn't, or so he believed) and be upset; he did not tell Mary Alonso, who had taken Dell's place as a source of gossip and information, and with whom he went out for drinks on occasion, usually along with Mary's partner, Roberta, a fey, freckly, dark-haired girl, because he didn't want to learn that the pale woman was a shrew or unstable—he preferred to let her remain a mystery (since we rarely feel compelled to mythologize the humdrum or the ordinary, his interest was likely more than casual). He began coming in early to work and staying late, using the time to practice his whistling in the reverb chamber of the third Dot, hoping to catch sight of her again. He worked on octave jumps, trills and ornamental phrasings, and developed a fresh repertoire of standards and novelty tunes. After a month he became sufficiently confident to essay a few numbers of his own composition ("fantasies," he called them), foremost among them a ballad that he entitled "Melissa"—he thought the woman looked like a Melissa.

Whistling, for Clyde, was its own satisfaction, but when Mary Alonso told him about the talent contest held at the Downlow every year and urged him to enter, he thought, What the hell? He devoted himself to perfecting "Melissa," adding a frill or two, reworking the somber middle passage, trimming the coda so the song fit within the contest's four-minute limit, and one afternoon in March, with the contest less than a month away, while he sat practicing on the ledge, with a circle of wintry blue sky overhead and shadow filling the sinkhole, all except for a slice of golden light at the brim, the woman, dressed in jeans and a burgundy sweater, came poling a skiff from the south, emerging from the darkness of the gorge with lanterns hung all over the prow and sides and stern. Something about her posture announced her even before he made out her face. She beached the skiff near the willow and climbed onto the ledge and took a seat about three feet away. Her flat azurine stare seemed as hostile as before, but Cliff saw curiosity in her face. Neither of them spoke for a couple of ticks and then she said, "That's a cool tune, man."

"It's something I'm working on," he said.

"You made it up?"

"Yeah."

"Very cool. What's it called?"

"'Melissa.'"

"Is she your girl . . . your wife?"

"I don't know why I called it that. The only Melissa I ever knew was back in grade school."

"It sounds classical. You ever hear the opera, *Pelléas et Mélisande*, by Debussy?"

"I don't think so."

She appeared to have run out of questions.

"What's it about, the opera?" asked Clyde.

"I don't remember much. This sad chick's married to this prince, but she's in love with his brother. She cries a lot. It's kind of a bummer. Your thing reminded me of it."

She kicked her heels against the rock and gazed out across the pond. Clyde realized that at this distance he should be reading her more clearly—he should have seen past the level of body language into her chaotic core, where need and desire steamed upward and began to solidify into shards of thought; yet he could find no trace of her fundamental incoherence . . . or else, unlike the rest of mankind, she was fundamentally coherent, her personality rising in a smooth, uninterrupted flow from its springs, a true and accurate extension of her soul.

"Not the notes," she said. "The feeling."

"Huh?" said Clyde.

"Your song. It reminded me of the opera. Not the melody or anything, but the feeling." She said this with a trace of exasperation and then asked, "Why're you staring at me?"

He was inclined to tell her that she had a smudge on her cheek (which she, in fact, did) or that she looked familiar; but she gazed at him with such intensity, he half-suspected that his inability to see into her basements signaled a commensurate ability on her part to see into his—afraid of being caught in a lie, then, he told her about his accident and its aftermath and explained how she appeared to be something of an anomaly, at least as regarded his hypothesis concerning light, intellect, and the chaotic underpinnings of human personality.

"Must be I'm in your blind spot," she said. "Because I feel pretty chaotic . . . at least most of the time." That he might have a blind spot disturbed him more than the thought that she might be a freak of nature. "Light-based intelligence," she said musingly. "What about Milton? He wrote great shit after he went blind."

"I haven't found a theory yet that explains everything or everyone. I suppose he's an exception, like you." He thought she might be losing interest in the conversation and asked if she commonly hung out in the third Dot. "Only during the season," she said in a fake upper-crust accent. Letting up on the sarcasm, she added, "I pass through when I go exploring down south. And when I need to be by myself, I'll stake out a spot next to the willow."

"So if I see you beside the willow, I should beat it?"

"Not necessarily," she said, and grinned. "You could whistle and see what develops. I've always had a thing for musicians." With an easy motion, she pushed up to her feet. "I've got to get back. See you around, maybe."

Clyde restrained himself from asking her to stay. "Hey, what's your name?"

"Annalisa."

She moved off and Clyde, watching the roll of her hips, knowing it was the wrong thing to do yet unable to suppress the urge, let out an appreciative whistle, an ornate variation on the wolf whistle that he had devised for just such occasions and often used to excellent effect, the intricacy of his embellishment compensating for the cornball tactic. Annalisa rolled her eyes, but he noticed a little extra sway in her walk as she went toward the skiff. He thought "Annalisa" was a much better title than "Melissa," and he decided then and there to break up with Joanie.

Usually Joanie was eager to go to his place, but that night, perhaps sensing trouble, she resisted being alone with him and they went for a drink at the Downlow, a labyrinthine nightclub excavated from the rock. Bass-heavy ambient music rumbled from hidden speakers. The rooms were lit by plastic boulders that shifted from dull orange to violet to blue-green, and served as tables; these were enclosed by groupings of sofas and easy chairs. There were decorative touches throughout—potted ferns; a diminutive statue that might have been Mayan or Olmec; a poster of Pet Nylund with his hair flying, face obscured, twisting the strings of his guitar—but not enough of them to create a specific statement. The overall effect was of a tiki bar in Bedrock whose interior decorator had been fired halfway through the job.

They chose an empty side room with an aquarium built into the walls, populated by fish with strange whiskery antennae and others without eyes. Clyde recognized none of them and asked Joanie what kind they were. She replied, "Who do you think I am? A fish scientist?" She looked sullen in the orange light, angry in the violet, depressed in the blue-green.

A waitress brought their drinks and, since Joanie's mood showed no sign of improving, Clyde got straight to the point. He had worked out what he felt was a tactful approach, but he had barely begun when Joanie broke in and asked, "Who is she?"

Defensively, Clyde said, "You think I've been unfaithful?"

She scooted an inch or two farther away. "Don't bullshit me. Men don't jump unless they got some place to land."

"I met this woman, all right?" said Clyde. "But we haven't done anything yet."

"Who is she?"

"If you weren't so goddamn negative about our relationship . If you didn't always. . . . "

"Oh, it's my fault?" She made a noise like the Prince did when he sneezed. "I guess I should have known from experience. I been dumped on more times than your toilet seat, so it must be me. . . . "

"See, that's what I'm talking about! You're always putting yourself down."

"It must be me and not the dickwads I go out with."

"Maybe all I need is a break," said Clyde. "A little space."

Joanie injected an artificial brightness into her voice. "What a good idea! I'll give you space while you cozy up to what's-her-buttass and I'll just hang loose in case things don't work out."

"Goddamn it, Joanie! You know that's not what I mean."

"Tell me who she is."

Reluctantly, Clyde said, "I only met her a couple of times. Her name's Annalisa."

For a second Joanie was expressionless; then she spewed laughter. "Oh, man! You hooked up with the willow wan?"

"I haven't hooked up with anybody!"

She put her head down and shook her head back and forth; her hair glowed orange as it swept the top of the boulder.

"What'd you call her . . . the willow what?"

Joanie's voice was nearly inaudible above a lugubrious bass line. "Wan. The willow wan. It's what everybody calls her."

"I don't get it."

"Because she's pale as birdshit and always acts crazy and hangs out by the willow tree and she does all kinds of crazy things."

"What's she do that's crazy?"

"I don't know! Lots of things."

"There must be something specific if everyone thinks she's crazy."

"She's all the time going down south of the Dots. You have to be crazy to go there." A look of entreaty crowded other emotions from her face, yet Clyde still saw anger and hurt. "She's gaming you, man. You don't want to mess with her. She games all the guys. She's Pet Nylund's ex-wife, for God's sake! She still lives with him."

"What do you mean?"

"Am I speaking Spanish? She fucking lives with him. In his house."

Some evidence of the disappointment he felt must have surfaced in his expression, for upon registering it, she snatched her purse and jumped up from the sofa. He caught her wrist and said, "Joanie. . . . "

She broke free and stood with her chin trembling. "Stay out of the Sub for awhile, okay?"

A tear spilled from the corner of her eye and she rubbed it frantically, as if trying to kill a stinging insect; then she said something he didn't catch and ran from the room.

Clyde had the impulse to offer consolation, but the weight of what she said about Annalisa kept him seated. Though they had established the frailest of connections, nothing really, he felt betrayed, hurt, angry, everything Joanie had appeared to feel—the idea floated into his mind that she might want him to suffer and had lied about Annalisa. But if it were a lie, it would be easy to disprove and thus it was probably true. He downed his drink in two swallows and went into the main room, a semicircular space with twenty or thirty of the boulder tables and a bar with a marble countertop and a stage, currently unoccupied, against the rear wall. Joanie was doing shots at the bar, bracketed by two men who had their hands all over her; when she saw him she gave her hair an assertive flip and pretended to be deeply interested in what one man (a big sloppy dude with long hair and a beard, Barry Something) was saying. He scanned the tables, hoping to spot a friendly face among the people sitting there. Finding none, he walked out onto the pier, sat on a piling under the entrance lights and listened to the gurgling of the Mossbach. Off along the bend, on the elbow of the curve, Pet Nylund's house staggered up the cliff face, three side-by-side, crookedy towers, their uppermost rooms

cloaked in darkness. Lights were on in several of the lower rooms. Clyde
toyed with the notion of going over and busting through the door and venting
his frustrations in a brawl. It was a bonehead play he would once have made
without thinking, and that he now stopped to consider the consequences and
hadn't simply acted out his passions with animal immediacy, never mind it
was the rational thing to do . . . it dismayed him. Carmine, he told himself,
might have been right in his estimation: maybe Halloween wasn't going to
work out for him.

Laughter from the doorway and Joanie emerged from the Downlow
arm-in-arm with the two men she'd been flirting with at the bar. The bearded
man caught Clyde staring and asked what he was looking at. Clyde ignored
him and said, "Don't do this to yourself, Joanie."

She hardened her smile and Barry Something put a hand on Clyde's chest
and suggested he back the fuck off. The touch kindled a cold fury in Clyde that
spread throughout his body, as if he'd been dunked in liquid nitrogen. He saw
everything with abnormal clarity: the positions of the men, Joanie's embittered
face, the empty doorway, the green neon letters bolted to the rock. He spread
his hands as though to say, no harm, no foul, and planted his right foot and
drove his fist into Barry's eye. Barry reeled away, went to his knees, grabbing
his face. Joanie started yelling; the other man sidled nervously toward the
entrance. Barry moaned. "Aw, fuck! Fuck!" he said. An egg-shaped lump was
already rising from his from his orbital ridge. Clyde grabbed Joanie's arm and
steered her toward his skiff. She fought him at first, but then started to cry.
Some onlookers stepped out of the bar, drinks in hand, to learn what the fuss
was about. Not a one of them moved to help Barry, who was rolling around,
holding his eye. Talking and laughing, they watched Clyde poled the skiff
into the center of the river. "Chickenshit bastard!" someone shouted. From a
distance, the tableau in front of the bar appeared to freeze, as if its batteries
had died. Joanie sat in the stern, her knees drawn up, gazing at the water. Her
tears dried. Once or twice she seemed on the verge of speaking. He thought
he should say something, but he had nothing to offer, still too adrenalized,
too full of anger at Barry, at himself, too caught up in the dismal glory of
the fight, confused as to whether it had validated his hopes for Halloween
or had been an attempt to validate them. When they reached her pier, Joanie
scrambled up onto it without a word and raced into her tiny, two-room house
and slammed the door.

Working alongside him the following daymorning, Mary Alonso, who had
gotten a buzzcut and a dye job, leaving a half-inch of blond stubble that he
thought singularly unattractive, filled Clyde in on Annalisa.

"She shares the house with Pet, but she's not with him, you know," she
said. "She keeps to her half, he keeps to his. Joanie was being a bitch, telling
you that without telling you the rest. Not that I blame her."

"For real? She's not sleeping with him?"

"She did once after the divorce, but it was sort of a reflex."

Clyde flipped a rotten walnut up with his rake, caught it in mid-air and shied it at the wall, provoking a stare from another worker, whom the walnut had whizzed past. "How'd you hear that?"

"Before me and Roberta got together, Annalisa had a girl crush on Roberta. She thought she might be gay, but. . . . " Mary strained to break up a clump of walnuts that had become trapped in underwater grass. "Turned out she wasn't. Not even a little." She scowled at Clyde. "Don't look so damn relieved!"

Clyde held up a hand as though in apology. "So Roberta told you about her?"

"Yeah. They stayed friends and she talks to Roberta sometimes. But don't get too happy. Her head's fucked up from being with Pet all those years. She tells Roberta she's going to leave, but she never does. There's some kind of bizarre dependency still happening between her and Pet."

Clyde went back to work with a renewed vigor, thinking that he might be the man to dissolve that bond. The weather was crisp and clear, and the sky crack showed a cold blue zigzag like a strip of frozen lightning that the ragged line of laborers beneath appeared to emulate. A seam of reflected light from the water jittered on the rock walls.

"I'm worried about you, man," said Mary. "I love you, and I don't want to see you get all bent out of shape behind this thing."

"You *love* me?" Clyde gave a doltish laugh.

Mary's face cinched with anger. "Right. Mister Macho. You think all love is is the shit that makes you feel dizzy. Everything else is garbage. Well, fuck you!" She threw down her rake and went chest to chest with him. "Yeah, I love you! Roberta loves you! It's amazing we do, you're such an ass-clown!"

Startled by this reaction, Clyde put a hand on her shoulder. "I didn't mean to piss you off."

She knocked his hand away, looking like she was itching to throw a punch.

"I wasn't thinking," Clyde said. "I was. . . . "

"For someone claims to have a problem with smarts, you do a lot of not-thinking." She picked up her rake and took a swipe at the walnuts.

The other workers, who had paused to watch, turned away and engaged in hushed conversations.

"You're so caught up in your own crap, you can't see anything else," said Mary, who had toned down from fighting mad to grumpy.

"We've established I'm a dick, all right?" Clyde said. "Now what're you trying to tell me?"

"Annalisa's not Pet's wife, and she's not his girlfriend, but she's his business because she lets herself be his business. Until that changes she's poison for other guys. That's the number one rule around here, even though they didn't write it down: Don't fuck with Pet Nylund's business."

"Or what? You go to the Tubes?"

"Keep being a dick. You'll find out."

Mary raked walnuts with a vengeance, as if she wanted to rip out the bottom of the Dot. Clyde rested both hands on the end of his rake and, as he gazed at the other workers, some intent on their jobs, some goofing off, some pretending to be busy, and then glanced up at the gorge enclosing them like the two halves of a gigantic bivalve, its lips almost closed, admitting a ragged seam of sky, at the gray walls stained with lichen and feathered with struggling ferns, he had an overpowering sense of both the unfamiliar and the commonplace, and realized with a degree of sadness what he should have understood long before: Halloween wasn't, as he had hoped, an oasis with magical qualities isolated from the rest of the country; it was the flabby heart of dead-end America, a drear crummy back alley between faceless cliff tenements where the big ones ate the little ones and not every dog had his day.

For almost a week he took to sitting each night beneath the dangling seventy-five watt bulb at the end of Ms. Kmiec's pier, hoping to catch Annalisa returning in her skiff from down south. He was a fool, he knew that—he had no reason to believe she felt anything for him, and the wonder was that he felt so much for her; yet he was unable to resist the notion (though he wouldn't have admitted it, because saying the words would have forced him to confront their foolishness) that they had connected on an important level. To provide himself with an excuse for sitting there hour after hour, he borrowed one of Stan Kmiec's old fishing rods and made a desultory cast whenever he sighted an approaching skiff. Briefly, he became interested in trying to land one of the silvery bioluminescent fish that flocked the dark water, but they proved too canny and the only thing he snagged was what he thought to be some sort of water snake, a skinny writhing shadow that snapped and did a twisting dance in midair, and succeeded in flinging out the hook . . . and yet he heard no splash, as if it had flown off into the night.

The sixth night, unseasonably warm and misty (it had been like that all week and the bugs and bats were out in force), he spotted a skiff coming from the south with no light hung from its bow and knew it had to be Annalisa. She paused when she noticed him, letting the skiff glide. He whistled the opening bars of "Annalisa." She turned the skiff, brought it alongside the pier, and said brightly, "What's up?"

"Fishing." He indicated the rod. "Thinking."

She smiled. "Ooh. That must be hard work. Maybe I shouldn't interfere."

She had on jeans and a turtleneck and an old saggy gray cardigan; her hands were chapped and smudged with dirt, and her reddish brown hair (redder, he thought, than the last time he had seen her) was tied back with a black ribbon.

"The damage is done," he said. "Come sit a while."

She looped a line over a piling and he gave her a hand up. She settled beside him, her hip nudging his. She let out a sigh and looked across the water to the houses on the far side, a game board of bright and dark squares, their walls barely discernable and their piers lent definition by diffuse pyramids of wan light and whirling moths at their extremities. She smelled of shampoo and freshly turned earth, as if she had been gardening.

"I see Milly's working late," she said.

"Milly?"

"Milly Sussman. Don't you even know your neighbors?"

"Guess not."

"You need to get out more. How long have you been here? Three, four months? I should think you would have noticed Milly. Statuesque. Black hair. An extremely impressive woman."

"Maybe . . . yeah."

With her hair back, her face seemed more Asian than before; her prominent cheekbones and narrow jaw formed a nearly trapezoidal frame for her exotic features, making them appear stylized like those of a beautiful anime cyborg. From all her tics and eye movements and the working of her mouth, he read a mixture of desire and fear. Something left a trail of bubbles out on the river. Three glowing silver fish hovered in the water beneath her Doc Martens. She peered at them and asked, "You catch anything?"

"Yep. I hooked me a nice-looking one."

"You're being clever again. I can tell." She kicked her heels idly against the side of the pier. "We missed out, not living in the age of courtly speech. I could say, like, uh, 'Hooked, sir? Thy hook is not set deep enough!' And you could. . . . "

He placed a hand on the back of her neck and drew her gently to him and kissed her. She pulled away and, with a nervous laugh, said, "Better watch it. You'll get girl cooties." The second time he kissed her, she displayed no reluctance, no resistance whatsoever. Her tongue darted out so quickly, it might have been an animal trapped in the cave of her mouth, desperate to escape, if only to another cave. He caught her waist, pulling her closer, and slipped his hand under the turtleneck, up along her ribcage to her breast, rolling the nipple with his thumb. Their teeth clicked together, they clawed at one another and sought fresh angles of attack, striving to penetrate and to admit the other more deeply. The kiss was a brutish, clumsy, an expression of red-brained lust, and Annalisa surfaced from it like a diver with bursting lungs, exclaiming, "Oh God!"

After a few beats they kissed again, and were more measured in their explorations, yet no less lustful. Clyde was about to suggest they move things to his bedroom, but Annalisa spoke first.

"I can't do this now." She tugged the turtleneck down over her breasts. "I'm sorry. Really, really sorry. But I have to go."

"Go where?"

"Home. I don't want to, but. . . . "

Despite himself, resentment crept into his voice. "Home to Pet."

Annalisa cut her eyes toward him and finished straightening her clothes. "It's complicated."

"You going to explain it to me?"

"Yes, but I can't now." She re-buttoned the top button of her jeans.

"When am I going to see you?"

"I'm not sure."

"I don't understand," he said. "You wanted me to kiss you."

"I did. Very much." She reached behind her head and retied her hair ribbon. "Since we're being candid, I want to make your eyes roll back. But it's dangerous. This was dangerous. I shouldn't have let it happen."

"How's it dangerous?"

"You could die."

She said this so flatly, he had to laugh. He wasn't sure whether she was telling the truth or attempting to scare him off. He stared at her, perhaps sadly, because she reacted to his expression by saying, "For God's sake! It was only a kiss." He continued to stare and she said, "Okay, the losing-consciousness part, that was new." She climbed into the skiff, undid the line, and held onto the piling. "I'm incredibly motivated to be with you. You probably sensed that."

He nodded happily.

"There's a safe way we can be together," she went on. "But you have to give me time to work it out. Weeks, if necessary. Maybe a month. Can you do that? If not, tell me now, because Pet is insane. It's not that he's suspicious or jealous. He is batshit crazy and he hurts people."

"I can do it."

A flapping of wings overhead, followed by long quavering cry that sounded like a man running out of breath while blowing trebly notes on a harmonica.

"If it takes a little longer even," Annalisa said, "promise you'll trust me."

"Promise."

"You won't do anything stupid?"

"I'll be cool."

"Shake on it."

She gave his hand a vigorous shake, but and trailed her fingers across his as she disengaged.

"All right. See you soon," she said, and made a rueful face. "I'm sorry."

It was slightly unreal watching her glide away into the dark and, after she had vanished, he felt morose and insubstantial, like a ghost who had suddenly been made aware of all the sensory richness of which he was deprived. The enclosure of the gorge, though invisible, oppressed him. Dampness cored his bones. It was difficult impossible to hold onto promises in all that emptiness. Whatever it was that made bubbles out in the river was still making them, trawling back and forth in front of the pier, closing the distance with each pass, lifting the water with each turn, causing swells. Clyde walked away from the pier, ignoring chased by the whisper of the water, the gleeps and tweetlings of frogs and other night creatures, and wearily climbed the ladder to his apartment.

They saw one another more frequently than he'd expected over the days that followed, running into each other in the bars, on the river, sometimes contriving to touch, and one afternoon, when Mrs. Kmiec sent him to Dowling's (Halloween's eccentric version of a supermarket and its most extensive building, four interconnected tiers of eight stories each) to pick up kitty litter, Annalisa accosted him in Pet Supplies, eighth floor, fourth tier, and drew him out through a door behind the shelves into a narrow space between the rear wall and the cliff face, and there she hiked up her skirt and they made violent, bone-rattling love balanced on girders above eighty feet of nothing, braced against rock that had been ornately tagged by generations of teenagers who had used the spot before them, swirls of orange, silver, blue, red, and fat letters outlined in black, most of them cursing the authority of man or god, whatever agency had ruled their particular moment, all their hormonal rebellion confined to this not-so-secret hideaway. Annalisa was sweet and shifty, cunning with her hips, yet she nipped his neck, marking his throat, and left a long scratch on his ribcage, and spoke in tongues, in gasps and throaty noises. It seemed less an act of abandon for her than one of desperation. Afterward he asked if this is what she'd had in mind when she mentioned a safe way of being together. "I couldn't wait," she said, staring at him with tremulous anxiety, as if the wrong word would break her, shatter the almost Asian simplicity of her face. He felt this to be the case, that she had put herself in physical and mental jeopardy by taking this step, and he realized that her strength and apparent independence was a carefully constructed shield that had prevented him from seeing what lay behind it—he still could not make out the roots of her trouble, but he sensed something restive, dammed up, a powerful force straining for release.

The week before the talent contest they held auditions at the Downlow. The stage was lit with a spot that pointed up the tawdriness of the glittery silver Saturns and comets on the dark blue painted backdrop; but there were amps and a good PA and professional quality mikes, everything a performer might need. Waiting to go on, through what seemed an interminable sequence of stand-up comics with no sense of timing, accordion players, twirlers, off-key vocalists, tap dancers, rappers, and a man who could put a foot behind his ear while standing and repeat everything you said backward (Clyde's favorite), he had several drinks to ease his nerves and oil his instrument . . . perhaps one too many, for when his turn came, following a sax player who noodled a decent rendition of "My Favorite Things," he announced that he would be performing an original composition entitled, "'Annali . . . uh, Melissa.'" A guy in the back asked him to repeat the title and he said, "Sorry. I'm a little nervous. That's 'Melissa Anne.'"

Pet Nylund was supposed to be in the audience and, as he adjusted the mike, adding a bit touch of reverb, Clyde searched for him (though he couldn't recall his face and wasn't certain what he would be like after so many years away from the limelight), but the spot blinded him. He warmed up with a scale, which drew catcalls, but after he had performed he received scattered applause, which was better than most had done.

Afterward he was given a packet containing an entry number and forms, and told he was in. His main competition was the sax player, a black chick named Yolanda who sang a wicked version of "Chain of Fools," and a young guy who did a one-man-band comedy act that was borderline obscene and a real crowd-pleaser. The singer and the young guy were one-two, he figured, but he stood a good chance for third place money, three hundred bucks and a Pet Nylund box set, enough to buy Annalisa something nice. He'd give the box set to Mary for Roberta, who was a fan.

He had another drink at the bar, looked around again for Annalisa and Pet, and talked to Spooz for a bit. Spooz complimented him on his whistling and said he should hang out—Brad would be along soon. Brad had a job topside that kept him running and was hardly ever around, and Clyde would have liked to stay and talk sports with him; but lately he preferred being alone with his thoughts of Annalisa to the company of others, so he begged off.

The lights were on in Ms. Kmiec's living room and, as he ascended the ladder, taking pains not to slip, because drunken ladder mishaps were a common occurrence in Halloween (only the week before Tim Sleight, whom Clyde knew from the Dots, had gotten a load on and fallen two floors, narrowly missing a granite outcropping and splashing in the river), Ms. Kmiec's door flew open and, framed in a spill of yellow glare, she leaned out and said merrily, "Clyde Ormoloo! Come have a drink!"

Her hair was pinned up loosely, riding atop her head like the remains of some blond confection, a soufflé that had fallen, a wedding cake that had been dropped. She had on a black lace peignor and a pair of matching panties; her unconfined breasts bobbled as she swayed in the doorway. She or someone had made bullseyes of her nipples with concentric circles of green ink. He assumed she was trashed and warned her to be careful.

"Clyde Ormoloo-loo!" She pouted. "You get in here right now! There's someone wants to see you!" She sang this last sentence and leaned farther out and beckoned to Clyde.

He scaled the remaining rungs, pushed past her and closed the door to prevent her from doing a half-gainer into the Mossbach.

The yellow room was as always, but for three notable exceptions: Prince was curled up on the sofa, his head tucked into his stomach, and the large framed photograph of Stan and Helene had been defaced by the realistic cartoon (also in green ink) of a stubby erect penis sticking out from the center of Mr. Kmiec's forehead. An aromatherapy candle that had gone out sprouted from a blue glass dish on the coffee table—the packaging, which lay on the floor, said it was Tyrrhenian Musk, a product of Italy, but it smelled like charred Old Spice to Clyde. He had the idea that he was interrupting one of Helene's private sessions.

"See!" Helene. She leaned into Clyde. "Princey's here!"

With some effort she lifted Prince, cradling him like a baby, and pressed him into Clyde's chest, as if expecting him to hold the animal. Prince yielded an annoyed, "Mrap," and struggled weakly. Clyde saw that the door leading to the adjoining house stood partway open.

"Is someone here?" he asked.

Helene buried her face in Prince's tummy and made growly noises, offending the cat still more.

A big, tanned woman with strong features, muscular arms and legs, several inches taller than Clyde, black hair tumbled about her broad shoulders, entered from the corridor, bottle in hand. Her face reminded him of the image of an empress embossed on a Persian coin that his dad once showed him, too formidable to be beautiful, yet beautifully serene and leonine beneath her ringleted mane. She wore a red Lycra sports bra and shorts that did their best to control an exuberant bust and mighty rear end. His first thought was that she must be a transsexual, but there was no sign of an Adam's apple and her hands were slender and finely boned—three rings, none a wedding band, adorned them, including a significant diamond nested among opals. "Hello," she said in a humid contralto. "I'm Milly. And you must be Clyde. Would you care for some apple brandy? It's sooo good!"

"Yeah . . . okay." Clyde perched on the couch beside Helene, who was still making much over the cat. Recalling Annalisa's description, he said, "You're Milly Sussman?"

"The same."

Moving with a stately grace, Milly took a seat in an easy chair and poured a dollop of brandy each into three diminutive glasses shape like goblets.

"I thought you owned the house across the way," Clyde said.

"I own two houses." She held up two fingers for emphasis. "One's basically an office. Helene?"

"Yes, please!" She scooted to the edge of the couch. Prince writhed free, fell with a thud to the floor, and waddled off to find a quieter spot.

"New friends," Milly said, lifting her glass.

Helene chugged the brandy; Cliff had a sip.

"It is good," he said, setting down his glass. "I notice you have a tan. That's unusual around here."

Milly examined her arms. "I'm just back from three glorious weeks in Thailand. Well, not just back, but I was there recently. A little island not far from Kosumui. You should have seen me then. I was nearly absolutely black. But now. . . . " She heaved a dramatic sigh. "I'm entombed in Halloween once again."

Helene went over to the portrait of her late husband and studied it with her head cocked.

"You must like it here," Cliff said. "I mean, two houses."

"It has its charms." Milly crossed her legs. "Lately, however, I find it limiting. And you?"

Helene hunted for something on the end table beside the easy chair, but was impeded in her search by the folds of her peignor and shrugged out of it. She located what she had been looking for—a Magic Marker—and stood sucking on the tip, apparently contemplating an addition to her work. Though for seven, eight seconds out of ten on the average, Clyde's thoughts turned to Annalisa, the sight of Helene almost naked was difficult to ignore.

Milly repeated her question: "And you?" Her smile seemed to acknowledge Clyde's distraction.

"I liked it better when I first arrived," he said. "I guess maybe I'm finding it limiting, too."

With a knee resting on the arm of Milly's chair, Helene drew on the portrait.

Milly ran a hand along her thigh, as if to smooth out an imaginary wrinkle in the skin-tight Lycra. "Perhaps there's a way we can help one another exceed those limits."

Choosing his words with care, Clyde said, "We're probably talking about different sorts of limits."

"Ah." Her face impassive, she sipped her brandy.

They endured a prickly silence; then Clyde asked, "So what do you do . . . for a living?"

"I have a foundation that funds cottage industries in the Third World. I was a lawyer; I suppose I still am. But the law. . . . " She made a disaffected noise.

"We could use some cottage industries here. This raking walnuts thing gets pretty old."

"Actually I was speaking to Pet about that very thing before I left for Thailand. Of course we don't need them, but diversity might infuse the people with a better attitude. Raking walnuts, packaging walnuts, shipping walnuts, all this ridiculous drudgery. . . . It reinforces the notion that he owns them. But he insists on running the town his way. Pet's an unpleasant little man. He's one of the reasons I'm thinking about leaving."

"Never met the guy."

"I did some legal work for him during the nineties. I liked him then, but he's changed a great deal since he stopped performing."

"There!" Helene backed off a few paces to assess her work. Atop Stan Kmiec's head she had created the line drawing of a parrot that, its head turned sideways, was threatening to bite the stubby appendage protruding from his brow.

"Very nice," said Milly. "Clyde and I were talking about Pet, dear. Anything you'd care to contribute?"

"Pet's an even bigger prick than Stan," she said absently, and cast about the room. "I think Prince went over to your place."

She headed off along the connecting corridor, weaving from wall to wall.

"Well," said Clyde, sliding to the edge of the sofa. "I've got work in the morning. Walnuts to rake."

"A question before you go," Milly said. "I realize that men—many of them— find me too Amazonian for their tastes. Is that why you turned me down?"

Clyde was startled by her frankness.

She smiled. "Be truthful, now!"

"It's more a case of my head not being in the right place," he said.

She put her glass on the coffee table, leaning close to him as she did. He became aware of the smallness of the room, and the heated scent of her body, and had a paranoid flash, recalling movies featuring women of her dimension and fitness level who served villains, generally of Eastern European origin, as paid assassins; yet he picked up nothing from her other than a gloomy passivity.

"I've got stuff on my mind," he said. "Life stuff, you know."

Milly sank back into the cushions, again crossing her legs. "Helene told me you were unattached."

A scream ripped along the corridor between the houses, followed by an explosive crash of glass breaking. Clyde and Milly sprang to their feet at nearly the same moment and, due to the cramped quarters, her head struck him on the point of the chin, knocking him back onto the sofa and sending white lights shooting into his eyes, and while she went down heavily between the easy chair and the end table. Milly managed to un-wedge herself and struggled up into a crouch, when Helene rushed in and bowled her over again. Helene yanked at a drawer in the end table, pulling it completely out and spilling a large pistol, a .357, onto the floor.

"Son-of-a-bitch got Prince!" she said tearfully.

She cocked the gun and, scampered across the coffee table between Milly and Clyde; she flipped a row of wall switches and threw open the door. Exterior lights bathed the granite cliff and the neighboring houses in an infernal white radiance, illuminating every crevice and projection. From the sofa, Clyde had a glimpse of something unusual. Traversing the cliff ten yards above them was a greenish black creature—at that distance it resembled an enormous cabbage that had been left out in the rain and rotted, losing all but an approximation of its spherical form, its leaves shredded and hanging off the central structure like the decaying rags of a homeless person. It moved rapidly, albeit in a series of fits and starts, growing taller, skinnier, pausing, then shrinking and becoming cabbage-like again, its body flowing between those poles, as if its means of perambulation involved muscular contractions and expulsions of air similar to those utilized by an octopus. Still groggy, Clyde sat up, hoping for a clearer look, but Helene blocked the doorway. She braced against the doorframe, adopting a shooter's stance, and squeezed off three rounds that boomed across the gorge and shattered the air inside the yellow room. Clyde stumbled up off the sofa just as she said, "Damn it!" and began fumbling with the gun. She tugged on the trigger, holding the weapon at such an angle that, if it hadn't been jammed, would have blown off her foot.

"Wait!" he said, going toward her.

A petulant expression replaced one of stupefied determination. She transferred the gun to her left hand and, playing keep away, thrust it out over the gorge, a clumsy movement that caused her to overbalance. She flailed her arms, clutched at the air, shrieked in terror and toppled out the doorway. Clyde made a dive for her and snagged an ankle, stopping her fall, but momentum swung her against the side of the house—she smacked into the wall headfirst and went limp. The edge of the doorway cut into the back of Clyde's arms. He eased forward, so his arms were free, his torso and head extended over the gorge, and firmed up his grip, paying no mind to Milly's hysterical advice. The dark river and the diminished pier and the strip of yellow-white sand beside it looked like really keen accessories to a toy model of the town. He closed his eyes to forestall dizziness. Other voices were heard. A man poked his head out the window of the house next door and told him not to let go. Someone else called from below, telling him to swing Helene out over the river and let her drop into the water, as if a forty-foot plunge were nothing to fear. Women's voices shrilled; thick, sleep-dulled male voices rumbled and children squeaked. It seemed the gunshots had waked half the population of Halloween and they each and every one were offering stupid suggestions.

"Milly! Get behind me," he said. "Grab my ankles."

She did as told and immediately began yanking him into the room.

"No, stop . . . stop!" he said. "Don't pull until I tell you. Okay?"

Inch by inch, Clyde worked his grip higher on Helene's leg. Sweat broke on his forehead. Helene was not a heavy woman, but he couldn't get his back into the lift and a hundred-ten, hundred-twenty pounds of dead weight took a toll on his arms. Her head kept banging against the house and he decided this was a good thing—if she woke and went to thrashing about, he might lose her. The lights gave him a headache and the small crowd that had gathered on the shingle below distracted him. Once he had secured a hold on Helene's knee, he told Milly to pull him about six inches back. She tugged on his ankles and Clyde twisted onto his side, a movement that swung Helene's free leg toward him. Holding her by the knee with one arm, he trapped the other leg and locked both hands behind her thighs. He told Milly to pull him six inches farther and when she did he heaved on Helene, shifting her up along his body to a point where he had a grip on her hips and buttocks, and a faceful of lace panties.

"Okay," he said to Milly. "Bring us in."

Once they were inside the room, Milly dragged Helene off him. The cheer that arose from the gorge was fainter than he might have expected, as if a sizable portion of those watching had been rooting against them. Blood smeared Helene's mouth and chin, most coming from her nose—Clyde thought it might be broken. While Milly ministered to her, he had a seat on the sofa and pounded the rest of his brandy. He poured another glass and knocked down the lion's share of that. The muscles in his shoulders burned. Helene came back to the world crying and carrying on about Stan, how ashamed she was for defacing his picture. She didn't remember a thing about the accident or Prince, but planted a bloody kiss on Cliff's mouth in gratitude after Milly brought her up to speed. Milly decided to take Helene over to her place, where she could better care for her, and said she'd be back to check on him as soon she made Helene comfortable.

Clyde closed his eyes and thought about the cat-killer (it wasn't the first inexplicable thing he'd seen here, but it certainly staked claim to being the headline on *Weird News*), and about Prince mrapping around Cat Heaven, and about Annalisa, what lay ahead for them and how it would be . . . and then he was being shaken awake by Steve Germany, a squat, shaven-headed man, all his features crowded together toward the center of his face, a walnut raker who worked nights as a bouncer at the Downlow, and another bouncer, Dan or Dave, he couldn't recall, sat next to him, and Spooz studied him from the easy chair, his double-chinned mug pale as an onion, and said, "Man, did you screw up," and there was a fourth guy, a scrawny, shriveled-up, narrow-shouldered geezer with a prunish face (except for a young man's sneering mouth) and his gray hair in a pony tail, wearing a midnight blue velvet jacket over a T-shirt bearing the design of a Chinese character on the chest and black jeans belted with a buckle in the shape of a P flocked round by silver birds (it looked as if he'd borrowed his grandson's clothes) and this enfeebled gangster of love, this Lilliputian Monster of Rock (Clyde knew he was Pet Nylund), produced a pocket tape recorder, clicked the play button, and Clyde heard his own voice say, "'Annali . . . Melissa,'" pause, crackle, and then, "Sorry. I'm a little nervous. That's 'Melissa Anne.'"

"Do you know who I am?" Pet asked in a sandpapery wheeze, and Clyde, realizing that he was in deep shit, understanding that it didn't much matter how he responded, answered, "George Michaels's dad?" Pet bared his teeth in a yellow smile. "Tube his ass!"

The tubes were situated at the opposite end of town from the Dots, occupying the summit of a sixty-foot-high granite mound and hidden by a high concrete block wall overgrown by lichen—it looked like an old WWII gun emplacement guarding the entrance to Halloween. That evening, however, it radiated evil energies visible to Clyde as pulsating streams of gray vapor and had the gargantuan aspect of an ancient citadel, a habitat fit for wizards and eldritch beasts. After the one-sided struggle to subdue him, someone had given Clyde an injection. Nothing calmative. His heart raced, his nerves twitched, and his thoughts flared like fireworks, illuminating one or another heretofore hidden corner of his brain before being dissipated by a new pyrotechnic display of insights and colors. Tattered glowing white wings without bodies, the relics of revenant birds and angels, swerved near and then vanished into the purple gloom; troll faces materialized from the coarse rock and spoke booming words, like the magic words in a children's book, and the black water acquired a skin of serpent scales. If he had not been trussed like a mummy, thin ropes pinning his arms to his sides and lashing his legs together, he could have gotten behind the hallucinations, and he would have offered a vociferous complaint if he hadn't also been gagged. As it was, he rolled about, rocking the skiff, until Spooz kicked him in the liver.

Making jokes at his expense, they lugged him up from the river and through a door and laid him down on a concrete slab lit by arc lamps, a penitentiary setting that had the industrial look and soul-shriveling feel and dry negative smell of an execution ground. A single star shone in the sky crack, its name unknown, so he called it Azrael, then Disney, then Fremont Phil or Capricorn Sue, depending on its sex. He lifted his head and saw six, no, seven perfectly round openings in the concrete, one of them covered with a piece of sheet iron, a winch mounted above each, and he flashed on the idea that perfectly round holes were a motif in Halloween, there were the Dots and the Tubes and . . . well, there were a couple of examples, anyway, and he imagined that some gigantic, perfectly round, acid-exuding worm or humongous beetle with diamond-hard mandibles had bored the holes, and pictured gaping mouths waiting at the bottom to be fed. A voice among other voices, Brad's voice, distracted him, and he tried to find him, craning his neck, rolling his eyes, a friend come to intercede, and Brad knelt beside him, his stubby dreadlocks looking like a tarantula hat, and hooked a chain to one of the ropes strapping his chest and said, "Sorry, man. Nothing personal." He measured the width of Clyde's shoulders with a tape and said, "Number Five'll do," and Clyde made eye contact with him and saw only a core impersonality—the man derived pleasure from being impersonal, from just doing his job and following orders, the glad-handing, Dallas Cowboy-loving torturer of Halloween town, and he couldn't fathom why he had failed to see this before and supposed that the blackness of Brad's skin absorbed the light and thus prevented him from . . . no, no, no, don't go there, he chuckled inwardly at the nuttiness of worrying about being politically correct, like a prisoner of the Inquisition fretting over his eczema, and then he was picked up and suspended over Number Five, and felt the chain grow taut, Brad steadying him as he was lowered, saying with relish, the last voice Clyde heard, "If you twist around too much, man, you'll rub off the chain and we'll have to fish you out with hooks," and Clyde, at eye-level with Brad's feet, envisioned hooks tearing off chunks of flesh grown too soft and rotten to impale, an image he carried down into the dark, the dank, claustrophobia-inducing dark of a pit that fit around him more tightly than a coffin, down, down, down, scraping the walls (the tube was canted at a slight angle), scarcely enough room to tip back his head and see the coin of lesser darkness above being devalued, dwindling and dwindling until it was the size of a half dollar, a quarter, a dime . . . and that was when he fell, bumping and battering his way to the bottom. A shred of instinct came into play and he bent his knees as much as possible to absorb the blow, landing with most of his weight on the left foot, the resultant pain so bad it seemed to fill his entire body until he forced it back, compressed it into a throbbing ache beneath his knee, shifting onto his right foot to alleviate it further, and yet the pain was still very bad, burning like a cancer in the bone, and something slithered, rattled, clinked down the tube and lashed him across the face, chipping a tooth, and he tasted blood (they had dropped the chain, or else it had torn loose from the winch) and he panicked and tried to spit out the gag and scream for what must have been a couple of minutes before he recognized the chain attached to his chest remained taut and they had flung down a second chain. Playing a trick. Having their little joke. Anger helped him deal with the pain, but he was incapable of sustaining it. Time grew sluggish, the seconds oozed past, each one a complex droplet of fear, agony, hope, fatalism, despair. He began to see and hear things that he hoped were unreal. Fish with fangs and cicatrice grins swam at him through the walls. The stone was a living depth of stone, breathing in and out, each contraction bruising his ribs, compressing his lungs. He couldn't think, poisoned by shock and trauma, and he wished they would finish him, drench him with scalding water or drown him in oil . . . it didn't matter. Ragged, grating voices doubled by echoes told him things about himself that he thought only he knew, things he hadn't known, and things he wanted to deny. He said her name as though it were a charm against them, Annalisa, and kept on saying it until it became as meaningless as rosary devotions. The voices persisted and told him lies about her. *That whey-faced bitch gamed you, man. Every night she goes home to that yellow smile and those gnarly bones. You know what they do? Think about it. What was she? His groupie? And she still lives with him? Come on! You think that's going to change? Look where you are. She gave up a little tongue, a little tit, and threw you a quickie . . . now she's laughing at you while Pet's hitting that big white butt of hers over and over and. . . .*

The voices became garbled, too many to hear, an inchoate stew of vowels and consonants that eventually faded, leaving only a single voice, that of a young man saying, "Holy Mary, Mother of God, pray for us now and at the hour of our death, amen," speaking so rapidly, the words ran together, and then, " . . . blessed be the fruit of thy womb, Jesus, Holy Mary . . . " repeating this fragment, this same broken prayer, again and again. It annoyed him that the guy didn't know the words and he tried to beam them at him (it sounded like he was right next door), and the guy must have received the transmission, because he began to say it correctly, Hail Mary, full of grace, the Lord is with theeblessedartthouamong . . . etcetera. Clyde got caught up in the rhythm of the prayer, in the sheer velocity of it. He seemed to be skittering across the prayer's surface as if it were a globe and he was a spider seeking to maintain his place by scuttling along the equator, but the globe spun too quickly and, dizzy from the spin, he lost traction and was blown off into the abyss, pinwheeling down into a noiseless, bottomless dark where there was a complete absence of pain and even spiders feared to tread.

A transformative thought visited Clyde, dropping down from the aether where it customarily dallied, occasionally occupying the minds of cosmic beings, the type of thought with which, if he could have mastered it, he might have comprehended the process of the world as though it were a problem in simple arithmetic, or affect the path of astronomical objects, or divine the future by the mere contemplation of a grape. Of course he was incapable of mastering it—it was too vast, too important, surrounding him the way a balloon night surround an ant. He inhaled its heady atmosphere, trying to absorb all the intelligence he could, but retained only fragments that translated into useless homily, some garbage about fitting a purpose to his life and finding (or was it founding?) a kingdom, and one item more specific, no less fragmentary, the phrase, " . . . below the fifty-seventh parallel." Yet he took these things to heart. He passed through the skin of the thought, clung to its outer surface until it wafted away, leaving him woozily awake and marginally aware of his surroundings, his leg aching (but the pain greatly diminished), watching a boatman—an indistinct black figure—thrust with his pole, making a faint splash and sending the skiff skimming beneath a dim sprinkle of white stars, dull and unwinking as breadcrumbs on a dark blue cloth. He lay in the prow, with someone breathing regularly beside him (he was too exhausted to turn his head and determine who), and flirted with the notion that the ancient Greeks had been accurate concerning their speculations on the afterlife, and old What's-his-face, Charon, had come to ferry them across the River Styx into the mouths of Hell. Though this was patently untrue (he smelled rotten walnuts and suspected they were crossing the third Dot), he had no doubt that the imagery was apt, that one of Pet's boys had been ordered to take them south and dump the bodies. He struggled to kindle a spark of rebellion, to resist this fate, but fatigue and whatever narcotic had been given him for the pain muffled his fire. He just wanted to sleep. Before passing out, the last question he asked (of whomever it is we ask these questions) was, he wondered if this was what had happened to Dell. . . .

They were crossing an underground lake, a stretch of water whose dimensions were impossible to judge—the walls and ceiling were lost in darkness, though lamps had been hung off the sides and both ends of the skiff, making them look, Clyde supposed, like one of those strange electric creatures that inhabited ocean trenches. Light from a lantern in the stern sprayed around the mysterious figure of the boatman, somewhat less mysterious now that he could see baggy jeans and a green down jacket patched with duct tape, a hood hiding the face. His leg throbbed and there was a considerable swelling beneath the knee (his trousers had been cut away). He eased onto his side and came face-to-face with a young brown-skinned man wearing a sleeveless T-shirt and clutching a blanket about his shoulders, gathered at the throat, a pose that made him appear boyish; yet his arms were thick and well muscled, those of a man. A gash on his cheekbone leaked a pink mixture of blood and serum. As if registering the weight of Clyde's scrutiny, his eyes fluttered open, murmured something, and closed them again.

"That's David Batista," said Annalisa. "Pet's editor. He was in the tube next to you."

She pushed back the cowl and shook out her hair; she had puffy half-circles under her eyes. Clyde wanted to ask a basic question, but his tongue stuck to his palette.

"Are you okay?" she asked.

He wetted his lips and swallowed. "Leg hurts."

"Yeah, Roberta says it's fractured."

"Roberta?"

"Mary Alonso's Roberta. I'll give you another pill."

At her feet, he noticed a tarpaulin covering someone wearing jeans and a pair of gray boots.

"And that," she said in a deliberate manner. "That is Pet."

Energy appeared to run out from her, rendering her a stony figure whose pallid animating principle stemmed from some un-alive source, as if the name pronounced had the power to transform warmth into cold, joy into hatred, every vital thing into its deathly opposite, and she stood motionless, frozen to her pole, with sunken cheek and haunted eye, a steerswoman dread and implacable, more so than Charon. Then, stepping back from the place where memory or emotion had borne her, she thrust with the pole, propelling the skiff into a channel with pitted walls like those of old castle. Clyde felt a cold brush of anxiety that, although triggered by her reaction, seemed a general anxiety springing from every element of their situation.

Annalisa fed him a white tablet not much larger than a pinhead, warned him to keep his hands clear of the water, saying, "There's things in there will take it off," and returned to her position in the stern. Batista woke and slid over to allow Clyde more room; then he sat up and Clyde asked him what was going on.

"All I know is these four women pulled us out and tubed Brad," Batista said. "Milly Sussman . . . you know her? Big, good-looking woman? She seemed to be the one running the show. She had the gun, anyway. She said she wanted us put somewhere safe until things got settled, so Annalisa's taking us south. I don't know what they've got in mind for Pet."

Annalisa was off in her own world, not listening to the conversation.

"If half the stuff in his memoirs is true," Batista went on, "they can drop him in the Tubes and leave him for all I care."

Clyde recognized Batista's voice as that of the guy who had said his Hail Marys wrong, if that were possible; he thought about inquiring whether or not he, Batista, had heard his advice, but decided it would be too much of a complication. "That's what you were doing?" he asked. "Helping him write his memoirs?"

Batista nodded. "Routing out a sewer would have been cleaner work. I told him I was quitting, so he tubed me." He shot Clyde an appraising look. "Did they give you drugs? This guy I know said they had drugs that made it worse."

"They gave me something nasty," Clyde said.

The white tablet kicked in. He felt warm, muddled, distant from pain. He luxuriated in the sense of bodily perfection that attended even the movement of a finger and admired the swelling on his shinbone for the subtlety of its coloration. A cloying vegetable scent infused the air and this, too, pleased him, though he was not able to identify it. The most apt comparative he could find (only this odor was far more acidic) was the incense his mom had ordered from a catalogue during her charismatic Catholic phase, Genuine Biblical Times Incense from Jerusalem, smell what our Lord and Savior smelled, and she had hated the stuff, said she couldn't get the stink out of her new sofa, so Clyde had appropriated the incense and used it to mask the smell of pot.

They emerged from the channel into another section of the gorge, skimming along beneath a gray-blue sky, a broad expanse in relation to Halloween's sky crack. The cliffs here were perpendicular to the river and higher than the cliffs in town. Some ninety or a hundred feet wide, the Mossbach had here acquired a murky greenish tint, meandering between steep, sloping banks from which sprouted dense tangles of strange vegetation: blackish green grass sprinkled with starfish-shaped white blossoms and stubby, many-branched trees that resembled a hybrid of bonsai and gorgonians; the majority of these were also blackish green, yet some of the fans were tinged with indigo. Dark globular bushes, each with thousands of tiny leaves, quivered as they drifted past, and vines, some thick as hawsers, others fine as wires, looped in and out like exposed veins feeding the micro-environment. The place had the dire atmospherics of a wicked fairy tale, a secret grotto poisoned by the presence of an evil spirit, and the early morning light held a pall that seemed a byproduct of the pungent odor (Clyde thought he recognized the base smell as cat shit, but doubted that could be right). Fat insects with wings like fractured blades of zircon wobbled drunkenly from shrub to shrub, giving the impression that the work they did was making them ill.

They rounded a bend and Clyde, glancing over his shoulder, was presented with a vista that to his eyes, grown accustomed to confined spaces, was a virtual Grand Canyon of confinements. Here the shore widened and the cliffs made him think of illustrations in children's dinosaur books, having a Paleolithic jaggedness, their summits tattered with mist. Bracketed to the rock was a Halloween house of black metal (two columns of six stories). The walls had a dull chitin-like finish that lent the rooms (quite a bit larger than usual) the aspect of twelve rectangular beetles crawling up the cliff in tight formation. Fifteen feet below the first floor of house, directly beneath it, tucked flush against the rock and fronted by a pebbly shingle that continued on to fringe the shoreline farther south, stood a flat-roofed, one-story building painted bluish green, a shade too bright to be called viridian. Clyde soon realized that paint was not responsible for the color—the structure was furred with lichen, the odd patch of raw concrete showing through. In one such spot the stenciled black letters MU AGE beneath a portion of a skull-and-crossbones added an indefinite yet ominous caption to the scene. Mutagenics, Clyde said to himself, remembering his conversation with Dell. The window screens were rusted but intact; the door was cracked open. To the left of the building lay a plot of fenced-in, furrowed dirt. Ordinary ferns sprouted from the rock above it, fluttering in the breeze as if signaling for help, hoping to be rescued from the encroachment of more alien growth. One thing distinguished the place above all else, verifying Clyde's suspicions concerning the odor: cats of every breed and description sunned themselves on the building's roof, peeped from thickets, crept along the margin of the water, perched primly in rocky niches and gazed scornfully down on those below. The shingle, their sandbox, was littered with turds. He took them to be feral descendants of the survivors of the cat-killer, yet they reacted with neither aggression nor fear and merely turned an incurious eye toward the intruders. There were hundreds of them, yet they made precious little noise, a scattering of miaows where one might have expected an incessant caterwauling. Some rubbed against Batista's ankles as he half-carried Clyde to the lee of the building and helped him sit with his back to the wall.

The derelict building; the house of black metal; the strangely silent cats; the unusual vegetation; the sluggish jade river winding between towering cliffs—these things caused Clyde to envision that they were characters in a great unwritten fantasy novel by Joseph Conrad, the ruins of civilization subsumed by elements of an emergent one ruled by the sentient offspring of our former housepets and, in this semi-subterranean backwater, the narrator and a handful of his friends were attempting to stave off the inevitable eternal night of their species by swapping anecdotes about mankind's downfall, individual tales of apocalyptic folly that, taken in sum, constituted a mosaic of defeat and sounded the death knell of the human spirit. He pictured a venerable storyteller, his gray-bearded jaw clenched round a pipe stem, rotted teeth tilted like old gravestones in the tobacco-stained earth of his gums, puffing vigorously to keep his coal alive and exhaling a cloud of pale smoke that engulfed his listeners as he spoke and seemed by this noxious inclusion to draw their circle closer. . . . Clyde laughed soddenly, amused by his ornate bullshit.

From the skiff, an outcry.

At the water's edge Annalisa stood over Pet, who was on his knees, his hands bound. He still had on his dark blue velvet jacket. She whacked him across the shoulders with her pole and he laboriously got to his feet. Clyde felt divorced from the situation and tracked the progress of a gray tabby as it sneaked near one of the globular bushes, made a sinuous, twisting leap, snatched a bug from mid-air and fell to tearing it apart. Another cat jumped down from the roof, eyed them with middling hostility, and sauntered off. Batista pressed his shoulder against the door of the Mutagenics building and forced it open—the swollen wood made a *skreek*ing noise. After a minute he hunkered down beside Clyde, who asked what he had found inside.

"A bunch of nothing," said Batista. "Couple of lab tables and a file cabinet. A door . . . probably leads up into the house."

Urged on by Annalisa, Pet came stumbling up from the shingle. Clyde thought of an old Italian vampire movie in which the main vampire had been exhumed from his crypt, a skeleton, but after a starlet's blood had been drizzled on his fangs, he gradually re-acquired sinew and flesh and skin—Pet appeared to be stuck partway through that process. Annalisa inserted the pole between his ankles, tripped him, and he went sprawling.

"Crazy bitch!" He wiped sand from his mouth with his coat sleeve. "Think this'll get you anything?"

"Don't worry about me," Annalisa said. "You're the one with the problem."

"I got no problem," said Pet with a smirk. "Brad and the guys'll be coming around the bend any minute, and you'll be on your haunches, begging for a bone."

"Watch your mouth!" Clyde had been aiming for belligerence, but the words were so slurred, they came out, "Wushamou."

"You don't know her, pal. She'd go down on a sick monkey if she thought she'd gain an edge." Pet chuckled. "Remember the tour with Oasis, honey? Man, you guys should have seen her. I told her. . . . "

Batista had been juggling some pebbles in his palm—he shied one at Pet, striking him in the chest.

"It won't be Brad coming," Annalisa said. "It'll be Milly."

"Milly?" Pet snorted. "That's crap! She wouldn't be involved in something this stupid."

No one said anything.

Pet looked at them each in turn. "What are you people fucking trying to pull?"

Annalisa sat next to Clyde and asked how he was doing.

"What's in those pills you gave me?"

"Morphine sulfate."

Clyde grunted. "I must be doing okay, then."

Pet shifted, trying to get comfortable. "This is all about him? This mutt?"

"Why not?" said Annalisa. "It doesn't have to be, but sure, let's make it about him."

She rested her head on Clyde's shoulder. The contact warmed him—he hadn't noticed that he was cold—and left him feeling dozy. For a minute or ten, the only sounds were the rush of the river and the cats.

"I'm hungry," said Batista.

"Me, too." Pet propped himself on an elbow. "What say we scrag a few cats and roast 'em? We can have a picnic. Got any mint jelly? I hear roast cat's great with mint jelly."

Annalisa leaned forward, trembling and tense. "You hungry?"

Uneasiness surfaced in Pet's face.

"I said: Are you hungry?"

That drained-of-life quality she had displayed earlier was back. Clyde had a hunch that she intended to kill Pet and caught at her arm; but she was already moving toward Pet. She strode past him, however, and fumbled with the garden gate; she flung it open, causing consternation among the cats trailing after her, and dug with her hands in the dirt, uprooting two big onions dangling from their stalks.

She brought them to Pet, pushed them at him. "Eat these."

"Fuck you!" He turned away.

"Don't be afraid," she said in a wound-tight voice. "They won't poison you any more than you've already been poisoned."

An inch of apprehension crept into his defiant expression.

"That's right," she said. "For over a year I've been bringing you treats from my garden. If you weren't afraid of doctors, a checkup might have revealed cancer. You must be riddled with it by now."

Pet tried to shrug it off, but he was plainly rattled.

"Of course you're such a toxic little freak," she went on, "could be you just absorb the shit. Maybe it's actually making you healthier."

She paused, as if giving this possibility its due consideration, and then swung the onions, striking Pet in the face, knocking him onto his back. She straddled him and hit him again and again, her hair flying into her eyes. Each blow thudded on bone. He tried to buck her off, but in a matter of seconds his body went limp. She kept on hitting him, taking two-handed swings, gasping with every one, like the gasps she uttered when she made love. The cats nearest her shrank from the violence, wheeling about and scampering off. Clyde yelled for her to stop and, in no particular hurry, Batista went over, threw his arms around her and pulled her away. She resisted, but he was too strong—he lifted her and whirled her about. The onions flew from her hand, bouncing and rolling to Clyde's feet. They were mushed and lopsided, dirt and speckles of blood clinging to their pale surfaces.

"Let me go," she said dully.

He released her and she gave him a little shove as she stepped away. She walked down to the river and pushed back her hair and stood gazing upstream. Flecks of onionskin were stuck to the blood on Pet's face. His eyes were shut and the breath shuddered out of him. Clyde couldn't tell if he was conscious. Batista hovered betwixt and between as if unable to decide with whom to align himself. One of the cats started lapping at the blood on the onions, ignoring Clyde's halfhearted attempts to shoo it away.

He called out to Annalisa—she backhanded a wave, a gesture of rejection he chose to interpret as her needing a moment. He felt the morphine taking him as his adrenaline rush faded and he did his best to keep his mind focused. He wanted to comfort her, yet he doubted that she could be comforted or that comfort was the appropriate medicine. He could relate to her outburst of rage against a man who had misused her. Everyone was mad that way; but mad enough to be a poisoner? To delight in secret over another's slow demise? That required a refined madness, a spiritual abscess that might prove to be untreatable. He drew in a shaky breath and was cold again. The landscape no longer seemed so epic and exotic, humanized and made paltry by her violent excess. Just a bunch of filthy cats, an abandoned building and some cliffs.

Batista came over and sat down. After a minute or two, so did Annalisa. Clyde draped an arm about her. She relaxed beneath the weight and cozied into him and he let go of his questions, persuaded by the animal consolation of her body. The cats, filling in the open spaces they had vacated, seemed emblems of normalcy, sniffing and shitting, batting at bugs, much in the way the world goes on following the hush created by an explosion, with people scurrying about, engines starting, all the noise and talk and bustle paving over a cratered silence, all the clocks once again ticking in unison.

The sun was not yet in view, but a golden tide had scrubbed the shadows from the top of the western cliff wall and, as the light brightened, some of the place's eerie luster was restored. About a half-hour after the beating, Pet sat up. He shot a bitter glance toward Annalisa and lowered his head. His left eye was swollen shut, his forehead bruised. Blood from his nose reddened his lips and chin, and he breathed through his mouth. No one spoke to him. He cast about, as though searching for something to occupy himself; then he lay back down and turned onto his side, facing away from them. Soon afterward the cats retreated, withdrawing swiftly into the underbrush to the south, a cat stampede that left nary a one in sight.

"Where are they going?" Batista asked.

Annalisa disengaged from Clyde, wearily lifting his arm away. She said something that sounded like "lurruloo," and peered south along the shore. Clyde heard a yowling, a cacophony of small, abrasive voices, and saw a greenish black something slide out of the brush and onto the shingle: the cat killer surrounded by a tide of cats. Whenever it shrank, spreading out into its rotted-cabbage mode, cats leapt onto its "skirts," clinging to them as it grew tall and spindly.

"Help me get him up!" Annalisa said to Batista.

Together they hustled Clyde into the building, a wide single room of unpainted concrete, dappled with lichen and reeking of mildew, empty but for lab tables and a filing cabinet, the floors littered with glass and other debris. A recessed black metal door set in the rear wall. They started to lower him to the floor, but he insisted upon remaining upright, propped against one of the tables. Pet scrambled inside as Batista shut the door. Out the window, Clyde saw the creature, utilizing its peculiar means of locomotion, slip along the shingle and come to a halt beside the skiff. Stretched to its full height, seven feet or thereabouts, it reminded him of a bedraggled Christmas tree that had been left out for the garbage and lost its pyramidal form, become lopsided and limp; instead of a plastic star, it was topped off by a glabrous, football-shaped, seemingly featureless head, dark olive in color. A few cats still clung to it, nibbling the fringes of its skin. The ground in its wake was strewn with half-conscious cats—some rolled onto their backs in a show of delight—and others could be seen wobbling off into the brush. The creature's body rippled, its loose flaps of skin creating a shimmying effect, and it produced a loud ululation, "Lurruloo," that had the throatiness and wooden tonality of a bassoon, deflating as the last note died—close at hand, now it looked less like a melted cabbage than an ugly green-and-black throw rug with a funny lump at the center. A bloated white cat that bore a striking resemblance to Prince waddled out from behind it and collapsed on its side.

"All this thing's doing is getting cats fucked up," Clyde said, peering around Batista, who was hogging the window. "It's not killing them."

"They love cats," Pet said. "The cats keep 'em groomed and the lurruloo turn 'em into cat junkies. It's people they kill."

"Because you and those idiot friends of yours were hunting them." Annalisa spat out the words.

"Uh-huh, sure. They were carrying peace signs and singing 'Kumbaya' before we came along. What do you think happened to the Mutagenics people?"

"Yeah, what did happen to them?" Batista asked. "Your memoirs are a little blurry on the subject."

"There's more than one of these things?" asked Clyde.

"Pet stranded them here," Annalisa told Batista. "They tried escaping through the caves. No one's sure what happened."

"The caves?" said Clyde.

"What was I supposed to do? Let 'em tell the world about their exciting new species?" Angry, Pet took a step toward her. "It would have been the end of Halloween, man. Soldiers and scientists all over the place."

Annalisa banged her fist against the filing cabinet. "If you hadn't poisoned their environment, you would never have known they were there. They would have never been motivated to visit the surface."

"Fuck a bunch of Greenpeace bullshit!" Pet affected a feminine voice: "You realize they're not animals, don't you? They steal cats and destroy TV cables. Surely you can see they're intelligent? They deserve our protection."

Pet was reacting, Clyde observed, as if the beating had never occurred, either because he felt equal to Annalisa now that she was onion-less, or because argument was simply a pattern they had developed. For that matter, she was reacting more-or-less the same. It made him wonder if beatings might also be one of their patterns.

"They don't like it here!" she said. "Why do you think they only send one up at a time?"

"If they only send one," said Clyde, "how can you tell there's more than one?"

Pet sniffed. "I don't fucking care why. But if they keep coming, I'll give 'em more than chemicals to worry about."

"I doubt that," Annalisa said. "When Milly gets here we're going have a discussion about them . . . and you."

"I'm still betting on Brad."

"We tubed Brad. By now some of the others are probably down there with him and Milly has the rest of your thugs doing doggie tricks. You shouldn't have gotten so tight with your lawyer. She knows all the right buttons to push."

"Hey!" Clyde yelled. "Does somebody want to answer my questions?"

Annalisa looked at him dumfounded, as if she had only just noticed his presence.

"What you said those about things sending one up at a time?" Batista turned from the window. "There's three outside now."

Pet and Annalisa crowded him out the way.

"I see one out front." Annalisa.

"There's one . . . behind the fence." Pet.

"Where's the third?"

The light from the window was suddenly blotted out. Pet and Annalisa backed away, and Clyde found himself looking into a maw of glistening, grayish meat that overspread the window screen. The lurruloo made a squelching noise—its flesh convulsed and it sprayed a thick, clear liquid onto the mesh, which began to yield a thin white smoke.

"Jesus Christ! That's acid!" Batista said. "Can it squeeze through there?"

"It's not real strong," said Annalisa. "It'll take at least ten, fifteen minutes to eat through the mesh."

With a sprightly air, Pet produced a prodigious key ring bearing a couple of dozen keys and shook them so they jangled. "Don't sweat it, man. I got this covered."

He crossed the room to the black door, fiddled with the keys, and unlocked it. Clyde continued to be fascinated by the lurruloo. Its insides were as ugly as a raw mussel, pulsing and thickly coated with juice. An outer fringe of its skin was visible at the bottom of the window—it was lined with yellowish hooks of bone not much bigger than human teeth that bit into the concrete.

Beyond the door a cramped spiral stair had been carved out of the rock. Though Batista helped him, ascending the stair started Clyde's leg throbbing again. Annalisa offered another pill, but he turned her down, wanting to keep his head clear. Opening off the stairs was a space twice the size of a normal room in Halloween, furnished with a pool table, a red-and-inky blue Arabian carpet, and a teak sofa and chairs upholstered in a lustrous red fabric splotched with mildew. The black metal walls were figured by a rack half-full of cues, an erotic bas relief and two louvered windows that striped the room with light, items that completed a modernistic take on American Bordello. Clyde lowered himself carefully onto the sofa, Pet sprawled in a chair, and Batista hung by the door. Annalisa climbed the interior stair, which corkscrewed up through the ceiling at one end of the room, returning after a brief absence carrying a pair of lace panties. She dropped them in Pet's lap and sat beside Clyde.

"I thought you quit using this place," she said.

Pet smiled—there were still traces of blood on his teeth. He tossed the panties onto the floor.

"You're such a shithead," she said.

"What do you care?"

"I *don't* care . . . but it pisses me off, you lying to me."

"It wasn't me, okay. It must have been one of the guys."

"You promised me nobody. . . . "

"What is it with you two?" Clyde pushed himself up against the sofa cushion and looked at Annalisa. "You just tried to kill him. Hell, you've been trying to kill him for a year! And now you're upset because he's lying?"

"I told you, it's complicated," she said weakly.

"Naw, this isn't complicated. This is deeply twisted!" Clyde inched away from her in order to get some separation. "We're in trouble here, and you two are carrying on like it's *Days of our Lives.*"

Annalisa's eyes filled. "We're not in trouble. The lurruloo can't climb metal."

"Great! Good to know. But that doesn't answer my question. I. . . . "

"How's this for an answer, tough guy?" Pet kicked the bottom of Clyde's left foot.

His eyes shut against the pain, Clyde heard a noise as of metal under stress and seemed to feel the room shift. Annalisa screamed and fell against him. Pet squawked and there was thudding noise, followed by Batista cursing. When he opened his eyes, he saw the room was at a severe tilt. Batista lay on the floor, rubbing his head. Pet still sat in his chair, gripping both arms, a confused, wizened monkey in a blue velvet jacket. Boosting herself up, Annalisa walked downslope to the nearest window and peered through the vents.

"God," she said. "There must be fifty of them outside."

Batista joined her at the window. "I thought you said the acid wasn't strong. It must be eating through the brackets."

"They had to have done most of the damage beforehand." She glanced at Pet. "Not intelligent, huh?"

The room sagged downward again.

"We've got to get higher." Pet headed for the stairs.

"Not a smart idea," said Batista. "If they weakened these brackets, they might have done the ones higher up, too. You want to fall from forty feet? Sixty feet?"

"Annalisa!" Wincing, Clyde stood, balancing on one foot and the sofa arm, in too much discomfort to worry about clearheadedness. "I need a pill."

"Let's go back down." Pet's voice held a note of panic.

"You're not opening that door," said Batista, blocking his way. "They're bound to be in the lab by now . . . and on the stairs. Give me the keys."

Clyde let the pill Annalisa handed him begin to dissolve under his tongue.

Batista motioned to Annalisa. "Help me turn the sofa over. Pet . . . get under a chair or something."

Ignoring Pet's dissent, Batista and Annalisa got the sofa turned and they crowded beneath it, Clyde first, Annalisa in the middle, facing him, and then Batista, the cushions muffling their bodies. Clyde put a fist through the cloth back of the sofa and grabbed onto a wooden support strut. He could hear Pet muttering and then it was quiet, except for the three of them breathing. He'd had no time to be afraid and now it was so unreal. . . . He thought people on an airplane in trouble might feel this way, that somehow it was going to blow over, that nothing was really wrong, that the hand of God would intervene or the pilot would discover a miraculous solution, all in the moment before the plane began its final plunge and hope was transformed into terror. Annalisa buried her face in his shoulder and whispered, "I love you." If she had spoken earlier he would have questioned the words, he would have asked how could she love him and be involved with a sickness like Pet Nylund? How could she be distracted from love by a petty hatred, even the greatest hatred being a petty indulgence when compared to love? Things being what they were, however, he repeated the words inaudibly into her hair and, as if saying made it so, he felt love expand in him like an explosion taking the place of his heart, an overwhelming burst of tenderness and desire and regret that dissolved his doubts and recriminations, a sentimental rush that united with the rush of the morphine and eroded his sensibilities until he was only aware of her warmth and the pressure of her breasts and the fragrance of her hair. . . . A shriek of metal, the room jolted downward once more and then came free of its brackets entirely and fell, slamming edge-on into the roof of the Mutagenics lab. It rolled off the roof, smashed into the ground sideways, rolled again. They managed to maintain the integrity of their shelter somewhat through the first crash, but when the room began to roll, the sofa levitated, leaving them clutching the cushions, and Clyde went airborne during the second crash and lost consciousness. The next he knew, Batista was shouting, pulling him from beneath a chair and some heavy brown fabric that he thought might be the carpet backing. He was disoriented, his vision not right. Sunlight spilled into the room, which was tilted, the furniture jumbled against what once had been a wall, half-submerged in water. Annalisa kneeled in the water, fluttering her hands above Pet, who lay partly beneath some bulky object. Her hands were red and her down jacket was smeared with redness as well. Clyde blacked out again and was shaken awake by Batista, who jammed a pool cue into his hand and yelled once again. He glanced up at the sun, the cliffs, and recognized that he was outside. Befuddled, he gazed at the pool cue. Batista, bleeding from a cut on his scalp, asked if he could deal with it. Clyde wasn't clear on the precise nature of "it," but thought it best to go along with the program. His vision still wasn't right, but he gripped the cue purposefully and nodded.

"I'll go get her," Batista said, and moved off down the slope, disappearing through a gash in the black metal surface the size and approximate shape of a child's wading pool.

Clyde realized he was sitting about a third of the way up the side wall of the room, and realized further that the room was in the river, sticking out of the sun-dazzled green water like a giant domino with no dots. What did they call blank dominoes? He couldn't remember. His head ached, the glare hurt his eyes, and his leg was badly swollen—he could feel a fevered pulse in it, separate from the beat of his heart. He started to drift, but a scream from below, from within the room, brought him back. Annalisa. He reacted toward the gash, but movement was not a viable option. Even morphine couldn't mask the pain that a slight change of position caused. He tightened his grip on the cue and, when Annalisa screamed again, he tuned it out.

Cats seethed along the shore in front of the Mutagenics lab; their faint cries came to him. They appeared interested in something on the opposite side of the Mossbach, but Clyde could see nothing that would attract such concentrated interest, just granite and ferns, swarming gnats and. . . . His chest went cold with shock. Twenty, twenty-five feet above was an overhanging ledge and a dozen or so lurruloo were inching along it, some of their hooks latching onto the cliff wall, some onto the ledge, unable to secure a firm hold on either. The extreme end of the ledge was positioned over the uppermost portion of the half-sunken room and, should this be their intent, would allow them to drop onto the metal surface one or two at a time. Gritting his teeth, Clyde turned in order to face those that dropped. More lurruloo were plastered to the cliff above the ledge, looking at that angle like an audience of greenish black sombreros with misshapen crowns and exceptionally wide, not-quite-symmetrical brims. Thirty or forty of them. *Goofy-looking buggers, but deadly,* said an inner voice with a British Colonial accent. *Saw one take old MacTavish back in '98. 'Orrible, it was!* He made a concerted effort to straighten out, focusing on the end of the ledge, and became entranced by the patterns of the moss growing beneath it.

A tinkly piano melody began playing in his mind, something his grandmother had entertained him with when he was a kid, and it was playing still when the first lurruloo slipped off the ledge, spreading its fleshy skirts (for balance?) and landed thirty feet upslope with a wet, sloppy thump. Its hooks scrabbled for purchase on the metal as it slid, doing a three-quarter turn in the process, trying to push itself upright, yet incapable of controlling its approach. Holding the cue like a baseball bat, he timed his swing perfectly, cracking the back of its bulbous head, served up to him like a whiffle ball on a post three feet high. He heard a crunch and caught a whiff of foulness before it spilled into the water. His feeling of satisfaction was short-lived—two more dropped from the ledge, but collided in mid-air, knocking one into the river. The other landed on its side, injuring itself. As it slid past, its skirts flared at the edges, exposing dozens of yellowish hooks, perhaps a muscular reflex in response to trauma, and one tore a chunk from Clyde's right thigh. Not serious, but it pissed him off.

"Batista!" he shouted, and a warbling, hooting response came from overhead, as if the lurruloo were cheering . . . or they might be debating alternative strategies, discussing the finer points of inter-species relations.

Two more skidded toward him, one in advance of the other. Clyde balanced on a knee, his bad leg stuck out to the side like a rudder, and bashed the lead lurruloo in the head, then punched at the other with the tip of the cue—to his surprise, it penetrated the lurruloo's skull to a depth of five or six inches. Before its body slipped from the cue, its bulk dragged him off balance, causing him to put all his weight on his bad leg. Dizzy, with opaque blotches dancing in his vision, he slumped onto the sun-heated metal. His leg was on fire, but he felt disconnected from it, as if it were a phantom pain. Human voices sounded nearby. He braced up on his elbows. Batista was boosting himself up through the gash and Annalisa sat beside it—she shook her head in vehement denial and talked to her outspread, reddened hands. Clyde couldn't unscramble the words. Batista rushed up the slope, pool cue at the ready, and, reminded of duty, Clyde fumbled for his cue, grabbed the tip, sticky with a dark fluid, and made ready to join the fray. But Batista was doing fine on his own, laying waste to the lurruloo as they landed, before they could marshal a semblance of poise, knocking the pulpy bodies, dead and alive, into the river. In his sleeveless T-shirt and shorts, Batista the Barbarian. Clyde chortled at the image—a string of drool eeled between his lips.

The lurruloo on the ledge broke off their attack and began a withdrawal, flowing up the cliff face, while those above offered commiseration (this according to Clyde's characterization of their lugubrious tones). Wise move, he said to himself. Better to retreat, to live and multiply and create the legend of the demon Batista, his Blue-Tipped Stick of Doom. Annalisa stared at him emptily and then, making an indefinite noise, she crawled up beside him. He caressed her cheek and she leaned into the touch. Her mouth opened, but she didn't speak. He cradled her head, puzzled by her silence. They weren't out of the woods yet, but they had survived this much and he thought she should be happier. *He* should be happier, excited by the victory, however trivial. But her silence, her vacant manner, impelled him to confront questions he couldn't cope with at present. Their future, for one. She seemed nearly lifeless, not like previously, her energies channeled into some dread purpose, but more as though a light had guttered out inside her, reducing her to this inert figure.

"Oh, wow," said Batista.

Hundreds of lurruloo had joined those on the cliff wall and they were wheeling as one, united in a great circular movement as though in flight from a predator, like a herd of wildebeest or a school of fish; but instead of fleeing, they continued to circle, creating a pattern that grew increasingly intricate—a great spiral that divided into two interlocking spirals, and this, too, divided, becoming a dozen patterns that fed into one another, each having a variant rhythm, yet they were rhythms in harmony with one another, the whole thing evolving and changing, a greenish black inconstancy that drew the eye to follow its shifting currents. It was a beautiful, mesmerizing thing and Clyde derived from it a sense of peace, of intellect sublimated to the principles of dance. He understood that the lurruloo were talking, attempting to communicate their desires, and the longer he watched them flow across the cliff face, the more convinced he became of their good intentions, their intrinsic gentleness. He imagined the pattern to be an apology, an invitation to negotiate, a statement of their relative innocence. . . . Shots rang out, sporadic at first, a spatter of pops, then a virtual fusillade. The pattern broke apart, the lurruloo scattering high and low into the south, twenty or thirty of their dead sinking into the Mossbach, the leakage from their riddled corpses darkening the green water. Clyde had been so immersed in contemplation, he felt wrenched out of his element and not a little distressed—he believed he had been on the cusp of a more refined comprehension, and he looked to see who had committed this act of mayhem. Two skiffs had rounded the bend in the river and were making for the wreckage of the metal room. Three men with rifles stood in the first and Clyde's heart sank on recognizing Spooz among them; but his spirits lifted when he spotted a tanned figure clad in sweat pants and a bulky sweater in the second skiff: Milly. They pulled alongside and made their lines fast to what remained of a bracket. Batista, appearing hesitant, as if he, too, had been shocked by the slaughter, helped Milly out of the skiff and gave her the digest version of what had happened, concluding with Pet's death, the battle, and its unusual resolution.

"The last bunch who were exposed to that hypnotic thing—I think it was about seven years ago—only one survived. You're lucky we came along when we did." Milly cocked an eye toward Annalisa. "How's she doing?"

Batista made a negative noise. "She's not communicating too well."

Milly nodded sadly. "I always thought she'd be what killed Pet."

Batista's eyes dropped to her breasts. "She gave it the old college try."

The river bumped the skiffs against the side of the room, causing a faint gonging; clouds passed across the sun, partially obscuring it; with the dimming of the light, as if to disprove his theories, Clyde felt suddenly sharper of mind.

Milly rubbed Batista's shoulder, letting her fingers dawdle. "Why don't you ride back with me? It'll give us a chance to talk about your situation."

She summoned Spooz and the other men. They hopped onto the half-submerged room and two of them peeled Annalisa away from Clyde. She went without a word, without a backward look, and that made another kind of pain in his chest, the kind morphine couldn't touch. Milly squatted beside him, Spooz at her shoulder, and asked how he was.

"Real good," he said. "For someone who doesn't know what the hell's going on. When were you people going to tell me about the lurruloo?"

"I'm sure Annalisa wanted to tell you. It's supposed to be on a need-to-know basis."

"It's obvious Helene didn't need to know."

Milly shrugged, but said nothing.

"Seems irresponsible to me," Clyde said. "Maybe even criminal."

"Things in Halloween are going to run differently, now."

"And you're going to be running them?"

"For a while."

He jerked his head at Spooz. "Is he part of the new order?"

"If he toes the line."

"What about Brad?"

"Brad's not part of anything anymore."

In her serene face he read a long history of cunning and ruthlessness—it was like looking off the end of a pier in Halloween and seeing all the grotesque life swarming beneath the surface.

"The king is dead, long live the queen," said Clyde. "Is that it? I'm getting the idea this whole thing fit right in with your plans. I mean, it couldn't have worked out any better, huh?"

"I'm not going to have trouble with you, am I?" she asked mildly.

"Me? No way. Soon as I'm able, me and Annalisa are putting this place in the rear view."

Milly mulled this over. "That might be a good idea."

With a sincere expression, Spooz extended a hand, as if to help him up. "Square business, guy. I was just doing my job. No hard feelings?"

"Get your damn hand out of my face," Clyde said. "I can manage my own self."

"Just below the fifty-seventh parallel . . . " included a lot of frozen territory: parts of Russia, Latvia, Lithuania, Bellarus, Sweden, Denmark, Canada, and Alaska. Ridiculous, to hang onto a fragment, a hallucinated phrase, a misfiring of neurons, out of all that had occurred, but he couldn't shake the idea that it was important. Clyde had yet not founded, or found, a kingdom, but he had fitted a new purpose to his life, and it was for that reason he had parked his pickup in front of the neighborhood Buy-Rite on a cold December Saturday morning in Wilkes-Barre, Pennsylvania, waiting for the pharmacy to open so he could refill Annalisa's migraine prescription. The migraines turned her into a zombie. She would lie in bed for a day, sometimes two days at a time, unable to eat, too weak to sit up, capable of speaking no more than a couple of words. Between the migraines and the anti-psychotics, they'd had maybe three good weeks out of the six months since they left Halloween. Those weeks had been pretty splendid, though, providing him hope that a new Annalisa was being born. Her psychologist was optimistic, but Clyde doubted she would ever again be the woman he originally met, and perhaps that woman had never truly existed. The knots that Pet Nylund tied in her had come unraveled with his death and they seemed to have been what was holding her together. Life in their apartment was so oppressive, so deadly quiet and gloomy, he had taken a job driving heavy equipment just to have a place to go. The guys on site thought him aloof and strange, but chalked that up to the fact that his wife was sick, and they defended him to their friends by saying, "The man is going through some shit, okay?"

His breath fogged the windshield and, tired of wiping it clear, he climbed down from the truck and leaned against the cold fender. The sun was muted to a tinny white glare by a mackerel sky, delicate altocumulus clouds laid out against a sapphire backdrop. A stiff wind blew along the traffic-less street, chasing paper trash in the gutters, flattening a red, white, and blue relic of the recent presidential election against the Buy-Rite's door for a fraction of a second, too quickly for him to determine which candidate it trumpeted. Not that it much mattered, The glass storefronts gave back perfect reflections of the glass storefronts on the opposite, sunnier side of the street. Quiznos. Ace Hardware. Toys 'R' Us was having a pre-Christmas sale. The post-apocalyptic vacancy of the place was spoiled by a black panel van that turned the corner and cruised slowly along and then pulled into the space next to Clyde's pickup. An orange jack-o'-lantern with a particularly jolly grin was spray-painted on the side of the van—it formed the O in dripping-blood horror movie lettering that spelled out HALLOWEEN. The window slid down to reveal Carmine's sallow, vulpine face. He didn't speak, so Clyde said, "What a shocker. Milly sent you to check up on us, did she?"

Carmine climbed out and came around the front of the van. "I had some business in town. She wanted me look you up. See if you need more money and like that."

"As long as the checks from the estate keep coming, we're cool," said Clyde. "How'd you find me?"

"I went over to your place. This woman told me you'd be here."

"Annalisa's nurse."

"Whatever." Carmine examined the bottom of his shoe. "How's she making it . . . Annalisa?"

"It's slow, but she'll be fine." Clyde waved at the van. "This is new, huh?"

Carmine looked askance at the jack-o'-lantern. "Milly's trying to encourage tourism. She's putting on a Halloween festival and all kinds of shit."

"You think that's wise? All you need is for a couple of tourists to get picked off by the lurruloo."

"They arcn't a problem anymore."

"What do you mean?"

"They're not a problem. Milly handled it."

"What are you talking? She wiped them out?"

"That's not your business."

Despite having less than fond memories of the lurruloo, Clyde found the notion that they had been exterminated more than horrifying, but was unable to think of an alternative way by which Milly could have handle it.

"Jesus, it's fucking cold!" Carmine jammed his hands into his pockets and shuffled his feet. "So what's life like in the republic?"

"Less benefits, little bit more freedom. It's a trade-off."

"Doesn't sound like so good a deal to me."

"That's your opinion, is it?"

Carmine gave a dry laugh. "I got to book. Any messages you want sent back?"

"How's Roberta and Mary Alonso?"

"They're in dyke heaven, I guess. They were married a few weeks back."

"No shit?"

"Milly made a law saying gay marriage is legal. Now she expects all the fruits to flock to Halloween." Carmine spat off to the side. "Got to hand it to her. She knows how to get stuff done."

"She makes the trains run on time."

Puzzled by the reference, Carmine squinted at him, then walked around to the driver's side of the van.

"Did Helene Kmiec kill her husband?" Clyde asked.

"How the fuck should I know?" Carmine started the engine.

"I'm serious, man. It's bugging me. It's the only question I have about Halloween I don't know the answer to."

"That's the only one you got?" Carmine backed out of the parking space and yelled, "Man, did you even know where you were living?"

Clyde watched until the black speck of the van merged with the blackness of the street, wishing he'd asked after Joanie. He reached for a cigarette, the reflex of an old smoker, and said, "Fuck it." He walked along the block to a newsstand that was opening up and bought a pack of Camel Wides. Out on the sidewalk, he lit one and exhaled a plume of smoke and frozen breath. Maybe Milly had blown up the entrance to the lurruloo's caves, sealing them in—maybe that was all she had done. What, he asked himself, would the penalty be for the genocide of a new intelligent species? Most likely nobody would give a damn, just like him. They had their own problems and couldn't be bothered. He thought about the 57th parallel and what might lie below it, and he thought about Annalisa's sharp tongue and wily good humor, subsumed beneath a haze of drugs. He thought about a local bar, once a funeral home, that now was painted white inside, every inch and object, with plants in the enormous urns and round marble tables, usually filled with seniors—it troubled him that she liked to drink there.

"Hey, buddy!" The newsstand owner, an elderly man with a potbelly and unruly wisps of gray hair lying across his mottled scalp like scraps of cloud over a wasteland—he beckoned to Clyde from the doorway and said, "You can smoke inside if you want." When Clyde hesitated, he said, "You're going to freeze your ass. What're you doing out there?"

Clyde told him, and the old man said, "She's always late opening on Saturday. Come on in."

With Clyde at his heels, the owner walked stiff-legged back inside, took a seat on a stool behind the counter, picked up a lit stogie from an ashtray and puffed on it until the coal glowed redly.

"Screw those bastards in the legislature telling us we can't smoke in our own place," said the owner. "Right?"

"Right."

There must have been a thousand magazines on the shelves: drab economic journals; bright pornos sealed in plastic; hockey, boxing, football, wrestling, MMA, the entire spectrum of violent sport; women's magazines with big, flashy graphics; *People, Time, Rolling Stone*; magazines for cat fanciers and antique collectors and pot smokers, for deer hunters and gun freaks and freaks of every persuasion; magazines about stamps and model trains, Japanese films and architecture, country cooking and travel in exotic lands; magazines in German, Italian, French. Clyde had patronized dozens of newsstands in his day, but never before had he been struck by the richness of such places, by the sheer profligacy of the written word.

"They tell you a man's home is his castle, but you know how that goes," said the owner, winking broadly at Clyde. "The little woman takes control and pretty soon you can't sit in your favorite chair unless it's covered in a goddamn plastic sheet. But a man's place of business now, that's his kingdom. That's how come I named this place like I did."

"What's that?" Clyde asked.

The owner seemed offended that he didn't know. "Kingdom News. People come in sometimes thinking I'm a Christian store, and I tell 'em to check out the name. Herschel Rothstein, Proprietor. I ain't no Christian. The point I'm making, shouldn't nobody tell a man he can't smoke in his damn kingdom."

Clyde wondered if the owner and his newsstand might not have been summoned from the Uncreate, perhaps by the same entity that had visited him after his ordeal in the Tubes, so as to pose an object lesson. He had been considering kingdoms in grandiose terms, a place requiring a castle, at least a symbolic one, and great holdings; yet now he recognized that a kingdom could be a small, rich thing, an enterprise of substance somewhere below the 57th parallel. A newsstand, a bar, a fishing camp—someplace quiet and pristine where Annalisa would heal and thrive.

A young woman dressed in cold weather yuppie gear came in to buy a paper and wrinkled her nose at the smell of the old man's cigar. He flirted outrageously with her and sent her away smiling, and they sat there, the owner on his stool, Clyde on a stack of *Times-Leaders*, laughing and smoking and talking about the bastards in the state legislature and the bigger bastards down in Washington, recalling days of grace and purity that never were, forgetting the wide world that lay beyond the door, happily cursing the twenty-first century and the republic in its decline, secure for the moment in the heart of their kingdom.

Lucius Shepard's *most recent books include* The Taborin Scale *and a collection,* Viator Plus. *Forthcoming are a novel,* Beautiful Blood *and a novella collection,* Four Autobiographies. *He lives and works in Portland, Oregon.*

Wherever you thought this story was going, it's my bet that it took more unexpected twists and turns in the darkness than you could have possibly dreamed. Only fantasy can offer a writer like Lucius Shepard the freedom to take you on a journey like this one—although few writers can equal his imagination or descriptive chops.

Halloween Town is a novella—too long to be a short story, too short to be considered a novel. It seems that novella-length works well for many fantasy writers and each year brings a number of notable ones. This novella was published in the esteemed *The Magazine of Fantasy and Science Fiction*, so at least it was widely available. Sometimes novellas are published by specialty presses as pricey hardcovers in limited numbers and only read (until, perhaps, republished in an author's collection later on) by a relative few. I'm thrilled to have the space to be able to showcase this and the other longer pieces in this anthology.

THE LONG, COLD GOODBYE

HOLLY PHILLIPS

Berd was late and she knew Sele would not wait for her, not even if it weren't cold enough to freeze a standing man's feet in his shoes. She hurried anyway, head down, as if she hauled a sled heavy with anxiety. She did not look up from the icy pavement until she arrived at the esplanade, and was just in time to see the diver balanced atop the railing. Sele! she thought, her voice frozen in her throat. The diver was no more than a silhouette, faceless, anonymous in winter clothes. Stop, she thought. Don't, she thought, still unable to speak. He spread his arms. He was an ink sketch, an albatross, a flying cross. Below him, the ice on the bay shone with the apricot-gold of the sunset, a gorgeous summer nectar of a color that lied in the face of the ferocious cold. The light erased the boundary between frozen sea and icy sky; from where Berd stood across the boulevard, there was no horizon but the black line of the railing, sky above and below, the cliff an edge on eternity. And the absence the diver made when he had flown was as bright as all the rest within the blazing death of the sun.

Berd crossed the boulevard, huddled deep within the man's overcoat she wore over all her winter clothes. Brightness brought tears to her eyes and the tears froze on her lashes. She was alone on the esplanade now. It was so quiet she could hear the groan of tide-locked ice floes, the tick and ping of the iron railing threatening to shatter in the cold. She looked over, careful not to touch the metal even with her sleeve, and saw the shape the suicide made against the ice. No longer a cross: an asterisk bent to angles on the frozen waves and ice-sheeted rocks. He was not alone there. There was a whole uneven line of corpses lying along the foot of the cliff, like a line of unreadable type, the final sentence in a historical tome, unburied until the next storm swept in with its erasure of snow. Berd's diver steamed, giving up the last ghost of warmth to the blue shadow of the land. He was still faceless. He might have been anyone, dead. The shadow grew. The sun spread itself into a spindle, a line; dwindled to a green spark and was gone. It was all shadow now, luminous dusk the color of longing, a blue to break your heart, ice's consolation for the blazing death of the sky. Berd's breath steamed like the broken man, dusting her scarf with frost. She turned and picked her way across the boulevard, its pavement broken by frost heaves, her eyes still dazzled by the last of the day. It was spring, the 30th of April, May Day Eve. The end.

Sele. That was not, could never have been him, Berd decided. Suicide had become a commonplace this spring, this non-spring, but Sele would never think of it. He was too curious, perhaps too fatalistic, certainly too engaged in the new scramble for survival and bliss. (But if he did, *if* he did, he would call on Berd to witness it. There was no one left but her.) No. She shook her head to herself in the collar of her coat. Not Sele. She was late. He had come and gone. The diver had come and gone. Finally she felt the shock of it, witness to a man's sudden death, and flinched to a stop in the empty street. Gaslights stood unlit in the blue dusk, and the windows of the buildings flanking the street were mostly dark, so that the few cracks of light struck a note of loneliness. Lonely Berd, witness to too much, standing with her feet freezing inside her shoes. She leaned forward, her sled of woe a little heavier now, and started walking. *She* would not go that way, not *that* way, she would *not*. She would find Sele, who had simply declined to wait for her in the cold, and get what he had promised her, and then she would be free.

But where, in all the dying city, would he be?

Sele had never held one address for long. Even when they were children Berd could never be sure of finding him in the same park or alley or briefly favored dock for more than a week or two. Then she would have to hunt him down, her search spirals widening as he grew older and dared to roam further afield. Sometimes she grew disheartened or angry that he never sought her out, that she was always the one who had to look for him, and then she refused. Abstained, as she came to think of it in more recent years. She had her own friends, her own curiosities, her own pursuits. But she found that even when she was pursuing them she would run across Sele following the same trail. Were they so much alike? It came of growing up together, she supposed. Each had come too much under the other's influence. She had not seen him for more than a year when they found each other again at the lecture on ancient ways.

"Oh, hello," he said, as if it had been a week.

"Hello." She bumped shoulders with him, standing at the back of the crowded room—crowded, it must be said, only because the room was so small. And she had felt the currents of amusement, impatience, offense, disdain, running through him, as if together they had closed a circuit, because she felt the same things herself, listening to the distinguished professor talk about the "first inhabitants," the "lost people," as if there were not two of them standing in the very room.

"We lost all right," Sele had said, more rueful than bitter, and Berd had laughed. So that was where it had begun, with a shrug and a laugh—if it had not begun in their childhood, growing up poor and invisible in the city built on their native ground—if it had not begun long before they were born.

Berd trudged on, worried now about the impending darkness. The spring dusk would linger for a long while, but there were no lamplighters out to spark the lamps. In this cold, if men didn't lose fingers to the iron posts, the brass fittings shattered like rotten ice. So there would be no light but the stars already piercing the blue. *Find Sele, find Sele.* It was like spiraling back into childhood, spiraling through the city in search of him. Every spiral had a beginning point. Hers would be his apartment, a long way from the old neighborhood, not so far from the esplanade. *He won't be there*, she warned herself, and as if she were tending a child, she turned her mind from the sight of the dead man lying with the others on the ice.

Dear Berd,

I cannot tell you how happy your news has made me. You are coming! You are coming at last! It seems as though I have been waiting for a lifetime, and now that I know I'll only have to wait a few short weeks more they stretch out before me like an eternity. Your letters are all my consolation, and the memory I hold so vividly in my mind is better than any photograph: your sweet face and your eyes that smile when you look sad and yet hold such a melancholy when you smile. My heart knows you so well, and you are still mysterious to me, as if every thought, every emotion you share (and you are so open you shame me for my reserve) casts a shadow that keeps the inner Berd safely hidden from prying eyes. Oh, I won't pry! But come soon, as soon as you can, because one lifetime of waiting is long enough for any man . . .

Sele's apartment was in a tall old wooden house that creaked and groaned even in lesser colds than this. Wooden houses had once been grand, back when the lumber was brought north in wooden ships and the natives lived in squat stone huts like ice-bound caves, and Sele's building still showed a ghost of its old beauty in its ornate gables and window frames. But it had been a long time since it had seen paint, and the weathered siding looked like driftwood in the dying light. The porch steps moaned under Berd's feet as she climbed to the door. An old bell pull hung there. She pulled it and heard the bell ring as if it were a ship's bell a hundred miles out to sea. The house was empty, she needed no other sign. All the same she tried the handle, fingers wincing from the cold brass even inside her mitten. The handle fell away from its broken mechanism with a clunk on the stoop and the door sighed open a crack, as if the house inhaled. It was dark inside; there was no breath of warmth. All the same, thought Berd, all the same. She stepped, anxious and hopeful, inside.

Dark, and cold, and for an instant Berd had the illusion that she was stepping into one of the stone barrow-houses of her ancestors, windowless and buried deep under the winter's snow. She wanted immediately to be out in the blue dusk again, out of this tomb-like confinement. Sele wasn't here.

And beyond that, with the suicide fresh in her mind and the line of death scribbled across her inner vision, Berd had the sense of dreadful discoveries waiting for her, as if the house really were a tomb. *Go. Go before you see . . .* But suppose she didn't find Sele elsewhere and hadn't checked here? Intuition was not infallible—her many searches for Sele had not always borne fruit—she had to be sure. Her eyes were adjusting to the darkness. She found the stairs and began to climb.

There was more light upstairs, filtering down like a fine gray-blue dust from unshuttered windows. Ghost light. The stairs, the whole building, creaked and ticked and groaned like every ghost story every told. Yet she was not precisely afraid. Desolate, yes, and abandoned, as if she were haunted by the empty house itself; as if, having entered here, she would never regain the realm of the living; as if the entire world had become a tomb. *As if.*

It was the enthusiasm she remembered, when memory took her like a sudden faint, a shaft of pain. They had been playing a game of make-believe, and the game had been all the more fun for being secreted within the sophisticated city. Like children constructing the elaborate edifice of Let's Pretend in the interstices of the adult world, they had played under the noses of the conquerors who had long since forgotten they had ever conquered, the foreigners who considered themselves native born. Berd and Sele, and later Berd's cousins and Sele's half-sister, Isse. They had had everything to hide and had hidden nothing. The forgotten, the ignored, the perpetually overlooked. Like children, playing. And for a time Sele had been easy to find, always here, welcoming them in with their bits of research, their inventions, their portentous dreams. His apartment warm with lamplight, no modern gaslights for them, and voices weaving a spell in point and counterpoint. *Why don't we . . . ? Is there any way . . . ? What if . . . ?*

What if we could change the world?

The upper landing was empty in the gloom that filtered through the icy window at the end of the hall. Berd's boots thumped on the bare boards, her layered clothes rustled together, the wooden building went on complaining in the cold, and mysteriously, the tangible emptiness of the house was transmuted into an ominous kind of inhabitation. It was as if she had let the cold dusk in behind her, as if she had been followed by the wisp of steam rising from the suicide's broken head. She moved in a final rush down the hall to Sele's door, knocked inaudibly with her mittened fist, tried the handle. Unlocked. She pushed open the door.

"Sele?" She might have been asking him to comfort her for some recent hurt. Her voice broke, her chest ached, hot tears welled into her eyes. "Sele?"

But he wasn't there, dead or alive.

Well, at least she was freed from this gruesome place. She made a fast tour of the three rooms, feeling neurotic for her diligence (but she did have to make sure all the same), and opened the hall door with all her momentum carrying her forward to a fast departure.

And cried aloud with the shock of discovering herself no longer alone.

They were oddly placed down the length of the hall, and oddly immobile, as if she had just yelled *Freeze!* in a game of statues. Yes, they stood like a frieze of statues: Three People Walking. Yet they must have been moving seconds before; she had not spent a full minute in Sele's empty rooms. Berd stood in the doorway with her heart knocking against her breastbone, her eyes watering as she stared without blinking in the dead light. Soon they would laugh at the joke they had played on her. Soon they would move.

Berd was all heartbeat and hollow fear as she crept down the hallway, hugging the wall for fear of brushing a sleeve. Her cousin Wael was first, one shoulder dropped lower than the other as if he was on the verge of turning to look back. His head was lowered, his uncut hair fell ragged across his face, his clothes were far too thin for the cold. The cold. Even through all her winter layers, Berd could feel the impossible chill emanating from her cousin's still form. Cold, so cold. But as she passed she would have sworn he swayed, ever so slightly, keeping his balance, keeping still while she passed. Keeping still until her back was turned. Wael. Wael! It was wrong to be so afraid of him. She breathed his name as she crept by, and saw her breath as a cloud.

If any of them breathed, their breath was as cold as the outer air.

Behind Wael was Isse, Sele's beautiful half-sister. Her head was raised and her white face—was it only the dusk that dusted her skin with blue?—looked ahead, eyes dark as shadows. She might have been seeing another place entirely, walking through another landscape, as if this statue of a woman in a summer dress had been stolen from a garden and put down all out of its place and time. Where did she walk to so intently? What landscape did she see with those lightless eyes?

And Baer was behind her, Berd's other cousin. He had been her childhood enemy, a plague on her friendship with Sele, and somehow because of it her most intimate friend, the one who knew her too well. His name jumped in Berd's throat. He stood too close to the wall for Berd to sidle by. She had to cross in front of him to the other wall and he *had* to see her, though his head, like Wael's, was lowered. He might have been walking alone, brooding a little, perhaps following Isse's footsteps or looking for something he had lost. Berd stopped in front of him, trembling, caught between his cold and Isse's as if she stood between two impossible fires.

"Baer?" She hugged herself, maybe because that was as close as she dared come to sharing her warmth with him. "Oh, Baer."

But grief did not lessen her fear. It only made her fear—made *them*—more terrible. She had come too close. Baer could reach out, he only had to reach out . . . She fled, her sleeve scraping the wall, her boots battering the stairs. Down, down, moving too fast to be stopped by the terror of what else, what worse, the dark lobby might hold. Berd's breath gasped out, white even in the darkest spot by the door. It was very dark, and the dark was full of reaching hands. The door had no handle. It had swung closed. She was trapped. No. No. But all she could whisper, propitiation or farewell, was her cousin's name. "Baer . . . " *please don't forget you loved me.* "Baer . . . " *please don't do me harm.* Until in an access of terror she somehow wrenched open the door and sobbed out, feeling the cold of them at her back, "I'm sorry!" But even then she could not get away.

There was no street, no building across the way. There was no way, only a vast field of blue . . . blue . . . Berd might have been stricken blind for that long moment it took her mind to make sense of what her eyes saw. It was ice, the great ocean of ice that encircled the pole, as great an ocean as any in the world. Ice bluer than any water, as blue as the depthless sky. If death were a color it might be this blue, oh! exquisite and full of dread. Berd hung there, hands braced on the doorframe, as though to keep her from being forced off the step. She forgot the cold ones upstairs; remembered them with a new jolt of fear; forgot them again as the bears came into view. The great white bears, denizens of the frozen sea, exiles on land when the spring drove the ice away. Exiles no more. They walked, slow and patient and seeming sad with their long heads nodding above the surface of the snow; and it seemed to Berd, standing in her impossible doorway—if she turned would she find the house gone and nothing left but this lintel, this doorstep, and these two jambs beneath her hands?—it seemed to her, watching the slow bears walk from horizon to blue horizon, that other figures walked with them, as white-furred as the bears, but two-legged and slight. She peered. She leaned out, her arms stretched behind her as she kept tight hold of her wooden anchors, not knowing anymore if it was fear that ached within her.

And then she felt on her shoulder the touch of a hand.

She fell back against the left-hand doorjamb, hung there, her feet clumsy as they found their new position. It was Baer, with Wael and Isse and others—yes, others!—crowding behind him in the lobby. The house was not empty and never had been, no more than a tomb is empty after the mourners have gone.

"Baer . . . "

Did he see her? He stood as if he would never move again, his hand outstretched as though to hail the bears, stop them, call them to come. He did not move, but in the moment that Berd stared at him, her heart failing and breath gone, the others had come closer. Or were they moved, like chess pieces by a player's hand? They were only *there*, close, close, so close the cold of them ate into Berd's flesh, threatening her bones with ice. Her throat clenched. A breath would have frozen her lungs. A tear would have frozen her eyes. At least the bears were warm inside their fur. She fell outside, onto the ice—

—onto the stoop, the first stair, her feet carrying her in an upright fall to the street. Yes: street, stairs, house. The door was swinging closed on the dark lobby, and there was nothing to see but the tall, shabby driftwood house and the brass doorknob rolling slowly, slowly to the edge of the stair. It did not fall. Shuddering with cold, Berd scoured her mittens across her ice-streaked face and fled, feeling the weight of the coming dark closing in behind her.

> *Dear Berd,*
> *I am lonely here. Recent years have robbed me of too many friends. Do I seem older to you? I feel old sometimes, watching so many slip away from me, some through travel, some through death, some through simple, inevitable change. I feel that I have not changed, myself, yet that does not make me feel young. Older, if anything, as if I have stopped growing and have nothing left to me but to begin to die. I'm sorry. I am not morbid, only sad. But your coming is a great consolation to me. At last! Someone dear to me—someone dearer to me than anyone in the world—is coming towards me instead of leaving me behind. You are my cure for sorrow. Come soon . . .*

Berd was too cold, she could not bear the prospect of canvassing the rest of Sele's old haunts. Old haunts! Her being rebelled. She ran until the air was like knives in her lungs, walked until the sweat threatened to freeze against her skin. She looked back as she turned corner after corner—no one, no one—but the fear and the grief never left her. Oh, Baer! Oh, Wael, and beautiful Isse! It was worse than being dead. Was it? Was it worse than being left behind? But Berd had not earned the grief of abandonment, no matter how close she was to stopping in the street and sobbing, bird-like, open-mouthed. She had no right. She was the one who was leaving.

At least, she was if she could find Sele. If she could only find him this once. This one last time.

She had known early on that it was love, on her part at least, but had been frequently bewildered as to what kind of love it was. Friendship, yes, but there was that lightness of heart at the first sight of him, the deep physical contentment in his rare embrace. She had envied his lovers, but had not been jealous of them. Had never minded sharing him with others, but had always been hurt when he vanished and would not be found. Love. She knew his lovers were often jealous of her. And Baer had often been jealous of Sele.

That had been love as well, Berd supposed. It was not indifference that made Berd look up in the midst of their scheming to see Baer watching her from across the room; but perhaps that was Baer's love, not hers. Baer's jealousy, that was not hers, and that frightened her, and bored her, and nagged at her until she felt sometimes he could pull her away from Sele, and from the warm candlelit conspiracy the five of them made, with a single skeptical glance. He had done it in their childhood, voicing the doubting realism that spoiled the game of make-believe. "You can't ride an ice bear," he had said—not even crushingly, but as flat and off-hand as a government form. "It would eat you," he said, and one of Berd and Isse's favorite games died bloody and broken-backed, leaving Baer to wonder in scowling misery why they never invited him to play.

Yet there he was, curled, it seemed deliberately, in Sele's most uncomfortable chair, watching, watching, as Sele, bright and quick by the fire, said, "Stories never die. You can't forget a story, not a real story, a living story. People forget, they die, but stories are always reborn. They're real. They're more real than we are."

"You can't live in a story," Baer said, and it seemed he was talking to Berd rather than Sele.

Berd said, "You can if you make the story real."

"That's right," Baer said, but as though he disagreed. "The story is ours. It only becomes real when we make it happen, and there has to be a way, a practical way—"

"We live in the story," Sele said. "Don't you see? *This* is a story. The story *is*."

"This is real life!" Baer mimed exasperation, but his voice was strained. "This story of yours is a *story*, you're just making it up. It's pure invention!"

"So is life," Sele said patiently. "That doesn't mean it isn't real."

Which was true; was, in fact, something Berd and Sele had argued into truth together, the two of them, alone. But Berd was dragged aside as she always was by Baer's resentful skepticism—resentful because of how badly he wanted to be convinced—but Berd could never find the words to include them in their private, perfect world, the world that would be perfect without him—and so somehow she could not perfectly immerse herself and was left on the margins, angry and unwilling in her sympathy for Baer. How many times had Berd lost Sele's attention, how many times had she lost her place in their schemes, because Baer was too afraid to commit himself and too afraid to abstain alone? Poor Baer! Unwilling, grudging, angry, but there it was: poor Baer.

And there he was, poor Baer, inside a cold, strange story, leaving Berd, for once, alone on the outside with Sele. With Sele. If only she were. *Oh Sele, where are you now?*

It seemed that the whole city, what was left of it, had moved into the outskirts where the aerodrome sprawled near the snow-blanked hills. There had been a few weeks last summer when the harbor was clear of ice and a great convoy of ships had docked all at once, creating a black cloud of smoke and a frantic holiday as supplies were unloaded and passengers loaded into the holds where the grain had been—loaded, it must be said, after the furs and ores that paid for their passage. Since then there had been nothing but the great silver airships drifting in on the southern wind, and now, as the cold only deepened with the passage of equinoctial spring, they would come no more. *Until*, it was said, *the present emergency has passed.* Why are some lies even told? Everyone knew this was the end of the city, the end of the north, perhaps the beginning of the end of the world. The last airships were sailing soon, too few to evacuate the city, too beautiful not to be given a gorgeous goodbye. So the city swelled against the landlocked shore of the aeroport like the Arctic's last living tide.

The first Berd knew of it—it had been an endless walk through the empty streets, the blue dusk hardly seeming to change, as if the whole city were locked in ice—was the glint and firefly glimmer of yellow light at the end of the wide suburban street. She had complained, they all had, about the brilliance of modern times, the constant blaze of gaslight that was challenged, these last few years, not by darkness but by the soulless glare of electricity. But now, tonight, Berd might have been an explorer lost for long months, drawing an empty sled and an empty belly into civilization with the very last of her strength. How beautiful it was, this yellow light. Alive with movement and color, it was an anodyne to grief, an antidote to blue. Her legs aching with her haste, Berd fled toward, yearning, rather than away, guilty and afraid. And then the light, and the noise, and the quicksilver movement of the crowd pulled her under.

It was a rare kind of carnival. More than a farewell, it was a hunt, every citizen a quarry that had turned on its hunter, Death, determined to take Him down with the hot blood bursting across its tongue. Strange how living and dying could be so hard to tell apart in the end. Berd entered into it at first like a swimmer resting on the swells, her relief at the lights that made the blue sky black, and at the warm-blooded people all around her steaming in the cold, made her buoyant, as light as an airship with a near approximation of joy. *This* was escape, oh yes it was. The big houses on their acre gardens spilled out into the open, as if the carpets and chandeliers of the rich had spawned tents and booths and roofless rooms. Lamps burned everywhere, and so did bonfires in which the shapes of furniture and books could still be discerned as they were consumed. The smells wafting in great clouds of steam from food carts and al fresco bistros made the sweet fluid burst into Berd's mouth, just as the music beating from all sides made her feet move to an easier rhythm than fear. They were alive here; she took warmth from them all. But what storerooms were emptied for this feast? Whose hands would survive playing an instrument in this cold?

The aerodrome's lights blazed up into the sky. Entranced, enchanted, Berd drifted through the crowds, stumbling over the broken walls that had once divided one mansion from the next. (The native-born foreigners had made gardens, as if tundra could be forced to become a lawn. No more. No more.) That glow was always before her, but never within reach. She stumbled again, and when she had stopped to be sure of her balance, she felt the weight of her exhaustion dragging her down.

"Don't stop." A hand grasped her arm above the elbow. "It's best to keep moving here."

Here? She looked to see what the voice meant before she looked to see to whom the voice belonged. "Here" was the empty stretch between the suburb and the aerodrome, still empty even now. Or perhaps even emptier, for there were men and dogs patrolling, and great lamps magnified by the lenses that had once equipped the lighthouses guarding the ice-locked coast. This was the glow of freedom. Berd stared, even as the hand drew her back into the celebrating, grieving, furious, abandoned, raucous crowd. She looked around at last, when the perimeter was out of view.

"Randolph!" she said, astonished at being able to put a name to the face. She was afraid—for one stopped breath she was helpless with fear—but he was alive and steaming with warmth, his pale eyes bright and his long nose scarlet with drink and cold. The combination was deadly, but Berd could believe he would not care.

"Little Berd," he said, and tucked her close against his side. With all their layers of clothing between them it was hardly presumptuous, though she did not know him well. He was, however, a crony of Sele's.

"You look like you've been through the wars," he said. "You need a drink and a bite of food."

And he needed a companion in his fin de siècle farewell, she supposed.

"The city's so empty," she said, and shuddered. "I'm looking for Sele. Randolph, do you know where he might be?"

"Not there," he said with a nod toward the aerodrome lights. "Not our Sele."

"No," Berd said, her eyes downcast. "But he'll be nearby. Won't he? Do you know?"

"Oh, he's around." Randolph laughed. "Looking for Sele! If only you knew how many women have come to me, wondering where he was! But maybe it's better you don't know, eh, little Berd?"

"I know," said little Berd. "I've known him longer that you."

"That's true!" Randolph said with huge surprise. He was drunker than she had realized. "You were pups together, weren't you, not so long ago. Funny to think . . . Funny to think, no more children, and the docks all empty where they used to play."

A maudlin drunk. Berd laughed, to think of the difference between what she had fled from and what had rescued her. All the differences. Yet Randolph had been born here, just the same as Wael and Isse and Baer.

"Do you know where I can find him, Randolph?"

"Sele?" He pondered, his narrow face drunken-sad. "Old Sele . . . "

"Only I need to find him tonight, Randolph. He has something for me, something I need. So if you can tell me . . . or you can help me look . . . "

"I know he's around. I know!" This with the tone of a great idea. "I know! We'll ask the Painter. Good ol' Painter! He knows where everyone is. Anyone who owes him money! And Sele's on that list, when was he ever not? We'll go find Painter, he'll set us right. Painter'll set us right."

So she followed the drunk who seemed to be getting drunker on the deepening darkness and the sharpening cold. The sky was indigo now, alight with stars above the field of lamps and fires and human lives. Fear receded. Anxiety came back all the sharper. Her last search, and she had only this one night, this one night, even if it had barely begun. And the thought came to her with a shock as physical as Baer's touch: it was spring: the nights were short, regardless of the cold.

She searched faces as they passed through fields of light. Strange how happy they were. Music everywhere, bottles warming near the fires, a burst of fireworks like a fiery garden above the tents and shacks and mansions abandoned to the poor. Carnival time.

Berd had never known this neighborhood, it was too far afield even for the wandering Sele and her sometimes-faithful self. All she knew of it was this night, with the gardens invaded and the tents thrown open and spilling light and music and steam onto the trampled weeds and frozen mud of the new alleyways. They made small stages, their lamplit interiors as vivid as scenes from a play. Act IV, scene i: the Carouse. They were all of a piece, the Flirtation, the Argument, the Philosophical Debate. And yet, every face was peculiarly distinct, no one could be mistaken for another. Berd ached for them, these strangers camped at the end of the world. For that moment she was one of them, belonged to them and with them—belonged to everything that was not the cold ones left behind in the empty city beside the frozen sea. Or so she felt, before she saw Isse's face, round and cold and beautiful as the moon.

No. Berd's breath fled, but . . . no. There was only the firelit crowd outside, the lamplit crowd within the tent Randolph led her to, oblivious to her sudden stillness, the drag she made at the end of his arm. No cold Isse, no Wael or Baer. No. But the warmth of the tent was stifling, and the noise of music and voices and the clatter of bottle against glass shivered the bones of her skull.

The Painter held court, one of a hundred festival kings, in a tent that sagged like a circus elephant that has gone too long without food. He had been an artist once, and had earned the irony of his sobriquet by turning critic and making a fortune writing for twenty journals under six different names. He had traveled widely, of course, there wasn't enough art in the north to keep a man with half his appetites, but Berd didn't find it strange that he stayed when all his readers escaped on the last ships that fled before the ice. He had been a prince here, and some princes did prefer to die than become paupers in exile. Randolph was hard-pressed to force himself close enough to bellow in King Painter's ear, and before he made it—he was delayed more than once by an offered glass—Berd had freed her arm and drifted back to the wide-open door.

It seemed very dark outside. Faces passed on another stage, a promenade of drunks and madmen. A man dressed in the old fashioned furs of an explorer passed by, his beard and the fur lining of his hood matted with vomit. A woman followed him wearing a gorgeous rug like a poncho, a hole cut in the middle of its flower-garden pattern, and another followed her with her party clothes torn all down her front, too drunk or mad to fold the cloth together, so that her breasts flashed in the lamplight from the tent. She would be dead before morning. So many would be, Berd thought, and her weariness came down on her with redoubled weight. A stage before her, a stage behind her, and she—less audience than stagehand, since these performers in no wise performed for her—stood in a thin margin of nowhere, a threshold between two dreams. She let her arms dangle and her head fall back, as if she could give up, not completely, but just for a heartbeat or two, enough to snatch one moment of rest. The stars glittered like chips of ice, blue-white, colder than the air. There was some comfort in the thought that they would still shine long after the human world was done. There would still be sun and moon, snow and ice, and perhaps the seals and the whales and the bears. Berd sighed and shifted her numb feet, thinking she should find something hot to drink, talk to the Painter herself. She looked down, and yes, there was Isse standing like a rock in the stream of the passing crowd.

She might have been a statue for all the notice anyone took of her. Passersby passed by without a glance or a flinch from Isse's radiating cold. It made Berd question herself, doubt everything she had seen and felt back at the house. She lifted her hand in a half-finished wave and felt an ache in her shoulder where Baer had touched her, the frightening pain of cold that has penetrated to the bone. Isse did not respond to Berd's gesture. She was turned a little from where Berd stood, her feet frozen at the end of a stride, her body leaning toward the next step that never came. Still walking in that summer garden, her arms bare and as blue-white as the stars. Berd rubbed her shoulder, less afraid in the midst of carnival, though the ache of cold touched her heart. Dear Isse, where do you walk to? Is it beautiful there?

Something cold touched Berd's eye. Weeping ice? She blinked, and discovered a snowflake caught in her eyelashes. She looked up again. Stars, stars, more stars than she had seen moments ago, more stars than she thought she would see even if every gaslight and oil lamp and bonfire in the north were extinguished. Stars so thick there was hardly any black left in the sky, no matter how many fell. Falling stars, snow from a cloudless sky. Small flakes prickled against Berd's face, so much colder than her cold skin they felt hot. She looked down and saw that Baer and Wael had joined Isse, motionless, three statues walking down the impromptu street. How lonely they looked! Berd had been terrified in the house with them. Now she hurt for their loneliness, and felt an instant's powerful impulse to go to them, join them in their pilgrimage in whatever time and place they were. The impulse frightened her more than their presence did, and yet . . . And yet. She didn't move from the threshold of the tent, but the impulse still lived in her body, making her lean even as Isse leaned, on the verge of another step.

Snow fell more thickly, glittering in the firelight. It was strange that no one seemed to notice it, even as it dusted their heads and shoulders and whitened the ground. It fell more thickly, a windless blizzard that drew a curtain between Berd and the stage of the promenade, and more thickly still, until it was impossible that so much snow could fall—and from a starlit sky!—and yet she was still able to see Wael and Baer and Isse. It was as though they stood not in the street but in her mind. She was shivering, her mouth was dry. Snow fell and fell, an entire winter of snow pouring into the street, the soft hiss of the snowflakes deafening Berd to the voices, music, clatter and bustle of the tent behind her. It was the hiss of silence, no louder than the sigh of blood in her ears. And Isse, Wael, and Baer walked and walked, unmoving while the snow piled up in great drifts, filling the street, burying it, disappearing it from view. There were only the three cold ones and the snow.

And then the snow began to generate ghosts. Berd knew this trick from her childhood, when the autumn winds would drive fogbanks and snowstorms onto the northern shore. The hiss and the monotonous whiteness gave birth to muttered voices and distant calls, and to the shapes of things barely visible behind the veil of mist or snow. People, yes, and animals like white bears and caribou and the musk oxen Berd only knew from the books they read in school; and sometimes stranger things, ice gnomes like white foxes walking on hind legs and carrying spears, and wolves drawing sleds ridden by naked giants, and witches perched backwards on white caribou made of old bones and snow. Those ghosts teased Berd's vision as they passed down the street of snow, a promenade of the north that came clearer and clearer as she watched, until the diamond points of the gnomes' spears glittered in the lamplight pouring out of the tent and the giants with their eyes as black as the sky stared down at her as they passed. Cold filled her, the chill of wonder, making her shudder. And now she saw there were others walking with the snow ghosts, people as real as the woman who wore the beautiful carpet, as solid as the woman who bared her breasts to the cold. They walked in their carnival madness, as if they had found their way through the curtain that had hidden them from view. Still they paid no notice to the three cold ones, the statues of Baer and Isse and Wael, but they walked there, fearless, oblivious, keeping pace with the witches, the oxen, the bears.

And then Randolph grasped Berd's sore shoulder with his warm hand and said, "Painter says Sele's been sleeping with some woman in one of the empty houses . . . Hey, where'd everybody go?"

For at his touch the snow had been wiped away like steam from a window, and all the ghosts, all the cold ones, and all the passersby were gone, leaving Berd standing at the edge of an empty stage.

"Hey," Randolph said softly. "Hey."

It was perfectly silent for a moment, but only for a moment. A fire burning up the street sent up a rush of sparks as a new log went on. A woman in the tent behind them screamed with laughter. A gang of children ran past, intent in their pursuit of some game. And then the promenade was full again, as varied and lively as a parade.

Berd could feel Randolph's shrug and his forgetting through the hand resting on her shoulder. She could feel his warmth, his gin-soaked breath past her cheek, his constant swaying as he sought an elusive equilibrium. She should not feel so alone, so perfectly, utterly, dreadfully alone. They had gone, leaving her behind.

"No." No. *She* was the one who was leaving.

"Eh?" Randolph said.

"Which house?" Berd said, turning at last from the door.

"Eh?" He swayed more violently, his eyes dead, lost in some alcoholic fugue.

"Sele." She shook him, and was surprised by the stridency in her voice. "Sele! You said he was in a house with some woman. Which house?" Randolph focused with a tangible effort. "That's right. Some rich woman who didn't want to go with her husband. Took Sele up. Lives somewhere near here. One of the big houses. Some rich woman. Bitch. If I'd been her I'd've gone. I'd've been dead by now. Gone. I'd've been gone by now . . . "

Berd forced her icy hands to close around both his arms, holding him against his swaying. "Which house? Randolph! *Which house?*"

My dearest Berd,

I'm embarrassed by the last letter I wrote. It must have given you a vision of me all alone in a dusty room, growing old before my time. Not true! Or, if it is, it isn't the only truth. I should warn you that I have been extolling your virtues to everyone I know, until all of my acquaintance is agog to meet the woman, the mysterious northerner, the angel whose coming has turned me into a boy again. You are my birthday and my school holiday and my summer all rolled into one, and I cannot wait to parade you on my arm. Will it embarrass you if I buy you beautiful things to wear? I hope it won't. I want shamelessly to show you off. I want you to become the new star of my almost-respectable circle as you are the star that lights the dark night of my heart . . .

4198 Goldport Avenue.

There *were* no avenues, just the haphazard lanes of the carnival town, but the Painter (Berd had given up on Randolph in the end) had added directions that took into account new landmarks and gave Berd some hope of finding her way. Please, oh please, let Sele be there.

"It's a monstrous place," the Painter had said. His eyes were greedy, unsated by the city's desperation, hungry for hers. "A bloody great Romantic pile with gargoyles like puking birds and pillars carved like tree nymphs. You can't miss it. Last time I was there it was lit up like an opera house with a red carpet spilling down the stairs. Vulgar! My god, the woman has no taste at all except for whiskey and men. Your Sele will be lucky if she's held onto him this long."

His eyes had roved all over Berd, but there was nothing to see except her weary face and frightened eyes. He dismissed her, too lazy to follow her if she wouldn't oblige by bringing her drama to him, and Randolph was so drunk by then that he stared with sober dread into the far distance, watching the approach of death. Berd went alone into the carnival, feeling the cold all the more bitterly for the brief warmth of the Painter's tent. Her hands and feet felt as if they were being bitten by invisible dogs, her ears burned with wasp-fire, her shoulder ached with a chill that grew roots down her arm and into the hollow of her ribs. Cold, cold. Oh, how she longed for warmth! Warmth and sunshine and smooth pavement that didn't trip her hurting feet, and the proper sounds of spring, waves and laughter and shouting gulls, rather than the shouting crowd, yelping as though laughter were only a poor disguise for a howl of despair. She stumbled, buffeted by strangers, and wished she could only *see*, if she could only *see*. But Wael and Isse and Baer were near. She knew that, even in the darkness; heard their silence in the gaps and blank spaces of the noisy crowd, felt their cold. And oh, she was frightened. She missed them terribly, grieved for them, longed for them, and was terrified that longing would bring them back to her, as cold and strange and wrong as the walking dead.

But she would not go that way, not that way, she would not.

Berd stumbled again. Under her feet, barely visible in the light of a bonfire ringed by dancers there lay a street sign that said in ornate script Goldport Ave. She looked up, past the dancers and their fire—and what was that in the flames? A chair stood upright in the coals and on the chair an effigy, please let it be an effigy, burning down to a charcoal grin—she dragged her gaze up above the fire where the hot air shivered like a watery veil, and saw the pillared house with all its curtains open to expose the shapes dancing beneath the blazing chandeliers. Bears and giants and witches, and air pilots and buccaneers and queens. Fancy dress, as if the dancers had already died and moved on to a different form. Berd climbed the stairs, the vulgar carpet more black than red after the passage of many feet, and passed through the wide-open door.

She gave up on the reception rooms very soon. They were so hot, and crowded by so many reckless dancing drunks, and the music was a noisy shambles played by more drunks who seemed to have only a nodding acquaintance with their instruments. Perhaps the dancers and the musicians had traded places for a lark. Berd thought that even were she drunk and in the company of friends it would still seem like a foretaste of hell, and she could feel a panic coming on before she had forced a way through a single room. Sele. Sele! Why wouldn't he come and rescue her? She fought her way back into the grand foyer and climbed the wide marble stairs until she was above the heads of the crowd. Hot air mingled with cold. Lamps dimmed as the oil in the reservoirs ran low, candles guttered in ornate pools of wax; no one seemed to care. They would all die here, a mad party frozen in place like a story between the pages of a book. Berd sat on a step halfway above the first landing and put her head in her hands.

"There you are. Do you know, I thought I'd missed you for good."

Berd burst into tears. Sele sat down beside her and rocked her, greatcoat and all, in his arms.

He told her he had waited on the esplanade until his feet went numb. She told him about the suicide. She wanted to tell him about his sister, Isse, and her cousins, but could not find the words to begin.

"I saw," she said, "I saw," and spilled more tears.

"It isn't a tragedy," Sele said, meaning the suicide. "We all die, soon or late. It's just an anticipation, that's all."

"I know."

"There are worse things."

"I know."

He drew back to look at her. She looked at him, and saw that he knew, and that he saw that she knew, too.

"Oh, Sele . . . "

His round brown face was solemn, but also serene. "Are you still going?"

"Yes!" She shifted so she could grasp him too. "Sele, you have to come with me. You must, now, you have no choice."

He laughed at her with surprise. "What do you mean? Why don't I have a choice?"

"They—" She stammered, not wanting to know what she was trying to say. "Th-they have been following me, Wael and Baer and Isse. They've been following. They want—They'll come for you, too."

"I know. I've seen them. I expect they'll come soon."

"I'm sorry. I know it's wrong, but they frighten me so much. How can you be so calm?"

"We did this," he said. "We wanted change, didn't we? We asked for it. We should take what we get."

"Oh, Sele." Berd hid her face against his shoulder. He was only wearing a shirt, she realized. She could feel this chill of his flesh against her cheek. She whispered, "I can't. It's too dreadful. I can't bear to always be so cold."

"Oh, little Berd." He stroked her hair. "You don't have to. I've made my choice, that's all, and you've made yours. I don't think, by now, there's any right or wrong either way. We've gone too far for that."

She shook her head against him. She wanted very much to plead with him, to make her case, to spin for him all her dreams of the south, but she was too ashamed, and knew that it would do no good. They had already spun their dreams into nothing, into cold and ice, into the land beyond death. Anyway, Sele had never, ever, in all their lives, followed her lead. And at the last, she could not follow his.

They pulled apart.

"Come on," Sele said. "I have your things in my room."

The gas jet would not light, so Berd stood by the door while Sele fumbled for candle and match. Two candles burning on a branch meant for four barely carved the shape of the room out of the darkness. It seemed very grand to Berd, with heavy curtains round the bed and thick carpets on the floor.

"A strange place to end up," she said.

Sele glanced at her, his dark eyes big and bright with candlelight. "It's warm," he said, and then added ruefully, "It was warm. Anyway, I needed to be around to meet some of the right people. It's such a good address, don't you know."

"Better than your old one." Berd couldn't smile, remembering his old house, remembering the street sign under her feet and the shape in the bonfire outside.

"Anyway." Sele knelt and turned up a corner of the carpet. "My hostess is nosy but not good at finding things. And she's been good to me. I owe her a lot. She helped me get you what you'll need."

"The ticket?" Berd did not have enough room for air in her chest.

"Ticket." Sele handed her the items one at a time. "Travel papers. Letters."

"Letters?" She was slow to take the last packet. Whose letters? Letters from whom?

"From your sponsor. There's a rumor that even with a ticket and papers they won't let you on board unless you can prove you aren't going south only to end up a beggar. Your sponsor is supposed to give you a place to stay, help you find work. He's my own invention, but he's a good one. No," he said as she turned the packet over in her hands, "don't read them now. You'll have time on the ship."

It was strange to see her name on the top envelope in Sele's familiar hand. He had never written her a letter in her life. She stowed them away in her pocket with the other papers and then checked, once, twice, that she had everything secure. *I can't go.* The words lodged in her throat. She looked at Sele, all her despair—at going? at staying?—in her eyes.

"You're right to go," Sele said. "Little Berd, flying south away from the cold."

"I don't want to leave you." Not *I can't,* just *I don't want to.*

"But you will."

She shivered, doubting, torn, and yet knowing as well as he that he was right. She would go, and he would go too, on a different journey with Isse and Wael and Baer. So cold. She hugged him fiercely, trying to give him her heat, wanting to borrow his. He kissed her, and then she was going, going, her hand in her pocket, keeping her ticket safe. Running down the stairs. Finding the beacon of the aerodrome even before she was out the door.

Out the door. On the very threshold she looked out and saw what she had not thought to look for from the window of Sele's room. Inside, the masquerade party was in full swing, hot and bright and loud with voices and music and smashing glass. Outside . . .

Outside the ice had come.

It was as clear as it can be only at the bottom of a glacier, where the weight of a mile of ice has pressed out all the impurities of water and air. It was as clear as glass, as clear as the sky, so that the stars shone through hardly dimmed, though their glittering was stilled. Berd could see everything, the carnival town frozen with every detail preserved: the tents still upright, though their canvas sagged; the shanties with the soot still crusted around their makeshift chimneys. Even the bonfires, with their half-burnt logs intact, their charcoal facsimiles of chairs and books and mannequins burned almost to the bone. In the glassy starlight Berd could even see all the little things strewn across the ground, all the ugly detritus of the end of the world, the bottles and discarded shoes, the dead cats and dead dogs and turds. And she could see the people, all the people abandoned at the last, caught in their celebratory despair. The whole crowd of them, men and women and children, young and old and ugly and fair, frozen as they danced, stumbled, fucked, puked, and died. And, yes, there were her own three, her own dears, the brothers and sister of her heart, standing at the foot of the steps as if they had been caught, too, captured by the ice just as they began to climb. Isse, and Wael, and Baer.

The warmth of the house behind Berd could not combat the dreadful cold of the ice. The music faltered as the cold bit the musicians' hands. Laughter died. And yet, and yet, and yet in the distance, beyond the frozen tents and the frozen people, a light still bloomed. Cold electricity, as cold as the unrisen moon and as bright, so that it cast the shadows of Baer and Wael and Isse before them up the stairs. The aerodrome, yes, the aerodrome, where the silver airships still hung from their tethers like great whales hanging in the depths of the clear ocean blue. Yes, and there was room at the right-hand edge of the stairs where Berd could slip between the balustrade and the still summer statue of Wael, her cousin Wael, with his hair shaken back and his dark eyes raised to where Berd still stood with her hand in her pocket, her ticket and travel pass and letters clutched in her cold but not yet frozen fist. The party was dying. There was a quiet weeping. The lights were growing dim. *Now or never*, Berd thought, and she took all her courage in her hands and stepped through the door.

My darling, my beloved Berd,
I wish I had the words to tell you how much I love you. It's no good to say "like a sister" or "like a lover" or "like myself." It's closer to say like the sun that warms me, like the earth that supports me, like the air I breathe. And I have been suffering these past few days with the regret (I know I swore long ago to regret nothing, even to remember nothing I might regret, but it finds me all the same) that I have never come to be with

you, your lover or your husband, in your beloved north. It's as though I have consigned myself to some sunless, airless world. How have I let all this time pass without ever coming to you? And now it is too late, far too late for me. But I am paid with this interminable waiting. Come to me soon, I beg you. Save me from my folly. Forgive me. Tell me you love me as much as I love you . . .

Holly Phillips *lives in a small city on a large island off the west coast of Canada. She is the author of the award-winning collection* In the Palace of Repose *and the dark fantasy novel* The Engine's Child. *You can visit her Web site at www. hollyphillips.com.*

Phillips has a knack for showing the reader both the beautiful and the ugly in her elegant, lyrical prose. Here she writes of a decision that must be made, a "door" that once Berd steps through it will close forever. There will be a new life beyond it, but there will also always be a great deal left behind.

WHAT HAPPENS WHEN YOU WAKE UP IN THE NIGHT

MICHAEL MARSHALL SMITH

The first thing I was unhappy about was the dark. I do not like the dark very much. It is not the worst thing in the world but it is also not the best thing in the world, either. When I was smaller I used to wake up sometimes in the middle of the night and be scared when I woke up, because it was so dark. I went to bed with my light on, the light that turns round and round, on the drawers by the side of my bed. It has animals on it and it turns around and it makes shapes and patterns on the ceiling and it is pretty and Mummy's friend Jeanette gave it to me. It is not too bright but it is bright enough and you can see what is what. But then it started that when I woke up in the middle of the night, the light would not be on any more and it would be completely dark instead and it would make me sad. I didn't understand this but one night when I'd woken up and cried a lot Mummy told me that she came in every night and turned off the light after I was asleep, so it didn't wake me up. But I said that wasn't any good, because if I *did* wake up in the night and the light wasn't on, then I might be scared, and cry. She said it seemed that I was waking every night, and she and Daddy had worked out that it might be the light that woke me, and after I was awake I'd get up and go into their room and see what was up with them, which meant she got no sleep any night ever and it was driving her completely nuts.

So we made a deal, and the deal said I could have the light on all night *but* I promised that I would not go into their room in the night unless it was really important, and it is a good deal and so I'm allowed to have my light on again now, which is why the first thing I noticed when I woke up was that it was dark.

Mummy had broken the deal.

I was cross about this but I was also very sleepy and so wasn't sure if I was going to shout about it or not.

Then I noticed it was cold.

Before I go to bed, Mummy puts a heater on while I am having my bath, and also I have two blankets on top of my duvet, and so I am a warm little bunny and it is fine. Sometimes if I wake in the middle of the night it feels a bit cold but if I snuggle down again it's okay.

But this felt really cold.

My light was not on and I was cold.

I put my hand out to put my light on, which was the first thing to do. There is a switch on a white wire that comes from the light and I can turn it on myself—I can even find it in the dark when there is no light.

I tried to do that but I could not find the wire with my hand.

So I sat up and tried again, but still I could not find it, and I wondered if Mummy had moved it, and I thought I might go and ask her. But I could not see the door. It had been so long since I had been in my room in the night without my light being on that I had forgotten how dark it gets. It's *really* dark. I knew it would be hard to find the door if I could not see it, so I did it a clever way.

I used my imagination.

I sat still for a moment and remembered what my bedroom is like. It is like a rectangle and has some drawers by the top of my bed where my head goes. My light is on the drawers, usually. My room also has a table where my coloring books go and some small toys, and two more sets of drawers, and windows down the other end. They have curtains so the street lights do not keep me awake, and because in summer it gets bright too early in the morning and so I wake everybody up when they should still be asleep because they have work to do and they need some sleep. And there is a big chair but it is always covered in toys and it is not important.

I turned to the side so my legs hung off the bed and down onto the floor. In my imagination I could see that if I stood up and walked straight in front of me, I would nearly be at my door, but that I would have to go a little way . . . left, too.

So I stood up and did this walking.

It was funny doing it in the dark. I stepped on something soft with one of my feet, I think it was a toy that had fallen off the chair. Then I touched one of the other drawers with my hand and I knew I was close to the door, so I turned left and walked that way a bit.

I reached out with my hands then and tried to find my dressing gown. I was trying to find it because I was cold, but also because it hangs off the back of my bedroom door on a little hook and so when I found the dressing gown I would know I had got to the right place to open the door.

But I could not find the dressing gown.

Sometimes my Mummy takes things downstairs and washes them in the washing machine in the kitchen and then dries them in another machine that makes them hot, so maybe that was where it was. I was quite awake now and very cold so I decided not to keep trying to find the gown and just go wake Mummy and Daddy and say to them that I was awake.

But I couldn't find my doorknob. I knew I must be where the door is, because it is in the corner where the two walls of my room come together. I reached out with my hands and could feel the two sides of the corner, but I could not find the doorknob, even though I moved my hands all over where it should be. When I was smaller the doorknob came off once, and Mummy was very scared because she thought if it happened again I would be trapped in my bedroom and I wouldn't be able to get out, so she shouted at Daddy until he fixed it with a different screw. But it had never come off again so I did not know where it could be now. I wondered if I had got off my bed in the wrong way because it was dark and I had got it mixed up in my imagination, and maybe I should go back to my bed and start again.

Then a voice said:

"Maddy, what are you *doing*?"

I was so surprised I made a scared sound, and jumped. I trod on something, and the same voice said "Ow!"

I heard someone moving and sitting up. Even though it was in the dark I knew it was my Mummy.

"Mummy?" I said. "Where are you?'

"Maddy, I've *told* you about coming into our room."

"I'm not."

"It's just not *fair*. Mummy has to go to work and Daddy has to go to work and you have to go to school and we *all* need our sleep. We made a *deal*, remember?"

"But *you* broke the deal. You took away my light."

"I haven't touched your light."

"You did!"

"Maddy, don't lie. We've talked about lying."

"You took my light!"

"I haven't taken your light and I didn't turn it off."

"But it's not turned on.'

She made a sighing sound. "Maybe the bulb went."

"Went to where?"

"I mean, got broken."

"No, my whole *light* is not there."

"Maddy . . . "

"It's not! I put my hand out and I couldn't find it!"

My Mummy made a sound like she was very cross or very tired, I don't know which. Sometimes they sound the same. She didn't say anything for a little minute.

"Look," she said then, and she did not sound very cross now, just sleepy and as if she loved me but wished I was still asleep. "It's the middle of the night and everyone should be in bed. Their own bed."

"I'm sorry, Mummy."

"That's okay." I heard her standing up. "Come on. Let's go back to your room."

"What do you mean?" I said.

"Back to your room. Now. I'll tuck you in, and then we can all go back to sleep."

"I *am* in my room."

"Maddy—don't start."

"I *am* in my room!"

"Maddy, this is just silly. Why would you . . . Why is it so dark in here?"

"Because my light is off. I told you."

"Maddy, your light is in *your* room. Don't—"

She stopped talking suddenly. I heard her fingers moving against something, the wall, maybe. "What the hell?"

Her voice sounded different.

"'Hell' is a naughty word," I told her.

"Shush."

I heard her fingers swishing over the wall again. She had been asleep on the floor, right next to the wall. I heard her feet moving on the carpet and then there was a banging sound and she said a naughty word again, but she did not sound angry but like she did not understand something. It was like a question mark sound.

"For the love of Christ."

This was not my Mummy talking.

"Dan?"

"Who the hell else? Any chance you'll just take her back to bed? Or I can do it. I don't mind. But let's one of us do it. It's the middle of the fucking night."

"Dan!"

"'Fucking' is a *very* naughty—"

"Yes, yes, I'm terribly sorry," my Daddy said. He sounded as if he was only half not in a dream. "But we have *talked* about you coming into our room in the middle of the night, Maddy. Talked about it endlessly. And—"

"Dan," my Mummy said, starting to talk when he was still talking, which is not good and can be rude. "Where *are* you?'"

"I'm right *here*," he said. "For God's sake. I'm . . . Did you put up new curtains or something?"

"No," Mummy said.

"It's not normally this dark in here, is it?"

"My light has gone," I said. "That's why it is so dark."

"Your light is in *your* room," Daddy said.

I could hear him sitting up. I could hear his hands, too. They were not right next to Mummy, but at the other end of my room. I could hear them moving around on the carpet.

"Am I on the floor?" he asked. "What the hell am I doing on the floor?"

I heard him stand up. I did not tell him "hell" is a naughty word. I did not think that he would like it. I heard him move around a little more, his hands knocking into things.

"Maddy," Mummy said, "where do you think you are?"

"I'm in my *room*," I said.

"Dan?" she said, to Daddy. My daddy's other name is "Dan." It is like "Dad" but has a *nuh*-sound at the end instead of a *duh*-sound. "*Is* this Maddy's room?"

I heard him moving around again, as if he was checking things with his hands.

"What are we doing in here?" he said, sounding as if he was not certain. "*Is* this her room?"

"Yes, it's *my room*," I said.

I was beginning to think Daddy or Mummy could not hear properly, because I kept saying things over and over, but they did not listen. I told them again. "I woke up, and my light was off, and this is my room."

"Have you tried the switch by the door?" Daddy asked Mummy.

I heard Mummy move to the door, and her fingers swishing on the wall, swishing and patting. "It's not there."

"What do you mean it's not there?"

"What do you think I mean?"

"For Christ's sake."

I heard Daddy walking carefully across the room to where Mummy was. Mummy said: "Satisfied?"

"How *can* it not be there? Maddy—can you turn the light by your bed on, please?" Daddy sounded cross now.

"She says it isn't there."

"What do you mean, not there?"

"It's not *there*," I said. "I already told Mummy, fourteen times. I was coming into your room to tell you, and then Mummy woke up and she was on the floor."

"Are the street lamps out?"

This was Mummy asking. I heard Daddy go away from the door and go back to the other end of the room, where he had woken up from. He knocked into the table as he was moving and made a cross sound but kept on moving again.

"Dan? Is that why it's so dark? Is it a power cut?"

"I don't know,' he said. "I . . . can't find the curtains."

"Can't find the gap, you mean?"

"No. Can't find the curtains. They're not here."

"You're sure you're in the right —"

"Of course I'm in the right place. They're not here. I can't feel them. It's just wall."

"It is just wall where my door is too," I said. I was happy that Daddy had found the same thing as me, because if he had found it too then it could not be wrong.

I heard Mummy check the wall near us with her hands. She was breathing a little quickly.

"She's right. It's just wall," she said, so we all knew the same thing.

But Mummy's voice sounded quiet and a bit scared and so it did not make me so happy when she said it.

"Okay, this is ridiculous," Daddy said. "Stay where you are. Don't move."

I could hear what he was doing. He was going along the sides of the room, with his fingers on the walls. He went around the drawers near the window, then past where my cloth calendar hangs, where I put what day it is in the mornings, then along my bed.

"She's right," he said. "The lamp isn't here."

"I'm really cold," Mummy said.

Daddy went past me and into the corner where Mummy had been sleeping, where I trod on her when I was trying to find the door. But he couldn't find it either.

He said the door had gone and the windows and all the walls felt like they were made of stone.

Mummy tried to find the curtains then too, but she couldn't. They tried to find the door and the window for a long time but they still couldn't find them and then my Mummy started crying.

Daddy said crying would not help, which he says to me sometimes, and he kept on looking in the dark for some more time.

But in the end he stopped, and he came and sat down with us. I don't now how long ago that was. It's hard to remember in the dark.

Sometimes we sleep but later we wake up and everything is the same. I do not get hungry but it is always dark and very cold. Mummy and Daddy had ideas and used their imaginations. Mummy thought there was a fire and it burned all our house down. Daddy says we think we are in my room because I woke up first, but really we are in a small place made of stone near a church. I don't know but we have been here a very long time now and still it is not morning yet. It is quiet and I do not like it.

Mummy and Daddy do not talk much any more, and this is why, if you wake up in the night, you should never ever get up out of bed.

Michael Marshall Smith *is a novelist and screenwriter. Under this name he has published over seventy short stories and three novels*—Only Forward, Spares, *and* One of Us—*winning the Philip K. Dick, HWA, August Derleth and British Fantasy Awards, as well as the Prix Morane. Writing as Michael Marshall, he has published six internationally best-selling thrillers, including* The Straw Men, The Intruders, *and* Bad Things, *and 2009 saw the publication of* The Servants, *under the name M.M. Smith. His new Michael Marshall novel* The Breakers *will be published in 2011. He lives in North London with his wife, son, and two cats. His Web site is: www.michaelmarshallsmith.com*

Unless you are *sure* you have a working nightlight—remember Michael Marshall Smith's cautionary tale the next time you wake up in the dark. Consider heeding its young narrator's advice. Obviously the author—probably thanks to being a father himself or possibly because he's still in touch with his inner child, as so many imaginative folks are—has learned that grown-ups can be so very stupid with their rules and their deals and their inability to understand about the dark.

G'night!

ACKNOWLEDGEMENTS

• The scope and intent of *The Year's Best Fantasy and Horror 2010* is unique. As the publisher allowed me a considerable number of pages to fill, I was able to select some longer works that, in a thinner book, might not have been afforded the space. And, with such a broad theme, I was able to select stories that do not fit anthologies more tightly constrained by definitions. Thanks to Sean Wallace of Prime Books for the lack of boundaries.

• Getting this assignment on short notice meant I was especially in need of assistance. I got it. Special thanks to Ellen Datlow, Stefan Dziemianowicz, and Sean Wallace's band of nameless (to me anyway) intrepid recommenders.

• Information about and the call for submissions for the next volume of *The Year's Best Fantasy and Horror* can be found at www.darkecho. com/darkfantasy. Contact: darkecho@darkecho.com.

—PRLG

PUBLICATION HISTORY

Kelley Armstrong, "A Haunted House of Her Own" © 2009. *Twilight Zone: 19 Original Stories on the 50th Anniversary*, ed. Carol Serling (Tor). Reprinted by permission of the author.

Peter Atkins, "The Mystery" © 2009. *Spook City*, ed. Angus Mackenzie (PS Publishing, U.K.). Reprinted by permission of the author.

Dale Bailey & Nathan Balingrud, "The Crevasse" © 2009. *Lovecraft Unbound*, ed. Ellen Datlow (Dark Horse). Reprinted by permission of the author.

Elizabeth Bear, "The Horrid Glory of Its Wings" © 2009. *Tor.com*, 12/08/09. Reprinted by permission of the author.

Deborah Biancotti, "Diamond Shell" © 2009. *A Book of Endings* (Twelfth Planet Press). Reprinted by permission of the author.

Holly Black, "The Coldest Girl in Coldtown" © 2009. *The Eternal Kiss: 13 Vampire Tales of Blood and Desire*, ed. Trisha Telep (Running Press Kids). Reprinted by permission of the author.

Nadia Bulkin, "Everything Dies, Baby" © 2009. *Strange Horizons*, 9/31/09. Reprinted by permission of the author.

Ramsey Campbell, "Respects" © 2009. *British Invasion*, eds. Christopher Golden, Tim Lebbon, and James A. Moore (Cemetery Dance). Reprinted by permission of the author.

Suzy McKee Charnas, "Lowland Sea" © 2009. *Poe*, ed. Ellen Datlow (Solaris). Reprinted by permission of the author.

Robert Davies, "Bruise for Bruise" © 2009. *Weird Tales #353*. Reprinted by permission of the author.

Kurt Dinan, "Nub Hut" © 2009. *ChiZine* 1/09. Reprinted by permission of the author.

Steve Duffy, "Certain Death For a Known Person" © 2009. *Apparitions*, ed. Michael Kelly (Undertow). Reprinted by permission of the author.

ABOUT THE EDITOR

Paula Guran is the editor of Pocket Book's Juno fantasy imprint and nonfiction editor for *Weird Tales* magazine. In an earlier life she produced weekly e-mail newsletter *DarkEcho* (winning two Bram Stoker Awards, an International Horror Guild Award award, and a World Fantasy Award nomination), edited *Horror Garage* magazine (earning another IHG and a second World Fantasy nomination), and has contributed reviews, interviews, and articles to numerous professional publications. She's also done a great deal of other various and sundry work in sf/f/h publishing. Earlier anthologies Guran has edited include *Embraces, Best New Paranormal Romance*, and *Best New Romantic Fantasy 2*. In addition to this anthology, she recently edited *Zombies: The Recent Dead* for Prime Books. Forthcoming anthologies for Prime include *Vampires: The Recent Undead* and *Halloween!* By the end of 2010 she will also have edited four dozen published novels and three collections.